A DOUBLE DOSE OF TROUBLE

A CASSIDY CALLAHAN ADVENTURE NOVEL

BY

KELLY RYSTEN

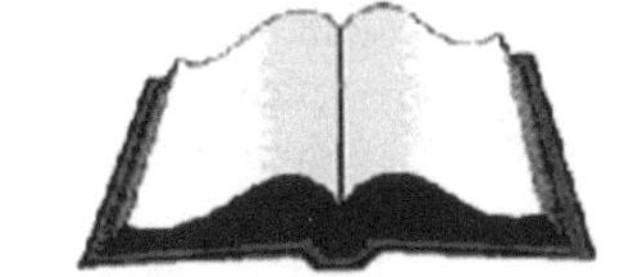

CCB Publishing
British Columbia, Canada

A Double Dose of Trouble: A Cassidy Callahan Adventure Novel

ISBN-13 978-1-77143-025-8
First Edition

Library and Archives Canada Cataloguing in Publication
Rysten, Kelly, 1960-
A double dose of trouble : a Cassidy Callahan adventure novel / written by Kelly Rysten.
ISBN 978-1-77143-025-8
Also available in electronic format.
Additional cataloguing data available from Library and Archives Canada

Cover artwork by Kelly Rysten: www.kellyrysten.com

This is a work of fiction. Names, places, and characters are a product of the author's imagination or are used fictitiously and are not to be considered as real. Resemblance to any events or persons, living or dead, past or present, is purely coincidental.

Extreme care has been taken by the author to ensure that all information presented in this book is accurate and up to date at the time of publishing. Neither the author nor the publisher can be held responsible for any errors or omissions. Additionally, neither is any liability assumed for damages resulting from the use of the information contained herein.

Publisher: CCB Publishing
British Columbia, Canada
www.ccbpublishing.com

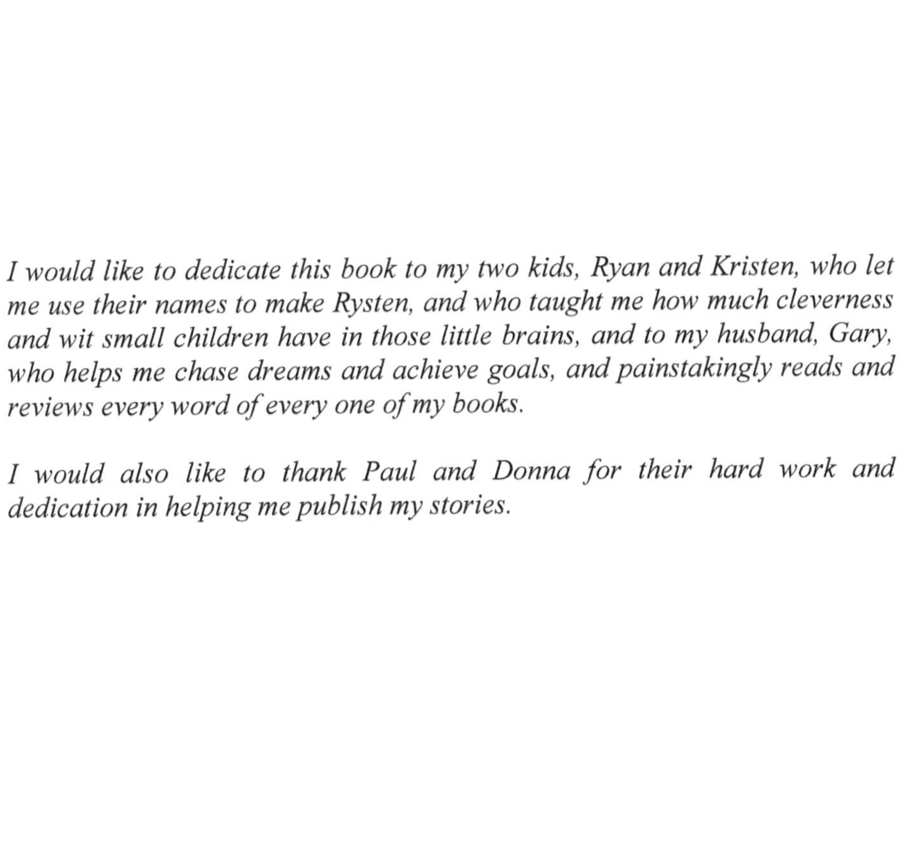

I would like to dedicate this book to my two kids, Ryan and Kristen, who let me use their names to make Rysten, and who taught me how much cleverness and wit small children have in those little brains, and to my husband, Gary, who helps me chase dreams and achieve goals, and painstakingly reads and reviews every word of every one of my books.

I would also like to thank Paul and Donna for their hard work and dedication in helping me publish my stories.

Other books by Kelly Rysten

Triple Trouble

Read about Cassidy Callahan's first tracking adventure with trouble at every turn.

Published 2009 – ISBN 978-1-926585-41-3

Car Trouble

Car troubles abound as Cassidy sets her sights on Police Academy. With a serial killer on the loose determined to send the police department a message, Cassidy's attendance is in question.

Published 2010 – ISBN 978-1-926918-03-7

A Cache of Trouble

A cache of banknotes lies hidden near Cassidy's canyon hideaway and a greedy criminal is determined to find the cache. Cassidy and the whole search and rescue team are drawn into the hunt, but while some seek riches, others just want Cassidy to survive.

Published 2011 – ISBN 978-1-926918-87-7

1

A PIT OF TROUBLE

Chapter 1

Sometimes I picture this character named B.T. Trouble. The B.T. stands for Big Time. He's a large, evil executive, in a huge, fancy office, with a padded, leather chair, facing a big computer monitor, and on the monitor is my life. He sits there watching me, and at his whim he tweaks my life, sending it into a tailspin of hopelessness and danger. Then he sits back and laughs as I struggle to escape my predicament. In a way there's a little optimism mixed in with the illusion. I hope that B.T. is just there for entertainment, and that he doesn't really want to kill me, after all that would end his fun. I do my best to keep the entertainment value going so he doesn't get bored and knock me off. But when I am living through the trouble-stricken times of my life I often wonder if it will be my last.

That's what happened after my storybook wedding. The day had been frustrating, humorous, and wonderful just like all weddings should be. Rusty and I were finally wed. All our family and friends were happy for us. We set out that evening on our honeymoon in wedded bliss and ended the evening in bedded bliss. We then flew off the next day to a series of adventures that I could never have imagined.

First we boarded a jet plane that took us from LAX north to St. Paul, Minnesota. I had no idea what we were doing there because Rusty had planned our trip. I didn't even get to pack my own suitcase. Given my penchant for survival, I'd brought my hunting knife and magnesium stick. I knew I couldn't take them on a plane so I packed them securely in my checked luggage. When we landed in St. Paul, Rusty rented a car and we drove out of town to a tiny airstrip. He had a computer printed map and got lost anyway, but we eventually pulled up to a corrugated garage with a windsock next to it. The airport. Most people would have backed out at the sight of the airport but, having been through the Marines and search and rescue, I was used to a variety of transport taking off in all kinds of conditions. However, we didn't board an airplane at the airport. Instead, we piled into a Jeep and drove away from the airstrip to a manmade lake. Minnesota has enough lakes, I thought. Why build another? But it turned out the lake was a landing strip too. We climbed aboard a small pontoon plane, and it whisked us across the lake until I thought we'd end up in the trees, and then it lifted into the air and breezed off to parts unknown.

I looked down. City gave way to country and country gave way to forest and still we flew. This was great! I wondered if there were moose down there. Was Minnesota moose country? What about grizzlies? I had tried to take a clue from Rusty's attire to determine where we were going, but he had dressed for the security of the big city airports, so he was just wearing jeans and a casual shirt. As a result, I wore jeans with a t-shirt for comfort and ease of travel. When I saw nothing but trees below I couldn't help it, I fell into survival mode and dug out my hunting knife and magnesium stick from my suitcase. These two items went with me anytime I ventured out of town, and they had saved my life more than once. I was lucky the plane was small enough that passengers and luggage rode together in the cabin.

"Cassidy, what are you doing?" Rusty asked.

"I can't help it. I was born a boy scout. 'Always be prepared.' That's a Boy Scout motto isn't it?"

"You're not worried are you?"

"No! This is great! I just feel naked without my knife when I'm in the woods."

"You're not in the woods."

"I could be in a few minutes. Where are we going?"

"I don't remember, but the pilot knows."

"Do you think the pilot would let me see out the front?"

"Don't count on it."

I made my way to the front just to see.

"Hi!" I said brightly, "Can I sit up here for a bit? It's been a long time since I've been up in a small plane."

He wasn't so sure he wanted company, but he gave me a nod so I sat quietly.

"Don't touch anything. You fly much?" he asked.

"Not much, only when I have to. I like flying, it's just that I'm more of a land lubber. I like to hike, and camp, and see critters, and there aren't many of them up in the sky. But I do fly occasionally for work."

"Oh, on business trips?"

"Not exactly. I do search and rescue. Occasionally we have to get a lift out with a missing person. That's about the only flying I do."

"Then you'll like where we're headed. Loon Lake. Have you ever heard a loon before?"

"No, we don't have them where I live. Are there loons at the lake?"

"Yeah, go out in the canoe. You'll see all kinds of animals and birds."

"How far is it to the lake?"

"It'll be a few hours to Lower Loon. We're going to Upper Loon Lake. That's where the cabins are."

"Cool! This trip was a total surprise, so I'm fascinated every step of the way."

I watched out the big windshield of the plane as miles and miles of dense woods slipped by underneath us. Occasionally a bright blue lake appeared in amongst the trees and I wondered what animals could be found down there.

After a while, I thought Rusty must be bored, so I made my way to the back of the plane and sat next to him.

"It's so cool, you ought to go take a look!"

"Are you having fun yet?"

"Oh yeah! I can't wait to get there, wherever there is. He said it would be a few hours. I hope we brought a lot of film. I want to take a picture of a moose."

My enthusiasm was rubbing off on Rusty. His eyes laughed at me, amused. He always silently laughed at me when I got excited about something. I looked like a kid walking into Disneyland for the first time. The woods of Minnesota were like Disneyland to me, new critters and trails and canoe rides and cabins. I pointed from the window.

"Look, there's a lake down there. I wonder if there's moose down there. I wonder if there are bears."

"Just sit down," he said, "There will be plenty to see once we get there."

"But, there's plenty to see right now. How can you just sit there?"

I sat next to him, but pretty soon I was drawn to the windows again. Half a dozen more trips to the window and he was no longer amused by my enthusiasm.

"Cass, you're going to wear yourself out before we even land."

"No I won't, it's just interesting to me. You can see woods and lakes and rivers and towns. It's cool!"

I sat down next to Rusty but the woods were calling to me. I started to get up but Rusty held me down.

"Just relax. We'll be there soon."

I sat listening to the droning of the plane engines. After a while they grew quieter and quieter. I started dozing off but suddenly my senses were jarred alive. No, it wasn't my imagination, the engines really were quieter. In fact, I couldn't hear anything at all from the left engine. I went forward and saw the pilot was furiously trying to maintain control of the plane.

"Go sit down and buckle in!" he yelled.

"Why? What's going on?" I asked, worried for our safety.

Before he could answer there was a loud pop and the plane lurched. A string of expletives came from the pilot.

"Go!" he yelled.

I went to the back of the plane but I wasn't buckling in yet. If there was something I could do, I'd do it first. I searched the back of the plane and found four parachutes. I took one to the pilot, and then gave one to Rusty.

"Cassidy are you nuts? What are you doing?"

"Go ask the pilot that!" I said urgently.

He went forward and took a look around, bracing himself as the plane bucked and lurched through the sky. He got the same response I did, an urgent command to buckle up. When Rusty came back he found me strapping on the parachute. It was a little different from the ones I'd used before, but I figured it out. I located the cords. Right hand first, left hand second.

"Cass! Sit down!" Rusty said nervously.

"Put that chute on!" I ordered. I'd never ordered him to do anything before, but my trouble radar was going off like crazy. I knew how to skydive, but I didn't know how to crash. So the chute was the winner in my mind.

I looked out the window. Fire leapt from the left engine. The plane fell steeply.

"Rusty! Put on the damn parachute! Have you ever jumped before?"

"No!" he called back.

"Do you think you can do it?"

"Only if I have to."

Curses continued from the cockpit. I went to the pilot.

"Buckle or bail?" I yelled.

He looked at me seriously.

"You know how?"

"I do, my husband has never done it, but I can tell him what to do. Which is the bigger risk?"

"This plane's going down! I'd like to try for a lake but I don't think she's going to make it. I think she's going to burn up before I get a chance."

"So, buckle or bail?"

BAM!

"Bail! If you know how, bail!"

"Tell him that!"

"Bail!" The pilot yelled, "Bail out!"

I went back to Rusty and helped him suit up. I adjusted everything so it was snug, but not too tight.

"What's our altitude?" I yelled.

"Eight thousand!" he yelled back.

"Here," I said, "count to thirty. Look at the plane, look at the ground, if everything looks clear pull the right cord. If the right cord doesn't work in ten seconds or so pull the left one. The reserve chute *might* open automatically but don't count on it. If it's going to open automatically it'll probably wait till you're at one thousand feet and one thousand feet looks awfully close! Can you do it?" He looked at me, his eyes wide with fear. I wasn't sure he could. I had to admit, it was a scary thing to do for the first time. "Can you do it if I go first?"

"If you're jumping, I'm jumping," he said with determination.

"It's going to be windy and noisy, just don't panic! Keep your head. The jerk is rough but tolerable. If your chute is square, you will have pretty good control steering and maneuvering. If it's round, just ride it down. Are you ready?" I called over the creaking, groaning airplane.

He squared his shoulders, took a deep breath then called back, "Ready!"

I silently prayed he could do it as I jerked the door to the plane open. I braced myself, looked down. That sure didn't look like eight thousand feet.

"Twenty, count to twenty! And don't jump feet first. Spread yourself out, face down, so you create more drag." I yelled hoping he could hear me. I took a deep breath, checked my bindings one more time, then bailed out. Oh man, I hated that feeling. It wasn't as bad as most people think. It didn't feel like a drop on a roller coaster. It didn't even feel like falling. It felt windy, and a little buoyant. I counted to twenty and then looked around. Rusty had jumped so I made sure he was well away from me as I pulled my cord. Nothing happened. I yanked twice more. I waited as my heart rate doubled. Nothing. I tried the left one. I felt some movement, and then the reserve chute slowly peeled out of the pack and wiggled around in the wind. Damn it! I thought, Mr. B. T. Trouble! Give me a break! This is not funny! I pulled at the cords trying to shake out the fabric, but it wasn't cooperating. The wind was too strong for me to do much. When I changed position the wind whipped me around, so I was tumbling as I fell. In the tumbling I managed to get a hold of the chute. I tried to spread it out, anything to get some wind in it! I frantically pulled at the fabric this way and that, hoping I wasn't tangling it worse. Any amount of drag at all would be to my advantage, so I pulled and tugged and tumbled through the sky. I'm not good with math but believed I had a little more than five minutes to figure this out.

I was tangled in the cords. My hair was flying in the wind. The fabric flapped around more loosely now. If I could just get everything back in its right place the chute might just catch. I worked my arm and legs loose from their tangle and when there was room to work I felt the cords tighten and the chute catch. One side of it was still stuck together, and I was falling awfully fast, but I had some measure of hope now. If luck was on my side, maybe I could work with the situation and come out of it in one piece.

I looked down. Minnesota is half water and I had lucked out. I was coming in for a very fast landing right into a lake. I felt a stab of fear as I approached the surface, then I hit the water and the cold almost took my breath away. Don't breathe, Cass, don't! I held my breath as long as I could, and then held it longer thinking all the time, don't breathe, don't breathe. My head stung from the water up my nose. My lungs burned! When my plunge slowed and then stopped, I kicked up towards the surface, frantically swimming toward the air above. When my head broke through and the air hit me again I gasped and coughed. Water was up my nose and in my eyes. I instinctively started treading water and coughing. I batted the parachute away and peeled off the harness. Rusty! Where was Rusty? I looked around and saw his parachute coming down in the woods. I then looked for a third parachute, but didn't see one. Where was the pilot?

I started swimming for shore, but was too exhausted, so I turned over onto my back to rest while floating. Then I swam a little more towards the area where Rusty had landed. He was going to be frantic by the time I found him. I swam some more. Come on, Cass, you can do it, just keep swimming, just keep on. My arms ached. My legs ached. I couldn't afford to let them cramp up, but I needed to get out of this cold water. I rested again, just a short rest, then I pressed on. Swim, rest, swim, rest. I was getting nowhere. It was too far, too far, no way could I swim that far. I shouldn't even be alive, and wondered why I wasn't some big splat on the ground somewhere. Then a stupid skydiving joke popped into my head, and it shook me out of my hopeless mood. I remembered it from my training in the Marines. The instructor had told it to me to help ease my fear during my first simulated jump.

"What's the difference between a golfer and a skydiver?" he'd asked.

I'd jumped but he caught up with me later.

"A golfer goes *whack*, shit. And a skydiver goes shit, *whack*."

Well, it wasn't a joke to me anymore. It was very much real. Now I was dealing with the results of my *whack*. Swim, Cass, just keep swimming. I swam and swam and finally I heard off in the distance Rusty's nearly panicked voice calling, "Cassidyyyy!"

I tried waving to show him my location, but I didn't know if he could see me. I swam faster. I hated doing these things to him. I put myself in swim mode, just like I did hike mode, and kept paddling. Any forward motion was acceptable, just keep paddling. Finally I heard splashing in front of me. Rusty was wading out and he reached out, pulling me up and out of the water. It was freezing!

"R-r-usty, build a fire. Please, build a fire." I was shivering so badly I couldn't stop.

I tried to stand but my knees buckled. Rusty helped me shivering and staggering out of the lake and up onto the shore. I collapsed just clear of the water, shivering uncontrollably. "Please," I said, "build a fire."

"Cass, oh babe, how did you do it?" he said rubbing my arms and shoulders to help me warm up, "When I saw your parachute not open I almost didn't pull my cord. It would have been so easy to just not pull it."

He wrapped me in a fearful hug and I would have hugged him back but I couldn't. All I could do was shiver.

"P-please Rusty. Just build a fire. I'm freezing and I'm beat. I can't do it."

"We don't have a way to light it, babe. We can't. Come on, come here."

"If you can build it we can light it. P-please." I got up trying to find the energy to gather the pine needles and sticks, but I couldn't. I just couldn't. I sat back down on the beach shivering and dug down into my wet pocket. The dirt clung to my wet clothes and the fabric of my pocket clung to my hand but I finally pulled out the magnesium stick.

"Use this. It's to start fires. Oh, it's s-s-o cold!" I unstrapped my hunting knife. Rusty built up a tiny stack of firewood but it wouldn't last long. "M-more wood," I shivered. When he had brought a small pile of wood, I shaved some magnesium into the tinder and struck the steel with my knife. I couldn't get a good solid hit in but Rusty saw what I was trying to do and took it from me. Three or four strikes and a spark hit the magnesium and the tinder caught.

"I always wondered why you carried that thing around." Rusty said. "It just looks like a hunk of metal."

"These two things are my survival gear. Where's your parachute?" I was still shivering but began settling down and started to think in survival mode. We might need that parachute. I didn't have the strength to drag mine out of the lake but Rusty's might prove useful.

"It's in the woods."

"We need to find it after I dry out. Is it really this cold or am I reacting badly to the fall?"

"You're lucky to be alive and you're worried about reacting badly?"

"No, I just need to know if it's really cold out. I can't tell if it's the weather or if it's just me that is freezing."

"It's just you. It's July in Minnesota. It's cold in Australia. Maybe you're working off an adrenaline rush. I know I would be if I were you."

"Well, my life didn't flash before my eyes. If it did I wouldn't have believed it anyway. I doubt anybody would, the c-crazy things that happen to me. Why c-can't I get warm? I need to shake this. We can't just sit around here. We need to figure out where we are. We need to find a town or a campground or the cabin. The cabin is north of here. But I don't know how far. It depends on what lake this is. If this is Lower Loon Lake then Upper Loon Lake isn't far. That's where the cabin is. Where's your parachute?"

"I can find it again. Why are you so set on finding the parachute? You're not going back up."

"Just in case you didn't notice, we are in the woods in Minnesota. We don't have any food or water and we have a long ways to go. We might as well consider ourselves in survival mode. The parachute has cords and material that might come in handy. I can make a snare out of the cords. We can make a net out of the parachute. It can help us a lot if we can find it. "

"We'll find it. Just take it easy until you get back to normal."

"Did the pilot jump? Did you see? I was k-kind of busy."

"I didn't see. I was busy too, deciding whether I wanted to pull that cord or not."

"Rusty, never, ever do that. You can't. I couldn't bear it."

I was still shivering and now my emotions were getting all jumbled up too, to think how close we came, both of us. It was too much. I climbed into his lap and put my arms around him, hunkered down and shivered until I was spent. I sat there limp and worn out until I realized I wasn't shivering any more. He held me, for his comfort as much as mine until I felt ready to tackle the next step of our adventure.

"Do you have your gun?" I asked.

"Yeah."

"Don't use it to hunt unless we have to. The pilot said there are bears up here. It'll be better to save it, unless we have a sure shot or we're desperate. Have you been on a survival trip before?"

"No."

"Okay, well, what you do is watch for food. Watch for anything that might work to our advantage, any little thing. We're going to get hungry. You can count on that. But we'll make it. First step is to find that parachute. Then we need to head north. We were getting close to the lower lake when the plane went down. We should be able to make it to the cabin. To head north we go the direction of the shadows. Have you had an orienteering class?"

"Only what they teach at academy. And that was years ago."

"We can tell direction by watching which way our shadows point during the day and by watching the North Star at night. I wish we had a way to carry water. That's going to make things tough."

"Are you sure you're up to this? Cassidy…"

"Hey, I've done this before. All we can do is our best. It's going to take patience and determination but I'm pretty sure we can get through this. Now where is that parachute?"

I followed him into the woods and we untangled his parachute from a low bush. I cut off the harness and saved the chute and the cords. As we were pulling the fabric loose I noticed berries on the bushes.

"I think we hit the jackpot," I said, and began picking berries and dropping them into the parachute. We picked several handfuls.

"What are these?" Rusty asked.

"I'm not sure, but I know the north is famous for berries."

"What if they are poisonous?"

"If they were poisonous, the animals wouldn't eat them, and animals have definitely been at them. There are tracks all over here. We need to head north, and we need to watch for a game trail. If we can find one before nightfall I will try to set up a snare to catch a critter. I don't like to do that but it's them or us at this point. Now, I know it's not something you like to do but we need to go back to the lake and drink before we head out. We can't carry water so we have to drink it when we can."

We went down to the lake and found the clearest spot we could and then drank our fill.

"If this was California there would be a bottle or a can or something floating on the shore, but I don't see one here. Don't they have people in Minnesota?"

We headed north. It was getting late so the shadows were long. I walked ahead of Rusty watching for game trails, footprints, animal tracks, edible plants, anything to make our situation easier. I knew there were animals in these woods. I hadn't seen one yet but there was evidence everywhere. Tracks, scat. Some of the tracks I was familiar with, others were new to me. I wanted to stop and study them but we didn't have time for that yet.

We hiked along through sun dappled woods, making pretty good time, under the circumstances. Then I found a nice busy game trail and could tell it was used frequently because the animals had worn a tunnel through the undergrowth. I stopped.

"Okay," I announced, "we're camping here for the night."

"Why here?"

"I'll show you. Watch how I do this so you will know how to do it. It's always handy to have a few survival tricks up your sleeve."

I searched the area for the things we needed to set a snare. First things first. I found a young sapling next to the game trail and took note of it. Then I turned my search away from the game trail and found another young tree, carefully choosing two branches.

"Rusty, can you break off this branch?" I could have done it myself, but I wanted him to participate in this, too. It would make him feel useful and I still ached from the fall. There was a crack and a peeling sound and a few yanks before he got the branch loose. "Now this one." I instructed. I whittled at the first branch while he wrestled with the second one. I made the first branch into a long stake with a hook on the end. The sturdier branch was the stake and the smaller branch coming off of it was the hook. I took the second stick from Rusty and whittled a smaller hook. This one didn't need a stake on it, but did need to fit with the first hook.

"What are you doing?" Rusty asked.

"You'll see."

We went back to the game trail and located the sapling I'd chosen. I looked at the set up with a critical eye. I found a rock and used it to pound the stake into the ground next to the game trail, hook down. Then I cut a cord from the parachute and tied one end to the sapling.

"Bend this tree down for me. I need to gauge the tension."

Rusty pulled the young tree down and I found a place along the cord to tie the trip stick. The rest of the cord was too short to make a noose out of so I cut another cord from the parachute. I fashioned a critter size noose and laid it on the trail. Then I tied the noose to the trip stick. It wasn't the best setup but it was what we had the equipment for. It was better to use just a single cord so the stick couldn't pull free when the sapling sprung up. I found other little sticks and pushed them into the ground next to the game trail.

"Now watch," I said. He pulled down the sapling and I carefully hooked the two hooks together. "Stand back and be careful of your eyes," I instructed. He stood back and I tried to trip the snare. Darn, too tough. I whittled at the trip stick a little and we reset the snare. "Stand back," I said again. I triggered it again and this time it released easily. We reset the snare and I arranged the noose at critter height. "Think you could make one?" I asked.

"Yeah, how long did it take you to learn how to do it right?"

"The first one took some tweaking. They almost always take some tweaking. But I'm getting better at it. I only use them when I have to now. I don't like killing critters but they are meat and we will need food. I'd rather save our bullets for defense. If we can snare our food we won't have to shoot it. Now, we need to camp a little ways from the snare. Sometimes animals avoid the place because it smells like people. Let's hope these critters don't know enough about people to be scared."

We found a place to camp and settled in. No tent, no sleeping bags, no jackets. It was going to be a long, cold night. I stretched the parachute out as flat as possible over our sleeping spot and tied the chords tightly to trees. It would keep the dew off and hopefully there would be enough water on it in the morning for us to drink a few sips.

"I'll split the berries with you," I offered.

He looked at the small offering. "You go ahead."

"Here, I'm not taking more than half. You forget, I've done this before. I'm used to this. There were times when a handful of berries was all I had for a whole day. Most times it was a handful of something that tasted a lot worse but it was edible so I ate it. Berries aren't so bad. Here, try one."

I popped one in my mouth. Ugh, it was sour! It was as sour as can be, but I chewed and swallowed anyway.

"Wait," I said, "find a ripe one first. That was awful!"

He laughed at me and started examining his berries. He found a softer one and popped it in his mouth. He made a face.

"Okay, so these berries aren't the best Minnesota has to offer. We'll find something better tomorrow. I'm still eating mine. Taste has very little to do with survival. Maybe we'll have meat for breakfast."

"How do you take things so matter of factly? Most people would be freaking out just from the jump. I am! But here you are, lost in a place you've never been to, no food, no water and you're snacking on awful berries and hoping for a meal tomorrow. And it all seems normal to you. How do you do it?"

"You forget I've parachuted before. And I've been on survival trips before. Is there any good reason to freak out?" I asked matter of factly.

"Yes!" he said.

"Give me one good reason to freak out."

"Well… because it's… normal. I still feel a little freaked out and my parachute opened!"

"Just in case you didn't notice I did freak out for a little bit back there. But it's over and now we need to think about food and water and heading north. So freaking out isn't part of the plan."

"Why north?"

"It's the one direction I know is right. Plus if we can make it to the cabin before our ten days are up we'll have a place to stay. You do want to finish the trip, don't you? I still want to try out the canoes. I want to see a moose. They have such funny expressions. I want to hear a loon." I could feel his smile in the dark.

"We need to sleep. We both need all the energy we can get for tomorrow."

Chapter 2

It was a very cold night. Neither of us were dressed for wilderness survival, so with little choice we just snuggled closer. The ground was rough, the noises unfamiliar, and I had a hard time getting sleepy thinking of all the new animals I might find. I was remembering all the tracks I'd seen that day and wanted to track the animals that had made them. Rusty drifted off beside me and I tried listening to his breathing to calm my thoughts. Everything here was new, and new to me was interesting, and anything interesting was something to explore, so sleep was a long time coming. I didn't even know I'd fallen asleep until I awoke in the morning. As usual, dawn was barely beginning when I stirred. I was torn between checking the snare and keeping Rusty warm. He must have been freezing, but practicality soon won out over warmth. If there was an animal in the snare I'd need to clean it, gather firewood, make a fire and start cooking it. That could take a few hours, and we needed to get as many miles behind us as possible. I wriggled free and rolled out from under the parachute, then noticed water had settled on top of it. That was good. We'd need that water, every little bit of it. I walked back to the game trail and checked the snare from a distance, nothing. Rats. I walked around looking for edible plants, but the forest here was unfamiliar to me. I avoided the area of the snare hoping something would wander down the run. Critters often moved around in the early morning hours, so there was still hope for a meal. As I wandered I found leaves full of dew and drank as I went. I decided to wake Rusty before the dew was gone so I made my way back to our camp. Slipping under the parachute, I sat quietly next to him, hating to wake him but knowing it was the smart thing to do. I shook him gently and he awoke with a start.

"What is it?" he said nervously.

"Nothing, you're not a cop today, just relax."

"I was."

"We need to get up before the dew burns off. It may be our only water today so we should get as much as we can while it's still here. Don't hit the parachute. You'll knock the water off it. Bad news this morning is that nothing tripped the snare. Good news is there is lots of dew. Water's more important so let's have a drink to celebrate."

"Some celebration, dirty water."

"It's better than no water. Here, pinch the parachute and tip it towards you. Some of the dew will run down and you can catch it in your mouth." He pinched and shook and a trickle of water started down the fabric gathering more dewdrops as it went. “If we get dew like this every night we ought to be fine, thirsty but fine. At least we are both desert rats and we’re used to less water than these northerners.”

After drinking from the parachute we walked around in the woods and I showed him how to spot dew in other handy places. When we approached the snare I saw a small movement ahead and froze. I held my hand up as a signal to Rusty. We stopped and watched. A rabbit was investigating the odd smells. I intended to remove the snare so we could set it up again when we stopped for the night, but maybe, just maybe…

“Freeze!” I whispered to Rusty.

I settled into a stalking crouch and silently made my way to the game trail behind the rabbit. The rabbit was very alert and sensed my approach. It froze, whiskers twitching. Rabbits usually freeze before they flee. If I could just get it to take off down the game trail I’d snare it. I kept my eyes on the rabbit, staying out of sight as much as possible. I crept, quietly following the tiny trail through the woods. I couldn’t just walk the game trail. It was just a tunnel through the undergrowth but I could follow along next to it. As I stalked the rabbit I wondered if I might have to catch it with my bare hands. It wasn’t moving. I didn’t want to dive for it. It would probably get away and even if it didn’t, it would put up a fight and I could get scratched or bitten. At last the rabbit gave me a nervous look and dashed forward. There was a *snap* as the trip stick released and a *whoosh* as the sapling straightened again, then the rabbit went flying up in the air and hung dangling on the end of the noose. Yes! In a way I was glad to have been there when the rabbit was caught. I hated the thought of animals dangling helplessly from the noose so I killed it quickly.

“Rusty, gather some firewood while I skin this critter. We have food!”

I took down the snare, saving the stake and the trip stick arrangement for use at the next stop. Then I skinned the rabbit and prepared it for cooking.

While Rusty turned the rabbit over the fire I scraped the skin clean. It wasn’t very big, but the night had been cold enough to make me appreciate every bit of the rabbit’s fur. Any little bit of insulation helps. If you know where to put a little warmth it can help warm the whole body.

Rusty patiently turned the rabbit this way and that, trying to prevent it from burning. I took down the parachute and rolled up the snare and rabbit skin inside. Then I fashioned the remaining parachute cords into straps so we could carry it backpack style.

The rabbit was good as far as survival food goes. When the outside meat was cooked we sat by the fire peeling off strips of meat and eating it, then roasting the next layer.

"Have you ever eaten rabbit before?" I asked.

"No, but I've seen it in grocery stores so I know people must eat it occasionally."

"I've eaten my share but never from a grocery store. It was usually like this, over an open fire, after a time of hunger. I have to admit it's a lot more fun being on a survival trip with you than it is alone."

"This is fun?"

"Yeah, this is fun. It would be better with more food but I like this, hunger and cold nights and all. I have to admit, I'd have preferred a working parachute. But I've thought of taking a trip like this many times. I think about being dropped in an unfamiliar place and what I would do to make my way back to civilization."

"Cass, this isn't a game we are playing."

"I know, but I'm not worried yet. We have a destination in mind. I think we'll do okay for water, if the dew comes each night. We can make it a few days without food. But don't worry, we'll find something. All we have to do is keep our heads on straight, watch for anything edible and we'll do okay."

"Does anything ever worry you?"

"Of course, and I'll be sure and let you know when I become worried. For now we're doing good."

When we'd taken all the meat off the rabbit that we could, I put out the fire and erased all the evidence that I could from our camp. I noted the direction of the shadows and we set out north again.

As we hiked, it was natural for me to lead. I watched for food, tracks, opportunities. When we went on search and rescue calls I was always the leader because I was the tracker. So we just naturally fell into that familiar formation, me leading, Rusty following. Sometimes he would track me as he followed along. It was good practice for him. Normally I hid my footprints as I walked but I wasn't hiding my footprints here. I wanted us to be found, if people were looking for us. So I left clear footprints and even marked our trail occasionally, just in case. If I saw rocks I'd stack them or place them in a line so people would see inconsistencies and watch for more. If there was a stick handy I'd even write Rusty's initials next to the rocks. I thought, since Rusty had made the travel plans, they would know his name. And so I tracked and walked and left a trail when I could. By noon I was hungry again, but we just kept walking. In the afternoon I spotted a welcome sight.

"Wait here," I instructed.

I stepped away for a moment searching through the undergrowth but was met by disappointment. I only came up with one small strawberry. I picked the leaves off of several plants and put them in my pocket. I palmed the one small berry and found Rusty again.

“I have a present for you,” I said, and placed the berry in his hand. He looked at it. “That’s all there was, sorry. We’ll watch for more plants. Go ahead, eat it. It’s only one berry.”

“Cass…”

“When we find a good water supply I’ll make tea. I saved some of the leaves. And we’ll find more strawberry patches, you’ll see.”

“How can you make tea? You don’t have anything to hold water.”

“If we can find a good water supply I’ll show you.”

We continued on. He ate the one berry, looking guilty about it. Finding strawberry plants was encouraging to me and I kept a sharp eye out for more. We walked and walked, weaving in and out of trees and brush, always following the shadows north. I saw lots of animal tracks, and that was encouraging too. The woods were alive. I could track the animals if the tracks were fresh. Each time I came across a very distinct track I examined it, deciding whether it was worth the time to track it. Most of the time the animal was too big, like a deer, or the track was old enough that I figured the animal was miles away.

I’d eat almost anything. If I could catch it, I’d eat it. The only problem was in the catching. I wasn’t hungry enough yet to take down an animal too big for my uses. I also imagined as soon as I brought down a deer some game warden would magically appear, arrest me and haul me off to jail. It just went against my principals to take more than I could use from the woods. I was trying to remember just how my woods lore had come about, why I had decided just when it was okay to kill and when it was not, how much to take, how much to give back, exactly what was the proper way to treat nature. I didn’t know when that had developed but I was very set on it. I’d have to be very desperate to break my own rules.

We were walking, and I was thinking, when I ran across a trail. It wasn’t a manmade trail but it was a very well used game trail. I looked at the tracks on it. Many deer had passed this way. I wasn’t looking for deer but wondered if they were headed for a source of water. If they knew the way to a stream, maybe the stream would lead to a lake. Any water source was worth investigating. I followed the deer tracks. Rusty followed me. We had to stoop and crouch down in spots but the tracks led me on. I worried a little that we were no longer heading north but water seemed more important. If it did lead to a stream I was hoping it would be deep enough to try a fish trap. There are all kinds of options in the woods, if you know what to watch for. These woods seemed more livable than the steep, dry mountains back home. What we weren’t prepared for on this trip was the cold. I continued following the tracks of the deer until we finally came to an open meadow. I was disappointed. I sat down under a tree and brooded.

"What's wrong, Cass?"

"I was hoping these tracks were leading to water. We don't need a meadow, we need water."

"Maybe if we followed them the other direction?"

"Maybe," I sighed. Well, there was one useful thing that I might be able to find in a deer meadow, and that was grass. Most grasses are edible but I was hoping for a certain kind that would make a good straw. If I was able to make tea, we would appreciate a straw to drink it with. I looked across the meadow, resting and watching for the plant I was hoping for. Rusty sat too. I rarely rested, so he was taking advantage of the situation.

"Wait here," I said, and headed into the meadow to look around for a stalk. A round, hollow stalk. I found some of the younger blades of grass and picked them. I chewed them and swallowed the juice. Not great, but not too bad. I doubted they were very digestible so I chewed until the grass was tasteless then spit it out. It wouldn't make our stomachs feel better, but maybe it would give us some of the nutrients we needed. I used my knife to cut a handful of young blades and brought them back to Rusty.

"Grasses are almost always edible. It doesn't taste great but if you chew it and swallow the juice it'll provide a little nourishment. Don't swallow the fibers. Just spit them out when you are done. I was looking for a straw. I'll be back."

I continued looking around the meadow and finally found a stalk that I cut off with my knife. I blew through it and air came out the other end so I stuck the stalk behind my ear so I wouldn't have to carry it. I cut another handful of grasses and then led Rusty back down the deer trail. We chewed, and walked, and chewed, and spat. When I reached our former trail the only way to recognize it was by tracking. We had never had a real trail to follow, so when we got back to where we'd turned west I was torn. I finally decided to give the deer a chance for a mile or two. I followed the deer in the other direction and this time I was rewarded with an immense, slow flowing stream.

"Yes!" I said enthusiastically. I turned to Rusty beaming.

"It sure doesn't take much to make you happy," he observed.

"We have water, and if we build it right, we can probably catch fish. Then we can follow this stream and maybe it'll lead to our lake."

"How are you going to catch fish?"

"Do you want to learn how to make a fish trap?"

"Sure, why not?"

"Okay, all we need is about thirty sticks that are longer than the stream is deep. So we need to start looking for those."

I studied the stream and guessed we'd need the sticks to be about four feet long.

"That's a lot of sticks."

"Yeah, but they don't have to be any particular size, branching is okay too. We are basically building a fish fence. They don't care what it looks like. And we can keep an eye out for one nice, long stick that we can use for a spear."

We started gathering sticks. After finding about a dozen of them I waded into the stream and began placing them in the water, stabbing them down into the creek bed a few inches apart. As Rusty brought me more sticks I arranged them into a wide V with a little circular fish corral at one end. The theory was that the V would herd the fish into the tip where we could catch them easily. It took work and time and patience. If there was one thing that came in handy in the woods it was patience.

"How do you learn these things?" Rusty asked.

"When I was a kid, I read survival books. Then I tried all the tricks in them over the years. There's a lot I don't remember, but the few things I do remember have been effective. Did you happen to see a large branch lying around? Or a log?"

"No, what do you need a big branch for?"

"Making tea."

"You've got to be kidding."

"Nope. A rock might work, too, if it had a bowl shape to it."

I walked around near our camp and found a dead tree that was leaning over the stream. Perfect. I got out my knife again and began hollowing out a bowl shape in the top of the log. It was rough going. The wood was old and hard, but I kept at it, pulling out the shavings and splinters and watching them float downstream. I scraped, and scraped, and dug until I had a rough bowl shape. I scooped up water and put it in the bowl and watched. The first bowlful was absorbed by the wood so I scooped more water in until the bowl remained full.

"Okay, I announced. "We need a fire."

Rusty built up a fire. I found several small river rocks and added them to the fire. Then I went to the stream to catch fish. I began up stream from the fish trap and waded around scaring the fish downstream.

"Cassidy, some of the things you do sure seem odd," Rusty observed.

"What's odd?" I asked.

"What are you doing?"

"Fishing. Get the parachute ready."

He untied and unrolled the parachute and I waded closer to the fish trap. I could see three fish swimming around in circles in the end of the trap.

"Ready?" I called, "Don't let them get away."

I waded closer to the trap with my arms dangling in the water. I slowly made my way closer to the fish. When I felt the slippery sides of a fish I closed my grip suddenly and flung it into the parachute where it flopped around. I went after the second fish knowing my day's food supply was trying its best to get away. This was easier to do the more fish there were in the trap. When they were crowded up it was harder for them to slither out of my grasp. I closed in on the second fish. It took patience. When I managed to touch it with one hand it would quickly dart ahead and fish are fast and slick. Finally, I had the fish swimming between my hands and I closed my grip as quickly as I could. I felt the fish flap back and forth, so I lifted my hands and flung the second fish into the parachute. One more to go. This one was smaller and the hardest to catch. I didn't really want a second fish but I knew Rusty might. Several tries later and I still hadn't caught it, so I waded up stream and scared more fish down and into the trap.

"How many fish can you eat tonight?" I asked.

"Right now, I could eat a grizzly bear, but after two fish I'll probably change my mind."

"So you want two?"

"Yeah."

"Okay."

I waded around upstream, and slowly made my way down stream again. This time there were four fish in the trap. They were all crowded together, so it was easy to grab one more for Rusty. I took out two sticks from the trap and released the rest of them. I left the trap in place hoping we would have fish for breakfast too.

When I got to shore Rusty had the first fish cleaned and he was working on the second one.

"Cut the head off mine. I can't stand to look my dinner in the eye as I eat it," I said.

"This from the girl that eats snake, and traps and cleans her own animals."

"Sorry."

We roasted the fish over the fire. They cooked quickly and we ate them off the sticks like corn on the cob. When we were finished I went to the log with the bowl hollowed out.

"Are you ready to try strawberry tea?" I asked.

"I'm ready to watch you make it. I don't know if I want any," he answered.

I put the strawberry leaves in the bottom of the bowl. Then I nearly filled the bowl with water. I went to the fire and used sticks to pull out the river rocks. I used the parachute as a hot pad and grabbed the hot rocks and rushed them over to the bowl. I dropped the rocks into the bowl with a small splash and a hiss of steam. The rocks heated the water, the water steeped the leaves, and in a few minutes we had strawberry tea. I took out the cooled rocks and added a third hot rock to make sure it really was steeping well. When the water had changed color, I handed Rusty the straw.

"Tea time," I said cheerily.

"Do we have to hold our pinkies out when we drink?" he asked.

"I doubt it."

"You first."

I climbed up onto the log and straddled it on one side of the bowl and Rusty climbed up and straddled it from the other side. I stuck in the straw and sipped. Not bad. I would have preferred it cold but it wouldn't stick around long. We needed to drink it while we could. It could use some sugar, too, but that was obviously not an option.

"Try it," I said. "It's not like the tea back home and it's good for you. It has lots of vitamin C in it."

When we finished the first bowl I added more leaves and water, then ran for a few more hot rocks. It was important to get whatever nourishment was available. We drank the second bowl of tea, and then ate the boiled leaves.

"It's getting dark and we need to find a place away from here to sleep. There's too many food smells here. I don't want any surprises in the night."

We followed the stream north for a little ways and found a sleeping spot. We doubled up the parachute and pulled it over us. There was no need for it to catch water since the stream was nearby. Instead, it would keep the dew off and insulate us a little from the cold.

"When I am off on searches and night falls and I am trying to get to sleep, I always wonder what you are doing. I know you are probably working or getting dinner, but I always wonder anyway. Now I wonder what Strict and Victor and Landon are doing. While we are up here looking for Upper Loon Lake and a single cabin, I wonder what they are doing. And I wonder if anybody is looking for us. And what happened to the airplane and the pilot. Surely, if the pilot had made it they would have sent people out looking for us, yet I haven't seen or heard a plane."

"Are you getting worried?"

"About us? No. I worry about the pilot. But I don't know that we could have done anything. He was heading for a lake, that's all he told me. He was hoping to land the plane, but he didn't expect to be able to. That's why I worry. But I know there's no use in worrying. I can't do anything."

"You're doing plenty right here. I still wonder how you know how to do most of the things you've done since we bailed out. How in the world did you learn to make tea without any tools? I'd never think to use a log for a cup or rocks to heat water. Where did you learn how to clean an animal?"

"I hunted with the ranch hands."

"And they made tea?"

"No, but they taught me how to field dress my deer and it's all about the same from one critter to the next. I learned how to make tea by reading about outdoor survival and then trying things on my own. That's how I learned how to make a fish trap, too. We need to check the trap in the morning in case there is breakfast waiting. And we need to take it down. Any kind of trap we make needs to be taken down before we leave the area. I don't want to leave critters trapped. I only take from the woods what I know I will use wisely."

"You've gone deer hunting?"

"Sure, the ranch hands go out hunting every season. They bring back two deer, although they could bring back one per hunter. We only take two because that's what they use in a year. Usually Steve and Randy each shoot a buck, but when I was a teenager Steve let me do it for the practice. At that point he was a better shot, but I could get closer to the herd. He made brownie points with the boss when he came back with a stalking story for my dad. I had a lot of pressure growing up to keep up with the hands, especially Steve. My dad considered him the stable one, so he was the one I was supposed to be like."

"Was your dad a hard man to live with as a kid?"

"Only occasionally. As long as I was out doing things he approved of, he let me do just about anything. Even when I got in trouble at school, he was pleased with me if I got in trouble for doing something he approved of, so he usually didn't give me a hard time. When he did, though, I sure knew it. When I wrecked a dirt bike I had to fix it myself. When I got stuck on the side of the road going to town because I hadn't checked the truck over I spent the summer rotating tires, checking oil, air filters and replacing everything that can be replaced on a truck. If I put Shasta up without brushing him down, I was assigned stable boy duties for two weeks and had to do all the horse care. So I learned a lot because of him. I got mad, but I never got vindictive. I knew I deserved what I got and now I'm glad I learned all the things I did."

"What did your mom think of all that?"

"She thought he was being hard on me, but he never asked me to do anything that would hurt me, so she let it go and sympathized with me."

I wondered why Rusty asked me so many questions, and then I wondered the same things about him, but we were all talked out and sleepy so I didn't take my chance to ask him.

Chapter 3

In the morning I slipped out from under the parachute and made my way back to the fish trap. After our fish dinner, I wasn't hungry and I enjoyed being in these woods far from the dry forest back home, so I quickly walked back to the fish trap without tracking. It almost cost me my life. Why is it the only times I don't track is when I should be? If I'd been reading the ground I would have been warned, but I was just strolling down to check the trap, thinking the water was going to be freezing, thinking I should probably take my jeans off so my clothes wouldn't get wet. It was too chilly to walk around in wet clothes. I didn't need to get sick, and lost, and hungry all at once. I came around a tree and nearly barreled into the backside of a bear. He was investigating the odors from where we'd cooked. Oh man! I backed off quickly and hid behind a tree, then, since Rusty had never seen a bear, I jogged back to our sleeping spot, now fully awake.

"Rusty! Quick! Come see what I found! Bring your gun."

He was alert in an instant.

"What is it?"

"Come see! But be careful. Stay behind me. Stay quiet."

This time I was tracking like mad but I hadn't crossed the bear's trail when I'd gone to check the trap until the last second. I approached the place carefully, all my senses aware. Now I could smell the distinct barnyard odor of a bear. I slowed and stayed behind trees until I located the bear foraging in the leftovers from our meal the night before, then he followed his nose down to the creek and investigated my fish trap. He shouldered the sticks aside and I watched helplessly as they floated downstream. I watched beside Rusty as our breakfast was caught and eaten raw. I was thrilled and angry at the same time. I'd never observed a bear for this length of time or from this close up, but there was a lot of work involved in cutting and whittling those sticks! It would take hours to replace them.

The stalker in me wanted to try to touch the bear but I knew there was little chance of that happening with Rusty here. The tracker in me wanted to examine the footprints, but I knew to wait until the bear had gone. So we stood silently and watched as the bear cleaned up camp and then waded across the creek and disappeared into the woods.

I turned to Rusty. "Isn't that cool!" I said enthusiastically.

"That was cool," he agreed smiling.

"I've never been so happy and so mad at a wild animal in all my life.

Look what he did to our breakfast."

"We'll figure out something. At least we got a good dinner out of it."

"You were lucky I didn't try and stalk it. Let's go look at the tracks!"

"Cass, do you know what time it is?"

"Yeah, it's daytime. That means we can see the tracks now."

It was, just barely. It had been nearly dark the first time I'd gone to check the trap. We stepped into camp and I cast around for some good tracks. There were some leading down to the stream, big round front paws and big wide, almost human looking back paws. If a bear was declawed, that's what Big Foot's footprints would look like, I thought. I pointed the tracks out to Rusty so he'd remember what bear tracks looked like.

"Do you think it's worth wading out there to see what I can recover?" I asked.

"No way. It's cold outside the creek, I don't want you down in that icy water."

"Oh well, being able to see a bear that close up made the whole trip worthwhile!"

When we got back to camp I shook off the dew and rolled the parachute up with the snare inside. We started walking up the creek, glad to have a ready supply of water. The food that day consisted of cattails. The young leaves, weird looking sprouts and the roots are edible, so we pulled several plants and harvested what we could use. It wasn't the best meal we'd ever eaten. I knew other parts of the plant were useful too, but we needed food and we used the parts most easily eaten. I set up the snare but didn't catch anything. The night was cold and damp and we clung to each other dejectedly. I knew the day had taken its toll on Rusty's positive outlook and I brooded over it, so we fell asleep with little to say.

In the morning I slipped away to check the snare and was pleased to find a small rodent. It wouldn't do much to fill us up but it was food. I was trying to guess what it was. A vole? Well, I wasn't going to be picky, food was food. I cleaned and skinned the animal then started a fire. Rusty woke up when he heard the fire crackling. He watched as I turned the animal this way and that.

"How did you catch an animal that small?"

"It was in the snare."

"I'm surprised it was big enough to trip it. What is it?"

"Meat."

"You know what I mean."

"Are you really that worried about it? To be honest I don't know for sure what it is. I'm guessing it's vole but as far as we're concerned it's just meat."

Hungry as he was, he still seemed dubious.

"It won't hurt you. I've heard that nearly all animals are edible."

So we ate vole for breakfast. We shared our meager meal and spent the day looking for edible plants, chewing on grass and hiking. I had Rusty set up the snare when we stopped for the night. I showed him the game trail and let him set and test the snare. Next I taught him how to spot a game trail. This was good practice for him. I thought I should really have him make his own snare, but it was easier to just use the one we had.

When darkness fell we found a sleeping spot and curled up together knowing it would be another very cold night. I had barely drifted off when I was awakened by the oddest noise. It sounded like weird laughter and it continued off in the distance.

"Rusty," I almost whispered, "What's that?"

"It's just a bird of some kind."

"I wonder if it's loons. The pilot asked me if I'd ever heard loons before. He said there would be some at the lake and that we should go out in the canoe to see them. Maybe the lake is close by."

"We'll see in the morning. Try and sleep."

It was like listening to coyotes back home. I never could sleep with coyotes howling. I wanted to go see them, and now I wanted to go see the loons. I needed the rest though and knew not to go wandering at night, so I lay there listening and before long the woods were quiet again and it was morning.

I slipped out of Rusty's arms and from under the parachute, then went to check the snare again. Empty. I was hungry after a day of eating nothing but half a vole and some grass. I wandered around in the nearby woods looking for edibles. A big piece of cheesecake would do nicely. I knew we'd run into more cattails along the creek but was hoping for something that tasted a little better. Berries would be nice. Blueberries, or strawberries, or blackberries would be wonderful. Fish, or rabbit, or squirrel. Anything. I thought about cutting more sticks for another fish trap, but it would take me half the morning to do that.

I crawled back under the parachute, found my place, and burrowed close to Rusty waiting for his day to begin. I thought over what had happened since our wedding day, how we came so close to losing each other, once to the plane, again to the parachute jump and again simply because of lost hope. I told myself to always hope. Always. If there was ever a hopeless situation we'd been through it.

Rusty smelled like the woods, like pine, and dirt, and smoke, and cooked fish. After a while he stirred, noticed I was still there, and hugged me close.

"You okay?" he asked.

"Yeah, I'm fine. The snare is empty. I looked around for edible plants and didn't see any so I came back to bed."

"To bed, the bare ground is back to bed?"

"It is if you're here sleeping on it."

"How far do you think a loon's call travels?"

"I don't know, not a mile. It sounded distant but even a distant call would be within a mile."

"What if it's another uninhabited lake?"

"We'll walk around it to be sure. You know, they really need to label their lakes up here. If we started out at Lower Loon Lake it makes sense that this would be Upper Loon Lake. But we don't know for sure what lake we started out from."

"I suppose you're ready to travel."

"Maybe, I'll check the snare one more time and take it down."

While Rusty shook out the parachute I went to check the snare and found it was still empty. Coming back empty handed, he looked at me like it was his fault.

"We'll keep to the stream. We should at least find more cattails."

He nodded. We bundled up the snare, the rabbit pelt, and the parachute, then Rusty slung it on his back. We followed the stream. If we didn't reach the lake by mid afternoon, I'd make another fish trap. I walked along tracking carefully, watching the forest floor for anything edible. Guess I could introduce Rusty to pine cones, I thought. We could make pine needle tea, too. Lists of edible plants were running through my mind as we walked, but I didn't know what many of them looked like and several of them came with warnings, "do not mistake for poison hemlock" and things like that. So, although I knew the names of many edible plants, I also knew to be wary. While walking along, heading north, and watching for food, something caught my attention. An irregularity. Something odd. I am always tuned to things out of place and most people wouldn't have noticed it at all. However, being a tracker, footprints are of special interest to me, so when I saw the aged footprint of a person I was brought up short. Could I follow this trail? It had to be at least a week old. It was fainter than the week old trails I'd followed in search and rescue. But, since it was a person's trail, it had to go somewhere logical.

I examined the footprint. I used my fingers to press it down and make the shape more distinct. It was small and narrow. A woman. A small footprint should have a short stride. I began looking for the next track, and the next. Rusty saw the transformation take place. He saw me slip into tracker mode, noticed the shift in my thinking and then my actions. He saw me switch from his little, enthusiastic, outdoors guide and wife, and turn into a wilderness detective. The trail took study. The ground was good, but the woman was light, and she moved easily in the woods. I felt like I was tracking myself. In many places the trail had been erased completely. It would appear faintly in the shelter of a tree and disappear where the tree had shed rain onto the tracks. I found a few tracks here, and a few tracks there, then followed the woman through the woods and down to a lake. A lake! Yes! But the footprints led to a rocky shore and vanished. I studied the shore for more footprints but didn't find any.

"Do you think she got into a canoe or something?" I thought aloud, "The pilot said we should get out in the canoes to see animals and birds. But you'd think there would be tracks going from the canoe as well as to it…Unless she was going some place in the canoe. Let's backtrack her."

We followed the tracks back through the woods until we reached the spot we started at. I then carefully tracked the woman back to her original starting place. It wasn't far. Her footprints cut through the woods and led to a small cabin which appeared to have been vacant for many weeks. We found the front door unlocked, and the inside neat and orderly. We could tell the place had only been lived in for a short time. We then looked around for evidence that this cabin may have been rented from the same company that Rusty had used to book our honeymoon cabin. The fact that it had only been occupied for a short time, and had a wooden number five on the front door, helped confirm our hopes. That wasn't much to go on. However it did give us hope of finding four more cabins, so we made our way to the lake and walked around it, keeping an eye out for buildings. Where the beach was rock we followed the margin between rock and vegetation hoping to catch footprints again. At last we found a path leading from the lake to cabin number four. Even though all the footprints on the path led away from the cabin we went up and knocked. An older woman answered the door. The scent from cooking came floating out the open door. Oh man! How could she do this to us? I didn't know what to say. I was too busy being hungry! Rusty slipped into detective mode.

"Good afternoon," he said calmly, "I was wondering if you could help us. Can you tell us who is in charge of the cabins up here and how to find that person?"

The woman stared at us open mouthed. "Normally there isn't anybody. The pilots hand out all that information when we land. But there was a man here going from cabin to cabin telling us to watch for a young couple. That was days ago. He was supposed to stay and watch for them, and he asked everybody to send them to cabin number two. It's the one with a dock. Are you the couple everyone is looking for?"

"It's very possible," he said, "Thank you for your help."

The woman looked as if she really wanted to hear our story but that would have to wait. Food and information were more important. If there were people searching for us they needed to know our location.

We went down to the lake, following the shore until we came to a dock, and then took the pathway to cabin number two. Before we reached the porch a man burst out of the cabin.

"Well, I'll be a monkey's uncle!" he exclaimed. "Never in a million years did I expect to see you two alive. When they sent me out here I thought it was pointless. Who could find this place? Who had the know how? Not city slickers from California, that's for sure. Searchers found the plane but there was no sign of you two. They sent out dogs, did flyovers of the crash site. Nothing. Come on in."

"We weren't on the plane when it crashed. We bailed out over some lake south of here," Rusty said.

"The pilot?" I asked, "Did the pilot make it?"

"Who, Pete? Shit. I think nothing could kill old Pete. He'll live. Again. I'm surprised he'll still go up, as many times as he's come down the wrong way. He's laid up pretty good but he'll make it. Twasn't 'til just recently we were able to talk to him. Come in. You folks need help. You've been run through the mill."

"I think we're fine. No injuries. Just a hell of a long time looking for this place. There will be time to talk later," Rusty said, "We haven't eaten much the past day or so and we'd like to wash up. Where can we get some food and a shower?"

"Cabin one. It's all yours. I need to get some information from you whenever you're ready. I'd like to head back to town in the morning. If you want a lift out, you can fly out with me. If you need medical attention I can get a plane over today."

"No!" I said quickly.

"Cass, you really want to stay after all we've been through?"

"Yes! I want to canoe and I want to see a moose and I want to see how loons make that weird noise. I want to track the animals around the lake and…"

"Okay, I get the point. We can stay." Then to the officer, "It's hard to keep this girl down."

We walked over to cabin one and were met with a nice cozy, romantic getaway cottage. There was a kitchen, living room and bathroom downstairs, and a loft with a big, soft bed. The place was fully stocked, ready for our use. We dug into the first junk food we could get our hands on, cookies. One whole package of cookies down and we were ready to get cleaned up. We then took turns showering in the little bathroom downstairs. I didn't have a hairbrush, hairdryer, clean clothes or make-up. I'd worn holes in my socks from hiking five days in the same pair, but I was happy and comfortable. I hoped to be able to sleep indoors after so many nights in the open in survival mode. It wasn't unusual for me to feel claustrophobic after a time of survival. It wasn't a fearful feeling, just too closed in. I liked to see the sky above me. In the end, though, the warmth of the cabin won out.

I found meal kits in the freezer. Not really instant meals but something that could be prepared with minimal fuss and mess. I pulled out enough for two and started figuring out the stove controls. There was a knock on the door and Rusty let in the officer we'd spoken to earlier.

"Have you eaten?" I asked, "It's just as easy to cook for three."

"Sure, if it isn't any trouble," the guy said, "By the way, I'm Bryce Buckner. Some people call me Bryce and some people call me Buck, just depends on the situation."

"Just like Strict," I said.

"Strict?" he asked.

"Yeah, he's our search commander. His name is Lou Strickland. He reminds me of a combination between my grandfather and a drill sergeant in the Marines. So, when he's all business we all call him Strict. But he has a hard time thinking of me like he does the other officers so more of the grandfather in him shows through and I end up calling him Lou a lot."

"You do a lot of search and rescue in California?"

"Yeah, a lot. If I wasn't on my honeymoon I'd probably be out there looking for some lost tourist in the Angeles Forest."

Buck looked at Rusty. "What about you?"

"Don't look at me, I'm a detective. We wouldn't have made it here without Cassidy's know how. She found food where I would have sworn there was none. She knew the lake was north of where we were and she found the cabins. All I did was carry the pack and gun. We didn't even fire the gun. She wanted to save it for defense."

"You see anything to make you think you needed it?" Buck asked.

"We saw a bear but we just observed it from a distance. There was no reason to shoot." Rusty said.

"It stole our breakfast though and that was two days ago. We haven't had much to eat since then," I added.

"Look, I've got these reports I need to fill out. If you can just give me the information I need I'll be out of your way."

"We don't mind. We know the drill, the paperwork involved. And we haven't had news since the plane crashed so it's nice to talk to someone. We had quite an adventure since we bailed out," I told him.

"I bet," Buck said.

"No, really, you wouldn't believe it. I barely do and I watched it happen," Rusty added.

Usually Rusty avoided talking about my near misses and I was surprised that he was willing to recount it all for Bryce. I was glad he was ready to talk about our close call. It meant he had come to grips with it. The two men talked while I cooked and occasionally Buck would steal glances my way.

Dinner tasted a little preprocessed but we exchanged search stories with Buck and helped with his paperwork. Finally he stood to leave.

"Okay, one more thing. The guys that own this company are a little worried about the legal aspects of your plane crash."

"They're worried about getting sued?"

He shuffled his feet, looked at the floor.

"They don't have to worry about that. We're not after their money. They can put their lawyer fees into buying new parachutes. Is there a town nearby?"

"Yes, but there's no road to it. The people that come up to this lake do it because they think it's remote. They get flown in and they only see the other campers up here, so it feels remote to a tourist, but there is a town about five miles east of here. Don't try to get to it on foot."

"Why not?" I asked. "All we have are the clothes on our backs and we need to arrange for new plane tickets so we can get home again. I'd hike five miles to be able to do a little shopping."

"Look, my office is in Taylor and I'm flying out tomorrow. Fly out with me and I'll make sure you have a way back."

"You think I'll get lost looking for a town?" I asked, "A town that's due east of here?"

"No, but I'd rather not set a precedence. You hike out of here and some other yahoo is going to try it and I'll never hear the end of it. I can get you a ride back. If Charlie can't do it the guys that own these cabins will certainly find a way. They owe you anyway. A five mile plane ride is chump change after what they were worrying about."

So that's what we did. Not wanting to go into Taylor smelling the way we did, that night I hand washed our clothes as best I could and let them dry overnight in front of the heater. They were still a bit damp in the morning but smelled better, and they dried out fast once we put them on and moved about. We boarded another small plane and got whisked over the mountain to a quaint, little town. Bryce took us to his office downtown and we visited all three stores in the four block downtown area. We bought toiletries, clothes, new backpacks and a camera. I was especially glad to find a camera. Now, if I saw a moose, I'd be able to take a picture of it. And I really wanted some pictures of my honeymoon even if it was just the last five days of it. I took a picture of beautiful downtown Taylor and then another of Upper Loon Lake from the air.

When we got back to the cabin Rusty took the toiletries to the bathroom.

"What do you think, Cass, should the beard stay or go?"

"I bought the razor for me, not you. Keep the beard for now. If you put on that plaid flannel shirt and get in the canoe you'll look just like a local. Kelly will get a kick out of a picture like that. It'll make him want to come up here for his anniversary."

Later I took a picture of Rusty in the canoe, and another one of him with the remains of his parachute.

"Save the parachute if you can. I have plans for it if we can bring it home with us."

The cabin was wonderful. It was snug and warm and outdoorsy feeling. We spent toasty evenings in front of the fireplace eating dinner at the coffee table just like we used to before Rusty got our dining room table back home. We went out in the canoe and discovered that loons usually make that weird noise when it is too dark to see them. We saw one moose while in the canoe, and I quickly snapped a picture in case that was my only chance. It was wading in the shallows at the north end of the lake. It reached into the lake with its mouth and pulled up plants so it was nicely distracted. I beached the canoe and then stalked the moose on foot. I didn't want to get too close because I didn't know the normal disposition of a moose. It was big and, if it turned on me, I could be in trouble. Each time it put its head into the lake I was able to get closer by several feet. Rusty watched me from the canoe with a disposable camera. I was fascinated by the moose's size. It was taller than my horse! I'd freeze while it looked around and then step carefully closer while its head was under water. It brought its massive antlers up out of the lake dripping with water and aquatic plants. I snapped a picture. This was so cool! Moments like this were what I lived for. The moose was maybe ten feet into the lake and I was on the shore crouched in the brush when a group of older teenage boys came paddling up in a canoe.

"Hey, Bullwinkle!" they yelled at the moose.

The animal grunted and turned, storming up the shore, and rushing right past me. I took a quick picture as it came my way and then dove for cover. It tromped through the brush and then disappeared into the woods. I was disappointed, and elated. I'd been this close to a moose! I returned to the canoe beaming and Rusty was shaking his head at me, his normal response to my minor close calls.

"Did you see that? If I wasn't jumping out of the way I could have touched it!" I said excitedly.

"I think jumping out of the way was the wiser choice," he said.

"Next time, you try it," I urged him.

"I'd rather watch you," he replied.

"I won't take you scouting unless you learn to move silently. Sneaking up on animals is good practice for you."

Rusty and I went back to the tracks and I showed him the moose's big hoof prints in the dirt. I tracked the moose a little way through the brush. I liked to get a feel for how different animals moved through the woods. This big guy didn't let anything stop him. He barreled through whatever was in his way, so it didn't take me long to give up and head back to the canoe.

We paddled around the lake watching the odd way the loons swam with just their heads sticking up out of the water. There were ducks, geese, and coots on the lake too. Deer came to the lake regularly. Unafraid of the campers, they wandered between the cabins. The campers either ignored them or ran around taking pictures of them. I had tried stalking the deer but they were on the move and just trotted off when I approached.

I was thrilled when we were out in the canoe one day and I saw a short wet head appear out of nowhere. Whiskers danced around on its furry face. What was it? I never saw more than just a wet head, lots of whiskers, and tiny ears. It swam at the surface briefly and vanished.

Our five days went by quickly. We were granted an extra five days to make up for time lost after the plane crash, but Rusty had to get back to work. We reluctantly packed our meager possessions into our new backpacks and were ready to meet the plane when it landed. Word had gotten around and many of the campers were there to see us off. We ended up in a storytelling time on the dock. Not wanting to cast fear, I didn't want to tell them that our plane had crashed because everyone would be taking the same kind of plane out of there. Mostly I told them about our trek north and of the different ways we had found food. The young people liked hearing about the bear, and they told us about the animals they had seen at the lake.

At last a red and white pontoon plane swooped out of the sky and skimmed across the lake sending loons and ducks scampering for the reeds. It putted over to the dock where a man jumped out and hooked a rope over a post on the dock.

"Are the two Michaels present and accounted for?"

"Right here," we said.

"Are you sure you want out? You have five more days due to you."

"We'd love to stay," I said, "but we both have commitments back home. We have to go."

We loaded up into the little red and white pontoon plane and once again were whisked up into the big blue sky and flew off to St. Paul. I was glad we had bought new clothes. Just thinking about boarding a jet in the clothes we wore on our trek north made me cringe. Something must be wrong with me, I thought. I was actually looking forward to getting home where I would have soap, a curling iron and make-up again. I had a blast on my honeymoon, plane crash and all, and was happy with the way we had come through our ordeal. I was confident that we would have found more food and could have survived for weeks if it had been necessary. I was also pleased to be able to take pictures of the old corrugated metal "airport" and its floppy windsock, but wished there had been a chance to photograph the parachutes and the bear.

The airport at St. Paul was busy. People rushing here and there, running to catch flights, so may people. This was the hard part of coming back to civilization for me. The crowds. Everything felt so crowded and busy. I felt pressed from every side and took Rusty's arm as he made his way through the masses to our gate. I was on sensory overload, forced to just follow. I fell into my seat on the airplane with a sigh of relief.

"I wonder if our bags were inspected." I contemplated out loud to Rusty. "If they were, I bet they were really wondering about us. Two sets of dirty clothes, a snare, an old parachute, my hunting knife and some basic toiletries. I hope my knife makes it through the trip. It's been through some interesting times with me."

"Maybe you should leave it at home if it means that much to you," he said.

"If I'd have left it at home we wouldn't have eaten for five days. I used it to make the snare, and to cut plants to eat, and whittle the sticks down for the fish trap, and to start fires. We wouldn't have even had a fire without the knife along. Sometimes you can get a spark off the magnesium stick with a rock but you can't count on it."

"Maybe we need to get you a cheap, new fangled knife that you don't care about losing for trips like this."

"No, I think my hunting knife leads a charmed life or something. I've had that knife since I was twelve, and it has never been lost, and it is always there for me."

"I wish some of that would rub off on you. You could use a charmed life."

"Maybe I've got one. Maybe that's why I'm still around. How do you know if you've led a charmed life if you don't test it every so often?"

"I'd rather not know. Stop testing it."

LAX was just as busy as St. Paul had been, even at eleven o'clock at night. We landed uneventfully and made our way to the baggage claim. The convenience stores, newsstands, and bakeries were all closed, and I gazed forlornly at the cases where cheesecake had been sitting all day long just waiting for me. Now that I was here the bakery was closed. We picked up our two backpacks and headed for the Explorer, left in long-term parking. I felt sorry for it sitting here in downtown L.A. while we went off on adventures without it.

The drive up the 405 and the 14 was uneventful and the house was cool, dark, and quiet when we finally entered in the wee hours of the morning. We set down our packs and both gave a sigh of relief.

Chapter 4

The next day we had to get back in the swing of things. Rusty drove into town to check in at the station. I restocked the house and picked up Shadow, my lively Shetland sheepdog, from the kennel. Lou Strickland called to make sure I had returned and would be at the search and rescue meeting at his house that evening. Fortunately he didn't ask me to tell him about the trip. I spent the day puttering around the house, pulling weeds around the corral and mowing the lawn. In the afternoon, I started dinner and when Rusty came home we ate quickly before heading for Lou's house. Rusty wasn't required to attend the search and rescue meetings, but liked to stay on top of things, and he knew everyone so he usually attended too. The meetings were not just for my little team. There were several teams that worked both together and separately in the area. My team was called when tracking was required but there were other teams trained in varied areas of expertise and Lou constantly worked at expanding the skills of the different teams so that they increasingly overlapped.

"Hey, hey, our little tracker has returned from the wilds of Minnesota!" Thez called out when we walked in. Their little tracker. I thought it was funny how they called me that, but it was exactly how I felt when I was with them.

"How was the honeymoon you two?" Victor asked.

"It was exciting. We had a blast!" I replied.

Victor, Landon and Thez exchanged glances. If I described something as exciting they knew something had happened. They knew my definition of exciting went way beyond the norm.

Victor broke first. "Okay, spill," he said grimly.

"Guys! We're happy to be back and we had a great time. Isn't a honeymoon supposed to be exciting?"

"We know your definition of exciting. Exciting to you is being hunted by lunatic serial killers and cornered by angry rattlesnakes. Let's see, they went to the woods in Minnesota. You got attacked by bears?" Thez guessed.

"Nope sorry, we did see one though." I answered, "That was great! I saw a moose too!"

"Good evening!" Lou announced as the meeting got underway. "If everybody can take a seat somewhere we will get started."

"Strict, you can't do this to us," Victor said. "Cassidy has another tall tale to tell us and she's not talking. We've got to pry it out of her or she'll escape and leave us all hanging until the next search."

"You guys need to wait. What are we going to talk about on the trail if I tell you the whole story at a meeting?" I asked.

"Out with it," said Lou. So we sat and I told them all about it but left out the part about my parachute not opening.

"So we dropped into the woods of Minnesota with no food and no water. Fortunately, Minnesota has a lot of water. We gathered dew and we found streams. We snared a rabbit and caught fish. One day we ate nothing but cattails. All we knew was our cabin was on a lake and the lake was north of us. We couldn't count on search and rescue because we were nowhere near where the plane went down. We didn't even know if the pilot was alive to tell people where to look."

"So what happened?" Thez asked.

"It took us five very hungry days, but eventually we found the lake and our cabin, and we had a wonderful time."

"Michaels? What is she leaving out?" Landon wanted to know.

"The part you won't believe. You'd think she was nuts, so she left that part out."

"This is Cassidy we are talking about. We don't believe that's all there is to it."

Rusty shrugged.

"These guys are getting harder and harder to keep entertained," I said. "What do I have to do, jump out of the plane without a parachute and live to tell about it?"

"That would be more up to your speed."

"Oh, come on guys, would you really believe me if I told you I jumped out of the airplane without a parachute? Would you?"

The room grew silent. They weren't sure. This was me we were talking about. Anything was possible.

Sigh, "Okay, I did have a parachute but it didn't open. There, is that better?"

More silence.

"I give up. Strict, the show is all yours."

"Wait!"

"Yes, Thez?" asked Lou.

"You didn't really jump out of the airplane without a working parachute, did you?"

"Yeah, I did, but I managed to untangle it on the way down."

"Michaels, what did you do?" Thez asked Rusty.

"I watched helplessly from my working parachute and couldn't do anything. I couldn't tell what she was doing tumbling through the air. Then the chute sort of opened but she was landing so fast. All I could do was watch. She splashed down in a lake and I landed in the woods. I ran down to the lake, but I couldn't see anything out there. I couldn't do anything and didn't know anything for what seemed like an eternity." Rusty paused. A very long pause, he took a deep breath, exhaled slowly, then got up and stalked out the front door. I found him standing outside trying to compose himself. He glanced at me forlornly.

"I'm sorry, babe, I lost it."

"It's okay, they all know how you feel. Well, my team does anyway. The others, they can guess. It's okay. You're allowed to have feelings too, you know. They may joke and push for stories but they do it so they can deal with it all. They hear it and joke about it so they can process it. You run into the same stuff at work. So don't worry about it."

He could accept that.

"Wait until you hear Lou talking and I'll get us back in without them noticing, and then we can sit in the back. Walk softly."

The meeting continued, something about a quicker response time on the Mathis search. I silently opened the door and we slipped in, walked softly to the back of the group and found a place to stand.

I wasn't familiar with what was being discussed in the meeting because it involved the calls that happened while I was gone. When I was in town word got around. We all heard about the searches second or third hand, but this time I had no background on a lot of what they were discussing. They had been busy. Fortunately, it had been more broad field searches and urban searches than tediously slow tracking searches.

"Cassidy, you'll be relieved to know Thomas Parker is once again safe at home. He's starting at college, majoring in business and accounting so maybe you won't see him for a while."

"Where did he get lost this time?" I asked.

"Guffy."

"You can't get lost from Guffy. It's on the top of a mountain. You go downhill to leave it. You go up hill to find it."

"Yeah, but this is Thomas Parker we are talking about."

"That's true."

I'd found Thomas Parker twice. I was curious how many other teams had found him. He managed to get lost every time he ventured into the mountains.

The meeting went on with questions, discussion and training days. I never got called to training days. Strict and Rusty didn't want me to get involved in aquatic rescues, rock climbing or apprehensions. So my list of training options was a bit limited. I always took the CPR class when it came up. I went to the rock climbing wall at the fire training station just because I was allowed and it was fun. I also practiced at the firing range and worked out at the gym.

"Cassidy, if some of us were interested in learning outdoor survival, would you be willing to teach us what you know?" asked Mark Hamil, a member of a different team.

That took me by surprise.

"Guys, you know as much as I do. You could snare a rabbit and catch a fish. You can read a book about edible plants. You just have to use your head."

"How did you know what to do on your trip?"

"I'd studied it as a kid and tried it on camping trips and then later I went on real survival trips. This was only the second time I'd been forced to use it."

"What would have happened out there if you didn't know what to do?"

"We still would have gotten by. We saved Rusty's gun for defense but we could have used it to hunt. You all carry. You could hunt for food."

"What if we'd like to try a trip out there where we had to get by on our wits alone?"

"Then you better make sure you've got a good supply of wits."

"Aw, come on Cassidy, you seem to know a thing or two. What could you teach us?"

"The first thing you have to do is learn to see things differently. You have to see the uses in everything. Instead of seeing a hillside you need to see the tracks and game trails. You have to look at a field and see the nutritional value of grasses, the uses for it. You have to see plants for what they really are. Some are edible and can help you, while others are poisonous and can kill you. Some you have to cook, some you can just harvest. Then there are others you can make things out of. You have to be able to see nature and see its uses, not just as pretty flowers, majestic trees, little furry animals. Flowers can be food, trees can too if you know what to do with them. Trees have many uses. Branches can be made into pieces for snares or a spear or a bow for hunting. Animals are food and if you are cold and know how to clean them you can use their fur for insulation to keep warm. Fine bones can be needles. There's more than one way to see almost anything in nature. You have to learn to see everything differently. Are you willing to change your perceptions of things that are seemingly set in your mind? You need to see manmade things in a different light, too. On our trip I was adamant that we find Rusty's parachute. Why?"

I looked around the room and received blank stares.

"We used the cords when we made the snare and we used the fabric to collect dew when we weren't near water. We could have also used the parachute for a fish net if it had been needed. So you see, you mostly need to change the way you think about things."

Judging from their reaction it appeared as if they had never thought of survival in that way before.

"Thez, what do you need to catch a fish?" I asked.

"Well, I guess for the most basic set up you need a hook, line and bait," he answered.

"What if you don't have a hook? What could you use?"

"A hooked stick? The right bone?"

"That's possible. Whatever it is has to be stronger that the fish's mouth. What if you don't have fishing line?"

"That's tougher."

"What could you use for bait?"

"Anything to trick a fish. A leaf?"

"Or some fur or something icky and smelly. Rusty, what do you need to catch a fish?"

"Thirty sticks," he answered, "and a quick hand."

"What if you don't have a quick hand?"

"Then we could have used the parachute to net them."

"Or?"

"Or we could have speared them."

"So with thirty sticks and another long stick you can have fish for as long as you stay near the trap. Game wardens aren't nice to people who use fish traps, though. Only use one in a survival situation. My point is, you can always find sticks in the woods. You can't always find a hook, line and bait. So you need to use the things you *can* find to your advantage."

Lou watched the discussion with interest. Maybe all this was showing him that I really did have a head on my shoulders. I was prepared when he sent me on a search. I wasn't just some kid girl who happened to know how to follow tracks. I knew a thing or two.

Chapter 5

We were home several days before the deer came down to our property. They grazed on the lawn and wandered past the corral. I was very excited but let them be in peace this time. I wanted them to know they were welcome at our home and that no one would hurt them. I would stalk them later, after they were used to coming and felt comfortable with people present. After Rusty went to work and I'd finished a few chores, I put some trail mix in the day pack, called Shadow to me and set out following the deer. I wanted to see where they came from and where they went. It was important to me because I wanted to study the route and see if this was a regular thing they did or if that morning had just been a fluke. I followed the tracks out the back of our property across the rolling, juniper covered hills and up into the forest. As the desert slowly gave way to forest I settled in, becoming more focused on what I was doing. The shade closed in around me and I studied the trail the deer had left behind. On and on it went until at last I saw the tan backs of deer up ahead. I'd caught up with the herd but didn't want to scare them so I fell back, just watching. They were still on the move but they were slow about it, grazing as they went. I ate trail mix as I went along and was so absorbed in what I was doing that I didn't noticed when the day had passed.

The sun was setting and I wondered how far I'd tracked from home. I wasn't worried about getting back because I could just follow the tracks, but I thought I better do it while I could still see them. I turned back and had no trouble following the deer tracks, but noticed I did have trouble finding my own tracks. It reminded me that I still had a tracking challenge from Chase to deal with, and wondered how hard he would be to track. I quit backtracking the deer and began backtracking myself for practice. I now realized that I had been hiding my footprints as I walked and had to look carefully to find them. Darkness fell and as the tracks became more difficult to see, I admitted to myself that I wasn't going to track my way back that night. Unsure of the distance, I started walking, heading in the direction of the house. I hadn't realized how far I'd gone. I had probably been tracking at a slow walk for several hours and could be four miles from home. So how far did I still have to go? I didn't know but I wasn't worried. I was actually more irritated with myself for losing track of time. Rusty would be home now and I should have started cooking dinner hours ago.

I scanned the homes below looking for familiar lights, but I didn't see any. I'd left home during daytime and couldn't remember if I'd turned on any lights so my house could be totally dark. Heading for the lights that were visible seemed like a reasonable way to find the road so I walked in that direction. Half an hour later I made my way around a house and stumbled up onto a road but I wasn't sure if it was mine or another one. There were no street lights out there in the hills and I had to stay on the road by feel. At last the one road I was following intersected with another and I was able to read the signs. Lost Hills Road and Juniper Road. I turned down Lost Hills Road, amused by the double pun, and eventually spotted my house in the distance with the Jeep and the Explorer parked in the driveway. I snuck around the house trying to determine where Rusty was so I could get in without a fuss. He was talking on the phone in his office so I snuck around back and silently slipped in the back door. I walked without a sound through the house and then peeked in his office door. I came up behind him and placed my hands around his shoulders.

"Sorry I'm late," I said quietly, not wanting to interrupt his conversation. I turned to go fix some dinner but Rusty held onto my hand and drew me onto his lap. He handed me the phone.

"Good luck, kid, you're gonna need it," said Lou.

"Why? What did I do this time?"

"I'm glad you're home. I'm going to bed."

"Okay, good night."

I snapped the phone closed and handed it to Rusty. He took it from me and then wrapped his arms around me.

"Rusty, you can't worry every time I turn around. I tracked the deer. I lost track of time. That's all."

"You can't track at night. It's been dark for three hours."

"It has? I knew it was getting dark but, by the time I noticed, I was way out in the hills. I tried to track my way home but it got too dark so I was just looking for the house. It just took me a while to find my way home."

"You should leave a note or something."

"I thought I'd be gone an hour or two. If I left a note and said I'd be gone for an hour or two and then didn't come home till after dark you'd just be more worried. Look, you knew I wasn't on a call because I took Shadow. You knew I couldn't have gone far. I left the Jeep. So I had to be close by."

"Tell me when I should start worrying. You can't. The longer I know you the quicker you get into trouble."

"How much trouble could I get into within walking distance of home? What's the worst that could happen?"

"You could have been attacked by a mountain lion."

"And what are the chances of that happening?"

"To anybody else? One in a million. To you? Fifty fifty."

"Very funny, I was tracking mountain lion bait and I still didn't see a mountain lion."

The next day Rusty came home with a magnetic white board. He posted it on the refrigerator.

"When you plan your day just write notes. Would it bother you to just write down your plans? I know you get distracted and I know you get stuck and unplanned things happen. I'd just like some clue what's going on."

The next day I dutifully wrote, "Backtracking mountain lion bait @ 2 PM," and then set out. This time I would be more conscientious and planned to keep track of the time. I followed the deer trail backwards to see where they had started from when they came to our house. I knew deer didn't exactly have a circuit that they walked but I also knew they were creatures of habit. If there was a meadow, a spring or a pleasant place to bed down on their back trail I wanted to know about it so I could meet them there some time. I also wanted to be able to take Rusty there. It would help his scouting abilities immensely if he could stalk deer on his own. So on I went. The tracking was easy. A small herd of deer leaves a lot of tracks. I followed the trail back into the woods. The deer had investigated several neighboring houses before they had reached ours. When the deer left the houses and their trail came down out of the pines I was rewarded with a very well grazed clearing in amongst the pine trees. Deer tracks were everywhere. Grasses were bent this way and that from deer wandering as they grazed. I'd hit the jackpot and had accomplished my goal. Well, the first step of my goal. I still didn't know when I could find the deer at the clearing but at least I knew they frequented the area. I arrived home and wrote on the board, "Mission accomplished," and drew a smiley face.

The white board came in handy. On Thursday I wrote, "Leave the Explorer, I need to buy wood." And so on Friday I had the SUV and drove into town to buy supplies to start my new agility course. I began with things that were quick to make, hurdles and jumps, but I bought some lumber for a bigger project too, the A-frame. I brought all the wood home and stacked it in the barn next to the table saw. I left the plywood in the truck so Rusty would help me unload it. I didn't mind unloading it but I knew he'd rather help me. I spent the afternoon happily making a jump for the agility course. I had one jump finished and ready for paint by the time Rusty came home.

On Friday I wrote on the board, "Backtracking mountain lion bait again tomorrow, want to come along?" And he wrote next to it, "Sure, but not before dawn."

Saturday we slept in. It didn't really matter when we left for the clearing since we weren't sure when the deer would be there. We took a leisurely shower, which meant we ended up back in bed and then back in the shower. We ate a leisurely breakfast, packed up the trail mix and headed out.

"You're not tracking the deer," Rusty observed as we walked along.

"That's because I know where they came from. I found a clearing that they like and I want to find out when they are there. So we are just trying to pinpoint their habits. We don't need to track them. If you want to track something track me. You wanted to learn how to do that anyway."

"I can do it when you let me but you forget and hide your tracks."

"If you really want to track me you're going to have to get used to me hiding my tracks. I can't help it. It just comes naturally to me. I do occasionally leave a trail on purpose. I did in Minnesota and I did when I was on the Troy search. A good reason will make me leave a trail but, you're right, I do tend forget and hide my tracks."

We came upon the clearing cautiously so we wouldn't startle the deer but they weren't there. I inspected the area carefully, examining the grasses for recent grazing. I found the edges of the grass had a serrated edge; a definite sign the deer had grazed there. Some edges were dry, from previous days, and some were more freshly cut. Maybe this was an early morning stop. I showed Rusty the grasses, explained my findings, and then pointed out all the other signs that indicated this was a favorite stopping place for the herd.

"Since the deer aren't here and there's nothing to stalk, stalk me," I suggested.

"You want me to stalk you?"

"Yeah, sneaking up on me at home is easy. Carpet absorbs the sound and walls block noise. If you really want to learn how to sneak up on me this is the perfect place to test it. You have dry grasses and branches to work your way through. Do you remember what I taught you about walking silently and stalking?"

"Yeah, but it's been months."

"I can't hear as good as a deer. I'll sit at that end of the clearing and you start from this end. If I can hear you I'll raise my hand so you know to be more careful."

"Cass, this is silly."

"You want to go scouting with me? You need to move silently. It might feel weird trying to sneak up on me but you're used to simulated exercises from academy. What's the difference?"

I sat at one end of the clearing with my back to him while he started out crouched in a stalk. Little telltale noises told me he wasn't comfortable. After analyzing them for a minute I realized he was leaning too far forward.

"You can stand upright to do this. You don't have to crouch to be quiet."

"How did you know?" he asked

"It's in the way you feel with your feet as you walk. If you feel something beneath your feet shift until you find a place that's silent to step. Take your time."

There was a moment's silence while he adjusted his attitude and then he started forward again. He was clumsy until he got into the flow of it, but then he began improving and continued for several steps before I raised my hand again. Then a few steps later I heard a similar noise from a different direction. I lifted my hand.

"You did not hear that," he said.

"You're right, what I heard was off to my right and you're coming in from the left. Now be quiet."

I heard the tall grass brush his jeans and raised my hand. Rusty stopped. Several more steps passed before I raised my hand again. Then I heard another noise off to my right and I tried to ignore it to better concentrate on Rusty. I raised my hand a few more times before sensing he was right behind me and then I turned around.

"Hey, you're doing better!" I said earnestly. "Do you want to try another exercise?"

"What kind?"

"Circle this meadow without me seeing you."

"You think I can do that?"

"You know the basics. Stay hidden or freeze when I look around, move when I'm distracted. Stay silent."

"You don't have anything to distract you and you'll know where I start."

"I'll give you a head start so you can find a different starting point and I can do something to provide a distraction. I can weave a mat out of grass while you try it."

"You're kidding, right?"

"No, you need the practice if you want to go scouting with me."

"When would we ever need to go scouting together?"

"There have been times when you wanted to go but I wouldn't let you. I wanted to scout out the canyon when Troy was up there but you wouldn't let me go alone. We could have gone together and found what he was looking for. I would have taken you with me if you had more practice. If we had scouted out the canyon we could have avoided the whole search and stand off. But if you don't want to that's okay. I'll just keep scouting alone."

He stood there, not wanting to play along but knowing I was completely serious. If he wanted to go into situations with me he would have to prove himself and the only way to prove himself was to try.

"All right," he said with a resigned sigh, "what do I have to do for this one?"

I went into the trees around the clearing and picked up four pinecones.

"These are shots. If I see you I'll throw a pinecone your way. Four shots and you're out. I'll give you a minute to find a starting place. Find it quietly or I'll know where you are anyway."

I sat in the clearing and started finding grasses for my mat. He went off to find a starting place. The clearing was not big, maybe half an acre. It was just a short exercise but it was good for him to practice. I was probably more likely to spot him than some unsuspecting criminal would be but more was on the line when we were on the job too. Then the shots were real and they were aimed.

Glancing up I was pleased that I couldn't see him right away. I picked long grasses and began weaving my mat, looking up when I thought I could catch him off guard. I looked behind me in case he had chosen an odd starting point. I scanned the woods around me. No Rusty, good! I weaved some more, glanced around, pretended to go back to my weaving and looked up instead. I perceived a movement off to my left and concentrated on that area. I glanced down as if to find more grass but picked up a pinecone instead. I located the tree I thought he would hide behind and glanced down again as if to weave. Then I reacted as if hearing a noise behind me and turned. There was that movement again. I looked carefully hoping he would stay hidden while I watched. Part of this lesson was stealth and part of it was patience. When I was convinced he wouldn't move until I looked down, I went back to my weaving.

I heard a twig snap and silently laughed at the following leaf crunches as he tried to correct his walk. I threw a pinecone in the direction of the noise then glanced around the circle noting places where he would run into trouble. There were some very wide gaps between cover. He'd either have to go deeper into the woods or be pretty sneaky to get by me. I was hoping he'd go deeper into the woods. I'd catch a movement here and a noise there but Rusty was doing better than I'd ever expected. I let him get away with little mistakes, though, and only threw a pinecone at him when he really truly gave himself away. When he got a pinecone he knew he deserved it and he got nearly around the circle when the last pinecone landed at his feet. He came out of hiding reluctantly.

"So, now it's your turn," he said.

I handed him my little grass mat.

"Will you finish it for me?" I asked.

He looked at the mat. "Not if you want it to stay in one piece," he replied.

"Do you really want me to make the circle? I can, but it's getting late and we still have a few miles to walk before we get home."

We headed for home idly backtracking ourselves. Rusty's tracks were plain and easy to read. Mine were subtle. In fact, mine were way too big. I stopped and examined the footprints. They were obviously moccasin footprints and clearly went in the right direction but Rusty had been following and occasionally the moccasin prints were over Rusty's. They were unmistakably too long and too wide to be mine.

"Look at this," I said, pointing. "What's wrong with these footprints?"

Rusty looked. "You weren't hiding your tracks. That's odd."

"It's not just odd, they're not my tracks."

He looked at me.

"What do you mean, not your tracks? Who else do we know who would be out here on our trail in moccasins?"

"It's still not my track. Look." I placed my foot inside the track and put my weight on it. I pulled my foot back clearly showing my small print within the lines of the larger one. I put my hands on my hips and looked around at the junipers surrounding us. Not many places to hide. "Chase Downing!" I called. "You can come out now."

Chase Downing was my tracking teacher at academy and he was an old friend of the Michaels family. He had served on the same force as Rusty's father, Bill. Chase considered tracking to be an art, and a dying one at that, so I kind of surprised him with my knowledge of tracking when I met him in academy. Ever since then he had kept tabs on me, through Rusty's family and police gossip. He was a quiet, secretive man, more tracker than officer. And now, I thought, he was here looking for a challenge.

"Cass, Chase is in San Diego. It would take a national emergency to drag him up here," Rusty said.

"Or he thought of a challenge for me," I answered, scanning the area more carefully, then I called out to the junipers, "If you want to get home in time for dinner, you'll come out. I'm waiting. I can wait here until tomorrow but we'll get awfully hungry."

I was going to feel really silly if Chase didn't come out. But he was the only person I could think of who would have followed us. Nobody else would have cared what we were up to. Any other person would be wearing regular shoes and wouldn't try to hide their footprints. Chase would have noticed both of our cars at the house and known we went somewhere on foot. He'd have circled the house and then easily found a trail leading away from it. Chase could easily distinguish our most recent trail from the older ones. He'd be curious about what we were up to out in the hills and he'd be sneaky enough to try and stay hidden. I only regretted taking so long to notice the difference in my tracks. I should have caught that right away. I was slipping.

Of course I had to give myself a little slack, though, because there was no reason to think anybody else was out here. So why question the trail at all?

"How curious are we?" I asked Rusty. "I can track him back to the clearing, then probably around it. He could lead us in circles forever if he wanted to, but I don't have the patience for this. He can only play games with us if we play along."

"So, game time? Or dinner? I vote for dinner, except for one small problem."

"What's that?" I asked.

"What if it isn't Chase?"

"I'd bet anything you want to name that it's Chase. Nothing else makes sense unless we have a very weird neighbor."

"We've never met our neighbors except for Hazel and Wally and they aren't capable of this."

"It isn't a neighbor," I said. "People like me don't buy houses like these."

"You did."

"Only because of you. You found it. You liked it first. And I'm glad you did. Now that I've been here a while I love it."

"So let's just go home and if Chase wants dinner then he'll show up."

"Okay."

About the time we walked through the backyard Chase stepped out from the barn.

"You two aren't much fun."

"We'll be more fun after we get some dinner in us," I told him.

"Good catch on the trail."

"Thanks."

He followed us into the house.

"You should lock your house when you go out," he said. "I read the note on the fridge."

I should have been mad at him for poking around but I knew he respected our home and hadn't harmed anything.

"We did lock it. Rusty's very careful about that. He's seen enough break-ins to know better. Even way out here where we never see a neighbor, he locks the house."

"Well, then you should burglar proof it. And teach Shadow to bark at strangers."

"Shelties usually bark at everything. If he didn't bark at you consider yourself lucky. He even barks at me."

"Yeah, with his tail wagging a mile a minute. Maybe you should get Rusty a Doberman."

"I don't think so. One dog is enough. Maybe you should show Rusty how you got in while I start dinner."

I put some steaks in the microwave to defrost and then wandered to the front windows, curious to see what kind of a car Chase drove. Parked at the curb in front of the house was an old, beat up VW Baja bug. It had oversized tires for off roading, a roll cage front and back with KC lights mounted on a sturdy rack up top. He was all set for the dunes. He hadn't gone out of his way on an expensive paint job. It was basic VW light blue. A spare tire was bungeed up top. I laughed, I hadn't been sure what to expect from Chase's car but somehow the contraption out front seemed right for him.

When the steaks had defrosted I placed them in five minute marinade. I then microwaved three big potatoes until they were baked and scooped out the insides. I mashed them with sour cream, cheese and butter, then added some chives and refilled the skins. Next I cut up a salad and started the grill. Before long we had dinner for three.

"It's good to see you've managed to stay out of trouble for three weeks," Chase commented.

"Yeah, right," I replied.

"That didn't sound like the kind of 'yeah right' that means I was right," he said.

"Well, it all turned out all right at the end. We just kind of had a rough start to our honeymoon. Rusty got some useful survival lessons in. Today's little exercises in the woods were nothing compared to that. If it had been planned, I would have considered it a great success. Unfortunately, it wasn't planned."

By the time I'd brought Chase up on the news it was very late, but I knew when he showed up he'd stay for the night. He challenged me to a tracking contest of some kind and I suspected we'd have his company until I could manage to get away and take his challenge. I showed him the guestroom and where the towels and blankets could be found.

"Chase, what are you going to tell Rusty's family when you get back to San Diego?"

"I'm going to tell them that you had a great time on your honeymoon and you seem to be doing fine. If they ask me point blank about anything specific I'll tell them the truth. Do you have a few extra pictures to back up my story?"

"How long will you be here?"

"A few days."

"We can print up a few for you. I got some nice ones of Rusty that they will like and some that show us at the lake having fun. I wish you could have seen the moose. I can't wait to see if I got some good pictures of the moose."

"Did you stalk it?"

"Yeah, but it was in the lake and I didn't venture into the water. But I snapped a quick picture as it was charging up the bank towards me. That picture is either a blurry piece of scrap paper or it is a really cool picture of a moose filling the whole frame. I'm keeping my fingers crossed on that one."

"You know why I'm here?"

"Yeah, I can guess. Do you think I can track you if you don't want to be tracked?"

"I don't know. Don't know if I can track you if you don't want to be tracked either. Got a destination in mind?"

"Let me think about it. Does it have to be someplace I am not familiar with? I've been all over these mountains."

"If you've been there before don't worry about it. Think of a place with differing terrains."

"I know a place but Rusty won't be pleased with my choice. It's a place I have only been to twice. It starts out meadow but there is a trail through it and then beyond the meadows there are rocks or a stream or mountains."

"Why won't Rusty like it?"

"Because last time I was there I was being chased by guys with rifles. He still has an aversion to that trail but I think it might be useful for our purposes. I can show it to you on a map. It's only fair that you know as much about it as I do."

"How much of it did you see off trail?"

"Not much. I was mostly trying to figure out how to get out of there alive. My decisions were instantaneous and I just dealt with what I met. I didn't have time to take much notice beyond my immediate needs."

"We'll look at it in the morning."

Breakfast the next morning sounded like an arbitration session.

"No erasing of the trail. The trail you leave is what you are stuck with," Chase said. "One day to find a camp and set up. It's got to be defendable. Once we find the camp we will circle it and close in. If you get shot you lose that round. Think of it like an apprehension, only you shoot first."

"Shoot?"

"Yeah, shoot."

"You wouldn't shoot me," I said.

"Paintball rifles. You ever try paintball?"

"No, but I'm a decent shot with almost anything."

"Good, so if you get shot you lose that round."

"Okay. So that means it needs to be physically possible to circle the camp," I pointed out.

"Why, what did you have in mind?"

"Nothing but if I make camp next to a cliff it would be pretty hard to circle it."

"You wanted to test your scouting abilities. I thought that ought to do it."

"You're right, it ought to. So I spend a day finding a place to camp. I set up camp. Then what? Do I have to wait out the next day while you try to find me? It can take more than a day to find someone who has been hiking all day and is hiding their trail too. How do we end this thing?"

"Show me the map," he requested.

I spread out the map and showed him. "There are meadows here and here. You see the trail, here. Once you get past the meadows you have mountains to the west. Down trail you have a big rocky mountain and to the east you have a very rough creek that leads to a wilderness area. There's a spring near this meadow," I explained as I pointed things out on the map.

"Looks dry. You sure the creek will be running?" he asked.

"No, but it was when I was there in the spring. No guarantees at this time of year."

He nodded.

"A day though? Either of us could travel a long ways in a day. This isn't going to be like tracking some lost city slicker kid. This could take some time."

"Yeah."

"Run it by Rusty when he gets home from work. And what if Strict calls? I can't put our little contest over a real search, even if it is for some damn fool tourist who should have known better. I just can't."

"Understood."

"No," said Rusty, grimly. "Of all the places in those mountains why did you have to pick Elk Meadows?"

"We need a place with lots of options. It's got meadows, mountains, rocks, the creek. Name a place up there with more to offer."

He thought about it, but didn't know the area as well as I did.

"Just a minute," he said and walked off.

"What's he doing?" Chase asked.

"He's either banging his head against a wall in frustration or he's calling Kelly, a ranger up there. He's hoping Kelly will recommend a different place."

When Rusty came back he started pulling out maps. I tried to reason with him.

"Rusty, Elk Meadows is just a campground. It just happens to be at the end of a trail that you don't like. But there's nothing wrong with the trail or the area."

"What about South Fork?"

"No. Poor choices. There's only a rocky creek and a rocky canyon."

"Springside."

"No variety."

"Buckhorn."

"Only one canyon with a trail down it or mountains that go straight up."

"Punchbowl."

"Only desert, it's too easy."

"Chilao."

"Rusty, what did Kelly say?" I asked.

"He wants to go too."

"He can't, this is just between me and Chase."

"What did he say about Elk Meadows?"

Rusty paused. "He thought it was a good choice."

"So there, see? Kelly wouldn't recommend it if he thought it meant trouble. He knows how easily I get into trouble so he would suggest another place if he thought there was a better one. I wish I could have talked to him. I'd like to know if the creek is running."

"You'll find out soon enough. He wants to hear all about this contest you've gotten yourself into."

"Oh no, then he'll want to go for sure."

"Why?"

"Paintball rifles. Big boy toys. You know how Kelly is, everything's a game to him."

"What are you doing with paintball rifles?" Rusty asked.

"Umm, shooting each other? You know we wouldn't use real ones."

"My wife, out in the woods playing war games."

When Kelly arrived it was like planning an invasion of a foreign country. He examined the maps pointing out different possibilities. Rhonda and Rusty just sat watching, shaking their heads in consternation, as Kelly, Chase and I pored over the maps.

"If you go up this fork it's like a fortress. Rocks guard the entrance and you can hide almost anywhere. Up here there's an old homestead but it's not good tracking ground around it. If you end up near there it makes a decent wind break so I've camped there on occasion." On and on he went while I took notes. It never hurt to know the area especially when I was up there so much.

"So," I said after Kelly had wound down again, "Elk Meadows still looks like the best choice."

"Sounds good to me," Chase answered.

"When are you going?" Rusty wanted to know.

"I'm ready to go right now," I said. "I've always got a pack ready for a two day search. All I need to do is pick it up and toss it in the Jeep. I think we should start on Monday though. Strict doesn't usually call me in the middle of the week so I'd rather be out of touch when he's least likely to call."

Kelly asked me, "You're going to spend a day hiking off trail with no destination in mind, just making things hard for Chase?"

"That's the plan. And when he finds me I need to shoot him first before he shoots me."

"Just don't forget to get your bearings every once in a while. Don't concentrate totally on your trail."

"Kelly, you sound like me when I do school lectures. I'll be fine. Then after he finds me I get to track him and we do it all over again."

"If he tracks you he'll know the area. He'll be able to plan his trail as he goes. You're giving him an advantage if you let him track you first. If you track him first you learn some of his tricks. You can get a feel for how he thinks so, when he is tracking you, you can use that information."

"Wow, who's the competitive one?" I asked. "This isn't a winner takes all contest. We're just having some fun. It is possible to win both rounds in different ways. I can win by shooting him first, or by being untrackable. Hey, if Chase doesn't find me how will I know it?"

"You really think Chase won't find you?" Rusty added.

"No, I guess I know he will. But in the unlikely event that he doesn't, how will I know? I'm not going to sit out there for a week waiting to get caught. We need to decide what to do, just in case. I once tracked a kid for three days and she wasn't even trying to hide her tracks. She'd only been missing a day and a half. So what makes me think Chase can find me in two days if I am hiding my tracks?"

"After the third night head for the car. I'll do the same. Same rule applies though, if you get shot you lose."

"Okay, that seems reasonable."

"Cassidy, are you sure you want to go through with this?" Rusty asked, climbing into bed and pulling me close. "You don't have to, you know."

"That's true, but I'd really like to know what we are both capable of, and there's only one way to find out. Chase is the best tracker and scout that I've met. If I can get past him then I'll know I can get past almost anybody."

"What if he beats you?"

"He probably will. He should be able to. I'm not going to worry about it if I lose. Maybe I need to know my limitations. One way or the other I mean to find out. I only wish I didn't have to spend three nights alone in the woods to do it. Then after we restock I'll have to do it again."

"Do you think you can find Chase if he hides his tracks?"

"I found Kelly when he was hiding his. I don't know about Chase. He is going to be tough and won't go easy on me. He might test me, and play tricks on me to see how I react. Either way he's going to be tough to track."

Monday was the hottest day of the year. I carried two and a half days worth of water, two days food, the stove, a change of clothes, my hunting knife and trusty magnesium stick, a very bulky paintball rifle, a small Ziploc bag of cookies and one slice of cheesecake which had to be eaten the first day. Too bad cheesecake didn't pack better; it was the one thing I craved but couldn't take backpacking.

Chase, Rusty and I stood looking out across Elk Meadows. Chase took in the scene noting what he could from the truck. It wasn't his turn yet.

"You take care of my girl out there," Rusty said.

"I will. It's just a camping trip with some odd hiking thrown in."

"Do you know where you're going?"

"I have some ideas. I don't know if they will pan out."

"Will you tell me?"

Chase took his cue and politely made himself scarce while I talked to Rusty.

"I won't touch the meadows, too easy to track. I'm not heading for the creek and the wilderness area. That's what he thinks I will do. I've got a route around the far end of the meadows that will lead me up into the mountains. So if anything happens I'll be in the mountains behind the meadows. I don't plan on being very far from the campground at any time. The end of the meadows is the furthest that I will be. You'll be able to see that clearly on the map."

"Okay."

"Take Chase out to Trujillo's and keep him up really late," I said sarcastically. "I'll see you in a few days."

I waited for the hug and kiss I knew was coming but he seemed reluctant to let me go. This always happened when I'd be gone overnight and I felt guilty leaving. I was grateful that our house felt more like home to him than the condo had. There was comfort within his surroundings, more evidence that he was no longer alone and that seemed to calm him a lot. He seemed to feel more anchored. He wasn't adrift anymore and to see that discomfort surface in him now only added to my guilt in leaving.

Chase appeared.

"I gotta go. I'll be back in a few days, hopefully paint free."

There was the hug. I knew it was coming and couldn't have left without it. I took it with me as I watched the guys get into the Explorer and drive away. Chase would be back in the morning to begin his tracking. I turned to the trail, examining it closely. I thought it was risky taking the trail but as I examined the sides of it I could see the plants were already very battered and worn. I looked around. No use venturing into the meadow. He'd spot the bent grasses before he got out of his Baja Bug. I headed down the side of the trail, placing each foot carefully to match up with the natural lines of the land, plants and forest debris that had blown in. This was normal walking for me. I did this as I walked all the time so I was able to keep up a fairly steady pace. Three quick miles and I came to the spot where the creek took off to the north. I hopped across the trail and then walked down to the creek. I made sure to leave a few clues behind to tell Chase I was heading up the creek where he expected me to go. They had to be very subtle clues because obvious ones would tip him off that I was up to something.

I then doubled back to the trail carefully hiding my tracks as best I could, hopping from rock to rock. I blended my footprints with the vegetation and followed a hollow log that ended in a bed of ferns. When I got back to the trail I followed it off to the side until I was forced back up onto it. Here was the big shale mountain. I remembered a place I had used when I was here before. I was being chased and needed an escape route and had found one straight up the rock. It was not a friendly climb. The rock was brittle, but I had found a wide crack in the rock that I could climb up easily. I walked several yards past the place I was looking for and then backed up carefully over my tracks. I found the crack again and carefully made my way to it, trying hard to keep my footprints light and soft. I then climbed up the crack to the ledge I knew was up there. The ledge hugged the side of the mountain and I followed it until it ended near the ground about a quarter mile off trail and beside the meadow. I was hoping that little twist in the route would throw Chase off. It would at least give him an hour's work trying to puzzle it out. I wondered how far he would go up the creek before realizing I hadn't taken that direction.

I had to hide my tracks carefully now. After Chase discovered my little trick he'd be particularly wary. I watched for things to help me hide my trail: rocks, roots, springy little plants, pine needles, all the things I hated to see when on a search. Of course whatever I used against him he would feel free to use against me. Maybe I should just go for stealth. He'd respect stealth and quick thinking over the simple use of a few rocks. I walked along thinking, placing my steps and watching for a place to camp. A game trail took off down the mountain and I followed it up the mountain hoping the deer would come through and confuse my trail.

The cheesecake was calling me from the pocket of my pack so I dug it out. My treat had melted and was stuck all over the inside of the Ziploc bag. I folded down the top of the bag and ate most of it. I ended up tearing the bag and licking it off the plastic. It was a mess. A sticky, gooey, cheesecakey mess but it was good and I licked the plastic as clean as I could without getting my hands all sticky. I looked back at my trail knowing I'd forgotten about my tracks while I was eating. I rolled up the plastic and stuffed it in a trash bag. It was time for some heavy-duty footprint hiding so I analyzed the lay of the land for further opportunities to trick Chase up again. I followed a patch of hard pack. That wouldn't fool Chase. He'd expect that. I considered climbing a tree, walking the branch and then dropping to the ground, but didn't want to do all that with a backpack.

After a while I stopped worrying about my trail because I was feeling lousy. If there was one thing I had learned in the Marines, though, it was to keep on keeping on. No matter what. If the mission wasn't complete you had to keep on. And my mission wasn't complete. I admitted I didn't have to keep going until dusk. I just had to find a place to camp that I could defend. Nothing in the rules said I even had to set up the tent and sleeping bag. I just had to "make camp". What if making camp meant finding a hidden place to sleep? I knew there had to be some evidence of my camp and something had to be done with my pack or critters would get into it. So I began watching for a good, defendable camp. The harder I searched the sicker I felt and then the cheesecake came up. A quarter mile later it came up some more. Arg, I felt rotten. I tried drinking water but not even that would stay down. Camp became more and more of a priority and I needed to rest. The more I moved the sicker I felt so I made my way to a thick part of the forest. I found a tall tree, pulled my tent off the pack and hoisted the pack into the tree. I opened the tent but didn't feel up to fiddling with all the poles and pegs. No way. I looked around and found a leafy place under some brush. After rolling up the tent so only the zipper showed I placed it in the leaves. I slipped inside through the zipper and pulled leaves over the tent. I then pulled the zipper nearly all the way before shaking the brush to drop more leaves on top of me. Finally I went to sleep, just me and the paintball rifle. The rolled up tent under me actually made a decent mattress and it didn't even feel like I was on the ground. It was comfortable as long as I didn't move. Movement brought uneasiness to my stomach so I laid as still as possible.

I awoke feeling even worse. My head throbbed and my stomach hurt. All I could do was lay still and wish for the third day. If I heard Chase my plan was to unzip the tent just far enough to take aim, fire my best shot, and then surrender. I was ready to quit. If I had the strength to move I would have headed for the car but that was now impossible. All I could do was wait for it to pass. I thought about what could have made me so sick. Flu? Food poisoning? Stupid cheesecake cravings, I never should have brought that cheesecake. Cookies were safe. I could have eaten the cookies, but no... I had to have cheesecake. Blah. It wasn't worth it this time. I quit thinking about it because thinking only made my head feel worse. Just lay still, Cass, it'll go away eventually.

As I lay still I realized I was losing track of time. It was dark and cold, then it was hot and bright. I slept, not caring what it was like outside, no longer even caring if Chase found me. Dark and cold again. At first I had to get up for necessities but as my system became more and more empty I didn't even need to do that. I pulled down the pack, grabbed the water bottles and hoisted it back. Then I crawled back in the tent, shook leaves over me and drifted again. And I dreamed, mostly reliving long lost memories. Some of them were scary while others involved everyday things. They weren't really nightmares, just memories. Being chased though these mountains, fighting Trent at Gear Up, being dragged by Shasta across the corral and down the road, the anger I felt at Peccati, hiking forever in the Marines, stalking deer behind the ranch, watching Jack fly at an air show.... Memories circling and twisting as I slept. Why was it cold? I shouldn't be cold. When I'd headed out on this fiasco it was a hundred and ten in the shade.

I thought I heard voices at one point but Chase wouldn't be talking if he was looking for me. I unzipped the tent just enough to peek out but didn't see anybody. I zipped back up. If there were people in the area I didn't want them to know my location. They were probably campers from Elk Meadows. They'd go away. I waited and time drifted again. I wondered how much I'd slept and how much I'd been awake. It was hard to tell the difference, especially when my only purpose was to tune out all feeling.

I was awoken by voices again but this time the voices were familiar.

Chase: "You know her better than I do. What would she do?"

And then Rusty: "She'd hide. You're the tracker. You know where she went. You found her pack."

"Yeah, and I thought I'd never find it, much less her. I circled the area, like I was supposed to. No shot. No movement. Nothing. No tent. I know she was here. I know she took the pack down again. She hasn't touched the food. She was easy to track towards the last because she wasn't paying attention and she was sick. But then she just disappeared."

"She'd hide. She's around here somewhere."

My hands shook as I quietly unzipped the tent a few inches. I wasn't sure I'd get a good shot off since I was so shaky. Why even bother, Cass? Why try? But I took aim anyway, with as little movement as possible, as little stirring of the leaves as I could manage. I aimed through the slit in the tent. I saw the larger form of Rusty and the shorter, wirier form of Chase and squeezed off one shot hitting Chase on the back of his shoulder. He spun around, alert, eyes piercing the brush around him. Ha, ha, I'd won, double time. He couldn't find me and I'd shot him! But I felt too rotten to really celebrate.

"Cassidy? The game's over, kid. Come out."

The game's over? How long had I been here? If Chase had found my pack, given up and brought in Rusty I must have really been out of it. I hadn't noticed when Chase circled my camp. I'd barely known day from night.

"Cass..." Rusty started but I wasn't there. He looked down the line of fire, looked through the brush, then at the trees close by. They still couldn't see me. They knew where to look and they still couldn't find my hiding place. Okay, I thought, time to go home. I shook the leaves off the tent and shakily unzipped it. Two sets of eyes narrowed as recognition took hold.

"Damn," said Chase, "I must have walked past this place a dozen times."

Rusty knelt next to the tent as I worked my way out. My head still throbbed and I was weak from being sick. I was glad it was just a walk down the mountain and across the meadow to get to the truck.

"I'm sorry Chase," I said, "I had to stop early. I didn't want to but I had to. I got too sick."

"I know. You should have stopped miles ago. Why didn't you?"

"I'm just stubborn. And the Marines would have been disappointed. I needed to finish. I had to meet my goal. But I didn't. I quit."

"I don't see anyone here calling you a quitter," Rusty said.

I stood up and the world spun around and my stomach felt queasy but there was nothing in it. My head throbbed with the spinning.

"Oh man, I am so sick. I can't even remember the last time I was this sick."

Rusty took down my pack and fished around inside it. He took out my stove and a backpacker meal.

"No," I said, "I don't want to eat. It'll just make me feel worse."

"Babe, you have to eat. You're barely there."

"When I get home. Backpacker food is gross second time around. I'll eat when I get home."

I pulled my tent out of the leaves and spread it out on the ground. I had to search around for the poles and pegs. After locating everything I started folding up the tent, getting it ready for packing but Rusty stopped me and did it himself. I sat beneath a tree, all worn out, and watched him work.

"Are you ready for a hike out?" Rusty asked.

"I don't have much choice."

I tied the tent to the pack and worked my way into the shoulder straps, pulled the hip belt snug and adjusted the weight so it settled firmly on my hips.

"Cass…"

"My pack doesn't fit you. I carried it in. I'll carry it out."

"You wanna fight me for it?" Rusty asked.

"I won't fight you. You know it."

"Then hand it over."

I stood there looking as defiant as I could under the circumstances. He knew he'd won. And he knew I didn't like it. But it was probably for the best. I pulled the quick release on the hip belt and shrugged out of the pack. He pulled the shoulder straps as loose as they would go, shouldered the pack and tightened them a little. He didn't bother with the hip belt.

I was determined to let the guys set the pace on the way back. I'd just put myself into hike mode and keep on. But they were taking it slow. When we reached the Explorer I curled up on the backseat. It was a bumpy ride leaving Elk Meadows. Every roll made my stomach hurt and every bump made my head throb. Eventually we hit pavement and I was able to ride peacefully. I fell asleep on the ride home and Rusty woke me gently when we arrived. Our home, it looked so good, so comfortable. I walked through the new living room to the comfortable, old, brown couch and curled up in a ball. It's funny, we had brand new furniture, a nice, new living room set, but when we wanted comfort we went straight to the old couch from Rusty's bachelor days. We'd watched lots of games on this couch and eaten many meals at the coffee table in front of it before buying our dining room table. It was comfort to me, it smelled like Rusty and it hugged me like Rusty, probably because it was so old it no longer had any particular shape. But I went to it when I wasn't feeling well and at that moment I was feeling just rotten.

Rusty sat down on the floor next to the couch.

"What do you think you can eat?"

"Anything, just not much of it. I'll find something in a bit. First I need to get rid of this headache. Then I'll be able to think more about food."

"Any idea what made you so sick?"

"Either cheesecake or a flu bug of some kind. I'm not taking cheesecake on the trail any more. It probably should have been refrigerated."

"Babe…" Rusty looked at me as if one of these days cheesecake was going to be my ultimate downfall. He got up and brought me a glass of water and something for my headache.

"I want to know how you got from the creek to the meadow without touching the ground," Chase said.

"Aww, Chase, that's my secret. I'm surprised you didn't figure it out. It was the only trick in my whole book and you're telling me it worked?"

"I only found your trail by making wider and wider circles until I found sign behind the meadow. I found sign at the creek, on the trail and beyond the meadow, but nothing linking the three locations."

"I knew not to touch the meadow. That would have been too easy. And you expected me to go for the creek so I couldn't do that. What else was there?"

"So, how did you get from the creek to the meadow?"

"I flew."

He glared at me.

"I'll show you some day."

"You know, when I saw how sick you were, how far you pushed, I thought I'd killed you with this contest. Then when you just vanished I didn't know what to think. Next time I'll have to define exactly what I mean by setting up camp. I didn't expect your camp to be a rolled up tent in a bed of leaves."

"Sometimes I don't bother with the tent."

"You don't have to track me if you don't want to. This could have been serious. This isn't fun anymore."

"Who said? Just give me a few days to catch up again. I'll track you."

"You're a glutton for punishment."

"I've heard that before."

It wasn't until the next day that I was able to keep food down and then I was eager to be out doing things. I put Shadow through the jumps I'd made and began cutting plywood for the A-frame I wanted to build. The sound of the saw brought Chase to the barn.

"What are you doing?" he asked after the noise from the saw had stopped.

"I'm making agility equipment. You saw the jump. I'm going to fill the backyard with obstacles. I had an agility course at my old house but it burned down. Then I didn't have space for one at the condo. One reason Rusty liked this house was because he knew I wanted to build a new agility course. So now that the wedding is over and I have time and a table saw, it's time to rebuild."

"I don't suppose you'd accept any help."

"I don't need it. But if you're looking for something to do you're welcome to chip in. I need both these sheets to be three feet wide. Then I need to cut two by fours the right lengths to make a frame on the back of the plywood."

I measured and drew a line along one edge of the plywood and Chase helped me channel it through the saw. We leaned the sheets next to a wall in the barn and cut two eight-foot two by fours and then four shorter boards to add support.

"Watch this," I said. "Shadow! Get the tool! Get the tool boy!" I commanded with enthusiasm. Shadow approached the tools on the ground, looked around for a likely candidate and picked up the screwdriver. "Good boy!" I praised. "Bring it here!" He dropped the screwdriver into my hand.

I used the screwdriver Shadow had fetched for me to attach the boards to the back of the plywood. After putting the two sections together I realized I should have cut the ends of the two by fours at an angle, so I penciled in lines and we sawed off the ends by hand. When the two sheets matched I fastened them together with a sturdy hinge. Once the A-frame was standing I attached furring strips to provide traction. Then I sanded the whole thing to prepare it for a test run and paint. We dragged the A-frame out to the yard and I called Shadow over.

"Shadow, heel." I walked over to the A-frame. "Shadow, sit." He sat. "Shadow, go up! Up, boy! Go up!" He looked at the A-frame. "Time to go back to leash work. He hasn't done an A-frame in a year so I knew we'd have to back up a little in his training." I tried a different tack. "Shadow, heel!" He heeled so I jogged over to the jump. "Shadow, jump! Good boy! Now jump again! Good boy! Heel!" I jogged over to the A-frame. "Shadow go UP!" He trotted half way up but didn't appear to like the feel of being off the ground. "Good boy! Go up! UP!" I stood on the down side encouraging him forward until he reached the top. "Good boy! Come down! Come DOWN!" He tentatively started moving along the down side but slipped a little. It was better to take the A-frame at a jog but Shadow was a cautious dog. He'd get the hang of it soon. It wasn't new to him, just unfamiliar.

"Do you ever sit still for a few minutes?" Chase asked me.

"Yes, I sat still for three days waiting for you to find me. Now I'm ready to do something. Building stuff like this keeps my hands busy. Are you ready to be tracked?"

"Are you sure you're ready?"

"Sure. I just want to run the plan by Rusty."

"Good luck."

I spent the afternoon painting the A-frame and jumps a bright blue. I left them to dry, hoping Shadow wouldn't get it into his head to do some work in his spare time. Just what I needed: a black, white and blue Shetland sheepdog.

When the A-frame was dry I planned to add a chain to make it more adjustable, and some carpet at the top so Shadow would be more likely to cross over. He didn't like seeing through the crack at the top. I could tell that just by watching him. He was a lot like Rusty, I thought. He could see through this contest of Chase's and, just like Shadow, was worried about falling through that crack. He was worried about what might follow for me once this contest was over. He knew if I showed up Chase I'd be in for some scouting and could be called on for advanced assignments, more than just finding lost hikers. That idea would never rest well with Rusty, so I expected some opposition to tracking Chase. There was no chance the outcome of our contest would stay under wraps. Strict knew what we were up to and he'd want to know how it turned out. Rusty's dad probably knew what Chase was up to as well, and retired or not word got around the police community. Rusty knew how word spread. He'd heard stories at the Joshua Hills station that had drifted in from LA and San Diego. The officers here waited for the next installment in the Adventures of Cassidy. I was sure my honeymoon had made the rounds of Joshua Hills and this would too, whether Rusty said anything or not.

I felt like it hadn't been fair to shoot Chase at Elk Meadows when he was talking to Rusty. I didn't really consider that a win. It had felt good at the time but it wasn't really fair. Chase wasn't prepared for my shot. He'd considered the contest over. Now, the fact that he didn't find me was another story. I could count that. He'd even had an extra day to figure that one out. It was time to go for round two.

Chapter 6

Rusty came home that night in a somber mood.

"What is it?" I asked over dinner.

"New case at work," he said shortly. "Two officers down."

"Oh no! Who?" I asked. "Are they going to be okay?"

"Yeah, they'll be okay but I don't like the way this was set up. Four guys hit a liquor store. They take off in four different directions. When the cars pull up the guys get out and they're fired on from two different directions. The store faces a vacant lot. We think they hid out at the houses around the lot but no one's talking. The take was almost nothing so the shooting had to be the motivation. The robbery was just a draw to lure the police in."

"Did you tape off the lot and the store?" I asked. "I can tell you the houses they headed for. Tracks in the yards might still be visible."

"Seems like everybody who went into that store cut across the lot to get there."

"It's okay, because customers' tracks are going to look different from robbers' tracks. Customers don't take off from a store running. And shooters have a particular stance they use. They plant their feet before they aim or, if they are on the run, their gait changes noticeably. What kind of guns did they use?"

"The store owner says three of them held handguns, one carried a rifle. He didn't know what caliber or make."

"Can I take a look around the area? I don't even need to get behind the tape to learn something. In fact, I'd rather not go onto the lot unless I have to."

He looked at me, aware that I wanted to help yet not wanting me to be involved.

"Just because Trent had it out for the police doesn't mean every criminal is going to stalk me because I visit a crime scene. It was probably gang activity and they got their two cop points and earned their tattoo, and now they're sitting back somewhere celebrating."

"You really do need one of us to go over the scene," Chase added. "Let's do it first thing in the morning."

Rusty looked relieved but I wasn't through with him yet.

"You don't want me to go just because I'm a trouble magnet."

"Cass, I told you, there's no such thing as a trouble magnet. I don't want you to go because…" His voice trailed off, unable to think of a good reason.

"I rest my case. I don't want to go just to be obstinate. Either I can help or I can learn something from the scene. Every time I track I learn something from it by studying the patterns and behaviors that go into the making of the tracks. Tracking is like building a library of clues in my head. It establishes patterns, so when I see something later down the line things add up more quickly. Either way some good can come out of it. So why can't I go?"

Rusty and Chase exchanged glances. "You can go," he said dejectedly. "Wear your uniform and your side arm. Can you two work together?"

Chase and I looked at each other. "I don't see why not," he replied.

I never liked wearing my uniform. It meant I was in Reserve Deputy mode and I did not consider myself police material. When Rusty and Chase spotted a suspect they responded quickly and with authority, while I stood there and thought, "Hey! That must be the guy we were looking for! Look! His shoes match the tracks and he's the same size I thought he would be. And oh, look, he's armed just like he was for the robbery." Maybe that's why I'm a trouble magnet. I'm just curious and friendly and trouble doesn't appreciate curious and friendly.

Fortunately, tracking the robbery scene didn't happen quite as I'd pictured while I was putting on my uniform and strapping on my 9mm. Rusty drove us to the crime scene and we met with a very upset owner.

"When are you going to take down this tape? Everybody who sees it shies away from the place. It's killing my business. I don't want people to think of robberies and shootings when they come here."

Rusty provided a vague answer that gave him some hope. "I'll see what I can do about that," he said.

Chase looked over the neighborhood. "The whole place is dirt roads. How did they expect to get away leaving a trail like that?"

"Welcome to the high desert," I said. "We have a lot of neighborhoods like this."

We stood at the door to the liquor store. The parking lot was rough asphalt surrounded by dirt roads and desert. I looked past the police tape at the vacant lot. There were hundreds of tracks in that lot and if we ventured in we'd have to sift through a lot of trails. Instead, we circled the lot until we found running tracks leaving it which I then compared to the tracks exiting the parking lot.

While Chase and I were examining the tracks a black and white pulled up.

"In case we uncover somebody," Chase told me. "Rusty's just watching out for you. Let him take precautions without making a fuss and he's more likely to let you in on these cases."

"So far his precautions haven't kept me from doing anything though. Either I am in the right place at the right time or I'm not. If we come across someone hiding in the bushes and they make a dash for it I'm not going to run back and say, 'Excuse me, Mr. Officer….' On the other hand if they are on top of things and ready for some action I won't get in their way."

"Look at this," he said pointing to the ground. "They stood behind this van. Took 'em long enough to set up for the shot. I'm guessing this was the guy with the rifle. The guys with pistols would stand straighter. The footprints look like this guy is more angled."

"Plus he is further from the parking lot. Makes sense to put the rifle further from the target. Do robbers usually plan like that? I thought they'd just make a run for it and shoot from wherever they ended up."

"Sometimes, but the angles are right for the rifle."

"I'm just thinking about how I shoot a rifle and guessing most people stand at an angle."

Chase was the senior tracker, so I followed him and learned what I could. Chase stepped away from the van and knelt down. He looked under the van then glanced around the scene.

"You got all the casings?" he asked Rusty.

"Yeah, two from this spot."

"Rifle?"

"Yeah."

"Caliber?"

"Forty-five."

"Did you find the other casings?"

"Yeah, 9mm."

We went after the forty-five shooter first. After taking his two shots he fled down the dirt road past chain link-fenced houses. After two blocks he hopped a three-foot fence and cut through a backyard. We caught up with his trail on the next street up. I kept thinking that if I had held up a liquor store and shot a cop I wouldn't be found anywhere near this neighborhood, but the tracks continued. They crossed the street then darted down another side street. All the time the houses got dustier and poorer looking until the neighborhood ended in some downtrodden apartments. Junked cars up on blocks sat around and puddles of old oil dotted the street in front of the apartments. A cracked sidewalk led between four dusty looking duplexes. Chase and I both circled the area looking for tracks leaving the apartments but found none that matched the man we were following.

Rusty got on his radio and called for more troops. We had four exits to cover. I was getting worried. I knew how easily this could turn deadly and I didn't want to see any bloodshed. And I particularly didn't want to have to shoot anybody. If trouble was heading my way I'd rather just let it run right over me than use my gun. And that wasn't the right attitude.

"Come on, kid, I've got orders," Chase said, interrupting my thoughts.

"What? We can't leave now!"

"I've still got orders. Are you going to come peacefully or am I going to have to throw you over my shoulder and carry you out?"

"Chase, I admit, I don't want to be in on the apprehension but can't I just sit in a patrol car? The whole force wants to get these guys. They don't need me. But don't make me leave. I want to be here for Rusty."

"And Rusty needs you to be out of here so he doesn't have to worry about you. He needs to be able to do his job, so how about we let him do it?"

I looked to Rusty and received his worried yet hopeful look back, just as I had expected. Okay, I really did need to get out of his way. I went over to him and asked, "You know how hard it is for me to just walk away from here?"

"Yeah, I've been in your shoes before, remember?"

"Yeah. I guess you have. *Please*, be careful."

"I will."

He handed me the truck keys. "I'll call when we're through."

I looked around at all the officers. I wanted to give Rusty a big hug and kiss but I couldn't so I just said, "Okay," swallowed the big lump in my throat, then hesitated again before I went dejectedly back to Chase. Together we walked back up the dusty road, through the dusty neighborhood and found the Explorer parked in front of the liquor store.

"Chase, can't we try and track the other guy? At least we'd be doing something."

"Nope, we could run into trouble and we can't ask the guys doing the apprehension to bail us out. We'll have to shelve it for now. Want me to drive?"

"Nah, I need to do something."

We both got into the Explorer and I drove to the station.

"What are we doing here?" Chase asked.

"You ever box?"

"Me? Yeah, of course, just for practice to keep my reflexes up, but I've done my share."

"I haven't, but the punching bag doesn't like me anymore. And it's going to dislike me even more when I'm through. I'm not very nice to it."

"That's good because I don't think I could hit you."

I let out a tension filled laugh. "You? You don't think you could hit me? Are you getting soft?"

"Yeah," he said, "I'm getting soft. I could pummel Rusty but I don't think I could hit you."

"It's okay, there's only one guy here that will box with me and I owe him a round. Last time we boxed I was recovering from the water skiing accident so I wasn't up to par."

We went into the station and I checked to see if Tom was in. I knocked on his office door. He opened it irritated but the look quickly turned to amusement.

"You ready for a rematch?" I asked.

"You're kidding, right?"

"No, but if you're busy that's okay."

"What have you been up to? Uniform? Sidearm?"

"You don't want me to tell you until after we box."

"Are you trying to prove something here? Two against one?"

"No, Chase won't box with me. If you don't want to I'll just take on the punching bag or the firing range."

"So what's with the bodyguard?"

"He's not a bodyguard. This is Chase Downing, tracking teacher and family friend. Chase, this is Tom. I don't know if he has a last name. You two can figure the rest out. If you want to box meet me in the gym."

I walked down the hall and entered the women's locker room. I didn't have a locker or clothes to change into but I found an empty one to hold my shoes, gun and everything from my pockets. I didn't usually box in uniform but this time I didn't have much of a choice.

I found the punching bag and took a few tentative swings at it. I pictured the apartments and what could be happening back there and as the tension rose so did my speed. The punching bag jumped and lurched. It was heavy but I needed something heavy to work off my frustration. I wasn't mad at Rusty, just frustrated with the circumstances. I didn't want to be a cop, however I didn't like being pushed aside as soon as the trail had finished either. I knew Rusty didn't want me to feel that way, but I also knew he needed me out of there. So the frustration mounted, and the punching bag took the brunt of it.

Tom handed me a pair of boxing gloves. I pulled them on and fastened down the Velcro.

"Same rules? Stay in the circle, feet are okay?" I asked.

"You sure you want to do this?"

"Yeah."

"Okay."

Poor Tom didn't know what hit him. He was smug starting out but I was plenty frustrated and I was quick. I never landed a punch that would actually hurt him but he had a hard time catching me. The few good punches he got in knocked me down but I was ready for that. I didn't want him to go easy on me.

Chase just sat on the little bleachers shaking his head at me, no doubt wondering at what point he should drag me out of there. He knew not to take me home bloodied but at that point I didn't really care. After yet another tumble across the hardwood floor Tom reached down to help me up but I lunged to my feet and rounded on him with a kick followed by a right hook.

"Are you mad?" he asked.

"No, but I'm good and frustrated."

"What would make you more frustrated than being kidnapped and beaten? Last time I saw you frustrated it was because of a kidnapping. So what happened that could be worse than that?"

"Rusty kicked me out of the apprehension."

"Ah, and you thought you should be in on it?"

"No," I said, delivering a punch to his shoulder. "I just wanted to stay, even if I had to sit in a patrol car. But he wouldn't let me."

"He loves you. You gotta give the guy some space."

Bam, bam bam! "You know you aren't helping much at all!" I said with more emotion than I wanted to admit. "He's there whenever something happens to me. I put the guy through hell and he keeps on keeping on, but one little apprehension and he won't let me stay. Anything could happen out there and all I wanted to do was be there."

Please, Tom, just knock me flat, I thought. I need to be beaten down. Just do it. It would feel better than this. But he didn't. He just kept up the boxing until I was too tired to lift a glove and then he called it quits.

"You've got your movement back. You're quicker than most. All you need is some power in those punches."

"A couple of guys might disagree with you. But I won't embarrass them by providing names. You want to try it without gloves?"

"No, you've had enough. I'm not going to send you home all bruised up."

Guess I knew that was coming. I should have been grateful, but I was a little disappointed.

"Chase? Will you take me on at target practice?"

Chase got up and slowly made his way down the bleachers. He looked me square in the eye, saw the frustration and said, "Sure."

I went back to the locker room and gathered up my things. I strapped on my gun again and put my shoes back on, then met Chase outside the locker rooms.

We went to the practice range and took turns at one station tallying our points with each round. In a way being frustrated helped because it made me feel edgy and I was always more accurate when I felt edgy. My reflexes were quicker and my mind was sharper. Chase managed to outshoot me but by focusing on my shots it had taken my mind off everything else that was going on.

"Can you shoot that good with a paintball rifle?" Chase asked.

"I doubt it. I never did care much for rifles. But I passed the test at academy and I hold my own against the ranch hands. I guess I really should practice with a rifle more often. When I was home at the ranch I went hunting a lot. I was used to the rifles my dad kept. Then I spent four years in the Marines and I learned a thing or two about rifles there too. But I still prefer my little 9mm. It fits my hand and it's simple to use. I've carried this same model ever since I was old enough to pick out my own gun. I only use the police issue guns when mine is out of commission. It tends to get stolen a lot."

"You know they were supposed to teach you in academy how to keep your weapon from falling into the wrong hands."

"I know but first it was stolen from my house. Then it was kicked out of my hand while I was pulling it out of the holster. It's just been a matter of bad timing."

"Maybe you should be working on your timing as well as your aim."

"Did Rusty really send you to keep me from going back to the apartments?"

"I thought you'd finally managed to put that behind you."

"I did. I just think it's odd that you have stuck with me. He didn't make you babysit me did he?"

"No, he respects you enough to do the right thing. He just knows how hard it is for you at times. And he really didn't want me there either. I'm not dead set on storming an apartment just to see some action. I see my own kind of action back home."

"I've never seen Rusty happy to get into the thick of things. He always has such a grim look about him when he has a potentially violent confrontation coming up. He can't hide it. I can read him like a book. Some of the guys you can tell, they love the action. But Rusty seems to like the thinking part of detective work more than the action part. He is capable and he knows what to do but he really would rather not have to raid an apartment building just to get at a suspect."

"He takes after his dad. Bill was the same way, but he did his job and he did it right."

"Okay, one more thing to do at the station and I'll be ready to do something else."

"What's that?"

"It'll only take a few minutes."

I went to Rusty's office and brought up his computer. I opened a word processor that had a paint program in it and made a silly little graphic that said "I Love You" and then saved it in a folder with his screensaver pictures. Some day when he was bored and his screensaver came on he'd get a surprise.

"Let's hope Schroeder isn't in here when that graphic comes up," Chase said.

"Just because he's the commanding officer doesn't mean Rusty can't have anything he wants on his screensaver," I said.

"It might be a bit embarrassing. Plus, it means you hacked a detective's computer system."

I peeked out the little window of Rusty's office to make sure the coast was clear and then we left the station.

"Where are we going now?" Chase asked.

"I don't know. I was hoping they would be through by now. I don't want to go home because it's a long trip back into town when Rusty calls. We have to stay findable, so we can't go tracking off into the desert." I thought for a bit. "Okay, I know a place where most guys don't mind killing time, but we need to stop by a department store first. I promise it'll only take fifteen minutes."

I pulled into the parking lot of a major discount store. Inside I bought a pair of jeans and a t-shirt. I was lucky since anything a size five or seven will usually fit. Before leaving I changed into my new clothes in the restroom. Then I jumped back into the Explorer and we headed for Sharky's, the local pool hall. They have twenty pool tables, dartboards, a couple of video games and a little grill where you can get burgers, sandwiches and nachos. It's a good place to kill time and I've never met a guy who didn't play pool. I thought I could count on Chase to have played many games of pool at Rusty's parent's house.

Chase racked the balls while I chose a stick. I let him break. Guys always like to break. Chase turned out to be a pretty good pool player. He had finesse and didn't scare the balls into the pockets. I was clumsy. I sunk my share of balls but didn't go about it gracefully. When he beat me twice in a row I switched him over to Nine Ball.

"What's this?" he said when he saw the balls racked in a diamond.

"Nine Ball. Do you know the rules?"

"Sort of. Hit the lowest numbered ball first. Sinking the nine ball wins the game."

We sorted out the ball-in-hand rule. I wanted to watch Chase think and Nine Ball is a thinking man's game. I watched him puzzle his way through all my defensive blunders. Seems like I always accidentally leave the cue ball hidden from the target ball, so Chase had to come up with some complicated bank shots. We ate nachos, Chase had a beer and we claimed music interference whenever we made a really bad shot. He claimed music interference for country songs and I claimed it for violent, screaming rock songs. We were halfway through our second game of Nine Ball when Rusty called.

"Where are you?" he asked.

"Hold on, let me get outside. I can't hear you."

When I was outside he asked again, "Where are you?"

"We're at Sharky's. Where are you?"

"I'm at the station."

"You ready to go home?"

"Give me half an hour."

"Okay, we'll finish our game."

The game stretched on and on. The stinkin' eight ball gave us a hard time. I think it suddenly developed an aversion to pockets. We chased that ball to every part of the table and we finally decided the only way to end the game was to use the eight ball to sink the nine ball. That made the shots even crazier and so it was well over half an hour before I accidentally sunk the cue ball and Chase had ball in hand and sunk the last two balls easily.

We pulled into the station parking lot and saw Rusty standing in the lobby talking to Tom. Oh boy. Chase and I exchanged glances. Well, there was nothing to do but go and face the music.

When we walked in the front door Rusty reached out with one hand letting me know he was ready for that hug. He pulled me close.

"You know, any other girl would have gone home, called their best friend and whined about how unfair their mean old husband was. You're the only girl I know who goes to his workplace and beats up on his coworkers."

"I did not! I owed Tom a rematch and he took me up on it. That's all!"

"I know, babe, I'm just kidding."

"How did the apprehension go? Did you catch him?"

"Yeah, we caught him and a lot more but the other three guys are still loose. Maybe we can pry some information out of this guy."

"We still have three more trails to track. I wanted to do it when we got back to the Explorer but Chase wouldn't let me."

Rusty and Chase exchanged glances then Chase nodded. A guy's version of "thanks," and "no problem, just doing my duty."

"Rusty, the tracks won't be visible much longer. Cars go up and down those roads stirring up dust. Dust fills the tracks. Car tread erases them. If you want to track down the other guys we need to get after it."

The guys were ready to go home but Rusty knew my curiosity would not let me rest until I had a chance at that trail, so we went back to the liquor store and he showed me the spot where the other shooter stood. I looked to Chase. He was the senior tracker. I thought it best to give him first dibs on the trail but he said, “This one’s all yours, kid.”

Unfortunately this second trail wasn’t nearly as interesting as the last one had been. The tracks led around the back of the store and then down the street a block or so before ending at the side of the road.

“Getaway car?” I asked Chase.

“Looks like it.”

I tried to track the car tread but lost it amongst all the other car treads on the road. I looked around. There were nearby houses. Maybe somebody saw the car. At least it would give Rusty something to go on.

“Cassidy, drop it,” Chase said. “You’re not going to track a car, at least not on roads this well traveled.”

I kicked rocks all the way back to the Explorer and gave up in defeat. I’d lost at tracking, boxing, target practice and pool. The day was just a waste. When we got home it was late and I puttered around dejectedly, wondering what to do about dinner. I wasn’t even sure Rusty had eaten lunch.

“Let’s just relax this evening. We’ve all had a rough day. I’m all for pizza and a ballgame,” Rusty suggested.

“Zeke doesn’t deliver way out here,” I reminded him.

“Then I guess we’ll have to go to his place.”

“No ball game. Call in an order and I’ll go get it.”

While Rusty called Zeke’s I headed out because it was nearly a half hour’s drive down out of the hills and into the city. It was dark by the time I arrived to pick up the pizzas, which included a big one for the guys and a little one for me. Driving back up into the hills, the scent of pizza, wafted temptingly through the Explorer. I’d taken the SUV because all my stuff was still in it and I wanted to take everything back into the house. As the road became darker I was looking forward to arriving home and settling down with the pizza and ballgame when I heard a *pop! Thumpa, thumpa, thumpa.*

Oh great, I thought, just the thing to top off my day, a flat tire. I looked around for a shoulder but they were all too slanted for changing a tire. When I finally found a spot to pull over it was in front of someone’s driveway. I looked at the peaceful house. The cars were all tucked away in the garage and no one was stirring. It seemed like a good place to change the tire. I got out and walked around the truck. Back tire, that was good news. The back of the truck was much lighter and the tire and jack were already back there. I searched for the lug wrench. Shoot, it was just one of those little ones. That was fine for Rusty but I needed some leverage. I yanked, and pushed, and pulled every which way, and the lug nuts stuck. I tried the long, firm pull that always worked for Rusty. I could have pulled on that thing for weeks and it wouldn't have budged. I set the lug wrench at an angle and brought my foot down firmly on the handle then tried putting my weight on it. Finally it slowly turned downward. It took me a half hour just to loosen the lug nuts on one tire. I took the jack out and heard a screen door slam then heard footsteps crunching over gravel. I looked and saw the beam of a flashlight weaving its way towards the Explorer.

"Need help?" asked a twenty-something-year-old guy. He was dressed in faded jeans and a greasy work shirt. He obviously knew cars.

"No thanks," I answered confidently, "I got it."

"Why don't you go wait in the house while I change that for you?"

"I don't need help. I'm perfectly capable of changing my own flat tire."

"Aw, come on, you know you don't want to do that yourself," he said, stepping closer. He reached out towards me and I stepped back. "No girl wants to spend their evening changing a tire."

He stepped closer again and shined the light on my face, then up and down my body. I felt like I was being visually stripped. I went to the backseat of the truck to strap on my 9mm.

"I don't mind, a flat's just a small inconvenience. I just need some space to work."

"Give me that lug wrench. You aren't using it right. I can have that tire off in a minute. Then we can go inside and have a drink…"

"Look, I don't know or trust you. The more you push the less I trust you. Right now the only way I'd let you help me would be at gun point and I don't think you'd like that. If you don't want this to go downhill really fast, just go back in the house and let me work. I've already boxed with a cop, put fifty bullets through the bull's eye at a firing range and lost four games of pool today. I'm just testy enough to give you trouble."

I pulled the gun from its holster and checked for bullets. He saw the glint of the metal and held up his hands in surrender.

"Okay, okay," he said, backing off.

Holstering the pistol, I went back to work. I jacked up the back of the truck and changed the tire fairly easily while the man continued to watch. It's amazing what a little incentive will do. I threw the flat into the cargo area, placed the jack in its little compartment and drove away with a terse wave.

I barged in the front door, tossed the cold pizza on the breakfast bar and flopped down on the old, brown couch.

"You'll have to microwave it. I don't want it anymore."

"An hour and a half to get pizza? No wonder they don't deliver out here." Rusty walked over and sat on the coffee table to talk. Then he saw the gun. I unbuckled it and handed it to him. He checked it, saw that it hadn't been fired, and set it on the coffee table. Then he flashed me a look that said, "Okay, spill."

"The flat is in the back of the truck. We need a longer lug wrench if I'm going to be changing tires. And we need those two-foot-long flashlights in both vehicles if we're going to live on a street with no lights."

"What made you worried enough to use your gun?"

"We have an overly friendly neighbor who I didn't trust. He thought I needed help. And I didn't use it; I only made it obvious that I was ready for trouble if he didn't back off."

"Did he back off?"

"Yeah."

"Why didn't you let him help you?"

"Something just didn't feel right."

"Why didn't you call me? I'd have changed it for you."

"I can change a tire myself. There was no reason to bother you. I'd feel better if you went and tightened the lug nuts down, though. I always feel like I can't pull them tight enough."

After changing into something more comfortable, I curled up on the couch with Rusty to enjoy the ballgame. I started hearing the pizza calling, and then my evening fell comfortably into place. Chase watched the ballgame and patrolled the grounds every once in a while. I couldn't understand exactly what he was doing but knew he preferred being outdoors. We should start planning round two of our contest so he could leave for home. I wasn't sure why he'd chosen to spend such a long time up here, but in Rusty's family they kind of just accepted whoever was around. Now I fell into a similar mindset with anyone associated with Rusty's family.

My family was different. I'd get a call from my mother or my sister saying exactly when they would arrive, what they wanted to do while they were here and when they would leave. I'd get a head count and sometimes even a request to prepare certain favorite meals. There were advantages to both ways.

This was weird, though. Chase was up here for over a week and Strict hadn't called. I'd been busy with the wedding, then off on my honeymoon and finally back home for over a week and still no call from Strict. Searches were usually a weekly occurrence for me, and an even more frequent occurrence for the other teams. I knew hikers didn't suddenly stop getting lost. Was this some sort of test or something? Was I on some training mission without even knowing it? My imagination started playing this up, and as it did my curiosity grew.

Chapter 7

The next day Chase and I went to Gear Up because he needed to restock his backpacking food. I hadn't eaten mine so I was in pretty good shape as far as equipment went. I looked at tents and decided I liked my old faithful one that I'd been using for years. I'd tried a new, more compact one, but when a frightened elk had thrashed it I was relieved to be back in my old tent again. I thought I was stuck in a rut, but I couldn't find anything I liked better than my old one. Chase shopped while I looked around at all the newfangled camping supplies.

Tuesday we were back at Elk Meadows dropping off Chase. Now that he knew about the creek, meadows, and mountains I wondered which he would choose to try and trip me up. I was hoping he'd go for the creek. If he really wanted to find out how I got from the creek to the meadow he'd end up somewhere in that area. Rusty and I drove away leaving Chase alone to pick his route unobserved. I worried. Would I be able to track Chase? I wasn't sure. I looked at this as a challenge, something to help hone my tracking skills and test my scouting ability. But I'd never tracked someone who truly knew how to hide a trail. Kelly had tried when I tracked him but he wasn't experienced at it. He had only practiced what he'd read about tracking in books, and although it may have worked for the casual observer, it hadn't posed much of a challenge for me. Chase, I thought, would be different.

Rusty dropped me off at the house and continued on to work. I emptied my pack and then repacked it, checking all my gear over and placing things so it would be easier to carry. I refilled my stove with fuel then made sure I had two and a half days worth of water, just in case the search took me into dry areas where water wasn't available. I tacked a target to a tree and practiced with the paintball rifle until I was hitting the target consistently from across the yard. I was wishing for a moving target but wasn't going to shoot at Rusty just for practice. I tried it the other way around, shooting at the still target while running across the yard and decided I better be standing still when taking my shot at Chase.

Rusty came home to a quiet house.

"Hey," he said, "we're alone again. We can do whatever we want."

"And what is it you want?" I asked.

"I want you. I don't care how or where but I want you before you go."

Out in the woods again, thirty pound pack, lousy food, lonely nights, barely a trail. Why did I think this was fun? Chase was good. I had to give him credit for that. He'd chosen a direction I never would have taken. In a way that helped my part of the game. If he'd have done the expected I would have had preconceived ideas about what he'd be doing to trick me. Since I'd never noticed this part of the woods I was relying simply on the signs he left behind. I tried to keep my mind on the trail but it was hard. After last night I was ready to just hike right back home, surprise Rusty and go for round two! Oh yeah, that would be fun, but here I was, just like I said I would be, tracking. I had a day to find Chase and he was doing his best to not be found. Besides picking a totally off-the-wall direction he was also doing things fairly predictably. But I guess I had done the same thing when I'd started out a week ago, done things predictably, that is.

There are both advantages and disadvantages to wearing moccasins when hiking. You barely leave a trail but on the other hand you can't blend in with the thousands of pairs of tennis shoes worn by campers and hikers. One step onto a treaded print and you leave a nice clean spot that is highly visible to the trained eye. And so that was what I watched for at first, an absence of pattern. Once I left populated ground I began watching for soft indentations, bent vegetation, any clue at all. Sometimes there were none. Usually there were some but I had to study and examine things carefully. Finding one track didn't guarantee me another track and sometimes not even a direction. Something didn't feel right about this trail. It was hard to follow but at the same time it was also too easy, appearing much like a hiker. I thought Chase would be attempting to hide his footprints and these footprints, although hard to see, were just hiking along. But who else would be wearing moccasins out here? The average person found them uncomfortable in the woods. They liked some cushioning when they stepped on sticks and rocks. It took a person accustomed to feeling with their feet, or someone with extra tough feet, to prefer moccasins off trail.

Chase's tracks led me behind the campground. He didn't exactly follow the road back out but had headed in that direction. Then he took off around the backside of the mountain. I knew there was a creek on the other side of the mountain but it seemed unlikely that he could get there from this side. I thought back over the drive in, trying to remember the lay of the land from the truck. What would Chase have seen on his way in that made him come back out this way?

Stop speculating, Cassidy, if you decide ahead of time what you think Chase did you will try to make his actions line up with that. Just keep your eye on the tracks. Shoot, where were the tracks? I backtracked myself for about twenty feet until I saw where I lost focus, then I started on Chase's trail again. Focus, Cass, focus.

He had been nice to me so far. His trail led through typical woodland, the ground neither too hard to take a print nor too soft, and it was easy to track on. Vegetation hid his tracks in places. Come on, Chase, I thought, do something interesting. About noon I came across a beautiful campsite. Someone had set up a tent under a tree. There was also a cooking ring with some handy rocks surrounding it. A stove was set out for cooking and a pack leaned up against a tree. Chase's tracks led right up to the camp and then went off in every direction. I didn't want to invade another person's camp but I was sure Chase hadn't set it up. It was too citified for Chase.

"Hello?" I called out. "Anybody home?"

No answer. I circled the camp hoping to pick up Chase's footprints leaving it when I suddenly caught a movement off to my side. I immediately slipped into stealth mode and made my way over to the area where I expected to intercept the person. Then I noticed his shoes. Damn.

"Excuse me," I said from the bushes. The man was immediately startled, jumping about five feet straight up.

"Damn it!" he cried. "What kind of a freaking place is this? It's full of crazy people! Sneaking up on me. Scaring me half to death!"

I smiled to myself. He'd met Chase.

"I'm looking for a friend of mine," I informed him. "Maybe you've seen him? Older guy, longish salt and pepper hair. He was backpacking and he carried a rifle like this." I held up the paintball gun for his inspection.

"I swear, the place is full of loonies! Yeah I saw him at Elk Meadows. He paid me fifty bucks to wear his old shoes for a day. I told him I wasn't going far, that I'd only be hiking for a few hours, that I had a favorite campsite away from the others. He said that was fine and would I wear his shoes anyway? Hell fifty bucks is fifty bucks and I'm an honest guy so I took the guy's fifty bucks and wore his shoes. See?" He held up his foot. Sure enough he was wearing Chase's old moccasins.

"Shit," I said quietly. "No wonder his trail was too obvious. I should have seen a trick coming." Then louder, "Thanks, for the information." Then I turned away thinking ARG!

As soon as I got a little distance away I broke into a jog back to Elk Meadows. There was no way I'd be able to catch up with Chase now.

"Hey!" the guy called after me.

"Yeah?"

"He also said to give you this," he said, jogging over tenderfoot style. He held out a piece of paper. It read, "Things aren't always as they appear, keep thinking."

"Would you hold the note against this tree?" I asked.

"Um, sure," he said hesitantly. I stepped back two steps, aimed at the paper and fired twice. Two neat little paint splats exploded on the paper. The guy jerked his hand back and the paper fluttered to the ground. I picked it up and waved it in the breeze to dry.

"When the guy gave you his moccasins what shoes did he wear to hike in? Did he say what direction he was going?"

"He had hiking boots on and, no, he didn't tell me where he was going."

"If you don't want the moccasins I'll return them to the guy they belong to. He only asked you to wear them to trick me so they accomplished their task."

We walked back to his camp, he took off Chase's moccasins, and gratefully pulled on his more comfortable shiny, white tennis shoes. I stuffed the moccasins into a side pocket of my pack.

"Thanks," I said and took off at a jog. I heard the guy mutter something about nutty Californians as I left camp. I came to a halt pretty quick though. Darn, the thought suddenly occurred to me that Chase wanted me to go all the way back to Elk Meadows. But what if he hadn't taken off from there in another direction? What if he'd followed this poor guy in different shoes and then continued on. He'd laugh at me from here to next Tuesday if I ran all the way back to Elk Meadows and started again. I was convinced our challenge had developed into a true battle of wits. If I ran all the way back to Elk Meadows I'd never find him in time and I was pretty sure he wanted me to be able to find him in a reasonable amount of time. So he was somewhere in this direction. I began weaving back and forth across the trail I'd come in on. I was almost positive I would run across hiking boot tracks off to the side of the moccasin trail. I better be right, I thought, I'm just guessing but I had better be right. I continued crossing and then crossing the trail again until I found it. A hiking boot print. Yes! I followed the boot print and was pretty sure this time I was actually following Chase. He wasn't thinking about tripping me up so much as staying out of sight of the other hiker. Once the two trails separated enough and he was no longer concerned about being spotted he turned off in another direction and began hiding his tracks in earnest. This was the Chase I had been expecting to see. His tracks blended and he had found difficult places to hike in, thickets of ferns where nothing could be seen from the knees down and rocky places, he had spotted them all. He was enjoying the hike too, watching for things to use in his favor. I watched for things I would have used, but also kept my eye on his tracks. As the day wore on I had to be more and more careful. If I accidentally stumbled upon his camp he'd shoot me before I could put two and two together. He could be lying in wait for me. The only problem was I didn't know if his camp was right around the corner or a mile or two away. I had no means of judging how fast he'd walked or how long he had traveled. All I knew was that he'd had enough time to con some guy into wearing his shoes.

Suddenly Chase's trail turned. Now this was interesting. What did he know about up here that would make him suddenly turn in that direction? I looked around and just made out in the distance two walls of rock that nearly met. Oh, wow, I hoped he'd gone in there. Even if it turned out to be the terribly defendable canyon Kelly had mentioned I still wanted to see it. I checked Chase's tracks, he wasn't hiding them now. Either he was in the canyon or he wanted me to believe he'd gone in there. I did not like this set up. Either I walked into a trap or I walked into the canyon and he could follow me in. A trap either way. I examined the entrance. Tracks led right up to the opening but then there were so many rocks I couldn't tell if Chase was up there. I watched for Chase's footprints around the entrance in increasingly bigger circles. No sign of him leaving. He wanted me to follow him in. How long was it? Was there space for a camp in there? Was it possible for me to circle it? What was at the end of the canyon? How many places were in there that he could shoot me from? A lot. Hoo boy, all I could do was go find out. At least this ambush was only a paintball trap and I'd been in worse situations in the past. In fact, I thought maybe I was taking this challenge a little too seriously. The worse that could happen was a paintball shot, and a lot of gloating on Chase's part. Maybe it would be better to get shot. It might limit my scouting and Rusty would be grateful. Okay Cass, onward and upward. I started up the canyon. It was more of a chasm than a canyon. If I stretched my hands wide I could touch both sides of it. It curved and twisted from rushing flash floods that had eroded away the walls. A few trees managed to grow in the bottom and rocks littered the floor. I kept to the side of the canyon inching my way up while watching for signs of Chase's passing. Make yourself small, Cass, stick to the shadows. I studied the floor of the canyon closely for footprints and then noticed something odd. It was a whittled stick propped at an angle. It held up a rock, which held up more rocks. Great, the canyon was booby trapped, not dangerously, but enough to give Chase some warning. It meant he was close and was paying attention. But it also meant he might be relying on hearing me rather than seeing me. I wasn't taking any chances. Now I kept hidden from sight, watching for tracks and for more likely booby traps that Chase may have set. It could be anything. A cord stretched across the floor of the canyon. A stick propped up. A branch pulled down taut, I had to be very careful to spot anything unusual. At this point I was glad in a way to have seen the warning trap. I hadn't seen a footprint for a while and it meant I was heading the right way.

I came to a pine tree growing out one side of the canyon. Its roots had been washed away and then a windstorm had tilted it until it leaned across the canyon and hit the top of the opposite wall. I considered the uses. One, the canyon was not a good camping spot. Two, Chase could use the rim of the canyon to watch for me. Three, if I didn't climb the tree he could easily shoot me from above. Had I been in Chase's position I would have climbed the tree and set up camp close to the canyon, so I climbed the tree. At the top I was rewarded with a few faint scuffs where Chase had pulled himself onto the ridge.

I knew I was close now, close enough that I took my pack off to make movement easier. I quietly unzipped the pocket containing Chase's moccasins and slipped them into a cargo pocket of my pants. Time to find that camp. I knew Chase's camp could be anything, a camouflage hammock between two trees. A bivouac sack under some brush. Chase was not used to luxuries on the trail. He had to set up camp as part of the plan but, just like me, it didn't have to amount to much. I concentrated on the tracks, striving to stay out of site from the direction the tracks were heading. I crouched low to get a good look at the ground and stay well hidden. I followed track by hidden track, wary, ready to hear that shot at any time. I was amazed that I stumbled upon his camp without so much as a sound or movement. He hadn't spent much time setting up and had done everything while standing in one place. It had required little set up and included a bivouac sack with his pack hoisted into a tree. Everything had been neatly camouflaged and stashed out of plain sight.

When I found his camp I thought I was still following a trail. It just suddenly stopped and when I looked around there was his camp. I quickly backed off, hiding behind a tree. How had I managed it? And where was Chase? I could be within feet of him. If I was, surely he knew it and was laughing at me. But, no, there was no sound, no movement. I dropped his moccasins on the ground where he would see them, then I circled the area. He wasn't there. Had I lucked out, or what? I circled it again finding his trail leading away, towards the canyon wall.

I smiled when I saw him, staked out overlooking the canyon, paintball rifle by his side. I hid behind a tree and watched. He hadn't expected me to climb the tree. He thought I'd keep going up the canyon. I could shoot him right now and put an end to the game, but decided not to, so I hid my tracks and went to stake out his camp. I found a place with a good line of fire on the spot where he'd find his moccasins and waited. And waited. And waited. It wasn't until nearly dark that he gave up on my coming up that canyon. He was walking to his camp, hiding his tracks and he stopped, looked around. He'd found the tracks from when I'd circled the camp. He followed my tracks, noting I'd made two passes around his camp. He followed my tracks back to where I'd observed him at the canyon and followed them to my present hiding place. Rats, I had wanted to shoot him right after I saw the expression on his face when he found his moccasins, but it wasn't meant to be. I stepped out of hiding and he grinned at me.

"Why didn't you shoot me when you had the chance?" he asked.

"Because, it isn't important to me. I don't need to shoot you to know I could have and you don't need to be shot to know I could have either. You saw where I stood. You know what I saw."

"What about Rusty?"

"I'm sure he'll drag the whole story out of us somehow."

"What about Strict?"

"Tell him whatever you want. Any idea why Strict hasn't called in three weeks? I need to get some hours in this month. I have to put in twenty-eight hours every month to stay qualified as a reserve deputy. Usually I have no problem putting in twenty-eight hours on one or two searches. But Strict hasn't called me in three weeks."

"Don't worry about it. You helped Rusty with the shooting."

"Wow, a whole hour's work. I don't think boxing with Tom counts as training time. Target practice might, but.... What bothers me more is that I know he has had work for me to do, so why hasn't he called?"

We'd gotten back to camp and he'd found his moccasins with the note slipped inside.

"There's your two shots," I said.

"Cassidy, I think Strict is having a hard time deciding how much he can risk with you. He knows you can follow a trail. You've definitely proven yourself there. Unfortunately you don't stop at tracking and it scares him, just like it scares Rusty. You can't blame them for that. They just care about you. Just like I couldn't box with you, they couldn't either. They can't hurt you and they feel responsible when you're put into dangerous situations. That's why we're out here. I thought it would be interesting and a challenge to track each other but Strict really wants to know the outcome. He wanted a good test of what you were capable of."

"If I don't go out on search calls I'll have to do ride-alongs. I don't want to be a cop. I can't follow procedure. I can't stand putting on the whole cop act. I hesitate when I should shoot and my first reaction to violence is to hide. Once I get my head on straight and analyze the situation I catch up quick. But I don't belong in a squad car and all the guys know it. If they wanted me along it would only be because they could count on some trouble, or cookies, or an interesting story or two. It definitely wouldn't be their overwhelming need for my proficiency as a cop."

"You're a good kid. I hope you never become a cop. And I think I can get Strict back on track. I know the guys are giving him a hard time. They want you back and not just for the tall tales and cookies. They know you can find people and you're a valuable part of the team. They feel it every time they go out without you. It's twice as hard and takes twice as long. So we want to put the team back together. I think I can help."

We heated up our stoves, prepared backpacker meals, and ate quickly so we could clean up. It was getting dark and neither of us liked eating after dark. I didn't expect bears in this part of the woods but you could never be sure. If they did show up it was usually just after sunset and they were drawn by the scent of food.

"Was it cold last night?" I asked.

"A little, not bad, typical California summer night."

"Okay." I tossed my pack on the ground for a pillow and spread out my sleeping bag.

"Cassidy…"

"Oh, no, not you too."

He grinned in the dark and let me be.

"Up at first light?" he asked.

"Yup. How far is it back?"

"Not too far. I spent more time on the canyon than I did on the trail."

"What else did you do down there? I found one trap that I thought you set up to warn you of my approach."

"We'll take them down on the way back."

"Did you booby trap the whole canyon and then climb up the tree?"

"Not the whole canyon."

"I didn't bother with the whole canyon. It didn't look like a decent camp was possible down there so I thought you'd camp up top and watch the canyon."

"You think too much. Bet you didn't go back to Elk Meadows either."

"Nope."

I was awake before first light but stayed in my sleeping bag until the sun started peeking over the horizon. I stuffed my sleeping bag in its sack, bungeed it to my pack and got out the stove. Oatmeal held no appeal and it was going to be a short day so I just made hot chocolate. Chase broke camp and skipped the whole stove business. He sat pulling strips off a big piece of beef jerky and watched while I paced and sipped hot chocolate. When the cup was empty I poured in a little water, swished it around and flung the water into the brush. Then I packed the cup and shrugged into my pack.

"You're too perky in the morning. Are you in a hurry?"

"Yeah, I know Rusty will be there soon. But we don't have to hurry. We need to take down the traps you set. If that guy you paid to wear your moccasins wanders up there he'll leave California and never return."

"Maybe we should leave them then."

"He was holding your note when I shot it. Thought he was going to lose a hand."

"Poor guy, jumped like a frog when I approached him at his camp at Elk Meadows."

"Yeah, he reminded me of Thez."

"You going to show me how you got from the creek to the meadow?"

"It depends on time. It's three miles from Elk Meadows."

"But it's not far from here. This canyon is part of the creek."

"Do you have a map?"

He dug it out. Guess he'd been planning his route for a while before we had a chance to finish the contest. Sure enough, the canyon went around the backside of a mountain and then almost hit the trail.

"Looks doable to me but I've never been over this part of the creek. Let's go for it. It's only a few miles. Then the rest is trails back to Elk Meadows."

We climbed back down the pine tree minus our packs. I climbed down first, then Chase lowered the packs down on a rope and climbed down last. We followed the canyon down to the first booby trap and Chase disassembled it. Then we followed the creek bed up and around the mountain. We were relieved when the canyon gave way to more open ground where we could walk without stepping from rock to rock. Chase took down two more traps designed to warn him of my approach and startle me a little.

When we got to the trail again I showed him what I had done. We were only going to do this once and it didn't serve any useful purpose to keep my actions secret. On the contrary, if he knew how I thought as I left a trail it might help him find me if he needed to in the future.

"Here's what I did. You'll have to follow me."

I walked down the side of the trail, then down to the creek, hiding my tracks just as I did before. I planted a clue, just as like I did before, then doubled back, keeping to the rocks and cover. When I got back to the trail I stayed under cover and made my tracks head down trail, then backed over my tracks. I hopped lightly over to the trail and made my way up the crack.

"Come on up, you have to see this," I told him. "This ledge follows the mountain down to almost ground level behind the meadow."

We walked the ledge until it ended and he stood there, hands on hips.

"Very clever," he said, "and you knew about this ledge how?"

"I was running from drug dealers who were after me with rifles and I needed a place to rest and plan, so I climbed that crack. They weren't trackers. They passed right underneath me and got stumped. See that big tree over there? The guy I wounded was sitting under that tree and the other guy was patrolling on a dirt bike, searching the trail for me. I climbed down out of their sight and stretched a rope across the trail. Then I fired a shot and the dirt bike came flying up the trail, right into the rope. Took out both guys with one trick. I stole their dirt bike and headed out. Got arrested for speeding and possession of stolen property, but I asked the officer to take me to Rusty's station and he bailed me out. That seems so long ago. Almost a year and a half ago. I was just a kid. What was I doing up here running from rifle toting drug dealers?"

"I have no idea. Sounds like you have lots more stories in that head of yours that I haven't heard."

"You don't want to hear some of them. Let's go home."

We climbed down again, I picked up my pack and we headed down the trail at a brisk walk. Three miles later Elk Meadows appeared off in the distance. When the Explorer came into view I couldn't help myself and broke into a jog. Rusty got out and stood there grinning, arms open wide. It's hard flying into the arms of the one you love with a backpack on. It's like two high school kids kissing and locking braces. So I removed my pack and leaned it against the truck tire and then got my hug. And my kiss. Then he held me out at arm's length.

"No paint!" he said.

"Nope, no paint."

"Did you find your man?"

"Yup, I found him. He just isn't as excited to see you as I am. He'll be here in a minute."

As I was putting my pack in the back of the Explorer and digging around for the trail mix a man walked over to Rusty.

"Don't camp here long," he warned. "The place is full of loonies!"

I smiled and came around the back of the truck.

"Don't worry," I said, "he knows, and we're leaving today. You can camp in peace." The guy blushed. "He met Chase and me the hard way," I explained.

"She's really very nice once you get to know her," Rusty said.

Chase walked up, "Hey man, thanks for helping out. And thanks for giving my shoes back."

Rusty raised an eyebrow.

"We'll tell you the whole story when we get home."

Home. It felt so good now. Rusty and I still needed to personalize it more and we still felt as if we rattled around in the spaciousness of it, but it was comfortable and it was ours.

Shadow tackled me as I came in the door. I was used to the ritual so I just sat on the floor in the living room while he jumped all over me. I tried to get a few pets in as he jumped around, but soon he raced off trying to turn it into a game of tag. This was my cue to do what I wanted so long as I pretended to try and get him every once in a while as he ran around trying to stay away from me. There was no need to really try and catch him because if I really wanted him to come to me, a firm "come" command was all that was necessary.

A quick shower and I felt much better. We spent the next few hours sitting around the table stuffing ourselves with chips and salsa, taking turns telling Rusty about the search.

"I kept telling myself that the trail didn't feel right for Chase's trail. But then I'd remember that the first three miles of my trail hadn't been too tough either so I kept on after the moccasin trail. I'm glad that guy didn't catch me scouting out his camp. He'd have really thought we were nuts."

"Why didn't you go back to Elk Meadows and start over?" Chase asked.

"Not enough time, so I weaved my way back until I found your boot prints. The boot print trail felt better. I could tell that trail was yours by how you hid your tracks."

We talked on and on. After a while I got up to start dinner while the conversation continued. Chase asked Rusty about the story I'd told him and Rusty filled in the background to it. I was glad he didn't continue with the rest of the story.

"Cassidy, you asked me why Strict has backed off on his calls for you. Remember that, when he was at your wedding, he didn't just see a bunch of people wishing you well. He saw you as Wayne and Betty's daughter, Jesse's sister, Bill and Bev's daughter-in-law. You're Tony, Sandy and Cody's sister-in-law. Now you're Rusty's wife. You're everybody's friend. You're not just this lone tracker that fell on his doorstep. And believe me, he saw all of their reactions when you walked down the aisle. He can't forget that moment. He can't put it behind him and just send you into who knows what. He knows you want to. He knows what you will do, how far you will go, so he holds back."

"That won't change if you talk to him," I inferred.

"No, you can't go back and he won't forget. Strict has to see you getting calls and tracking again to remember the real you again."

"The real me? That bride at the wedding was the real me too."

That statement certainly got Rusty's attention but he didn't say anything.

"You'll get a call from him eventually, and when you do it'll be a straight forward tracking case. Take it. Things will click. You'll click with the guys; the search will be easier with a tracker back on board. Just give it time."

"Yeah, and while I am giving it time people are wandering around out in the hills, running out of water. I've had some close calls. I've seen situations where people wouldn't have made it another day. What happens to those people while Strict is sorting out his emotions?"

"I'll talk to him tomorrow on my way out of town."

"But how will I know anything about it if you go back to San Diego?"

"Strict will call."

I had to be content with that.

The next morning I awoke and wandered over to the bay window to see deer on the lawn. They were nibbling peacefully so I quickly brushed my hair, and pulled on jeans, a flannel shirt and moccasins. I slipped out the back door and inched around the side of the house. Four deer. The yard was wide open, no chance of making myself shorter than the grass. They would just have to get used to seeing all of me. I knew it would take time. I didn't expect to get close to them the first time. They needed to get to know me but this was a good way to do it. I slowly made my way out to the yard to introduce myself deer style. I made myself visible to them and then I just froze there, letting them become comfortable with me. A few more steps, freeze. They headed for the trees so I stopped. That was far enough. Introductions had been made. Once they were no longer fearful I sat down cross-legged in the grass and just watched them. After a while they moved off around the corral and wandered away. I stood, pleased with the little bit of progress I'd made. I went inside to find Chase standing at the window.

"I'm not pushing myself on the deer. I want them to accept me as a regular part of their day. I want them to come out of the trees even if they see me working outside. So they need to get to know me a little bit at a time. They'll come around. The deer near my hideout were becoming used to me before they were chased away. Why are you up so early?"

"I heard the door," he said simply, like that explained it all, which it did, but only because it was Chase who said it.

I started straightening the breakfast bar. Wiping off the top, putting glasses in the dishwasher.

"Do you want some breakfast? Or do you want to wait for Rusty?" I said, picking up a thick envelope. Oh yes! Why didn't that man think to tell me these things? I'd been waiting anxiously to see my honeymoon photos and he just leaves them in an out of the way spot.

"I'll wait for Rusty."

"Good, let's sort through these pictures. I had Rusty order three of each print. One for each set of parents and one for ourselves." We sat down at the dining room table and I sorted the pictures into stacks, one for Bill and Bev, one for Mom and Dad, and one for ourselves.

"Rusty's got a beard," Chase observed.

"Yeah, that's what happens when you spend five days without a razor. Then when we finally got one I told him he could keep the beard until we headed home."

"You liked the beard?"

"It just seemed to fit the setting. I think he looks good in the pictures but I like him better without one. Oh look! Here's the one of the moose charging up the bank towards me. Well, it's not worth framing but you get the idea," I said, handing the picture to Chase. It showed the moose's right nostril and eye, a strong neck and blurry body fading off to the left of the picture. "Here's what the moose really looked like," I said, handing him the picture I'd taken while I was stalking it. There were pictures of us sitting in Adirondack chairs on the cabin porch. There was one of me cooking in the little kitchen in the cabin, one of the loft area and another of the living room area. We laughed at a picture of me wading in the lake. My expression was funny because the water was freezing.

I opened the next packet to find a picture that Rusty had taken from the canoe showing the moose nearly running me over. I put that one in a separate pile for Jesse. There were several peaceful canoeing pictures that were placed in the stacks for the parents. I debated about the parachute picture.

"Chase, what is this a picture of?" I asked.

"It's Rusty holding a parachute," he stated.

"Would you have recognized it without hearing the parachute story?"

"Yeah, a parachute is a parachute. Nothing else looks like it."

"You decide. How do you think Bill and Bev will react if they see this picture?"

Chase picked up the stack I'd set aside for Bill and Bev. There were several nice shots of Rusty, a couple of me.

"Keep that one," he said.

I added a picture of the cabin to each stack. The next picture made me blush, as did each one that followed until I had counted five. Five pictures and I had no idea when Rusty had taken them! Chase looked at me amused. I put them face down on the table.

"I didn't even know he took those!" I said. "I am really slipping, before I know it I'm going to have to take him scouting. I told him he couldn't go scouting with me until he could sneak up on me without being seen."

"And I can't see those pictures?"

I looked at them again. I had been nude when they were taken but they didn't really show much.

"I'm not going to show them to you! If you want to see them you'll have to be either very sneaky or convince Rusty to show you."

I actually thought the pictures looked very comfortable and romantic and it didn't bother me that Rusty had taken them. I only wish I had a little warning rather than stumbling across them with Chase.

There were pictures of Taylor's main street, the town from the air, Upper Loon Lake from the air and a picture of me getting out of the little pontoon plane. All in all I was pleased with the pictures.

Rusty walked in wearing boxer pants, a t-shirt, tousled hair and a very sleepy expression.

"Did you see the honeymoon pictures?" I asked.

"No but I picked them up," he answered.

"Chase and I were just looking at them," I said.

He paused.

"So," he said cautiously to Chase, "what do you think?"

Chase grinned at him enjoying his embarrassment. "*Lucky man*," he said with a wily look.

"Cass, I thought we'd be looking at those pictures together. I never thought you'd show them to Chase first! I…"

Chase and I cracked up.

"Here," I said, "Chase hasn't seen them yet. You decide."

"You don't care?"

"He'd see more of me in a swimsuit. It was just the circumstances that took me by surprise. Promise me you are not putting those pictures on your screensaver."

He flipped through the pictures.

"I like this one," he said, handing me a picture. It showed me wrapped comfortably in a big red and black plaid buffalo blanket, sitting on a fur rug in front of a fire. The fire had warmed things up so the blanket was not exactly wrapped tight anymore. The picture showed a lot of bare shoulder and a lot of leg but it was the comfortable warmth within the picture that made it such a good one.

"Me too," I admitted.

"I want to talk to you before I head back," Chase told Rusty. He pocketed the pictures for Rusty's parents and Rusty pocketed the pictures of me. They both headed for Rusty's office and I started breakfast.

Once I had sausages, omelets and toast ready I went to call the guys. They were in a deep, serious conversation about the scouting aspect of the contest.

"She walked right into my camp. Circled it twice and tracked me to where I was staked out. Cassidy could have shot me any time she wanted. She could have been there an hour or more before I gave up on her coming up the canyon. She was there all that time and I didn't even know it. She came out of hiding when she was ready, no sooner. I'm willing to bet she could have watched me until dark, set up her camp just out of sight of mine and watched me the next day without me knowing, had she wanted to."

"Breakfast is ready guys, come and get it."

"Thanks," Rusty said. "We'll be there in a minute."

Chase continued, "She found my trap, identified it for what it was and avoided it. She reasoned out where I was and found me instead of continuing up the canyon like I expected her to."

I left. It sounded like I had an ally in Chase. I thought it wise to let him be. They were still talking as they came down the hall.

"So, how much of a camp did she bother with?" Rusty asked.

"Not much." Chase answered. Rusty smiled and shook his head. Chase continued, "I started to protest but decided it was better to keep the peace. She seemed very comfortable with her pack for a pillow and her sleeping bag rolled out on the ground."

"At least she used a sleeping bag," Rusty said. "She doesn't always."

"The reason I told you all that is because I'm going to Strict's place on my way out of town. I wanted your reaction."

"You knew she was there, how?" Rusty asked, giving me a look. He didn't want to be talking in front of me but couldn't break it off without excluding me. I let the guys talk. This was my future in search and rescue they were discussing and I wanted Rusty to be comfortable with whatever was decided so I kept my silence and just let them continue.

"I found her tracks. Only a tracker would have caught them. You would never have known she was there. Strict might have, maybe. He's tracked before but only easy trails. He knows a thing or two but he has to be watching for clues and doesn't catch subtle things. I doubt if he'd have known she was there either."

"What bothers me is that scouting usually involves firearms."

"That's why I threw in the paintball rifles but she didn't shoot me. If I would have tried to shoot her she would have let me."

"Why?" Rusty asked, turning to me. "If you had been shot, then you would have lost. It would have marked Chase as the better tracker and scout. Would you have let him shoot you?"

"Yeah, I would have. He's more experienced. If he came out looking like the victor it wouldn't bother me. I'll always be the junior tracker as far as I'm concerned."

"Why didn't you shoot him?"

"I didn't need to."

"It was just paint."

"No, it was an understanding. He knew he could have been shot. He knew to shoot me would have been dishonest. So we settled for a silent understanding."

"What we need to know," Rusty said, "is if it came right down to it, could you? If it were him or you, could you take him out?"

"No. I don't think I could shoot Chase, even if it was in self defense."

"What if it was someone you didn't know? If it had been a real apprehension and the guy discovered you, could you shoot him?"

"I think so. In cases like that my instincts take over. If I knew it was self-defense I could do it. If taking out one person would save others, I could do it. But you know how it would affect me. Both of you know."

Yup, I could tell by the looks on their faces, they both knew.

After breakfast Chase went to Strict's house, but I would have to wait to find out if the tracking competition had affected the men's opinion of me. I thought I had proven my abilities, but I also thought they would hesitate more, knowing I had to be pushed beyond their comfort zone before I would act in a violent way against an attacker.

Chapter 8

Several days later, just as I was getting out of the Explorer at a home improvement store, my cell phone rang. It was Rusty.

"Hey!" I said brightly. "What's up?"

"Are you ready for a search?" he asked.

"Yeah, it must be something different if Lou ran it through you this time. Got any details?"

"A few. It ought to be interesting anyway."

"Why?"

"Ever tracked a motorcycle before?"

"Not since I met Lou. And I kept tabs on the dirt bikes when I went after Kelly, but that wasn't really tracking. It was just me being cautious. I've never had to find a motorcycle track in amongst other motorcycle tracks. A lot of ground can be covered on a motorcycle though. How am I supposed to catch up with a motorcycle on foot?"

"You won't. Ever rode an ATV before?"

"No, but it can't be much tougher than a dirt bike and I've ridden those."

"Are you willing to give it a try?"

"Sure, you know I'll try anything."

"Wear your uniform. I'll pick you up in half an hour."

"I'm not home. I went to the store to buy wood, but I'll go home instead. We ought to get there about the same time."

"Okay, I'll meet you there."

I climbed back into the Explorer and drove home wondering exactly what would be involved in tracking a motorcycle. It couldn't be that different from tracking people but I worried about distinguishing one motorcycle track from another. Well I'd give it a try anyway. When I got to the house I went to the garage and found our packs, emptied them, and refilled them with food and water. If this was desert tracking, it meant carrying our entire water supply for the whole search. I packed my tracking tools. I took anything that might help the search. Sketch book, measuring tape, magnifying glass… I was sometimes surprised how often I needed just a bit of help.

I changed into my uniform wondering what it would look like after riding around in the dust and dirt for hours. I strapped on the 9mm since it was part of the uniform. I hoped I didn't need it. If I was asked to wear the uniform, though, I had to be prepared to act like an officer.

Rusty rushed through the front door and went to change his clothes. He returned wearing swat team black. He noticed the gun, the uniform and paused. He knew why I was wearing it, yet from the expression on his face I knew it bothered him.

"Why the uniform?" I asked. "I know it should be worn every time I go out, but Strict doesn't push it unless I'm supposed to be representing the force in some way. So what's the deal?"

"Hopefully nothing. It's just a precaution."

"Usually precautions are a signal for trouble to me."

"This may turn into more of an urban search, we don't know, it just depends on which direction the kid went. We have a nervous mother and a serious health situation with a kid who doesn't take his medical condition seriously. He could be out in the desert, at a friend's house, at the corner market, we don't know and no one has seen him. They've questioned the locals. There is a motorcycle track going off into the desert and the guys tried to follow it but Strict called them off before they could make a mess of things. Strict thought we ought to get your input."

"Let's go give my input then."

Rusty drove out to a little bedroom community near Joshua Hills and then to the outskirts. We wound around on dusty roads and saw many dusty front yards full of mesquite and cactus. Occasionally someone went out of their way and installed a sprinkler system and grass, but nearly all the houses were sandy tan with sandy yards and Spanish tile roofs. I noticed with dismay that most of them also displayed a dirt bike or two in a side yard or shed. Rusty pulled up to a house surrounded by rescue trucks and cars. I pulled my pack from the truck and headed for the area with the most action. A group of men stood over a patio table intently focused on a map of the area. I slipped in between them and listened, trying to get a feel for what they were doing.

"Look, we can speculate all we want, but we have to go by what we know, and all we know is the trail gets real confusing right here," Victor said, poking at the map. "No matter what direction the trail goes from there, it doesn't matter where it looks logical for a kid to go, there's hundreds of miles of bike trails and he could have been over half of them. We won't know anything until Cassidy gets here and takes a look. We've been over and over this and it's not doing us any good."

I couldn't resist. "Maybe if you go over it one more time, Cassidy might figure out what you're up against," I said.

They all stared at me like they'd seen a ghost, not that cops are afraid of ghosts. They just don't usually enjoy surprises as much as most people, especially when they are on the job. The two men standing on each side of me took a step back.

"Cassidy, don't do that to us," said Ben Tomlin. He'd given me a ride back to town once when I got my Jeep stuck. He wasn't used to my silent ways.

"Let's go," said Landon.

"Wait, you haven't shown me what I'm doing. All I know is it involves motorcycles and it's all new to me."

"Come here Cass," said Rusty. "Strict knew what you'd need." He took me to a picnic table where I found another dirt bike, several pairs of shoes and a picture of the missing kid. I picked up the picture. It showed a thin boy, almost grown, bright intelligent eyes, no hair, and a captivating smile. I also sensed an attitude lurking beneath the friendly face.

"His hair was just growing back," a woman standing beside me said. "I got him the dirt bike because he finally seemed strong enough to handle it. He's been through so much; I just know he'll come through this too. He has to."

"Can you show me some of his tracks?" I asked, examining the soles of his shoes. I was sad, but grateful, to see distinctive wear marks on his soles. The wear marks of a weary kid who wanted to run and play but only had the energy to walk. A kid who tried no matter how badly he felt. It would make tracking easier but it saddened me at the same time. The dirt bike was similar to all the other dirt bikes I'd seen up and down the street. The woman took me to the side of the house. There were many footprints surrounding the house, which was one reason I didn't like getting called in hours after the rest of the team had formed.

"He wanted to try and chop firewood this morning before it got hot. I didn't want him to but he seemed focused on it. I think he only managed to split one log but maybe you can find some tracks over here."

There was a large log set up for splitting firewood, an ax was propped up against the side and one freshly split log had been added to the stack. I glanced at the ground trying to pick out the right tracks. The spot was littered with woodchips, and grass was invading the area. Most of the tracks headed directly from the front to the backyard and were probably from the searchers and police officers. I focused on the area around the log and singled out the tracks of our missing boy.

"What is your son's name?" I asked the woman.

"Garrett, and I'm Lydia. All these men here and they call in a young girl to do their tracking for them?"

"It's what I do best. They're better at the real police work. Me? I follow a trail, but I can follow trails that they lose so they keep calling me. Looking at the tracks I know I could find Garrett if he was on foot. I'm a little worried about tracking a dirt bike. The tread is the same as the two-dozen other bikes on your street. Have you heard a lot of dirt bike activity since Garrett disappeared?"

"No, not much, the kids on our street usually go out riding on the weekends. Garrett goes during the week so he doesn't have to try and compete with them, but he has been working to the point where he would be comfortable trying."

"That's good news to me, not as many other tracks confusing the trail. Was Garrett still wearing these same shoes when he went out riding?"

"Yes, he probably was. He tends to have one pair of favorite shoes and wears them constantly."

"Okay. I think I'm ready. Try not to worry. I'll find Garrett and I know my team can handle the medical aspects if anything comes up. We'll keep in touch by radio and Lou Strickland will fill you in whenever he knows something."

I joined the guys, all ready to jump on their olive drab all terrain vehicles and speed off. Big boy toys. Unfortunately I needed to go slow for a bit. I needed to figure out how this machine worked and I needed to get a feel for the trail. As soon as things clicked a little I'd be right up with them until tracking took over and speed had to be sacrificed.

"Think you can wrestle this machine around in the desert?" Lou asked.

"Yeah."

"Would you rather ride with Rusty? You can double up."

"I need to be able to see the trail. If I rode behind Rusty I wouldn't see a thing."

I took the pack off the front of my ATV and moved it to the rack on the back. I really needed to see everything I could. I bungeed it down in case things got rough then sat on the seat looking at the controls. It appeared to be semiautomatic, not like the dirt bikes I had used before. If they gave me this one to simplify things it was a mistake, but I thought I could handle it. I fiddled with the three different brakes. I turned the key and pushed the button until I found all the gears. I settled on first but could probably have started out in second. I rode around in a circle while the guys all jumped on their ATVs.

"Wait!" I yelled above the roar. I walked the dirt bike trail a short distance on foot, taking in what few mannerisms I could. Garrett started out with both feet planted on either side of the bike. He gave it some gas and walked with his feet, not yet comfortable with the bike. These things were good to know. It would easily distinguish him from other bikers if he stopped. I found the wobbly start and the drag of his foot as the bike took off, then the steady straight track of a dirt bike in action. I walked back to the guys and climbed on my machine. The officers looked like they were ready for a race.

"Guys, I don't care what you do out there, but don't mess with my trail. I need to be able to read it without other tracks in the way. Show me how far you got."

They roared off in a cloud of dust and I followed behind, slower. I'd catch up but I wanted to get a good feel for how things worked. I couldn't see a thing for all the dust so I stayed back figuring things out on my own, confident the dust trail would always tell me their location. Within minutes the dust trail stopped so I headed for the spot where the dust was settling.

The guys had gathered at an intersection of two trails. I stopped my ATV and got off. These things were always easier on foot. If time and distance were not important I'd have preferred to do the whole search on foot but we needed the ATVs for the sake of time. I found the trail entering the intersection but the motorcycle track hadn't just breezed through it and kept going. Garrett had run circles around the intersection, like a roundabout, before he chose a direction. The land here was flat with plenty of room to ride in circles as he made his decision. They weren't nice neat circles. Several of the wobbles that hit the trail could have been the right one. All four directions had seen recent use. I found a place where he'd taken the circle a little too fast and put out a foot to catch himself. I walked a bigger circle around the intersection trying to find the trail with the most recent track. I studied the four trails from both sides to catch them in different lighting. They were so similar. Okay time for Plan B. I'd call in the reinforcements. I went to my pack and pulled out a magnifying glass. The tracks were plain but sometimes when I magnified them the edges became starker or rounder to my eye. Maybe rounder tracks would be older and sharper tracks more recent. I had to keep in mind the way they were made too, but any little hints helped the decision making process.

An ATV pulled up. "Oh no, she's got out the magnifying glass. This is serious," said Victor.

I knew which track came into the circle so I examined that one first, then compared the other tracks to the first. When I thought I'd found the newer track leading out of the intersection, I stepped back and climbed up on the seat of my ATV to get the big picture. I pictured Garrett coming into the intersection, pulling into the circle, pictured the bike going around once, twice, losing a little control, sticking his foot out, catching himself and buzzing off in the first stable direction. I walked down the chosen trail to verify if the bike trail remained fresh. It did. I was ready to declare a direction. I hopped on my quad and started it up, put it in second and took off down the chosen track. Pretty soon I had three dust trails following me. I kept an eye on the motorcycle track as I rode next to it, watching to make sure Garrett had stayed on the trail. Whenever a track left the trail I stopped to make sure it was an old track. If it was Garrett heading off trail I followed along but for the most part he kept right to the trail.

There were hills that the other kids had taken at high speed and then sailed over in long jumps. Garrett didn't do that. His wheels rarely left the ground, and the few times they had I celebrated the free feeling with him sensing his need to be just a little more like the other kids.

I followed the trail across broad expanses of desert, up and down arroyos, up and down hills. The intersections were always tricky but most of the time Garrett seemed to take the most obvious route. I stopped at every intersection and got off my ATV to examine each direction. Every so often one of the guys would buzz up to check on me. I think they were having more fun than they were supposed to on a search of this magnitude, but there was really no way for them to help me so I left them to their fun.

Further and further into the desert the trail led me. I was glad we had the ATVs because it would have taken weeks to track all this ground on foot.

I came to a place where Garrett's tracks followed a wash through a little canyon. There was no way out of the canyon so I knew he had to ride the length of it. I hit the gas sending the ATV leaping ahead, sand spraying out behind me. Weaving in and out of mesquite and rocks, I wrestled the quad up over little hills while climbing up the canyon. I zipped down the straight-aways and ground my way through tough rocky places, always keeping an eye ahead for Garrett or his bright yellow dirt bike. I spotted Rusty on the hill above and waved, then had to stop as the sand took a sharp left and then a right. There was a quick, bumpy dip that was tricky and then I was off again to meet the guys at the top of the canyon. I checked often to make sure I was still on Garrett's trail even though there wasn't any exit from the canyon. A tracker is never completely sure without sign so I confirmed my sign and continued tracking.

The next mile was just a straight shot across the desert, which led me to believe it was headed for another area of hills and steep dips and turns. All I had to do across the desert was make sure that Garrett had stayed on the trail. I took off again, riding fast enough to eat up some ground but slow enough that I wouldn't miss a departure from the trail. I was intently concentrating on the track just ahead when I heard a long *kaaazing* and the guys all pulled up. I was so focused on the trail that I didn't even think about what had made the noise. After watching them come and go all day it wasn't surprising to see them doing something different. I kept to the trail until I saw a man stumbling along through the desert, rifle in hand. His clothes were ragged and dust covered. His hair was gray and unkempt. His shirt was only half buttoned and half tucked into his pants. His shoes had holes in them.

Kaaazing! Another bullet went flying. It was my turn to pull up.

"Stupid off roaders! Git offa my property! Git! Git!" he yelled. The guys closed in on me. We slipped off our ATVs and crouched behind them, then drew our guns and waited to see what would happen. Rusty stood at the head of our little ATV pack, looking official, which was odd because he was the only one not wearing an obvious uniform.

When the man came within hailing distance Rusty called out to him, "Mister, put your gun down. You are this close to being arrested and hauled off to jail." He flashed his badge and the old man pulled up short, wary. "We're looking for a lost boy. We'll be off your property as soon as his trail leads us off. Have you seen him? Sixteen, tall, thin, no hair, yellow dirt bike? He was alone."

The man instantly turned from angry to concerned. He nearly dropped his rifle and his expression softened.

"Yeah, I seen him. He's the only one of them kids worth knowin'. Most of 'em make fun of me. They throw things at my trailer just to make me mad. Garrett stops by my place and brings me stuff his mom bakes. He knows I gets lonesome out here… He's gone missin'?"

"Yeah, when did you last see him?"

"This morning, later, well after breakfast. He likes my dogs too. He comes to pet the dogs and visits. He don't have nobody to talk to 'cept his mom and a mom don't always know what's in a boy's head. Doctors don't got time for conversation. They're all business. A kids gotta have hopes and I let him have hopes so he keeps comin' here."

"What direction did he go when he left?"

"Just continued on down the trail like he always done. You want a dog? I got a dog what can find him. All's I gotta do is tell 'im go find Garrett and off he goes. Cause sometimes Garrett will take him for runs."

"Thanks, we'll keep that in mind. Could you point the way?"

"Jus' go the way you're headed, just up ahead you'll see a barbed wire gate. He'd come in and go out through that gate. You'll see."

"Thanks, for your help. Next time don't be quite so anxious to blow away off roaders. It's likely to get you in trouble."

"How you gonna find him in all that desert?" the man asked, concerned.

"We've got a tracker. We're still on the trail. We'll find him."

Everyone holstered their weapons and mounted up again, relieved that the shooting had been all show.

"Well," said Rusty, "we're lucky Garrett is a friendly kid. That was a good tip. It means we've been headed right all along."

"Somebody ought to radio that in to Strict so he can tell Garrett's mom we've found proof that we are still on track," I said as I headed out. I found the gate, then Garrett's footprints walking up to it. He stood fiddling with the latch trying to open it. He was conscientious about closing the gate behind him as he left. I followed his trail away from the hermit's gate and into the hills beyond over trails, up and down the hillsides, and around tight corners. Anything and everything a kid could think of to try they had made a trail over. I followed Garrett's trail in, out, round about, up and over. He was doing pretty well considering his strength. If I had a chance to talk to Lydia I'd tell her that her son was capable of more than she thought.

I followed Garret's track up hill and down, up hill and down, then up hill and over until suddenly there it was! Garrett's yellow dirt bike! He'd ridden up over the hill and smack dab into an old washing machine that someone had dumped in the desert. The front wheel of his bike was bent, making it useless. Garrett was now afoot.

I shut off my quad and climbed off. I saw that the wreck had pushed the washing machine a good six feet down the hill. I circled Garrett's bike on foot looking for signs of injury. He had taken quite a spill, landing on the other side of the washing machine. He'd lain where he had fallen for a long while before he felt able to stand. I closely examined the tread of his shoes before starting to track him on foot. He had checked out his bike, and discovered the bent wheel. I followed his footprints away from the scene.

If the ground had been soft, I might have been able to drive the ATV and track at the same time, but it wasn't. Instead the dry ground was hard and the tracks were not plain. It took close scrutiny and a lot of patience. I followed the tracks up over a hill and down the far side. His trail looked like it was headed back towards the hermit's old trailer. That made sense. I didn't like the look of his trail though. It was erratic, showing a kid in pain but with his head on straight. He knew he needed help and knew help was far away, but he was trying. After a while Garret started stumbling. Rocks turned under his feet, but he got back up and pressed on. Sometimes the trail was confusing and I had to stop and study the ground but I inched along.

"Victor? Landon?" I radioed. "I'm getting close."

"Ten-four. On our way."

I came to a spot where Garrett had stopped to rest. He had sat, not laid down. That was a good sign. When he started again his walk appeared stronger. He made his way diagonally down a hill and headed across the desert. I followed, watching the trail deteriorate again as Garret's steps became erratic. His strength faded so fast, I knew this kid was in trouble. I caught a glimpse of blue in the distance and starting running in that direction. It was Garrett. I felt for a pulse and found one but he looked very pale. I'd never seen anyone that pale before. I stood, searching the hills for dust trails. Come on guys!

"Ten-sixty-five found," I reported.

"Ten-forty-five?"

"Ten-forty-five B," I sent back. I was just guessing, but it would bring the guys on the run. Missing person found in serious condition.

"What's your twenty?"

I scanned the hills and found a dust trail.

"South."

The dust trail turned and pretty soon they topped the hill and headed in my direction. I knelt next to Garrett feeling helpless. I knew first aide but I was afraid to move him. There was gravel embedded in his arms and I worried about broken bones, but he was alive and his breathing was steady. Victor and Landon knew the rest. As the guys closed in I found a place out of the way and sat watching, a helpless feeling hovering over me like a cloud. It was always like this whenever I found an unconscious person. When I was able to speak to them it gave me a purpose but this silent waiting always left me feeling helpless and lost. I was grateful that Rusty was here and knew how I felt. He'd help the guys, then he'd come over to help me. Rusty took over the radio while Victor and Landon consulted between themselves. They decided Garrett ought to be delivered to his own doctor, so Rusty requested an air ambulance from L.A.

I noticed off in the distance the old hermit looking on. I made my way down the hill as he made his way up, rifle still in hand. It made me wonder if he slept with it and if he had ever shown Garrett how to shoot.

"He'll be okay," I told him. "He's in good hands. These guys will do all they can and then some."

"When'll he come back?" the old man asked forlornly.

"I don't know, his bike is broken and if that's his only way out here it might be a while."

"Where is it? I cin fix it. I cin fix anything."

"We'll have to bring it back to his mom's house. I'm afraid we aren't allowed to leave it with you. If I get a chance to talk to his mom, I'll tell her that Garrett's more capable than she thinks. Maybe if she has a little encouragement she'll fix his bike up faster."

"She don't got the money, nor the know how. Guess I'll have go get all gussied up and pay her a visit. Only she don't know 'bout me. I'll have a lot of 'splaining to do."

"She's going to be wary. You can't blame a woman for being wary. You'll have to be kind and patient and let her know you're just thinking of her son."

He planted his hands in his pockets and stood there uncomfortably, shuffling his feet in the dust.

"Maybe I won't."

"It's worth a try. If you're careful, maybe you'll make another friend."

"I don' need friends."

"You need Garrett and he needs you."

He turned and walked slowly toward his trailer. He turned around again and called out to me, "Thanks for findin' him."

"I'm glad we did," I called back.

There was a long wait for the air ambulance because it involved calling up a whole new team. They had to fly over the mountains and find us in the middle of the desert.

Rusty gave me a lift back to my ATV. I showed him where Garrett's bike was and he lifted it onto a frame on his ATV so we could bring it back with us. When we returned to the group Garrett's coloring had improved. With Victor and Landon on site things were more in control.

The ambulance landed on the trail below and Victor and Landon spent some time passing along information to the crew. Hospital names, doctor's names, medical details, treatment details, paperwork. They handed everything off and the ambulance lifted into the sky clattering away and back over the mountains. Everyone stood around preoccupied with their own thoughts. Mission accomplished, time to go home.

I needed something to do, some activity to chase away the helpless feeling. Usually that meant going home and waiting for Rusty's warm hug but here I was with a group of guys trying to fight it off and still appear in control. I needed some action, but knew what followed would be a long ride back to base camp, and a lot of paperwork before Rusty and I would finally get home.

"All work and no play makes Cassidy a dull girl," said Victor. "I'll return the bike. You two try and have some fun on the way back. See what these things can really do."

Victor took the ATV with the bike and piled on the packs then hopped on. Landon followed. They both took off. Rusty and I exchanged glances.

"I'll race you!" he declared.

"You'll win. You've done this before."

"You were doing pretty good back there in the canyon. I bet you can hold your own."

"You're willing to put on the speed. I don't know how fast is safe on these things."

"Now's the time to find out," he said, gunning his engine.

"You'll never live it down if I beat you, you know."

"I'll risk it."

Okay, I couldn't deny him his fun. I'd race him. And I'd lose, but it would be worth it. I jumped on my ATV and took off, testing the machine, testing my willingness to push it, keeping track of the thousands of small bushes that seemed to jump in the way. I was beginning to think the arroyo was the way to go if I wanted to get up some speed. The narrow one was tricky but I thought I remembered a big broad one that led in the right direction. I headed for it and found a way down, then opened up the quad and hit the gas. Pretty soon I lost sight of Rusty, but knew if I came up out of the arroyo I'd see his dust trail off in the distance somewhere. He'd be finding his own quickest way back. I skipped the tempting hills and banks that the kids liked to ride their dirt bikes on. If we hadn't been racing it would have been fun and good practice for me, but I wasn't willing to take time out for that. I followed the arroyo for more than a mile. When I found a way up out of it I got my bearings and headed for Garrett's house. Looking around, I saw a dust cloud off to my left so I hit the gas again and bounced off across the desert. I discovered a dirt track and really put on the power, pushing the machine as fast as I dared, more for my own knowledge than to try and win any race. I took it down into a small wash to try my hand at wrestling the quad through the twists and turns. Whenever I saw the dust cloud off to my left it was in the distance, no real threat to the race, so I felt a little freedom to experiment. It seemed to be going mighty slow for Rusty in a race, but I knew he would give me a run for my money and wouldn't purposely let me win. The next time I looked I didn't see a dust cloud. He must have cut behind a hill. I raced to the end of the wash and then across the open desert. I saw houses in the distance. Still no dust cloud closing in. I started racing for Garrett's house for a different reason. I wanted Rusty to be there, gloating at me. But when I got there I only found Strict and a few guys shutting down base camp.

"Where's Rusty?" I asked.

"He was with you," Strict answered.

"No. He raced me back. He should have come in first. Landon's with Victor and he has all the gear so they were going slowly. Rusty should have been here already."

I scanned the horizon for a dust cloud but there was nothing, not even the dust trail I had seen earlier.

I puttered around base camp waiting impatiently. Taking a manila envelope of papers to the Explorer, I began my report. Three forms later, I heard an engine and went out to see who had arrived. Victor and Landon pulled up. One of the volunteers started to load my ATV onto a big trailer.

"No wait. I might need that," I called out.

I approached Lou. "Ask him for his twenty."

"Cassidy, I'm sure…"

"Just ask him to report in."

He gave me an impatient look.

"Ask him to report in before I go back out."

He went to the radio. "Michaels? What's your twenty?"

A long pause. All the guys gathered around the base station.

"Does he have a radio?" Lou asked.

"He always has a radio," I answered.

Lou repeated his radio call, "Michaels, do you read me?"

We waited again.

"Okay," I said nervously, "what do we do now? I'm going back out. Victor, you've done enough. Your family is waiting for you. Landon? Will you go with me?"

"Yeah, you know I will."

"Do you know the quickest way back to where we started?"

"I know a way that's faster than you tracked. You got back pretty quick."

"I fooled around a lot on the way. I saw your dust trail and thought it was Rusty's so I experimented in the washes."

"We'll just take one quad. Less to deal with."

"I'll need to drive to track."

"I know."

Back into the desert we drove. Landon knew a quicker way and drove the ATV fast too. I didn't want to put my hands around his waist but when the going got rough he called out, "Belt loops work too." I stuck a couple of fingers through his belt loops and rode it out. When we got to the place where we had started I leapt off the ATV and walked the area on foot. I remembered the direction I'd taken off and the direction Victor and Landon had taken off so Rusty's trail had to be the middle one. I walked it a little on foot. He was going fast, faster than me. I could tell by the amount of sand scattered by the tires and the less distinct tread marks. I got a good feel for his speed and thought about what his plan would have been. A cop with a challenge was like a hound on a hunt. He wouldn't be like me, finding ways to make the race interesting. If he was going to make it interesting he would have stuck to me, pushing me to go faster. No, he was simply finding the fastest route and pushing his machine to the max. Hopefully that meant he had left a plain trail through open ground.

When I returned to the ATV Landon had shifted position to the rear knowing I'd need to see Rusty's track clearly. I hopped on the ATV and took off driving it as fast as I could and still follow the trail. I found several curves where Rusty had skidded in his haste to beat me. "You can really follow his trail this fast?" Landon asked.

"It's open ground and his is the only track. I can't lose it here. If he followed the road he would blend in too much and I'd have to slow down, or even track on foot. If he went over hard pack or rocks I might not be able to see it. If he takes off down a wash I'll have to slow down. Believe me, I'll slow down if I need to. For now I'm fine."

Landon stood behind me trying to see the trail ahead and I kept the vehicle's bouncing to a minimum so I wouldn't toss him off.

I was focused on Rusty's tracks when Landon suddenly yelled, "Whoa! Cassidy! Brakes! Brakes!"

I slammed on the brakes and skidded to a halt. Landon grabbed my shoulders to keep his balance and then sat down hard.

"What is it?" I asked, jumping off. I followed Rusty's trail on foot and it went up over a rise and sailed off into nothingness. At least it was a short drop but my blood ran cold. I ran to the arroyo wall and looked down. Two sections of the drop off crumbled away where the weight of the ATV had caved it in. Rusty's ATV was on its side. I could see gouges in the sand telling me it had rolled over several times. Hopefully he'd been tossed off early in the accident. Rusty lay next to a scrawny desert tree. The top had been snapped off about five feet up. I examined the drop off and saw soft, loose sand below so I took a run and leapt off, landing ankle deep in the sand.

"Cassidy!" Landon yelled after me.

I ran over to Rusty. He'd taken a blow to the head and had a goose egg of a lump. That was bad news. At least I had plenty of experience with getting hit on the head, so I didn't panic.

"Rusty? Hey, it's me. Come on. Can you hear me?"

I felt for his pulse. It was strong and faster than I remembered it but not too fast.

Landon joined me, placing a hand on my shoulder. When I didn't acknowledge him he knelt down.

"Cassidy, look at me, I need your help and you have to stick with the plan. We need to get Rusty out of here and we're not far from Garrett's house. Let me tend to Rusty. I need you to go get some guys and a stretcher. We can meet an ambulance at Garret's house. Take the ATV and bring back help.

"You want me to go? But…"

"No buts, the quickest way to get Rusty out of here is on foot. It'll be at least an hour to get a helicopter out here. You know that. We're only about half a mile from Garret's house. If he comes to I'll radio you. He'd be glad to know you're able to stick with the plan."

I couldn't leave. I had to, though, and Landon had to stay because he was the EMT. My heart and brain were at war.

"Go. The sooner you get down there the sooner you can get back."

"Did you talk to Strict? Does he know why I'm coming back?"

"Yeah, he'll have the guys ready when you arrive, now get going."

"You're just keeping me out of your way so I won't think."

"It still needs to be done and you'll be the first to admit that you shouldn't stop to think."

He had that right. If I stopped, the icy feeling would take over everything until I was paralyzed with fear. So I moved. I raced that ATV down the wash as quickly as I could and was relieved when I discovered just how close we really were to Garret's house. Three guys and a stretcher were waiting as I pulled up on the ATV.

"Cassidy, are you okay?" Lou asked.

I couldn't even answer him. No, I wasn't okay but if I said anything I'd be left behind and I wouldn't stay. I had to get back. I didn't have to answer though; he could read me like a book.

"Can you lead the guys back?"

"Yeah, it's not far. Let's go."

I was in shock, unaware of who was with me, simply doing what had to be done. I had probably met these volunteers before and should have thanked them for helping, but I was too busy internalizing the whole situation and too full of fear to think about it.

Walking back seemed to take forever. We fought the sand in the wash until it got tiring and then headed for the firmer ground beside the wash. With easy walking we made good time. When Landon and the tree came into view I jogged off to see how things were going. Rusty was still out.

Landon intercepted me. "Try not to worry, he'll be okay. I can't find anything that makes me think this is serious. His pupils dilate evenly. He's stable. They'll run lots of x-rays at the hospital and we'll know something pretty quick. Did you notice his arm?"

I shook my head. "I knew you wouldn't want me to move him."

"I think he put his arm up when he saw the tree coming at him. Hopefully his arm took most of the blow."

"It's been a long time and he's still out."

"Don't think about that. Think positive. Can you ride Rusty's ATV back? If you can do that it'll save Strict another trip out here. Go see if it's drivable."

The guys all converged on Rusty and all I could do was watch or right the ATV. I looked at the vehicle lying there on its side. Landon could have done it while I was gone but probably had left it for me to do. I checked the machine over and it didn't look like it was broken in any way so I grabbed the handlebar and pulled hard. The machine was heavy but I didn't have to lift it, just pull until its weight took over and the soft sand gave way. It fell over in a cloud of dust. I drove around testing it while the guys got Rusty strapped onto the stretcher. Slowly we made our way back to Garret's house. The guys walked the desert beside the wash while I drove the ATV down it. I couldn't get back up because of the steep walls so I rode below, far away and blanketed in my isolation. Sadness enveloped me, I felt lost and petrified with fear.

Landon kept me busy until the ambulance arrived, then we were whisked off to the hospital. At that point the reality of Rusty's condition caught up with me and it became a constant battle to keep everything in check. I couldn't take it. I had to do something. When I get stressed I do one of two things. I either become analytical and figure out my options, or I withdraw until the situation becomes small enough to handle. In the ambulance, the more I analyzed the situation the more worried I became, so this time I withdrew.

In the hospital I was shoved off to some obscure waiting room and was left wondering if any of the staff realized I was Rusty's wife. How could I be informed of my husband's condition if I was just one face in fifty in a waiting room filled with other worried faces? After Landon finished his paperwork he searched until he found me waiting, then knelt down to talk at eye level.

"Cassidy, you need someone here with you. Who's your best friend?"

"Rusty."

"Who's your best girlfriend?"

"Nobody."

"Where's your family?"

"Up north."

He stood and began pacing around in a circle thinking, then asked, "If Rusty needed someone to help you, who would he call?"

"Kelly," I said automatically.

He disappeared for a little while, and I curled up into a little ball in the chair. If I could just make myself smaller the feeling of helplessness would get smaller too, I told myself.

I was sitting there, a little numb ball of misery when Kelly entered the waiting room. I didn't even see him until he was right in front of me.

"Cassidy, I swear you're a chameleon. Some custodian is going to walk by your chair and say, 'What's this blonde wig doing on the back of this chair?' And he's going to grab you by the hair and yank you out." I knew he was trying to be funny, trying to draw me out, but I was too far gone. "Come on. Walk with me. Cassidy, girl, come on."

I burrowed deeper, knowing that if I moved I'd come apart.

"What can I do?" he asked squatting down to my level.

"Get me news. I need to know something."

"Kiddo, they'll bring news when they know. I already made sure of that. Come on, you need to do something. Where's Shadow? Is he still at home?"

Shadow. "Yeah, he's at home," I said still numb, still curled up in a little ball of self protection.

"Cassidy, it'll help to stay active, distract yourself. When was your last meal?"

"I'm not hungry. I'm okay."

"No, you're not. Look at yourself, you're barely here. I keep thinking, if I blink, you're going to vanish. You're like a blonde Cheshire cat without the smile. Let's get you something to eat. Even if it's just junk from the machine."

"Kelly, I can't. I just can't. Please don't make me."

"Can you tell me why? Why can't you?"

I was going to cry. I knew it. If he didn't stop, then everything would come crashing in, and that was something I couldn't handle. I hid my eyes from him. I wouldn't let him see me cry.

A woman opened the door of the waiting room. "Mrs. Michaels?"

I looked up, fearfully acknowledging her voice.

"The doctor would like to talk to you," she said softly.

I paused, uncertain if I'd be able to move, but I needed to hear the news. I gathered my strength, stuffing my emotions safely away. I'd told Rusty I couldn't compartmentalize my feelings like the officers could, but now I realized I did it, too. I was aware that my self control wouldn't last long and the woman was waiting. I unfolded myself carefully and stood, checking my actions, my emotions, making sure everything was hidden away just right. I followed the woman, feeling like a zombie. Reaching the door I turned, looking for Kelly. He seemed relieved that, at last, he could do something, so he followed us into the stark hallway. The woman glared at him.

"It's okay, he's Rusty's best friend. He should know too."

She led us down the hall, and through a door. I stopped when I realized Rusty was there, still unconscious. I felt Kelly's hands on my shoulders, felt his concern seep through. I didn't know if I could manage enough control for the both of us. The nurse walked around the bed checking Rusty's chart readings and IV settings. I went to Rusty's side. He had a big bruised lump on his head. I brushed the hair away from it. Ouch, that was going to be tender for a while.

"Hey in there," I said, "I don't know if you can hear me, but I'm here, as much as they'll let me be. Kelly's here too." I could feel the strain in my voice but tried not to let it show. I remembered his arm and was relieved it wasn't in a cast. He had a long, deep scrape down the side of his arm but that would heal quickly. It was the stillness that bothered me.

How many times had Rusty been in my place? How many times had he stood helplessly by as I was doing now? He's the strong one, I thought. But was he? Or had he just survived like I was doing now?

"Rusty, please. Please move. Say something. Anything. It doesn't have to make sense." I looked for a chair in the room but it was void of anything not medically related.

"Cassidy," Kelly said, "it just takes time. What I see in here is encouraging. No big machines, no beeping monitors. If the doctors were really worried there'd be all sorts of things in here and they aren't here. It's all just the standard stuff."

"I know you're right. I'm just having a hard time listening to my head right now."

"At least you're talking. That's better. We'll hear something soon and it'll be good news, you'll see."

The doctor came in and I followed what he said at first but then I got lost in all the medical terminology. I began grasping at small, encouraging phrases like "no swelling" and "good as new in no time" and "lucky he was in good shape".

"How long?" I asked. "When will we know more?"

And, just as Kelly had predicted, the doctor said we just needed to give him more time. He said they were moving Rusty to a room. We were asked to leave for half an hour or so but later we'd be able to stay. I went back to claim my chair in the waiting room only to discover all the chairs had been taken. Now what? Was there a corner somewhere? I didn't mind the floor. Just give me a little corner. But Kelly drew me aside, and before I knew it we were in an elevator, and then standing in line at the cafeteria.

"I can't eat when I feel like this. Eating just loses its priority and gets shoved aside."

"Then get it to go and you can eat it later. At least you'll have something. And they have chairs down here. We can sit while they move Rusty to a room."

I tried to eat, I really did, but I couldn't taste anything so I wrapped it back up again and took it along. Not even the cheesecake looked good. We took the food up to Rusty's room.

"You're looking better," Kelly said. "That's good to see. Can you tell me what happened?"

"You know what happened. Landon told you when he called."

"He didn't say much. He just said that Rusty had been hurt in an ATV accident and you were at the hospital. He seemed more worried about you than he was about Rusty, said he'd never seen you like this before."

"That's because the only other time I'd seen Rusty unconscious Landon was trying to restrain me. I wasn't going to get in their way. I just wanted to be there. I told Landon to let me go and warned him that if he didn't I'd let him have it. He laughed at me and that made me so mad that I slugged him. Bet he didn't tell you that."

"You slugged Landon?"

"Yeah."

"Wilson, right?"

"Yeah."

He laughed. "I'd like to have seen that."

"I wouldn't do it again. We weren't exactly the best of friends then. We get along better now. In fact, when he was asking me who he could call, I got the impression that he would have preferred staying himself, but he knew it wasn't his place."

"So what did happen?"

"We'd spent the day tracking down a kid who went out dirt bike riding and disappeared. After we found him Rusty challenged me to a race back to base camp. It was my first time riding the ATVs, so I didn't expect to win, but I got back to base camp first. When the last team arrived with all the gear and Rusty still hadn't shown up, I asked Strict to radio him but there was no answer. Strict wanted to give him more time but I knew Rusty should have been the first one back. He would have answered his radio if he could have. So Landon and I backtracked and I found Rusty's trail. He'd gone over a rise and went off the side of an arroyo and into a tree." My voice caught in my throat. "And he's been out ever since." I automatically pulled my feet up into the chair.

"Nope, no going back," Kelly said firmly, pulling down my feet. "Relax. Come on. It'll be okay. Relax. How did you like the ATVs?"

"I liked them a lot, until Rusty crashed. Now that I've tracked on ATVs I bet I get called to ATV training. That ought to be interesting."

"It sure is good to see you talking. When I first got here you scared me."

"Sorry. If they had a gym or a punching bag I'd have felt better. Usually a good run or a fight with the punching bag helps. When I can't exercise it off I tend to hide. If I can't hide in the woods I make myself small."

"You were almost small enough to slip through the cracks in the chair and disappear… please, don't do that again. When Rusty comes to he doesn't want to see you curled up in a little ball. You need to be able to talk to him, get him to focus and think."

"I'll try."

We talked and Kelly helped lighten the mood in the room. We talked about the honeymoon and the contest with Chase. He laughed when I told him about Chase paying that guy to wear his moccasins. I laughed at my reaction to the trick.

"Do you know how many Greens it takes to change a light bulb?"

I smiled, "I don't know. How many Greens does it take to change a light bulb?"

"Only one, we're pretty bright. You just need to give us the green light first."

"That's awful," I replied.

He knew it, and grinned. "How do Greens feel when they are sad?"

"I don't know and I'm afraid to find out. Turquoise?"

He laughed. "You're pretty bright yourself."

"So, I was right?"

"You were right."

"Do you feel as turquoise as me right now?"

"No, I don't think that's possible. But you're doing better."

I felt Rusty stir beside me.

"Hey, can you hear all these rotten jokes?" His hand gave a quick squeeze, more like a twitch, but it was encouraging.

When Kelly thought I'd worked my way back to a semi-normal state he went home to catch some sleep. I knew his wife Rhonda would be worrying about him so I told him to go.

It wasn't until the wee hours of the morning that Rusty really began coming around. I couldn't sleep. I was worried that I wouldn't wake up if Rusty needed me so I stayed awake, watching him carefully. All those weary guard posts in the Marines had taught me a thing or two. It really is possible to stay awake for two days straight even after hiking for ten hours while wearing a forty pound pack. I felt another twitch and squeezed back, then felt a more controlled squeeze. "Rusty? It's okay, take your time. It'll come with time. I ought to know… You scared me there for a while but it's okay now. You're going to be fine. I'll be here. I'll always be here… You taught me a thing or two through this. I found out I love you even more than I thought. I need you. I really, truly need you. I thought I was going to curl up and die yesterday. I was so scared. But then I learned we have good friends. They were there for me. Landon called Kelly and he was so patient. Remember after I got out of the mountains when I found Kelly, and all I could do was curl up in your office chair? It was like that. I was so scared for you, I couldn't move. Kelly was so patient and kind. Tell him I'm sorry I put him through that. I know it was awkward for him, best friend's girl and all that. But I'm back and I feel sane again and we'll get through this together."

I rambled on and on. I don't know how much he heard or understood and it really didn't matter. I guess it was more important that I say what was on my mind than it was for him to hear it. If he understood me, that was okay, too. He could hear in my voice that the hard part was over and I was ready for the next step.

When his eyes finally opened he was confused at first. I stood up so he could see me.

"Hey, you, how are you doing?"

No answer but I could see the wheels turning. I smiled at him, thankful I was capable of a smile.

"What happened?" It wasn't the deep, thundery voice I knew so well, but it would return along with his attitude.

"You learned that ATVs can't fly. You don't remember the accident?"

"Vaguely."

"It'll come back."

"How long?"

"I don't know, let me think. It was late afternoon when we finished the call. So you probably arrived here about six yesterday and it's about three AM. So you've been out about ten hours. I don't know exactly when you crashed. I was off trying to beat you back to base camp."

"You won."

"No, I didn't. Winning implies a victory. There was no celebrating yesterday. From the time I got back I thought something had happened. Strict didn't send me back out until everybody had come back in and you didn't answer your radio. I had to push him to check on you. He thinks nothing could possibly happen to one of his big, strong detectives."

"How'd you find me?"

"You know the answer to that one even if you aren't thinking straight yet."

His eyes smiled. "You tracked me down. What are you doing up at three a.m.?"

"Pulling guard duty. It's okay, I've done it many times. Maybe I'll take a nap when Kelly gets here. How do you feel?"

"I've got a killer headache. Other than that, okay."

"Do you want something for the headache?"

"How long has it been since a nurse came through?"

"A few hours."

"They're due back any time. Just wait. You can sit down."

"I can't see you if I sit down."

He tried scooting over only to discover his new found aches and pains. I was relieved to see him able to move around. Everything appeared to be in working order.

"Stop, Rusty, don't hurt yourself. Just lay still, here, I've got a solution." I turned the chair around and sat on the back of it, placing my feet on the seat.

"Cass, you don't need to babysit me."

"I'm not. I'm treasuring minutes."

"You're what?"

"I just want to be with you. Can I do that?"

"Sure, but what did you say?"

"I'm treasuring minutes. When you proposed to me you said you wanted every minute I'd give to you. Well, maybe I want some minutes too. I don't mind that they are at three in the morning. I just want to be here with you. I know your nights and days are turned around. You've been out for ten hours so it feels like daytime to you. That's okay, it can be daytime to us. Let the rest of the world sleep. We can do whatever we want."

"Did you call Schroeder?"

Oops. "No, I haven't even thought about calling anybody. I didn't even call Kelly, Landon did."

"I know."

"You heard? I didn't know if you could hear me. I just needed to talk, I guess. Could you hear us while Kelly was here?"

"No, I missed that."

"So you missed hearing his Green jokes."

"It's okay, I've heard them before. Where do Greens go for a good time? The Green Light district. Yeah, I've heard them."

I laughed. "He didn't tell me that one."

"Well, when he does, pretend it's the first time you heard it."

"Okay."

"Have you talked to a doctor?"

"The doctor only said enough to reassure me. If you want the technical jargon you'll have to wait. You're not going to lose a leg and you're not going to have to relearn how to tie your shoes. Just have patience."

He grew quiet and after a little while I figured out that he'd drifted off again so I moved the chair back and found a position I could sleep in and dozed.

I woke to the sound of footsteps. A nurse and Kelly entered the room at the same time.

"Cassidy? You're still here?" Kelly asked.

"Of course."

He looked concerned.

"It's okay, I think he's only sleeping. I talked to him last night."

"And?"

"And he'll be fine. He made sense and he was thinking clearly. He'll be okay."

"And you?"

"I'm okay, thanks."

"I fed Shadow and let him outside. You need to put in a doggie door."

"We don't have a fence and I'd worry about him wandering off. I guess I need to figure out where our truck is. I rode in with the ambulance and they won't let Rusty out of here without a ride."

"Where did you leave it?"

"At base camp. Strict will be able to tell me where it is."

After tracking down the truck's location I was told it had been left at the police station. Returning to Rusty's room, I found Rusty and Kelly having a conversation.

"Are you going to stick around for an hour or so?" I asked Kelly.

"I can. Why?"

"The Explorer is parked at the station so if you are going to be here for a little while I'll run down there and pick it up."

"It's a mile and half to the station."

"I know. I'll be back in an hour."

"I can give you a lift."

"Why? It's only a mile and a half. I walk a mile just to find some tracks to follow. It's no big deal."

It took me half an hour to hike to the station and another half hour to give everyone an update on Rusty. There must have been a guard set on the Explorer because as soon as I approached the driver's door three cops descended on me wanting the whole story.

"A mile and a half is longer than you thought, wasn't it?" Kelly asked when I returned.

"No, the walk was fine but then I got cornered by officers wanting to know what happened. So I had to tell them all about it. There was more talking than walking."

"Well, I lied, I do have to get going. I'll see you two later," Kelly finally said and then took off.

Rusty and I sat in relative silence for a few minutes, but he had a pensive expression on his face.

"What is it?" I asked.

"Nothing, just some things Kelly said."

I didn't push for more but turned the chair around and sat on the back of it where I could see him.

"Have you talked to the doctor yet?" I asked.

"They want to run some test today just to check things out and make sure I didn't do any damage. It sounded like that would happen in the afternoon and he warned me I'd probably be stuck here until morning."

"Now that I have wheels again, can I get you anything?"

"You need to take care of Shadow. While you are home you can get the files from my desk and a change of clothes."

"Okay."

"Cassidy, was what Kelly said really true?"

"I don't know what he said but, yeah, it probably was."

"Oh, babe, come here," he said, reaching out.

I pushed the chair aside and sat down on his hospital bed to give him the hug he needed, wishing I could just climb in bed with him and snuggle.

"It's okay. I was scared. I've never been so scared in all my life but it's okay. I think I'll stick to being stalked by crazy murderers. It's easier than seeing you hurt. But it's over. We're still us. We're still together, treasuring minutes."

Now that Rusty was awake and everything was looking up I knew he'd be bored stiff. I went home and picked up the files he'd asked for. I fed Shadow then ran him through the jumps and the A-frame. Stripping out of my very dirty uniform I took a quick shower and shaved my legs. I chose a sundress with cheerful flowers on it, which I knew Rusty would like, quickly curled my hair and put on some make-up. I tried thinking of some other activity that Rusty could do at the hospital but I'd never seen him read a book and he did all his puzzle solving by working on cases. I chose some comfortable clothes for him to wear home, grabbed our honeymoon pictures, and went back to the hospital feeling much better about the whole situation.

I was feeling perky in my cute, little sundress so when I cheerfully turned the corner into Rusty's room and came face to face with Schroeder he did something very uncharacteristic by smiling broadly. Usually Schroeder was all cop, all business. I knew he could relax because Rusty had stayed friends with him, but I'd never seen him behave that way. He looked me up and down.

"Well, well, that's one way to get a guy out of the hospital," he said. "Keep it up."

"Hi, Schroeder," I said cheerfully. "Do you have a first name? I think I even sent your wedding invitation to just 'Schroeder'."

"No, you sent it to Mr. and Mrs. Schroeder."

"Oh, okay."

I entered the room and set the files down on Rusty's table.

"Your files and the honeymoon pictures. I don't think you saw the rest of them because you went off to talk to Chase."

"Want to see where we went on our honeymoon?" Rusty asked Schroeder.

"Sure, I was wondering where a cop and a tracker would go on their honeymoon."

I turned the chair around so I could be at Rusty's level. He took one packet of pictures and handed the other one to Schroeder. Pretty soon polite comments began flying across the bed. Rusty and I started through our batch, talking about the trip, while Schroeder made comments on his stack of pictures well aware that we weren't paying much attention to him.

"Pretty lake," Schroeder said. "Where was this?"

"Minnesota," Rusty answered absentmindedly.

"Look," I said excitedly, "it didn't turn out very good but here's the picture of the moose. At least it shows how close it was. Isn't that cool?"

"Looks like you had fun," commented Schroeder.

"I like this one of you," I mentioned to Rusty. "You look like a real Minnesotan."

"Nice legs," said Schroeder.

Huh? What did he say? I glared at Rusty.

"Did you put those pictures back in with the others?" I said accusingly.

"I thought we should keep them together," Rusty replied.

"Then you just handed them off to Schroeder?" I asked.

"I didn't know they were in there. I just handed him the ones we weren't looking at."

"Schroeder, I didn't even know he took those. This is getting embarrassing!"

"There's nothing wrong with these pictures. You have nothing to worry about," Schroeder said.

"I don't want the guys thinking of me like that. They only see me in khakis or camouflage, occasionally in uniform. The only time they have seen me in any other way was at the wedding and then I had a good excuse. A bride can't wear camouflage to her wedding!"

"Believe me, the guys know you're a woman. I like this one," Schroeder said, handing it to Rusty.

"Me too," Rusty agreed.

"Did Chase see those pictures?" I asked.

"He liked that one too," Rusty answered.

I knew Chase would have, but I thought that would be the end of this.

"Cassidy," Schroeder said, "you hand a bunch of pictures like this to a guy and you might get some raised eyebrows but for the most part they expect to see a few risqué pictures from a honeymoon. At least they hope to.

Look, hand these pictures to the next guy who walks in and I bet you hardly get any reaction at all."

As if on cue, Landon walked through the doorway. He looked around the room and his eyes finally settled on me when he saw that I was wearing a dress. He winked at me. I was sure he'd come to the hospital to see if I'd survived the night but I sure didn't want him to be the next guy through the door. Rusty and Schroeder looked at me.

"No!" I said adamantly. "Not Landon!"

"What makes Landon so different from any other guy?" Schroeder asked.

"I have to go camping with Landon on a regular basis, that's what," I countered.

Landon looked puzzled. The poor guy didn't know what he'd walked into.

Rusty conceded.

"I'm glad to see everybody's feeling better, but what are you talking about?" Landon asked.

"Give me those pictures," I said.

Rusty handed them to me.

"These," I told him. "You can see those but you can't see these."

"What are you going to do with them?" Rusty asked, looking like a little kid who just had a favorite toy taken away and knew he might never see it again.

"I'll take them home and, when we go to the ranch for Thanksgiving, Jesse will help me scrapbook *all* the honeymoon pictures and you'll have them to look at whenever you want."

He had to go along with my wishes for now and reluctantly let it drop.

Landon began flipping through the honeymoon pictures.

"Nice place," he said. "Looks like you had fun. Didn't you take any *interesting* ones?"

Chapter 9

I had three wonderful lazy days at home with Rusty. We slept in late and enjoyed luxurious showers together. I was beginning to think he ached worse right before we showered just so he'd get a massage out of it.

The deer came down to our yard more frequently now. When we'd been considering buying the house Rusty thought he'd enjoy sitting in the bay window of our bedroom and watching me stalk the deer. I wasn't quite to the stalking stage, but he sat in the window watching me make friends with them. They were still skittish, but I was making progress by not pushing myself on them.

I got an email from Rusty's parents:

"Cassidy, thank you so much for the wonderful pictures you sent home with Chase. I'm glad you and Rusty had a memorable honeymoon. I'll show the pictures to Sandy when she comes over. I don't think she's seen her brother with a beard before…" Bev rambled on and I politely replied to it, telling her we were all doing fine and looked forward to seeing them again.

Then Rusty received an email from his younger brother, Cody:

"Hey Rusty, great pics. I want to see the ones Cassidy wouldn't send to Mom and Dad. Cody."

This triggered a quick email from me to Jesse:

"Jesse, help! I need some scrapbooking done. Everybody wants to see some pictures Rusty took on our honeymoon and I don't know how to make them rated G. I have to admit they are only PG13 right now but I'm embarrassed and they keep falling into the wrong hands. What can I do? Cass."

And then from Jesse:

"Dear Sis, if the pictures are only PG13 don't worry about it. All these people are over 13, right? So who cares? I wish James would take some PG13 pictures of me! BTW Did you take any PG13 pictures of Rusty? If so you better not hold out on me. Seriously though, if you want a scrapbook done just send me the pics in the order you want them in the book and I'll get started on it. If I'm not done by Thanksgiving you can help me finish it up. Bring an album with you when you come so we can put it all together. Love ya, your sis."

Rusty was amused by all the emails.

"So, if Jesse thinks the pictures are okay can I have them back?"

"It depends. If I'd taken those pictures of *you* would you want me to show them to Jesse? She said I better not hold out on her. If I knew women at the station, what about them? You wanted to show those pictures to Landon. I work with Landon. I have to camp with Landon. So, if the women at the station wanted to see pictures of you, should I show them?"

"No, you shouldn't, out of professional consideration. If it was just you and Jesse or some girlfriend and it was just a girl thing I wouldn't care."

"Now, there's the glitch. What exactly defines a 'guy thing'? You never know who I'm going to end up working with. I don't want to go out on a search with guys who remember me from bedroom pictures. With Chase, okay, it was a guy thing. He knew the pictures existed. He knew they were only mildly entertaining. I didn't mind that. It was embarrassing when Schroeder came across them."

"Only because you were there. Even people who might see the pictures wouldn't admit they had seen them. That's like privileged information. You just don't ask people for privileged information. Either you get it or you don't and you never brag about it. The guys are used to that. So think of it that way."

I tried to ease up and he tried to be considerate, but we never came to an agreement. It was difficult because I didn't want to know who had seen the pictures, but also wondered who might have seen them. I tried to keep a loose hold on them and trust Rusty, but my curiosity would get the better of me. I'd open the envelope to check and see if the pictures had been rearranged from the last time I looked at them, but then I couldn't remember their order. It was frustrating.

I made copies of all the pictures to be scrapbooked and sent them to Jesse stacked in the order they were photographed, or in the order I wanted people to think they were taken. The questionable pictures I asked to be placed on just one two-page spread so it could be skipped over easily. When Jesse got the pictures I received another email:

"Cass, I am so jealous. There is absolutely nothing wrong with those pictures. They are beautiful. Mom thought so too and you know what a prude Mom is. I didn't show Dad. Randy wants extra copies. I said no. Before you get mad, I didn't show Randy, James did. I can't wait to go to the scrapbooking store and buy cute paper to go with the pictures. When are you going to get your wedding pictures back? I'll KIT, Luv, Jess."

I covered my face with my hands and counted to twenty. Then I looked at the calendar because the day to pick up the wedding pictures was fast approaching. Two days. Yay! I couldn't wait to see them.

I was trying to reply to Jesse's email when Rusty got home from work. I dropped what I was doing and went to start dinner. When he came in a short time later he appeared a little hesitant about bringing up the subject of our honeymoon pictures again.

"If you need the computer just close that program. I'll answer it later," I said as I rushed around.

"Now can I have the pictures back?" he asked.

I froze in place. He'd obviously read the message from Jesse that had been on the screen. Rusty looked pitiful; big, round, hound doggie eyes, hands in pockets, head bowed, as if waiting to be released from a timeout. I'm sure he wasn't doing it on purpose, which made it even worse. Okay, I admit it. I fell for it.

"Rusty, that's no fair," I laughed. "Can you wait two days?"

"What difference does two days make?"

"We pick up our wedding pictures in two days. I got copies for the people in the photos and once they've all been packaged up we'll make a set for you to show everyone. I'll give you back the pictures then and I'll just have to trust you to be considerate."

His mood brightened and his eyes changed from recalcitrant kid to grateful husband in an instant. He wrapped me in a hug so suddenly I had to be careful I didn't hit him with the spatula I was holding. I sure hoped, if we had kids, they didn't have eyes like that. I'd be a sucker for sure.

"I can't help it if I'm proud of you," he said seriously, but his eyes were still smiling.

"Me? You're proud of me? What have I ever done to make you proud?" I asked, genuinely surprised.

"Cass, I was proud of you in the first five minutes I talked to you. You had me from day one. Any girl who would take on a bank robber and carjacker, choose to stay there and reason her way out of being kidnapped when help was standing on her doorstep had my admiration. I wanted to yank you right out the door but I didn't know what could happen if I did. So I had to trust you. You had spirit, from day one, and it hasn't dimmed in the least."

"What does that have to do with the pictures?" I asked.

"You take all that spirit and your big heart and put it in someone as beautiful as you and any guy would be proud. I like the pictures because they show the real you. No tough girl camouflage, no guns, they just show your true self and you're more beautiful that way."

Gosh, if he wanted dinner he sure better be quiet, I thought. I was very close to abandoning the whole idea and going for him instead. He removed the spatula from my hand and looked around the kitchen. He didn't see much in the way of dinner preparations, but that was because he'd come home early and surprised me. He opened the microwave and poked at the meat. It was still mostly frozen so he put it back in the freezer. He then led me to the couch and sat down. When he held out his arms I climbed into his lap and gave him a big kiss. He hesitated.

"This can't end up in bed," he said. "We have a dinner invitation. You're not going to like it."

"What do you mean?" I asked warily.

"Hazel and Wally. Do you remember them?"

"Yeah, our neighbors up the road. They invited us for dinner?"

"Hazel caught me on my way to work this morning. I know. I should have called you. I told her we would come unless work interfered and that I'd call if something came up."

"Aw, can't something come up? I'll call in a tip for you."

"We ought to get to know them a little. It can't hurt to be on good terms with the neighbors."

I took a look at my clothes and then Rusty's. As usual, he looked great in a coat and tie and I was wearing old blue jeans and a t-shirt.

"I should change clothes if we're going to be dinner guests."

I dragged myself away from the couch. Even if I put on my good casual clothes I'd feel underdressed next to Rusty. I decided to dress up a little and picked the blouse and slacks I'd worn to start academy, then started feeling just as awkward as I had the first day of class.

Hazel and Wally were not the happy hosts I had expected. There appeared to be a strained atmosphere to the evening and it didn't come from unfamiliarity. We made small talk about the weather, where we were from and how long we had all lived in the area. Still the tension hung in the air. The casserole was good. I got the idea that Hazel and Wally probably lived on casseroles. When Hazel and I were getting drinks to go with the meal I noticed three old casseroles in the refrigerator. She must make a new one for dinner and then eat leftover casseroles for lunch. As the meal started winding down Hazel and Wally looked at each other uncomfortably. There appeared to be a silent exchange between them as to who would begin the uncomfortable topic of conversation that had been looming between them all evening. As expected Wally lost but Hazel quickly took control when she thought he wasn't expressing himself adequately.

"We couldn't help but notice there were a lot of policemen at your wedding," Wally said.

"We know a lot of officers," Rusty answered simply.

"We've been trying to get the police to look into a matter but they haven't been helpful," Wally continued.

"Have you ever heard of Mark Mireau?" Hazel interrupted.

"Yes!" I answered, curious as to how this tied in with the topic of the local police. "He's a nature photographer."

Hazel beamed, pleased that I had recognized the name. "He's our son. We have two sons and a daughter."

Wally interrupted enthusiastically, "Mark was doing a series of photographs about the animals of the Channel Islands because there are several species of animals that are indigenous to the island chain."

The thought occurred to me that Mark must have used the word 'indigenous' around Wally a lot.

"He's traveled to Africa and down the Amazon and explored the Sahara Desert, but he saved this project close to home for one reason. He wanted to be at his brother's fiftieth birthday party. He said it was easy to catch a boat back to the mainland the day before the party, and he chose to photograph the islands so he could be at the party," Hazel continued.

"The only thing is," Wally took over, "the party was two days ago and there's been no sign of Mark. To rearrange a busy schedule and make plans to be here was not an easy thing for Mark to do, so we are sure he definitely planned on attending… and yet he didn't show."

It was Hazel's turn, "The police told us Mark was a very capable, grown man and unless we could come up with some evidence of foul play they couldn't help us. We don't know what happened to prevent him from being here. We only know he would have been here, or called, and we haven't heard anything."

"It's unlikely he could call from the islands," I suggested. "Cell phones don't work from there and if he was photographing animals he wasn't near any buildings."

"We know, but we were just hoping you could ask your police friends what our next step should be. How could we find someone to go over there and ask around? Maybe the rangers on the island could hike the trails? Maybe… we just don't know what's possible but we need to find out what's happened."

Hazel was wringing her hands now, the worry evident on her face.

"Hazel," I said, "there isn't anything on those islands that can hurt a person. There aren't even any poisonous snakes. There are no large carnivores. There's nothing dangerous there. So I doubt he is hurt. What could possibly have happened?"

They didn't know but that didn't lessen the worry.

Hazel and Wally didn't know anything about our professional lives and we were very tempted to keep it that way. I argued with myself about whether to go over there and look around. I decided I required more information, but I needed to get it in such a way that they wouldn't get their hopes up.

Rusty saved me temporarily by saying, "The Joshua Hills police won't get involved with things going on in the Channel Islands. You need to contact someone with jurisdiction there."

Hazel replied, "Nobody will do anything until he's been missing a week. But anything could happen in a week. If something prevented Mark from coming it would have happened two days ago."

I was getting warning glares from Rusty.

"Do you know what island he was on?" I asked.

"No, but we know he had already spent time on Anacapa. He did that in the spring when the birds were nesting. He got some excellent photographs of baby birds, spectacular photographs. They made me want to hug the poor little things," Hazel said.

"Where did his boat take off from? Does he have his own boat or did he hire a boat to take him out there?"

"He just hops on a tourist boat. He gets whatever permits are necessary and explores on his own. So many of those islands are nature preserves so he has to be very careful about where he can and cannot go. His reputation is good though. His name helps. Most people know his motto to 'never leave a mark'. You know the old phrase 'take only pictures, leave only footprints'? That's Mark. He takes it very seriously."

Rusty gave them some tips, suggesting they look into what company provides boat trips to the Channel Islands and then call them to see if they could pin down what island their son might be on. Once they knew which island, they could find the people in charge of the comings and goings on that particular island and start asking questions. The more information they had when they contacted the authorities the more they would be taken seriously.

While Rusty had been speaking, I was doing my best to stay quiet. It took tremendous effort because I really wanted to go hike around the Channel Islands. If I did, I would just be considered a tourist there, relegated to the trails. To do any real tracking I'd have to convince the authorities I had reason to and so far Mark was not considered a missing person, just a photographer late for an appointment. The tracker part of me said the trail would be dead in a week. The humidity and wind would destroy the trail quickly. It was hard to stay quiet but Rusty was right; they needed to learn more first. I was sure as soon as they reached a dead end I'd hear from Hazel.

As we were walking back to our house down the pitch black road Rusty said, "I'm proud of you again. The whole time Hazel and Wally were talking I expected you to rush out the door and hop on the next boat for the Channel Islands."

"I was tempted but it's not that simple," I replied. "Knowing which island he is on would help. But you were right, they will feel better and the authorities will take them more seriously if they do their homework first. It's just so hard to turn my back on it. I'd love to hike the Channel Islands."

"At least give them a few days to uncover what they can. It really would be better if people on the island handled this. They know better where to look. They may have even talked to Mark and just need to be tipped off that he hasn't shown up. This could all blow over in a few days. Hazel and Wally are probably just over reacting."

"If anybody can weasel the information out of the tour company Hazel can. She'll push all their wrong buttons until they give up in self defense," I added.

In spite of our discussion and the decision to let things ride for a few days I couldn't wait. That evening I used the computer and did a search for the Channel Islands to learn what I could about them. By the time I'd read through a couple of websites I knew the company Mark had probably used to reach the islands and also where to board a boat to go there. However I waited to see what information Hazel and Wally were able to uncover.

Chapter 10

A few days later Hazel came huffing and puffing up the road.

"I forgot how far it was!" she gasped. "I needed the exercise though, just look at me."

Although she did need the exercise I only smiled and invited her in.

"Oh my," she said, "the house looks so different from when Bernice lived here. She was always a little stuffy though and had to have everything just so. This is much more comfortable. I feel like I can actually walk on the carpet without taking my shoes off! You aren't a stuffy housekeeper, are you?"

"I don't think so," I answered, unsure exactly how she had intended her comment to be taken. "I still need to do something with the walls. Before Rusty and I moved in we were living in a tiny condo and he hadn't bothered much with decorating. So I am still looking for ways to personalize the house. Come in and sit down."

I led her into the living room and sat down on the couch, wondering if I had ever sat on it since having it delivered. Rusty and I always went to the den when we wanted to sit. It was warmer, cozier and more familiar while the living room felt like part of someone else's house.

"Can I get you anything?" I offered.

"No, I'm fine. I just wanted to tell you what I found out about Mark. He went to Santa Cruz Island a week and a half ago. He got off at Prisoners Harbor and as far as they know he didn't return with any of their boats. He had bought a camping permit and filed the waiver required to hike through the Nature Conservancy. They wouldn't tell me any of this over the phone though. I had to take all the documents I could to their office and spoke with them in person. I suppose I'm glad they don't release information about their visitors to just anybody. I guess it's a good thing, but I had to throw a royal temper tantrum to get my way."

I was sure Hazel was quite capable of throwing a royal temper tantrum. In fact, I had been counting on it.

"So Mark has been on the island for a week and a half and he only planned on being there a week?" I asked.

She nodded pitifully.

"The islands are a national park. They have rangers there. Did you talk to any of them?"

"I talked to a nice man in a uniform at the museum. He was trying to be helpful but I could tell he never went out to the island. His job was to sell t-shirts, postcards and nature books. He could answer all kinds of questions about the islands but not about tourists. Oh, I take that back, he did know something about the people but it was the Indians who first lived on the island. He told me a lovely story about the Indians there, the Chumash, but nothing about where Mark could have gotten lost."

"Mark didn't get lost," I said. "It takes talent to get lost on an island that size. The mainland is to the east and the ocean is to the west so that automatically defines north and south. Mark knows his directions and knew the trails even before setting out. He didn't get lost. Wild animals wouldn't have attacked him and the scariest animal on the island is a skunk. Maybe he got skunked and wouldn't board the boat."

She laughed nervously.

"If he saw a skunk I hope he got a picture of it." I continued, "Skunks are really cute and the skunks on the island aren't afraid of people at all so he could get a really good picture of one."

"I think he was looking for a fox," Hazel said. "There is a fox that only lives on that island. It's on the endangered species list and he was determined to find one and photograph it. He had a short list of animals he was looking for but admitted that a week wasn't much time to find them. He knew he probably wasn't going to find them all but he really wanted to photograph a fox."

"So he had food and water for a week? There's no potable water on the island. His pack would have been heavy if he was carrying a week's worth of water."

"How do you know so much about the island?" Hazel inquired suspiciously.

"I don't. I looked it up on the Internet and I have done a lot of backpacking so I know how much water weighs. I've had to pack my own water many times."

"What should my next step be?" she asked.

"You need to talk to someone who has actually been out there, the rangers or campers. Ask them if they talked to Mark. Find out if anyone has seen him and how long ago it was."

"I can't do that. I'm just an old lady. I can't go hiking around an island. He was staying at a campground three miles from the pier. I can't manage a climb like that. It's impossible."

I agreed, if the walk between our houses had winded her she shouldn't venture out to the island. I was grateful Hazel was a talker though. She was giving me plenty of information whether she knew it or not. I was planning the search in my head while at the same time vehemently denying that I would go out there at all. Rusty would not be happy. Strict would definitely discourage me. The authorities would not like me taking matters into my own hands, but I planned anyway. My mind was just too active to sit idle with so much fresh information to work with. I had to do something with it so I planned silently while using polite conversation to encourage Hazel to continue talking.

"Oh! And I almost forgot," she exclaimed, "the nice man at the museum sold me this map! I thought I could figure out where Mark went if I saw a map, but I'm not very good at reading maps and it is terribly confusing to me."

Now *this* interested me. This was something I could work with!

"Can I see it?" I asked enthusiastically. "Let's go to the dining room where we can spread it out."

Yes! I thought as I saw the details unfold. I found Prisoners Harbor and located a couple of camps that were about three miles from the pier. I then pinpointed where the ranger stations were located. This was doable, I thought. It was a lot of land to cover and the tracking would be next to impossible but I wanted to try it. I could talk to the rangers. I could hike the trails. I was fairly certain I could spot where a person had left the trail. The only thing that I didn't like was that I had expected Mark to head for the interior of the island in the Natural Conservancy while all the ranger stations were in the national park area of the island. It would be a long hike for help if I needed it. In fact, as I studied the map the trails in the two sections of the island didn't appear to connect. I would be cut off from help by a half hour boat ride and the boats only came twice a day.

"Tell me about Mark," I said. "If he were photographing animals where would he go? Would he take his time in one area or would he try and cover as much territory as he could in the hopes of stumbling across more animals?"

"He would find a central location, away from people, where he thought there might be animals, and then stay there unless someone pointed him in another direction."

"What about the coastline? Do you know if he was planning on investigating the coast, maybe photographing the seals and sea lions?"

"Anything is possible with Mark. If he did photograph the sea lions he would rent a kayak to get in closer but he wouldn't spend a lot of time with them since he can take pictures of sea lions and harbor seals any time. He was looking for animals that were harder to find and possibly endangered."

"Can I borrow the map? I want to show it to a friend of mine and see what he thinks."

"Of course, if I need it I know where to find it."

Rusty sat patiently while I explained my thoughts.

"My plan is to get on the boat in Ventura and get off at Scorpion Canyon. I can talk to campers and rangers there. If Mark rented a kayak to photograph sea life he probably did it at Scorpion landing. There are a couple of miles of coast right near the pier where sea lions and seals hang out. I'd rent a kayak and paddle up and down the sea lion rocks for a day. Then the next day I'll hop on the boat and go to Prisoners Harbor. Hazel said he was planning on staying at a camp three miles from the pier at Prisoners Harbor. There are only two camps and the one in the central valley has several trail loops he could have taken to look for wildlife. The other one is on a trail by itself and there aren't as many options there as there are in the central valley. Plus the vegetation is more varied in the central valley. You have woods and grasslands both. I think if he were looking for animals that's where he would go. Look," I said, pointing out the area on the map, "four days worth of loops right from this one camp. If I were him that's where I'd go."

"But you're not him," Rusty pointed out.

"Okay," I countered, "what would you do?"

"Okay, that's what I would do too. But on the way back I would take this longer trail back to cover more ground."

"What should I do if he needs help?" I asked. This was a major concern for me. It looked like help would be a long time coming.

"All you could do, unless the rangers can outfit you with a radio, is catch the next boat, make arrangements with the authorities and then lead them back."

"But that could take a whole day if the boat isn't going back to Scorpion landing!"

"Exactly. That's what makes this whole search a complicated mess. That's why you should leave it to the teams there."

"Can't we just go to Scorpion Canyon, talk to the rangers, and see what can be done? If we can't do anything at least we'll be able to rent kayaks and have fun. We can see some nice coastline and maybe some seals and then have lunch at the picnic grounds. Hazel can't go over there. She barely made it to our house when she walked over. I'd feel better for having done something and maybe we can get the ball rolling. Then we can at least say we tried to help them and it might turn into a fun day."

"Cass, if they say 'no' then you won't have a fun day, and if they decide to do something you'll want to be in on it. You won't patiently kayak up and down the coast. As long as there is a chance you can help, you'll want to be in on the action."

"Well, can we just kind of wander over there as tourists and do some looking around?"

"You're talking about a seven day trip. No, I can't take off seven days on short notice right after a two week honeymoon. It can't be done."

"Can you take off one day, kayak Scorpion Point with me until I leave from Prisoners Harbor? You can pick me up in six days."

"You're really set on this, aren't you?"

"I'm sorry, Rusty, I can't just let this drop. I need to at least try. There's nothing there that can hurt me. There's no way to get into trouble on the island. I don't know how to scuba dive so I won't become shark bait."

"Then what happened to Mark?"

"I don't know, but I'm going to find out."

Chapter 11

The next morning I was at Hazel and Wally's house bright and early. Hazel answered the door with her hair in rollers and wearing a bathrobe.

"Oh dear," she said, embarrassed, "I wasn't expecting company this early. Cassidy, come in. Just don't look at me or my house."

"Don't worry about it. I won't be here long. I need a picture of Mark. Do you have one?"

"I don't have a recent one, but I have one that is a few years old. Why?"

"Tomorrow morning I plan to take a ride over to the island to see what I can find."

"Oh dear! You'd really do that? For me?"

"And for Mark. I just feel like I have to do something. I looked over the map and I have a plan. I think I know which camp he went to and there are several hiking loops he could have taken from there. I'm going to hike them and keep my eyes open."

"You can't do that alone! Rusty's going with you, isn't he?" she asked as she began searching through a drawer of her china cabinet. Then she walked down the hall and removed a picture from the wall.

"He'll be with me the first day, then he has to get back to work. But I've camped alone before. Don't worry about me."

"Here," she said, holding up an eight by ten portrait, "this is my Mark, and here's a snapshot because this is probably what he'll look like if you see him. The portrait is a professional one he had taken to help advertise his work."

She was right, I'd never have recognized him from the portrait, especially considering he'd probably have week's worth of stubble, too.

"Thanks, I'm going to copy them and then you can have them back. I don't want to take the originals with me camping. I need to run and pack up a week's worth of camping gear. I have tickets to buy and permits to file. I won't have phone access on the island, so don't worry if you don't hear anything. I'll come over afterwards and tell you all about it."

"Oh dear, oh dear, when I told you about Mark I didn't mean for *you* to go looking out there all by yourself! You can't do that! Dear, leave this to the real search people."

"It can't hurt for me to go hike around the island. I've gone camping by myself many times. While hiking I can talk to other campers, maybe the rangers. The least I can do is try. So don't worry."

"I have to," she stated as if it were written in stone, "it's what mothers do best and you're young enough to be my granddaughter."

As I closed the door behind me I heard her wail in the background, "Oh, Walter, what have I done?"

I laughed silently to myself. Maybe I should have told her that looking for people is what I do best, but I was afraid she'd have gotten mad at me for not going out there sooner. Okay, let her worry. If she became too anxious then Rusty would hear about it and he knew the plan. He could show her there wasn't anything risky in it.

I got in my Jeep and drove to town. First stop was Kinko's to make color copies of the photos. Next stop was Gear Up where I bought fourteen backpacker meals, hoping I wouldn't need them all. I only planned on cooking lunch if I had to have something hot. Every cooked backpacker meal required some of my very limited water supply. I preferred to get by on trail mix and beef jerky. I bought a light weight climbing rope. I would have to put my pack where animals couldn't invade it. According to my research they could even figure out the zippers so I bought paperclips to hold the zippers closed. I didn't think a seagull or a skunk could figure out how to get a paperclip off a pair of zipper pulls. At the grocery store I finished by picking up hot chocolate and oatmeal. I could tell already that my pack was going to be heavy, and I hadn't even started packing. Water was going to be the killer because it was so heavy. At least I'd only be carrying the heavy pack for three miles. Once I got it to the camp I'd be hiking without the pack.

When I got home I bought boat tickets and made reservations for the camp online. I didn't think there would be other people in the central valley so my reservations were probably unnecessary. Only seasoned backpackers would want to venture inland because most people preferred the coast where they could kayak and scuba dive. I printed out the waiver, signed it, then packed my search pack for the long trip. Stove, fuel, food, water, water, more water and one set of clothes. I might have to spend several hours in Ventura so I'd save the extra set of clothes for the last minute.

I set aside an empty daypack so Rusty could take back what I wouldn't need: extra silverware, trash, empty water bottles. Anything I could send back with him was less weight to carry on the trail. I made sure I had the map and planned to get Hazel a new one while I was in Ventura. Her old map was going to be marked up as I hiked the loops.

When I was ready I hefted the pack. Oh man, I thought, I'd better load this in the Explorer myself. If Rusty picked it up I'd catch some flack. At the last second I tossed in a camera. Maybe I'd see one of those foxes and have a chance to take a picture of it too.

Rusty came home early and then we went back out to pick up the wedding pictures. I brought them home and labeled envelopes for each person in the wedding party and for each family member. Then I stacked photos on the envelopes. I sorted the honeymoon pictures and separated out the pictures Rusty had taken of me. When each stack had a few wedding pictures and a few honeymoon pictures I put them in their envelopes and handed them over to Rusty.

"You can hand these out while I am gone. It'll give you something to do. If anyone asks to see wedding pictures please show them these. They have been labeled so you can't possibly mix them up. After I'm back I'll mail pictures to family out of town."

We left town early because the boat took off from Ventura at nine in the morning. It was a sunny and pleasant drive through miles of orange groves. We arrived early so we could stow our camping gear before the other passengers boarded. After a short walk along the waterfront I pulled on a jacket. The breeze off the harbor was already cold and it would get colder when the boat came up to speed. As the craft pulled away from the dock and putted out to the open sea we heard a brief welcome message from Captain Jed. It sounded like an amusement park ride, "No running. Keep your hands and arms inside the boat at all times." We were also informed that, since this was a family educational experience, they would attempt to locate and observe any marine life on the way. Half of me said, "Yes! Maybe I'll see a whale!" and the other half said, "No! We need search time!"

Reading one of the crew member's name tags I called out, "Jim!" as he went by seemingly in a hurry. "I'm going to Santa Cruz to look for this man. He went there twelve days ago, but didn't show up to a family event. He made this trip specifically so he could attend his brother's birthday party. Do you recognize him?"

Jim looked at the picture. "We see a lot of people come and go from this boat. I don't even notice faces anymore."

"You might have noticed this guy. He is a well known nature photographer, Mark Mireau. He would have been carrying a lot of camera equipment and might have asked where on the island he could find the Island fox."

Jim wracked his brain for a moment then grabbed the cook as she went by.

"Dolores, does this look like that guy we took over to the island a few weeks ago? Remember, he was taking pictures of the dolphins at a thousand frames per minute?"

"He would have checked in camping gear too," I added.

"Yeah, yeah, I think I know who you're talking about, although we get a lot of those too. And we get all kinds of questions about the wildlife there."

"Do you remember if he took the boat back to the mainland?" I asked.

"No, we never saw him again."

"Now I remember," Dolores said, "I was taking tickets for the trip back and checking off campers on the clipboard. Remember? We waited and waited for him and double checked the names but he never turned up. It put us late getting back. People were upset because we didn't stop for wildlife. They weren't too worried about being late, but they wanted to see whales and we couldn't take time to stop."

"What do you normally do when a passenger doesn't show up?"

"We don't worry too much. Passengers meet up with people who come over on their own boats. They may have gone exploring with a friend and rode back with them. It's the tourists on day trips we need to keep track of."

Rusty and I exchanged glances. If Mark had ridden back on another boat Hazel and Wally would have heard something.

I thanked Jim and Dolores for their time and they continued on with their duties.

When the island came into view I heard the engines change speed as the boat turned north. Off to starboard the sea birds had gathered over one area of the ocean. Gulls and pelicans dove into the water and other birds floated on the surface. Suddenly the ocean exploded in a frenzy of activity. Dolphins leapt out of the water and the birds that had been feeding on the surface flew into the air. The sky filled with birds while the ocean seemed full of dolphins leaping around the boat.

"Oh Rusty look!" I shouted with excitement. "I've never seen so many dolphins!" There must have been thousands of them and I had to ration my pictures. He was enjoying my enthusiasm, but as usual remained calm while I reacted like a kid in a new toy store. I could tell when he really got into it because he would place his hands on my shoulders to steer me in the direction he wanted me to look. He pointed to the water directly below the side of the boat where we could see gray forms swimming swiftly through the water below us. Occasionally the gray would rise to the surface, then a dolphin would come out of the water for a second and disappear again. All the passengers were crowded on the side of the boat with kids clamoring to see and pressing themselves up against the rail. We remained in the thick of it for a while enjoying the dolphins until I motioned toward the deck above. We left the press of people and headed to the top deck. Rusty followed me up the metal ladder. From there we could see all around the boat and enjoy just how vast the pod of dolphins was.

"Okay, maybe I *will* learn how to scuba dive," I said wistfully.

"Is there anything you don't want to do?" he asked.

"There are lots of things. I don't want to be a snake charmer and I don't want to wrestle alligators. Although if trouble finds us in Louisiana I might have to learn how real quick. Oh, one more thing, I don't want to learn how to tap dance."

He laughed. "Okay, I get the picture."

Eventually the boat engines started and we headed for the island again. Although I could have watched the dolphins forever I was relieved because we needed the search time. A number of passengers appeared grateful for the boat to be moving again because while the engines had been off the bobbing of the craft made several people seasick.

When we landed at the dock the boat bucked and lurched with the ocean swells. A seal was swimming close to the pier with just his nose and eyes poking above the water, avoiding the boat but watching the passengers disembark. We would wait for an up swell and then hop on a metal ladder and climb a few rungs to the top of the pier. I looked down from the pier into a kelp forest. Okay, maybe I did want to learn how to scuba dive, shark bait or not. When Rusty and the camping gear were both offloaded, I shouldered the pack and we headed for the ranger station. Jim had scheduled to lead a guided tour and was waiting for everybody to disembark from the boat. We asked him how to get to the ranger station and were directed to continue up a dirt road where we'd find the station on top of a hill overlooking some historic buildings. Had we taken the guided tour we probably would have been told about the history and present use of the buildings. I watched the road as we walked. The soil was dark with bits of shell and gravel in it and didn't take tracks well. As we reached the broad plateau that makes up most of the island I gazed out over vast grasslands with tall yellow flowers swaying in the breeze. I thought that if Mark were anywhere on top of the island I'd be able to see him from the ranger station. I knew the island was twenty-plus miles long with mountains and valleys but the grass seemed to go on forever. I thought, if there was a fox out there, how would you ever see it under all that grass? I would just have to hike out there and find out for myself.

We knocked on the door to a building displaying a flag in the window. A young ranger answered the door. I noticed his nametag. Austin.

"May I help you?" he asked routinely.

"Yes," I answered, "we're looking for a man that was on the island twelve days ago. He took the boat to Prisoners Harbor but we thought he might have stopped at Scorpion Canyon to photograph sea life and ask questions. Ultimately he wanted to photograph the Island Fox so I was hoping he might have stopped here to find out where he would be most likely to find them. Have you seen this man?" I asked, showing Austin the pictures of Mark.

"Can't say that I have," he answered. "Why are you looking for him?"

"His parents are friends of ours. He was supposed to be in Joshua Hills for a family get-together and didn't show up. That was five days ago. I work search and rescue in Joshua Hills so I came out to take a look around. I can show you on the map what he may have done and I plan to go to Prisoners Harbor to look for him."

"Hold on," Austin said. He went out the door and returned with two other men. They were talking quietly amongst themselves and I was hoping Austin had informed them of our mission. "Okay," he said, "go ahead."

I spread out the map and explained everything in as much detail as I could. We passed around the pictures but nobody recognized Mark from the photos.

"Cass, why don't you go down to the campground and set up. I'll be down in a little while."

I didn't want to go. He was planning to give them the old lecture about his poor little wife determined to take off into the wild unknown all by herself. But I had to admit it worked on some guys, so I took my leave.

The campground was a pleasant grassy area shaded by trees. The beach was a short walk away and three trails led up the cliffs to the top of the island and lookout points along the coast. I could hear meadowlarks off in the distance, their song slightly different from their mainland cousins. I found a good area for camping and set up my old familiar tent. The ground was moist enough that I could just step on the pegs to drive them into the ground. I put the poles through their sleeves and bent them into the little pockets. The old tent was so worn some of the pockets had holes through them but I was still using it because it was comfortable and familiar. I stuck my pack inside the tent and fastened the zipper closed with a paperclip. No critters allowed.

I found a picnic table and waited for Rusty to come from the ranger station. He finally made his way down the hillside and sat opposite me.

"No luck," he reported, "no radio. They doubt Mark is on the island. They say help is not hard to come by even in the Nature Conservancy and that, if something happened to him there, other hikers would have been around. There is nothing dangerous out there. The worst thing they could think of was maybe he fell off the island. The cliffs do tend to be brittle. They keep tourists away from the edges, but they suspect he just found another way back to the mainland."

"But, if he had, he would have shown up at Hazel and Wally's house. Do you think he stopped at Scorpion Canyon?"

"No, but we are stuck here for the day. You won't get a lift to Prisoners

Harbor until late tomorrow morning."

"So, what do you think would accomplish the most for today? Kayaking? Hiking? I think hiking would give me a good idea of what I might be up against. But kayaking sounds like more fun. It won't take long tomorrow to decide the best way to go about tracking. From what I can see, there is almost no point in tracking besides looking for places where Mark might have left the trail. Would you like to try kayaking? I've never done it before but I'd like to try. It'll give us a chance to question the guy who rents out the kayaks."

"Doesn't anything slow you down?" he asked.

"I did slow down. I was slowed down all the way out here."

"You were not. You had your eyes peeled the whole time for whales or dolphins. I saw you. You weren't slowed down for a second. You might have been sitting still but you were still active."

"I can't help it. All this is new to me and new things are interesting! I have to know more, so I look. Sometimes I just end up looking and not seeing much, but sometimes I end up seeing really cool things. I'm so glad we got to see the dolphins together. If I'd seen them by myself I would have just wished you were there. I enjoyed it so much more with you along."

"So, now I suppose you want to go paddle around and see some seals together."

"Can we?" I asked eagerly.

"We'll have to watch the time since I need to be on the boat at four."

It was a short hike down to the beach where bright green, orange, and yellow kayaks were stacked. I asked about Mark.

"I wouldn't have been on the island twelve days ago," the woman renting out kayaks said. "We switch off weekly so I would have been home then. I meet a lot of photographers who rent kayaks. Everybody with a big camera wants to go get pictures of the sea lions. Even kids with kiddy cameras want to go take pictures of the sea lions. They get the pictures developed and wonder why all they can see are rocks. It's cause sea lions look a lot like rocks, know what I mean?"

"Yeah, I know what you mean. We'd like to go out for a few hours," I said.

It seemed as though we were hitting mostly dead ends as far as Mark was concerned, but I was hoping for better luck at Prisoners Harbor. Now, it felt as though an entire search day was going to be wasted at Scorpion Canyon but there was no other access to Prisoners Harbor. I tried not to dwell on it as I paddled up the coast. Rusty insisted that I set out first so he wouldn't leave me behind. I'd never paddled a kayak before and it was slow going until my arms got tired and then it was even slower going. The kayak girl had been right, the sea lions did resemble rocks. We saw many rocks but not until one of them moved were we able to distinguish the difference between the rocks and the sea lions. Then we started noticing the seals too. What we enjoyed the most though, was watching them swim. On land they were awkward but once they got in the water they were graceful and nimble. There didn't seem any point in taking pictures of sea lions that looked like rocks but I did take a couple of Rusty kayaking.

A whiskered nose poked up out of the water and sniffed the air beside my kayak. I pointed it out to Rusty. He stayed at a distance so I'd have time to watch it. After a minute or so the nose came further out of the water and then the sea lion rose, curved into a graceful arc and dipped back under the surface again. A few flaps of its flippers and it was gone, but I was thrilled.

As we paddled up the coast I kept watching for people, stray kayaks or anything that might hint that Mark had been this way. As I paddled along I saw very little chance of finding Mark here and Hazel had been right; he wouldn't spend much time on these animals, not when there were more interesting and harder to find animals inland.

We found a tide pool and sat above it watching crabs and small fish scuttle and dart about while starfish lay nearly motionless on the rocks.

We were both getting tired and hungry so we headed back to the beach then walked to the campground to cook lunch.

"You take care camping up there in the valley," Rusty admonished.

"You know I do. I know my limits. I know to conserve my water and where to catch the boat if anything comes up. Everything will be fine. This is about the most unlikely place for someone to get hurt. You know, I can see how people get turned around in the mountains. After a while all the trees look alike, you can't see landmarks off in the distance to verify directions. But how could someone get lost here? Everything's so obvious."

"Mark's not lost. We already decided that."

"Yeah, but there's nothing here to hurt him, no way to get lost, so what happened?"

"That's why I wondered about your motivation for coming out here."

"I just need to find out. Even if I don't find anything, at least I'll be able to tell Hazel I tried."

"What if Strict calls while you are gone?"

"Tell him I'm off bending the rules a little bit, then fill in the back story."

"He won't be happy with you."

"If I thought he was likely to call me I'd be more inclined to stick around."

"You've seen less trouble since he backed off."

"But it wasn't his fault I ran into trouble before. I think trouble is just waiting for me to get close to something risky so he can really zap me."

"He? Trouble is a *he* now?"

"No, of course not."

Chapter 12

The boat docked as scheduled at four o'clock and so I walked with Rusty back down the pier. We sat on a bench on the wharf while all the day hikers boarded.

"On the way back, while you are enjoying fancy seafood in Ventura, think of me out here eating bland spaghetti from a pouch."

"I refuse to feel sorry for you. You chose this."

"I know. I'll call as soon as I have a few bars on my cell phone. Don't forget, if you get bored, there are wedding pictures to be delivered to the people who live in town."

The last of the passengers had boarded the boat so Rusty gave me a warm hug and a deep kiss then reluctantly followed them down the ladder. I sat on the pier and watched the boat as it headed out to sea. When it was a little speck in the distance I walked the beach and then hiked to the top of the cliff to sit and watch the ocean. It was going to be a lonely week. I followed the trail a short distance watching the surrounding brush for game trails. I understood how Island Foxes could easily survive out here. Mice and other small animals flourished running beneath the tops of the waving grass and small foxes would thrive on this ample food supply. Birds flitted over the grasslands and, although I never saw one, I continued to hear meadowlarks. As the sun began setting I walked back to the campground, made dinner and went to bed as soon as it got dark. I pictured Rusty driving back through the orange groves then dejectedly walking into a dark house. It was a depressing thought, so I turned over and stopped thinking.

Although I awoke with the sun there was no need to start rushing as the boat wouldn't leave Ventura until nine. It also wasn't expected to dock at the pier until well after ten, eleven if they followed a pod of dolphins through the channel again. That left me plenty of time to eat breakfast, break camp and have my pack down at the pier by the time the boat came. After breakfast I cleaned up and paced the camp, ready to be on my way to Prisoners Harbor. I wanted to hit the trail and had three miles to hike with no idea of how hard it was going to be. I couldn't hike it quickly because I needed to watch for signs of Mark, so I found myself getting antsy by the time the boat arrived. I'd spent time hiking to the cliff tops again and had also circled the buildings that were fenced off from the tourists. It left me wondering who had lived there and what their lives had been like out on an island with no game to hunt. They must have farmed, I thought, but how would they have brought farm equipment over from the mainland?

When the boat arrived, another load of day hikers disembarked. I knew Rusty was at work but found myself watching the faces anyway. After all the tourists had gotten off they began checking bags for returning campers. The crew stowed them away so I made sure they were aware I would be getting off at Prisoners Harbor. I didn't want my gear buried beneath all the packs returning to Ventura.

I watched the sandy beach of Scorpion Canyon recede as the boat found deeper water and then saw the cliffs and points go by one after another until we pulled into Prisoners Harbor. I waited for the hikers to disembark and then waited while my pack was offloaded. I took the map out of a zippered pocket and got my bearings, then headed south down a dusty Jeep trail towards the central valley. I was glad I wore my hiking boots because the road was rocky. I watched for footprints and although there were some I had no idea what Mark's footprints were like so I watched for men's footprints and footprints leaving the road. I also watched for odd prints in the dirt that didn't make sense. And, since tracking was a habit ingrained into me, I also watched for fox tracks. It was a slow hike watching the whole width of the road for so many things. I did see a man's footprints and studied them, trying to pick up any clues that I could about them. The rocky road didn't help at all. I caught part of a print here, another there. I wanted to study this man's prints because it was definitely one man, traveling alone as Mark would have done.

I imagined the central valley to be green, since the map showed wooded areas and grasslands. I thought I wouldn't see another person until I met Mark, so what I encountered in the central valley came as a complete surprise. There was a field station there with a laboratory, dorms and students coming and going in Jeeps and conducting studies on the weather, the flora and fauna. They had odd equipment coupled with an eager determination to learn. And they had seen Mark! He had camped nearby a week ago. When I located the camp, though, there was no tent, no pack, no photography equipment and Mark was gone. However, I did manage to find footprints that matched the footprints on the road. There was a flattened area that could have been left from his tent but there was no sign of Mark. I circled the camp looking for footprints leading away from it when I noticed a young woman watching me with interest.

"What are you doing?" she asked.

"I'm looking for a man who camped here a week ago and has been missing for the last five days. His family is worried, so I came out here to see if I could track him down. So that's what I'm doing. I'm tracking."

"Wouldn't it be easier to just ask around? If you track Mark you'll run around in circles for a week. He was looking for animals to photograph, and he did take some pictures, but then he went home."

"Are you sure he left for home? He didn't go to Campo del Norte?"

"Mark didn't have time and it would have taken him all day to get there. He was supposed to catch a boat out of Prisoners Harbor and it's six miles to Campo del Norte. It would have taken him all day to get there. Going there would have added at least two more days to his trip and I know he didn't have that much time to spare."

"But he didn't take the road back to Prisoners Harbor. I would have seen the tracks going in both directions if he had taken the road."

"There's another way back. He could have taken the road, but if he was looking for wildlife he probably took the trail. It's longer but he'd be more likely to find animals to photograph by taking the trail."

"Did you talk to him much?"

"Yeah, he was interested in our studies and some of the kids had heard of him, so it was like having a celebrity in house. So we *all* tried to talk to him."

I abandoned my tracking and got out the map instead.

"So, you think he took this trail?" I asked.

"Or the road. He left pretty early. Only a few of us saw him leave. He said he'd be back though."

"When?"

"He didn't say. Not for a while. I doubt I'll still be here when he comes back."

"And you're sure it was *this* man?" I asked, wanting to make sure we were talking about the same person.

"Yeah, the larger picture doesn't look much like him. Mark was friendlier looking, more like the snapshot when I talked to him. I have a poster at home with one of his photos on it. Where'd you get his picture from?"

"His mom."

"You actually talked to Mark Mireau's mom?"

"Umm, yeah, she's my neighbor."

"That is so cool! Wait till I tell the other kids I talked to Mark's mom's neighbor. They are going to be so jealous."

I folded the map and began setting up my tent in a different area in order to preserve all of Mark's tracks. My tent was halfway set up when I heard a scratching noise and turned to see a black and white visitor trying to open my pack. It was a skunk! I rarely saw skunks back home and wished the camera wasn't in my pack. After setting up the tent, I started wondering how I'd cook dinner as my stove and food were also in the pack. I decided as long as the skunk considered me friendly it was probably safe to get closer so I approached cautiously. The skunk didn't even seem to care. I put my hand on top of the pack and shook it gently thinking the skunk would jump off. Any normal critter would have run away in fright, but the skunk didn't budge, so I unzipped a pocket and removed the camera. The skunk immediately investigated the open pocket of my pack. I smiled as I zoomed in on my backpack with the skunk furiously fishing around in the pocket for goodies. I took a few pictures of my friendly guest but still couldn't cook dinner. If I opened up the main compartment he'd have a feast.

"Shoo!" I said, waving my hands around. "Go check out some other camper." But I was the only camper there and the skunk wasn't budging. "Come on, buddy, move it. I want my dinner!"

What can you do with an animal that won't be intimidated? I couldn't pick it up or chase it away and I couldn't hurt it. Finally I just picked up the pack and dumped the skunk off. It stamped its feet with indignation and followed the pack like a puppy dog after a treat. I propped the pack up on my leg while I fished around for the stove, water and backpacker food. When I set the packet of food down next to the stove the skunk tackled it and tried to open the packet but I was able to quickly and cautiously retrieve it. After heating just enough water to cook the meal, I poured the hot water into the pouch and then carried it around while the lasagna cooked. If I had set the pouch down the skunk would have had my dinner in no time. I then realized my fork was still in the pack so I had to hold the pouch with one hand and manipulate the zipper with the other, all the while fending off a fearless skunk. This was getting ridiculous. I held the pouch in my mouth, trying not to burn my face, while I opened the pack up again and found my fork. It was like a circus act. Let's see how many things Cassidy can do at one time! Victoriously pulling out the fork I looked up and in the dusky shadows of the brush I saw an Island Fox. Yes! I thought. This might be my only chance. So, holding the pouch of food still in my mouth I pulled out the camera and quickly snapped a picture. Then I stalked closer, closer. I took another picture and stalked a little closer. This time I slowly knelt down and zoomed in on it. The fox seemed to be watching the skunk and waiting for his own chance at my pack. Sitting down on the ground, I opened the pouch and began eating the contents while still watching the fox. It was small, even for a fox, and was mostly salt and pepper gray with some tan points on it. It looked at my dinner hungrily. Sorry, boy, a rule's a rule. Do not feed the animals. I wondered, if I sat with my dinner, maybe he'd stick around, like the skunk did, but when I sat I ended up with the skunk in my lap. What was wrong with the animals in this place? When I stood to get rid of the skunk the fox dashed away into the trees and vanished.

I paced the camp eating my lasagna noodle dinner from the pouch while keeping a step or two away from my black and white friend. I wished I could get a picture of him while he was climbing on me and then the answer came to me. I looked the camera over and figured out how to use the timer. I counted the number of seconds it would take me to set the timer, find the best place to sit and finally get attacked by the skunk. I figured fifteen seconds ought to do it. I set my pack on its back, set the camera timer, placed the camera on my pack, dashed to a spot about ten feet away from the camera and sat down on the ground. Within a few seconds the skunk was playfully climbing up my leg and trying once again to get into the pouch of lasagna. I was holding the pouch out of his reach when the camera shutter clicked. I could only hope that I'd been sitting in a good spot for the picture. After finishing my dinner, I packed up my trash and closed up all the zippers on my pack with paperclips. I circled Mark's camp again and found some footprints leading away from it. He had come and gone from camp a lot. Heading in the direction of the trail back to Prisoners Harbor I weaved back and forth looking for footprints. I finally picked up some faint ones that I thought were his so I remembered the spot. I'd start out there first thing in the morning.

As the sun began setting I picked up my cell phone hoping for a signal, but didn't get one. I pictured what I thought Rusty might be doing. He'd be working or eating dinner, but I also hoped he'd be delivering our wedding pictures to Kelly and Rhonda.

When the skunk decided the food was gone and he wasn't going to get any, he chattered at me a little longer and then wandered away. I went into my tent and lay in my sleeping bag thinking. At least this trip seemed easier than I thought it would be. Getting some information about Mark's whereabouts had helped tremendously. I wouldn't get to hike all those loops, and I wouldn't see as much of the island as I had wanted, but it was necessary to follow where Mark had gone. Tomorrow I'd hike the longer trail back to Prisoners Harbor and… and then what? What if I didn't find Mark? I'd backtrack to make sure and then study the map again. It's all I could do on my own.

Chapter 13

Dawn found me breaking camp. I started up my stove and made oatmeal and hot chocolate. My water situation had improved. I no longer had to spend four days hiking those loops as originally planned and could be more generous in my water usage. The island was a chilly place. I nursed my warm cup of hot chocolate and paced, then thought I'd be warmer hiking. After finishing breakfast I hit the trail. I found my starting place from the evening before and picked up the tracks. It was going to be another trail where all I could do was verify tracks as I hiked and watch for places where Mark might have left the trail. I was grateful that I got a good look at his tracks at his camping spot. They were eroded and faint, but were similar to the tracks I'd find on the trail. I thought I should be able to recognize them again now that I was pointed in the right direction. The tracks led down a rough dirt road and when the road forked I stopped to examine both roads. I found Mark's footprints on the left fork, which made sense. It was the one heading north to Prisoners Harbor, the more remote trail that would lead to more wildlife opportunities.

About a quarter mile down the left fork, I was encouraged to see something that was almost certainly a sure sign I was following Mark's footprints. The tracks suddenly stopped and I found sharp indentations in the shoulder of the road of a pack set firmly down and then close by the square indentations of tripod legs. I wondered what he had seen that caused the flurry of activity. His tracks continued forward in an odd pattern. The angles of his steps were suddenly different and I tried to picture what would have caused that to happen. Maybe he was sneaking up on something. The footprints angled forward, milled around, then stepped off the road and into the grass. I followed, knowing he had returned to his pack and continued down the road but the whole trail was worth investigating. I learned a little more with every action Mark had taken, and more patterns fell into place as I tracked. Whenever Mark left the trail there was a chance of finding him so I had to be certain to cover his entire trail. I wouldn't go back to the road until I was certain I'd found all the sign I possibly could. Glancing around in the grasses, trying to find the next track, I saw a dirty, curled up piece of paper and picked it up; it was attached to a small spiral bound notepad. On it was scratched dates: #1-6 10-5 skunk, #7-8 10-5 scrub jay, #9-12 10-7… no note yet about an Island Fox. There were numbers in a column under f-stop and

ASA but they didn't mean anything to me. I read the column under distance with interest. He'd been very close to the skunk, which I knew was easy to do. The scrub jay was thirty feet away, so he must have had a good zoom lens. I wish he had found an Island Fox. I was curious how close to one he could get. The page had a good coating of dust and the ink was running a little from the damp. Placing the notepad in a pocket of my pack, I was thankful for this clue which confirmed that I was on the right track. I followed the tracks back to the road and returned to the place where Mark had left his pack. He continued down the road but I remained curious as to what picture he had taken. Had the trail been fresh and I had more time I might have figured it out, but after several days I didn't expect to find any visible animal tracks.

When the trail turned off the road and headed north again I followed the tracks. The trail grew narrower and still narrower until it was just a parting of the grasses. Other plants bent over the trail and I noticed seeds scattering as I brushed them. I wondered what plant I was sowing. Wildflowers? Some weed from the mainland they were trying desperately to control? There sure was a lot of it and I hoped it was something native.

The trail followed the ridge bordering Eagle Canyon and I followed the shallow canyon ever closer to the sea. Walking along, the only person in a sea of dry grass and spent plants, the island felt remote. I knew just three miles behind me was a lab full of science teachers and college students, a hub of activity, but not a hint of the busyness reached out to this canyon. Only an occasional meadowlark and the sighing of the wind could be heard. Small brown birds flitted from plant to plant, but they never stood still long enough for me to get a good look at them. I found another place where a person had left the trail and then returned, but no sign of anything other than maybe a call of nature. Guess Mark felt alone out here too.

I found a new place where it looked like someone had left the trail, except after following the bent grasses I saw no indication the sign had been left by a person. As I parted the plants no familiar lines from a human footprint could be found, only sharp indentations, almost like a deer. Or a pig. A pig? Like a domestic pig? Or a javelina? This was interesting. I examined the tracks and decided the gait was too long to be javelina. What kind of animal made these tracks? I wished there was time to follow them, but then I remembered that I wasn't supposed to be off trail at all. After returning to the trail I saw that the animal had crossed the trail; it hadn't been on it and turned off. It was traveling cross-country. I'd have to remember that and research it when I got home.

Eventually the trail met another road and Mark had turned west towards Prisoners Harbor. I was just looking forward to a quick hike along the top of the cliffs and down to the pier when another trail departure caught my eye. I looked to the left to see if the grasses on the other side were bent, like they had been before. No animal had crossed the trail this time, but the change was abrupt and the grasses had been trampled in haste. I continued down the trail looking for signs of Mark's footprints, but couldn't find any. If Mark had left the trail at this point he hadn't come back, so I followed the trampled vegetation in the direction of Eagle Canyon. I studied the footprints beneath the plants. The soil underneath felt much softer than the soil on the road. I discovered a man's footprints sunk deep into the loamy earth. Suddenly a large form appeared under the vegetation and at first I feared that it was Mark. My heart sank as I thought of him laying out here for days, but as I rushed closer I saw that it was a backpack. On closer examination I noticed the tripod strapped to the pack underneath the tent. I stood gazing over the wide-open land before me. It went on a short way and then dropped off into the canyon and down to the ocean. Where the canyon met the ocean, the walls became steep and treacherous. I followed the bent plants, no need to examine each track. Only one thing could have left this much of a trail, a photographer with a subject in his sights. When I did examine the footprints I could tell Mark was crouched. More weight was placed on the front of his foot. His tracks led to the edge of the cliffs overlooking Eagle Canyon and then slowly picked their way closer and closer to the edge. The soil turned to rock, eroded, crumbly rock. Dangerously crumbly rock.

"Mark! Mark Mireau!" I called out, hoping he could hear me, but there was no response. I examined the rock where the footprints had disappeared, no sign of passage at first and then the distinct look of a rock misplaced. A rock that has stood in one place for a long time is usually the same color and texture as those surrounding it. Break off a piece of it, though, and the rock beneath can be very different. That is what I saw, the difference between a rock that had sat there for eons and one that had moved recently. No seagull or fox had jarred that rock loose. I crept closer to the edge. More rocks had been torn loose; most of them had fallen off the cliff to the bottom. I prayed Mark wasn't with them. It was a long drop to the bottom. Nobody would have survived that fall. I looked around for a bush or a tree to tie my rope to and found a scraggly manzanita bush firmly anchored close to where I'd last seen sign. I unzipped the bottom compartment of my pack and pulled out the rope I'd stashed there with my one change of clothes. I tied it firmly to the bush, hoping the roots went deep, and then wrapped the rope around me for a body rappel. I was taking this slow, though. I didn't want to jar rocks loose that could fall on someone and I didn't want to harm any nests that the seabirds had built. They weren't nesting this late in the season but I was still cautious. I walked down the cliff letting out a little rope as I went along.

"Mark! Mark Mireau!" I called as I descended, but all I could hear was pounding surf.

I didn't want to go down too far because I had to climb up again to get back to my pack. When I'd descended as far as I was comfortable I walked the cliff side to side, calling out Mark's name. I didn't know if anybody would be able to hear above the noise of the ocean, but I called anyway.

"Hey!" I heard faintly above the ocean's roar. I looked around frantically. Where did it come from? "Hey! Over here!" A man's voice! I couldn't see anybody. Where was he? A rock hit the cliff near me and I headed in that direction. I didn't trust the rock so I used the rope to support myself. "Over here!" I heard closer. Then I saw him. Just a man, on a ledge, up Eagle Canyon, out of sight of the trail and the ocean. Only seagulls knew he was there. I worked my way over, letting out more rope to give me distance.

He was terribly sunburned and his arm hung in front of him in such a way that I knew he'd broken something.

"Oh," he said as I climbed onto his ledge, "I was hoping for a rescue but God sent an angel."

"Not quite," I answered. "Looks like you could use a doctor but I'm afraid I'm not a doctor either. All I can do is help you up off this crag. I'm not here with a team of professionals. Your parents tried to get a real search going, but had no luck at it. I promised your mom I'd come look for you, so here I am. She didn't actually know she was talking to a tracker when she told me you were missing. Can you climb?"

"If I could climb I wouldn't be stuck here," he answered.

"If you had tried to climb this rock you'd have ended up down there," I pointed out. "It crumbles too easily. But you can trust this rope. Think you can climb up the rope?"

"No, my left arm is useless. I've been who knows how many days without food and water."

"Okay, hold on, I'll be right back." I started up the rope but he stopped me.

"You're not leaving me here, are you?"

"Right now I'm just going to my pack for food and water. We'll decide whether I'm staying or going after you decide if you're climbing or staying. If you are climbing I'm staying to do my best to help you. If you're staying I'm hiking back out for help. I can hike to Prisoners Harbor, or I can hike back to the field station and see what they can do. Looks like either way it's going to be a wait for you if I take off. But… food and water first. I'll be right back."

I climbed the twenty or so feet up to the cliff top and found my pack again. I strapped it on, then lowered myself back down the cliff, this time hitting the ledge more accurately. When I got down to solid footing again I carefully wriggled out of the pack because there wasn't much space on the ledge with the two of us there. I started opening the top compartment of my pack and suddenly the pack came alive! There were scratching noises and frantic scrambling, and once the zipper was opened a foot or so a black and white blur climbed swiftly out the top and up my front! I gave a startled cry and jumped back, slamming into the rock behind me. The skunk jumped from my shoulder onto the rocks, scrambled upwards, knocking small rocks down in his fright as he scuttled over the edge to safety. Mark laughed out loud, then quickly stopped when the movement caused him pain. I sniffed the inside of my pack and decided it was safe. I handed Mark a water bottle.

"I was right, you *are* an angel. What's a kid like you doing out here anyway?"

"I'm not a kid. I'm a tracker and I was looking for you because you needed to be found." I handed him the Ziploc bag of trail mix and then pulled out my little one burner camp stove. I pumped it up and tried lighting it but the wind blew out the match. I tried again shielding the match from the wind. This time the flame caught and the little stove came to life. I heated enough water for backpacker food and hot chocolate then held up several packets for his inspection.

"Beef stroganoff," he said.

"What is it with guys and beef stroganoff?" I asked. "Whenever I rescue a guy who has been without food for a while they choose beef stroganoff."

"You do this often?"

"Yes and no, not like this. I do find people fairly regularly. It's what I do best. I volunteer my tracking skills with the search and rescue operations in Joshua Hills. Your mom didn't know that when she talked to me about you. In fact she still doesn't know. You should have seen the look on her face when I told her I was going to come look for you. I hope she isn't too worried."

"Worrying is what she does best," Mark informed me.

I poured boiling water into the pouch and then into the cup of hot chocolate mix.

"Sorry , I only have one fork. I thought I'd be out here a week so I cut back on weight. Water was more important than silverware. Tell me what kind of shape your arm is in. What do you think is wrong with it?"

"It's not my arm. It's something in my shoulder. I hit this rock good and hard when I fell but I count my blessings that I did hit it and that I bounced in this direction. If I'd have fallen the other way I'd be a goner."

"Think you can climb up the rope if I help? Do you know what a belay is?"

"It's a rock climbing term but I don't know what it is."

"It's a way for a rock climber to help another climber ascend a rock face safely. Basically, I tie myself to that tree up there and make myself an anchor. I'll find a nice stable place where I can brace myself in real good and wrap the rope around my body to provide friction. The friction will make your weight easier for me to bear in case of a fall. Ideally, if you fall, it will only be the length of the tightened rope. Then you get your bearings on the rock and try again. My job is to either give you slack to climb or tighten the rope to keep the fall minimal."

He looked at me skeptically and I didn't blame him. I was skeptical about it myself, that's why I wanted to talk him through it.

He looked me over, all hundred and twelve pounds of me.

"*You're* going to keep me from falling?"

"Got a better plan? If I hike out for help it's going to mean another night on this rock. I can leave you with food, water and a sleeping bag. It's up to you. Another night or a slightly risky climb."

He weighed his options as he hungrily gulped down his beef stroganoff and drank hot chocolate. I imagined it got pretty cold on that rock at night.

"No," he said, "I can't risk it. One slip and you could be worse off than me."

"I won't fall, no matter what you do. I'll be tied to the tree. You'll be tied to the rope. I can manage the rope. All you have to do is climb."

He thought some more.

"I'll give it a try," he finally said.

"With only one good hand?" I asked.

"There are plenty of handholds and footholds. I just need to test them to be sure they are stable. I can hold the rope for balance."

After Mark finished eating, I packed the stove, cup and trash away, then made sure everything was secure. I fashioned a harness at the end of the rope for Mark then climbed back up the rope. I untied it from the tree then took up some of the slack. I tied the rope around my waist, anchored it once again on the tree, and found a place where the rocks were deeply imbedded in the cliff. I sat down and put my feet against the rocks. I positioned the rope to come up smoothly between my feet, around my back and back down through my feet again.

"Pull hard on the rope!" I yelled over the cliff. "Let's test this a little first!" I took up the slack in the rope. No pull, he couldn't hear me. Okay, hmm, I pulled up the slack tight and gave three hard tugs. I thought he might take that as a signal I was ready. I felt the rope go slack and gradually pulled up the rope, always making sure I had a firm grip. I wished I could see Mark as he climbed, but the rock close to the cliff was very flaky and it would be just as flaky for him. I hoped he was testing each hold on the rock before trusting it. When the rope went slack I pulled until it tightened up again and slowly, ever so slowly Mark made his way up the cliff face. Slack, tighten, slack, tighten, wait, wait, slack. The rope gave a sudden hard pull and every muscle in my body reacted on instinct. I tightened my knees and leaned back, holding onto the rope tightly with both hands. A yowl of pain echoed off the rocks. I held tight, feeling the tension in my shoulders, my hands, my knees, the tightness of the rope around my back. Come on Mark! I thought. We're proving this works but it's time to get on with it! I felt the rope move about but the slack was painfully slow in coming. The climb went even slower after his fall. Maybe he was more cautious. Maybe he was in pain. Sometimes it took him a while to search out a way up, but I just waited while he searched and finally the rope loosened a bit and I pulled it up some more. I imagined the jagged rocks at the bottom of the cliff and my determination set in and my patience grew. At last I saw the top of his head appear, then he crawled over the top of the overhang and onto firm ground guarding his injured shoulder and only grasping with the uninjured side.

"I never want to do that again as long as I live," he gasped. He sat down on the ground, clearly exhausted by the climb.

I was starting to untie the rope from the bush when I remembered my pack. I wasn't leaving my pack behind. That was a gift from Rusty.

"I need the rope one more time," I said.

He struggled out of the harness and handed it over.

"What are you doing?" Mark exclaimed.

"We left my pack down there. My husband gave it to me. I'm not leaving it behind. I'll be right back." I rappelled back down, tied the end of the rope to the pack and then climbed back up. I pulled my pack up the cliff and with a sigh of relief brought it up to where I could untie it and carry it back to the bush. Then I untied the rope and stuffed it back in my pack.

"You sure must like that pack a lot to go over a cliff for it," Mark observed.

"Yeah, it's got lots of memories in it. Rusty gave it to me for my twenty-fifth birthday. I've used it many times since then. It's seen a lot of rescues. If we are going to catch that boat we need to hurry. What time does it leave Prisoners Harbor?"

"Three-thirty."

"I don't think we'll make it."

"Me too," he admitted, "but if we camp there we'll make the boat for sure tomorrow."

I led him back to his pack and he looked at all the gear forlornly.

"We'll have to leave it here," he said. "There's no way I can carry that to

Prisoners Harbor."

"It's only a mile or so, I'll come back for it in the morning. We can't get a ride to the mainland until the boat leaves in the afternoon. I can run back for it tomorrow. How much does it weigh?"

"Too much for you. With all that camera gear I barely had space for food."

"You'll need your tent and sleeping bag tonight," I said.

After sorting through our combined supplies I repacked what we needed with the essentials for one night. Tents, sleeping bags, the stove, dinner packets and breakfast packets. I didn't push the oatmeal for breakfast. We had plenty of food so backpacker food would be the fare for mornings too. After we got the essentials I added photography gear until I was left wondering if I'd manage to carry it all. Mark attached his camera to his tripod and carried it propped on his good shoulder.

"I feel the same way about this old camera as you do about your pack. It fell with me over the cliff and it stays with me in all my travels. I may have better cameras but it will take a lot for me to replace this one."

"Did you get a picture of the Island Fox?" I asked.

"I don't know. You never know about photos until you develop them. Sometimes I think I took the perfect photo only to find out it is scrap paper. And sometimes I take a picture I think will be useless and it turns out to be everybody's favorite."

"I have a picture that is both. It's of a moose in Minnesota. It's a lousy picture but it will always be a favorite of mine because it shows just how close I got to the moose. When you visit your parents stop by and I'll show it to you."

"You're really Mom and Dad's neighbor?"

"Yeah, it's a really funny story how we met."

We enjoyed talking as we walked. I told him how we met Hazel and Wally while he shared what it was like to be raised by them. I told him about growing up on a quarter horse ranch and he seemed fascinated with the life of a ranch kid. He asked me about search and rescue, so I traded stories with him. Seems like every search reminded him of a photography expedition, and his expeditions reminded me of search stories. I found there were a few searches I still couldn't talk about. I still couldn't admit I'd killed a man even after several months; even if it was the right thing to do, even if not doing it would have harmed many more. I still couldn't talk about it. It was like a tarnish on my life. Like most people, he couldn't believe I'd done so many things in such a short time.

"Some of the things that happened to me are still hard for my husband to recall. If he seems distant at times, when we are telling these stories, it's just because some of the memories are hard for him to handle. He's been through so much with me."

"He's invested a lot. So he feels a lot," Mark observed, wisely.

As we were walking along we saw a movement off the road. I froze, hoping it was a fox, but the movement seemed too big, noisy and clumsy for a fox. An animal always meant a stalking opportunity to me so I automatically went into stalking mode.

"I'd go after it if I had the energy," Mark said, "but I just can't. I need a rest."

"Do you mind if I try? You can stay here. I like to see how close I can get and I'm curious what it is."

"Sure, but you won't get a good picture with that little camera."

"It's okay, it's the experience I like more than the pictures."

I took off my pack and stuck the camera in my pocket, then set off into the grass, my eyes set on the rounded form rooting around in the brush. I crouched low and approached from behind. It was busy looking for something. When the animal raised its head I froze. It was a pig. What were pigs doing loose on the island? It turned its head back toward the ground and I advanced slowly. It looked at me with beady eyes then went back to rooting around. I stepped closer, closer. I knelt down in the grass making myself a smaller profile. Then I advanced in a low crouch. I thought this probably looked rather odd to Mark but, surely, he was used to stalking animals if he was a nature photographer. I got my camera ready and then made a noise that I used to call birds out of the brush, *"fsk, fsk, fsk, fsk, fsk,"* I said rapidly and then repeated the call. The pig glanced up and I pressed the shutter release. I waited while it looked me over and then took a few steps away. I remained still for as long as it was wary. It contemplated its next destination and began trotting away. I followed, still in a crouch, then gave up the hunt. I turned to make my way back to Mark and he stood there, camera in hand.

"I hope you don't mind," he said apologetically, "I've never seen anybody move like that. Where did you learn to do that?"

"I've always stalked animals. From the time I was old enough to notice them I snuck up on anything that moved."

"You should see yourself stalking. Does it feel as natural to you as it looks to someone watching you?"

"Yeah, it does," I admitted.

"If I could move like that, I could get much better photos than I do now."

"I just assumed you stalked animals."

"I can't stalk like you. My stalking is more like a quiet walk, hiding behind trees. You don't require trees. You can stalk an animal anywhere like that and it still doesn't notice you."

"They notice me. You just have to convince them that you aren't a threat. You could learn to do it. Practice on the deer near your parent's house. That's what I do. They come to my yard sometimes to graze."

We followed the road along the ridge overlooking the ocean and then Prisoners Harbor came into view below. No sign of the boat. We were stuck for the night and most of the next day. I found a flat spot and set up both tents. Mark tried to help but his shoulder pained him to move. My tent was no problem. I could set it up with my eyes closed. His tent had different poles with different configurations and I wrestled with it. When I finished it wasn't a pretty sight, but it would stand for the night. I tracked around camp finding more skunk tracks. There were tourist tracks everywhere. I caught Mark with the camera again.

Before the sun set I started up the stove and prepared two more pouches of backpacker food. This time Mark chose chicken with rice. I wished I had some fruits and vegetables but the closest thing was the trail mix with dried fruit in it. I handed him the bag, knowing he needed all the nutrients he could get. As I sat cross legged in front of the stove heating water for hot chocolate I heard the sound from Mark's shutter over and over.

"Do you take pictures of everything?" I asked.

"No, just things that work well as subjects. If you want me to stop I will. You just seem at peace in this setting and it shows in everything you do. You were even comfortable climbing up and down the cliff. I seldom meet someone so at home away from home. Besides, it isn't often you get a set of pictures to remind you of your rescues."

"Then can I take one of you? It's the people that I remember from my rescues. The calls all run together. Three miles tracking, six miles, three days of tracking, they all run together but I remember each person. Lee, the Downs child; Kelly, the ranger who'd been missing a week and had been shot and dumped over a cliff; Trevor, the boy I was trapped in a mine with for three days; Thomas, the boy scout who gets lost whenever he goes to the mountains; Jake and Douglas, who led me into a trap where their boss shot me; Garrett, the boy with cancer who took a spill on a dirt bike. It's always the people I remember."

"Sure," he said thoughtfully, "you can take my picture." He stood and found a spot that would work as a background then adjusted all the settings on his camera for the lighting and shutter speed. He focused it and showed me the button to push, then sat down with his back to the tents and the stove still heating water in front of him. I aimed and pressed the button. Then I took one with my own camera.

As we were sitting quietly, taking turns with the cup of hot chocolate, he looked at me and said, "I still don't know your name."

"I'm Cassidy," I responded.

"I've never met a Cassidy before."

"My dad is an old west buff. He named me after Butch Cassidy. I'm glad he didn't name me Butch. My sister is named after Jesse James."

"I was named Mark because my mom thought it went with Mireau. Not too original but it'll do. It's getting dark. You don't know how good that sleeping bag is going to feel after all those cold nights on that cliff."

"Yeah I do, I've spent many nights out in the open. I bet you froze. When we get to Ventura you're going straight to the hospital. I'll call an ambulance to come meet us at the harbor."

As we turned in I warned him, "I'll take off at first light to go retrieve your pack. I'll be gone for a few hours. Help yourself to what food there is."

"Okay."

We were in our separate tents, laying in the dark trying to get to sleep when I heard from the other tent, "Cassidy? Why'd you really come all the way out here?"

"I told you. You needed finding."

A long pause. "Thanks."

Chapter 14

At dawn I jogged back to Eagle Canyon to retrieve Mark's pack. I wanted to get there and back as early as possible. He seemed to be in good health considering what he'd been through, but I felt uncomfortable leaving him alone. I knew he couldn't pump up the stove without two hands, so I needed to get back to cook our breakfast. I hoped he was a late sleeper so he wouldn't be awake and hungry for long. It didn't take me long to find the pack but it was a long, slow, heavy hike back to camp. How had he managed to carry such a heavy load? I had to stop and rest several times. Experience had taught me not to remove the pack. The process of taking it off and putting it on, then getting used to the weight again was harder than just resting with it on. The pack was too big for me and, though I was able to rest it on my hips, I couldn't get it well balanced, so it grated on me the whole time I was hiking.

Mark grinned at me marching along under his heavy pack. I bet he took a picture of that, too.

"I wondered if you'd manage all that weight. You're one tough cookie."

"Yeah, that was even worse than the packs we carried in the Marines!" I said, setting it down with a sigh of relief. "At least those packs fit."

I cooked breakfast and we ate and watched for boats. I took down my tent and left his standing in case he needed to rest during the day. We walked down to the pier and watched the seagulls. When the catamaran appeared in the distance we silently celebrated its arrival. We knew it wouldn't head back to the mainland until late afternoon, but we had a ride.

"Do you have your return ticket?" I asked Mark.

"No, it was in a notebook, but I lost it on the hike. I'll take care of the fare when we get to Ventura."

"Oh yeah! You mean this little notebook?" I asked, pulling out the notepad I'd found.

His face brightened. "Yes! I'm glad you found it. It has notes on all the pictures I've taken for the past few weeks."

"I'm glad I found it, too. It meant I was on the right trail."

He flipped to the back of the notepad and pulled out his ticket from a manila pocket.

The boat pulled up to the pier and we watched all the cheerful hikers disembark, full of energy, ready to take their guided tour of the harbor. When all the passengers were off the boat, I approached the crew.

"We need to get back to Ventura. What's the quickest way?"

"We'll be taking off from here about four o'clock." A crewmember named Dave answered.

"There's no quicker way?"

"How much quicker?"

"This guy has been stuck out here for two weeks. He's been stranded on a cliff with no food or water and he has a broken shoulder. He needs to have it looked at."

"We could radio someone to come out but it would take them a few hours, then it would be a few hours back. You're only looking at an hour or two's difference."

I looked to Mark. He said, "After sitting on that rock for days I'm not going to whine about a couple of hours delay. I'm just glad to be here at all. Do I smell hotdogs?"

"We've got a little kitchen. We sell sandwiches, burgers, hotdogs, chips, fruit. Simple stuff in case people don't bring a lunch."

Mark followed his nose onto the boat and although he'd just eaten a big breakfast I had to admit even a hotdog sounded better than more backpacker food. Dave made a gesture to stop him but didn't have the heart.

"Margaret!" Dave called, "you've got a customer!"

"How can I have a customer? They all left." A fiftyish woman wearing a blue polo shirt and tan slacks came down a ladder.

"Have a heart," Dave said, "he's been stranded on the island. He needs junk food."

Mark ate four hotdogs loaded with ketchup, mustard, relish and cheese. Anything they had to go on hotdogs he piled on. They dripped and fell apart but he enjoyed every messy bite. After a while I left him in their charge and returned to take down Mark's tent. I strapped everything to the packs, then I shouldered my pack and carried it to the pier. I hauled Mark's pack down the pier and set it near mine. When I climbed back aboard the boat, Mark was telling the crew stories about photographing eagles in Canada. I took my change of clothes to the head and washed as best I could then put my clean clothes on. I wouldn't smell great but at least I'd feel better.

Dave brought the packs aboard and then I heard the engines start up. They brought the boat out into the bay where it could lie at anchor more comfortably. We rested in climate-controlled comfort while Mark dozed, then woke and laid down on a bench in the dining area and went to sleep. I couldn't possibly sleep. I was on a boat and when things got boring I started getting antsy. I walked the dining area, looking out the windows at the island and ocean, then went out onto the deck and climbed the ladder to the upper deck. I could see the mainland off in the distance, so near and yet so far. It was a lazy, boring day, trapped on the boat, but Mark had a good rest, for which I was glad. While sleeping he wasn't moving around and in pain. The crew was kept busy performing their chores while the passengers were enjoying the island. I waited, paced, and looked around wishing I was back on the island tracking. I sat on the upper deck and watched the tourists on the island, then realized they were making their way back. Yes! I was ready for the next leg of this journey. I wanted to see Mark in the hands of people who knew what they were doing. And I wanted to see Rusty. As soon as I called he'd know Mark had been found and I was coming home early. Rusty knew that I'd leave no stone unturned, and I wouldn't give up on Mark, until I completely ran out of resources. He might worry at first, knowing how hard it was for me when a search did not end well, but he'd brighten after hearing the outcome. And I couldn't wait to be wrapped in that hug, that old familiar Rusty hug that I couldn't get anywhere else. I was hoping that he'd come from work and be wearing one of his old brown coats, especially the soft tweed one. A hug from Rusty in his brown tweed coat was the most comforting thing in the world. He'd worn that coat when we'd first met and he wore it often. When I pictured Rusty I always pictured him in the old tweed coat. Stop it, I scolded myself, you're going to make yourself homesick before you know it. Then I realized it was too late.

The tourists began gathering on the end of the pier and I was thankful when the engines started again and I heard the anchor being pulled up. The boat motored over to the pier and it became a friendly chaos as all the hikers boarded and found seats for the ride back. They were more inclined to sit on the way back, having spent the day walking on the tour.

I found Mark sitting with a group of hikers. He'd slid to the end of the bench and placed his broken shoulder to the wall to prevent anyone from bumping it. He kept up a friendly stream of conversation but I could see the care he took and the pinched expression when he forgot to put on his friendly face. He needed to get to a doctor and he needed it yesterday. If I'd just hiked faster, if I'd just found him sooner, we would have been back a day earlier. I went to the captain.

"When we get close to Ventura can you radio for an ambulance to meet us at the harbor? My friend is in pain. He's been dealing with that shoulder for several days. He'll be mad at me for requesting an ambulance but it's the quickest way for him to see a doctor."

The Captain looked me over to determine if I was serious then nodded his assent; he didn't stop for wildlife viewing either. It was a quick ride straight across the channel. As the buildings of Ventura came into view I checked my cell phone and placed a call to Rusty as soon as I could.

"Hi!" he said brightly when he answered on the second ring. "You're early. I hope it's because of good news."

"It is. We're coming into Ventura and I'm going with Mark to the hospital. Call when you get close to town to find out where I am and, if you talk to Hazel and Wally let them know Mark will be fine."

"Hazel's been driving me nuts," he confessed. "She thinks she sent you to your death out there. She's never been camping and she just knows you're going to be attacked by man-eating squirrels or something. When she isn't going on about wild animals she thinks of you as some poor, lost girl out there all alone and vulnerable and that doesn't help at all."

"It was skunks, not squirrels. Did you tell her this is what I do? It's my job to find people?"

"No, maybe I should have. The upside is she feels like if she can't do anything for *you* she can at least look after me so she comes over every evening with a different casserole. She says she makes a big one for her and Wally and a little one for me but even the little one is enough for three meals."

I smiled. Maybe Hazel and Wally weren't so bad after all.

"I made a big mistake," I said. "I let my thoughts wander and now I miss you like crazy."

"I'm just finishing up and then I'll come get you."

"Are you still at work?"

"Yeah."

Yes! What coat are you wearing? But I didn't ask. I could hear sounds of activity in the background as he tried to finish his day. I wanted to talk, but knew the longer I kept him the longer it would take him to hit the road, so I reluctantly told him to drive carefully and that we'd see each other in a few hours. I hung up and watched the buildings grow closer and closer until we were motoring through the breakwater. We saw other boats lined up in the harbor parked serenely in their berths, and then our empty dock appeared ahead and the boat slowed even more.

I was right, Mark was not happy about the ambulance. He had a rental car to consider and his camera gear to keep track of. After loading our packs into the rental I got directions to the hospital and then drove the rental car there. It was a long wait in a busy emergency room and I was still waiting when Rusty called for the name and address of the hospital.

"I'll meet you in the lobby," I said.

I quickly went down to the lobby to wait. I knew when Rusty got there because a woman a few chairs down from me said, "*Mm, mm, mm* would you look at what just walked in the door!"

When I saw him wearing his old brown coat my heart leapt. I was home again. Wherever he was, that was home. I'd never get tired of that hug, the smell of his coat, the feel of his chin resting against my head. How he could stand to hug me after I'd been camping for four days, I didn't know, but he didn't seem to mind and I let his presence soak into me.

After checking on Mark and being advised it would be several more hours, we dropped off my film at a one hour photo lab. Then we went to a restaurant for dinner where I told Rusty all about the search. Later we picked up the pictures and returned to the hospital to check on Mark.

"What am I going to do?" I asked after being turned away again. "I need to get my gear and make sure Mark has the car keys. I can't just take off."

"Let's go get your pack. That'll take care of half the problem."

I led Rusty to the rental car where I very carefully sorted out Mark's photography gear from my camping gear.

"We were trying to even out the load so I could carry both packs," I explained to Rusty as I sorted. "Cameras are heavy! I never packed such a heavy pack before and that was after we balanced it all out."

He carried my pack to the Explorer while I made sure Mark's pack and photography gear were locked securely in his trunk. Then we went back to the emergency room to check on Mark again.

The nurse, annoyed with my persistence, said, "I tell you, missy, he'll be fine."

"I know. I know he'll be fine but I have his car keys and I'm leaving town. He at least needs these keys."

The nurse stared me down but I didn't give in so she led us down the hall. After peeking in a room, she entered, then she came out again.

"You have two minutes," she told me.

"Thank you," I replied, and Rusty followed me in.

"Hi," I said quietly as I approached the bed. "My ride's here and I need to go home. I'll have to talk to your mom and dad in the morning. What should I tell them?"

"Hey, Rusty, good to meet you. Next time it'll be under better circumstances." Then to me he said, "Tell them I'll be up to visit as soon as they let me out of here."

"Okay, here are the car keys. I sorted out the gear and it's all safely locked in your trunk."

"What color's my car again?"

"Silver."

"Great, there's probably a dozen silver cars out there."

"It's under a tree out in front."

"Thanks Cassidy, I'll see you both when I'm up that way."

"Okay. Can I see your pictures from the island?"

"Sure thing."

"Even the ones you thought wouldn't turn out?"

He wasn't so sure about that. "Why?"

"While I was tracking you I wondered what you were stalking and I am curious if I'm able to match the pictures up with the tracks. It's an educational thing. I like to match track patterns to the activity associated with them. It's just a tracker quirk."

"You got it. Take care and I'll see you as soon as they let me out of here and I can get up to Joshua Hills. It better be soon. You know how my mom can be."

Once back home I walked from room to room enjoying the homey feel of it. I started wondering if I was getting soft and turning into a regular housewife. I told myself that I better watch out, next I'd be noticing babies at the stores. I wasn't sure how I felt about children, though. I knew Rusty would make a great dad, but I wasn't so sure about myself as a mom. It wasn't the day-to-day nitty-gritty things I worried about. I just didn't want to be tied down. When I needed to get up in the mountains, I wanted the freedom to go. If Strict called, I didn't want to arrange for a babysitter for possibly several days and work out all the little details. It was important to hit the trail as soon as possible to increase our chances of success. Nope, children were definitely not in the picture any time soon.

"Cass, are you all right?" Rusty asked as I walked through the house.

"Yeah, I'm fine," I said sitting down on the couch next to him. He held out his arms and I snuggled into them. "I'm just glad to be back. Even with all the unexpected people and twists this search threw at me it was lonely. The island felt remote. The animals were strange."

"Strict called while you were gone."

"Did he have a search for me?"

"I don't know. He seemed hesitant, like he didn't want to send you, so it's probably just as well you were off doing something safe like hanging off a cliff. Cass, why didn't you just go for help? You didn't have to climb down there by yourself."

"It would have added another day to the search. The closest help was either three miles behind me or a mile and an overnight wait in front of me. I didn't feel I was risking much. The climb didn't scare me. I had a rope. Helping Mark back up was the scary part. I couldn't pull him up because he was too heavy. He couldn't climb without help. So I helped him the only way I knew how."

"What made you think up that plan with the rope?"

"I'd read your rock climbing books and it made sense. I need to go through a training day on cliff rescues. It would really help if I knew the proper way to do things."

"Oh! Oh my! Dear, you're back!" Hazel squealed with delight when she answered her door. "Come in! Come in! I made a casserole for Rusty but he wasn't home last night."

"He was in Ventura picking me up from the search. Mark will be fine. He's in the hospital right now but it's nothing serious. We think he broke his shoulder and we know he was dehydrated, but he was in good spirits when I left. He said he'll be up to visit as soon as he's released."

"You have to tell me all about it!" she said and dragged me into the kitchen. It was painted in a barnyard theme and Hazel collected chickens. She had chicken wallpaper borders and a chicken cookie jar that crowed when it was opened. The thought occurred to me that if my cookie jar crowed whenever I opened it I'd definitely eat fewer cookies!

"Hazel, before starting I want you to know that I'm a tracker. That's why I was able to find Mark. I've tracked people all my life and I do tracking here for the search and rescue operations in Joshua Hills. That's why Rusty and I know so many police officers. I found Mark by following his footprints. Considering his location, I doubt anybody else would have found him in time. He couldn't be seen from the ocean or from the trail so he's lucky you made such a fuss. If you hadn't followed your heart and instincts, he wouldn't have survived. As it is he will be here in a few days, with his arm in a sling, maybe a little skinnier, too."

"If you're a tracker, what does Rusty do? I always thought he should be a male model, like in the JC Penney catalog."

I laughed. "No, I don't think that would be the kind of life for Rusty. He works with the police department, too but it would be great for his kid brother." Then, before getting into further details about Rusty's job, I told her all about the search. It was foreign to her and she couldn't imagine a woman wanting to follow a bunch of tracks. She couldn't envision carrying a heavy pack over miles of trail, cooking on a stove with only one burner and then eating food from a foil pouch with only a fork. She cringed after learning I only had two sets of clothes for the entire trip and covered her ears when I told her about the cliff. I didn't go into detail about how we got Mark back up off the cliff side, but simply said that we met the boat and that he was in the hospital impatiently waiting to come visit them.

"I don't know how to thank you. How can I repay you? I want to do something."

"Nothing. There's nothing for you to do. I find people because they need it. Mark needed finding, so I found him. It's what I do best, and I think it's good for people to do what they enjoy for the benefit of others, not for some material benefit. If it were money or material things I was worried about I'd have a career. But I don't. That's not what's important to me."

"I'll think of something," she said, "just you wait."

Chapter 15

A week later I was in the barn planning Shadow's next obstacle for the agility course when he began barking and racing around the house like crazy. Barking at everything in a friendly way is normal sheltie behavior, but it also served as a warning. Following Shadow around the house, I came to an abrupt halt. It was the guy from down the street who had tried to help me with my flat tire. He wasn't standing at the door waiting for a friendly response. Instead I caught him walking around the house and peeking in our windows. I shrank back behind the bushes, then made my way in through the back door. I locked it behind me, then made sure the other doors were locked too. I went to the closet, got out my 9mm, and checked to make sure it was loaded. Then I found a spot in the hall that was out of sight of all the windows and prayed the guy would go away.

I worried about Shadow out there. I was almost sure Shadow wouldn't leave the property. He would either follow the man around or look for me. I just hoped he didn't follow the guy home.

I jumped when the doorbell rang but decided not to answer it. Then I heard a noise at the back of the house. Who would be at the front of the house while this guy was at the back? I went to the front door concerned that a friend might meet up with this guy.

"Who is it?" I called out.

"It's Mark."

"Damn it Mark, you've got lousy timing," I said. "Get in here."

I opened the door quickly and he stepped in, then I stepped out, gun drawn. I looked in both directions and then stepped back into the house. I pulled Mark along into the hallway. I was willing to take this guy on by myself but I wasn't willing to endanger others. I thought Mark would be safer inside with me than outside. Pulling my cell phone from my pocket I hit Rusty's number.

"Hey there," he said brightly, answering on the third ring.

"Can you send an officer up here to drive by the house a few times, maybe walk around the property?"

"Sure. Are you okay?"

"It's that guy I had trouble with when I had the flat. He's prowling around out there, looking in windows. I've got my gun and I would have confronted him but Mark showed up. I'd feel better if somebody else checked this guy out."

"I'm on my way."

"Rusty, no..." but he was gone. "Like I said, Mark, you have lousy timing. Just sit tight. We're sitting here in the hall because we can't be seen from any of the windows."

"You have spots like this planned out ahead of time?"

"Not exactly, I just notice and file odd facts so when things like this come up solutions fall into place more easily. Would you feel better armed?"

"I don't think so. I'd be more likely to shoot your house than an intruder. Are you a good shot?"

"Yeah, if need be. I won't shoot unless I'm forced to, though. I've been forced before and it's no fun."

"You've actually shot someone?"

"Yeah, but I don't like to talk about it. How's your shoulder?"

"Better, but useless. I'm stuck in this sling for eight weeks."

"What was your mom's reaction when she saw you?"

"You don't want to know. Basically she broke my shoulder again in the biggest hug of my life. Then she cried and dragged Dad into the whole thing. And, of course, she had to hear the whole story from my point of view."

I glanced towards the kitchen and thought I saw a movement outside. "I'd offer you something to eat, but we'd need the kitchen and I don't want to be spotted."

"Hey, don't worry about it. Is your life always this exciting? Searching for missing photographers? Hiding from prowlers?"

"You don't even know the half of it. Actually, the past few months have been rather peaceful for me."

The doorbell rang again. This was starting to feel like grand central station. I didn't know whether to move or not. Then there was a pounding on the door that made me jump.

"Cassidy?" an unfamiliar man's voice called through the door.

Mark and I exchanged glances, then I went to the front door.

"Who is it?" I asked.

"Police."

That was quick, but I guess an officer could have been in the vicinity. I opened the door and there stood the guy looking as smug as can be.

"Well, well, I see you're still armed. You don't trust anybody, do you? Mighty suspicious aren't you? Why can't a neighbor make a friendly call on you?"

Shadow rushed in the door looking like he'd done his duty by greeting our visitor and showing him inside. Then Shadow sniffed around a bit and headed down the hall.

"Don't take another step," I warned. "Friendly neighbors don't prowl around houses peeking in windows or lie their way inside. So far you've done nothing to make me believe you're a friendly neighbor."

"Aw, come on," he said, taking a step closer. "You can trust me. You want me on your side. You don't want to get on my bad side."

"I'm likely to get on your bad side real quick unless you turn around and get out of here. You don't want to be here when the police arrive. They'll haul you off and find something to pin you with."

"No, they won't. I haven't done anything wrong."

"You take one more step and you'll have done something wrong. Now go."

"I don't think so. I think you should let me in. I think we need to talk on friendlier terms." He made his way forward and I drew my gun. "You won't shoot me. I can see it in your face. You don't want to hurt anybody. All your tough talk is just a big show. I bet you'd take a beating before you'd pull that trigger." He was right but I'd never admit it.

I was praying Mark had stayed put, better yet, I wanted him to lock himself in the bathroom.

"You really don't want to be here when the police arrive. They are used to seeing me in tense situations. They'll shoot first and ask questions later. You may not be able to answer if you give them a hard time."

"I'm really scared. Maybe if you were a little friendlier you wouldn't get into tense situations. Did you ever think of that?" he asked, advancing.

"Damn it!" I said. "I really don't want to shoot you! Why can't you just go away? What do you want?"

"I just want to be on friendly terms with my neighbors, some friendlier than others. The more you spurn me the more determined I get."

"You're crazy. Why would anybody want to get to know you more if you intimidate them and terrorize them? You can't treat people like that and get anywhere. With your attitude even an offer of help is turned away."

"Yes, which is why I came. All I wanted to do was help you with your car. Why did you refuse?"

"If you want to help people you need to sound sincere, not like you're setting a trap for them."

"I'll have to remember that. I've been watching for the Explorer. I came over a week or so ago but you were gone for several days. Where were you?"

"None of your business."

He stepped forward and I switched the gun to my left hand. He stepped forward again and I kicked him in the groin and then slugged him in the nose. He staggered back and blood spurted from his face.

A black and white drove up and came to a halt in front of the house. Jayce Thompson stepped out shaking his head.

"Cassidy, can't you at least manage to stay out of trouble in your own home?"

"I try. Some people are just persistent," I replied nervously.

Jayce came to the front door and looked at the guy who was now curled up in a ball on my porch. He tried to stand but was still too sore. Jayce gave the man a moment to recover, then handcuffed him and put him in the car. "Are you okay?" he asked me.

"Yeah," I answered, rubbing my sore knuckles. "You will probably end up turning him loose. He didn't do anything to break the law, yet."

"Trespassing, there's always trespassing."

"Call Rusty and find out where he is. He might want to talk to this guy before you haul him off. Do you want to come in and wait? A friend stopped by but we haven't had a chance to visit yet."

"Let me get Rusty's twenty first. If he's going to be a while then I'll come in."

Jayce returned to his cruiser and radioed Rusty while I went inside to find Mark still sitting in the hall. "You can come out now," I told him. "Can I get you something? Coke? Tea? Cheesecake?"

He followed me to the kitchen and watched while I added ice to two glasses, filling one with Coke and the other with tea. There was a light knock and Jayce came in quietly.

"Rusty's at the foothills. He'll just be a minute. Is one of those for me?"

"Sure."

He took the Coke and Mark grabbed the tea, so I reached for another glass and filled it with ice and tea for myself.

"Jayce, this is Mark. He's a photographer and the son of a neighbor."

"What happened to your arm?" Jayce asked him.

"I took a tumble down a cliff. Five days before Cassidy found me."

Jayce looked at me. "He's one of your ten sixty-fives?"

"Yeah, sort of," I answered. "Not officially."

"I wondered why I hadn't heard about it," Jayce said. "Usually Rocky and Cliff handle cliff rescues."

"You're kidding. Rocky and Cliff? That can't be their real names."

"Rocky is short for Robert MacKay, and Cliff is short for Edward Heathcliff."

"Oh, yeah, Bob and Ed. I knew that. Well, this wasn't in our jurisdiction, and the police there didn't consider Mark a missing person. I told his mom I'd go look for him, so I rode the tourist boat over, and while I hiked and camped, I also tracked. That reminds me, Mark, I got my pictures back from that trip. I don't usually carry a camera on searches but I thought your mom would want to know what happened and I brought the camera in case I needed to collect evidence. Then I ended up taking pictures of animals."

I went to the bedroom and found the packet of pictures, then handed them to Mark. He flipped through them well aware they had been taken by an amateur.

"If I'd really been there as a tourist the pictures would have been better. I'd have taken the time to stalk the animals and get closer, but since you were missing I felt pushed to search."

"You got a picture of an Island Fox," he said, impressed. "The skunks weren't too hard to photograph, were they?"

"I think I got a couple of pictures of them. They sure were persistent critters."

"What's this?" he asked, handing me a picture where half of me had been cut off.

"I tried setting the timer on my camera. I wanted to get a picture with a skunk climbing on me but I sat in the wrong place."

Jayce made a face. "You let a skunk climb on you?"

"It was a very friendly skunk and it didn't act like it would spray me. I never met an animal quite like that one before."

"Next time mark a spot on the ground, focus on the spot and make sure the camera can actually see the spot before you set the timer. A few degrees off and you can miss the subject altogether."

"Easier said than done when you have a skunk following you around like a puppy."

I heard a car door and then another car door. I went and peeked out the front window, but didn't like what I saw. Rusty had the guy pinned up against the squad car. He was livid and if there was one thing I avoided it was seeing Rusty angry. It was like watching a violent storm. He rarely lost his temper and I'd only seem him strike a person once, when they had clearly deserved it, but still… I closed the curtain hoping he didn't notice me.

"Rusty's home," I announced. Jayce headed for the front door. "I wouldn't go out there yet if I were you," I warned.

Jayce turned around and came back to finish his Coke.

"I wanted you to see my pictures from the island," Mark said. "So I developed them and brought them along. I have something for you, too, but it's out in the car. I wanted to give it to you when Rusty was here."

I opened the envelope and looked at the first few pictures. "Are they in order?"

"Yeah, I kept them in the same order they were taken."

"I like the skunk ones, weren't those the cutest animals?" I flipped to the pictures of the scrub jay.

"Not bad for being thirty feet away. I'm surprised they let you get that close. You must have had a zoom lens."

"How did you know I was thirty feet away?"

"I was tracking and looking for sign. When I found your notebook I read a little to verify that it was yours. If the notebook was yours, the footprints were yours, too."

"You remember my notes days after the trip?"

"I remember the oddest things. I wondered what you had been stalking when you lost your notes, and what had made you venture over the side of a cliff. That part was missing from the notebook."

"Keep going," he advised.

I continued through the pictures. Some were very good, and some looked like I'd taken them. Flipping over the last picture of a scrub jay I saw that Mark had, indeed, gotten his picture of the Island Fox.

"You saw one during the day?" I asked. "No wonder you left the trail. This is a wonderful picture!"

"Look at the next couple. I was able to get closer before it ran away."

The next two pictures were close-ups. You could see individual hairs on the fox's face. Jayce looked over my shoulder. "Wow, those are almost professional! You should have copies printed up! Sell them to wildlife magazines or something. You could make money off pictures like that!"

Mark and I exchanged glances but didn't say anything to Jayce.

"I like the one that shows the whole fox though. I prefer seeing an animal in its natural environment. This shows the texture of the grass and the way the animal is at home there."

There were several pictures that showed the fox running off through the brush. Then there was a picture of a bird I'd never seen before. As I flipped through the pictures I asked Mark what it was.

"I don't know either. That's what made me follow it. That's what led me over the cliff."

"It sure is a pretty bird and you got some great pictures of it. I just wonder what it is!"

"I'm going to take the pictures to a friend of mine at the University of California. I bet he can identify it for me."

"Where are the rest of them? I know you took some after I found you."

"I'll show you when Rusty is here. I want him to see them too."

I peeked out the front window again and Rusty had the guy back in the squad car. He was talking to him through the open driver's side door.

"I think it's safe to go out now," I told Jayce.

Jayce went outside and there was some talk between him and Rusty, then Jayce got in the cruiser and took off while Rusty came inside. He opened the door and stood there for a second. I was worried he was still mad. Seeing his big form filling the doorway didn't help the image. When he'd gotten his attitude adjusted and decided how to tackle the situation, he entered the room.

"Cass, you can't take on a man with your fists. Why did you do it when you had a gun in hand?"

"I didn't want to shoot him. I wouldn't shoot him unless it was absolutely necessary. I hit him because I didn't want to harm him."

"If you were close enough to hit him he was close enough to take your gun," he said evenly. "He could have killed you!"

"He might be strange, but I don't think that was his intention."

"What was his intention?"

"I don't know, but he sure gives me the creeps. His actions and his words constantly contradict each other. I think he just enjoys scaring people. I hope he doesn't get bored trying to scare me and get more intimidating."

"Mark?" Rusty said.

"Well… I *thought* we'd be meeting again under better circumstances," Mark began. "I didn't see the guy but, from what I heard, Cassidy's right. The guy's like a rattlesnake. He was pushing her to let him in, and she was right not to trust him."

Rusty turned, running his fingers through his hair. I'd learned that gesture was a sign of frustration for him and sensed he'd rather not make a big deal of this with Mark in the house. However, he also needed to gain an understanding about how this situation could progress.

Trying to lighten the mood, Mark said, "I brought something for you. It's in the car."

He went out to his car and Rusty followed. They returned carrying two long thin packages.

"When I saw the photos from the island, I knew I had to do something with them. Open them up," Mark said.

Tearing the protective paper off the outside I could tell they were framed prints, but I wasn't prepared for the impact of the photos. They were all of me, but Mark had edited the photos somehow. They weren't color pictures like the photos of the animals. One set was framed vertically, the other horizontally. The vertical one showed me climbing the rope up the cliff. It was black and white and a little stylized, the outside edges pixilated to bring out the roughness of the rock, the toughness of the climb. The other panel showed me stalking the pig. These were not rugged, pixilated pictures but smooth, soft-edged pictures. He captured the focus, the concentration, the fluid movement, the patient study of a good stalk. None of them showed the pig. It was just me, in a totally natural manner being myself. Each frame held four, eight by ten, progressive pictures. They were matted, framed and autographed. He turned one over and there was a picture of himself, unshaven, dirty, and hurt sitting in front of his tent with my little backpacker stove in front of him. Below it was a handwritten note:

"To Cassidy, whose willingness to help a neighbor brought her to a lonely outpost. Whose keen eyes brought her to me when I needed help most. Whose firm determination and bravery brought her to a successful rescue. I thank you from the depths of my heart. Mark Mireau"

I didn't know what to say. Rusty was studying the photos. Of the stalking pictures, he swallowed a big lump in his throat and said softly, "That's my girl." When he turned to the climbing pictures he had a different reaction. "Cass, you're not even anchored to the rope!"

"I was just climbing and it was tied to a tree. It wasn't going anywhere. I had to go up and down that rope six times without using any fancy climbing equipment. I'd never even done a belay before. I'd only studied your rock climbing books. I had to use what was on hand and that was my brain and a rope."

"Well," Rusty admitted, "that's my girl, too. You did it, Mark. You captured Cass' spirit in pictures."

Mark humbly accepted the compliment silently, then turned to me. "You'd never done that before?" he asked.

"No," I confessed. "But I knew the theory behind it. Mark, thank you for this gift. You didn't need to do anything for me. Tracking people is what I do. Just seeing you back on the mainland in one piece was enough for me."

"I know, but it wasn't enough for me. Neither is this," he said motioning to the pictures, "but it's what *I do* and I hope you enjoy it."

"I will…thank you."

Chapter 16

The next day when Rusty came home from work, he dragged me away from dinner preparations, led me to the couch and sat down. He held out his arms so I climbed into his lap. Open arms, that was Rusty. If he was happy, he wanted to hug me. If he was sad, he wanted to hold me. If he happened to be feeling playful, he would hug me until his fingers became distracted, then they would tease and tantalize me. Sometimes while we were hugging I ached, waiting for that first touch.

"Gotta get my minutes in," he said. His voice rumbled with my ear pressed against his chest.

"Uh oh, why? What's going on?"

"Strict will be calling in the morning. The guys are out there now but Strict knew you couldn't see enough to track. You'll have to catch up with them in the morning."

"Do you have any details?"

"Old man. His daughter thought he'd like to go camping like in the old days so she picked him up from the nursing home and they went out in her RV, a nice easy camping trip, just to get up in the mountains. He wandered away. He's got Alzheimer's so it might take some patience on your part. He couldn't have gotten far. Maybe the guys can find him tonight. They're walking the area with headlamps on. Maybe he'll realize people are looking for him and come back."

"It's going to be cold out there for an old man. And he might be unsteady. He could fall. If they're tromping around in the mountains there's going to be footprints everywhere."

"Cass, try not to worry about it. I just wanted to give you a heads up."

"Strict is worried or he wouldn't start out a search like this."

"You're right, he's plenty worried. He's grasping at straws right now. Maybe you can help him out in the morning. He recommends wearing blue jeans, a blouse and tennis shoes. If Albert thinks you look like his daughter he'll be more likely to listen to you. If he calls you Katherine just call him Pop and quietly tell him what he needs to do. He'll act confused at first, but then he'll usually do as he's asked."

"Sounds like you talked to Strict for a long time."

"Yeah, long for Strict."

The wheels in my head started turning. I couldn't help it. I thought about the old man wandering around in the woods, unsteady on his feet. If the searchers hadn't destroyed his trail he should be easy to follow.

"Cass, don't worry, I know you can do it. I just wish it wasn't necessary."

I couldn't sleep that night. Scenarios kept flitting through my mind. It never served any purpose to dwell on a search until I saw exactly what I was dealing with, but sleep refused to come.

First thing in the morning I drove up to base camp. Strict greeted me with a worried hug. Landon grinned, glad to have his little tracking buddy on board.

"How'd the search go on the island?" Strict asked.

"How'd you know about that?" I countered.

"Rusty told me where you were."

"As well as it could under the circumstances, but I need technical rock climbing classes, Strict. I was only guessing how to get an injured two hundred pound man up from a cliff. It worked, but we were lucky, too. If he'd been more seriously injured then I'd have had to hike for help and it would have added another day to the rescue."

"I'll keep that in mind. You should be able to keep your feet on the ground for this one."

Strict was well prepared for this search and had everything I needed handy. He introduced me to Katherine and she told me a little about her father's mental state, how well she expected him to be managing out there and what he was capable of physically. She didn't look anything like me except that she was short and wore blue jeans, a blouse and tennis shoes. I had dressed accordingly, but wasn't sure how anybody could mistake me for Katherine. When Strict showed me a pair of Albert's slippers I thought I'd be able to track him easily. There were not just wear spots on them but it looked as if Albert never raised his feet to walk. Strict had also taped off an area with distinct footprints. As I examined them I thought, this should be a cinch.

In a way it was. Finding Albert wasn't difficult. Landon followed me, pressing for the story of Mark's rescue, so I told him the whole story and rambled about the trails, the odd animals and my discoveries as I searched for Mark. We found Albert standing in a copse of trees, taking a leak. His clothes fit his thin frame loosely. He was wearing an old, faded flannel shirt and old slacks cinched up tight with a belt that fit him a little better than his pants. He was also wearing an old fishing hat with flies sewn onto it.

"Can't a man even use the loo without being spied upon?" he asked with a quavering voice. Landon smiled. We let him zip up and come out but when Landon tried to take his arm Albert wriggled loose. "I'm not ready to go back!" he cried. "I just want to find out if the fish are biting. I know the lake was this way. It was always this way before."

There wasn't a lake within ten miles of this place, but in his confused state he didn't know that.

"Pop," I said uncertainly, "the lake is this way. I passed it when I was looking for you."

"It's not that way. Anybody knows the lake is downhill. I may not know much but I know water goes downhill. I just want to see the lake and talk to the fishermen. I remember so many times the people at the lake weren't catching until I told them the bait to use. I never had trouble catching fish."

I took his arm with the pretense of leading him downhill, while actually gently steering him back towards the RV.

"The lake was always so pretty this time of year," he rambled on. "I remember when we used to catch more fish than we could eat. Do you remember going out in the rowboat and catching so many fish we had to start throwing them back?"

"Yeah, Pop," I agreed, "that was a great trip."

He followed along for a little while before trying to turn in the wrong direction again. I gently steered him back but he began getting agitated.

"Aren't you hungry, Pop?" I asked. "You haven't had breakfast yet. Let's go back to the camper and I'll cook you some breakfast. We can go down to the lake later and talk to the fishermen." I didn't know what I was doing. I just knew I didn't want to frighten him. If he was wary of me he wouldn't cooperate. We had to stay on friendly terms and at the moment that meant living in his world. It saddened me to see him so physically active and yet mentally not quite there.

"It won't take long. The lake is just down this hill. I know it is. I've been there so many times." Then Albert suddenly changed the subject and asked, "How is Elizabeth doing?" I didn't know who Elizabeth was, much less how she was doing.

"Fine, Pop, Elizabeth is fine."

"That's good. I miss her so. Has it been years?"

"It's been a long time," I agreed.

He found a log and plopped himself down. "I'm so tired, so tired and lonely. Where's Elizabeth?" he asked. "Where's your mother? She loved camping. She was always the first one up in the morning. When we got up early to go fishing, she would have a pan of scrambled eggs and a pot of coffee ready for us. She was always so happy when we came back with strings of fish because she liked them wrapped in tin foil and cooked on the fire. And…and I haven't seen her in so long. I hate this getting old stuff. I know how it was, and I know how it is, and nothing matches up anymore."

I looked to Landon but there wasn't much he could do. If he interfered, Albert would probably rebel again. This was becoming a miserable situation for me and I didn't know how much more I could take. I was only twenty-six years old and this experience made old age look very frightening and discouraging. I was feeling just as lost and helpless as Albert. Would there be a day when I walked off into the woods looking for tracks, missing Rusty? I forced my thoughts away from the subject so I could deal with the problem at hand.

"Pop, please, I've got scrambled eggs back at the camper. You need to eat something. You've been out here all night. I've been looking all over the place for you. Please come back with me. The lake won't feel so far away with a good breakfast in you."

"Did you fix 'em like your mother did?" he asked, hopeful.

"She taught me how to do it, you know that."

Alfred stood and began following me, but then halfway to the camper he suddenly froze and started backing away from me shouting, "You're not Katherine! Who are you? Why are you trying to trick an old man?" He began crying, frustrated and confused in his uncertain state of mind. Alfred looked around for an escape route, but being an old man and limited in his mobility, he obviously couldn't run and didn't stand a chance.

"Pop! Stop! It's okay. I'm just here to help you. Don't be afraid. I'm just here to take you to Katherine. Please, Albert! I'm not going to hurt you. I'm not trying to trick you."

Landon moved around behind Albert to head him off just in case he tried to run. But, how do you stop an old man? A young man, hell, I'd tackle him, but I wouldn't use force with Albert. I took his arm because he seemed used to being led, and I pointed him towards the campground.

"Come on, let's go get some of those scrambled eggs."

"Scrambled eggs sounds good," he said as though he'd completely forgotten about the lake and was resigned to just accept his present circumstances. I fought tears all the way back to the campground, listening to him rattle on about Katherine's first birthday and the curtains that Elizabeth had saved up for when they had been living on twenty dollars a month.

"They were so cheerful, and to think she saved for months a penny here and a dime there, to put a little cheer in our house. It was almost a shack. We had lots of scrambled eggs because we had chickens. We could always eat because of the chickens but we had so little. Those were tough days. Our son's first bed was a dresser drawer. And he grew so fast. I had to make a crib..."

I listened to a life gone by. Now it only existed in fragments of this one old man's memory, who had inadvertently shared his thoughts with me. I was left wondering what to do with his stories because it seemed wrong to let them die, a life almost forgotten. But that's what happens, I thought, no matter what kind of a life you lead, eventually it's forgotten. It felt so empty, so sad.

When we returned to base camp, it was no longer a base camp to me. It was now Katherine's camper and it meant Albert was safe with his family again. And it probably meant a quick trip back to the nursing home. I kicked myself. No scrambled eggs, no trip to the lake. I'd lied the whole day through and it felt rotten. I went to the Jeep, laid down on the backseat and cried. When I finally sat up Landon was standing there looking at me, but I didn't care. I pulled my feet up and put my head on my knees and counted to twenty, composed myself, then opened the door and climbed out.

"I got the paperwork. You want me to drive?"

"You've got another car you need to take back."

"Rosco will do it. He wants to go home anyway."

"I'm not going home. I'm going to the station."

"You and Rusty have plans?"

"No, we never have plans on search days. I need to vent. I'm going to go cream the punching bag. Maybe I can find someone to box with."

I don't know why he came along, but I was pretty sure he wouldn't box with me. He talked on the way, mostly about Strict and what could be done to get me back on board. I was too emotional to hear most of it. I think I answered him but I'm not sure.

When we arrived at the station I looked into Rusty's office, but he wasn't there. After placing a sticky note on his door saying that I'd be in the gym, I then went and took on the punching bag. I let my thoughts flow and it didn't take long before the emotions overwhelmed me again. I slugged the bag. I punched it and kicked it and fought all the feelings built up inside of me. After Landon had made the rounds talking to the officers he knew, he came in and held the bag for me. The bag was harder to move with Landon on the other side so I put more force into my punches and by the time Rusty walked in I was pretty much worn out. There were several guys in the gym working out but I ran over anyway and grabbed him in a tense hug. He held on, looking to Landon for any clues.

"Babe, what is it? Did you find your man?"

"Sort of… I found him physically, he's safe and back with his daughter."

"There you go, that's what counts, right?"

The emotions welled up again. "I don't know. I don't know what counts anymore. Please, don't let me get that old. I don't ever want to be that old."

"Cass…"

I went back to the punching bag and attacked it again. Rusty stood on the other side, holding it steady for me.

"Babe, I do. I want you to grow old. It's not the same for everybody.

You're going to live to be a hundred and your grandkids are going to be like Patrick sitting around asking you for tall tales. If I know you, you're going to go skydiving on your seventy-fifth birthday. But no matter what happens, it's us. It'll happen to us, together. Babe, stop, please."

"I can't." *Bam, bam.* "I spent today lying through my teeth to an old man. I did it because he didn't know any better. I spent the day as his daughter fifty years ago. I promised him scrambled eggs and a fishing trip. That guy will never go fishing again. All he could look forward to was a quick trip back to the nursing home. Runny eggs and old memories. I feel like a heel."

"Old memories are priceless. Cass, Albert needs those memories, he's happy in them. You gave him more time to enjoy remembering his past. Some people you track down so they can build more memories while others you track down so they can live in them. No matter what happens, giving someone more time is a precious gift."

With tears in my eyes I looked at him and said, "That's your dad talking. You even use his inflections."

"Yeah," he admitted, "I suppose it is. I've just never had to say it before but, now that it's out, you're right. And maybe he got it from his dad. Maybe it goes on and on and on and I'm telling you, no matter where you spend it, time is precious. Babe, don't lose that thought."

I felt worn out. I always felt that way after a bout with the punching bag but it wasn't a physical tiredness, it was emotional weariness. I just felt all wrung out. I left Rusty to his work while Landon and I drove out to the compound to retrieve his car. Usually we met at the compound and took the search and rescue vehicles out to the site. This time I'd left my Jeep at base camp in order to catch up with the team.

We were driving down a street with heavy traffic. It was up against the foothills and frequented by a lot of commuters detouring around the busy downtown area. I had stopped at a red light when suddenly, three cars ahead, there was the sound of screeching brakes followed by the smack and crash of an automobile in the intersection. Since Landon was an EMT and I, theoretically, had first aid training we were obligated to stop and assist. Landon flipped open his cell phone and quickly called in the troops. I signaled and inched my way over to the shoulder. After parking the Jeep we got out to survey the sad scene before us. It didn't look good. Car parts and broken glass were everywhere. No doubt there were injuries, too. Landon ran to one car while I went to the driver's window of the other car. I noted the airbag. That was good. I opened the door to speak to the driver who was looking confused and agitated.

"It's okay," I reassured him, "help is on the way. Just stay in your car until someone can check you out." I looked into the back of the car for passengers, but there were none. The man started to release his seatbelt. "No, no," I told him, "just stay there. We've got a police car and a rescue squad on their way. You'll be okay."

At the mention of police the man started frantically searching for his seatbelt latch. He pushed the button and reached for the door but I barred his way. He had a wild look in his eyes as he frenetically searched for a way out. Although it was a good sign that he appeared strong enough to be so agitated, something didn't feel right. My training from academy clicked into place and I went into automatic gear, reciting learned instructions for him to sit down, it was for his own safety… The old police lines spilled from my mouth, but fell flat on the pavement, unheard. As the man tried pushing his way past me I steered him back to his seat. As long as there was no threat of fire, and traffic was easing around the scene it was best that he remained in his car. From the corner of my eye I saw men directing traffic while Landon was having a hard time in the other car. He was coping with a frantic, injured woman and a passenger, both requiring attention. I wondered if I should help Landon since he looked like he could use it.

"What's your name?" I asked the man

"Alfonso," he answered.

"Alfonso, you have to stay here. There are cars everywhere. It's rush hour. Just wait for the rescue squad."

Off in the distance I heard sirens. Yes!

Suddenly Alfonso rushed me and I stood my ground but he barreled into me, lifting me into the air, and tossing me out of the way. There was a screech of tires followed by a crushing blow and then nothing.

I wasn't out for long and awoke to the flashing lights of the police cars. Rescue personnel were trying to determine what had happened. They thought I had been the driver of Alfonso's car, but where was Alfonso? Shoot. This was a mess. I tried to stand but was gently held down.

"Look, I'm not part of this wreck," I insisted. "I was trying to keep the driver from leaving his car and, when he heard sirens, he freaked out and threw me into the traffic. I'm fine. Let me up." It occurred to me that I was acting very much like Alfonso had earlier, but with good reason. I needed to find my missing driver. By leaving the scene, he had immediately turned the accident into a hit and run, and that was a punishable offense. "Where's your little waiver form?" I asked. "I want to refuse treatment. I need to find the driver of this car and I'll do it if you just let me go."

"Don't give it to her," Landon said evenly.

I glared up at him, if there had ever been a call I wished I'd worn my uniform on then this was it. If they'd seen the uniform the Emergency personnel would have a totally different reaction.

"Landon, tell them I'm not the driver of this car." Then to the officers I said, "If you'll run the plates on that Jeep over there you'll know I'm the driver. I stopped to render aid and the driver of this car didn't want to receive assistance. He threw me into traffic. I'm fine. Give me the stupid form so I can get on with this."

They ran the plates on the maroon Intrepid, then on my sand colored Jeep. After attempting to persuade me to go in for an examination, they finally handed over the release form and I signed it.

"Now," I said, "I'm only an out of uniform reserve deputy, but my job so far has been tracking. You guys have a missing driver. Last I saw him he was dazed and confused, but able to lift and throw a hundred pounds. So he is somewhat able-bodied. I am going to track this guy. If you want to back me up, fine. If you don't, then just consider me a pedestrian."

I looked around for a direction to start, found the path of least resistance, and waited for traffic to stop before wading through it. On the side of the road there were tracks from a dozen gawkers. I remembered Alfonso had been dressed as a businessman. Crisp pressed shirt, tie, and slacks, and he probably wore loafers. I searched the side of the road for dress shoe prints. Landon caught up to me with another officer in tow.

"You better be right," the officer admonished Landon.

"Right about what?" I asked, still tracking.

Landon answered, "That you could find the guy, that you were crazy enough to do it, and that someone better be prepared to subdue him or you'd be back on the ground again."

"That sounds about right to me," I answered. I broadened my circle but I didn't think Alfonso had gone this way any more. I crossed the road and began walking the soft sand just beyond the shoulder. I picked up the distinctive trail of a hurried man wearing dress shoes. He followed the shoulder of the road at a brisk walk for about half a mile and had briefly tried jogging but quickly gave it up. I noted he was favoring his right foot. When an intersection appeared in the distance he began angling towards the side street, and then cut across the desert. The neon lights of a bar and grill beckoned. I followed the tracks up to the graveled parking lot and then circled the building looking for Alfonso's tracks leading away. I didn't find any. Alfonso had gotten thirsty and I hoped he hadn't gotten drunk. As I started to enter the establishment Landon stopped me.

"Cassidy, leave this to the cops."

"How are you going to recognize him?" I asked, addressing the officer. "I talked to the guy, know what he looks like and could ID him by the soles of his shoes, but could you? I'll point him out to you and then the show is yours. I'll go back to my Jeep and you can do whatever you want."

The officer held a quick radio conversation and then he followed me in. I noticed out of the corner of my eye three, sleek black and whites cruising up the street. I thought they were taking this capture very seriously, considering the man had only left the scene of an accident, but dismissed it and concentrated on the bar and grill. The place was crowded. The bar area was full and most of the tables were taken.

"Find a seat anywhere," a barmaid called out. The room fell silent as the uniformed officer entered the room. "I'm supposed to meet someone," I said, walking around the establishment as if looking for a friend. Alfonso wasn't at the bar. I walked in and out amongst the tables but didn't see him there either, so I started an outer circle of the place. There was one row of dimly lit booths against a long blank wall. I walked the circle examining the tables in the middle of the floor. Suddenly a man jumped out from one of the booths. He grabbed me from behind, wrapped his arm around my neck and held a used steak knife to my throat.

"Now, that wasn't a very smart thing to do," he said calmly.

Landon flashed me a look that was half fear and half a sarcastic, "Oh no, not again." Funny, that's exactly what had crossed my mind too.

"I suggest that anybody who doesn't want to remain a hostage pick up your drink or your dinner and quietly leave the restaurant," Alfonso said loudly.

The tables nearest us began clearing out, and as those patrons left the others began taking note of the situation. We were soon left with Alfonso, Landon, one officer, myself and a lone bartender crouching behind the bar. He might have thought he was hidden but the mirror made it obvious he was still there.

"Alfonso, what do expect to gain by this?" I asked. "All you've got is a steak knife. The police aren't going to let you go. You're racking up charges left and right."

At the mention of the name, Alfonso, the officer stiffened noticeably. Alfonso grinned, enjoying the recognition.

"Hand over your weapons or the girl gets it," he instructed.

I signaled him not to. He hesitated, then reached for his sidearm.

"No, don't," I told him. "Don't give him any more advantage than he's got. Let him get out of this on his own."

The grip tightened.

"You don't seem to notice who you're dealing with here, but *he* does," Alfonso said, indicating the officer. "He knows I'd slit your throat just to get you out of my way. Right now you're useful. I think I'll keep you around. Now give me the gun," he demanded in a calm voice.

“Do you know what the cops out there are going to unleash on this place?” the officer asked. “First they’ll try and talk you out. Then they’ll start launching things in here.”

“Yeah, ever been pepper sprayed before? I have, and it’s no fun,” I commented, getting everyone’s attention. Of everyone present, I was the least likely to have been pepper sprayed but I always had fun surprising people. “Believe me, you don’t want to be pepper sprayed. Close your eyes. Don’t breathe. It hurts like hell. You don’t want that… or to be stun grenade, or…”

“We get the picture,” Alfonso said, bending my arm behind me and tightening the grip with his knife hand. I wasn’t going to squirm. This guy wanted to see me squirm but I decided not to give him that satisfaction. Thinking the situation through, I concluded that Alfonso didn’t stand much of a chance. There was one weapon inside the bar and an army outside. The officer inside the restaurant had stayed to protect me and so I decided if he was ready to take charge, I would give him that chance. I was just about to provide a distraction when there was a mechanical noise near the door followed by the sound of some mechanical clicks.

“Oh shit,” the officer swore softly.

My cell phone rang, startling everyone in the room.

“Would you stop that infernal thing?” Alfonso snapped.

I froze, even though the ringing was irritating and distracting. Then, as the sound began to dominate the situation, I decided I better do something about it. Alfonso hadn’t said to turn it off. He said to make it stop, so I answered it.

More mechanical clicks.

“Hello?” I said.

“Babe, I’m going to be late getting home. Don’t wait up for me. It’s important we get this guy while we can. I’ve been on this case for a month and we finally got a lucky break.”

Oh man, I hoped it wasn’t *this* case! “It’s okay, Landon and I ran across an accident on our way back and we’re kind of tied up, too. We’ll catch dinner later, although there’s a bar and grill I wouldn’t recommend for dinner tonight.”

Anxious pause. “Are *you* in there?”

Alfonso released my arm and snatched the phone from my hand. I could hear Rusty saying, “Cass? Cassidy, this is no time to play games.” Alfonso grinned while the officer started looking even more concerned. He knew where those mechanical sounds were coming from. They were from the bomb squad robot and he had been nervously counting the seconds before the bar turned into a war zone. Alfonso was distracted. The officer was all eyes and ears. Now was the perfect time. I brought my heel down hard on

Alfonso's right foot, hoping he had been favoring it for a good reason. He howled with pain and I grabbed the knife as Alfonso reacted to sudden retaliation. I spun around, twisting Alfonso's knife hand and the officer stepped in, gun drawn. One, two, three and Alfonso was on the floor being cuffed. I took my phone back and listened for a few seconds.

"Yeah," I said, a bit breathless, "we're in here, but I think it's safe to come in now."

All the doors opened at the same time and the place was suddenly full of cops with no job to do. Rusty just stood there with his arms folded shaking his head.

"Hey, Michaels!" Someone teased, "How does it feel having your wife bring in your felons for you?"

Tom appeared behind Rusty and asked, "Does she do this to us on purpose?"

"I don't think so," he replied.

We spent the next few hours sitting in a booth rehashing the day's events.

"Today was not one of my better days," I said, laying my head down on my folded arms. "Landon, Strict is not to hear about this."

"How are you going to stop him with half the force whining about you spoiling their capture?"

"Oh man, I didn't think about that. I should have just let them stun grenade the place."

"You've already been knocked out once today. I don't think twice in one day is good for anyone's health. And I bet you still won't go and get checked out."

"No, I'm fine. It's just been one of those days."

"For most people one of those days means they got a speeding ticket or the dog threw up on the carpet."

"Oh God, I hope the dog didn't throw up on the carpet! That would be just the thing after a day like this."

Rusty dropped me off at my Jeep then drove Landon to the compound so he could pick up his car. I knew he'd question Landon and drag the whole story out of him and my partner would fess up because he really was worried about the tumble I'd taken into the traffic. I knew just how worried Landon must have been by the way Rusty busted in the front door when he finally got home. He found me quickly and gathered me close. These things always seemed to affect Rusty more than they affected me. I was used to trouble by now. As long as there was no ongoing danger I put it behind me and kept going. It wasn't as easy for Rusty. I could see I'd be living in a protective bubble for a few days.

That night when we went to bed Rusty didn't watch me undress for the fun of it. He was observing with a critical eye. I was bruised and sore, but I'd endured worse so I wasn't complaining. I still wasn't exactly sure what had happened and Landon probably didn't know either. I just remembered flying through the air and a hard bump. I had a tender spot on my head and it would twinge when I brushed my hair, but in general I felt pretty good.

"Cass, please don't trivialize these things that happen to you. I know you don't want me to worry, but I need to know."

"Why?" I asked.

"Well, from a detective's point of view it could mean the difference between the guy being held or released. It could be ten years difference in his jail time. If the judge thinks the suspect is safe to let loose, he'll set a bail amount. If Alfonso can come up with that amount, and believe me he can, he'd be free again. If the judge finds out he assaulted an officer, left the scene of an accident and then held someone hostage he won't let the guy loose. He'll consider him a danger to society and Alfonso was a danger. We lucked out that he got in a wreck and you just happened to be there."

I knew all that, of course, but I'd just never actually thought it out.

"But babe, from a husband's point of view I just need to know for my own peace of mind. If you play down everything that happens, you might be hiding something important. I have to trust that you'll always tell me the truth, especially with something like a head injury. You might think you're fine when you're not."

"It's hard for me to make a big deal out of it. I don't remember it happening and my head doesn't hurt. I'm more worried about Strict hearing about this. Here I am trying to get back into the team and then something like this happens... At least the search went as well as could be expected. Oh, and I'm glad I had to track Alfonso to that bar. He favored his foot when he walked so I even knew which foot to stomp. I didn't mean to get involved in the capture. I only went in there to point the guy out. Then I was supposed to leave. It just didn't work out that way."

"How do you manage to get into trouble so fast? One moment I think you're safe at home and the next I find out you're being held hostage by a violent criminal. And to think what we were planning to do." He pulled me closer. "If we'd have gone ahead with the plan I'd have felt so guilty. I'd have been a basket case."

"You can't think like that. I heard the sounds and knew what they were. In a way I didn't want you to know where I was. I wanted you to do what was necessary. Luckily you didn't have to use the robot. It would have wrecked the bar."

"You were more worried about the stemware than yourself?"

"No, I knew it would be unpleasant, but I also knew it would work."

Chapter 17

Landon stopped by the next day, presumably to make sure I survived the night. I was wearing a short sleeved t-shirt and the bruises were plainly visible. I was trying to hang the pictures Mark had given me, and Landon stood in the middle of the room advising which way to tilt the frame so they hung straight.

"Those are cool pictures. Where did you find prints like that? I didn't know Mark Mireau had a studio around here. I've never seen pictures by him that weren't of wildlife."

"He showed me the wildlife ones he took, too. He got some great shots."

"These are really appropriate for your house. They have you written all over them."

"Thanks, that's because they *are* me. Normally I wouldn't put pictures of myself on a big, plain wall in the living room, but I want Mark to know how much I appreciate them, and his mom and dad will like seeing his work when they visit."

He examined them more carefully.

"Well I'll be, they *are* pictures of you. How did you meet Mark Mireau?"

"When I went to Santa Cruz Island?"

"Yeah?"

"I was looking for Mark. He took these pictures while we were there and gave these to me as a thank you gift."

"Do you realize how much these are worth? People would pay a mint to have a one of a kind picture from his camera."

"I don't value a gift in dollars. I value the intent of the gift. There's a picture of Mark with a handwritten note on the back that makes the intent very clear. I took the picture of him when we were camped out waiting for the next boat home. It's kind of cool, it shows him just as he really was, injured, dirty and scruffy. I wish that picture didn't have to face the wall all the time."

I took the print down and showed Landon the picture and inscription.

"So, you rescued a celebrity!"

"He isn't a celebrity, he's just a friend. My neighbor's son."

"Maybe to you."

"Landon, I don't think of people that way. He's just a man who needed to be found. I would have done the same for anyone else. And I didn't ask for this gift. I was dumbfounded when he gave it to me, but I would have felt the same if a five-year-old had given me a crayon drawing for my fridge."

"I know. That's one of the things I like about you."

The next few days were calm, peaceful, and irritating. I began pacing the house, weeding the yards, planting fall flowers in the containers on the front porch, gazing out at the hills, and planning woodworking projects. I went to the home improvement store and bought more wood, screws, and nails. I measured and cut the pieces for a new agility obstacle, the dog walk. It consisted of a raised narrow walkway with ramps going up and down. We had tackled the jumps and the A-frame. I thought it was time for something new and Shadow was ready for some real instruction. The challenge would be in training him to walk the plank while he could see the ground below. So far Shadow wasn't comfortable with a drop off. The A-frame was wide and sturdy and Shadow had adapted to its height. The dog walk would be different. It was narrow and flexed a little. Agility training involved exposing the dog to new things and encouraging him to focus and think.

In order to train Shadow to think I needed to build the course first. I enjoyed working with my hands, and building stuff, but the logic behind some of the construction didn't come naturally to me. I measured twice and cut once. Well, if I measured right twice I should only have to cut once. Sometimes when starting to put things together I realized that it was necessary to cut twice, but despite any setbacks the obstacles would eventually get built.

I laid the strip of plywood on the floor of the barn and lined up the two by fours that would support it and make it sturdy. I drilled screw holes and began attaching the boards. I really need to buy an electric screwdriver one of these days, I thought. Kneeling over the boards and twisting away at the screws I noticed a movement in the yard. I froze. Movement was okay, it could be Shadow or possibly a deer. I hadn't been working with power tools or making much noise, so the movement could have been a deer. I hoped it was a deer, but it wasn't. A deer wouldn't go towards the house. I flattened myself against the dark wall of the barn and made my way out the back door and into the junipers behind the house. I moved from tree to tree until I had worked my way to the side of the house. I watched as a man walked around the house looking, for what I didn't know. He went in the barn, came out and examined the hills. He went to the back door, opened it and entered. Just thinking about him walking around inside my home was giving me the creeps. I wasn't armed and didn't have my cell phone, so it was better to remain in the trees. My anger grew. I found a vantage point from where I could see both the front and back doors, and remained hidden until the man left. After I saw him leave and drive away I went into the house. Our home had been searched, but nothing appeared to be missing. Even my gun, which had a blazing sign on it that screamed "steal me," was still there. I called Rusty.

"Hey," he said after the second ring. "What's up?"

"We had a visitor today. I was in the barn and he was looking around the outside of the house so I slipped into the trees and hid. When he thought no one was home he went in through the back door and searched the house. I can't find anything missing. I don't know what he was after or if you can pin anything on him. I just thought you should know."

There was a long pause. "Are you okay?"

"Yeah, I didn't go near the house until I saw him drive away. He didn't know I was here."

"Thank you," he said.

"For what?"

"For staying away from the house. I know you were tempted to confront him but I'm glad you didn't. Was it the same guy?"

"Yeah, what's his name? I'm sure they got his name when they took him in for questioning. Despite insisting he is so friendly, he still hasn't told me his name."

"Teague Stern"

"Does he have a record?"

"He's a troublemaker but so far he's only been charged with misdemeanors. That doesn't mean he hasn't done this before. It just means he has never been caught."

"I think I'll pay Hazel a visit. If anybody would know the comings and goings in this neighborhood it would be her. I need to ask her if there's any point in hanging around for Halloween, too. With a quarter mile walk from house to house I doubt there are many trick or treaters on our street."

"Oh! If it isn't my most favorite neighbor in the whole world!" Hazel squealed as she dragged me into her house. Guess my status rose a notch with Mark's safe return.

We visited, catching up on the news. Mark was at home recuperating and putting together an article about the Island Fox. He'd already received an offer from a travel magazine for an article about the Channel Islands, but had turned it down until he could visit the other islands. He was aiming for an article in a wildlife publication, preferring to protect the wildlife rather than send scores of tourists there to encroach on it.

After the conversation with Hazel had died down a little, which took some time, I approached the topic I'd actually come over to discuss.

"Have you had any trouble with prowlers in this neighborhood?" I asked.

"Oh… no! Have you?" she asked, clearly distressed with the idea.

"A little," I confessed. "You haven't seen anybody driving up and down the street keeping an eye on the houses, watching to see if someone is home?"

"I barely see the road from my front window," she pointed out. "I wouldn't notice something like that."

An idea came to me. "Do you mind if I walk around your house? If he came to your house too, then there would be footprints all over the place. I'd be able to tell if someone was prowling around out there recently."

"Oh dear, please do! If someone has been here I certainly want to know about it!"

We went outside and I looked at the ground around the house. Hazel followed, watching me with interest.

"What can you possibly see down there? It's just dirt."

"It's not just dirt to me. It's information. I don't see anything that looks suspicious. Wally was walking around in the backyard this morning. He stubbed his toe on the barbecue grill, then got mad and kicked it. I hope his foot feels better now."

"How did you know that?" she asked, incredulous.

"I can see what happened in the dirt. See his footprints leading up to the barbecue? This scrape mark here shows how the wheel slid on impact and then the footprints get all screwy because he was walking off the pain and then there's another scrape mark where the barbecue grill scoots in the other direction. He shouldn't have kicked it. Now I bet he has more than one sore toe."

"That's amazing. How do you do that? That's precisely what happened."

"I've been studying tracks since I was a little kid, it's just what I do. I don't see any footprints of prowlers though. That's good. You don't know of any troublemakers in the area?"

"Oh, these neighborhoods off from town always get their share of wild teenagers. They get bored out here with no access to friends, and a long drive to town. Then boredom turns to mischief."

"What kind of mischief?"

"Have you noticed the street signs out here all have bullet holes? Kids run around with guns and shoot things, usually harmless things. If you value your house you will post *no hunting* signs around your property."

"Do you know of any specific kids that were particularly violent or acted odder than the rest?"

"Yes there was one, but I don't know who he was. He was mean to animals. He wouldn't just hunt them, he hurt them. He had a cruel streak.

When he was a teenager he got kicked out of his house and I don't know whatever happened to him. He had a weird name, not John or Tom or Greg. It wasn't a name I'd heard before. Now that's going to drive me nuts until I think of what it was! I hate when that happens. Wally!" she called across the house. "What was that mean kid's name, the one who pulled wings off flies and tried to shave the Axtell's cat?"

"How should I know? I'm not the nosey neighbor! You're nosey enough for both of us!" Wally yelled back.

"Was it Teague?" I asked.

"That's it!" she beamed. "I sure am glad you thought of it so I wouldn't have to wrack my brain for the next week! But how would you know?"

"We've met. He tried to force his way into my house and I called the police on him."

"Oh dear, he wouldn't like that, and you don't want to make him mad. He's got an awful temper. He could be as sweet as could be and would volunteer for odd jobs around the neighborhood, but while he was doing them things would disappear. If he was pet sitting, the animal would die of some mysterious cause. It happened so seldom, and to different people, so nobody really connected it to him. But I tell you we wouldn't let him take care of our pets. No siree!"

This did not bode well for me, I thought. We visited a little longer and Hazel confirmed there wouldn't be any trick or treaters at our door this year.

"The few families with kids take them into town to a church carnival or they go trick or treating in neighborhoods where the houses are easier to get to. You won't get anyone at your door unless you personally know a family with kids. Then they might stop by on their way into town."

It took me over an hour to make my way out of Hazel and Wally's house. I almost felt trapped by hospitality but eventually I broke free and walked home.

It was a quiet evening and I was deep in thought. Rusty watched me, aware that it might not be wise to let me think for too long. Put too many puzzle pieces together and I was likely to do something rash. I made dinner in a distracted manner then picked at the food on my plate. Eating was usually not very high on my list of priorities and it didn't take much to bump food off the list completely.

After dinner I puttered around the house then went outside to look at the tracks Stern had left behind. I studied them, wanting to be able to recognize his tracks if I ever saw them again. They were boots of some kind but not cowboy boots. They had a more rounded toe and a wider rounded heel. Not work boots, the tread was too smooth. Not a hiking boot. I followed the footprints letting Stern's little quirks and mannerisms sink into my memory. I found quirks and mannerisms were more of a subconscious thing. They would surface when something matched up but I didn't really think about them as I tracked. When Rusty asked me to profile while tracking I always had a steady stream of ideas about the person, never really knowing where those ideas came from, and they usually turned out to be true. I had circled the house, noting that Stern had been here more than once, had looked in all the windows more than once, had spent an unusual amount of time outside the bay window in the bedroom. Rusty stood on the back patio watching me.

"Learn anything?" he asked.

"Yeah, I learned that I don't want to have anything to do with this guy."

"Tell me about it."

So I told him about the tracks and I told him about what I'd learned at Hazel and Wally's. He stood there, hands in pockets, grimfaced.

"And Hazel recognized the name, Teague Stern?"

"Right, the neighborhood troublemaker kid who steals stuff and makes pets mysteriously disappear."

"Only now he's turned into a dangerous troublemaker grownup."

Chapter 18

Halloween arrived and, no longer feeling obligated to stick around for the trick or treaters, we followed Rusty's Halloween tradition of meeting with a group of officers and SAR volunteers at Trujillo's. Although we dined in this restaurant frequently, it had taken me a while to realize it was also the local cop hangout. Benny greeted each officer by name and even knew most of their orders ahead of time. Occasionally an officer would stop him to change their order from their "usual" to a different choice, which always sent Benny jogging back to the bar to get an order book so he could write it down.

When we arrived I noticed a lot of familiar faces, but I also saw a few people I needed to meet. Thez, Landon, Tom, Kelly and Rhonda were there. Schroeder had brought his wife to the party. I had never met her but I had heard good things about her from Rusty. Schroeder was actually smiling and I found out that Mrs. Schroeder had a first name. He introduced me to her without telling her that I was the station's official trouble maker. Her name was Nancy and she seemed very nice. There were several others who spoke as if they were also on the force and a few EMTs who I didn't know. Landon seemed to know everyone. After the normal trick or treat hours passed the place swelled with even more people. Strict and his wife Dee stopped in for a drink, along with Victor and his wife, Natalia. Big John almost filled the place with his booming, contagious laughter. The music was loud, the food was good, the mood was festive and we stayed half the night.

"What's going on with you these days?" Strict asked me.

"I need work," I replied. "I have to get out of the house."

"What does Rusty think about that?"

"Right now, he'd probably agree with me. He doesn't like me to be gone for days at a time, but these days the woods are feeling safer than our house."

He looked to Rusty.

I went on, "It hasn't gotten dangerous yet, but there was the potential for it to turn that way. We've had a prowler at our house. The first time I met up with this guy, I strapped on my gun and warned him that I was prepared to use it. So basically I got off with just a threat. The second time I ended up slugging him."

"She's got a mean right hook, too!" added Landon from a few tables away.

"Ha, ha, I heard about that!" called an officer from another table. "She didn't just slug him, she kicked him in the balls!"

"Ouch," Landon added.

"He's entered our house when he thought no one was home. He prowls around peeking in windows. He just generally makes things feel unsettled. I have to keep the doors locked and I'm armed when I work in the yard. If you're not calling me out on searches to keep me out of trouble, it's not working. Trouble finds me no matter where I am."

I suddenly regretted saying anything. My festive mood vanished and I found a quiet corner to sit and watch the others. The women wandered by to exchange pleasantries and Rhonda stopped to thank me for the wedding pictures.

It was nearly one a.m. when we arrived back home. Rusty parked the Explorer in the driveway and we casually walked up to the front door. Rusty reached to put the key in the lock and I froze, then swiftly moved to stop his hand. Anger flared and I turned away. Then Rusty saw it too. We immediately backed away from the front door.

"Stay with me," he said.

Together we inspected the outside of our house and then looked in the windows, just like Teague Stern probably had earlier. When we got back to the front door I was repulsed by the sight of it. Although I'd seen plenty of dead birds before, it was the malicious intent of the act that infuriated me. It violated my beliefs to ever harm an animal unless I needed to. I'd killed animals for food or in self-defense, but I couldn't ever imagine killing a living thing just to scare somebody. He had shot it and then nailed the poor bird to the front door. It was a raven. A pesky bird to say the least and an appropriate choice for Halloween, with its jet black feathers and sharp, open black beak, but still the act infuriated me. A handwritten sign in black magic marker said "Trick or Treat".

"Stay here," Rusty ordered. He unlocked the front door and went from room to room, checking for intruders, gun ready. He turned on lights as he went and once the whole house was beaming with cheerful light he returned to the front door to let me in. Shadow gave me his usual greeting, dashing in and out trying to tempt me into playing. It wasn't working this time. We sat together in the living room in tense silence.

"I'll take care of the bird," Rusty said. "Where do we keep the hammer now?"

"It's in the barn with the woodworking tools."

He found a flashlight and went out back to get the hammer then returned a short while later and began searching the house for something else.

"What are you looking for?" I asked.

"The camera. I think we need to start documenting this stuff."

I found the camera in the drawer where I always kept it and handed it to him.

"Cass, please be careful. This guy is sick. There's a noose hanging in the barn."

I wore my gun outside the house now but wasn't sure if I'd use it. Should push come to shove, though, it was there if I needed it. I entered and exited the house through the front door so it could be locked behind me and kept the back door locked at all times. I wondered about the wisdom of locking myself out of the house, but if I had to hide from Teague I'd prefer to do it in the trees where there was room to maneuver. I wore moccasins so I could move with stealth.

I finished constructing the dog walk, then sanded and painted it. As I worked with Shadow, teaching him what he needed to do to complete the obstacle, he balked at the height so I ended up starting him out closer to the ground. He knew the "go up" command and the "go down" command, it was the part in the middle that he had trouble completing. When the dog walk was high he didn't like being up off the ground. When it was down low it was too easy for him to jump off. We worked and worked. "Go up, Shadow, go up, good boy! Now walk, come on walk, good walk!" When he felt the board bend and looked down, he'd stop. I was working with him one afternoon when he paused in the middle of the dog walk and I noticed he had stopped because of a distraction near the house. An uneasy feeling crept over me. Shadow leapt off the dog walk and ran around the side of the house. No!

I started to go after him but stopped, slinking into the trees instead. I needed time to think and to be out of sight. I snuck around the house again to confirm it was Stern, and watched as he knocked on the front door and then quietly moved around the house. If I went down there it would mean a confrontation. Getting anywhere near Teague Stern was bad news for me. Rusty would kill me if I went down there.

"Cassidy!" he called out. "I know you're here somewhere. You wouldn't leave your dog loose outside unless you were home."

Stern walked the property looking for me. Shadow, not knowing any better, followed him, prancing around excitedly, welcoming him to our home. Everybody was a friend to Shadow. Every once in a while Shadow would glance around for me. "Come on Mom!" he seemed to be saying. "We've got company!"

I kept to the trees.

"Damn it Cassidy, you're pushing me! I'm losing patience with you. I like your dog. He'll make a nice snack for *my* dogs." He waited to see if that would get a reaction. When it didn't, he walked back to his car. "Come on boy," he ordered in a gruff tone of voice.

Don't do it! I thought.

Shadow backed away from the low, angry tone. He was hearing a reprimand, not a command. A command came in an encouraging voice. It might be firm, but it was still friendly. Stern pulled a thick, heavy leash from his car. When Shadow was close enough Teague grabbed him by the ruff and clipped the leash onto his collar. Shadow set his feet, bracing against the tug as Stern dragged him to his car. Stern lifted him by the scruff of the neck and stuffed him in the car. Shoving him onto the passenger's seat, he drove away. I watched as he drove down the street, pulled a U-turn and then abruptly stopped. Stern turned off the engine and waited, watching the house.

I didn't know what to do. I couldn't go into the house but needed to do something. I was scared for Shadow. How would I get him back? Nailed to the front door? Hung in the barn? Would I ever see him again? Sitting there, hidden, I was tempted to shoot out Stern's tires but that would only make him more unstable and I didn't need any additional trouble. I worried what Stern would do in the event of a real threat. Unable to return home, unable to help Shadow, I retreated to the woods feeling sick inside. I walked to the deer clearing but the deer were still gone. I'd had more luck finding them at my home than at theirs. Huh, I thought, same way with Stern. Seemed like he was always turning up at our house. I wondered what his place was like, so I followed the road, staying in the junipers, and made my way to his house. When I found it, I hid at a distance and watched. Pale yellow, stucco, dirt yard. There was no movement. I circled the place taking mental notes. I didn't see any dogs but they could be in the house. Taking a chance, I walked up the gravel walkway and rang the bell then ducked back into the trees. Nobody answered, no barking dogs. I wasn't learning much and didn't feel safe so I headed back to the woods again. I snuck up on our house from the trees then looked down the road. Stern was still there. I went up into the hills and tried calling Rusty. He answered on the fourth ring with a very distracted, "Hello?".

"Rusty…"

He tensed immediately, knowing I wouldn't call him at work without a good reason.

"Stern took Shadow. I can't go home. He's watching the house."

"Where are you?"

"I'm just in the trees near the house. I'm okay. I'm armed. He doesn't know where I am. Stern's tires are just *begging* me to shoot them."

"Just stay put."

"I guess I was hoping something could be done, but I just don't know what. He's probably hoping I'll go after my dog."

"Don't! It's not worth the risk."

"This is ridiculous, he's been here for a couple of hours. Doesn't he have anything better to do than watch our house?"

"You've been out there for two hours?"

"Yeah, I walked down to Stern's house. He threatened to feed Shadow to his dogs, and I couldn't do anything here, so I walked down to his place. I didn't see any sign of dogs and I didn't hear barking when I rang the doorbell so maybe he was just trying to goad me into coming out."

"Cassidy… you're taking big risks. What if he had gone home?"

"I was watching the road and knew he hadn't. I just wish there was something I could do. He won't be nice to Shadow. He doesn't know how to treat anything with kindness. I could see that just from the way he grabbed him. Shadow is too friendly. Anybody could take him any time because he trusts people."

"Babe… I can't leave now. I wish I could but I can't set this aside for a dog. Will you stay safe? I need to count on you to stay safe."

A long pause. "I'll stay away from Stern. I won't let him see me."

"That's not what I asked. Will you stay safe? Can you go to Hazel and Wally's?"

"No, I need to keep an eye on Stern. Once I know he's gone then I'll be able to go home, but I can't even trust him to leave. When he left the last time he only drove down the street and watched the house from a distance. I need to keep him in my sights to know when I'm safe."

Rusty wasn't satisfied with my answer, but it was a truthful one.

"I'll be there as soon as possible but I don't know how long it will be."

Bummer, I thought as I hung up, so I settled in for a long wait. I watched Stern's car and knew Shadow was getting bored. He had tried climbing onto Stern's lap to watch for me more easily but Stern had batted him away. Shadow jumped back with a startled look. My anger flared. I'd never hit my dog. He played rough and enjoyed a good wrestling match but I'd never struck him.

As the sun set it started getting cold and still I sat, pulling my legs up close, hunkering down to conserve heat. This guy was stubborn. Finally when the sun was down and the hills were pitch black and he couldn't see our house anymore he started the car and drove away. I followed as best I could but couldn't see a thing in the blackness. I watched the tail lights fade and disappear at the end of our street. He was gone but I was still afraid to go home, and I'm sure it would be just what he was hoping I'd do. If he were smart he would come back in half an hour or so. I thought about walking down to his house, but it was too dark and difficult to tell one car from another by their headlights. I could get caught on the road and it was too dark to walk off the road. I was stuck. I found a place in the darkness where I wouldn't be seen and watched the front of the house. After Stern was gone I was alone with my thoughts so the worry grew until I couldn't sit still anymore. I got up and walked, feeling the ground with my feet while keeping the house in view. I'd left the house in the daytime so very few lights had been left on, just enough for me to know where it was in the darkness. By the time Rusty got home I'd been bored, worried, cold, hungry and uncomfortable for hours. I saw the headlights down the street and shrunk back. Was it Stern? Was it Rusty? Was it some neighbor further up the street? The headlights pulled into our driveway and came to a sharp halt. Rusty bounded out of the Explorer and eyed the dark house.

"Cassidyyy," he called nervously into the darkness.

"I'm here," I told him. "It's just too dark."

He went to the Explorer, brought out a large maglight, and cast the light around until he found me. I picked my way out of the trees and across the side yard, cold, shivering and miserable. He met me halfway.

"Have you been out here all this time?" he asked, wrapping his coat around me.

"Yeah, Stern only left about an hour ago and I couldn't count on him staying away."

When we were finally in the house and had turned on the lights I noticed he wasn't in his usual work clothes. He was dressed for action. I wondered what I had interrupted earlier in the day. I knew he would turn his cell phone off when necessary but I still regretted worrying him on an already stressful day.

"The house feels too empty. Rusty, I can't just leave him there. Stern's mean. He hit Shadow. Sitting there all day watching that car just made me more and more angry. A hundred plans went through my head but I didn't come up with anything I could act on."

"So you kept your promise?"

I nodded sadly.

"That's my girl. I keep telling you if you don't go looking for trouble you'll get into less of it."

"Then why is Stern here? He's been nothing but trouble from the very beginning. What about you? Did you get your man?"

"I had about the same luck you did today. Made some good contacts. Maybe it'll lead to something."

That was about all the information I ever got from Rusty. He didn't want me to worry so he never elaborated.

He wrapped me in a comforting hug and I felt his chin move against my head as he spoke. "I'm sorry I couldn't help you today. I know Shadow means a lot to you. Stern won't hurt him while he's using him for bait. We'll figure out something. How much is he worth?"

"Rusty, you can't measure his worth like that. He's an animal. I already decided I wouldn't endanger a person to save him. But I'd also do just about anything to get him out of there. He's worth anything I've got."

"Babe, I know. I know what he's worth to you. What's he worth to a judge?"

"Well, he's not show quality. He's too big. But he has potential in obedience and agility. I paid four hundred dollars for him."

"To a judge Shadow is property, stolen property. If you have anything that documents his worth then we can add that to Stern's rap sheet."

"I think I do. I keep all that stuff in a folder because I have to be able to find rabies certificates and things like that if animal control stops by. I kept the receipt because it had the breeder's address on it and I might need a new dog someday. He's a great dog and good breeders are hard to find, so I wanted a dog from the same place. I sure hope I don't need a new dog soon. If something happens to Shadow, I don't think I could get a new dog. It would feel wrong to replace him. Now look at me, I'm getting all worked up again."

I felt lousy from worry and grungy from being out in the hills all afternoon, and Rusty was still in work clothes, so we both changed into casual clothes then headed for town. As we drove by Stern's house I stared at it, watching for any sign of man or dog, but the house was dark and I saw no signs of life. Where were they?

Zeke's was busy even late in the evening. It seemed ironic that Zeke's had been where I went the day I met Teague Stern. By now all the waitresses knew us, and tonight Becky was our waitress.

"You going to have the usual?" she asked.

"We'll share a large of Rusty's usual," I replied. I wasn't in the mood to enjoy my food anyway so it didn't really matter what was on the pizza for me. I sat back, took advantage of the distraction, and let the busyness of the place flow around me. Zeke's was the first restaurant Rusty and I had visited after we met, and I still remembered that day. I had been bruised and beaten, but what I remember most about it was trying not to stare at Rusty. After losing my husband six months before I felt guilty looking at another man, but I didn't feel guilty now. It hadn't taken long for Rusty to work his way into my heart, but it took him a while to see the walls come down and for an easy relationship to start building. If there was one thing Rusty had it was patience. He had never forced anything on me but eagerly accepted my growing loyalty to him. He'd probably had me from day one, but it took me a long time to come to terms with that fact and to accept it.

"Quit thinking," Rusty admonished. "If you don't stop worrying you're going to jump out of the truck as we pass Stern's house and then I'll have to drag you home."

"I wasn't thinking about that. I was remembering all the times we've been here before. Seems like it always marks some kind of trouble. First time was…"

"After Silva," he interrupted.

"Yeah. And the last time was when I met Stern."

"I don't understand what set him off. Refusing his help hardly seems reason to stalk you like he has."

"He doesn't think like most people. Maybe he has done this before and just needed a new victim."

"I sure hope not. If he has, and there's no pattern pointing us to him, it means he's awfully good at what he does. Most people are either careless or too consistent and then they get caught. If he's done this before, and there's nothing to incriminate him then he's been watching his tracks and planning ahead. But so far, judging from what he's done to us, it doesn't feel that way to me. It seems more like he gets bored so he wanders our way to goad you some more."

"Then what does he want with Shadow? The only reason I can think of for him to take Shadow is to lure me. And as much as I hate to admit it that's not going to work."

When we drove home again Stern's house was still dark.

"It doesn't make sense," I said. "If he's trying to lure me to go after Shadow, why isn't he home? How can I be lured if I don't know where to go?"

"So far a lot of this guy's actions haven't made sense. They just show how warped he is."

Chapter 19

The next day, to prevent myself from personally breaking down Stern's door and storming his house, I wrote on the white board: "Gone tracking in the hills, ETA 5 PM". I hopped into the Jeep and headed out feeling angry and very lonely to be tracking without my four-footed friend.

My poor Jeep was being neglected. I used to take off into the hills regularly but ever since the wedding I had been feeling more settled, less apt to roam, more likely to listen to Rusty's voice inside my head and be more careful. That day, though, it seemed far safer to be away from the house and away from Stern. My immediate goal was two-fold: I needed to track and I wanted to know the roads near our house better. I wanted to search out a way into town that didn't involve going by Stern's house. Even if that meant driving miles out of my way I'd like to be able to come and go without him recognizing my Jeep or the Explorer. When I left the house I turned right and headed deeper into the hills. I passed Hazel and Wally's place and everything looked peaceful. I was pleased to discover that the road eventually led up into the pines and then circled back down. There were more homes nestled back in the hills and the further I drove the more rustic the homes became. I discovered elaborate log cabins and quaint bungalows hidden in the pine trees. There were porches lined with birdfeeders and firewood stacked in neat rows, covered with tarps to keep off the rain. I followed the road until it hit another and was dismayed to realize the road it intersected was Stern's street. I turned the Jeep around before reaching Stern's house and headed back up into the hills. There was a dirt road I'd passed a couple of miles back that might lead to good tracking ground. Once there, I studied it cautiously. The road almost looked like someone's driveway but I couldn't see the end of it so I turned and followed it deeper into the hills.

The road narrowed to one lane and then to two wheel ruts. This was interesting to me. It was precisely the kind of road that led to barely known places in the mountains. Places without people were areas where animals felt free to roam without fear.

The passenger's seat felt empty because I usually brought Shadow along on these trips. He loved going up into the hills and would tag along while I tracked. He followed smells and stayed within sight of me at all times. It was a lonely tracking day and my thoughts kept returning to the problem of how to get him back. I found a place to pull off the road and got out hoping for a distraction. I cast around for tracks but didn't see any close to the Jeep so I continued wandering through the woods with my eyes on the ground.

Tracks were not easy to spot. Small, common animals were light and barely left a trail while larger, heavier animals were rarer. I settled for a game trail and judging by the size of it there might be rabbits or foxes on it. Frequently game trails were not judged by width but by height. A deer and a rabbit were capable of leaving the same width of a trail but a deer cuts a taller path through the brush. A person frequently had to stoop to follow a deer trail through thick woods. The game trail of rabbits and foxes, a person couldn't crawl through. And most people didn't even see the game trails of mice and voles. I was stalking silently along the game trail when a movement caught my eye. Movement out here was good, it was something to focus on and stalk.

Crouching low I headed towards the area where I'd seen the movement. I wasn't sure what animal I was sneaking up on yet so I had to use every trick in the book. Different animals required different stalking methods. Stalking a coyote was much different from stalking a deer or a rabbit.

As I grew closer to the movement I became more cautious. This was a large animal and they usually possessed power. I knew it wasn't a bear, because the color of the movement had been tawnier, like a deer. I hoped it wasn't a deer because if it was I'd immediately back off. This was hunting season and stalking deer in the woods during hunting season was generally a bad idea.

I was puzzled. The movements continued but stayed in one place. Usually a movement meant animals traveling. The movement rose and fell, then paused, then rose again and paused again. Then I discovered the animal and was simultaneously elated and terrified. It was a mountain lion. I'd never seen a mountain lion in the wild before. It was distracted because it was feeding on a partially buried carcass. This was one animal I didn't want to get too close to because it was dangerous, but I couldn't take my eyes off it. It was thrilling to observe one so closely, and I wished I could have taken a picture of it for Mark. I hid, not moving a muscle as the huge cat gorged itself. The breeze must have shifted because the cat caught an odd scent in the air and shifted its position. Oh great, now I really couldn't move. I was surprised how little blood was on the mountain lion's face. Then I thought that this must be its second feeding on this carcass and the blood had all drained away. When the cougar had finished eating, it scratched dirt over the carcass and lay down beside it. Now I was really trapped although not dangerously so. I couldn't move without being spotted but so far the mountain lion had not been aggressive in any way. I didn't feel very safe testing that point, though, so I stood statue still waiting for my break. I finally got it when the huge cat, lazy from its big meal, dozed off. Although I was tempted to try and touch it, I knew one touch could cause more trouble than I could handle, and I just might end up shooting the cat. I didn't want to do that, so I refrained and quietly made my escape while it was sleeping. I was thrilled, though. I had seen a mountain lion fairly close up and had been able to observe it for a longer period of time than I'd ever thought possible. I went back to the Jeep and quickly drove home, pleased with my day. I still missed Shadow, but there was something else niggling in the back of my mind.

A part of me was glad that Shadow had not been with me that day. He could have easily ended up as the mountain lion's next meal. But that wasn't what was bothering me. Something didn't match up and I couldn't figure out what it was. What was there to not match up about a mountain lion sighting? But still…

While driving home I kept a careful eye out for Stern's car. I approached our house with caution and was happy to see Rusty's Explorer already in the driveway. I parked, jogged up to the front door, flung it open and went inside. Rusty was at the front door in an instant, relief clearly written across his face.

"Cass, we need to rethink this white board idea. I've been worried sick."

"Why? I wrote down what I was doing. I didn't know exactly where I was going but I thought I told you enough so you wouldn't worry."

"I was wondering if you were too specific. Look at it."

Under my message to Rusty a second note had been added: "Thanks for the tip." Then there was a bullet hole through the whiteboard that had passed into the refrigerator and another note below the bullet hole: "Thought I'd even the game a little."

"How did he get in the house?" I asked. "I made sure it was locked up!"

"I haven't figured that out yet. We went to Stern's house this morning. We found nothing to incriminate him. He denied being at our house and there was no evidence he had Shadow or any other dog. I think this," he said, indicating the bullet hole through the refrigerator door, "might be in retaliation. He's mad that the police are involved so he feels he has to do something to put more pressure on you."

"Great, just what I need, a Teague Stern who is armed."

"Where did you go today?"

"I followed our street into the hills to see where it went. Unfortunately it hits Stern's street on the other end too. Then I followed a little dirt road up into the mountains and did some tracking. I didn't have much luck on the tracking but I want to go back tomorrow. I saw a mountain lion and I want to follow its tracks and get an idea how they move through the forest. It was so cool. It was eating so it was distracted and I got to watch it for a little while. I couldn't track it today because it was too close. I wish you could go with me tomorrow."

"Why?"

"Something isn't adding up for me in this mountain lion sighting."

"Why? You knew there were a few mountain lions up there."

"I don't know. I was surprised to see one just because they are so rare but that's not what's bugging me. I don't know what it is, but it doesn't feel right. Something is just off about it."

"How long will it take to go out there in the morning?"

"Maybe an hour. It's only ten minutes away. I can't track the mountain lion straight to the animal. They are just too dangerous, but I want to get a feel for the tracking. It's something else that is bugging me. Maybe if I go up there I'll figure out what it is."

We got up early and Rusty dressed for work so he could drop me by the house afterwards, then continue on to the station. It was chilly out. I layered my clothes because I didn't know how long I'd be out. I gave him the simple directions and we drove up into the mountains. When the dirt road turned to one lane and then into a rough track he began to wonder.

"What would you have done if Stern had followed you in here? You'd have been trapped."

"No one was following me."

We arrived at the place where I had stopped before and I asked Rusty to pull over. We left the Explorer and I led him to the place where I had seen the mountain lion.

"I was hiding behind this thicket and I saw it right over there. It was distracted so I was able to sneak around this way." Rusty followed me around the thicket to the same tree I had hidden behind. "I watched it for a long time while it was busy eating. Now that it's gone, let's go over to where it was sitting. I'm interested in seeing the size of its paw prints in relation to the size of the cat I saw yesterday. I've never had a chance to match them up before." I led the way over to where the mountain lion had lain. I was pleased to note the texture of the soil changed as we neared the spot. Paw prints would show up easily in soil this soft and I began casting around looking for tracks. I walked up to the partially buried carcass and the sight of it made my blood run cold. My heart rate doubled and I felt the color drain from my face. I couldn't move but I had to get out of there right away. I turned, bumping into Rusty.

"Get me out of here," I gasped. "Rusty, please, I can't stay here!" I stumbled around him and jogged back to the truck but I couldn't sit. I paced quickly back and forth. It gave me the feeling of escaping even if it didn't accomplish the goal. Rusty stopped me and I buried my eyes against his shoulder. "Take me home, please take me home. Now I know what didn't match up. I can't track this place. Just take me home and come back with your team. I can't stay here."

"Cass, what is it? What could possibly have you this shook up? You've seen animal carcasses before."

I just shook my head unable to form the words. It felt so wrong. And I knew that the mountain lion had not killed his meal. He had found it. A mountain lion wouldn't bury his prey this close to a road. Only a person would bury something near a remote road. The mountain lion had found it. The thought of it turned my stomach.

"Rusty, the carcass the mountain lion was eating… it's human. And the soil is soft, unnaturally soft, because there's more than one grave… I can't stay here. If you don't take me home I'm going to start walking. I have to do something."

I didn't know what was wrong with me. I was shocked to my roots and I shouldn't have been. I'd been in a war zone. I'd seen dead people before. It always saddened me, but not like this. This place just felt wrong. I had to get away from it, the sooner the better.

"Okay, babe, one minute and I'll take you home." He kissed me on the forehead and gave me a comforting squeeze, then quickly walked around the area, trying to get a feel for what he'd be dealing with. Then he took me home.

The scene we left behind was sickening and I felt unable to process it. How had it come to be? Of course, if I allowed my mind to process everything I'd know the people had been murdered and disposed of, but my emotions were getting in the way of reason and I just wanted to hide. I needed to believe the world didn't really have people in it that would kill a person and then just bury them on a lonely mountain road to be found and devoured by passing animals. It was too overwhelming for me so I just crawled into bed, pulled the covers up to my chin and hid in my sadness. Rusty was worried. He'd seen me freaked out before but had been able to stay with me. This time he was obligated to call the station and get a crew out to investigate the site right away. He wanted to stay, but we both knew he had a job to do.

"Are you going to be okay?" he asked, concerned.

"Just lock me in and come by on your way back to work."

"Okay. I'll be here for a little while. It's going to take some time to contact all the right people."

He went to the kitchen and called the station. I heard the pacing, the quiet explanation, more phone calls. Then he sat with me, gently rubbing the covers so I could feel him close by. It was unbearably hot under all those covers but I wasn't coming out. After a while the doorbell rang and Rusty went to answer it. Gradually officers and investigators began gathering in our living room. I heard footsteps coming down the hall, then Rusty's stern voice, "Schroeder, leave her alone. She'll come around."

Yeah, I'd come around as soon as the sadness and the shock battled themselves out, as soon as my icy heart thawed. I burrowed deeper. I was getting soft, I told myself. In the Marines we'd been trained how to kill. People. Women weren't sent into combat but we were trained what to do if combat came to us instead. I'd gone through the drills. I'd toughened up inside and had just done it. Then I'd been taught again in police academy. I knew how to take a man down. Hell, I'd done it, but emotionally it had hurt me badly and I was still mourning. Mourning the man I had to shoot, and now I was mourning these unknown people. I was getting soft, but I didn't think that it was a bad thing. I thought maybe I'd gotten too hard for my own good and now I was just finding my own heart again. Rusty came in to tell me they were leaving. He knelt down to eye level and pulled the covers back gently so he could see my face and then brushed the hair from my eyes.

"Try not to think about it. I'll be back as soon as I can." Those eyes, those caring eyes. I wanted to grab him, pull him in, and make him stay but I knew it wasn't possible, so I just accepted what he said with a sad nod. "I'll lock up. Don't answer the door. If someone wants to find me they'll call my cell phone."

When I heard everybody file out and I heard the last click of the front door deadbolt falling into place, I let my feelings go and I cried until I was empty and couldn't cry anymore. Still too hot, and buried under the covers, I hid from a world where people killed people. The doorbell rang and I ignored it. A long pause and it rang again. Go away, I thought, call the cell; they're up in the hills. It was quiet for a long time and then I realized I heard sounds coming from within the house. Quiet stealthy sounds, like Rusty made when he was trying to sneak up on me. I thought he'd given that up. But it wasn't my husband. Rusty was up in the hills and he'd be gone for hours, probably most of the day depending on what they uncovered. The sounds continued. I lifted the covers just high enough to see the room. Teague Stern was leaning against the doorjamb.

Chapter 20

"Well, well, well, I knew you were hard to catch so I never expected to find you like *this*! Today must be my lucky day."

I counted the steps to my closet where my 9mm hung waiting for a call. It was too far. If I ran for it I wouldn't have time to get there, draw it and fire before he caught me. He swaggered over to the bed. He reached down and I batted his hand away. He smiled.

"Oh, come now, you're not shy are you? A girl like you should have plenty to show a guy like me."

"Afraid not," I said.

He grabbed the sheet and threw back the covers and there I lay in all my fully clothed glory. Jeans, t-shirt, sweatshirt, even shoes, hair tousled, red eyes.

"Your poor husband. What does he have to do to get any?"

Well, I thought, there's this certain look… but I wasn't going to give him the satisfaction of a response. I just glared at him.

"Does he have to put you at gun point and ask you to strip… like this?" he said evenly pointing his pistol at me. Forty-five. It would put a good sized hole in me.

"No. I'm not taking anything off for you. You've got a fight on your hands if you think I'm going to cooperate with you in any way. You won't shoot me. If I know your type, and believe me, I've come against your type before, you won't shoot me. Using the gun is no fun. You want to toy with me and shooting spoils that. Plus you don't want to make a racket. Shooting draws attention and you don't want anybody calling the cops again."

He cocked the gun.

"A bullet hole through the wall only leaves evidence," I warned him. "You don't want to leave behind any evidence. No blood on the floor. Nothing. So holster your gun."

"There are worse things than getting shot," he replied. "You need a lesson. Ever been beaten?"

"Yeah," I said ready for a fight, "it's no fun."

"I like a good fight. By the way, your dog, he's not much of a fighter. He's holding his own but he's a wimp. He's lucky he has all that fur and a good sense of hierarchy. Both have come in handy where he is. But he isn't a fighter. He'll never make it to the pit. But maybe *you* can. Get up."

Getting up sounded like a good move defensively so I rolled out of bed and stood there defiantly, all five foot four of me.

"Now, show me what you've got," he demanded smoothly.

"Again? You didn't like it last time I did that. Seems like you ended up in a bit of pain."

"That's not what I meant," he replied. "Now, show me what you've got."

So I launched myself at him, since I wasn't going to strip for him. I came at him with my nasty right hook that Landon still remembers. I leaned into it and Stern staggered back. He pointed the gun at me with both shock and amusement registering on his face. I ignored the gun. I knew it wasn't exactly a wise thing to do. He could have blown me away but I trusted him to enjoy the fight enough to not shoot. I sent a kick his way and he jumped away knocking things off the dresser. That was good, even if I didn't connect, Rusty would know something had happened here. And he'd know where to go looking. He already had a team of cops handy. I thought, backup-wise, I was in good shape. Only problem was my backup was about eight miles away and very busy at the moment. Stern and I circled each other. He was watching for a chance to nab me. I was looking for a way out. If an escape failed to present itself, a good solid hit would do. I tried imaging he was Tom, but this time I didn't hold back on my punches. I moved in with a jab and then jumped back. He took it, but I wasn't sure if he was pleased or surprised. He advanced. Watch for his weakness, Cass. Fighting styles have patterns. Find his pattern and throw him off. He kept the gun trained on me, but as far as I was concerned it was an advantage because he held it in his right hand, and only fought with his less coordinated left. Since he was determined to advance on me and I had room to maneuver, I backed into the hallway. When he followed I threw all my weight into him sending him falling into the back wall of the hallway. I had learned to throw my weight around early on. It took a lot of force for a hundred and twenty pound woman to budge a large, stubborn male. His head hit the wall with a thud. I followed him down punching, hitting anything I could connect with. He let out a roar and stood up dumping me off of him in the process. His face was red and the veins stood out on his neck as he took a furious step toward me. I thought I'd probably crossed a line right there and made a mental note to be more careful. I ran down the hall with Stern in hot pursuit. He pushed me and I fell against the corner of the coffee table. The pain overwhelmed everything and then Stern planted his knee in the middle of my back. He twisted my arm behind my back. Where was the gun! He needed both hands to pin me down. Where was it? I looked around, frantically looking for the weapon nearby, but as I turned I saw the butt of the gun coming down. I rolled just enough to avoid the blow.

"No!" I yelled. "Don't knock me out. I'll go. Shit, those gun butts hurt like hell. You'd think my brain would be scrambled by now."

I needed to keep thinking. If he knocked me out I'd be powerless. At least if he took me conscious I could take notes. I could see and react. He might over power me but, if I could just keep thinking, I'd find a way out of this situation.

"I have a nice place reserved for you. I think you need a little lesson."

He dragged me off to his car. I was glad to note the front door was left unlocked. That would tip Rusty off right away. I could feel my left eye getting puffy and my shoulder was hurting like crazy. His twisting didn't help at all. When he stuffed me into his trunk I would have been scared except I knew we weren't going far. I felt the movement of the car and kept track of the stops and turns. I kicked at the tail lights. Even if I couldn't use the trick to escape, maybe I could scatter some pieces that could lead Rusty in the right direction.

"Damn it Cassidy! If you tear up my car you'll regret it!" he yelled as he drove.

Stern drove to the end of my street and turned left, just like I thought he would. Then he went down Sunset, his street, and turned right, just as I had been expecting. Only problem was he kept going. His driveway was short, but this trip was too long. Where was he taking me? After perhaps a half mile he stopped. So, we were still fairly close to his house, I thought. He opened the trunk and hauled me out. When I regained my feet I saw junipers, a large cleared area and a big, tan corrugated metal building. I noticed there was no external damage to the tail lights, no plastic trail to tip off Rusty.

"When my parents died they didn't know they left me a gold mine," he said. "This old barn is a gold mine. I make more money off this barn than I ever did working. Let me show it to you. You can see your dog, too."

I looked around for any sign of Stern's house but there wasn't a house in sight. As he slammed the trunk shut I heard a cacophony of barking. After a few barks and loud woofs there was snarling and sounds of a scuffle.

"My dogs," Stern explained. "I wouldn't run if I were you. All I have to do is open that door and you're dead meat."

He pushed me towards the barn. There were no big, wide doors like a horse barn. These doors were meant for people. As we entered the stench of it hit me like a blow. There were rows and rows of cages made out of chain link fencing. I estimated each cage was about four feet square because all the cages were made from the same width of fence. Cages four by four by four and roughly half of them held a dog. Some of the dogs were big, some were medium sized, all were tough, scarred, and battle worn. There was a large arena in the middle of the barn that had been cleared with about six dogs sharing the area.

"Call your dog," Stern ordered.

I hesitated. "Shadow?" I called tentatively. A black and white blur raced around the large pen and then up to the fence. He was filthy, matted and leapt at the fence excitedly. The other dogs caught up with him and attacked, dragging him down. He struggled with a startled *yipe!* He tried again to reach me but the pack assailed him again and he withdrew, then paced at the back of the pen clearly cowed. His eyes sought me out even as he paced.

"Call your dog," Stern ordered.

"No. I won't." At the sound of my voice Shadow started planning, looking for a way past the pack but he wisely stayed back.

"See, he knows his place. He knows the bigger, stronger dogs are superior. You, on the other hand, haven't learned your lesson yet. See, I have a front row seat reserved to teach you a lesson. He shoved me down the row of cages until he found one positioned between two large dogs. "This is Brutus and Tyson. I suggest keeping your fingers on this side of the fence. On the other side is your dog. I'll let you have some time to see how things work around here." He shoved me towards the cage. I looked at my options. There was no way I was going to get out of here by fighting with Stern. But I was not going to go in that cage.

"No." I said flatly. "I'm not going in there."

Stern stuck his gun in his pocket and came toward me. I backed against the cage and he grabbed me by the shirt front flinging me over the cages. I skidded with a rattle across the chain link and landed with a *thunk* on the other side. The snarling pack raced toward me. I jumped up and back onto the cages inches before the lead dog slammed into the fence. Brutus and Tyson went nuts. When I landed back on the aisle side of the cage Stern said, "I see you're learning. Now get in the cage."

"What keeps the dogs in that area?" I asked. "They could easily jump out."

"The penned dogs. They've all fought the penned dogs. The dogs in the middle are rookies. They haven't earned their place in the pens yet. They're still fighting for the privilege. Now get in there. Maybe in a few days you'll learn who's superior around here."

I was sick, sick of the violence and the false pride. I hated what Stern was doing with these animals, turning them into something they shouldn't be and hurting them in the process. I couldn't do anything about it now, but maybe I'd think of something. In the meantime the pen was my only option. I went in and Stern slammed the gate then padlocked it shut. He went to the corner of the barn and put on pads to protect himself from the dogs. Then he entered the arena and the pack attacked him with a vengeance. He got a bucket and scooped up some dog food, brought the bucket to the middle of the area and set it down. A few dogs continued to attack him, but he kicked them off. Shadow had learned the bucket was food. He stood at the back of the snarling mass of dogs and stared eagerly. The bucket was overturned in the mayhem and a few kibbles rolled his way. He snatched them up and retreated. I ached for him. How many times had he been attacked for trying to get his share before he'd learned to retreat?

I quickly discovered that the only wall of the cage I could lean against was the side with the gate. Brutus and Tyson were very protective of their space and they charged the fence if I brushed up against it. If I leaned against the arena side the whole pack charged up, snapping and snarling until Brutus put them in their place.

Stern left the arena, closing the gate behind him. He removed the protective padding and returned to my cage. "When you're ready to show me what you've got, let me know," he said then left, locking the barn door behind him.

After Stern's departure I sat with my back to the gate watching the arena for Shadow. So far he seemed to be okay. He'd learned to stay out of the way, a quiet presence in the pit, unnoticeable, just like me whenever I felt scared or threatened. After a while I became aware of a sound and it wasn't a dog sound. It was a person crying softly.

"Hello?" I called out. The pack raced over to my cage snapping and biting, charging the fence. There was no response so I tried a different tactic. "Who are you?"

"Don't do that to the dogs," a girl sobbed. Several dogs charged in the direction of her voice. I watched as they raced to a cage across the arena.

"Who are you?" I repeated.

"Marissa," she answered, "and you'll get along a lot better here if you just do what Teague says. If you make him mad you'll be sorry. Please don't make him mad. He does evil things when he gets mad. Please don't. Please... I can't even watch it anymore. If he's just angry then he goes after the dogs. Says it makes them better fighters. But if he gets really mad he will go after you... or me."

"What do you mean, he goes after them?"

"He has an electric stick and it hurts. Please don't make him mad."

"How long have you been here?"

"I... I don't know anymore. I gave up counting. I haven't stood up in so long, it hurts to straighten up. At least the dogs over here are nicer. They don't mind me being close anymore. I can pet them now."

"Marissa, have you found any way to get out?"

"Out of the cage? Yeah, you just gotta do what Teague asks. But if you tell him you will then he takes you to a house, and if you don't do it you'll be sorry. It'll hurt bad. Maybe he won't feed you that night. Maybe he'll use the electric stick on you. If you choose to do what he says then you better be prepared to do it."

I questioned Marissa until I couldn't think of anything else to ask her. I found out Stern's routine and learned we'd mostly be eating dog food. She said he treated people the same as the dogs. But when a person or a dog was deemed useless they suddenly disappeared. Finally after all the questions had wound down and quiet had settled in Marissa asked, "Who are you?"

"I'm Cassidy," I answered. "You can always talk to me. Don't be scared. We'll figure a way to get out of here."

I watched Shadow. As long as he lived up to his name the pack ignored him. He seemed to only move around when the pack wasn't riled up. Once they became aggressive they turned on the weaker dog.

When the barn began to dim Stern came in and dumped a scoop of dog food in each bowl, including Marissa's and mine. Then he went through and filled each water bowl until it overflowed. I guess I should have been grateful for all the water but having it overflow infringed on my living space. I ate some of the dog food. I was used to eating unsavory things in order to survive. It wasn't degrading to me. It was to Marissa, however, and she whined at her captor for some real food, but he just grinned and enjoyed watching her beg. Stern would never get that satisfaction from me. But he had news.

"You owe me a new door," he announced. "Your fucking husband knocked mine in and searched the house. He tried to arrest me but he didn't have enough evidence. You better hope I don't get hauled off to jail again or you may rot here."

Rusty. He must be frantic. How long had he known I was gone? There was no way of knowing.

Darkness settled over the barn. The dogs slept and Marissa and I tried to sleep, too. I was jerked awake in the night when a noise startled the dogs and they all began barking at once. It made me wonder if Rusty was outside, but that was unlikely since he had no way of knowing where I was.

In the morning Stern fed each of us again using the same routine, a scoop per bowl and an overfilled water dish. He knelt by my cage.

"I don't want to see you like this," he said. "Are you ready? I'm not asking much. Just show me. Show me what you've got and I'll let you out of here."

"No," I replied. "It's going to take a lot more than a cage and dog food to get to me. I'm used to doing without. I can be content in almost any situation."

"Content? Huh! I don't think so. Do you want to test that?"

That day I spent time examining my surroundings. There wasn't much to see, but I did manage to learn a few things. The fence was held to a frame with galvanized wires which were thick and unbending. Still, they had been bent to construct the cages so I knew it was possible to bend them. I worked at them. Where was my hunting knife when I needed it? I hadn't seen much use for it when I was just doing a half hour's worth of tracking with Rusty. He was armed and dangerous and I was only showing him an area I'd tracked, so the knife had been left behind. If I only had it though, I knew those wires could be bent.

I talked to Marissa and learned she was only eighteen and had met Stern at a party. After being charmed into leaving with him, she later realized how erratic he was, capable of changing at a moment's notice. When she had demanded to be taken home he'd imprisoned her here instead. When Stern fed her in the evening he asked her if she was ready and she began to cry, but then said yes. He let her out of the cage and she walked slowly, stooped over. He seemed almost kind as he followed her outside. They were gone all night and she came back the next morning even more broken than she was before. She held no hope of rescue. I didn't expect rescue either, so I watched for opportunities.

Chapter 21

Once the pack got used to me, I was able to visit with Shadow through the wires of the cage. It didn't upset the other dogs for him to be near me so he slept by my cage for comfort.

"I'm sorry, boy, we're going to get out of this, don't you worry. We're smart, we'll find our break and we'll make use of it."

"Why do you talk to that dog?" Marissa asked wearily.

"Because he's mine. Stern stole him from me, hoping I'd go after him. I didn't, but he managed to get me anyway. He's a smart dog. He sits, lays down, stands up, fetches, jumps hurdles. He can do lots of things."

"At least he's nice. Do you think Teague will make him mean?"

"No, I don't think Shadow has a mean bone in his body. If anything the treatment will just make him fearful. He's already become fearful living with the other dogs picking on him."

I shared my dog food with Shadow since he wasn't getting his share when the pack fed. I'd tell him to sit and then I'd toss the kibbles through the holes in the wall and he'd catch them one at a time. He was a good catch. I tossed them gently so they would always land within reach.

During the day Stern came to the barn and worked with the dogs. Sometimes he placed the pack in cages and then brought out two veteran fighters. He would sic the two dogs on each other and watch them fight, taking notes of their injuries and tactics as if he was planning a big fight, matching up opponents. Sometimes he wore the padding and would enter the ring with a chosen dog and shock it until it attacked him in a rage. He seemed to want the dogs to hate him. The more they hated him, the more he would dote on them, punish them and shock them. A hate-filled dog only meant money to him.

After each work session with the dogs he approached me and asked, "Are you ready? Come on Cassidy, show me what you've got."

"No." I almost said *stick it*, but then I thought he'd take it literally and I'd be in even more trouble.

"It's just a little thing."

"So why would you want to see it?" I asked sarcastically.

The conversation varied a little. The results of my refusal varied a lot depending on his mood and how well the dogs had preformed. I now understood how Marissa felt when she tried to straighten up. A couple of times I had been jerked from the cage and shoved up against the wall. Stern's anger was unpredictable. A simple no could result in a fist to the face. Once I ducked and he slammed his fist into the wall of the barn. That earned me a fist to the stomach.

Another day, after Stern had been in the pit with two veteran fighters, he had a hard time returning the dogs to their cages. He had a pole with a loop on the end for moving the dogs from place to place without being bitten, but the dog charged him and he wrestled it down the row of cages. After Stern left I finally saw it, my break! The scuffle must have uncovered it. In the dirt of the floor a short screwdriver with a yellow handle was half buried. If only I could reach that tool, I could free myself! That night I called Shadow quietly to my cage.

"Shadow, come. Come boy! Good Shadow, good come! Now jump! Come on jump UP! GO UP! Come on boy, what a good dog! Shadow JUMP!" He paced nervously, whining, looking at me, wanting to obey but frightened to do so. Finally, he tensed nervously and then, to my great relief, jumped and hauled himself unsteadily onto the top of my cage. He didn't like being up off the ground. The chain link was hard to walk on and then Tyson went nuts lunging and barking. That scared Shadow. "Good boy! Now walk! Walk, Shadow! Good boy!" He tried to bolt but his feet kept falling through the chain link. He struggled to get his leg loose, then walked unsteadily and fearfully across the roof of my cage and jumped down into the walkway. Yes! "Good BOY! What a good dog! Good Walk! Now, get the tool! Get the tool boy, good tool. Go get it!" Shadow started looking around on the ground for a tool. He found the screwdriver but he couldn't pick it up because it was buried in the dirt. He scratched at it, and then stepped on the tip lifting the handle out of the dirt. He picked it up and carried it to my cage. Yes! Yes! I had a tool! I reached through the wires and took the screwdriver, then went to work on the wires of my cage. They were thick and bent slowly. I worked feverishly while trying to hide my progress from Stern. When I heard a noise I would hide the screwdriver, sliding it down my sock and under the leg of my pants.

In the morning when Stern came to feed us Shadow was sleeping by my gate.

"Cassidy, how'd your dog get loose?" he grabbed Shadow by the scruff of the neck.

"Leave him alone! He only wanted to be with me. You hurt him and I'll, I'll…" I didn't know what I'd do, but it wouldn't be nice.

He released Shadow, opened my cage and dragged me out. "Come on Cassidy. Why do you have to be so hard headed? I'm not asking much. Show me."

"You'll get nothing out of me!" I replied. "You can do what you want to me, but I will not strip for you!"

Shadow started bounding around us happy to be free. Stern grabbed him and shoved him into my cage, slamming the door shut. Tyson and Brutus went nuts, lunging and snapping at the walls of the cage. Shadow paced frantically, looking for an escape.

"I can do what I want? You don't know what I am capable of or you wouldn't tell me that. Come here." He grabbed me by the arm and hauled me around to the gate of the pit. He put padding on my arms and legs, none on my torso, then he shoved me through the gate. The pack charged across the arena snarling, lunging, working themselves into a frenzy. I was glad they were just rookies, mostly attacking the padding. I blocked and kicked at them, anything to keep them away from my sides and face. A large dog lunged and knocked me over and I cowered as they went for my face, hiding in the padding as they jumped all over me, yanking my hair and tugging at the padding on my arms. Stern laughed. When he thought I'd had enough he yelled at the dogs, then waded in with the cattle prod forcing them to back off. He hauled me out of the pit and removed the pads from my arms.

"I can do anything I want. And I'd rather be nice to you so, now, Cassidy, show me."

I looked him straight in the eye and said, "No."

He removed the padding from my legs and the screwdriver fell to the ground.

"Where'd you get this?" he accused.

"I don't know what you're talking about," I lied.

He backhanded me. "You lying bitch, where did you get this?"

He snatched the screwdriver from the floor and I started backing away. He raised the screwdriver like he was going to stab me with it but I dodged around him and made a dash for the door. He threw the screwdriver at me, hitting me on the head. I grabbed the doorknob, but it was locked. Stern grabbed me and spun me around, but I planted a fist right into his nose then stomped his instep. His eyes narrowed and he dragged me off tossing me into a different cage. I lay there shaken, no food, no Shadow, no water, no screwdriver, just two more angry dogs and a furious Stern.

Chapter 22

What hurt me the most through this horrible experience was thinking about Rusty. He was a detective. What could he possibly unearth about this place? I knew he was putting his all into trying to find me, but I couldn't think of a single lead that would bring him to this barn. Many times I'd seen him unable to sleep and up in the middle of the night worrying over some case that particularly touched him. Imagining him worried, determined and angry only made my situation worse. I decided my time would be better spent finding a way out.

Every day at feeding time Stern asked the inevitable question, "Come on Cassidy? Are you ready to show me what you've got?" He bribed, threatened and sometimes hit me, but I refused to give in to him. No matter what he did I'd never lower myself to his level. He thought that by beating on me and throwing me to the dogs he became superior, but in my mind it didn't work that way. I tried to maintain an analytical attitude about my situation, watch for opportunities, and take advantage of the smallest ones; but there were moments when I had to admit I was slipping. The loss of the screwdriver had been a hard blow. Now Shadow was in a cage where I couldn't see him and I didn't know if he was getting fed. I hoped he was.

The afternoon of the fourth day, Stern showed up at the barn. He tied and gagged both Marissa and myself then led us around the side of the barn and in through another door. It was an office much like the office next to the barn at my parents' ranch, except this one was full of dog fighting equipment as well as paperwork. I saw heavy leashes, another cattle prod and spiked collars. Stern forced us to the ground and we lay side by side on the office floor. He tied my feet together, then Marissa's.

"What's going on?" I asked through the gag.

"Big fight," Marissa answered, "stay quiet."

"Why?"

"If anybody suspects we'll get the shock treatment."

I started working on the ropes, pulling my feet back and forth. They loosened a little bit but not enough for me to get a foot loose.

We heard the sound of cars pulling up outside and people moving about, their footsteps next to the door.

"Help! Help!" I yelled through the gag.

Marissa stared at me in shock, desperate for me to be quiet. Judging from her reaction she must have experienced Stern's shock treatment.

"Help!" I yelled anyway.

Stern rushed through the door, slamming it behind him. He glared at Marissa who squirmed away from him whimpering. He jerked me up and said in a low, threatening voice, "One more peep and it's the pit for you!" Then he slammed me back down on the floor and began jabbing me over and over again with the cattle prod. Then he really became enraged and started hitting me with it, like a bat. The tip stung when it hit and sometimes he'd hit the button when he brought it down giving me a welt and a shock at the same time. After he'd left and I was able to focus again, I could see Marissa was nearly hysterical. It left me wondering what horrors she had seen in her time here.

"It's okay," I said, still shaken. "It's my own fault. I had to try."

After a while we could hear that Stern's gold mine was really paying off. We heard the cheers of victory and the moans of despair as people were parted from their money. There were several fights that night but then the sounds changed. There was a wild scuffling like people running for the exits and then Stern rushed into the office. He went to his desk and pulled out a gun.

"Your fucking boyfriend has brought his fucking police buddies in! Damn it Cassidy! There won't be a dog alive when they get through! And they won't stop at the dogs either!"

He unbound my feet, removed the gag and stood me in front of him. He held me in front of him and started to open the door. He was going to use me as a shield. My heart sunk. I wouldn't let him use me against Rusty. He could beat me to a pulp, but I wouldn't allow him to use me to get out of this. I spun around to face him.

"No. You're not getting any help from me! I *refuse* to go out there."

He glared at me, grabbed my arm and tried dragging me out of the room, but I twisted loose before he could open the door wide enough. His anger flared. He advanced on me until I was up against a wall, then he began hitting me. I dodged but the office was small and my hands were still bound. He knocked me to the floor and began stomping and kicking me. When he almost lost his balance, he switched to pummeling me with his fists. All his rage was focused on me, all the fear of losing his gold mine, all the fear of what the police would do to him was being inflicted on me and I couldn't do anything about it. I felt a jab of pain from each blow. When would it stop? It seemed to go on forever and then after a while the pain from them grew less and less. I was fading. I could feel the darkness closing in and I fought it. I tried to hide from the blows, turn my face under the desk so he couldn't reach my head. If only I could use my arms. I had to focus, but it was getting harder and harder to keep track of it all. I squirmed and pulled away. I rolled, hoping he couldn't kick me in the stomach again. I cried out, but it only came out a mumbled, "No, stop." The last I saw of Teague Stern was a hate filled, bitter face and a bloodied fist coming at me. I heard a door bust in and then gunfire.

"Oh God." A pause. "Michaels, get over here." Longer pause. No, don't let him see me like this. Marissa crying. A call for the medics. Ten forty-five C. Critical. I imagined what the single letter meant to Rusty. No, I thought, don't tell him that.

"Cassidy?" Jayce Thompson. I knew the voice, but I couldn't recognize him under all the riot gear. "Hold on kid. It's going to be okay."

I couldn't respond.

"Look at me, come on, Cassidy, I need you to look at me. Show me you're there. Come on."

Nothing. He reached out and I flinched away, instinctively.

A scuffle. Rusty. I could see him. I could see all the pent up rage, all the overwhelming sadness, the fear. I could see it but it barely registered. I wanted to reach out to him, but I couldn't. He wanted to hug me and he was afraid to touch me. I was so broken. He couldn't even speak to me. He tried, but the words stuck in his throat, and then someone pulled him away, and the medics filled the room. My hands were untied and the pain of moving my arms took over everything. I pulled my hands up to protect my face from an imagined blow and the pain from that movement sent me over the edge. Tumbling, tumbling in a sea of pain.

Chapter 23

The physical blows played over and over in my mind. At times it was realistic, sometimes just a sensation, always a stab of fear. No! A flinch. A sense of motion approaching me. A jerk. The blows. The blows wouldn't stop. Please… stop. I don't know how long it continued but I watched it playing endlessly before me. Every needle jab became another shock from Stern. Every movement was a swinging fist. Every touch became another hit.

Again. The blows, the flinch. I couldn't move. My arms wouldn't move. He was killing me. Please, stop… the flinch again.

I drifted, unfeeling. At least the drifting was peaceful. But it didn't last.

Voices. Pressure next to me. A perceived threat. An attempted jerk away. Gentle voices. The pressure changed. I struggled. I couldn't move right. What was wrong? Sad voices. A hand on mine. A perceived threat and another jerk away.

More drifting. Yes, the drifting helped. Much needed peace.

"He's broken her. Kelly, what if her mind is gone?"

"You can't think like that…"

"I can't even get near her. She fights anything. Anything real, anything imagined."

"Give her time. She's been through hell."

Someone moved and I instinctively flinched. Why couldn't I move my arms? Must shield my face. He's broken her. He's broken her. Can't think like that.

How long… please, somebody… Rusty… a movement, a flinch.

He's broken her… no… no Stern's going to break me. I'll beat this. No satisfaction for Stern. I will not give in. I'll fight it… Fight it. Wait. Logical thoughts. I've got real thoughts! I tried opening my eyes, nothing. I tried my fingers, nothing. I tried speaking, but couldn't form words.

"Cass?"

It was like a shock. I flinched. Gradually I calmed again. Try to form a word, Cass. Just one word.

"Rus…"

"Okay, it's a start. Babe, it's a start. Come on, think. Don't think about fights. The fight's over. Just think happy thoughts. What do you want to do when you get out of here?"

Too much. Too much at once. Fight's over.

"You still there?" he asked.

Form a word, Cass.

"Rus… can't."

"It's okay, someday you will. We're going to get you out of here and do something just for us. You need to ride at the ranch again to get your balance back. You need Cody to play practical jokes on you."

No, stop. "Short… too much."

He backed off.

"Can't move."

"It'll come with time."

"Arms."

"Babe, your arms are tied down. Don't worry about your arms. Try your toes."

Toes. No toes, but my feet moved.

"There you go. Can you open your eyes? I want to see your eyes."

I tried but only saw through slits.

"Can you see me?" he asked.

"I see… not you."

He moved and came into view. I pulled away, then stopped. Rusty, it's Rusty. I tried to smile.

Consciousness came then left, my mind drifted then came back. It became confusing and I was unable to distinguish a difference between the two states. I was drifting again and my hand flinched. Rusty took hold of it gently.

"Come on, babe, show me you're there."

Nothing. He squeezed a little.

Then another familiar phrase "Cassidy, are you ready? Come on, babe, show me what you've got."

I stiffened immediately and yelled, "No!" I couldn't form the whole response but I turned and pulled away desperately! "Won't!… No!"

"Babe, shhhh, oh Cass, what did I do? It's okay. It's okay. It's just me. Cass, please, trust me. It's just Rusty. Don't move. Don't hurt yourself. Oh, Cass, what did he do to you? What did he do?"

He had to back off. Every touch was Stern. I came to, crying. Or maybe I woke up. I no longer knew one from the other. I opened my eyes.

"Cass? Oh babe, what did I do? Are you there?"

"Rusty?"

"Okay. We're okay again. Babe, what did I do wrong?"

It took me a while to realize I was still struggling, fighting the bindings, and trying to get away. When I finally calmed down I could only mumble, "Don't have… words… later."

Later was a long time coming. I had visitors. Landon stopped in almost every day. He sat for an hour or so trying to encourage me to talk but I couldn't process my thoughts well enough to form sentences. He was patient. He flirted with me when Rusty wasn't there, but I didn't have the strength to tell him off. Strict came. He stood silently by the door watching Rusty talk to me. Watched me try and form sentences. Victor came once. He knew I wasn't up to much but he told me search stories, saying how much easier it would have been if I'd been there. Cody and Chase even showed up from San Diego. Cody called me his little sis and joked around. Chase wanted the facts. Who did it and were they dead yet? He brought get-well wishes from Rusty's parents. Kelly came often. Sometimes he was there with Rusty when I woke up, but one day when I awoke Kelly was there alone.

"Hey girl," he said, "I sent Rusty out. He needed a break, but he'd never admit it. He's going to be mad if he finds out he missed visiting with you."

"I'll try and… stick around," I replied weakly.

"That's better."

"I want… my arms back."

"That's going to take time, kiddo. You've got broken bones in there and you still react too violently when you see a threat coming."

"What's broke?"

"I haven't talked to the doctor. That's Rusty's job. But at least your collar bone."

"Cattle prod… probably from the cattle prod."

Kelly studied me in stunned silence, then asked, "What? Cassidy, did he use a cattle prod on you? No one knows what you've been through. This is the first clue we've got."

"Shocked me… hit me with it."

"Can you talk about it? Anything… any clues at all to help us understand?"

"Don't know… Where to start?"

"It doesn't matter. Anything. It'll help you to get it out and we need to know."

I tried to think through what had happened but it brought on flashbacks.

"Black eye… from push into coffee table."

"Cassidy, your whole face was swollen when they brought you in here."

"Lived in a cage… ate dog food."

The beatings flashed through my mind. No! Don't! I flinched away from an imagined blow.

"Hey! It's okay, Cassidy, settle, settle, it's okay."

"I'm sorry," I cried.

"It's okay. Stop. I didn't mean to push you that far. And that's why you can't have your arms back. They're trying to keep your arm still, but it's not working very well."

He gave me some time to calm down before continuing.

"Let's talk about something safer. I know Rhonda already did but I wanted to thank you for the wedding pictures. Sorry to be biased, but I'm especially glad to get a portrait of Rhonda and me. We'll never be able to afford to go have one taken and it means a lot to see it on the mantle."

"Wanted you… to have it."

"Rhonda takes it a little differently. She remembers what it felt like to be all fixed up. She's been buying things here and there to try and get a look out of me. So thanks for that, too," he said with a wink.

"She needs to go… oh shoot. She needs to go… shopping… with Sandy."

"Rusty's sister?"

"Yeah, Sandy knows… oh Kelly, I can't…"

"It's okay, rest. You don't have to talk."

"Knows what… looks good on a girl."

"Shhh, rest. Just rest. Try and be awake when Rusty gets back."

"K."

"A lot of people are rooting for you. You've got more friends than you know…" he kept talking and I think I faded out, but I faded back in, too, and I heard when Rusty walked into the room. I opened my eyes.

"Let me talk to him for a minute, then he's all yours."

"K."

He steered Rusty out of the room and then they returned a few minutes later.

"Just keep it upbeat," Kelly said as he left.

Rusty sat on a chair next to the bed. After his conversation with Kelly he didn't know where to start.

"Can I sit up?" I asked.

"Tell me if it hurts." He found the control and pushed the button to raise the head of my bed.

"Stop, okay… maybe the feet?"

He pushed the button and raised my feet a little.

"Thanks."

He smiled but it didn't reach his eyes, he was still looking troubled.

"Don't think about it."

"About what?"

"What Kelly told you."

"I can't help it. How do you feel?"

"I hurt… I want my arms back."

"I'll ask the nurse. You need to try to control your reactions. Can you tell me what set you off? I don't know what I said but you panicked. I need some clues here."

"Rusty, I was only half conscious… when you said it…. If you said it now… I wouldn't react... the same way."

"Still, babe, what was it?"

My breathing quickened. Why that? Why did he have to ask me that? It meant I had to say the words. I pictured Stern standing in front of me again and asking, "Are you ready to show me what you've got?"

"Cassidy, stop, whatever is going on inside that head of yours, please stop. You've got to get a handle on it."

Once I'd calmed down he tried again. "I want you to tell me what triggered it, and don't let your thoughts get carried away. If you have to stop, it's okay. Just get the explanation out without panicking. Control your thoughts. I don't care if it takes all day. Just try."

"I can't… too many words… Can't find the words."

"Just try. Take your time."

I took a deep breath. My thoughts were already racing ahead of my ability to speak. I had to focus. "Stern liked using psychol… psychol…"

"Psychological?"

"Yeah, tricks… He didn't ask for much… but I knew to give in… to give in to one..." I could feel my breathing quickening again.

"It's okay, babe, you're doing good."

I shook my head no.

"I knew to give into one… would just invite another."

He understood and knew it was true, too.

"He broke into the house… after you left… so he found me still in bed…. He was really disappointed," slow down, Cass, slow down, "when he pulled back the covers and I… was fully clothed."

I could picture Stern standing there when he said, "Your poor husband…"

"Cass, hey." Rusty waved a hand in front of my eyes. "Focus."

"He asked me to… to take my clothes off… and I refused. So he used that again… and again. That was the first thing he wanted me to do to get better… treatment out of him." My head was spinning from the effort of talking so long, corralling my thoughts. "Marissa said… if I did it he would treat me better… but I knew it was a trick." I had to stop. I could feel the words coming, hear Stern's voice when he said them. "A couple of times a day he would ask me and I would refuse… sometimes he just liked seeing me be stubborn…" Make it stop, Cass, don't go on. But I did go on, for Rusty's sake. "And sometimes he would… get mad and beat me." I needed my arms! I needed to curl up in a little ball where it was safe. "The phrase he always used was… was 'Are… are you ready… to… to show me what you've got?'"

When Rusty heard the phrase something inside him clicked.

"Oh Lord," he said softly, "I didn't know."

"He'd say it… and I'd refuse and… and I never knew what kind of a reaction I'd get… but I refused anyway."

"Okay, babe," he said softly, "it's okay, you can stop. If it hurts you can stop. I know now."

"Rusty? How is Marissa? She seemed like a city kid. She shouldn't have been in a place like that. She wasn't coping. She was only existing."

"Hon, are you sure you want to know?"

"Why? It's got to be better than how I ended up. Stern blamed me. At the last he went after me. Then the shots..."

"Cass, Marissa was there a lot longer than you. She... needs help. Real help. But... let me just say, she's as shell shocked as you are, but more subtly. She can't walk right. She's meeting with detectives but it's hard. She's assigned to a female officer, because she doesn't trust men. She was abused, yes, but she gave in to Stern. As she put it she 'earned her keep'."

I wondered what she had to do to 'earn her keep' and decided I'd done the right thing, even if I'd taken the brunt of Stern's anger. I lay there shaking. All my energy had been spent in detailing Stern's behavior. Rusty sat with me, mulling over everything he'd learned that day.

"Rusty," one last question. "How did you find me?… How did you… know about the barn?"

A long pause.

"The graves," he answered quietly. "They held mostly dogs. Two recent additions were battle-scarred fighting dogs. The bodies were two women and we were able to identify one of them. I questioned her family and they expressed concern about their daughter going to the fights. I got some connections, made some calls. I arranged for an undercover cop to talk to Stern in a bar. He acted like he was addicted to gambling, said he did the horses and had lost a small fortune in Vegas. Stern welcomed him into his little clique, invited him to the next fight and even gave him directions. So the officer went to the fight, took some notes, lost some money, and then called us in. When I saw the place, I couldn't stay in the barn. To me, knowing Stern, I saw it as a prison. An inhumane prison. I hurt thinking of you there. And I knew you wouldn't be in the barn if it was full of people attending the fight. Then Jayce called me to the office. The code said critical. Critical. I kept telling myself it might not be you. I'd heard the gunfire and knew it could be Stern. But when I walked in I couldn't deny it anymore. Babe if I hadn't known it was you I'd have never recognized you. You hung by a thread. They wouldn't let me in the ambulance. Landon spoke up for me, but they still wouldn't let me. Then they whisked you away. Schroeder sent me with Ben and we took off after the ambulance. Landon somehow recognized Shadow in the cages and took him before animal control went through the barn. Every day when I sat with you I wondered what might have happened if something hadn't tipped you off about the mountain lion. What if I hadn't gone with you? What if I had no clues to go by? How long would he have kept you? How long could you have survived under those conditions? All those questions and more. People would come and worry with me and…"

I faded out.

The mountain lion. My first mountain lion sighting and it had saved my life, just barely. I wondered later what would have happened if the police hadn't raided the fight. Would I have been beaten? Eventually, yeah, I would have. Stern never wasted any opportunities for violence.

Chapter 24

"You're going to kill yourself if you push much harder," Lou said as I struggled to cross the room.

"Over thinking is more… dangerous… than pushing myself."

My knee gave way and Lou jumped to my aid. I saw the quick movement, the hand coming and ducked instinctively. Down I went. "Damn it, Lou… you can't move like… that around me yet." He offered me a hand up. "No, don't. I have to do it myself."

"Who says? In case you didn't notice you have a broken collarbone and if you fall on it wrong you'll be back in bed again."

"Rusty's taking me home, to … the ranch, in a few weeks…. I need to be strong enough to ride."

"Riding is easier than walking."

"Not the way I do it."

"I should have known. Do you do anything the easy way? If you survive your trip to the ranch, I'd like you to track again."

"Really? What happened … change your mind?"

"You. You deserve a place on the team and have proven yourself as a tracker and a scout. You're clearly not staying out of trouble on your own. So there's no reason to hold you back. Plus, the guys are driving me nuts. Victor and Landon are getting some much needed practice but they really miss you and, I have to admit, I do too."

"Big tough search commanders aren't supposed… to get soft like that."

I started back across the room. I hadn't realized how close a call I'd had until I tried to walk. During my first attempt, in a physical therapy session that I thought was unneeded and unwanted, I couldn't even stand erect. My balance was so off I listed to the side. I needed to retrain my brain a little bit. After building up strength and practicing for hours with parallel bars for support I was able to maintain a standing position and eventually walk short distances.

When the hospital finally turned me loose and I was able to go home I thought I'd be happy, snug and warm. I looked forward to my own soft bed and being able to eat anything I wanted any time I wanted. Rusty surprised me by asking what he could do to make the house feel safe again. Stern's gone, what's not safe about our home, I thought. But as I lay in bed next to Rusty I could only picture Stern standing there, sneering at me. That first night I couldn't sleep and turned my back to the dresser. I crept closer and closer to Rusty, needing his touch. I hid in his arms but I couldn't lie on that side for long because of my shoulder. We finally switched sides of the bed, but then we couldn't sleep because everything felt backwards to us. Unable to sleep and with no energy to get out of bed we naturally started touching. At first it was comforting and playful. He was gentle, aware I didn't have much energy and knowing it could hurt. He allowed me to progress at my own speed and everything appeared to be going fine until he moved over me, entering me. Seeing the male face moving so close, the stimulation of sex, increased the conditioned response and flashbacks took over. I cowered and cried. I didn't want this to happen, but I couldn't help it! He backed off.

"It's okay, babe, don't worry. Shh, I knew this could happen. I'm sorry I pushed you. Here's where we get creative. Hush, come on, it's just me." He spoke quietly so he wouldn't intimidate me and started again, from the beginning. Then he unexpectedly stopped. "Come here," he said, coaxing me out of bed. He led me to the den where he lit a very fake looking fire in our gas fireplace. He laid a blanket on the floor and drew me down onto it, then started from the beginning. "We're back at the cabin," he whispered. "Can you feel the fire? Can you hear the loons? We just had dinner and it's too dark out to go anywhere. It's just us." A few touches. "Mmm, I love you so much. I want this to be good for you. Just relax. Feel the fire?" I closed my eyes trying to take pleasure in his touch. Just feel, Cass, don't think. Listen, it's Rusty. Rusty's magic fingers, playing, teasing, oh man, okay. Touching, touching, mmm, yeah. Then a finger inside and the thumb, rubbing, rubbing. Come on, Rusty, come here. Please, come here. Oh! He waited until I was just on the edge and then he twisted around and lifted me and before I knew it I was on top. I wanted to be touched so badly! "You're in control, babe. Now I can see you. I love looking at you. You look so good in the firelight."

I didn't look good. Though the swelling had gone down and my appearance was returning to normal, I looked awful. I was also developing an attitude. There was one thing that I would defend with every fiber of my being. I refused to allow Stern to come between Rusty and me. We had a need, both emotionally and physically, to be close, to reach beyond everyday sex and grasp at life, pure, simple and free. Teague Stern was not going to steal that from me. I drove Stern from my thoughts and reached for Rusty, reveling in those shivery, tantalizing sensations that drove my body crazy. It was a struggle. Pain and joy mingled. Flashbacks threatened and Rusty excited me, fueling a night I would never forget. I longed for the culmination, the climax, that would tell me Stern had not won, but to win the battle required action on my part. Rusty watched eagerly and touched a little too gently. More! Rusty more! My breathing quickened as I gasped with gentle moans. All of a sudden I climaxed, my back arched and I grabbed hold of his arms for balance. I moved, up and down, up and down on top of him as he thrust inside me, driving my climax to new heights. Just when I thought I couldn't keep it up anymore, when I thought I was going to collapse in a heap on top of him, Rusty suddenly came inside me. It was the culmination of physical ecstasy and emotional triumph blending until, at last, total exhaustion forced us both to stop. With the blanket beneath us, we lay on the floor in a wet, tangled heap. He held me close worried he'd pushed too hard, too fast.

"It's okay," I cried into his shoulder. "It's a good cry… just stay with me…. Don't go away."

"I won't, where would I go? Only to you, shh, babe, only to you."

The next day the doorbell rang and I peeked out, still wary of visitors at the house. It was Landon. I heard a loud *woof* on the other side of the door and opened it wide. Shadow bounded into the house nearly knocking me over.

"Whoa boy, gentle, be gentle," Landon said, but it was no use. He hadn't used a commanding voice, or words Shadow understood. "I didn't know what you usually fed him," he began.

"Thank you."

"But I fed him grocery store dog food. I hope that's okay."

It wasn't what Shadow usually ate but I couldn't complain. I threw my good arm around Shadow's neck, but he squirmed loose. He didn't like to feel confined.

"Landon, how... can I thank you? You saved him... from the pound. They would have kept... him for me, but it would have been..." memories of the pit threatened, "as bad as Stern's barn... to him."

"My landlord wasn't happy, but I told him it would only be for a few days."

He was back. Shadow was back. I'd wondered if either one of us would survive that adventure and here we were together again.

"Cassidy? Are you okay?" Landon asked.

"Yes," I sniffed. "I'm okay. I'm more okay now... than I was before. Thank you... for bringing him back.... I don't know what... I'd do without him."

After Shadow explored every nook and cranny of the house and confirmed that Rusty was all right, too, he came back and curled up at my feet. I painfully lowered myself to floor level where I could reach out and pet him. Landon watched us for a minute before he unexpectedly excused himself.

"Do you... have to go?" I asked, "Tell me about the calls... I miss work..."

"Cassidy... no, not yet. Just let me leave here seeing you and Shadow like this. That's the best thank you I could get. You know, I'd never experienced the devotion of a dog before. He waited by my front door all day, every day. When I came home he would follow me around for a little while. He'd eat if I fed him, but then he would always go back to the front door. He was just waiting. Waiting for *you*. That's why I'm here. To show him he wasn't waiting in vain."

He got up to leave but then he turned around.

"I guess we're all like Shadow. When something happens to you, we wait. We know you'll be back, because you always come back." He walked over and offered me a hand up, then clasped me in a gentle hug, careful of my shoulder. "You just keep doing that, okay?"

"O... kay," I answered.

"I'm going to steal a cookie," he declared walking into the kitchen. I heard the sound of the cookie jar lid being lifted, the dry sound of cookies being sorted. He then reappeared examining the cookie for nuts and gave me a quick wave before walking out the front door. It would be a long time before I would be seeing Landon again. I had to work my way back to the call list and that would take patience, time and hard work.

We decided to rearrange the furniture in our bedroom so the dresser would be less visible from the bed. We moved the coffee table to the den temporarily. After Shadow came home, I spent several days trying to brush him out before giving up and calling a groomer. Rusty went to work and I attempted to become more active by learning to weed and cook one handed. At times I was able to manage and then there were times when the process of doing simple activities eluded me. Finally it was time to pack for the ranch but even that proved to be difficult.

"Rusty, why is my brain… so fuddled? What happened to me? I can't even decide what… to take to the ranch."

"It doesn't matter. The doctors have a name for it but what's important is that it'll get better with time."

"What if I… can't track anymore?"

"That would be very sad, but it's such a part of you, I don't think you'd lose that ability very easily. Go out back. See if the deer have visited. See if you can find Shadow's tracks. I bet you can."

I was too fearful to find out because at the moment nothing felt natural to me anymore. I had to think about everything I did.

The trip to the ranch was exhausting. I tried to be cheerful when we arrived but I also quickly escaped to my room and fell into a deep sleep, awaking later to the dinner bell. I couldn't eat and only picked at my food. My mother looked on, concerned. The table grew very quiet.

"So, what kind of trouble have you gotten yourself into since the wedding?" Randy asked, attempting to lighten the mood.

I tried to form a response but my thoughts and emotions got all jumbled up until all I could do was flee. I pushed my chair back in such a rush it fell over with a bang. I set it up right and left a very surprised family behind me as I fled the house. I made my way down to the barn and looked in on Shasta, the quarter horse I'd had since I was a teenager. His big head swung my way in recognition. With my emotions all a jumble I ducked in fear, then kicked myself for letting my reactions get the better of me again. I walked from stall to stall and each time a horse poked its head out at me I'd jump back, duck or flinch. Returning to Shasta's stall I tried petting him one handed. I'd learned very early that the horses never demanded an explanation when things weren't right. They accepted me with all my flaws and hang-ups. It was easy to turn to them when I needed a little distance from people.

I used the wall of the stall as a ladder and when I reached the top it was high enough for me to reach over with a leg and slide carefully onto Shasta's back, then I lifted the chain holding the door closed and eased my horse forward. The gate swung slowly open. It generally wasn't wise to ride without a saddle or bridle but I wouldn't have been able to lift the saddle and bridle high enough. After giving him a gentle kick with my heels he moved forward and I kept him moving until we were out of the barn, then I let him wander. He saw activity at the house and since his trainer, Randy, was there he trotted up to the porch. As I bounced up on horseback my mom took one look at us and frowned.

"Cassidy, what is wrong with you? You barely said, 'Hi, good to see you.' when you arrived and you didn't eat dinner. You've barely spoken three words. Now here you are riding with no control whatsoever. All this is not like you at all!"

Steve, Randy, Martha and Mom all stood there like a firing squad and I was doomed. Dad and Rusty came out the front door. I gave Shasta a kick and he startled forward and then turned. I kicked him again, needing to go anywhere to avoid the inevitable trouble magnet story. I should have known better.

"Steve, put a saddle and bridle on that horse before she kills herself," my dad boomed.

Steve started walking toward Shasta and I gave the horse another kick but Steve whistled and Shasta immediately obeyed his trainer. Steve caught him easily and walked us back to the barn. At least it was Steve, I thought. If there was a ranch hand I could talk to, it was him.

"Cassidy, your mom's right, something's wrong." I slid off Shasta and tried to make a run for it but it didn't work. I was too emotional to do two things at once. "Hold up, kid, you're not going anywhere until I get to the bottom of this." We walked into the barn and he confronted me. "Do you really want to ride or is this a way to escape?"

It felt as though I was back in the hospital again, trying to form sentences.

"Steve… I can't… I can't talk… I try but it gets stuck."

He gave me a strange expression, put Shasta in his stall then turned and asked, "Okay, why?"

"I… I… was in hospital. I got beat up. Stern… Stern did it."

"When?"

"I… I don't know… I've been awake three weeks."

"What do you mean, awake?"

"I… don't know. Steve, I lose words…. When I get emotional. Or need my brain for physical… I lose words."

"Because you were beaten up?"

"Rusty brought me… to find peace… to ride, get my balance… I just need peace."

"Oh, kid, the troubles you've seen," he said sadly and reached out to hug me but I flinched away.

"I'm sorry!" I cried, "Try again."

He wrapped me in a hug. "I'll talk to your mom and dad. You don't need to try and do this again. Maybe it'll come out more naturally if you can relax."

"Steve? I'm scared…. What if I can't track?"

"Of course you can track. If you can eat, you can track."

"Took me… while to eat. Steve, one more… no, two more."

"What's that?"

"Don't make Rusty… tell it."

"And?"

"Can't use my… left arm… collar bone broke. Saddle and bridle… can't do it. Think I can ride."

"Okay, kid, you need anything, just holler."

He brought me around the side of the barn and drew a big X with the toe of his boot.

"I'm going to go talk to your folks. I'll leave a nice clear trail and when you get to the end of it you'll know if you can track. I won't hide my tracks, but I won't make them obvious either. You'll see. You can track. Give me a few minutes head start."

He started out but I had no concept of how much time had gone by. I waited and waited then started tracking when I got tired of just standing around. Cowboy boots aren't difficult to track. They usually leave a good heel print and so I was able to follow Steve's trail fairly easily and arrived at the ranch house rather pleased with myself. I found Rusty, but he looked at me with concern.

"I can track Steve," I announced in a whole, complete sentence. It was short but it was there.

"Why'd Steve rush in here to talk to your mom and dad so fast?"

"I told him… enough so… they understand. They still… have questions. But… they'll understand why it's hard."

"You were doing really good for a while. What happened?"

"I can do one thing… at a time. Emotions, try to do something physical and I lose words. See? I sit quiet and calm, I can talk."

"What threw you off?"

"I can't talk about the… beating without flashbacks… then my emotions… go haywire and my words disappear."

"You told him you were beaten?"

"Barely. I could hardly get it out."

Things became a little tense for a while. My mom didn't know how to talk to me. She wanted to know more but she was afraid to ask.

"You should have called," she said.

"I couldn't... call," I countered.

"Then Rusty should have...."

"He was... with me. Mom... he sticks with me every minute."

"A parent needs to know these things," she said. "If you had kids you'd understand."

"I know, Mom... but at first I couldn't... and then... to tell it... I couldn't... just remembering... makes it all come back... Maybe that's why... Rusty didn't push... me to call... He knows... what I see... I just want... to be normal. And you see... now... what happened."

There isn't a whole lot a parent can do when their kid insists on doing things on their own. Sometimes they just have to hope they raised them smart enough and tough enough to make it through. She decided it wouldn't do any good to push the matter. She had made her point and things calmed down a little bit.

"Mom, I'll talk… just have patience. I talk better when I'm calm… But I'll try to talk about anything."

"I have to admit, this isn't as bad as Steve made it sound."

"I was very emotional... when I talked to Steve. Emotions will wipe out my words really fast."

"You've got a broken collarbone?"

"Yeah, it should be in a sling, but… But I had my arms tied down for two weeks and I refuse to use one. I just try not to use it."

"Can you try on clothes?"

"You want to go shopping?"

"Yeah, there's this dress that I think might be perfect for you."

"Why do you only find dresses?"

"I don't know. I like them, even though I never wear them. They make a girl feel pretty."

"I might need some help with my left arm. I do wear dresses on dates with Rusty."

"Is Rusty good to you?"

"Oh yeah, he's so good for me, Mom, nobody else could… could put up with the… things I go through. See, there goes my words. As soon as I get emotional."

Shopping seemed to relax us a bit, although trying to talk while walking and struggling to get into outfits was hard. Mom explained to Jesse what to expect so Jesse slowed down, listened carefully, and kept her questions nice and general. Patrick, however, didn't know any better.

"Aunt Cassidy? Why are you talking weird?" he asked.

"Something bad happened to me… and it hurt my brain," I answered.

"What happened?"

"Patrick, leave Cassidy alone," Jesse interrupted.

"A bad man beat me up."

"How does that hurt your brain?"

"I… don't know, Pat…. It just does… if it's bad enough."

We had a very successful shopping trip, which is a good thing when you are shopping with my mother because she makes up for lost time and buys everything. This also makes me very careful about what I choose to really like. She loves to shop and has enough money to buy whatever she wants, but I've always been careful to not take advantage of her generosity. We bought the dress and several sweaters.

"Woo hoo, Casssssidyyyy, you're buying boyfriend sweaters for Rusty?"

"Boyfriend sweaters?" I'd never heard the term.

"You know, sweaters meant to attract a boyfriend."

"Did I? I just… thought they were cute."

"Oh yeah? You watch Rusty and you'll know what kind of sweaters you bought! That reminds me, we can finish scrapbooking your honeymoon photos if you want to. There's only about four more pages to go."

"Sounds like fun… what did you do… with the boyfriend photos?"

"I think you'll like it. I'll show you when you come over."

At the rate we were going I'd be shopping and scrapbooking until it was time to head back home. I really needed to be working on my riding and tracking. The combination of talking while trying on clothes, and walking around a busy mall was very wearing. Mom could tell it was taking its toll on me, so we called it a day after lunch and returned to the ranch.

When we got home Jesse dug around in my shopping bag and pulled out a deep green sweater.

"You put this on for dinner and you'll see what kind of a sweater this is."

I found Rusty talking with my dad.

"I need… a rest. I'm going to nap."

Rusty followed me upstairs and sat with me while I put my things away.

"Do I get to see the dress for dinner tonight?"

"Nope, Jesse insists... you have to see the green sweater first. I'll wear the dress for Thanksgiving." Oh, no! Duh me! If Thanksgiving was coming, it was now November and I'd missed most of the month! "Rusty! I… I missed… I'm sorry."

"Hey, hold up. Calm down and you'll talk better. Come on," he said, rubbing my shoulders gently. "What's so important that you missed?"

"I missed… your birthday… I didn't mean to… I even have a plan… I just couldn't do it."

"My birthday? My birthday means that much to you?"

"Of course!"

"Babe, you were unconscious on my birthday. And you did give me a present. Lie down and let me tell you about it." Once I was comfortably settled he laid down and scooted close to me. "I'd been at the hospital since they brought you in. I was afraid to leave. You were right on the edge at that point. Nobody could tell me anything. The doctors weren't committing to any prognosis yet. They didn't want to get my hopes up. You were having a rough time of it. You would stir a little, but then as soon as I got a glimpse, a flicker of hope, it seemed like something closed in and you'd fight it. Kelly came to the hospital and insisted I needed a break. He wanted to take me out. I couldn't, though, I couldn't leave you. We sat for a long time talking. Then Landon came to see you and Kelly told him about my birthday. I hadn't even noticed it was my birthday. Landon said he'd stay with you and he'd call if anything happened. They insisted, even if it was only an hour, that I had to get away. I asked Kelly if we could stop by the station to pick up a few things. I turned on my computer, logged in and was going to download my email and gather up a few files. I was sitting there trying to think of what I needed but I couldn't focus on work. I tried, but it was no use. All of a sudden Kelly goes, 'Rusty look!' and when I looked up, there on my computer screen in bright, colorful letters was 'I Love You'. It was only there for a few seconds and then the picture changed to a photo of you and Shasta in the barn. It was like you were reaching right out through the monitor, and just like at the hospital I only got a few seconds here and maybe a glimpse there." He paused, attempting to keep his emotions in check before continuing. "I couldn't stay away. We picked up a pizza and went back to the hospital and shared it with Landon. I felt better for being there. So you see, you did give me something on my birthday, a little ray of sunshine and just a little bit of hope."

"Kelly was there for your birthday?"

"Yeah, he spent the evening with me in your room."

"I don't know what day it was, but the first time I heard your voice you were with Kelly. The lines still pop into my head and I don't know why. You said, 'He's broken her, Kelly, what if her mind's gone?' and Kelly said, 'You can't think like that.' And …"

"Cass stop, please stop!" he said, clearly bothered by what I'd heard. "I didn't know you could hear me."

"I didn't know either…and you said, 'I can't even get near her… She fights anything'… I'm sorry. I'm so sorry… I didn't mean to fight you. I spent ages in flashbacks."

"Hush, I know. I know. How do you remember that?"

"I… just do… but in a way it helped… my first thoughts… that I knew were thoughts… were in response to those words. I told myself I was *not* broken… I was going to beat this… and… and I'm still trying. I'll have your birthday present finished a few days after we get home."

"I've got all the birthday present I need. Right here. My little fighter."

Chapter 25

Later I awoke feeling much better and decided to wear my new green sweater with a more stylish pair of jeans. I freshened my make-up, curled my hair a little, then slipped out without waking Rusty.

Jesse, her husband, James, and their two sons came for dinner. Jesse jabbed James in the ribs. "What do you think?" she said, pointing at me. "Boyfriend sweater?"

"Definitely. Why didn't you buy one?"

"Because on me it looked like a 'my big, fat boobs don't fit in this sweater'."

"You're not fat."

"Do I have this guy trained or what?" Jesse asked me. "Watch this, does this blouse make me look fat?"

James rolled his eyes and recited, "That blouse couldn't *possibly* make *you* look fat."

I hoped I never had Rusty that well trained. Jesse wasn't really fat; she was a mom and had gained a little weight with each child. She might not fit into her old clothes as she once had, but she wasn't fat.

"Where's Rusty?" Jesse asked.

"I laid down for a nap and he's still asleep."

"Mmhmm, yeah, right. You showed him the sweater didn't you?" she accused teasingly.

"I did not. He hasn't seen it yet."

"You're talking better now!" said Patrick brightly.

"That's because I'm rested."

"Will you tell me a story?" Patrick always wanted to hear a story. I was glad I had a couple handy. He especially liked stories involving animals.

Just then the dinner bell rang. I didn't feel ready to climb all those stairs again so I was glad when Rusty appeared on the top landing. He came down the stairs and looked at me approvingly in the new sweater. Jesse gave me an "I told you so" look as Rusty hugged me close right in front of everybody.

"Mmm, nice sweater," he said. "Why haven't I seen it before?"

"Because we just bought it today."

"I'll have to send you shopping with your mom more often."

"Please, Aunt Cassidy, can you tell a story?" Saved by the kid.

We all gathered around the table and Patrick watched me, ready for the adventures to begin. Jesse's eyes glanced from me to Patrick and then back again.

"Pat wants to hear a story," I announced to everyone. "Do you have the patience for it?"

"Cassidy, you don't have to if it's too hard for you," Jesse said.

"I'm doing good for now. I can get through one. Do you want to hear the airplane story or the bear story or the moose story or the mountain lion story?"

"Start at the beginning!" Patrick said enthusiastically.

"Okay, that would be the airplane story. When Uncle Rusty and I went on our honeymoon we flew to Minnesota and then we got on a little airplane that can take off and land on water. The pontoon plane took off from St. Paul and it was really cool watching the forest and lakes go by. I even got to sit up front with the pilot and he told me about all the animals I might see at the lake where our cabin was. When we were almost to the lake our airplane had engine trouble! At first the pilot told us to sit down and buckle up, but since I had parachuted in the Marines I chose to strap into a parachute instead. I thought I could always buckle up *after* I put on the parachute. As it turned out, though, the pilot said the airplane was going to crash and so Rusty put on a parachute and we both jumped out of the plane over the woods of Minnesota. There was only one small problem! My parachute wouldn't deploy! I was falling through the air and I couldn't get my parachute to open."

"I don't want to hear this," my mother said. "You shouldn't tell this to your parents. We're both going to die of a heart attack."

"Speak for yourself," my dad said. "I think it's fascinating, she obviously made it, didn't she?"

"I tugged and pulled on the parachute trying to get the fabric to catch in the wind and I was tumbling through the air thousands of feet above the ground. I figured I had about five minutes before I was a big *splat* on the ground. Finally my parachute opened part way, but I was falling awfully fast. I came in for a very hard, fast landing on a lake. Fortunately, I was able to see where Rusty came down and so I swam in that direction. It felt like I was swimming forever and when I finally got to shore I was so cold. I couldn't get warm no matter what we did! We had to spend five days in the woods with no food. We snared a rabbit and made a fish trap. One day we only ate cattails and we even made strawberry tea without a pot or anything. Rusty thought that was really weird that we could make strawberry tea without any tools."

"How did you do it? Mom has teabags and a whistling teapot and a pitcher and everything. How do you do it with none of those?"

"Some day I'll show you… how to do it."

"Cool!" said Patrick. "Too bad I don't like tea."

"It's good for you in a… survival… situation. It has lots of vitamins in it. One day we ate a vole."

"What's that?"

"Have you ever seen a guinea pig in the pet store?"

"Yeah, they are noisy."

"Voles are… kind of like that except smaller… and brown."

"You're talking funny again," Patrick observed.

"Patrick!" Jesse said. "That is rude. You apologize to Cassidy. She can't help it."

"It's okay, Jess, he's… just being a kid. I wish… adults would be that honest sometimes."

"Uncle Rusty?" Patrick asked, and although it sounded strange to me it was true, Rusty was his uncle now.

"Yeah, Pat?"

"Did you arrest the guy that beat up Aunt Cassidy?"

"The police did. I went to the hospital to take care of Cass. He was shot in the raid and he is still in the hospital, but if he lives he will spend the rest of his life in jail. He did a lot of bad things."

"I'm glad you catch bad guys," Patrick said.

"I just wish I could catch them quicker," Rusty added.

Scrapbooking. Who would have ever thought there were so many gadgets just for pasting pictures in a photograph album! And it can't be just any photograph album either. It has do be acid free, linguine free, super duper, extra creative, bradded, journaled, embossed, and decorated photograph albums. I was shocked at the amount of work Jesse had put into arranging my honeymoon pictures. We sat down, each with our two page spread and went to work.

"Here's ribbon, die cuts, stickers, brads, eyelets, paper, scrap paper, fancy scissors, rubber stamps and embellishments. Help yourself."

"What… do I do?" I asked, not knowing where to start. She handed me my five photos.

"Find paper that goes good with the theme of the pictures."

I had the airport pictures. Red, white and blue airplanes. The old corrugated airport with its floppy orange windsock.

"Red?" I asked.

"You can do better than that. What do you remember most about that particular memory?"

"The old, broken down building of the tiny airport."

"Okay, well, I think we have some tin roof paper. That would look like an old corrugated metal building. Then you can add travel embellishments."

"Now is not the best time for me to try and get creative."

"It's okay, just ask before you stick and I'll tell you if it looks good."

It took me half an hour to leaf through all the hundreds of sheets of scrapbooking paper, but she was right, there was one that looked like an old tin roof. Why would anybody need paper of an old tin roof? Or spaghetti noodles, or grass? I couldn't believe the weird paper Jesse had available.

The tin roof paper was too busy for a large area so I decided to use it as accents with rust colored paper for the background. Then I cut out a windsock shape from a scrap of orange. Jesse cropped the pictures before I started piecing things together. She actually cut them up! But they were focused better once she was finished.

Fiddling with all the little pieces of paper taxed my brain and I became weary rather quickly, but finally we both had the last two-page spread done.

"Wait," Jesse said, "I have brads that look like rusty nails. Add those and it'll tie it together better."

"Jess… I gotta quit. I need a nap. I just can't…"

"That guy really did a number on you, didn't he?"

"Yeah."

"Here, it'll only take a second." She fished around in a plastic bin and brought out a little Ziploc bag of brads. She poked a few through some corners of my photo mats, bent the tabs back and declared the book done. "Now you can see the whole thing."

We looked at the book page by page and I exclaimed in broken sentences what a good job she had done then told her about each of the pictures. She had placed the boyfriend pictures on a two-page spread as the centerfold and then added ribbon with the word *romance* running down it so I could even tie them closed if I wanted. I wasn't sure how she managed it but the pages were formally masculine as well as casually feminine all at the same time. She'd picked up colors from the picture she knew Rusty liked, and that added a rustic charm to the pages, but there was also a feminine wispiness about them too.

"Jesse, how… can I thank you? You put so much… work into this."

"Just get better. A mom's got to do something when the kids drive her nuts. I do crafty things."

"I need to go home… and sleep."

"You want a ride?"

"It's only… quarter mile….Yeah, I want a ride."

I walked into the ranch house and looked at the stairs. No way. I wasn't tackling those stairs.

"Mom? Where's Rusty?"

"He went out shooting with Randy. He'll be back in an hour or two."

"You have a… blanket handy?"

"There's one in your closet."

"Too far… okay."

I stumbled out the front door and lay on the porch swing. The wood was freezing but I didn't have the energy to find a better place. A blanket soon appeared and my mom went back into the house with a *tsk, tsk.* I wrapped myself up in it, lay back down again and was out like a light. After a while I awoke with the slight jiggling motion from the swing, heard shoes on wood, then a gentle, "It's just me. Don't jump. Okay? It's just Rusty."

"She knows that," Randy said.

"Not always, and you should see her when she doesn't. She'd likely hurt both of us."

He picked me up, blanket and all and carried me inside.

"Babe, you were freezing out there. You need to be inside on a day like this. Come on, up to your room."

The next day we decided to go riding. Steve saddled the horses for me. Rusty didn't enjoy riding yet, but it was because he wasn't at home on a horse yet. He was able to make his way through the gaits and would remain seated, but then dismounted awfully sore. A trail ride would be good for him and an easy way to get more experience in the saddle. We rode out to the wood where the fox den was, and I showed him the site where the mother fox had attacked me for getting too close to her babies. I found old fox tracks but they weren't using the den at this time of year. I showed the tracks to Rusty and we followed some for a while. I was relieved that I was able to follow a fox trail. Tracking was difficult because I had to walk, focus on the trail, and concentrate all at the same time. My brain still felt scrambled and it didn't take long to wear me out. I tied Shasta's reins to Rusty's horse.

"Can I… ride with… you?"

"You okay?"

"Think I… overdid it."

Rusty climbed into the saddle and left me a stirrup so I mounted the horse behind him.

"Nope, I want you in front. You look like you're about to crater."

"You need… stirrups."

"I'll be okay."

So I slid off and barely remounted in front of Rusty. He said the magic words, "Let's go home Mac." And his horse headed back to the stable. I leaned back into Rusty and the warm familiarity made me feel comfortable and sleepy. I was so used to the movement of a horse that I just rode with it naturally in my sleep with Rusty's arms wrapped around me.

"Cass, don't push yourself like this. What if you'd been out here alone?"

"Got to push to… go anywhere."

The ranch hands rushed up when they saw a riderless horse. Randy took Shasta and came back quickly.

"What happened to her?" Randy demanded of Rusty accusingly. He'd always been over protective of me. He had lived on the ranch since he was fourteen and thought of me like a little sister, even though I was two years older. He'd outgrown the mad crush he once had on me but his protective nature never let up.

"She's just tired. She went too far and overdid it. She'll be fine."

I threw a leg over Mac's head and slid to the ground where Randy promptly caught and steadied me. I led Mac to the barn.

"No way, Cassidy. We'll take care of it."

"It's… my job."

"Not if you're fired. When you can talk clearly you can groom horses all you want."

"Did Dad… give you orders?"

"He doesn't have to. By now we know."

I walked into the ranch house, Rusty following. I looked at the stairs with disgust. I didn't have the energy to climb all those stairs and the living room was starting to look more appealing, especially if the fireplace was lit. I went to the back porch and took a log off the stack. Rusty promptly took it from me with a glare.

"All you need to do is say something."

"Doing… saying… about the same effort."

We brought the wood around front and Rusty went inside with an armload of logs. I turned and noticed Jesse's old pickup coming slowly down the road. It was weaving around strangely and suddenly veered to the side taking out a corral fence post. That section of fence tipped in and fell over. Where was Jesse? Or James? And then it hit me, it had to be Patrick! As the truck came coasting around the corner and went by the front of the house I could see him standing on the seat, looking out the windshield and then glancing down again at the pedals.

"Rusty!… Help!" I managed to shout as I dashed after the truck. I ran after Patrick, praying he wouldn't hit the gas. I was getting winded really fast but ignored it and put on a burst of speed. I managed to grab the door handle and yank it open. I pulled myself up and in, shoving Patrick to the passenger's side and stomped on the brake. The truck slid to a halt and I shifted it into park. Things were swimming around as I slid out of the driver's seat. "Who… told him… story 'bout… me an'…tractor?" I mumbled as I slumped to the ground.

Crackling. I could hear the fire and felt the warmth seep into me. I lay there drifting, unable to move for what felt like a long time. Rusty noticed I was awake and took note of the change. He didn't push me to move and since I was comfortable on the couch he just sat with me, not even broaching the topic of the truck.

"Thank you… for putting me… on my right side. How long… have I been… out?"

"We're on our fourth log."

"Funny… couldn't climb… stairs… but I can chase… down a truck."

"Old Frank told Patrick about the tractor."

"Figures… today… right?"

"Yeah, it doesn't take Patrick long. Now rest. Try and sleep. You're trying to do too much."

I slept for most of the afternoon and Rusty kept the fire going. I faded in and out but never really had enough energy to move. He'd talk to my dad, then to Steve. The subject of Stern and the beating never came up. I knew it meant Rusty wasn't dealing with the aftermath very well and it was still a tender spot.

"Cassidy? Dinner time. You need to eat something. You're wasting down to nothing. When I carried you in I was shocked. Can you eat dinner with us?"

"Yeah, I'll try."

"Aunt Cassidy, I'm sorry I drove the truck," Patrick said as I took my seat next to Rusty. I knew Jesse put him up to it.

"Did… Old Frank tell you… what happened to me… when I drove the tractor?"

Old Frank suddenly looked guilty.

"I had… to mend… the fence… wash the tractor… and did extra chores for a week."

"I don't know how to mend a fence!" he said, worried.

"If… you're going to be… a cowboy like… your dad… it's about time… you learned. But that's… up to your parents. Having been… in your shoes… I'd let you off easy."

"You're talkin' weird again. I'm sorry I hurt your brain."

"Pat… you didn't… I just have to rest."

I knew from the expression on Patrick's face that he blamed himself. I'd told him that my brain hurt and he had come to associate my speech with the severity of the condition, so it was a logical conclusion for a small child to come to. He jumped down from the table and ran out the back door. I got up to go after him.

"Where'd… he go?" I asked Jesse.

"Probably the tree house."

Shoot. "Okay."

I started out the door and followed the road to Jesse's house. I could see Patrick up ahead running toward the tree house and I started smiling. The tree house I'd built myself and it was where my nephew ran when he was feeling sad. It took all my energy just to walk down there and then I would have to climb up too. You can't talk to a sad kid by yelling up at a tree house. There was a rule about that somewhere. You have to be like a kid yourself when you're with them, at least aunts who look like little kids do. I took the ladder slowly and crawled up into the tree house, all the time trying not to use my left arm.

"Did you… climb… the rope to… get up here?" I asked.

He was sniffling and red eyed. "Yeah. I tried and tried until I learned how, but I can climb up the rope easy now."

"I knew… you could do it. Pat… you didn't hurt… my brain. It just takes time… and… you know what?"

"What?"

"I bet… no one's really mad… at you for driving… the truck. You have… to learn to wait… until you're… the right age to do things…. Grandpa and Grandma and Steve… they are all… saying, oh, no, not again! Not another Cassidy… we barely lived through the first one…. See… you're a lot like me…. At the same time they admire… your inde… independence and quick thinking… you've got spunk… and they like that…. If they punish you… for taking the truck… take it like a man…. Do what they say… and learn from it…. But you didn't hurt my brain. I know you… wouldn't treat a person like that mean man… did to me. You care… about people… or you wouldn't be sad… for me."

On the way back to the ranch house I told him in stuttering, broken sentences about seeing the bear on my honeymoon and how it stole our breakfast. By the time we got back I was barely standing, could hardly talk and needed to eat something, but I was only able to manage a few bites. I made sure to eat a few vegetables and a little meat. I stayed at the table for Patrick's sake, but when everyone began dispersing I headed to my room and quickly fell into a deep sleep. Rusty jiggled me a little before he went to bed and again in the morning to make sure I was actually sleeping. It was very unusual for me to sleep past him, but when he decided I was just tired he showered, dressed, and started the day. It was Thanksgiving.

I slept on and on, my body apparently demanding rest after the previous day's excitement. A few hours before dinner, my mom came into the bedroom causing me to jump in fright.

"Are you okay?" she asked as she sat next to me on the bed.

"Rusty, should have warned you. I've been jumpy."

"I thought you'd want some time to get dressed for dinner. Do you need help?"

"Come back in an hour. I'll shower and do my make-up before I put the dress on."

"You're sounding better."

"Yeah, the sleep helps. Don't let Patrick ask for the mountain lion story over dinner. If he asks, encourage Rusty to tell him about the moose."

"What's wrong with the mountain lion story?"

"It involves human body parts."

"Oh, right. Cassidy, how do you get mixed up in these things?"

"I just went out tracking. I saw a mountain lion. I'm lucky I did, too, or Rusty wouldn't have found me."

"Huh? You lost me somewhere."

"It's a long story."

I got up feeling better than I had in days. My head felt clear and I was able to shower easier, nearly one handed. I put on make-up, curled my hair, then took out the dress. As with most of the fancy dresses that looked good on me, this one was woodsy colored. My cute dresses are colorful and perky while my fancy dresses have muted tones with textured fabric that that tend to hug my body a little. My mom could spot a dress for me from across the store. She had clothing radar or something. She came in later and helped me slip my left arm through the hole and then zipped up the back of the dress.

It was time to find Rusty. I was sure he'd been bored stiff for most of the day but when I found him he was visiting with a group of guys in the living room. He noticed me at the top of the stairs and I felt very self-conscious as I walked down. He stood when I got to the bottom of the stairs.

"Who's this stranger posing as my wife?" he asked in a teasing voice.

"Careful, that one's trouble," Randy commented.

"Trouble in disguise," added Zack.

I let them have their fun.

"I'm glad you're feeling better, but you really do look different and it isn't the dress. What have you done with yourself?"

"I didn't do anything. Did you see the scrapbook of honeymoon pictures? I helped Jesse finish it up."

"You'll have to show me. But really, Cass, something's different."

"I promise, nothing's different. I'm not stuttering but that's because I just had a long rest. But other than that I don't know what you're talking about."

"Are you pregnant?" my mom called out from the kitchen. "If you were that would account for it."

"Mom! No, I'm not pregnant. That's a silly thing to ask!"

"Why? You've been married four months. Lots of couples get pregnant sooner than that."

"Well, I'm not. I don't know if I even want kids. We haven't even talked about having kids."

"You don't need to talk about it to do it," Randy commented, and then quickly blushed in embarrassment.

"Well, I'm not pregnant and I'm not planning on getting pregnant and I don't know what you think is so different except that I do feel much better today. Can't we just be glad of that?"

"Of course we can dear," my mom replied.

The conversation turned to the safer topic of horseracing.

"Cassidy, you're about the size of a jockey," my dad observed. "Would you test out a new colt we've got in training?"

"No," Rusty stated adamantly.

"*What* did you say?" asked my dad in disbelief.

"I said no. Cass shouldn't be racing." Uh oh. Did Rusty know what he was doing? Rusty continued, "And if someone asked Betty to do something dangerous I would hope you would say no, too."

The ranch hands immediately stood back to watch the action play itself out.

"Cassidy?" Dad said, turning to me.

"You're not putting me in the middle of this debate. If I ride the colt I'd be going against Rusty's wishes and if I don't then I'd be going against you. Either choice is wrong." Wow, I couldn't believe I just did that!

"Harrumph," Dad said. "I can't believe, my own family."

"Mr. Gordon, you're asking more than you know. You didn't watch Cassidy just two weeks ago trying to walk again. One spill on the racetrack could cost her months and I'm not willing to risk that."

"Is it safe to ring the dinner bell?" Martha asked, sensing fireworks.

"There's no need. We're all here except Jesse and we know they are on their way," Dad replied.

As we were sitting down to our huge Thanksgiving dinner Jesse and her family arrived with the kids dressed in slacks, white shirts and bolo ties. Jesse was wearing a new outfit that we just bought on our shopping trip. All the ranch hands wore pressed jeans, colorful western shirts, string ties and shiny black boots. Dad and Rusty were both wearing sport coats and ties. The mood turned festive again and we all sat down to steaming plates of turkey, roast beef and leg of lamb with all the fixings. This year, I told myself, I was going to have more pumpkin pie. Last year I had spent my whole trip working on academy homework and had nearly forgotten about pie, but not this year. I was determined to get my pie. Plates were passed and conversation became quiet for a while until Patrick had cleaned his plate and then asked the inevitable question. Would I tell another story? So I told him about stalking the wild moose, making it sound a lot more dramatic than it actually had been. He asked for the mountain lion story, too, but I told him that would have to wait until after dinner.

"It ties into several other stories that some people might not want to listen to, so we don't want to tell it when everyone is at the table. Plus some of it is a little bit gross."

Rusty mentally went through the whole story as he remembered it and started looking worried. He wasn't sure he wanted to hear it either.

After dinner everyone settled in the living room with pie and Patrick persisted.

"Pat, it's a very long story. And the mountain lion portion is only a short part of it. And some of it is gross…"

"Cool!" he interrupted.

"Not cool, sad, and other parts are sad too. Do you still want me to start it? What about everybody else?"

I received numb stares in return. Nobody was sure with the exception of Patrick.

"Okay, well, if you get up and leave I won't be offended." I then started way back with the flat tire and the mean man who had been trying to make me believe he was nice. I told them about Stern prowling around the house and the bird nailed to our front door. I told them about seeing the mountain lion and something being wrong about the sighting. I then mentioned how we watched the mountain lion eating people at the graves and how much it had upset me. I explained how Rusty had gone back to investigate and the mean man coming back and kidnapping me. I didn't delve into all the psychological aspects of the experience because there were some things young boys didn't need to hear. Then came the part about getting stuck in a cage and being with the fighting dogs and getting thrown in the pit with the dogs biting at me… I tried to skim over the violence, and then I suddenly realized Rusty didn't know about the pit. I abruptly cut the story short. Oh man, I should have been more careful. Everyone listened as I continued explaining how Rusty had made the connection between the mountain lion and the dog fighting ring, how the police had raided the barn, and how Stern had taken everything out on me and I realized Rusty didn't know that information either. Perhaps Rusty was protecting me from flashbacks, but he hadn't heard the whole story, and now everyone knew. Finally, I told them about waking up in the hospital and having to basically learn how to talk and walk again and about all the friends who had been there for me.

"Stern beat you because the police showed up?" Rusty asked. I heard the real question, though. He was blaming himself. He'd set up the raid. He'd sent the undercover cop in and Stern had seen Rusty there.

"Stern wasn't thinking straight," I told him. "It's not your fault that he beat me. I could have prevented the beating. All I had to do was let him use me as a shield and he would have tried that, but I refused and *that's* why he beat me. I wasn't going to let him use me against you, and then after it started I couldn't stop him."

Rusty's anger flared and I could see the storm clouds brewing. He excused himself and started for the door, obviously needing some time alone to think. Then Patrick's little boy voice suddenly piped up, "Don't be mad! You've never been mad at each other! *Please*, don't be mad! You should be glad Aunt Cassidy's brain doesn't hurt anymore! You should be glad!" Patrick suddenly leapt to his feet ready to flee from the room. Everyone else remained seated obviously shocked by everything that had just transpired. Rusty scooped up Patrick as he ran by and the young boy lashed out at him.

"Hey, buddy, settle down, it's okay. I'm not mad at Cassidy. Stop. Patrick stop. You said something that's very important. How you can tell that Aunt Cassidy's brain doesn't hurt any more? Please tell me. I need to know. You can hit me all you want, but I just need to know."

Patrick settled down when he realized that Rusty wasn't angry with him. He wiped his nose on his sleeve and looked down at me from way up in Rusty's arms. Patrick then sniffed out his reply. "She doesn't talk weird anymore, even when she's sad and scared and... and her eyes are pretty again."

"What? Her eyes are pretty again?"

"Yeah, when her brain hurt she didn't see right. It looked like she was looking behind me when she was looking at me, and it looked weird, and now she doesn't do that. She's got pretty eyes again. And I thought, I thought her brain was better. And I was glad for her and then everybody got mad."

Rusty paused. He took a couple of deep breaths.

"Out of the mouths of babes," he said softly, the storm clouds dissipating. "You're right Patrick. You saw what nobody else did. I've been trying all night to figure out what was different about Cassidy and I couldn't. Thanks for showing me that. You've done more for me than you'll ever know. You've given me reason to be happy again."

Rusty set Patrick down and he ran over to his mom and hid, obviously ashamed of his outburst. After a while he shyly returned to Rusty. "I'm sorry I hit you and yelled at you, Uncle Rusty," he said in a rather rehearsed tone of voice.

"That's okay, Patrick. You were just standing up for what you thought was right. It takes a brave kid to stand up to me."

Patrick was right. My brain didn't hurt anymore. It felt wonderfully free to be able to think clearly again. I could talk and walk at the same time. Patrick and I enjoyed quiet activities together that wouldn't get him into further trouble or over tire me. We stalked the rabbits in the paddocks and tracked the ranch hands and dogs. I rode Shasta through a barrel racing cloverleaf and even took him over some low jumps. Rusty was finally able to see the album of our honeymoon pictures, though I had to get over my embarrassment of knowing the ranch hands had seen them all, too. I really wanted to finish Rusty's birthday present but I had to go home to complete it.

For Rusty's birthday, I decided to make a collage of memories and souvenirs from our honeymoon that didn't fit into the scrapbook. I bought a poster-sized shadow box frame. I hung the parachute, snare, and rabbit pelt inside. Then I chose six favorite photos and attached them framed inside the display. I didn't have an artistic eye, but I hoped with some experimentation that it would resemble a miniature museum exhibit of our trip. Gradually the project took form until, at last, nearly a month late, I presented it to Rusty. We decided to hang it in the living room because it complimented the photos that Mark had given us. When we had guests they would pause in the living room, intrigued by the display. They could identify each of its components but were unable to decide why I'd gone to so much trouble to make it. With this quirky display, our honeymoon adventure would always be a great conversation piece in our home.

After the visit to the ranch I had very little stamina, but I knew that would improve with time and hard work. So I walked knowing it would still be weeks before I'd have the endurance to go out on a call. I had to be able to hike and carry a pack before Strict would call me again, so I pushed for that goal. Tourist season was over in the Angeles Forest but winter was coming and with it the inevitable snow rescues. First things first, though. Hiking. Then backpacking. I could do it. I'd get there. Eventually.

MERRY TROUBLED CHRISTMAS

Chapter 1

I stood statue still while the deer eyed me warily. Rusty watched from the bay window. Two steps closer. *Click, buzz.* The ears of the deer swiveled to the area of the barn. Two steps closer. *Click, buzz.* What *was* that? After a moment the deer all started grazing again so I crouched lower. Three steps closer. *Click, buzz, click, buzz.* Again the deer's attention focused on the barn. Two more crouched steps. *Click, buzz.* I chose a doe who seemed more peaceful than the others. Step, step, freeze. *Click, buzz.* I knew that sound. That was Mark, then I too focused on the barn. I was determined to touch the doe. I hadn't planned on that until Mark showed up but I wanted to show him how close he could get to wildlife if he really put his mind to it. I felt my foot come down on a stick and shifted it to land silently on grass. Inch by inch. When I was twenty feet away I waited until the deer were grazing and quietly sat down in the grass, giving them a few minutes to get used to me. Then I smoothly went from sitting to a very low crouch position and closed in. *Click, buzz, click, buzz.* Fifteen feet. Ten feet. It seemed to take forever. I'd only touched a deer once in my life but I'd come close several times. Most of the time I just enjoyed being with the herd. Eight feet. Crouch lower. Wait, wait. Six feet. Six feet was really close and I should have been content with that distance, but why stop? *Click, buzz.* Eyes on the barn. Step, five feet. Step, four feet. I reached out cautiously, cautiously, very gently. One more step. *Click, buzz.* Reach out, coarse hairs. Barely a touch, lightly, so lightly, like a leaf floating by. I touched the doe. *Click, buzz. Click, bzzzzzzzzzzzzzzzzzzzzzzzz*... The deer's ears perked up, it focused on the barn and then leapt away into the junipers.

"You can come out now," I called to Mark.

"Sorry, I ran out of film."

"What are you doing back here so soon?"

"Studying stalking. I took your advice and checked out Mom and Dad's house for deer. I haven't seen them there so I came over to ask where I could find them. Guess I found out."

Mark Mireau was a very well known nature photographer I'd rescued after he'd fallen over a cliff. His parents were Hazel and Wally, my next-door neighbors. Mark had been intrigued the first time he saw me stalk an animal. If something interests Mark, he photographs it and his efforts were now displayed in our home, a welcome addition to our bare living room walls.

"Come on in," I said as I led him through the back door and into the den.

Rusty came down the hall, having changed out of boxer pants at the sight of our unexpected company. He was now dressed in jeans and a flannel shirt, looking very rugged and outdoorsy. Hazel had thought Rusty looked like a male model. Today he looked like a model for an outdoor adventure brochure. In reality, he was a detective on his day off. "Can I get you anything?" I asked.

"Got coffee?"

"I will in a minute."

I got my good morning hug from Rusty. "Did you touch it?" he asked.

"Barely, I didn't want to scare it."

I put a filter in the coffeemaker and added coffee, then measured out the water and added it to the machine. I flipped the switch to start the pot brewing.

"I've had a few requests for the photos I took of you on the island. I keep telling people they aren't for sale. I didn't think you'd want your picture to be hanging in other people's homes and offices. But other people see in the photos what I see in you. I made up a set to hang in my office and people notice them even before the nature pictures, maybe because the subject is so different. I end up telling the story behind them about once a week and people are attracted to them. Do you think we could come up with a set that you would allow me to sell in my studio? If so, I'd cut you in."

"You're kidding. Right?"

"I'm completely serious. I've had offers of over five hundred dollars for a set similar to the one in your living room. Think about it."

"Why would anybody want a picture of me?"

"Because they see the same thing I did when I took them, a comfortable ease in unusual surroundings. It appeals to people. Nobody expects to see a girl so at home in the outdoors. I wish you could see some of the reactions."

"What kind of pictures did you want to take?"

"Just the things I know you do best, tracking, stalking. If you are open to the idea, camping, rock climbing."

"Hold it. I am not a rock climber. If it's rock climbing pictures then Rusty is the one you want."

"Everybody expects pictures of a guy like Rusty in a setting like that. The *unexpected* is what draws the eye. I'd take pictures of Rusty for the Marines. For nature lovers I take pictures of you."

Rusty laughed quietly to himself, because he knew I'd been in the Marines and he hadn't.

"It's not having my picture for sale that bothers me. I'd just rather people not know who I am, unless I am needed for a search. Rusty will tell you I don't like a lot of attention."

"So, choose a name. Do you have a nickname?"

"Yeah, lots of them but I guess most people call me Trouble."

"You? They call you Trouble?"

"Yeah, well, only people who have known me more than a week."

"To really get Cassidy in her element, you need to go on a search," Rusty commented.

"You mean a real call? Like search and rescue?" Mark asked, "Could I?"

"That would be up to Lou Strickland and the other members of the team," I replied. "Are you looking for search and rescue photos or photos of me tracking? I don't know what Landon and Victor would say about being photographed and I'm not sure what Lou would think of a city slicker tagging along on a call. We see some rough territory, occasionally we need to be picked up by helicopter."

Marks eyes became larger and his grin broader as more options were opened up before him. Uh oh, I thought, he's stuck on the idea.

"Do you expect opposition?"

"Perhaps at first. Lou isn't too keen on rescuing the rescuers. We have enough trouble with the victims."

"What about the others?"

"Landon admires your work and has an arrogant streak. He'd probably be honored to think he might end up in your pictures. Victor is more humble. He'd rather stay out of the pictures or be unrecognizable in them. He wants to do his job, and serve others quietly. Both are very capable EMTs. I'm proof of that. They follow me wherever I lead them without complaint and will take over as soon as they are needed. We make a good team. Depending on the availability there are two other guys who could end up going. You really don't want to photograph Thez and Roscoe. Roscoe isn't really shy but he disappears when the press arrives. He is knowledgeable and capable but a very private person. Thez is the opposite. Thez dramatizes everything. He isn't very comfortable in the outdoors and overreacts to everything. A call with Thez is never boring, always entertaining, and a bit frustrating. You wouldn't get any candid shots with him around. He'd know just the right angle, just the right lighting. I think he would drive you nuts."

"So, how do I contact these people?"

"Lou and Landon shouldn't be a problem. They could show up here most days, given some notice and no emergencies. Victor has a job and a family. He can get away for calls because his hours are flexible but he has a life outside the team."

"Do you think we can make a go of it?" Mark asked.

Rusty and I exchanged glances, wondering if we even wanted this to happen. A call was inevitable and I guess I didn't really mind being photographed tracking if Mark was capable of keeping up with the team. I was looking forward to seeing Landon's reaction to meeting Mark. Landon considered Mark to be a bit of a celebrity.

As it turned out Lou was a bit hard to convince.

"No," he said, "no civilians on searches."

"What about me? You sent me on searches before I went through academy. And Mark isn't going to do any rescuing. He's just following along to take pictures of me. All he wants are some candid photos of a real life search."

"We needed you. We don't need a photographer." Then turning to Mark he asked, "How far can you hike in a day?"

"You won't have to worry about me. I've hiked in every environment you can think of and I'll carry everything necessary to fend for myself. Just tell me how long to plan for."

"That's not what I asked," Lou pointed out. "How far do you expect to lug that equipment in a day?"

"I'd gauge the weight of the pack by how far I expect to go. If we're looking at five miles I can pack heavy, ten miles I'd have to pack light."

"There's no telling how far we will get in a day," I told him. "It depends on the trail. If the tracks are easy to read it goes faster. No matter what, you will spend all day on the trail until we find our missing person. We start at first light. We eat lunch on the trail. We stop at dusk. I think the furthest we have hiked in a day was eleven miles. We did eleven miles in a day on the Brewski search."

"You can drop everything at a moment's notice? When we call we expect a response immediately."

"You betcha."

"No guarantees," Lou said. "Maybe. If it's a straightforward tracking call, maybe. No apprehensions, no scouting. I don't schedule the calls either. They come in at all hours of the day and night. If you're going with Cassidy, the call could come anywhere from five a.m. to five p.m. any day of the week. Pack for three days. Pack light. Pack all the water you need for all three days. Sometimes there's water on a search, more often there's not."

"That's a good sign," I told Mark as Lou drove away. "By the way, tracking is not really an exciting thing to watch. It can get very tedious and slow if the tracks are hard to find. When the tracks are easy to see, it is still a slow walk. I have to be sure before continuing on and it's also why we have such a good success rate. I have never lost a trail yet. A search might take an hour. It might take three days. I never know when starting out."

The phone rang four times and there was loud rock music blaring in the background when Landon answered.

"Hello?"

"Hi, Landon, it's Cass. A friend of mine is in town and would like to meet you."

The music quickly faded until it became a tolerable racket.

"Is she cute?"

"It's not a she. It's a he."

"So you're not setting me up with a date."

"Well, he does want to go out with you but not like that. It's Mark Mireau. I thought you'd like to meet him and we have a question for you."

"I'm on duty right now. I'll get off at six. What's for dinner?"

"I haven't decided yet." I wracked my brain thinking of what I had ingredients for. "Spaghetti? Roast beef? Chile Verde?"

"Sounds good, if I don't get a call I'll be there around six-thirty."

"Okay, thanks, see you then." I hung up the phone. "I can't believe it, he got a dinner out of it! What about you? Landon will be here at six-thirty. Rusty will be here at seven. You're welcome to eat with us too."

"Sounds good. I'll have to see if it'll hurt Mom's feelings too much if I bail out. I can only take so much casserole. Maybe it'll be tuna. She knows I don't care for tuna casserole. About once a week I take them out to eat just out of self-defense. Mom thinks I love steak but the fact is I just need something besides noodles."

That settled it, roast beef was the easiest meal to prepare and the most unlike a casserole. I thawed out a roast. Mark went back to Hazel and Wally's to visit for the afternoon and I planned a dinner for four.

Mark must have been anxious to go on a call because he arrived at six-twenty wanting to talk to Landon. He brought the pictures he'd taken earlier and the ones he'd taken of me when I'd rescued him on the island.

"I don't know how you do it. You capture the moment, not the person. When I look at your pictures I don't see myself. Instead I see the concentration and focus of the stalk. How are you able to achieve that?"

"It's not me, Cassidy, you just radiate that to the camera. When people watch you stalk they're not seeing some cute girl trying to touch a deer. They see what stalking really feels like. It makes them want to try it too. That's why people ask for my images of you. When they see the pictures they think they feel the way you do when you are stalking."

The doorbell rang. Landon was still in his work uniform: navy twill pants and a white uniform shirt with ambulance company patches on the sleeves. I always wondered why an ambulance company would have white uniform shirts but Landon's was always stark white when I saw him. His navy blue jacket had the same patches on it and he draped it over a chair as he came through the door.

"You're looking great," he said. "You really had me worried after that last bout of trouble."

"Yeah, it's been a struggle," I admitted. "I'm still not one hundred percent, but I've been exploring the hills, Christmas shopping, and going to the gym. Here, I want you to meet Mark."

"You went Christmas shopping and still managed to stay out of trouble?"

"Very funny, Landon. This is Mark Mireau. Mark, this is Landon Wilson. Landon is the guy I get paired up with the most on searches."

"It's good to meet you," Mark said.

"Likewise," Landon replied.

"And Mark is a photographer in need of a subject," I said, hoping to spark one of them into taking over the subject.

"A whole big wide world out there and you come *here* looking for something to photograph? Why?"

"Have you seen the pictures I took of Cassidy?"

"Yeah, they're really good. When I first saw them I knew they were perfect for her house. It took me a minute to realize they were pictures of *her*."

"I made a set for my office, a souvenir of my trip to the islands, and people have been trying to buy them from me ever since. So I'm here to take some more. I'd like our two sets to remain unique but I'd also like to tackle this from a more professional perspective and offer them for sale in my studio. Here, I'll show you the pictures I took the other day." He handed Landon the photos. "I'd like to take more out in the woods if possible. These were just taken in the backyard but I may use them anyway because…"

"You actually touched it?" Landon exclaimed.

"Barely, I only tried it because I knew Mark was watching. I wanted him to get interested in stalking so he could move in closer on his subjects."

Mark laid all the pictures out in order, then chose four progressive shots of me closing in on the doe and finally touching it.

"I take a set like this, stylize them a little, then enlarge them so they're visible from across a room, like the ones in the living room, and for some reason people are drawn to them."

"What made you branch out into photographing people?" Landon asked.

"I've always taken pictures of anything interesting, mostly just for my own enjoyment. People have always interested me, and I have sold a few portraits here and there, but this is the first time people have approached me to ask for the story *behind* the pictures. I've been hearing about the emotion of the pictures rather than the person. When I take a picture of an animal people admire the detail, the beauty of nature. With these pictures of Cassidy it seems like I've touched on something quite different. A whole new level of photography."

"So how do I fit into all this?" Landon asked dubiously.

"I wanted to take some photos of Cassidy tracking and Rusty suggested I go on a search."

"You want to follow us on a call? What did Strict say?"

Since I knew how to read between the lines of Strict's response I answered, "It didn't sound as if he liked the idea, but he advised Mark about how to pack."

"Then it's a go?"

"Only for a straight forward tracking case. What do you think of it? Would you mind being photographed on a search?"

"Hell no, it sounds like fun. There's this one second that you have to catch though. It's like Cassidy morphs or something. One second she's this cute kid and the next she… I don't know, she just becomes something else. You have to see it."

I jumped on that quickly, "Landon, you are exaggerating."

"No, I'm not. All the guys watch for it. You do it when you track, when you stalk and when you're scouting. It's a little different each time but it's amazing the transformation that takes place."

"He's exaggerating," I told Mark.

"No he's not," Mark said. "It's like unveiling something. You can see what it is even when it is covered up, but you really only receive the full impact and purpose of it once it's been unveiled."

"You guys are getting weird on me here. You're getting all philosophical. Are you okay?"

When Rusty came home I set the table, took the roast out of the oven and made gravy.

"What's up with Landon and Mark?"

"They *were* discussing photography and now they are trying to define exactly what happens when I morph from Skipper to Tracker Woman."

He laughed, but his eyes told me he had seen it, too. He went to the living room, curious if they had figured it out yet.

As I entered the living room to ask what everyone wanted to drink I heard Mark say, "The Incredible Hulk was a good guy. He just *looked* like a bad guy."

"Well, that's sort of the way it is except she stays cute, but she turns from pert cute to dangerous cute."

"That's enough, guys."

"Don't pay any attention to her. Cassidy's just never heard this conversation before, but I've heard it many times," Landon said.

"It's a mental shift, but there's nothing physical about it," I told them.

"We'll see," Landon said. "I bet it shows up on film if Mark is able to catch it."

"Dinner's ready," I announced, hoping that food would end the conversation, but now Rusty had latched onto it.

"I think the place where it's the most obvious is at the firing range, but the weapon might have something to do with the illusion. Have you ever seen Cass shoot?" Rusty asked Landon.

"Only once, and she was definitely dangerous at the time," he replied.

"Okay, stop. This discussion is going to lead to the apprehension in the canyon. Any more than a minute on that topic and I'll be reliving the shooting and will feel guilty for the next week, so let's not go there." I suddenly realized I had introduced the very subject I had intended to avoid. Rusty and Landon both looked at me in disbelief then silently dropped the subject.

"You actually shot a guy?" Mark asked in disbelief.

"It's debatable whether it was my shot that killed him or not because five seconds later the grenade went off and he was blown to smithereens. It just stopped him from blowing up other people."

"The grenade went off?" Mark asked in surprise. "So you're a hero."

"Mark, you should be aware that sometimes these calls don't always turn out as we hope they will. Most of the time we track down a lost hiker, Landon patches them up, and then we send them to the hospital to be checked out. Sometimes things aren't quite what they seem. Once I had to shoot a tiger before it attacked a guy. Once I had to shoot a suspect before he blew up my team. Then there was the time when I was shot because the search was really a trap. Lou won't let you go unless he believes it's a very simple matter of tracking down a missing person. But even then we can't guarantee the outcome."

"Who would shoot *you*?" Mark asked.

Rusty and Landon each gave a nervous laugh. Landon summed it up pretty well by saying, "Cassidy seems to be on the bad guys' most wanted list."

Chapter 2

Strict called three days later. I quickly got the facts, then called Rusty and Mark. The call came in the afternoon, so we were nearly guaranteed an overnight search. We only had two hours of daylight left but two hours could be a significant start depending on the trail.

"Mark? Ready to roll?" I asked when he answered his cell phone.

"Really?"

"If you're packed up and ready for three days I'll pick you up in fifteen minutes. Layer your clothes, it's going to get cold tonight."

"This is a real search and rescue call?" he asked, sounding like a little kid.

"Yeah, straightforward tracking call. A family broke down on a mountain road. The dad went for help. Rangers found the wife and kids in the car but the dad left the road, probably thought he could save time going cross-country. That never works in these mountains. The reason the roads wind around so much is because the mountains are so steep. Once you leave a road you are stuck in a canyon, often with no way back up."

We drove to the compound where Victor and Landon were picking up the search and rescue vehicles. Since there were four of us with four packs, we took one of the SUVs. Victor drove.

After introducing Mark and Victor, I asked if Strict had informed him of the search's details.

"Yeah," Victor replied

"And?"

"It's a normal call as far as I'm concerned."

Victor drove up to base camp and we checked in with Strict. He gave us directions, and we followed them up a narrow dirt road until we came to a rescue vehicle and ranger truck parked on the side of the road. A group of men stood around talking and waiting for us. We left the SUV and strapped on our packs.

Kelly Green walked up. "Hey, Trouble," he said giving me a warm hug. "It's good to see you again. You on this call?"

"Yup, I brought plenty of backup. You know Victor and Landon. This is Mark Mireau."

"Hey, like the famous photography guy!" Kelly said enthusiastically.

"Yeah, just like him," Mark said.

"Mark, this is Kelly Green. You both have something in common. You have a bad habit of finding the wrong end of a cliff."

"Here's your tracks, kiddo. We started you out on the road where the tracks are plain. I knew you'd appreciate a nice clear start. Your ten sixty-five is Carl Cranston. He's got a little outdoors experience, warm clothing. He's physically fit, young. Good luck."

"Thanks, we only have a couple of hours left today so I better get started."

I tried to ignore the team as I located the beginning of the trail. The tracks along the road were surprisingly clear. I profiled as I tracked. Medium sized man, shoes on the small side, worn spot on the right side of the right shoe, distinctive tread, short stride. I followed the tracks along the road, gathering facts, ignoring the guys as they waited for the morphing they expected.

"Wait," said Landon, "it'll start as soon as she hits the first tough tracks."

"Hey," Kelly exclaimed, "you really are Mark Mireau!"

"Wait," whispered Landon to Kelly, trying not to throw off the morph.

Kelly tagged along. I felt like a mother duck with her tagalong ducklings; I was followed by Mark, camera at the ready, and then Landon who was attempting to coach Mark. Kelly followed, watching the scene with growing interest, while Victor followed last, just taking it all in with a sense of amusement. He knew all he had to do was keep me in sight and everything would be fine.

Once I got a feel for the tracks I jogged along looking for the location where the tracks had left the road. Darkness was coming which meant I'd have to stop. When that happened I wanted to be as far down the trail as possible. As I headed off-road I heard behind me, "Now watch, keep watching…"

Click, buzz, click buzz.

The tracks went into the trees and disappeared when they crossed a bed of pine needles. Okay, time to buckle down.

"Now…" whispered Landon.

Okay, I had to admit, he knew me. I could feel the change almost cloaking me as I had to slow and focus on the tracks.

Click, buzz, click, buzz.

At least Carl had been in a hurry. Usually pine needles were notorious for hiding tracks but these needles had slid underfoot leaving a clear message to me. It felt good to be on a trail again. Tracking was the most natural thing in the world to me. I loved the continuing puzzle that the ground presented. I read and thought and followed. I pieced together the tough parts and continued at a very slow walk. Once I fell into tracker mode I was better able to ignore the camera and the guys. A scuff here, a track there…

"Cassidy," Kelly interrupted, "I'm heading back. I'll call Rusty after work and let him know you got off to a good start.

I put a mark next to the last good footprint and gave Kelly a hug before he left.

"Thanks Kelly, he hates these overnight searches. It'll be good for him to talk to someone."

"What did you mark?" Mark asked.

"The last footprint I found. It just tells me where to start back up again."

"I don't see anything," he said.

"I do," I answered. "See?" I outlined the part of the print that was visible. "Let's go, we want to cover as much ground as possible today. Nights in these mountains are murder on lost people."

Victor appreciated the stop because he was curious about my last trouble attack. I told them the story as we walked. I paused when I had to concentrate. Victor and Landon were used to that. They knew I'd continue when I could easily track again. Searches often turned into storytelling for me, partly because I always had an adventure to draw a story from and also due to the local gossip at the station. It eased the boredom as we walked miles and miles of rough terrain, cross-country. The footprints led downhill, ever downhill. Occasionally Carl stopped, questioned the wisdom of his decision and decided it was either go back the way he came or continue into the canyon. From time to time I heard the *click, buzz* of Mark's camera.

When dusk settled over the mountains we set up camp. It wasn't easy finding flat spots for four tents but we managed. We began the evening routine that Landon, Victor and I had developed by working together. Mark watched and tried to fit in. A pot of water was heated for everyone to use for backpack food, and then a second pot of water was heated for coffee or hot chocolate. When the meal was finished, the leftover water was used for washing dishes. When Mark had a few idle minutes he wandered out of camp to take more pictures.

"Are you ready for a very cold night?" I asked Mark.

"This is southern California. How cold can it be?" he asked.

"Uh oh, I hope you're ready for a cold night. What's your sleeping bag rated for?"

"Twenty degrees."

"Well, sleep in your clothes and keep your jacket handy. It could easily get colder than that."

As the sun dipped behind the mountains the temperature plummeted. Everyone pulled out their jackets and gloves then started pacing the camp to keep warm. Victor and Landon did their nightly circuit with flashlights in case Carl could see the lights. Victor then checked in with Strict, giving him our location. Finally, we decided to turn in.

"Why don't you just light a fire?" Mark asked.

"It's against park rules. Too much risk of forest fires in these dry woods. If there's one thing we don't want back here it's a forest fire," Victor answered.

"Up at first light?" I asked as I entered my tent.

"Ten-four," answered Victor and Landon in unison, but I just got an odd look back from Mark.

I explained to him, "We track while it's light. So we wake up with the sun. Somebody's counting on us out there. It's not nice to keep lost, freezing people waiting so we get up at first light. You're going to bed early. You'll get your sleep."

During the night I heard a tent's zipper being unzipped. "Don't go south, you'll mess up the trail."

I heard a sleepy, "Okay," from Mark as I drifted off again. Then came the sound of brush crunching, leafs rustling, a few mild curses and a lot of shivering as Mark attempted to find his way in the pitch-black forest.

"Cassidy! Say something. Where are you? I can't see a thing!" he whispered loudly.

"Mark, please go back to sleep. We have a long day tomorrow."

I heard a brush against tent fabric.

"Okay, here we are." A tent was unzipped, zipped shut again, and then everything became quiet. My thoughts wandered to home but I checked them quickly knowing I'd start missing Rusty. I'd never get back to sleep if I let that happen.

We awoke to frost on the ground which wasn't a good sign. I was determined to find Carl that day. I didn't know how many nights he could survive out in the open. Every overnight search, I found myself cursing the darkness. I would track all night if it was possible to see, but tracking was hard enough during daylight; there was simply no way to do it in the dark.

In the morning we started our meal routine in reverse, with hot chocolate first to warm up stiff hands, then food. While the food was rehydrating I took down my tent and packed it for travel.

Mark shivered, rubbed his cold hands together and stomped around camp trying to stay warm.

"Hot chocolate does wonders. Put something hot in you and you'll feel better."

Victor and Landon went through the motions without complaint and were ready to hit the trail quickly.

"Mark, you miss some good photo opportunities in the early mornings."

"You are not a typical female," Mark said as he stood shivering.

"Thank you," I responded.

"All the women I know turn the thermostat up until everybody in the house is roasting. Then they complain about the cold as soon as they step outside, yet here you are as comfortable as the wildlife that lives out here."

"Who said the animals out here are comfortable? They might be cold too. I come up here prepared for the cold. If you plan ahead and expect it be cold, then it comes as no surprise. Grab something to eat and let's go. The sooner we hit the trail the sooner we find our ten sixty-five."

"Wh…where's your coat?" he asked.

"I don't need one, I have thermal underwear, a t-shirt, flannel shirt and sweatshirt on. I bet in a mile I take off the sweatshirt. The layers trap heat. I'm perfectly fine like this. Now grab your pack and let's go."

"She sure is impatient."

"I want to find Carl today. You've never been on a search before, so you don't know how critical time can be. I don't think I have to remind you what it feels like to be out in the wilderness alone, not knowing how you're going to get back home again. You've been there. Now Carl is in your shoes and he's counting on us."

That convinced him. "Right, so let's go," he said.

I looked around for Carl's footprints and found them covered with frost. I hoped the cold had frozen the footprints into the dirt but the thawing would deteriorate them, making it a mixed blessing.

Downward, ever downward we tracked until we were on the floor of the canyon. It seemed like I was always tracking in canyons but that's because these mountains were mountains from the floor up and canyon from the top down. So either way I was either above or inside a canyon of some kind.

Mark must have liked the scenery in the bottom of the canyon, or maybe I was tracking better, because I heard the *click, buzz* of his camera a lot. The trail became more difficult to read because the canyon was very rocky. I had to watch for sandy spots in between the rocks and ended up having to backtrack. Rocks were the curse of tracking. They offered very little information. I was frustrated at the slow pace of the search.

Once Victor figured Strict was up and about he checked in via radio. "Put Cassidy on," I heard Strict say.

"Hey, Strict, how's it going on your end?" I asked.

"Okay. You doing okay?"

"Yeah, I'm fine."

"It wasn't that long ago you were laid up pretty good."

"Strict, I'm fine, frustrated with the tracking, but fine. It sure is rocky here. Why do missing people always have to go for rocky places?"

"What's your twenty?"

"I don't know, that's Victor's job," I turned to Victor. "What's our twenty?"

Victor read the coordinates off the GPS and I relayed them to Strict.

"Hell," Strict said, "what's he doing there? You're doing great, kid, just stay on his trail."

"That's the plan."

Staying on Carl's trail was easier said than done. Occasionally he'd leave a partial track but any track at all gave me a rush of hope. I'd memorize the shape and direction and then head that way. The heel had a shape, the toe, the instep, the outer edge. They were all different so I could tell which part of the footprint I was seeing and imagine the rest, imagine what the step looked like, what the action looked like, where the next step should be. I was so focused on the faintness of the trail I didn't even notice the guys or what they were doing unless they spoke directly to me. They had to call me by name or I'd assume they were talking amongst themselves.

"Cassidy, lunch," Landon called out, aware that I'd track until I dropped unless he said something. On an easy trail, the subject of mealtime just came up naturally in our conversation. On a tough trail I'd become so absorbed in the tracking that I'd forget to eat. Without taking my eyes off the trail I reached up to a zippered side pocket and took out a stick of beef jerky and a sandwich bag of trail mix. Lunch. I tracked as I ate.

Carl had bedded down for the night under a low overhang. It had been an uneasy night but I was relieved he had made it through. I spent a little time trying to get a feel for his physical well-being. It was nighttime when the cold settled deep into the bones and the darkness seemed to last forever. I'd never been out in the woods needing help in the winter but had experienced it in the spring. I'd also camped out in the open in the winter. I knew the cold and how it pressed in and seemed to freeze a person from the inside out. Come on, Carl, I thought to myself, find a place to stop and just wait for us, your family is fine. They are in good hands. You could be out Christmas shopping for your little boys.

"Cassidy, quit thinking," Landon called out.

How did he know? He was getting as bad as Rusty. He knew as long as I stayed Dangerous Tracker Woman we'd be in good shape but if I thought too much my emotions would come into play. I needed to focus on the trail, only the trail. For some reason Victor never reminded me of lunch or admitted that he could read me like a book. I thought Victor and I made a good team, too, with slightly different interactions. Mark must have given Landon some questioning look because Landon started talking about our tracking mannerisms.

I got back on track, found Carl's footprints and followed easily for a little while. At least he hadn't headed straight for the rocks again. Carl's tracks were significantly different leading away from his sleeping spot. Maybe he was hiking in the cold but I feared it might be something worse. After a short time tracking I figured it out. Carl's feet were numb. He had tried stomping around to get some feeling back but that hadn't worked, so he continued stumbling along on unfeeling feet.

"Victor, Landon, we're looking at bad news here. I don't like this trail."

"Okay, how old is it?" Landon asked.

"A day. I found where he spent the night, but when he took off in the morning the trail was totally different. I think he's lost all feeling in his feet. Why is it the more urgent the trail, the harder it is to read?"

"It isn't, it just feels that way to you," Landon pointed out. The thought occurred to me that Landon knew me a little too well. I read the tracks, careful to pull all the information I could from them. They were erratic, clumsy, out of kilter. I followed them for a few hours as Carl's tracks began to wander aimlessly. He had found a place to sit, and seemed to gain some purpose as he rested because his trail straightened out for a bit, but as it deteriorated again I began to despair. At the end of a search wandering tracks indicated a lack of concentration, and this could be brought on by several physical problems, hypothermia and dehydration leading the list. I forced myself to slow down, watch the sign, but sensed time was growing short. This was important and couldn't be rushed or something might be missed. My tension began to trickle back to the team. We were all silent, tense, following the tracks with diminishing hope until we came to an end. Suddenly the tracks just ended at the bottom of a long drop off. Up above, the highway curved in a big hairpin turn, and where we were at the bottom, Carl's tracks had abruptly stopped. I examined the foot of the mountain but Carl's tracks went into the rocks and the only way to go was up. We looked above, listening to the cars as they zipped by far overhead. So near and yet so far.

I began climbing, watching for sign, even in the rocks. Victor and Landon spread out on either side of me, aware that if Carl had climbed he probably had not climbed straight up. The bank consisted of boulders meant to cut down on erosion. Maybe it did that, but it also made for risky climbing. We weren't sure whether to trust the rocks to stay in place or not, so we tested each one before using it.

"Cassidy? I'm onto it," said Victor from my left, and Landon and I both started climbing left.

"What have you got?" Landon asked him.

"Blood on the rocks."

Victor was the one who found Carl. He'd found a place in the rocks to rest. His hands were scraped and bloodied. His expression spoke volumes, not of physical pain but more of fatigue coupled with failure. He was stiff and cold. I stood there in amongst the rocks, numb with my own kind of cold. It was that icy feeling that crept in when I couldn't do anything, when fate was taken out of my hands. Mark stood at the bottom of the rocks, camera in hand. Victor and Landon had the situation under control so I climbed back down to Mark.

"And that's why we get up at daybreak," I said quietly. I set up a partial camp at the bottom of the canyon using my tent for shade. I opened up my stove and set out trail mix and water in case volunteers grew hungry. I cleared an area where people could talk and rest. As I was working, I heard the call go out to Strict. Ten sixty-five found. Ten forty-five D. Coordinates that gave our location. Confirmation that we were just off the highway. A request for a coroner. I walked in amongst the trees, waiting. I knew I'd have a job soon but right now I was fighting off that icy feeling that kept threatening to overwhelm me. Keep moving, Cass, just keep moving. Mark followed helplessly, unsure of what to do, wanting to help me, but aware I needed my space, too.

"What are we doing?" he finally asked.

"It's going to take a while for the coroner to get here," I told him. "We need an investigator and the coroner on scene. Once they arrive Victor and Landon can leave the body. We'll have a camp full of people. I'll make sure Victor and Landon get something to eat. They can rest in my tent if they need to trade off."

"What are they doing up there?"

"Guarding the body. Making sure predators don't get to it. One of them will stay up there until the others arrive. Maybe I'll take a turn. We'll be here for a while. Sometimes the coroner has to come up from LA. Make sure and eat dinner before it gets too dark."

It was a long afternoon. Landon climbed down to eat an early dinner and then climbed back up. Victor climbed down. I ate dinner with him and then grabbed a rifle and climbed up to take my turn on guard duty.

"You don't need to do this," Landon told me when I arrived at the body.

"I know, you'd stay up here all night rather than make me do my share. Go on. Nothing's coming after this body with a camp below and a highway above. We're just following procedure. I can sit here with a rifle as well as anybody else can."

I chose a rock and sat, rifle in hand, thinking about Carl, wondering how I could have gotten there sooner, and why tracking had to be so time consuming. I knew all the answers and with every call I'd been assigned, I asked myself the same questions. No matter what the condition of the person, I'd tell myself I could have tracked faster, could have gotten there sooner. The truth, of course, being that had I rushed we may have lost the trail completely.

Lights appeared up on the highway and men soon rappelled down. Finally a coroner's van parked behind the rescue squad and fire truck. It didn't take long for a news van to find the action.

I wanted out of there. My job was done. There was nothing I could do now but dwell on the situation and for me that kind of thinking was bad. Tracking required a lot of thinking, but once I hit the end of the trail it would change. Instead of analyzing and categorizing minuscule clues it reverted to a more emotional thought process. I needed something to occupy my mind, give it a job to do. I wandered in and out of the trees, staying within sight of the camp. I was trapped with my thoughts which were spiraling out of control.

"Stop, blaming yourself," Landon said out of the darkness.

"That's what I always do," I answered sadly.

"It wasn't your fault. It never is."

"It doesn't stop the feelings from escalating. I can't help it… If…"

"Nope, don't start with the 'what ifs'. You did your best, it's more than anybody else could have done. You got us here just like you were supposed to. So stop blaming yourself."

It was late at night when the four of us were finally able to follow the coroner and the other volunteers up onto the highway. Then we needed a ride back to base camp and to our vehicle. After returning the SUV to the compound we finally picked up our own cars and headed for home. It was quiet as we drove through the foothills and the junipers. I finally dropped Mark off at his parents' house.

"Sorry this call turned out for the worst," I said.

"There's nothing you could do to change that. I did manage to get some pictures although Landon is going to get on my case. He really wants to see if we can catch that morphing thing on film."

I almost smiled and said, "Mark, it's just a change in focus. Nothing is going to show up on film. If it does I'll… I don't know what I'll do except be really surprised. You didn't take any pictures of Carl, did you?"

"No, I didn't even go up there. But I did get some pictures of the reactions. You have my permission to take any pictures you don't want printed. If something looks or feels too personal to you, simply take it. I don't want to invade your privacy."

"Thanks. It's late and I need to get home."

"Good night."

I waited until he found his way inside and then drove home.

The house was dark when I arrived. Rusty hadn't heard about the search or he would have stayed up. I left my pack in the Jeep and quietly let myself in. I went to the bedroom and undressed in the dark, then remembered that I'd been camping for two days so I started the shower and got in. I had a head full of shampoo when Rusty came in and sat on the counter naked, waiting for me. I sure wished I didn't feel all jumbled up inside. Usually I invited him to join me, but emotionally I was still processing the aftermath of the search. He watched me quietly, an array of emotions crossing my face as I battled through the conflict in my mind. I rinsed off and without drying I went for my Rusty hug. I was so sad. Carl had been a little older than Rusty. His boys were five and seven. And he was gone… gone from their lives forever.

Rusty held me all wet, cold and depressed before wrapping me up in a towel. I dried off and then crawled into bed where I snuggled in close to Rusty, absorbing his comfort. He understood that I'd talk when I was able. He knew I was blaming myself but would get over it. It was pointless trying to convince me of anything until I worked through the emotions. How had I lived without him for so long? The only person who really understood me. The only person who unconditionally accepted and loved me anyway. How did I manage without him? It was hard to believe that we'd only been married four months.

"Oh, babe, it's okay, shhh, you just need sleep. It's so late. My dangerous tracker woman is back from the wilds," he continued, allowing me to listen to his voice, letting the peaceful sound of it seep into me. I cried quietly, working my way to a calm place where I could relax enough to sleep and in the morning when I didn't stir and he had to leave for work, he knew what a toll it had taken on me. The news was not good and he'd hear the basic story at work. Rusty would get off work and return home as soon as possible, well aware that I'd still be kicking myself.

It didn't help when Carl's story was splashed all over the news. "Trackers yesterday discovered the body of Carl Cranston just a few hundred feet from a nearby highway…" I was glad they hadn't filmed me in amongst the rescue party. Victor and Landon were shown for a moment. Mark was there for a brief second, looking a lot like a shabbily dressed cameraman. As usual, the flashing lights and uniforms showed up to the public eye while the dirty, backpack laden searchers faded into the background. When Carl's wife was shown I had to turn off the TV.

In the afternoon I tracked up into the hills. Shadow, my Shetland sheepdog with boundless energy, ran circles around me as I walked. I found the tracks of ground squirrels. They were short trails that ended at a hole in the ground at the base of a large juniper bush. Every so often I saw the squirrels sunning themselves in the sand, watching me pass by. I found deer tracks but already knew where they led and didn't plan to track them any further. It was peaceful wandering the hills, focusing on the ground. I came across an old coyote trail and followed it a little ways just to be tracking, aware I'd never find the animal as the tracks were at least a day old. Determined to cook a homemade meal for Rusty I went home early and found myself looking forward to eating some of my own food, too. Backpacker food couldn't take the place of real home cooking and I always returned from a search craving vegetables and sweets.

When Rusty came home stir-fry was sautéing in my big Texas skillet and the rice was cooking. I combined the sauce ingredients and then poured it all into the vegetables.

"A man came to the station looking for you today. I sent him to Strict. I didn't think you wanted Carl Cranston's family knocking on our door today. Did you watch the news?"

"Did you?" I asked him.

"Yeah, the guys called me in to watch it when they heard what the news announcement was about. I suspect you stopped watching about halfway through but you missed something."

"What's that?"

"You missed seeing the Cranston family thanking the mysterious search party who vanished at the sight of TV cameras."

"Victor and Landon were both on the news. I did see the first part."

"They were looking for you but thought they were looking for a man. Phillip Cranston was very surprised when he walked into the station and was sent to my office. He started thanking me for finding his son but I stopped him, turned the wedding picture around that sits on my desk and pointed to you. 'This is the guy you're looking for,' I told him, 'but she doesn't like a lot of attention and prefers to remain invisible.' He was shocked and sat on the chair in front of my desk. I told him how sorry I was about his son, that you felt it even more than me. We spent about half an hour talking about search and rescue, how a kid like you got into a job like that. He wanted to do something and I knew you didn't want anything from him so I sent him to Strict. I figured if he wanted to give something he could give it to the organization. They can always use donations to help buy better equipment."

"Good thinking. I wouldn't have been up to talking to Cranston's family today."

"I just wish you were able to see the good in what you do. Grieving family members don't track down the officers or volunteers involved unless they really care. It would have been so much easier for Phillip Cranston to sit back and do nothing but he wanted to thank you personally. That should tell you something."

Chapter 3

I don't often attend funerals but felt a need to attend Carl Cranston's and witness the family moving on. I only owned one suitable outfit, a little black dress that I'd been saving for a date with Rusty. I wore a black sweater over it and attempted to blend in with the others crowding the church building. As Phillip Cranston stood before the gathering speaking about his son, his eyes scanned the congregation until finally settling upon me. I shrank from his gaze but knew he had me pegged. A video was shown depicting Carl's life and I laughed and cried along with everyone else. A five-year-old in his dad's work boots, a ten-year-old holding up his first catch, Carl's high school graduation, then the pride on his face while holding his first son. When a picture appeared of Carl with his older boy the voice of his younger child suddenly piped up, "There's Three!" followed by the older brother arguing, "I'm not Three, I'm Carl the Third!" Their mother quickly shushed them both. Carl's sister read a short letter she'd written to her brother then a pastor spoke to their family and friends. It was comforting to see the family had a lot of support. They would be okay.

While filing out to leave, a man standing next to me asked, "How did you know Carl?"

"I didn't," I replied, not really knowing where my answer actually came from. "I guess I came to get to know him a little bit. I only knew him through his footprints, but I sensed a firm determination to help his family." Then I stopped or I'd have lost it again.

Phillip Cranston wasn't one to stick to formalities. Instead of lining up to shake hands with everybody who attended the service, I found him leaning back against my Jeep. I should have removed the JHSAR sticker in the window. A yellow fire hat was depicted on it and the letters stood for Joshua Hills Search and Rescue. As he stepped away from my vehicle there was a dust colored spot on the back of his black suit.

"Your husband was right, you do prefer to stay invisible. You're good at it, too. I never would have guessed if I hadn't seen your picture. You? You're the one who spent two days looking for my son? You're the tracker?"

"Yes, sir," I responded. Phillip Cranston had that authoritative look about him that made me immediately revert to my Marines background. He just looked like people called him *sir*, so I called him *sir*, too.

"Why? Why'd you go out?"

"Carl needed to be found. I find people."

"So I see. Did your husband tell you why I was looking for you?"

"Yes, and he was wise to send you to Lou Strickland."

"I'd still like to do something for you."

"We don't find someone hoping they'll hand over money, or do something for us. We are just trying to help people, and sometimes… sometimes we get there too late. I'm so sorry. I tracked down Carl hoping he'd be spending Christmas with his family. While tracking I imagined a father playing slot cars with his boys under the Christmas tree. I didn't know what Carl looked like or even if his sons liked cars. That's just the image that played through my mind. If Carl had been able to spend Christmas with his family that would have been the best reward I could ever receive." My voice trailed off and I felt myself close to tears again. At that moment I wanted to jump in my Jeep and take off, but the parking lot was full of people.

Mr. Cranston studied me. Standing before him I felt trapped and needed to do something, anything to work off the emotions. He decided to back off.

"Cassidy, thanks. I think this evening I'll go play slot cars with my grandsons. They don't really understand that their dad won't be back. But I'll be there for them. You can count on that."

I quickly decided to give up on the punching bag at the station. A cute blonde in a little black dress taking on the punching bag just sets the guys off for some reason. I received whistles, a few winks and smiles. Nobody ever took me seriously in a dress except Rusty, and that's because he knew I would only wear one for him. He understood it was an invitation, and he respected it by guarding and cultivating the mood.

"I need a locker. I really need a locker. I need to keep gym clothes here," I said, storming out on my way to Rusty's office. He wasn't there but I waved through Tom's window as I went by.

I put on the sweater as I crossed the parking lot.

"Cassidy!" I heard yelled from the station door. Rusty jogged up, and after quickly assessing my mood refrained from winking at me. He knew I wasn't at the station to lure him away. He might have been hoping, but he knew better. Perhaps he'd talked to the guys. Maybe my attitude showed through. "Will you stay in town?" he asked.

"Why?"

"Because… if you go home you'll change into jeans and cook dinner, and then we'll spend a long quiet night puttering around the house…"

"When will you get off? And what am I supposed to do in town dressed like this?"

"Can you Christmas shop, for just a little while? Then meet me at

Trujillo's at, oh, sixish?"

"Trujillo's? The bar or the restaurant?"

"The bar, we'll figure out the restaurant afterwards."

"Wow, I didn't know the power of a little black dress when I bought it."

"Will you?"

"Sure, maybe I can find something for your mom. Any ideas?"

"Forget Mom, she likes anything. Go to the antique mall and look for the most obscure band you can find on records."

"You're kidding! Who is this for?"

"Cody. He collects old records. Thirty-three and a third, seventy-eights, it doesn't matter; just find the oddest one in the bunch that's still playable."

"Rusty, records are before my time. I don't know what to look for!"

"Me, too. That's half the fun of it. Just see what you can find."

"Okay."

"Obscure bands? Sure we got obscure bands. Everybody in this place is obscure now, except maybe the Beatles and Elvis and we got them, too."

An old guy with gray, frizzy hair and thick glasses led me to a corner of the antique mall and showed me a booth full of boxes of thick vinyl records. The boxes were so heavy I couldn't move them.

"How do you know if the music is any good?" I asked.

I read his nametag. *Henery* is what it said. Odd name.

"You play it."

"Do you have a way to play it?"

"Sure, I got a 1954…"

"No, I mean just to test it out. I've never heard of these artists. How do I know what to buy?"

"You said obscure bands. You aren't going to find much good in obscure music anyway. I'll let you look. If you need any help flag down me, or Rhonda or Miss Molly. Don't know that we can help in your case but everybody's got an opinion."

I flipped through dozens of dusty old records until a title caught my eye. The Chocolate Watch Band. I smiled, how could you not like a group with a name like that? I slid the record from its sleeve and looked for scratches.

The Electric Prunes? Bubble Puppy? The Replacements? What were they replacing? How about Question Mark and the Mysterians? The Dixie Cups? Iron Butterfly? Okay, Cassidy, an odd name doesn't mean a group is obscure. Still…

The old, frizzy guy passed by on some errand, "Oh, Henery…" I called after him.

Hurrying off down the aisle he called back "No, he's the author. I'm

Henery the Eighth from Herman's Hermits."

Herman's Hermits? I looked through the box and found one of their records. Sure enough, there was a song called Henry the Eighth.

A woman wearing a pink sweater ambled by, and taking note of her name tag I said, "Help me, Rhonda. I don't know what I'm looking for."

"Sounds like you do to me," she answered.

This was puzzling. I knew I was blonde but normally I was pretty much with it.

"You still haven't found what you're looking for?" Miss Molly asked.

"Yeah, I mean no. I found it but I don't know what to buy. I'm supposed to find something for my brother-in-law who collects obscure music."

"I Had Too Much to Dream Last Night," Rhonda said.

"Me too," I agreed, "but this place is helping to get my mind off it."

"No, it's a song. By the Electric Prunes. Guess they thought they could get something moving with that one."

"I Ain't No Miracle Worker," said Miss Molly.

"I'm not expecting a miracle, I just need to make a choice."

"No, no, that's a song too. By The Chocolate Watch Band."

"Okay, I give up," I said totally befuddled. "I'm buying The Chocolate Watch Band, The Electric Prunes and Herman's Hermits just so I can tell Cody about this crazy conversation. It probably won't even sound crazy to him but he'll get a laugh out of watching me tell it."

It was dark when I left the antique mall so I drove to Trujillo's. I sat at the bar in my little black dress and nursed a margarita while I waited for Rusty.

"Hi, there," a man said as he sat down next to me. "Are you alone?"

"I'm waiting for someone," I answered.

"Can you talk while you're waiting?"

"I don't see why not."

"So, what do you do for a living?"

"I put dinner on the table every night by seven."

"You don't have a job?"

Rusty entered the bar and took a seat two stools down to listen.

"Yeah, I have a job, sort of. It's more like a vocation."

"Interesting. What do you sort of do for your job?"

"I lead guys on."

"You know, in some states that's illegal."

"Not the way I do it. Besides, most of the guys I lead on carry badges."

"Now you've got me curious. What kind of a job could a girl like you have that would lead the cops on? Undercover cop?"

"Who said they were cops? Lots of people carry badges. If I was an undercover cop do you think I'd be sitting here telling you about it? I don't think so."

"Right. So I guess it's safe for me to talk to you, if you aren't an undercover cop."

"Right."

"So what is it that you do?"

"You wouldn't believe me if I told you."

"Try me."

"You first."

"Okay, I sell things," he stated.

"What kinds of things?"

"Things that make the stresses of big business easier to handle."

"Oh yeah? Sorry if I'm being naïve here but it sounds like your job might be a little riskier than mine, if you know what I mean."

"I trust you. You just have that look about you. Now, what do you do for your job?"

"I'm a tracker."

"You're kidding."

"That's what everybody says. Look, if I wanted to fabricate a glamorous job for myself I'd say I was a movie star. Who would choose a tracker as a fake job?"

"Okay, you're right there. So you *are* a tracker?"

"Yeah, I lead guys on and find people. I follow tracks and bring in help when someone is lost in the woods."

"O…kay."

"Oops, I see my husband is here now, so I have to go. It was nice talking to you…"

"Stan. Stan the High Way Man."

"Um, right."

"And you are?"

"Cassidy. Have a good evening."

"You too."

I picked up my barely touched margarita and moved down two stools behind Stan.

"Rusty, next time you agree to meet me, *please*, just meet me! Having you hang around and wait is nerve wracking."

"And useful," he said quietly. "How do you do these things?"

"I didn't do anything. I just sat at the bar and he came up and talked to me."

"You're right, maybe you *are* a magnet for trouble." While Rusty was speaking he watched Stan behind me. He appeared nervous, which was unusual for Rusty. "These tall stools are uncomfortable, let's go find a table," he suggested, leading me away. We took a corner table where Rusty sat with his back to the wall so he could watch the room. I drank my margarita slowly while Rusty sipped his beer. He was obviously waiting for something.

A waitress set down chips and salsa.

Stan left the bar and approached another woman who was by herself. Rusty watched as he was turned away. Stan roamed the room socializing with several different people. Most of them were well dressed: people on their way home from work, including stressed out businessmen and career women.

The chips and salsa on the table magically disappeared even though I didn't remember eating any. If Rusty ate any he did it without looking at them, because he never took his eyes off the room.

A businessman approached Stan and there was a complicated handshake. Stan spoke to the man in an animated manner before leading him out the door. As they left Rusty relaxed.

"Where'd the chips go?" he asked.

"I don't know. Are you hungry?"

"Yeah."

"Me too, maybe the tortilla chip elves ate them."

"Tortilla chip elves make chips, they don't eat them," he pointed out.

"Thanks for sending me to the antique mall for the afternoon. That was just what I needed to get my mind off this morning."

"Did you find something?"

"I think so. We won't know for sure until we talk to Cody."

"What's with the black dress?"

"I went to Carl Cranston's memorial service. I wore a sweater over the dress."

"Much to the disappointment of the guys there."

"Rusty! It was a funeral. Guys don't watch for girls in little black dresses at funerals!"

"They don't?"

"Okay, maybe they do. I wore the sweater over it because it seemed more appropriate. I found out Phillip Cranston has eagle eyes. He spotted me right away."

"And?"

"He's going to play slot cars with his grandsons."

"Well, at least you didn't have a boring day at home. I think you ought to avoid bars though. Pretty soon Tom's going to ask you to finish academy and go undercover. All you have to do is enter a bar and the most wanted person in the place hones in on you. I could have sat here with you for an hour and never recognized Stan, but you sit and talk to him for ten minutes and get his life story."

"I didn't mean to."

"I know, that's just my point. You do these things without even trying."

"Get me a permit to carry concealed and I can just hang out and reel in the felons."

"No. You'd put me out of a job."

"Yeah, right."

"Okay, then, no, it's too dangerous."

"Forget about Stan. We're both here, all dressed up, ready for a night on the town, so what do you want to do?"

"Let's get a bite to eat, then there's someplace better we should go."

"Really? Where?"

"Nancy Schroeder throws a Christmas party every year. Since we're in town and all dressed for a party we ought to go. It'll be fun."

"You think I might catch Schroeder smiling?"

"If you leave the sweater in the car," he said teasingly. "He's not as gruff as you make him out to be, and despite his attitude he really does like you. He says you're good for me. Before I met you, he used to call me at the office late at night and tell me to go home. He used to yell at me for being too impulsive."

"You? You're about the least impulsive person I've ever met."

"When there was only myself to consider, it didn't take much thinking. If something needed to be done, I did it," he said dipping a taquito into nacho cheese sauce. "When we met I felt like I should watch out for you. Widow, living all alone. You needed a man to call on. I didn't know at the time that you knew more about cars than I did or that you were as good a shot as me. At first Schroeder thought it was a good thing. Then, when he realized you got into a hell of a lot more trouble than I ever did, he got worried. He'd seen his share of women trouble makers, embezzlers, bank robbers, drug dealers, hookers, women just on the wrong side of the law. You didn't fit into that mold. Eventually, he concluded you were on our side and that your talents were needed on our side, too."

I finished off my share of the taquitos.

"So, what kind of conclusion did he come to?" I asked, wondering how Schroeder thought of me now.

"He hasn't. Nobody has. You are an ongoing mystery with two sides that are as different as night and day. One side is a very capable tracker, scout and outdoorswoman. The other is this adorable young woman who all the guys want to guard and protect. They see a darker side of the city, full of people and situations they don't want you involved in. As soon as there's a crime that involves tracks everybody's all gung ho, ready to watch you in action. Then just as quickly they stop to reconsider. If it's a scene of violence they don't want you exposed to it because that reminds them of the violence you've already seen. If it's an apprehension, they don't want to bring you into a potentially dangerous situation. Schroeder knows you'll never be a cop, and neither one of us wants to see that happen. He almost kept you out of reserve academy but knew you had talent and he realized to really tap into that talent you needed to complete academy. You convinced him that you needed the training. So basically, where we stand now is you have the qualifications if Schroeder needs you and the training and authority to defend yourself if put in a tight spot. Now the goal is to make sure you don't get into any tight spots. But Schroeder does like you and says you are good for me. He's also glad to see you working with Strict. So," he said, standing and reaching for his wallet, "you ready to go party?"

"Sure, but do you really think this dress is alright?" I asked, turning this way and that.

"Ooo yeah," he said with a mischievous gleam in his eye. He wasn't very convincing. Rusty's reaction made me wonder who else would be there.

The Schroeders lived in a large, two story home surrounded by neatly trimmed and rounded landscaping bushes and a seasonally dormant flower garden. A wreath hung on the door and Christmas music could be heard playing inside. A young boy dressed in Superman pajamas greeted us at the door.

"Scotty! It's your Grandma's party. She gets to answer the door," a woman's voice scolded. Scotty ran off, taking a flying leap and landing square in the middle of the living room sofa. "Good evening, Rusty, come on in." Rusty showed me in the front door where introductions were exchanged.

"Linda, this is Cassidy. Cassidy, this is Linda, Schroeder's youngest daughter. Last I heard you had two boys."

"Scotty and Nate, and as soon as I get them upstairs to bed the party can really get started. Dad told me you recently got married, Rusty. He didn't tell me you robbed the cradle!"

"I didn't," Rusty said a little defensively. "Cassidy is your age and the wedding was in July. That's hardly robbing the cradle."

"I think last I saw Dad he was letting Nate run his train. Mom is in the den with the others."

"Thanks. Cassidy, you've gotta see this." Rusty grabbed my hand and led me to a room that would have been a library or a study in anybody else's house. We stood in the doorway and watched.

"What's this?" Schroeder asked his little grandson. Nate was maybe two.

"Chain!" he said enthusiastically.

"Good boy! Make it go. Not too fast, it'll crash." The train slowly moved around the track, *clickety clacking* along but much too slowly for Nate. Schroeder stood holding the boy close. He pointed to the town, carefully laid out on the train board. "Can you find a doggy? Where's the doggy?" Nate pointed. "Good boy! Now where's the horsey?" Nate squirmed to get down and ran over to the country side of the board. Three tiny HO scale horses stood in an HO scale corral. "What does a horsy say?"

"Neigh, neigh!" said Nate.

"And what does the doggy say?"

"Woof, woof."

"And where's the boy? Do you see a boy like you?" Schroeder asked.

Nate looked and looked. Tiny HO people walked the sidewalks of the town. This was like *Where's Waldo?*

"Up!" Nate called, needing a bird's eye view.

"He rearranges all the people when we come so they are never in the same place," Scotty informed us. "I have a store named after me in Grandpa's town. It says *Scotty's Toy Shop* on the sign. Nate has an ice cream store named after him. Nate, look for the boy in the park! There's always kids in the park."

Rusty led me away. "So much for gruff old Schroeder," he observed. We went to the den and joined the group. I knew Landon was there before I actually saw him. I felt his stare from across the room. Landon's gaze felt much different from Rusty's. When Rusty looked at me it felt as if he was savoring the view. It was slow, sensuous and pleasurable, making a woman desire more. Landon's look was piercing and intense. I blamed the little black dress.

"Rusty! Cassidy! I'm so glad you could come!" Nancy gushed. She was wearing an emerald green sweater dress adorned with bright red jewelry. The Christmas tree was just as colorfully coordinated as she was. Shiny gold and red balls hung amongst antique ornaments. Shimmering tinsel and garland spiraled down in neat, precise drapes. Plates of divinity, fudge, sweet breads, brownies and other homemade candies dotted the tabletops. Nancy pinned two little, homemade Christmas pins to my dress and another set to the lapel of Rusty's coat. "For the benefit of those not in law enforcement we are playing a little game. If you talk in codes or acronyms and someone catches you, you lose a pin. If you catch someone talking in codes they have to give you their pin."

"Okay!" Linda announced. "The kids are officially in bed with orders to stay upstairs. You are welcome to spread out and make yourselves at home. I'm taking the hors d'oeuvre out of the oven."

The doorbell rang and Nancy rushed off to answer it while her guests started milling around the room. The Christmas cards placed on the mantle drew my attention and I admired several depicting nature views. What really intrigued me though was the possibility of learning Schroeder's first name. At last, some clues! Surely someone had written a greeting and called him by name. I reasoned that, if the Schroeders wanted their cards to remain private, they wouldn't have them on display. Besides, I wasn't planning on reading the notes, I just wanted to see the names written inside. "Schroeder and Nancy," "Nancy, Schroeder and family," "Nancy, Schroeder and anybody else who might be reading this…" that last one kind of caught me by surprise. No one, not one person, had called Schroeder by any name other than Schroeder.

"Good evening, Cassidy," came a voice from over my shoulder. I jumped. I thought it was Rusty, since he knew how curious I was.

As I turned around I said pleasantly and a bit nervously, "Hi, Schroeder, I am dying of curiosity. Is there *anybody* who calls you by your first name? Anybody at all?"

"No."

"Not even your mom? What does your mom call you?"

"Schroeder."

"Even your mom calls you by your last name?"

"Yes."

"What does she call your brothers and sisters?"

"They actually have first names. If I show you *why* she calls me Schroeder will you quit looking for my first name?"

"I doubt it. I know I could find out what it is if I really wanted to dig. I just don't like to pry and it feels invasive to search for it. I'm a tracker, not an archeologist. I was hoping someone might have left a few tracks on your mantle."

"Follow me."

"If this involves a picture of a little blonde boy at a toy piano…"

He suddenly turned around.

"You're kidding," I said apologetically, "just like in the cartoon strip?"

"I took lessons real early," he said, leading me back to the room with the train set. "In those days they didn't start teaching kids until much older. I started at six and kept at it through elementary school. In junior high sports took over. It wasn't cool to play piano. Football was cool. I only played the piano for my own pleasure until I grew up and then I relearned the value of it. I branched out, still for my own enjoyment, but at least I didn't lose it. I mostly play classical, a little rag, some of my favorite popular tunes. I never cared much for complexity as long as I could perfect an easier version, so I'll never be a master piano player."

"Will you play for us?"

"No. Maybe someday if it's just for you and Rusty. Even though I enjoy it, and others do too, it doesn't fit in with the job description. The name still fits because the guys call each other by their last names a lot anyway. So I'm just Schroeder. Even Nancy calls me Schroeder. Here," he said, handing me an old black and white photo. Pictured was a full sized piano and there he was playing as a young boy with slicked back hair and wearing an intelligent gleam in his eye. He was dressed in a white button down shirt and tie, pressed black slacks and shiny black shoes. "It was my first recital. I had to play three pieces."

"There's no music."

"We were required to memorize all our recital pieces. Actually, now I credit the memorization I did at such a young age with helping me to easily recall descriptions and numbers at work. I remember details much easier than most people my age. I think it's because I started early."

"Did you play Beethoven?"

"Yeah, I know several works by Beethoven. And, yes, I can play *Linus and Lucy*."

"Schroeder?"

"Yeah?"

"Thanks. It's nice to know you're a real person. I'm surprised you told me, though."

"I trust you."

"The last guy who said that to me probably got arrested for it."

"Oh yeah? Who was that?"

"Stan. I don't know his last name. Sells drugs at Trujillo's, well, he did until today. Based on Rusty's reactions, they brought him in nice and quiet."

"We've been after that guy for weeks, only had a general description of him from people who didn't want to snitch. I've got to hear this."

"Ask Rusty, I'm not sure exactly what happened except that I talked to the guy for about five minutes and then Rusty watched the room very carefully. Rusty can probably tell you what really happened."

Linda brought a tray of stuffed mushrooms to the buffet table, so I made my way across the room. The aroma of Italian cuisine was coming from the kitchen. No wonder Rusty only wanted an appetizer at Trujillo's. Rusty was standing with a group of guys, a plate full of Christmas candy in one hand. Schroeder had joined them. I selected a couple of stuffed mushrooms, placing them on a small snowman plate.

Glancing up, I realized Landon was near, his eyes resting on my body, studying me up and down.

"Ten eleven," he said quietly.

"Landon, you said that on purpose."

"So I did." He removed his pin and stepped forward, glancing at the dress, wondering where he could pin it. I saved him the trouble and I took it from him.

"What do you mean, ten eleven?" I said, handing it back.

"Think about it."

Ten eleven meant, "identify this frequency", oh, duh. At least his sense of humor was intact.

"Rarely," I replied.

He fiddled with the pin. "I heard about your ten fifteen," he said, stepping closer. A ten fifteen was a prisoner in custody. So Stan *had* been picked up.

"He wasn't mine. I just talked to him for five minutes. Ten three," I said nervously. Stop transmitting. I handed the pin back to him. Nancy, this game of yours isn't working for me at all, I thought.

"Ten one," he replied. "Ten nine." Reception is poor, repeat last transmission. He removed another pin. Now I had to come up with two ten codes.

"Landon, ten three or you are going to be a ten ninety-one D." Stop transmitting or you'll be a dead animal. Okay, so it was lame.

"Ten four," he said, smiling. He looked at me, amused now.

"Okay, one pin, just one, your game is over."

As Landon stepped forward, Rusty asked, "Did I hear a ten sixty-seven?" A call for help?

"Not quite," I answered, "he's just a ten twenty-nine M." Wanted for a misdemeanor.

"Ten twenty-nine H," Rusty warned Landon, tossing him a pin. Caution-severe hazard potential.

Landon stepped forward, attached one pin to my dress gently and left with a smile.

"I'm glad he didn't get into the penal codes. He'd have lost me," I commented as Landon walked away.

"Why do you let him pull things like that?"

"He knows his limits."

"Does he still give you trouble on the job?"

"No, I think it's this little black dress."

Landon worked the game to his advantage collecting pins from the guys, and then "accidentally" needing to pin them on the girls. I think Nancy was onto his little pursuit, but everyone was having fun, so she let him be. The game backfired royally. Codes and acronyms flew and little Christmas pins were being actively exchanged. I'm not sure who won the game. Landon certainly scored, but Terry Brooks ended up with the most pins, probably because she enjoyed Landon's slips.

"That dress is just begging to come off," Rusty whispered as he brushed past me. A shiver went up my spine. That rascal, he knew exactly how to tease me. I thought of the long drive home through the dark hills. Okay, two could play at this game. I found my purse and brought it to the powder room where I locked the door behind me. Then I quickly removed my underwear and balled up my bra and panties small enough to stuff into my purse. I turned this way and that, studying my reflection in the mirror to make sure it wasn't *too* obvious. I freshened my make-up to convince anyone who might be watching that my visit to the powder room had been for a legitimate reason. Later in the evening as I passed Rusty I took the opportunity to plant my bra in his right hand coat pocket. He was standing with a group of officers. I didn't see his initial reaction but I stood off at a distance and watched as he fingered the lacy, slinky material in his pocket. Occasionally he'd glance around searching for me.

"Why are you hiding?" Nancy asked.

"I'm playing games with Rusty," I admitted.

She scanned the room until she found Rusty. "So I see!"

"You do?" I blushed. I didn't realize it was *that* obvious.

"That man is going to jump your bones before you get home."

"Nancy!" I gasped.

Rusty glanced around the room again, hand in pocket. He turned back to the group, but it was obvious that he wasn't listening.

"Don't be mean to him. The poor man. What did you do?"

"Nancy!"

"What? Just because I'm fifty-five doesn't mean I can't act like I'm twenty again. A woman my age needs a few tricks up her sleeve, too."

"I'm sure you've already thought of most of them. I slipped my bra into his pocket."

"Oh, you *didn't*!" she said laughing.

"He started it."

Rusty glanced at his plate, downed the last two hors d'oeuvre and headed back to the buffet table, all the while casually glancing around the room.

"You get out there," Nancy insisted. "I'm going to check the tortellini. You'll be lucky to make it through dinner."

I sauntered up to the buffet table. Rusty ran a hand up my hip as he moved past me, noting the obvious lack of underwear.

"You want them?" I whispered.

He didn't have to answer. His eyes said it all. He wasn't interested in the panties. He wanted more.

"You sure know how to torture a guy," he whispered back.

"You want me to stop?"

"I didn't say that."

"I don't have much more I can take off," I revealed quietly.

I absentmindedly placed a couple of hors d'oeuvre on my plate and walked away. Let him stew. Just knowing I was walking around with nothing on under my dress was enough to get his imagination going. He abandoned the food and sat on the couch watching the room. I mingled between each group of guests. Sometimes it was small talk: who are you and how do you fit in here? Sometimes it was cops deep in shop talk. The officers were exchanging stories of odd pullovers. There was the guy who insisted he had to get his wife to the hospital but there was no woman in the car. He'd been in such a rush he'd driven off without his wife. She had to call a cab, but the driver wouldn't take her since she was in labor, so an ambulance was called. The expectant father was frantically trying to track down his furious wife, and the baby was nearly born by the time he reached the hospital. Then there was the woman on her way to work at a bikini bar. The officer asked for her ID, but it was in her purse and locked in the trunk. She was too drunk to even tie a knot and her bikini top kept popping loose. She ended up in detox wearing only half a bikini to sleep it off.

"There was this one guy I pulled over," Ben Tomlin started. "He was driving a rental car erratically down Desert Boulevard. Claims he just got out of the hospital and that he was attacked by a tiger. A tiger? I said, 'Yeah right, like tigers run loose in the middle of the desert,' and I gave him a ticket for reckless driving and speeding. Can you imagine trying to get away with that?"

Everybody laughed with the exception of Rusty, Landon and myself. We still clearly remembered the tiger loose in the desert. Rusty caught my eye and patted the couch beside him. I made my way across the room and joined him.

"Let's get out of here," he said.

"We can't. Nancy's betting we won't last through dinner," I answered quietly.

"We won't."

"Aw, come on, you can make it through a plate of tortellini. Just think what could be done with all that sauce. We've never done it Italian style before."

"Cass... do you know what you're doing?"

"Yeah, I'm stalking."

"Stalking."

"Yeah, just wait until I finally get to touch you. It'll be worth the wait."

I've never seen a man so anxious to get his hands on a plate of tortellini. I laughed quietly as he pretended to eat slowly and make conversation. He politely turned down Black Forest cake, insisting everything had been so good, he didn't have room for dessert. Then he did his best to herd me out the door while making polite comments about the great party.

I heard Nancy mutter, "I gotta give him credit, he made it through dinner."

I slid onto the passenger seat of the Explorer and Rusty gave me a long look before starting up the engine. The lights of the Schroeders' neighborhood passed by slowly, cheerful Christmas lights shining in the night.

The mood in the truck was not cheerful. It was charged. It was seriously charged. It was find-a-dark-place-and-park charged. The only problem being that there wouldn't be any dark places until after we left town and started up into the hills. Rusty pulled off onto a lonely dirt road, bumped along it a little ways then parked. Oh man, those eyes spoke volumes.

"You're sure? You don't mind?"

"Fold down the seats."

He jumped out and pulled the latch, quickly folding the backseats down. Rusty took off his coat and crawled into the Explorer's expanded luggage compartment. It was like being in the hideout. No headroom, barely enough floor space, but it didn't matter. I crawled from the front seat to the back giving him a full view down the front of my spaghetti strapped dress.

"Cass, come here. Every swish of that dress, every touch of that bra in my pocket, every look across the room... What am I going to do with you? You drive me crazy."

I'd never seen him quite so aroused before. Rusty seemed to be at odds kneeling in the back of the truck gazing at me with so much longing, it looked as though he was going to explode. Yet he seemed to be holding back. I had been prepared for an all out attack. Hell, I wouldn't have asked for one if I wasn't prepared for it. I motioned him closer. As I started unbuttoning his shirt he went straight for the belt and then the clasp. We didn't even wait for him to undress. His loose, half unbuttoned shirt provided caresses and the cold belt buckle sliding up and down my side delivered a shiver of stimulation. The change in his pockets clunked with every movement and the force of his lovemaking filled me. I clutched at him, as the waves grew stronger. He looked at me in surprise as I lifted him off the floor of the truck in a sudden flurry of excitement and then we both laughed as we lost the rhythm. The Explorer rocked and the movement flowed through and around me in a rough and tumble romp in the back of the truck. Afterwards I realized I was still halfway in the dress, too. The spaghetti straps were down around my waist and the skirt was bunched up in a wrinkled mess. The smell of sex was everywhere. The windows were fogged. The night was freezing and we were torn between making a quick drive for the house or snuggling closer. I popped the driver's seat forward and Rusty rested against the back of it. Then I climbed into his sticky, wet lap, snuggling close. He pulled his coat over us and we lay there just enjoying the closeness, the warm dampness, the moment.

Only being married four months didn't seem to lessen the desire to learn about each other more intimately. We enjoyed the familiarity of our relationship in some ways, but in others each experience was new and exciting. We had sex, nice polite, consensual sex. Hot, steamy, touchy sex. Playful couch sex. We always knew what the other wanted but we were still actively exploring the other side of our relationship.

"Why did you hold back?" I quietly asked into the folds of his loose shirt.

"I could hear my dad's voice, his words were echoing through my brain during the party, 'Don't let the act become more important than the person,' he'd warn me."

"If the person flat out begs for the act, it's okay," I gently advised him. "I won't give you mixed signals."

"Still, I don't want it to be one-sided."

"Rusty, I'm yours. Whenever you want me, I consider myself yours. I wouldn't have married you if I hadn't made that commitment."

He pulled me closer, carefully mulling over my words.

The cold of the night seeped through the foggy windows and forced its way into the truck. Rusty opened the side door to get out and pop the driver's seat back into place, but a chorus of raucous barking erupted nearby. I instinctively shrank into Rusty. I knew the bark of a dog wasn't necessarily bad and it probably came from a pet confined to a nearby backyard. I knew dogs were usually friendly but a large, barking dog now struck terror into me. Understanding my fear, he slammed the door shut.

"Come here, it's okay," he said gently.

"I know. It's all right. Just a first reaction."

"Can I take away those memories? Just slip them out of your head and give them to me."

"I wouldn't consider it even if it was possible, not even for a minute."

He crawled into the front of the truck and pushed back the driver's seat from the inside. I wriggled out from my wrinkled mess of a dress and pulled on his sports coat, then crawled into the front seat. We drove home, heater blowing, toes still cold, hearts warm. After a short while the truck became toasty warm and I let the coat fall loose.

"Don't get in a wreck or we'll never hear the end of this," I joked.

He pulled into our driveway and parked the Explorer next to my Jeep. I was grateful that our nearest neighbors lived a quarter mile away as I left the truck wearing only Rusty's sport coat. I tender-footed it to the front door and stood on the warmer doormat. He unlocked the front door and we made our way to the den where Rusty lit a quick fire while I let Shadow outside.

"We should buy one of those soft fur rugs for cuddling in front of the fireplace," I commented. "We sure enjoyed the fireplace on our honeymoon, partly because of that soft rug."

I found a blanket and laid it out in front of the fireplace and curled up in it. Rusty changed into lounge pants and lay down behind me. Pretty soon his hands wandered. I turned so I could see him.

"Again?" I asked playfully.

"My hands are jealous," he answered.

"Your hands can do anything they want. You have magic fingers. Anything is possible with magic."

"You seem so comfortable without clothes. Were you always that way?"

"No. Not at all."

"Why?"

"It wasn't acceptable. In the real world clothes are required."

"Oh come on, surely Jack…"

"No, Rusty, don't. That was another life. I don't want to live in that life anymore. I prefer this one."

My words appeared to catch him by surprise. I'd spoken about my first husband before. It just felt so long ago, so far away. I barely remembered what Jack looked like, especially after his pictures had been destroyed in a fire. There was no way to bring back the fading memories so it seemed best to let them go.

"You're willing to talk about being beaten, shot at and stalked, but not about Jack? Was he mean to you?"

"No, not at all. He was kind and dashing and… regimented. I guess regimented is the best word for him. We were in the service. Everything is regimented in the service and he fit in well with that, in his personal life as well as his work. He never understood my yearning for the mountains, the need to feel earth beneath my feet. The military was his life and he was comfortable as long as he was in his military bubble. So I'd go off to the mountains where I could think and breathe. He never hurt me, he was always kind to me, but I never felt free with him. I would never have been free with him. You free me."

"He didn't know what he was missing."

Chapter 4

The next morning Mark stopped by for a visit but he appeared to be preoccupied, not his typical easygoing self. He spread out the tracking pictures on the kitchen table in the same order as they'd been taken. My first impression was they appeared to be nothing special, but Mark didn't see them that way. He was used to spreading out a series of boring pictures then selecting the good ones. What I saw captured on film was a woman either staring at the ground or squatting down, puzzling over something she was studying. I'd warned him that tracking wouldn't be interesting to the viewer. He pulled out nine pictures and arranged them in a three-by-three grid. The nine he'd selected had been well chosen, starting with the rescue trucks on the road with a group of searchers in conversation, then a shot of Victor, Landon and myself while on the trail, photographed from the back with our bodies leaning forward beneath heavy packs. There were several of me tracking, then another shot of the three of us again, followed by an image of the fire trucks and coroner's van parked at the top of the drop off. The last picture showed me sitting alone. He had really zoomed in and it was obvious that he wanted the dirt, the grime, the sadness, and dedication to the job to come through this one picture. I was sitting with my back against a rock, my feet propped up, a rifle across my knees. My face was dirty. Sweat and tears streaked the dirt. My hair was windblown and my eyes spoke volumes about hard work and defeat. I took a moment to stuff away the memories it brought to mind. It may not have been a pretty picture, but it certainly was a truthful one.

"Do you really think people will buy pictures like these?"

"I think the stalking ones will go over better but I'm not sure about the ones from the search. They might be a bit too emotional for some people, especially since I think some word of explanation should accompany the pictures. Better yet, I think these pictures would make a good documentary article about search and rescue, something that really demonstrates what it's all about. There are several publications who would buy it."

"Strict would like that. Any plug for search and rescue helps our efforts."

"How's that?"

"The county supplies us with basic equipment. If we want something better, it comes out of our own pockets or from donations. It's a tight budget and we always know what piece of equipment is next on our list because something breaks or a new technology emerges, or we just find we need something that isn't available to us yet. Most search and rescue teams work the same way, so an article like that could help search teams nationwide."

"What piece of equipment is your team looking at right now?"

"Strict would be the one to ask about that. There are many different teams in our organization and mine has minimal requirements. Personally, I've got my eye on a bulletproof vest and a rifle."

"Why would you need a bulletproof vest?"

"Because I tend to get shot at. So far I've been hit twice. I was wearing a borrowed Kevlar vest the first time."

"And the second time?"

"The second time they got me." I shrugged it off. "It was minor compared to most of my misadventures, but it scared everyone and I don't like scaring the team."

"The article wouldn't pay as much to you personally."

"You know I'm not trying to make money off this and I'd prefer as little recognition as possible."

"You want to buy something that could save your life but you aren't interested in the money you could get out of this?"

"Mark, as far as I'm concerned this is your work. You should get the pay for it. A vest will turn up eventually. In the meantime… I just need to be careful."

"I'll have to get permission from Victor, Landon and Kelly to use their pictures."

"That shouldn't be a problem. Victor is the one you should be the most concerned with, but he hardly shows up in these pictures. You know Landon will say 'yes' and Kelly is a lot like Landon except he's more easygoing and would enjoy the idea of being in some of your work."

"So you agree an article would be the way to go?"

"I think an article would do the most good and reach the most people. Some people don't even know there are teams they could call on. It would be educational and would benefit the search and rescue volunteers too."

"Okay, now, I want to show you something else, in these same pictures. Can you see it?"

"What am I looking for?"

"Some of the pictures are different."

This was supposed to be one of my stronger suits, finding the oddity amongst the ordinary. I ruled out all the middle pictures taken of me just following the trail. It had to be at the beginning or the end of the search. And then it hit me: the morph. Oh, man. I went back to the start of the search. There I was speaking with Kelly, followed by me tracking along the road, then finally climbing over the bank where Carl had left the road. I remembered the feeling of doom as I followed Carl's tracks down his trail further and further away from anything safe and familiar. Why don't people stay where they know it's safe? Following the road would have taken Carl time but he surely would have survived the walk. Leaving safety often leads to trouble for the inexperienced. Studying the pictures shot after stopping at the pine needles, I took out the three pictures taken before and then after. Then I took out two more. Mark smiled, it was almost a mischievous, Grinchy-type smile. It looked eerie on him.

I studied the pictures. Something did seem odd between the two sets. The whole mood of the picture changed. But the only thing that changed in the pictures was me. I went from cute Cassidy to Dangerous Tracker Woman but there were no *visual* differences, only a distinct subconscious shift which had taken place between the frames. But it was there and there's no denying it had happened. I wasn't alone in my assessment. Mark had seen the change or he wouldn't have pointed it out to me.

"Has Landon seen these pictures yet?"

"No, Mom and Dad looked at them but they couldn't see it, couldn't see why I had wanted to take pictures of you tracking. Couldn't see why you would wander around in the woods staring at the ground. They are just tuned differently. They are jolly old people and I love them like that, but they will never understand the life you lead. They liked the stalking pictures. They asked who has tame deer around here. They thought it was nice that you got to pet them. They had no idea how much trouble you went to just to touch that doe."

"So you, your parents and I are the only ones who have seen them?"

"Yeah, now that I think about it Mom did comment about one picture." He looked through the photos spread across the table and chose one that had been taken after the search was over. It was the one of me with Victor's rifle across my knees, tears running down my cheeks through the grime from the trail, a lost and lonely expression on my face. "She said, 'How could they do that to her? It breaks my heart to see Cassidy like that.' I told her, 'Mom, they don't do that to her. She chooses to do it so others won't feel like that.'"

"Maybe that's the picture you should use if you write an article. If your mom understood it, maybe that's what the average person will respond to as well."

"It depends on the publication that prints it. Print that picture in a family magazine and the anti-gun people will hit the roof."

"Yeah, okay, I can see that. Can you figure out what changes the mood in these pictures? I can't see anything different. Same me, same trees, same trail but it's totally different."

"I know. I'd like to see what Landon and Rusty see in them."

"Hello?" Landon asked.

"Hey! Mark has some pictures he'd like to ask you about. Barbecue at seven?"

"Barbecue?"

"Mark is tired of his mom's casseroles so we are having anti-casserole."

"Ah, I see."

"In this case barbecue doesn't mean drowned in barbecue sauce. It means cooked on the grill."

"Okay."

Before dinner Mark showed Landon the tracking shots he wanted to use and asked him to sign a release form granting permission to use his picture. They discussed various angles the article could cover, while I was in and out of the conversation, getting dinner ready.

"What do you call this dish?" Landon asked.

"Well, on the trail I call it mayo-jar steak, but when I'm at home and it hasn't been packed in a mayonnaise jar I guess it's just plain teriyaki steak. It's a lot better after being packed around in the mountains and cooked over a campfire. I'd bring it on a search but I usually have to grab my pack and run when Strict calls."

Landon pushed back in his chair with a contented sigh. "Can I see the rest of the pictures?" he asked Mark.

"Yeah, when we have room to spread them out. I want you and Rusty to both look at them."

I got up to clear away dishes. "Wait for me, I'm dying of curiosity, too," I said.

After rinsing the dinnerware and putting it in the dishwasher, I left the pots and pans in the sink to wash later.

Mark placed the pictures on the table in the order they had been taken. Rusty and Landon bent over them. Landon was immediately drawn to the beginning of the search.

"Whoa, that is so weird," he said softly.

"What is?" asked Rusty.

"Look, cute Cassidy, cute Cassidy, cute Cassidy, dangerous Cassidy."

"What makes them different though? Mark and I can't figure it out. One set is cheery and adventurous while the other is almost gloomy but nothing in the picture has changed."

"How far apart were they taken?" Rusty asked.

"Only seconds. You're only looking at maybe thirty seconds total in these six pictures," Mark replied.

"That *is* weird," said Rusty. "You're sure a cloud didn't block the sun or something?"

"The lighting looks the same, it's just the mood that changes," Mark said.

"But I can't see any mood change. Everything looks the same, it only *feels* different," Landon added.

"That's what's weird about it," Mark said.

"Something's got to be different. Cassidy, where's your magnifying glass?" Landon asked.

"In my pack," I answered. I left the table to go to the garage and retrieve it.

The guys pondered over the pictures, and theories were tossed about, but we couldn't decide exactly what the difference was between the cute me and Dangerous Tracker Woman.

"Do you think you got some ill vibes off the trail?" Landon asked. "You piece things together as you track. Did you have some idea even at that point that Cranston wasn't going to make it?"

"No, it wasn't until he bedded down for the night that I began to lose hope. I was still very positive at this point."

"I mean subconsciously," Landon said. "Maybe your mind knew something even though you weren't actually thinking it on purpose."

"I don't think so. Is that even possible?"

"Just as possible as you morphing from cute Cassidy to Dangerous Tracker Woman," Rusty suggested.

"But look at this," I said, picking out the photo that Hazel had noticed. "Two days of grime, rifle in hand, totally miserable but it's back to normal old me."

"Let me see that," Rusty said. "What were you doing?"

"Guarding the body."

"Wilson, I ought to wring your neck."

"No, Rusty, I went up to fill my post, and he offered to stay, but I needed to do my share. I would have felt the same no matter where I was."

We examined the pictures through the whole search. Dangerous Cassidy faded when I wasn't tracking, but the more intense the search, the more it appeared that a cloud hung over me. When I was tracking, though, I hadn't felt gloomy. I felt comfortable. Tracking was what I did best and it came most naturally. So the cloud of doom felt rather odd when I studied the pictures.

We never solved the mystery. We just agreed that there was something visible in the pictures, yet not one of us were able to identify the source.

Chapter 5

The next day I drove into town after leaving a note for Rusty on our new white board, "10 am Gone grocery shopping, ETA 1 pm". Then I hopped in the Jeep and took off for town, thinking about what to cook for dinner and if there were any ingredients I needed to buy. I drove down Lost Hills Road, noting there was still frost on the ground then turned left on Sunset Road heading towards town. As I rounded a hill, I saw smoke in the distance. Smoke was bad news in the foothills and wildfires were common. I needed more information about the situation before I'd be comfortable spending several hours in town. I stayed on Sunset until a road veered off west which I took heading towards the fire. As I closed in I could see the source of the smoke was a house fire but the fire department hadn't arrived yet. I pulled my Jeep off the road well away from where the fire trucks would need to be positioned. Then I jogged over to the house only to be met by a puzzling sight. There was a woman, still wearing pajamas and slippers, with tears streaming down her face, attempting to push a car towards the burning house.

As I ran up to her I yelled, "Is there anyone in the house?"

"No!" she wailed.

"Did you call the Fire Department?"

"The damn phone is in the damn house. Help me push his damn car closer. I want it to burn! If he's gonna do this to me, he can just as well lose his car, too!"

I got out my cell phone. On this side of the foothills there should be reception. I placed the call requesting both the fire and police departments since it was obvious there was some kind of unlawful behavior going on. I hadn't decided yet if she was burning down his house or he was burning down her house and the car was just in retaliation. When I got off the phone the woman had given up on the car. It was a lost cause. It was too heavy and an uphill push all the way to the fire. She was walking around in the front yard cursing a mile a minute, crying as she watched the house burn.

"You're sure, there's no one inside the house?"

"Yes, we got out but it's gone. The whole house is a loss."

"What do you mean 'we'? All I see here is you."

"My daughter, she ran away soon as she heard my ex go ballistic, she took off into the hills." Her tears started up again. "I just hope he don't catch her. He's bad news, real bad news."

"Should someone go help her?"

"Not me! I couldn't catch her for one and for another if my ex even sees me he'll kill me. Shit, I just can't help but hate that guy, what he done to us."

I ran to the Jeep and pulled out the daypack and my 9mm then returned to the house.

"Whatcha doin' with that thing?" the woman asked.

"Hopefully, nothing. Is your ex-husband armed?"

"*Don't* call him that. I don't even want to think about being married to that animal."

"Still, I need to know if he's armed."

"He's probably only armed with his fists, but that's enough. He can do more with his fists than most people could with a gun."

"How old is your daughter?"

"Thirteen."

"Does she know her way around the hills?"

"Jade knows one trail real good. She runs it every day for cross-country practice. If she stuck to the trail, she'll be back soon. If she's not back in an hour or two then I'd be scared for her. I'd be real scared Dontrell got to her. If she had to leave the trail, then I don't know. She'd only leave the trail to get away from Dontrell."

A plan was forming in my mind. If Jade wasn't back by the time the police arrived I'd go after her. I was really hoping for some backup, especially if I was going to be dealing with an angry ex. I called the police station and asked that the responding officer call me on my phone. After a few minutes the phone chirped its cheerful little tune and I answered.

"Thompson here, what's up?"

"Jayce?"

"Cassidy? What's up?"

I had to revert to codes because I didn't want to talk about Jade in front of her mother. So using mostly codes I gave him the Reader's Digest version. "I've got a possible arson and a possible missing person. The missing person is not in the structure. She's fled the scene and is being pursued by a suspicious person. We need backup. I might need to go after the girl and we need an officer to report to the fire. Where are you?"

"I'm at Palm Drive and Prairie Road." Still at least fifteen minutes away. "Can you find her?"

"Easily."

"Ten-four, I'm calling for another car."

I could hear sirens in the distance being transmitted through Jayce's phone. As I hung up a juniper near the house caught fire.

"Are you a cop?" Jade's mom asked me.

"Sort of. I work for the police when they need me as a reserve deputy, but technically I'm not a cop unless I am working with a senior officer."

By the time Jayce pulled up in his black and white two trees were burning brightly. Right behind him were two big, shiny hook and ladder trucks and a rescue squad.

"How long has Jade been gone?" I asked. "I arrived about 10:20. It's a little after eleven now."

The house was nearly cinders now but the two trees were burning brightly.

"It's been over an hour, maybe an hour and a half."

"How long is her running trail?"

"I don' know, I'd guess five miles."

"And she jogs it?"

"She tries to run it but she paces herself."

"So if she were running five miles per hour she should be back. Five miles per hour is a steady jog. Could she do all five miles at a steady jog?"

"She's number two in her class. She can do it. I jus' hope Dontrell can't catch her."

"Does Dontrell know the trail?"

"Yeah, he knows it, he's jogged it before. He used to help Jade train, only I think he was doing more'n training her, if you know what I mean. That's why she run when she saw him."

Jayce took all this in, getting a picture of the situation. I looked to him.

"I can find her," I said.

"Wait," he told me.

"Why?"

"We might need more backup and they can't find us if we take off."

"How far behind is backup?"

He radioed in a request for the responding officer's ETA.

"Twenty minutes."

"Well, we should know for sure if we need to go out by then."

I am not a patient person. I watched the firemen rushing around and tried to stay out of their way. They almost evacuated me until they realized I was working with Jayce.

"Calm, down," he admonished me.

"Sorry, Jayce, it's just that I've been in this girl's shoes before. I know what it feels like to be chased through the hills by someone you're scared of. I know how fast things can turn ugly."

"Things can turn uglier if we go up there unprepared."

When we finally saw a black and white cruiser down the road I headed out.

"You fill them in. I'm going to find the start of the trail."

I started at the road and walked a wide circle around the house. When I got to the back I was alarmed to see several more trees were engulfed in flames.

"Where do you think you're going?" Antonio Rodriguez called to me.

"I'm tracking our ten sixty-five. We'll be out of the area in a few minutes. I need to get the direction before we set out."

Antonio was an occasional volunteer on the team when a call involved water rescues. In this area, that usually meant pulling cars out of the aqueduct.

I had been hoping to pick up the trail closer to the house. If I could have started at the back door I bet I could have just followed Jade's tracks straight to the trail. There was no way the firefighters would allow me behind the fire line. I knew that much, which meant I had to circle the property staying well away from the fire. I found the trail leading away from the house, marked it and then went back for my team.

"I've got a lead," I told them.

I looked at my two backups, Jayce Thompson and Kent Jacobsen. I had worked with Jacobsen as a reserve deputy on an apprehension, so he was going to be wary. Kent knew that I'd walk into trouble in the blink of an eye and Jayce knew I didn't even need to walk; trouble came knocking on my door. Great.

"Are you ready?" I asked.

They looked at me in my pack and noticed the gun. They didn't want to do this. Both men sensed this search would be a Cassidy calamity in the making.

"Look, my job is just to find the kid. I won't do anything but track unless you tell me to."

The two officers looked resigned. "We have to at least bring him in for questioning on the arson case," Jayce pointed out. "Question is do we take Cassidy along?"

"I thought she was taking us along."

"She said it was an easy trail."

"Easy for her."

"Oh, yeah."

"That doesn't mean easy for us."

I waited, arms crossed.

"Okay," Jacobsen said reluctantly, "lead the way."

They followed me back to the start of the trail, which was almost behind the fire line now. We left behind Kent's partner to question Jade's mother about the fire and set off in search of the missing teen.

"How fast can you guys follow?" I asked.

"How fast can you track?" Jayce answered.

"This is a cross-country jogging trail. All I have to do is watch for footprints leaving it. I can jog it but I don't want to leave you behind."

"Like you could jog in that pack."

"Hey, I have water and trail mix. At least I'm a little bit prepared for a five mile hike."

Jade had jogged this trail many, many times. Unfortunately, so had Dontrell. I saw the girl's footprints covered by Dontrell's footprints, both moving at a sprint. I walked faster and broke into a gentle jog. I suspected Jade would stick to the trail as long as she could stay well ahead of him. I kept close tabs on the footprints. If there was any irregularity I would stop to study it out. I wanted to know what was in this girl's head. It might be important to know how her mind worked. If she found herself in a tight spot she would have to think and act, and if that happened any hints I'd gathered would help.

The guys hiked steadily behind me. I'd get ahead while the trail was clear but they would catch up when I had to stop and study. It was important to finish this trail today. I wasn't prepared for a night on the trail and although I could do it I knew the guys wouldn't let me. I quickened my pace, grateful for being only a few hours behind Jade but I couldn't maintain her pace. If she was still running I'd never catch her. Seeing her footprints on the trail was both encouraging and disheartening at the same time. It meant she wasn't in immediate danger but it also meant she was gaining ground on me.

The stress of the situation appeared to be telling on Jade. Where she normally could run and jog the whole five miles, she now sprinted a short distance and then stopped to catch her breath. I read each stop. It was generally the same. She'd find an area with a good view and stop to look at her back trail. A couple of steps to rest as her breathing steadied and she was off again. Dontrell ran and walked, ran and walked. His stride was much longer than Jade's, whereas she was even smaller and lighter than me. Dontrell was fit and close to six feet tall. When he ran, he ate up ground. I expected, when I finally caught up with them, to find two very athletic and handsome people. Jade quick and wary. Dontrell quick to anger, ruthless and ill-tempered.

I looked back at the smoke rising from Jade's house. I'd made good time. I hit the trail again, time pushing me on. I noticed angry, heavy clouds gathering over the mountains and hoped they stopped there like they frequently did. If there was one thing I didn't need right now it was rain or snow.

Jade's next stop took a different turn. I studied the trail. She had suddenly stopped, needing a rest, but Dontrell was close. She turned quickly and bolted. I followed each move as she tried to keep an object between herself and Dontrell. She tried to make a dash for the trail but he headed her off and she just missed capture by heading uphill and sprinting as fast as she could to gain ground. This was what I had feared and wondered how long ago it had happened. So many bad things can occur in an hour, I thought. I'd learned that lesson time and time again. Luck can turn bad in a split second. Bad luck was harder to control, too. Once trouble hit, you were stuck with it until it gave up or won, and you couldn't let it win. I hoped Jade knew that. She couldn't let Dontrell win.

"Cassidy! Wait up, where are you going?"

"No," I called back. "You want to talk, catch up. This trail is turning bad. We don't have time to chat."

I could count my blessings though. This desert sand was about the easiest tracking I could have asked for. Jade's and Dontrell's trails had separated for a bit and that made reading Jade's footprints easier. I jogged up the hill, quickly noting each step. The tracks were erratic. She was trying to run and keep track of Dontrell's whereabouts. I stopped suddenly as Jade's tracks made a sharp turn and I looked around to find Dontrell's footprints, running tracks coming up from the side. I turned back to Jade's tracks. She'd stumbled and caught herself with her hands. There was a deep toe print in the sand as she rushed forward from her crouched position, but Dontrell had caught her. There was a mess of tracks that indicated a scuffle between the two. I followed each of Jade's footprints. The guys caught up as I was figuring out the scene.

"Her mom might not know much about picking men but she knew a thing or two about her daughter's situation. Jade's had self defense classes and she's putting up a pretty good fight. The more she fights him the slower they will go."

Jade's footprints gave a quick twist and a leap and then Dontrell fell backwards. I had to laugh. This kid definitely had spunk. She sprinted away. Dontrell rolled to his feet, shook off the attack and followed. The next time he caught up he tackled her and forced her to the ground. And that's where Jade's footprints ended. There was nothing I could do. He'd gotten her. Now, what would he do with her out here in the sticks?

I paused to collect my thoughts. Okay, I needed to track Dontrell now. Much as I didn't want to meet up with the guy, I knew it would eventually happen. I followed the tracks. Dontrell's added weight and the fact that Jade was still fighting made him easier to track. I walked quickly, the tension mounting. They were headed back to the house, and Dontrell's car. Hopefully on the other side of the fire we could count on more officers stepping in if needed. Smoke still billowed over the hills where Jade's house had stood.

Dontrell still didn't know the police were involved or that he was walking into a trap, if we could spring one on him. I motioned the guys forward.

"He's got the kid and he's heading back to the house, I assume, because his car is there. We have to stay on his trail, just in case Jade manages to get away but we ought to radio some warning about what might happen."

The clouds over the mountains were dissipating due to the wind picking up and as we walked into it, the biting cold and acrid smoke made our eyes water. It whipped my hair around and made tracking difficult. Gusts brought up dust, reminding us just how dry the hills were. The smell of smoke was strong and the sky grew hazier as we walked. Ash began falling like snow and we realized the fire had gotten out of hand. I looked into the wind judging the size of the fire.

"Cassidy, we've got to get up higher and go around. You're heading right into the fire," Jacobsen called out.

"I'll see it long before we need to worry about it," I replied.

"You can't know that, not with this crazy wind," he said loudly.

We watched the clouds skim across the sky, low and threatening. They were moving too fast to be a worry concerning rain or snow, but it also meant the fire had plenty of help spreading in our direction.

"There's no way to track if I leave the trail," I told them.

"To hell with the trail. This place is going to be in flames soon. Jade and Dontrell's trail has been obliterated by fire."

"Not yet, it hasn't."

"Cassidy, do we have to hog tie you and drag you out before you kill yourself?"

"Dontrell has to decide something about this fire, too. What did he do?"

"I don't know and we may *never* know and we for sure won't if we don't get out of the way. I am *ordering* you to abandon the trail and go around the fire."

I set my hands on my hips and glared at Jacobsen. One of them was my senior officer. The more I thought about it, either one of them could give me orders because they outranked me. When I chose to find Jade and Dontrell, I put myself under their command. I had to obey, that was it. I didn't have a choice. I guess my Marines background paid off this time because I backed down. This wasn't my decision. It was his, he had made it and there was nothing I could say to change his mind. I looked to Jayce and he stood firm. I watched as hope flew away on the wind and got caught in all the smoke and died. I followed the guys uphill and around the fire. At one point we could see fire cresting a hilltop close to us. We quickly headed south around the hill.

I heard Jacobsen communicating with his partner. He was trying to get an idea of what we were up against.

When we'd started out it was still cold, nearly freezing, yet now I was wishing I didn't have a heavy coat to deal with. I kept it on anyway. The coat might be uncomfortably hot but it was protection from the fire too.

"We're heading in the right direction," Jacobsen announced, "keep heading south."

We picked up the pace but the smoke forced us to slow down. The harder we pushed the more smoke we breathed in. A steady hike in a planned direction was our best bet. The fire crested a nearby hill and we took note of its progress as we hiked quickly toward the end of the line.

Suddenly a figure dashed away from a pocket of fire that had flared up nearby. It was Dontrell! The smoke quickly brought him up short and he bent over in a fit of coughing, dumping a very angry Jade into the ash and dirt. Instead of running away from him, she jumped to her feet and rounded on him with a kick to the head that sent him flying.

The officers sprang into action. They dashed forward, guns drawn. I ran towards Jade. She backed away, crouched, ready to escape.

"Please, Jade, don't run. We need to get away from the smoke. The fire is our immediate danger. We have to deal with that first. Come on, it's okay, look; Dontrell will be in cuffs in just a few minutes. He can't hurt you anymore."

She had a wild look to her and panicked. She rounded on me with a punch and a shove that sent me sprawling in surprise. Guess I should have been expecting that reaction.

"I am not going back!" she yelled. "Restraining orders don't work. Nobody's safe long as he's around. I'm not going back! The only safe place is a long, long ways away from his sorry face and that's where I'm going. You can't stop me!"

"He's not going to be around," I quickly shot back. "He's going straight to jail. He'll be booked for arson and kidnapping, maybe child endangerment. We'll throw the book at him. Just stop for a second. Stop and calm down and you'll see the fire is the big threat now. You might be a kid but you've got a good head on your shoulders. Slow down and think this through."

She stopped when she heard something good about herself. She wasn't used to that and my words caught her attention.

"We've got radio contact with the police and the fire department," I explained. "We can get out of this. They will help us any way they can. Right now we know to head south. So let's do that. Focus on the first goal, getting away from this fire. The rest will take care of itself."

We turned to the guys. I had been so focused on Jade that I wasn't aware of what had happened behind me. Jayce was nursing a bloody nose but Dontrell stood there cuffed and cowed. I opened my pack and rummaged around inside. Usually it held a day's worth of trail food, water, a change of clothes, a hunting knife and a magnesium stick. I removed an old t-shirt and poured water onto it until it was completely damp. I gave it to Jayce to use on his nose. The damp material would also filter out smoke.

Jade took one look at Dontrell and almost made a run for it.

"No, don't do it. We have a better chance if we stay in a group. If they have to send a helicopter back here we need to be findable. A group is a lot easier to locate and pick up." Judging from the look on her face, I hadn't convinced her yet.

"Jade, the officers will shoot him before they'll let him get to you again. You're safe."

Jacobsen gave Dontrell a push in a southerly direction and Jayce took his place on the other side. Jade and I followed. I knew she'd feel better if she could keep an eye on Dontrell. We pushed towards the road. Jacobsen's partner radioed for an update and seemed satisfied with the progress.

The fire was spreading fast. I noticed that we weren't behind the fire anymore. There were little pockets of fire all around us. Sometimes the ground under our feet was blackened, sometimes ash. I had the feeling that one freak wind could bring it all down on top of us. I felt scared, but I wasn't letting on. Fear is contagious. If I showed any fear, Jade would get scared and things would go downhill really fast. I had to put my worries aside and follow the plan. All we could do was our best, so we hiked south watching for a break.

By the time the road came into view we were all ash covered and dripping with sweat. My feet were blistered from walking on burned ground in moccasins. The road appeared between two pockets of fire. The passageway was closing.

"I'm not going in there," Jade said adamantly.

"It's that or continue south. We don't know how far we'll have to go or what the conditions will be there. If we're quick, we can make it." I dropped my pack and took off my jacket. "Here, put this over you. If the fire gets close it'll get the jacket first and you can throw it off when we reach the road. Come on, I'll go with you."

I urged her forward holding onto her shoulders to offer some physical support.

"Okay, ready? One, two, three… go!" I took off running, almost dragging Jade with me until her feet caught up and then she ran, too. There was a sharp pop next to us and Jade screamed, jumping to the side. I had hold of her but the sudden change in direction threw me off. Down I went, face first into the ash, as Jade rushed through. I got up just in time to see the guys run past.

"Cassidy!" I heard as they went by. There was ash in my eyes and I couldn't see. Everything felt hot. I rubbed at my eyes as I ran, but I couldn't see and I tripped. Okay, it made no sense to hurry and without my sight I had to go slowly. I felt with my feet. How far was it to the road? Fifty feet? The heat was closing in and I imagined the fire leaning my way, flames licking at my path, teasing me, threatening. I could be walking right into the fire and not even know it. Was I even walking in the right direction? I stopped, mentally examining what had happened and convinced myself I was still pointed toward the road. I continued walking until, with a rush of relief, I felt the downward slope to the road and firm hands guiding me out of the fire's path.

"Drop and roll!" I heard. "Drop and roll!"

I didn't realize that they were talking to me until I had most of the ash cleared from my eyes. Jayce tackled me, using my coat to smother the flames. The guys were so covered in ash and grime I had a hard time telling them apart. Which one used to have a mustache? I couldn't remember, and neither one of them had eyebrows anymore, either.

Jacobsen got on the radio and a rescue squad was sent out, followed by a police car. The EMTs checked out all five of us. The firemen approached me with reservations. These guys knew I'd likely refuse treatment. I was surprised they didn't have one of their handy little medical release forms ready. I went through their quick checkup and monitoring process just so I could tell Rusty they had given me the all clear.

I located the t-shirt. It was dry again but I turned it inside out and found a semi-clean spot then scrubbed at the dirt on my face.

"Stop by the station and fill out your paperwork," Jayce told me. "You'll get credit for your hours."

"This wasn't a call, this was an attempted trip to the grocery store."

"Fill it in anyway. We need all the evidence we can get on this guy."

"Can I get a ride in?"

We took a head count and divided everyone between the two cars.

"Have you ever ridden in a squad car before?" I asked Jade, attempting to start a conversation.

"Unfortunately, yes, but it wasn't my fault. I was with a friend who decided a CD was more important than the next few years. What are we going to do at the station?"

"First we will find your mom. Then you will have to tell the police what happened to you. They will assign a woman officer to you. Don't be afraid to tell her everything. Believe me, they have heard it all. They will understand and the more information you give them the more they can use against Dontrell."

"Just today, or other times, too?"

"Just make sure you specify when each thing happened. You can go back as far as you want to, but make sure you at least go through the events of today as clearly as you can remember them. And don't worry if your emotions get in the way. They are used to that, too."

"Why can't I talk to you?"

"Because I'm just a wife on her way to the grocery store."

"You carry a gun to the grocery store?"

"No, I carry a gun in my Jeep, in case I get a call. I work search and rescue. You really want to speak with an experienced officer. She will know what to write down and how to say it so it has the most impact."

"Why are you going to the station then?"

"I have a few reports to fill out, and my husband works there. He'll give me a ride home."

"He's gonna be mad when he sees what you've been up to today."

"He won't be mad. I doubt he'll even be surprised. He's used to things like this happening to me. Do I still have my eyebrows?"

"Nope."

"Rats, last time he was the one who lost his eyebrows. I was hoping I'd managed to keep mine. You should have seen him, though. Usually he is the most handsome guy in the world but when he lost part of his hair and his eyebrows in an explosion, he had to get a haircut and his hair was cut *real* short. He looked like a hit man. He looked all tough and I felt like I was being followed by a bodyguard whenever we went someplace together."

Girl talk, it calmed her to talk girl talk. I wondered what Jacobsen thought about it all. He'd occasionally glance in the rearview mirror while driving and I thought I saw a smile once or twice, but I couldn't be sure.

"Is he, like, really cute?"

"I wouldn't say he's 'cute'. He's a hunk."

"Can I meet him when we get to the station?"

"That's up to Officer Jacobsen. Hey, Jacobsen, can Jade stop by Rusty's office while she's at the station?"

"You want to show off your hunk of a husband?"

"Oh come on, it's just a girl thing. I'm not showing him off. I don't even know if he's there. Rusty could be on some ten-hour long stakeout somewhere for all I know."

"Why don't you call him and see?"

"Because if I call him I'd have to explain the whole thing over the phone.

You're a guy. You can do the same thing in ten words or less."

Jacobsen got out his phone.

"Watch this. I bet he uses ten words or less," I told Jade.

"Michaels? What's your twenty? Okay, stay put." He closed the phone. "Okay, he's at the station."

"See? Now I won't have to spend the rest of the trip on the phone. How many words did he use?"

"Are contractions one word or two?"

"It doesn't matter; even if you count it as two he used less than ten words."

Rusty was waiting in the staff parking lot when we pulled up. He didn't even recognize us when we drove past him and parked.

"Is that *him*?" Jade asked in awe.

"Yep, that's him. But watch his reaction. I bet he is hardly surprised at all."

Jacobsen parked and got out before Rusty recognized him. Jade got out staring up into Rusty's bright blue eyes. He looked embarrassed.

"Just think if he was in uniform!" Jade exclaimed.

I climbed out and Rusty gave me a look that was halfway between deep concern and quiet amusement.

"Babe, what happened?"

"Jade, this is Rusty."

"Hi, Jade," Rusty said politely.

She grinned at him like a lovesick junior high kid.

"I'll be inside whenever this 'girl thing' wears off and she can think again," Jacobsen said sarcastically.

"Did you get a call today?" Rusty asked me.

"No, I tried to go grocery shopping," I explained.

"Are you okay?"

"Yeah, I'm fine, I even let the EMTs do their quick check on me."

"It was *that* close a call?"

"It was pretty smoky."

"I don't suppose you want to go out to dinner."

"Like this? No way. Get me a locker and I'll keep a change of clothes here. I bet there are a dozen empty ones in the women's locker room."

"Want me to go check?" Rusty asked, smiling.

Jade blushed. "*Please* tell me I don't look as bad as you," she said.

"You still have your eyebrows," I said encouragingly. She really did look as bad as me except for her eyebrows. Guess my coat got the worst of it. "Come on, I'll get you a soda from the machine and then you have some work ahead of you. Officer Jacobsen will show you what to do and then a woman officer will lead you through the rest."

I limped to the station. Oh, man, I didn't even want to look at my feet.

Jacobsen led us to a room where Jade met Terry Brooks. Jade took one last look at me and said, "You're right, he is a hunk."

"They're all hunks," Terry said. "Put a guy in a uniform and tell them they're a hunk and they get hunkier by the minute."

"But he wasn't even wearing a uniform," Jade said.

"Who was that?" Terry asked, amused at the immature naïveté of a thirteen-year-old girl.

"She met Rusty," I replied.

"Oh, well, Michaels is different. He's got a head start on all of them in the hunk department. Someone put a uniform on that guy and told him he was a hunk when he was a baby."

"It sure worked," Jade said as she disappeared into the interrogation room.

"What was that all about?" Rusty asked, surprising me.

"Nothing calms a teenage girl more than talking about boys. So, how is my hunk today?"

"Obviously better than you. What happened?"

"I tried to go grocery shopping. Jade's ex-stepfather tried to burn down a house and kidnap the kid. So Kent, Jayce and I attempted to round them back up. The fire got out of hand and we ended up making a run for it and here we are. Kidnapper, kidnappee and officers all in one piece. Oh, and we still need toilet paper."

Picking up the necessary forms, I limped to Rusty's office. I peeled off my shoes and socks to examine the soles of my feet. Blisters, blisters and more blisters. It was going to be painful walking for a while. I took my time filling out the forms, knowing how much weight my statement could carry. I wanted everybody to know exactly what happened. Dontrell should to be kept away from that family for as long as possible. Jade needed to grow up without the fear of Dontrell showing up again. I couldn't stop a mom from making poor choices, but I could help by putting one of those poor choices behind bars.

Chapter 6

I could make polite conversation and talk girl talk for Jade's sake. I could joke about the experience to ease Rusty's worry, but it didn't take away the reality of it. When Jade had wanted to back out and go around the fire I had wanted to even more than she did. I saw the road as safety and the corridor of flames as a death trap. I had to force myself to focus on the road, only on the road, or I wouldn't have been able to face the fire. Then I felt compelled to give Jade my coat, my only layer of protection. As I counted down the seconds to our dash, I was trying to psyche myself up.

At night I'd face that flaming corridor and in my dreams it would close. I'd never been burned badly so I didn't feel the pain in my dreams, but the fear was very real and on the first night my reaction took Rusty totally by surprise.

"Whoa, babe! It's okay!" He pulled me close and I was trapped. The fire was there and I couldn't move! "Cassidy, hon, wake up." Every brush against the sheets made my face sting and so I was trapped in a stinging, scorching chaos. My feet burned, adding realism to the sensations. "Cass, oh babe, shhh, hush, wake up, come on, wake up." He rubbed my arms until I could tell one world from the other. I was home. I was home again. I let the familiarity and the peacefulness settle in and become reality before I turned to Rusty. "Maybe now would be a good time for you to tell me about it," Rusty said gently.

I recounted the story as well as I could remember it, which was all pretty general until we got close to the fire.

"The guys just left you there?"

"No, it happened so fast, we were all running. They ran past me before they knew I was down and when I got up I couldn't see. I've practiced walking without seeing the ground, so the fact that I couldn't see didn't send me into a panic. But not knowing where the fire was really scared me. Maybe it was good that I didn't know how close it was. I didn't even know my pants leg was on fire until Jayce tackled me."

"Babe, don't do that again."

"I didn't even do it this time. I was looking for a kid who ran away from a house fire. We had no way of knowing how large the fire would grow in such a short time. I waited for backup because I didn't know how dangerous Dontrell was. I used my head. I didn't rush into it without thinking things through."

"Are you sure you're okay?"

"Yeah, for now, I'm going to have to stay off my feet until the blisters heal."

"What blisters?" he asked, switching on a bedside lamp.

"Rusty, they'll go away and I'll be fine."

"I thought you said the EMTs checked you out. They let you go with this?"

"They didn't ask me to take off my shoes. The bottoms of people's feet aren't a big priority for them. It's the middle of the night. We need to try and sleep. No more nightmares."

"Does it hurt?" he asked as we settled down again.

"My face, hands and leg just feel like a bad sunburn. My feet hurt to walk on them. They sting when anything touches them."

"And yet you walk on them anyway."

"I'm just stubborn that way."

Rusty refused breakfast in the morning. He said he'd get something on the way but I knew he just wanted to save me the pain of walking. My feet still burned and the blisters were worse. I hobbled to the den and turned on the TV then placed my feet up on the coffee table to prevent them from rubbing against anything. The doorbell rang and I started to get up.

"Who is it?" I called out.

"It's Mark," he called back.

"Run around to the back and come in through the den," I called to him.

Mark's face soon appeared at the sliding glass door and I motioned him in. He opened the door quietly, came in, and sat down on the other end of the couch.

"It's going to be a while before we go out stalking," I told him. "How long are you going to be in town?"

"Through the holidays. At least Mom doesn't make a casserole for Christmas dinner. What happened to you?"

"I burned my feet."

"Looks like you burned more than your feet."

"The eyebrows will grow back fast."

"Hey, you weren't involved in that fire near here, were you?"

"Yes and no. I came across the fire on my way to the grocery store. It started at a house so I stopped to make sure everyone was out. I called the fire and police departments and that started a long day of tracking. The fire was small when I started out."

"You should contact the TV station. They had calls all day. They knew people were back there but it was a tense day in the news because nobody heard anything. People would phone in saying, 'Yeah, I can see the smoke from my house,' just so they could get on the news but nobody had any useful information."

"Well, I'm not calling. They would all faint if that happened because they're used to me running from the TV cameras. Plus, if I did call they'd want details which I can't provide because it would affect the case."

"So, you're not going stalking for a while?"

"Not until I can walk comfortably again. Now would be a good time for you to practice on the deer in the yard though. They usually appear about six in the morning or four in the afternoon. It would be good practice for you."

Since Mark was not an early riser he showed up behind the barn a little before four each afternoon. At first he came with his camera, then decided he needed to work on stealth. After the deer had bolted three times in a row before he'd hardly started, he dejectedly came and knocked on the back door.

"What am I doing wrong?" he asked.

"First, you need to relax. The deer will sense nervousness. Second, go slow. Patience is your best friend when it comes to stalking. Only move when the deer are distracted. When they are eating or paying attention to something else, you can move slowly. Third, move smoothly and think small. Picture a bush between your target and where you are. Pretend you need to hide behind the bush. When I have time, I like to just lie on the ground near the deer, letting them get used to me. And I don't start a stalk unless I have a couple of hours to put into it. I know this sounds silly but it would help if you didn't smell like your parents' house when you come over. The deer know the yard isn't supposed to smell like apple/cinnamon candles. Go buy a camouflage outfit and keep it outside so it smells like the outdoors. It might look awful and get dirty, but the deer will respond better to you. If you don't want to buy new, then wear anything with a pattern, like plaid, to break up the view when the deer see you. Thrift stores and Army Surplus might have used ones that are already soft and will be quiet when you move. That's another thing to think about. Being quiet when you stalk. It's pretty easy to do on grass, but out in the woods it's much tougher."

"I feel like I just got Stalking 101 condensed down into five minutes."

The telephone rang.

"Do you mind if I get it?" I asked Mark.

"No, don't. I'll get it. Then you won't have to juggle the crutches." He walked over to the breakfast bar and picked up the phone. "Hello? Michaels' residence… It's your sister," he said handing me the phone.

"Hey, Cass, you're getting an early Christmas present this year," Jesse said. I listened, trying to figure out if she sounded excited or apprehensive.

"Oh ya? What is it?"

"I can't tell you, Patrick wants to."

"Oh, no, not already. Please tell me he didn't tag a rabbit!"

"Aunt Cassidy! Guess what! Guess what I did!"

"You got to see Santa at Disneyland? You beat Steve at a quarter horse race?"

"No!"

"You got your driver's license?"

"No! Are you making fun of me for driving the truck?"

"No, I'm just guessing what you were going to tell me."

"I tagged a rabbit! I wasn't even going to try 'cause I was wearing my cowboy boots but then it just *begged me to* so while Mom was unloading Dad's Christmas presents I sneaked up on it very, very carefully."

"That's great Pat! I'm so proud of you! Did it see you coming?"

"Yeah, but I froze, just like always. And this time I sneaked all the way to it! And it was so soft! I was so excited I scared it away but I tagged him. I really tagged him! When do we get to go deer stalking?"

"Pat, I'm supposed to go to San Diego for Christmas."

"Can you come *before* Christmas?"

My poor feet were screaming at me, "No stalking!" But I had a six-year-old who just met a goal he'd been working on for a year, maybe more. A sixth of his life, anyway. I couldn't say no.

"I'll have to talk to Uncle Rusty and your mom. How would you like to spend a weekend at my house? I get deer at my house, too."

"You mean come stay the night? By myself?"

"It's up to your mom and dad."

"Talk to Mom! I can't wait to go deer stalking!"

"Hi," Jesse said.

"Jesse, this is a really bad time to take Pat out deer stalking. I want to go. I really do and I will if it's possible, but I was wondering if you could bring him down here to stay for a few days. I have deer that visit my backyard and it would be so much easier than riding out to them and then walking a half mile just to sneak up on them. Patrick could stalk deer every day right next to the house and I wouldn't have to try and walk much."

"What did you do this time? Usually a half mile is a stroll in the park for you. I remember you running laps on the racetrack to get in shape and now you don't want to walk half a mile."

"I burned the bottoms of my feet on a search that involved a brush fire. I'll be okay, no need to tell Mom anything. And if I have to walk half a mile to stalk deer with Patrick I will but… if you can bring him down we'll drive him back."

"Okay, I'll check with James and you talk to Rusty and I'll call you back tomorrow."

Mark listened with interest. I hung up with a frustrated sigh.

"Oh, no!" I groaned. "My nephew stalked a rabbit. I had a deal with him, when he tagged his first rabbit I'd take him deer stalking, and he did it. Arg! I thought I had at least a year to go. What am I going to do?"

"Don't worry, he'll be fine. Just give him the same pointers you just gave me and send him out."

"Ha!" I said, then quickly lost the urge to laugh. This was *not* funny. "The kid is only six."

"Six? And he stalked a rabbit?"

"Yeah, that's what I get for having a nephew who takes after me and then encouraging him. That's one reason I'm scared to have kids. What if they take after me? I don't know if I can put up with a kid who takes after me. It's kind of fun visiting Patrick a couple of times a year, but to have a kid like that full time? No thanks!"

"It sounds like you need to call Rusty and quietly have a nervous breakdown. I'll see you later."

"Okay, go find some old, quiet clothes with a pattern and leave them outside. That'll help."

"Okay, good luck with the kid."

"Thanks."

Rusty wasn't at his office when he answered his cell phone. I could tell by the noises coming through the phone that he was outdoors somewhere.

"Hey," he said. "What's up?"

"I have some very, very bad news."

Stone, cold silence.

"Okay, it's not *that* bad."

"You're conscious, that's good."

"Nobody died, everything is status quo… but… Patrick tagged his first rabbit. You know what that means."

"You can't go stalking with him now!"

"Why?"

"Well, because of your feet, for one. And there are only two weekends before Christmas. We are supposed to spend Christmas in San Diego. You aren't thinking of spending Christmas at the ranch are you?"

"No, we promised this year to your family and we'll be there for Christmas. Do you think we could drive Pat back if Jesse and James bring him down here? Would you mind having a kid in the house for a few days?"

"Let me see what I can do. Can you even stalk?"

"Not well, but I'd mostly be instructing. I can do that with Patrick in the backyard if he comes to our house. Plus, it might be an adventure for him to come down here all by himself. Maybe you could show him around the station, let him sit in a squad car. He'd be real excited to do that."

There were tense voices in the background.

"I can't talk now. I have to go, but thanks for letting me know. I'll check at work and see about a day to go to the ranch."

"Okay, be careful."

"Will do."

It was agreed, Jesse would bring Patrick to our house the Monday before Christmas and he would spend the week with us. Then we would take him home on Friday, spend the night, and head for San Diego on Saturday. Christmas was Monday. It would work. I wouldn't have to ride for miles and hike a lot and Patrick would have more time for stalking in the safety of our backyard.

"I get to stay at *your* house?" Patrick asked excitedly.

"Yup, what do you like for dinner?" I asked, intending to fix things he'd actually eat.

"Spaghetti, pizza, we never get to eat pizza here 'cause the only pizza place is a long ways away. Grilled cheese sandwiches, macaroni and cheese, chicken nuggets, French fries. We never get French fries because we have to go to town to get fast food and Mom doesn't believe in fast food."

"Well, if your mom doesn't believe in fast food then we shouldn't eat a lot of it here either."

"Aw, rats."

"Bring warm clothes, don't forget a coat. Bring your moccasins and tennis shoes. Your boots and cowboy clothes won't fit in very good down here. Just bring your usual play clothes."

"But I play in my cowboy clothes," he complained.

That didn't surprise me at all.

"Okay, just bring clothes you can get dirty in."

"Yay," he said mischievously. Jesse didn't like dirt. To me, six-year-olds and dirt were almost synonymous.

I hung up with a huge to-do list rattling around in my head. At least Patrick seemed pretty easy to please.

What was I going to do with a six-year-old boy in the house for five days? I'd never been around Patrick for more than a day and those times he had seemed very much like an immature ranch hand. He knew what needed to be done around the ranch, but he just wasn't big enough to do any of it. He didn't seem to play like normal kids his age. His idea of play was adventuring. If he couldn't go on real adventures he made up his own in the yard. The tree house became a fort or a hideout or a cabin. His favorite pretend adventure since starting school was being a trapper in the old west. The tree house was his home and he'd go "trapping animals" around the yard. That consisted of tracking the dogs and the rabbits that frequently crossed the yard. Then he'd gather his pretend furs. The ranch was "town" and he had other great adventures as he walked the pretend miles into town, all one quarter of them. Well, I had plenty of pretend places here. I had a house, a barn and a gazebo that he could turn into whatever he liked.

Patrick did well in school. He was reading and, not surprisingly, did well when it came to spatial analysis. He enjoyed working with maps and drawing and understood his directions before he could even spell them. I was expecting good math skills coupled with bad handwriting and spelling. Patrick had a love of learning as long as he could apply it to his own interests and an aversion to learning anything that didn't interest him such as grammar. His interest in history and science would depend totally on how it was taught. If the teacher gave him interesting hands-on work he would thrive, and if they lectured about things that didn't interest him he'd daydream. So I expected him to be an excellent student until he hit junior high. That's when a teacher's lecture would probably take the fun out of everything he'd been interested in during elementary school. At least that was how it was for me. Junior high had been tough because I'd just gotten old enough to really explore, so my imagination was full of things to do; yet I'd be trapped in a boring lecture. My imagination was a lot more interesting than school. Okay, Cass, back up, the kid is only in first grade.

I decided to have at least one book a day to keep him busy. I needed to make Christmas candy. He'd like helping with that, especially since I'd let him snitch. All the candy making at the ranch was done by Jesse and Martha in the big ranch kitchen and then it was put away for special occasions. Not so at Aunt Cassidy's house. Things were made to be snitched except for the things put in gift boxes. Those were off limits. That's why we made double batches, so there'd be plenty to snitch. I decided to wrap presents before Patrick arrived and then made a list of what was needed in town. Rusty went with me. We took advantage of the extended holiday shopping hours since living out of town made it hard to get to some stores while they were still open.

"Help me find books for Patrick to read at our house. I'm not going to let him be lazy. He's going to read while he's here. If I can find books he likes then he'll enjoy reading."

We both looked until I found a few old-time stories about a dog on a ranch. They were short chapter books and Rusty found easy readers.

"Those are too hard for him," Rusty pointed out.

"You're right. He doesn't have to be able to read all the words as long as he *wants* to. If he wants to he will figure out how to read the story."

"You're sure it won't be frustrating to him?"

"We can always fall back on the easy ones and I'll read the harder ones out loud to him. But I bet if it interests him he'll ask for help reading the hard ones."

When Rusty saw all the macaroni and cheese and the other kid-friendly food in my shopping cart he began questioning what the next week was going to be like.

"Don't worry, dinners will be pretty much like usual. Patrick and I will eat the mac and cheese and hotdogs for lunch."

"What's all the baking stuff for?"

"I'll be making fudge, peanut butter balls, Rice Crispy treats, and cookies. You can take some to share at work and Patrick can snitch some, too. Christmas goodies are better when they've been snitched. Maybe he'll leave some for the trip to San Diego."

"I thought he was coming down here to stalk deer."

"He is, but I can't schedule a deer herd. He might stalk in the mornings and afternoons but I can't guarantee deer in the yard every day. We need something to keep us busy during the day when the deer are elsewhere. If I don't keep him busy he's going to want me to take him tracking."

"You think a six-year-old boy is going to want to cook with you?"

"I bet he's used to it. He's Jesse's kid. I'd say he'll bring his favorite toys along but I haven't noticed him playing with any toys. It's Wyatt that has trucks and cars and talking stuffed Elmo dolls. Patrick has never been interested in toys."

"What do they get him for Christmas if he doesn't play with toys?"

"They buy him toys anyway and when he loses interest, then Wyatt grows into them. It's okay. It was the same way with me. I'd rather have time to ride or some tracks to follow than anything my parents gave me, so Jesse ended up with most of my gifts. Maybe that's why she grew up to be more materialistic than me. I inadvertently spoiled her rotten. Once in a while I'd grow into something useful, like a BB gun, or archery equipment, or a new saddle and then I did put the gifts to good use, but toys? Dolls? Jewelry? All that stuff was for other kids. My mom gave me dresses and dolls while my dad bought me hunting knives, BB guns, outdoor survival books, and a compass. I got many hours of entertainment from that compass. I tried to get lost so I could use it to find my way back, but I couldn't because I knew the hills too well and looked at my back trail too often. I'd ask myself, 'Am I lost yet? Am I lost yet?' It was frustrating trying to get lost but being unable to do it."

Rusty laughed. "How old were you when you did that?"

"Well, if I'd been exploring the hills for a while then at least eight years old, but I'm guessing I was more like ten or eleven. At first I thought, who cares if the gadget can tell you which way north is? North is that way! But then I applied it to map reading. While I was horseback riding I could put some distance between myself and the house I figured out how the compass worked."

I was an odd kid and I expected Patrick to be an odd kid too. It would be easier if he was a normal kid, but I'd just have to wait and see.

Chapter 7

Patrick arrived with his parents a week before Christmas. Jesse was a basket case. Maybe it was because I'd never had kids myself, but I didn't see why they were making such a big fuss about it.

So the kid was spending a week with his aunt and uncle. It wasn't anything to cry over, but Jesse definitely did her share. Patrick was embarrassed.

"She does this whenever I do something for the first time. She cries every year when I start school. She cried the first time I got on the bus. Sheesh, Mom!"

"It's okay, Pat, moms are allowed to do stuff like that. If you learn to put up with it now maybe it'll be easier later on when your wife cries at the drop of a hat," I informed him.

"Do wifes do that, too?" he asked with a look of disgust.

"It depends on the wife," his father replied. "They generally outgrow it. Then they have kids and it starts all over again."

"I'm not gettin' married," Patrick declared.

"Now, remember to wear your coat when you go outside. And you must obey Cassidy and Rusty. And don't go stalking without Cassidy there. And no tracking outside of the yard. No driving of any kind! Don't stay up too late. When Cassidy says it's bedtime you go to bed without a fight. Be respectful…"

"Yes Ma'am," Patrick interrupted.

"And don't be a wise ass," Jesse continued.

"And don't cuss?" Patrick asked.

"Okay, I think we're ready to go," Jesse said in a huff.

"You don't want lunch before starting back?" I asked.

"We need to get home. James has work to do and Mom wants help decorating the house. We're going to wind white twinkle lights around the front fence of the ranch and I bought inflatable snowmen to put next to the gate."

"I heard it could snow. Then your snowmen will match the rest of the ranch."

"It won't snow. It hardly ever snows, you know that."

"I know. I just heard it somewhere."

Jesse gave Patrick an embarrassing kiss and hug then got into the car, teary eyed again. She rolled down her window.

"And eat your vegetables. French fries don't count. And brush your teeth every night."

"Jesse, enough already," said James to his wife.

"And if you want to call home you know the number, right?"

"Yeah, you made me say it over and over again all the way here."

"Good boy."

James started up the truck and Jesse waved all the way down the street until they turned out of sight. I imagine she then burst into tears, had a good cry and was fine until they arrived home.

Patrick turned to me and said, "Mom didn't want lunch because we already ate."

"Oh, really? Where did you eat?" I asked, making conversation.

"It was like when I buy my lunch at school."

"You mean a cafeteria?"

"Yeah, only, I don't get it. People eat there so they can pick just what they want, but Mom made me eat lima beans, broccoli, chicken and milk. So I guess it doesn't work for kids."

"You don't like lima beans, broccoli and chicken?"

"I do, but I'd rather eat a corn dog with lots of ketchup and French fries. I guess I don't mind milk. Most of the kids at school like Coke. They say I only like milk because I live on a farm. I keep telling them we don't even have a cow but they are just being mean. They don't know nuthin'."

"You're right, they are just trying to be mean. You only have to give them the amount of respect they deserve, so just ignore their rude comments. Come on, I'll show you where your room is."

"Wow, that's a big bed!" he exclaimed.

"I bought it for Grandpa and Grandma to use when they visit. Your bathroom is right across the hall. It's all yours unless we have company and I'm not expecting anybody. If you need anything at night, I'm right down the hall and through those doors. Leave your suitcase in your room, and I'll show you something." I led him through our bedroom to the big bay window overlooking the backyard. "This big window here is a good place to watch for the deer. When they come down out of the hills they come from that way," I said, pointing. "There's a window in the den that you can see them from, too. The deer don't come every day and, when they do, they could come early in the morning or about four in the afternoon. Do you know how to tell time?"

"Sort of. I can read numbers and I know the bigger numbers are closer to the next hour. So three fifty is close to four but three fifteen isn't yet."

"Right. There's a digital clock on the coffee maker, microwave and the alarm clocks. So, when do you need to watch for the deer?"

"Early in the morning and three fifty in the afternoon?"

"Yeah, I'll be watching too. If you see deer out there just come get me quietly and I'll show you what to do."

"Can you show me what to do before I have to do it?"

"Well, it's sort of the same as stalking rabbits only deer run away instead of freeze when they get scared. So you have to be very careful not to scare them. You have to move smoothly and silently and only move when the deer are distracted or eating. When they look up, freeze. When they look away, stalk slowly and smoothly closer. There's a spot in the backyard we will start from. The deer are used to seeing people there so they won't be as scared if that's where you begin. Do you know what deer tracks look like?"

"I know they have pointy hooves."

"There are deer tracks by the barn. I'll show you. Let me grab my crutches."

"Why do you have crutches?"

"I hurt my feet tracking behind a fire. That's why we're stalking deer here, close to home."

"Can I see?"

"Yeah. It looks better now. The blisters are almost all gone but they are still real sensitive and the rocks outside are hard to walk on."

"Ewe," he said when I sat down and began pulling on slippers.

"I need to make a new pair of moccasins. Do you want to make a pair of moccasins while you're here?"

"You can do that? I thought a big machine made them."

"It does, but you can make your own. I won't say it's cheaper to make your own but you can choose leather that you like, and you can fit them to your feet. Let's go look at the deer tracks. If you see them here, you will recognize them when you see them in the hills back home."

I carried my crutches to the back door and then used them to make my way over to the corral. The deer always fed on the lawn and then moved off past the barn. I'd learned to keep the corral gate closed because deer would wander in there and then get trapped. If I ever wanted venison during hunting season, I had the perfect deer trap. But, no, I'd never shoot any of them, these were my deer and I wanted them to feel welcome at my house.

"Patrick, here you go. These are the front hooves and those are the back ones. See how close together they are? Now, follow this doe. See if you can track her."

He squatted down and studied the tracks. I wasn't going to hurry him. Everybody learns tracking in their own way. He had to categorize the tracks in his own mind and rushing him would only interrupt the process.

"These are the front?"

"The back hooves often overlap the front ones because of how deer walk."

He rose and squinted down at the tracks then slowly moved forward. As I followed along I thought of the many times Victor and Landon had followed me in the same manner, with patience and never interrupting. Now I was wondering if they had been partnered with me because of their infinite patience. It took all my own patience to slowly follow along with Patrick.

"What's this mark?" he suddenly asked.

"Good catch!" I praised. "That's a dew claw. You know how dogs have a pad and a claw up on the side of their leg?"

"Umm, no," he answered.

"Shadow, come!" I called. Once the black and white bundle of energy was sitting in front of me I asked for a paw. "Here, feel Shadow's dew claw. It's like a pad. Deer have them too, and they only show up on tracks as they move through soft sand or when they are leaping or running." As I released Shadow's paw he gave me a quizzical look. "Good boy," I said, petting him.

"So this deer was walking along until something made it jump or run? What made it jump?"

Oh, man, this kid was going to keep me hopping.

"I don't know, but maybe we can find out. Which way did the deer go when it jumped? Picture a horse startling. I'm sure you've seen that. Remember how they lean back right before they jump a little?"

It felt odd going into so much detail with a little kid and made me wonder how Chase would have handled Pat's question. Somehow I thought that, if Chase had been here, it would have pleased him to find us out here puzzling over which way a deer jumped.

"I think it jumped that way," he said pointing, "but I don't know why."

I bent over the track and used a piece of dry grass to point.

"See, the dew claw? It moved just a bit after it hit the ground. It hit right here, and then when the deer jumped the angle changed. Now look at the points of the hoof. There is a deep print. It shows you how the deer's weight was distributed during the jump. All the weight is right here and it was pushing against that spot. So… where did the deer jump?"

"How come you talk to me like an adult?"

"Huh? I don't. I talk to you like a tracker. Do you understand what I'm trying to explain?"

"Yeah, but Mom would never expect me to. She'd try and figure out some wimpy little kid talk and I'd have to try and figure out what she really meant."

"Sorry, I've never had kids, and I haven't learned wimpy little kid talk yet. So, where did the deer jump to?"

"She pushed this way. So she jumped that way. How do you know it's a she?"

"Well, I don't. I just see a lot more does than bucks so I assume it's a she."

He walked in the direction of the push and found where the doe had landed.

"She landed here and then her tracks go that way."

"Now let's go see what scared her. She wouldn't jump *towards* a scary thing so she must have been jumping away from it."

We followed the opposite direction looking for any clues as to what might have startled the doe. I found a footprint but didn't mention it to Patrick.

"Look this way," I advised him.

"Did you find it? What was it?"

"It was a man eating cow."

"Na uhh, there's no such thing as a man eating cow. You're trying to trick me."

"Then find what I found. We need to go home. If we are out in the hills when the deer come they might stay away."

He began trotting over but I stopped him. "Nope, don't do that. You might be destroying just the information you need to solve this mystery. Watch the ground as you walk slowly. I'm not standing near it. I want you to find it. It could be a wolf or a coyote or a person or a mountain lion or a man eating cow… widen your search just a bit. It doesn't have to be close to scare a deer. Deer are very alert. Do you see any tracks, anything at all?"

I watched as he got closer and closer to the man's tracks. When he saw them he was disappointed.

"Aw, it was just a person."

"But what do we know about this person? And he really was a man eating cow. Look, he dropped a piece of beef jerky in his surprise."

"How do you know it was a he?"

"With people it's fairly easy to tell. Look at his track, and then look at my track. Now compare the two. What's different?"

"The man's track is lots bigger, but women can have big feet too."

"That's true, but men's feet are usually wider, even if they aren't longer. Once you've been tracking a while, you will notice men walk differently too. You have to do a lot of tracking to get all these quirky little facts into your head. Then, when you see tracks, you'll know right away if it's a man or a woman, even when the prints are big or small. There's a list of things that you can run through in your head to narrow down the description. For instance, I can tell just from these tracks that this man was almost six feet tall. He wore brand new hiking boots. He had almost black, curly hair and brown eyes. He likes beef jerky. He carries a camera."

"You can't know all that from these footprints," he admonished me.

"I can't? Look. Back up on his trail just a bit and then track him. See? Footprint, footprint, footprint, he's walking along…oops! A deer! Now look at his tracks. One foot here, the other there. A very stable standing position. I'm betting he stopped and tried to take a picture of that doe. Yesterday, afternoon."

He still looked at me doubtfully.

"We need to go home. Do you need a snack before the deer come?"

"I can snack?" he asked, like it was a foreign word.

"Yeah, you can snack. You can even help me make Christmas goodies. I need to send some to work with Rusty and I was going to bring some on my trip to San Diego."

"Why are you going to San Diego right at Christmas time?"

"Rusty's mom, dad, sister and brother live there."

"I wish you could come to the ranch for Christmas."

"I will next year."

We entered the warm house not realizing how cold we'd been outside. Days were a lot chillier in the foothills than they were in town. I showed Patrick how to measure and add the ingredients one at a time to make cookie dough. Our cookies were made with a little extra vanilla for flavor because Patrick had tipped the bottle a bit too fast. We mixed up the dough and then tasted it.

"What do you think?" I asked. "Too much vanilla?"

"I like it."

"Okay, now for chocolate chips. What kind do we want? Peanut butter? Dark chocolate, milk chocolate? Swirls?"

"Let's use peanut butter and milk chocolate, then it'll be like Reese's peanut butter cookies."

"Okay, then our fudge will be made with the dark chocolate."

We added the chips and mixed it all together.

"It's three thirty, time to start watching for deer. Let me give you a few tips." I went to the den window. "See those trees right over there? Watch that area. Don't just look for a deer. Watch behind the trees for any movement, any deer colored movement. If you look for hints of deer then you'll see them sooner. And don't rush out there. We should only sneak out there after they come all the way in."

Patrick sat by the window waiting for the deer.

"Don't stay in the window, you'll get tired of waiting real fast and the deer might see you. Just check the window every ten minutes or so."

I put a test cookie in the oven. When I saw that it was baking well, I had Patrick fill a cookie sheet with dough balls. He checked the window and then we filled another cookie sheet. I could tell I was going to do most of the baking myself. Pat ran down the hall and into our bedroom to check from the big window. I switched the cookie sheets when the timer went off and put the cookies on the cooling rack then checked the window in the den. No deer. Rats. Each time I switched the cookies sheets I checked the den window, too. Three cookie sheets later it suddenly occurred to me that the house had become way too quiet. I went to the bedroom expecting to see a discouraged six-year-old sitting in the bay window. Instead I saw…nothing. The room was empty.

Chapter 8

"Patrick?"

I looked around the bedroom and master bath and noticed that there were little kid knee prints left in the fabric of the seat inside the bay window. I checked Rusty's office and the guest bedroom, living room, dining room, kitchen, and den. Pat knew not to go outside because he wouldn't want to scare the deer away. Outside remained my only option unless he was hiding, but there was no reason for him to hide since he wanted to watch for deer. I looked at the time. Four fifteen. He knew the deer could show up anytime. Glancing out the back window, the yard appeared to be still and peaceful. I turned off the oven and went outside, quietly circling the house, watching for little kid footprints. It wasn't hard to find Patrick's trail. He knew exactly where he was going. He'd slipped out the front door and snuck around back. He stood for a while at the corner of the house. Why was he stopping? I examined the footprints. They didn't show up well in the grass. Only the fact that they were fresh gave me any clues. Most of his weight was on his toes, indicating he was leaning forward. He quickly ran to the corner of the barn and stopped again. This was little kid sneaking, like he'd seen on TV. Run to a hiding place and freeze there. Look for the bad guy, or the deer? What was he hiding from? He'd snuck around the backside of the barn and crouched in a hidden corner for some time. He leaned forward on his toes, watching. It looked like he was hoping to see the deer, but I had been looking for them as well and hadn't seen any. I was glad my yard was mostly dirt as the whole barn and corral area made for easy tracking. I was glad I could track, too. I imagined most aunts with a missing child would panic and have no clue of where to begin looking. At least I had clues.

I followed Pat's footprints, trying to figure out what was going on in this kid's head. It had to be something important. He had been told in no uncertain terms not to go tracking outside the yard or stalking without me. Whatever made him leave the yard must have been more important than a punishment. I knew from his steps that he wasn't tracking. If he were tracking, his footprints would have followed another set of tracks closely. He was in a sort of stealth mode, at least as much as a six-year-old could be. He was keeping an object between himself and his target while watching it very carefully. His walk was not always straight. He faced whatever he was watching and some of his steps went sideways. It all depended on the nature of the object he was hiding behind and the angle he had to look to keep tabs on whatever had interested him. I had to give the kid credit; he was going to make a great scout some day.

I didn't have to track him far. If I hadn't been so focused on his tracks and looked around more I would have known and thought, "Oh duh me!" When I finally found him he was crouched behind a bush, cell phone in hand, talking quietly to someone.

"Yeah, I'm hiding, they don't know I'm here… yeah, that's right… okay, I'll stay here."

"Patrick!" I said a little too sharply. He jumped.

"Aunt Cassidy! Just go home! I got it taken care of."

"You have what taken care of? What are you doing way out here? I've been worried about you! You just disappeared!"

"Yes, I'm okay," he said into the phone.

I could hear sirens in the distance.

"It's my aunt. She's a tracker, so she found me. The bad guy is still in the house. I haven't seen anybody come out. Okay, here she is." He handed me the phone.

"Hello?"

"Are you Patrick's aunt?"

"Yes, who am I speaking to?"

"This is Marlee Davis. Are you aware your nephew called 911 to report a prowler?"

"He what?"

"He said there was a suspicious man sneaking around your house. He kept an eye on the man and called 911 to get the police out there."

"How do the police know where to go? He doesn't even know an address!"

"He is a very smart little boy. He read your address off the sign on your house."

"But we haven't had a prowler!"

"Yes we did, Aunt Cassidy! He was sneaking around the barn and he was wearing camouflage so he could hide and everything! When he saw that people were home he left and you get into so much trouble with bad guys I wanted the police to get him before he could hurt you! He's in that house! He won't get away! They'll catch him. I know they will!"

I looked at the house. Hazel and Wally's house. I should have known. ARGH! I should have guessed.

"Okay, the guy my nephew saw was *supposed* to be sneaking around my house. He comes to my house to practice sneaking up on the deer. He wasn't doing anything wrong…"

The sirens screamed to a halt and an officer bounded from the vehicle.

How Big John was able to bound, I'd never know. He must have a soft spot for little kids and thought Patrick was in danger.

"The police are here," I told the woman, "and I have a lot of explaining to do. I've got to go."

Bam, bam, bam. Big John pounded on Hazel and Wally's door.

More sirens in the background.

I headed for the house.

"Who is it?" Hazel asked uncertainly.

"Police, open up!" Big John bellowed. Why did it have to be Big John? Hazel was going to faint.

"John!" I called. "This whole mess is just a misunderstanding."

"I have a report of a prowler…"

"Yes, at *my* house. But he wasn't a prowler. He's a friend. Don't take him in. He is welcome to prowl around my backyard. He is learning to stalk deer and the deer visit my house. My nephew hadn't met Mark and he mistook him for a prowler. John, you know how much trouble I get into. Patrick thought he was saving me from a bad guy. He followed Mark here hoping you would arrest him before he could hurt me. But Mark wouldn't hurt me. He's a friend."

Another police car drove up. Jayce took one look at me and rolled his eyes.

"I should have known," Jayce said as he got out of his patrol car. "Cassidy, what have you gotten into this time?"

"Nothing! It wasn't me this time, I swear!"

"Then what are you doing here?"

"Tracking down a missing nephew. Patrick? Where are you?"

Patrick stepped sheepishly forward. "I'm sorry, Aunt Cassidy, he looked like a prowler to me."

"Patrick, this is officer Jankowski and Thompson. They want to take my friend to jail. Tell them what you think happened."

Hazel was cowering behind a barely opened door.

Patrick explained to the officers what had happened while I went and told Hazel that everything was fine. I asked if Mark wouldn't mind stepping outside for a minute.

"Patrick, is this the man you saw at my house?"

His eyes got real big. "It's the man eating cow!" he exclaimed.

Hoo, boy! Now I had even more to explain.

"How did you know he had dark hair and brown eyes?" Patrick glared at Mark. "Do you have a camera?" he asked Mark seriously.

Hazel invited everyone into the house and for the next hour we sorted it all out. I think it took an hour for Big John to get enough divinity. He took a piece as a favor to the hostess, but within minutes he began mindlessly taking one candy after another.

Hazel's Christmas tree was decorated in neon ornaments. There were pink flamingos and beer commercial ornaments, glowing palm trees, surfboards and woody cars. Where she found all the neon ornaments and why she would collect them was beyond me, but it was kind of cute in a Hazely sort of way.

The officers finally wrote off the call as a misunderstanding and left on a sugar high, waddling back to their cars. I stood outside and waved as they drove away.

"Now, Patrick, this is Mr. and Mrs. Mireau and their son Mark. They're my neighbors and are welcome at our house anytime. Mark sneaks around the backyard a lot and I forgot to tell you. He's studying stalking, too. The deer don't come to his house, so he comes to our place. I think you owe them an apology. People don't like having their homes invaded by the police."

"I'm sorry Mr. and Mrs. Mireau, and Mark, too. You don't look as scary when you're at home."

"Cassidy, did I get this right, that kid followed me all the way home talking to the police the whole way because he thought I was a prowler?"

"Um, yeah."

"Wow, buddy, you're good! I didn't even know you were there! Cassidy ought to teach you how to track and you could work for the police too!"

Patrick stood taller after hearing Mark's praise. "She already is a little bit," he said. "That's how I know you were the man eating cow!"

Mark gave me one of those looks that said, "Help, he lost me somewhere!"

"When you walked to my house yesterday did you startle a doe and try to take its picture?"

"Yeah! How did you know?"

"We were tracking the doe and I gave Patrick a puzzle. He had to figure out what had startled the doe and we determined it was a man eating beef jerky, hence, the man eating cow, and that you tried to take its picture. We figured out that much from the tracks. Then I added that the man had dark curly hair and brown eyes just because I figured it was you and I could surprise Patrick when he found out I was right."

As we rode home in Hazel's old Buick Patrick eyed the house with concern. "You aren't going to tell Uncle Rusty about this, are you?"

"No," I answered truthfully, "I won't have to. Those two officers called him before they got to the end of the street and told him all about it. Things like that get around the station *real* quick. But don't worry; it won't be as bad as you think."

“Ha!” said Hazel.

“It’s really hard to punish a kid for doing what he thinks is right,” I added, attempting to get my point across to Hazel. I wondered if I was the only understanding grownup around, or maybe Patrick was enough like me that I simply understood his thinking too well.

Hazel pulled up into the driveway. “Good luck, Patrick,” she said grimly.

“We have to use the back door,” I said to Patrick as we waved to Hazel. “I took off thinking I was just looking around the yard so the back door is unlocked.”

Hazel backed the Buick out of the driveway, across the road, and over a small sagebrush before pulling forward again to head for home.

I opened the oven and took out the little bricks trying to pass for cookies. I threw them away and preheated the oven again.

“You missed the deer for today,” I said.

“No, I didn’t,” Patrick replied.

“You didn’t? How did you stalk the deer if you were stalking Mark?”

“There were lots of deer between your house and Mr. Mireau’s house. They hid from us but I could see some of them. They blend in with the bushes really good, but I could see them moving around trying to stay out of our way. They didn’t even run away very much. They just kept moving like they had somewhere to go.”

“You could see them? Did Mr. Mireau see them?”

“I don’t know. He didn’t stop and try to stalk them.”

“Tell me how you look when you want to see deer.”

This was getting eerie. If he gave me a good explanation of scatter vision I was going to throw in the towel right now.

“How I look? You mean, how I see or what do I look like?”

“How you see. Right now you see me. Is looking for deer different than looking at me?”

“Yeah, I have to look, like, at a whole, big picture. I see big. But blurry. Well, not really blurry, it’s like I only see what I mean to see. I watch for animals moving and when I watch for animals moving everything else is less noticeable. Does that make sense?”

“Yeah, it makes perfect sense to me. Did you know most people don’t use that kind of vision at all? They don’t know how to do it, so they don’t see animals. They can be standing right next to an animal and not see it because they are not looking at it right.”

“But it makes sense to you. You do that, right?”

“Yeah, I do that. You stalked Mr. Mireau, watched the deer and talked to the police all at the same time?”

“Yeah, I didn’t tell the police about the deer, though.”

I was shocked. What was I going to do with this kid? He was like a tracking sponge. He understood tracking in a way I hadn't learned until much later. It made sense to him. Now it felt as though we were wasting time by only stalking deer in the yard. Patrick could be out learning even more advanced tracking techniques. I reminded myself that Patrick was only six years old. He wanted to stalk deer. Even that was advanced for a kid his age. When we went to San Diego maybe Chase could give me some advice.

I baked two more sheets of cookies before Rusty walked through the door. He was holding back a grin, but only half succeeding.

"I heard Patrick got here okay."

"Yeah, he arrived around lunchtime. By four thirty he was at Hazel and Wally's, then about half an hour ago he made it back here again. I spent my time tracking him down and explaining what really happened to Big John and Jayce. It's taken me all day to bake these cookies."

"Did you stalk any deer?"

"We need to talk about that later."

"Oh."

"Chase doesn't happen to want to work on a quarter horse ranch, does he?"

"No, I don't think so. You sound… distressed. Have you had a talk with Patrick yet?"

"No, he knows what he did right and what he did wrong and I believe he really did very little wrong. He showed wisdom beyond his years. It definitely needs some fine-tuning, but I was impressed. If he'd just talked to me *before* calling the police everything would have been fine."

"Do you mind if I talk to him?"

"No, he's expecting it. I think it's a ranch thing. Back home he'd hear about it from his mom and dad, then Steve, then Old Frank, then Grandpa. So he's not exactly looking forward to it. Sorry, but I'm having trouble finding fault with what he did. He thought he was helping me and I hate to punish a kid who was just trying to help. I know he broke the rules. He left the yard, went out without me, and should have talked to me before jumping to his own conclusions, but he still did remarkably well at everything else."

"Okay, I just want to talk."

"I recommend not talking in the office. Going to the office is a bad thing. If you really just want to talk take a walk or build a fire or something. Doing something while talking is easier for a ranch kid. I had a lot of talks while training horses and painting fences. Waiting for a filly to be born is a good time to talk, too."

"I'll keep that in mind."

Rusty walked down the hall, looking for Patrick. Later, I heard the sound of the front door opening and closing. Once I had finished baking the rest of the cookies I started looking around for dinner ingredients. I'd bought them specifically for Patrick's visit. For some reason at that moment though, Zeke's Pizzeria was calling me all the way from in town. Should I answer the call of Zeke's pizza or actually cook something?

Rusty came back looking rather… distressed.

"We better see about Chase taking that job on the ranch," he said. "Someone needs to spend a lot of time with that kid and his parents aren't going to do it. Jesse will educate the talent right out of him."

"Rusty! What an odd thing to say! Jesse might be a little overprotective…" His look silenced me. "Okay, you're right. But it's not like he has to be a tracker just because he has the talent and understanding. Pat can be whatever he wants."

"They'll try to make a horse trainer out of him."

"And if he takes after me and his dad he'll be a good one. And training horses would leave him free for searches if he stays interested in tracking…Why, what did he say?"

"He kept getting distracted and when I asked him what he saw, he started profiling Mark's tracks. He didn't know that's what he was doing. He just started talking about Mark like he knew him. He said something like, 'Mr. Mireau wants to stalk deer but he learned too much. I think he must have gone to one of those big, fancy schools for rich kids. You can't act all snooty with deer. You have to act like you belong with them. He needs to sit in the yard and listen to the deer, then he could stalk them better. If he would listen to the deer instead of trying to get them to do what he wants, he would do better. And he needs shoes that don't feel clumpy….'"

"We don't know if he's right, it's just his subconscious putting little things that he reads together."

"Why would a set of tracks make him think about Mark's schooling? How does he know Mark's boots make his feet feel clumpy?"

"He doesn't, but there's one way to find out. And it is possible to see that a person's shoes are uncomfortable. There is a certain way people normally walk and if their shoes feel clumpy they will walk awkwardly. He might have noticed an odd pattern in Mark's tracks."

"You want to ask Mark?"

"You know Mark is somewhat at home in the outdoors but he isn't real seasoned to it. A lot of his travels involve people carrying everything for him and he follows guides. In places where he is well known Mark doesn't have to tell them his name at the hotel desk or even need to wait for a taxi. He has a secretary that keeps track of all his comings and goings. So it doesn't surprise me at all that Patrick saw that as a rich kid mentality."

Patrick came into the kitchen carrying an armload of pinecones.

"Do you have any peanut butter?" he asked.

"Yeah, why, are you hungry? I think I hear Zeke's calling. You said you liked pizza."

"Yeah! But I didn't want the peanut butter for me. I put peanut butter on pinecones and then birdseed sticks on them. I hang them by my bedroom window and the birds come eat. I watch them and find them in my book. I have a list of birds. See? I checked off House Finch and House Sparrow and White Crowned Sparrow and Oregon Junko and Dark Eyed Junko. I thought maybe you might have different birds at your house."

"I'm sure we can find some peanut butter and bird seed around here somewhere. How about some pizza?"

Zeke's was quiet when we arrived, probably since everybody was out Christmas shopping and not thinking about pizza. Zelda was our waitress this time and I watched as a Ziggy and a Zeus passed by our table. I could have sworn Zelda used to be Brenda.

"What's with the Z names?" I asked Zelda.

"Zeke thought it would be cute if we all had Z names, kind of like the fifties diner downtown has waitresses like Bubbles and Barbie and BobbyJo. Zeke went with Z names, but it's a little confusing because we just pick up a name tag when we come in and then we have to remember who we are all day and sometimes there are only guys names left and I hate being Zack or Zed or Zechariah all day!"

"Can I play Area 51?" Patrick asked.

"Does your mom let you?" I asked.

"No, but if I go with my dad we play it. He beats me all the time."

"Well, that's to be expected. He practices with real guns. Rusty and I have to keep in practice too. Why don't you guys play? I'll let you know when the pizza gets here."

They went to the game room and pretty soon I heard the sounds of fake gunshots and fake screams followed by a voice calling out, "Don't shoot the civilians."

"What's a civilian?"

"Only shoot bad guys. You lose points if you shoot good guys."

It didn't take long for Patrick to lose. I think Rusty quit with some shots left over.

"So what's a civilian?" Patrick persisted.

"If you were on the police force it would be anybody not in law enforcement. If you were a soldier it would anybody not in the military. It's the normal, everyday people of a country. The moms, the kids, the pizza waitresses, the teachers and delivery boys and lion tamers and… just people outside the organization."

"Is Aunt Cassidy a civilian?"

"Technically, no, she was in the military and she could still be called back if they needed her. And as a reserve deputy she could be called into service at any time. So, even though she looks like a civilian, she isn't."

"Then how can you tell, on the game, who to shoot and who not to?"

"The game is a little more straightforward than real life."

"Do bad guys try to shoot Aunt Cassidy because she's not a civilian?"

"I wish it were that simple."

"Mr. Mireau looked like a bad guy. He acted like a bad guy. How do you tell a bad guy from a good guy?"

"Ask a grownup. Don't trust anybody unless you ask a grownup you know and trust. If you would have asked Aunt Cassidy about the man in the backyard she would have told you who he was and why he was there."

"Is Mr. Mireau a civilian?"

"Yes, he's a photographer," I replied.

"He looked like an Army guy."

"That's because I told him he could stalk deer easier in camouflage clothes."

"This is confusing. You look like a civilian but you're not and Mr. Mireau looks like an Army guy but he's a civilian."

"Are you this curious about everything?" I asked.

"Yeah, my mom gets tired of it and tells me to be quiet. She hardly ever knows the answers to my questions anyway. Like how do you tell a coyote track from a dog track and how come Zack's footprints always leave sand scattered? And do snakes leave tracks?"

"Yes, snakes leave tracks in sand and Zack's tracks leave sand scattered because he can't keep still. He rushes a lot. Have you ever noticed how he rushes and then tries to force himself to slow down? When he's in slow mode his tracks look more normal and when he's back to normal, nervous Zack, his tracks will scatter sand because he's always in a rush. Coyote tracks are a different shape than a dog's tracks and they almost always trot. When we get home I'll show you in a book the difference between a coyote track and a dog track."

The questions from Pat never stopped all the way back home. If he tagged a deer what could he stalk next? What if a person switched shoes? Did the person's tracks look the same in different shoes? Did I ever see tracks that I didn't recognize and what did I do? How do you stalk birds and squirrels that could climb up into trees?

By the time we reached home it was bedtime. After Pat had changed into pajamas I sent him to bed with one of the easy books. Although he needed a little help with a few words, it pleased me to see him sounding out words, even words with a silent *e* in them. When he'd read the address off of Hazel and Wally's house he'd known how to read the word *road* as well as *lost* and *hills*.

Later I sat down on the couch next to Rusty with a relieved sigh. Rusty smiled. "Not ready to be a mom yet, are you?"

"Not if they call 911 just because a neighbor is stalking deer in the backyard. Not if they stalk people away from the house and try and have friends arrested."

He laughed. "Jankowski and Thompson had fun with that one. They called me before they got back to town."

"I thought they might. Patrick was real worried that I'd tell you about it, but I warned him that you'd know whether I told you or not. He thought he'd really get punished for this. I guess he would have back home."

"You understand him because he thinks like you did. When I heard about today it was just like hearing Old Frank tell stories about when you were a kid."

"Gee, thanks."

"It shows he's a thinker. He knew, if he didn't do something, that bad guy was going to eventually hurt you. He didn't care that he was only six and that, if the bad guy discovered him, he could be in a world of hurt. Patrick saw what needed to be done and he did it. The fact that Mark is a friend had very little to do with it. You should have heard the comments at work. I heard, 'You're starting your nephew out early, Michaels. Starting him off on prowlers so he'll be ready for felons by the time he hits academy?' and 'Your wife nabs the tough ones, you send your nephew after the easy ones?' They were just kidding, but it would help if I could bring in just one guy without your help."

"I don't mean to!" I said.

Crossing paths with the men Rusty had been looking for was totally by chance. It was out of my hands. I blamed the trouble magnet. Only the trouble magnet could cause something like that to happen twice in the past few months.

"Are you ready for bed?" Rusty asked.

"No, it's still early and Patrick isn't asleep. He only promised to stay in bed."

"Will he?"

"He knows that only means to give himself a chance to get to sleep. If he gets scared or lonely he's still allowed to get up. I expect another question or two before he knows I'm really serious."

The house felt quiet and still. It seemed like it was just the two of us curled up on the couch together, waiting for that small voice to call out from the bedroom down the hall.

"Did you ever lie under the Christmas tree when you were little and look up into all the layers of lights and shiny ornaments? I used to think it was magic," I said.

"What was magic?"

"I don't know, just the Christmasy feeling I got from watching the lights twinkle. It was a warm, fuzzy and comfortable feeling and it just felt like magic."

"Do you want to go lie under the Christmas tree and watch the lights again?"

"I don't think it's magic anymore. Magic comes in other forms now."

"Aunt Cassidy?" a hesitant voice called from down the hall.

"I think he can hear us. What do you think?" Rusty asked quietly.

"What is it Patrick?" I called back.

"Does Santa leave footprints?"

Hmm, I didn't know. If Santa were magic he might not.

"I don't know, Patrick, I've never tried to track Santa before."

"I'll try to track him this year. Then we'll know," Patrick replied.

"You do that Patrick."

"Can you stalk Santa? If he knows if you're bad or good he might know he was being stalked."

"Plus he has all those reindeer keeping watch over things too. He might be a little hard to stalk."

"Good night, Patrick," Rusty called out.

A few minutes later, "What about owls? Can you sneak up on owls? They can see behind them."

"You'll be lucky if you ever find an owl to stalk. They hide during the day and only hunt at night. Stalk them like you would a person who can turn around at any time. Now go to sleep."

"I can't, I'm not sleepy and then I think of questions and I can't sleep with unanswered questions."

"This sounds all too familiar," Rusty observed.

"I'll be back in a minute, I hope."

I went into the guestroom. "Pat, we can't answer questions all night. If I start that, one question will just lead to another and you'll never get to sleep. The deer show up really early and if they come you'll have to be ready. That means waking up while it is still dark out."

"But I can't sleep," he complained.

"Yes, you can, it just feels like you've been in here forever but it's only been fifteen minutes. When you think of a question, start trying to think of an answer. Think of all the facts you know surrounding the question. Ask yourself more questions and what those answers might be. Eventually you will get to sleep."

"How do I do that?"

"Well, give me a question."

"Mice are so little do they have tracks too?"

"Okay, now reason it out. Where would you find mouse tracks, if they did leave tracks? How big are mice? They are really, really little so they have really little tracks. How would you go about finding a mouse? Just ask yourself more and more questions. When you answer the questions you know the answer to, you sometimes will answer your original question just by thinking instead of asking. So, answering those few questions, you think, mice like the barn. They like oats. If you look in the barn near the oats, you will see if mice leave tracks. See, you can answer your own questions if you just think. If a question pops into your head, just think of more questions on the same topic, and answer the ones you can and I bet you get to sleep and wake up smarter, too."

As I plopped down onto the couch again I asked Rusty, "What am I going to do with that kid?"

"Just ask yourself more questions on the same topic and maybe you'll answer your own question."

"Very funny."

"No, you were right. And you were right to tell him that. You're good at getting him to think for himself."

"I hope he doesn't think for himself *too much*. It can be dangerous."

Chapter 9

My alarm went off at quarter to five. I wanted plenty of time to shower, get dressed and cook breakfast before the deer arrived. According to the thermometer it was sixteen degrees Fahrenheit outside. Hopefully Patrick brought some warm clothes for stalking. He wandered out from his bedroom, sleepy eyed and still wearing his PJs.

"What are you doing up so early?" I asked.

"You said the deer get here at six and I am used to getting up early because the rabbits are on the grass when the sun comes up. Then after the rabbits finish, the birds visit my window. Then after the birds have been there a while, Mom wakes me up for school. I have to get on the bus on the big road at seven thirty. After the deer come can we make bird feeders?"

"Sure, or you can just watch the birds at my bird feeders. The birds are different depending on what I put out there. If I put regular birdseed out then I get the same birds you have checked off on your list. If I put out peanuts I bet we can get some Stellar's jays, gray jays and scrub jays."

He ran back to his room and dug through his suitcase then returned with a field guide to North American birds, a book way beyond his reading ability.

"What's a jay look like?" he asked.

"Look for the Stellar's Jay. The others should be on the same page. It's blue but it fades to black at the head. It has a pointy head."

He leafed through the book until he found the page showing the jays.

"Cool! They will come to the feeder if you give them peanuts?"

"The Stellar's will. The others only show up once in a while. I'll show you where the feeders are after Uncle Rusty gets up. What do you want for breakfast? Pancakes? Eggs? Bacon?"

"Pizza?"

"You want leftover pizza for breakfast?" I asked doubtfully. I'd had my share of cold pizza breakfasts but it was only because I was lazy and hungry at the same time.

"Can I? It has meat and milk and vegetables and bread. I learned that from Mom. She was eating chocolate cake for breakfast. She said it had milk and bread and eggs in it so it was just like eating a regular breakfast. Dad said it was like eating Count Chocula with extra sugar."

I hadn't planned on hearing the family secrets, but this was kind of fun.

"Sure, you can have pizza today. Not every day, but this morning it's okay. Do you want it microwaved?"

"Do I have to eat it at the table?"

"It would be better, then you don't have to worry about dropping it and giving Shadow a pizza feast."

"Then I guess you can microwave it."

He ran to the window but it was still dark outside.

"The deer will start moving around as the sun comes up."

"Can I go outside for a little while?"

"You need to dress warm. It's below freezing out there."

"Only two minutes? I won't freeze in two minutes."

"At least put on some shoes and your coat." If Jesse had been here she'd have had a fit.

He ran to his room, pulled on his shoes and coat and ran outside through the back door. He jogged across the yard, knelt in the frosty grass and stared at the junipers. He looked this way and that, while he quietly sat. He then ran back inside, obviously happy, and dropped his jacket onto the back of the couch.

"What were you doing out there?" I asked.

"Inviting the deer to come," he said in a matter of fact manner, as if I should have known.

"How do you do that?"

"Just like you would a friend, except you don't have to talk. You talk deer talk to them."

"And what does deer talk sound like?"

"It doesn't sound like anything."

"Where did you learn that?"

"I just decided it was the polite thing to do. Deer don't like to be told what to do, just like kids, but they like to know they can come."

"Do you think they will come now?"

"Yup," he said cheerfully.

I set down a warm slice of pizza and a fork.

"What would happen if you invited a coyote?"

"I wouldn't invite a coyote if the deer were here. The deer would think I was tricking them."

"But if the deer weren't coming and you wanted to see a coyote, would it work for a coyote?" I was really curious now. What thought processes made him think he could just go out there and invite the deer over for breakfast?

"Coyotes don't listen very well. They do what they want no matter what people say."

"What about the dogs at the ranch? Do they come when you invite them?"

"No, they got used to being talked to, so you have to talk to them."

It made perfect sense to me except for the part about the deer listening.

Pat ate the pizza, debating each time he came across a bell pepper. Holding up the peppers for inspection, he remembered he had stressed the importance of vegetables being on the pizza, so he had to eat it. This was one odd kid. When he was finished, he ran to the window to see dawn just starting to color the sky on the horizon.

"You've got plenty of time. Why don't you go pick out some warm clothes to wear outside? You'll want jeans, a warm shirt, socks and warm shoes. When you go out, wear your coat and gloves if you brought some."

Patrick ran off, ready to start stalking, and returned wearing jeans, moccasins and a sweatshirt that read "Barn Brat". It had a picture of a bunch of cowboys in a barn with a little kid tagging along. He ran to the window again.

"They won't be here until it gets light," I told him.

"They're on their way. They're coming. How far do they have to come from?"

"I don't know. There's a little meadow that they like about a mile away, but I don't know if that's where they come from in the mornings."

"Well, they're coming. I'll see them when they get here."

"What makes you think they're coming?"

"I asked them to."

Just like that. He asked politely, so of course they were coming.

"Let me show you some hand signals we can use to stay quiet, because talking will scare the deer." I held my hand up, palm out. "This means stop." A push down motion. "This means get lower. The more I do it the lower you crouch." The universal hush sign. "Be quiet. Freeze when the deer have their heads up, stalk slowly and silently when they aren't looking. I'll go with you at first so you can copy me. If I think you are doing good and you can continue alone I'll give you a go-ahead signal. I won't speak unless it's really important. Uncle Rusty might be watching but if you notice him don't let on. He knows to stay back and out of sight."

"Come on," he said, pulling my hand.

"Pat, what's the hurry?"

"They're coming."

"And?"

"And I want to meet them. I asked them to come and they'll expect me to be there."

I started to say it didn't work that way but decided to go along with him.

"Get your coat and gloves."

I headed to the bedroom for my own coat and gloves and found Rusty was awake so I asked him, "Have you heard Patrick talking out there?"

"No, why?"

"I'll tell you later, after I see if it really worked."

I gave Rusty a kiss then met Patrick back in the dining room.

"You're sure. If we go out there the deer are going to come and they are expecting you?"

"I think so. Come on."

"If we have to wait out there we're going to freeze."

"Come… on!"

"Okay! I'm coming," I said as I followed him out the door. "Quiet, stop and look first. If you see deer, stalk quietly for the corner of the barn."

Pausing, we looked into the junipers, glanced around, then quietly walked to the barn watching the junipers as we went. I opened the barn door slightly so we could get out of the wind.

"The deer are used to me working in here so they won't worry if they see us coming from this direction. Are you sure you want to be out here? We could wait in the house and stay a lot warmer."

"They're on their way."

"Pat, you can't know that."

"Shh…" All right, I'll stand in the barn waiting for some deer to answer the call of an overconfident boy.

Peeking around the barn, his eyes suddenly lit up and he glanced back at me. He pointed the way before slipping out of the barn. I reached out to stop him but he stood out in the open showing himself to the deer. Pat then knelt down again just as he had when he first invited them over. I stood quietly at his side. A doe walked out of the trees. I half expected her to bow in acknowledgment but she bent to taste the frost-covered grass. Patrick just knelt there. When three does were standing in the yard he carefully stood and looked to me. I gave him a "ready?" look and he returned a "not yet" look. He watched the yard, waited for the deer to feed and then stepped forward, alert, while carefully observing the deer. With his eyes he pointed left. I followed his gaze. The buck.

Step by smooth and silent step we inched out to the yard, Patrick as my little shadow, copying my movements, yet somehow remaining detached. He was quick to freeze and surprisingly patient waiting for the deer. He stepped forward a little too soon and the deer's heads all snapped up. He froze and waited for a long while until the nearest doe trotted off a bit and stopped. The buck stepped out onto the grass, making his presence known. Patrick knelt down again, seemingly acknowledging the buck's position within the herd. Where had he learned this stuff? When Pat saw it was safe, he rose and stepped toward the herd again with stealthy, quiet steps. Freeze. Heads down. Two more steps. Freeze. The deer peered over our shoulder. I imagined them looking Rusty in the eye as he took his place in the bay window. We waited for them to accept the change and go back to feeding. I sensed Patrick's impatience. I knew standing in the field motionless when you were literally freezing wasn't always fun. There was no complaining or shivering allowed. Pat could have given this up at any time and I wouldn't have faulted him for it. However, the longer he stuck with it the more credit I had to give him. I didn't expect him to get very far this first time. The deer were still fifty or sixty feet away. He was close enough to get a good look at them and likewise, the deer could now get a good look at us. Sixty feet was plenty close. In the deer clearing near the ranch it would have taken us a few hours to get this close.

The deer took their time relaxing and Patrick was having trouble staying still. No nose itches, no sneezes, no flexing sore muscles. We had to freeze. The deer's heads went down, step, step, pause, cautious step, freeze.

We were down to forty feet and for no apparent reason the deer suddenly had better things to do, so they wandered off. I watched Patrick as he allowed himself to relax. He walked quietly behind the deer as they moved off to their next destination. He knelt one more time and then got up and followed me into the house. We stomped around the house, hands in pockets waiting for the warmth to take hold. Rusty appeared at the end of the hall in boxer pants and a t-shirt.

He came in and took a seat on the old brown couch.

"Patrick, come here," Rusty said. "You did great! I was watching from the bedroom window. You got a lot closer than I did on my first try stalking."

Patrick looked thoughtful.

"I guess I can't expect them to know me so soon," he said.

"What do you mean?" Rusty asked.

"I talked to them. I asked them to come and they did. I guess I should just be glad they came. It's not like they had to. They could have stayed away."

"Patrick, whether the deer show up or not is purely chance. They come when they think the grass here is worth the trip. Sometimes we see them frequently; sometimes they stay away for a few days at a time," Rusty said.

"Next time they will know me better. Did I scare them away?"

"Not that I could tell," I said. "Usually, if you scare them, they suddenly look at you very alert and then they move quickly away. This time it just seemed to be time to move on."

"I don't want to scare them. I know what it feels like to be scared and I don't want them to be scared."

"The fear deer feel is different from the fear people experience," I told him. "They don't dwell on it. They don't think about what could have happened. It's more like when you are startled by something and then jump away, 'Yikes!' and then you don't think about it much anymore because what scared you is gone. If you stay nice and quiet and move gently and smoothly, you won't make them afraid to come here. If deer stayed away from any place they could meet predators, they couldn't live in the mountains. They know dangers lurk so they stay alert but they don't worry about things like small boys trying to stalk them in a yard."

"What do deer worry about then?"

"Animals don't worry like people do. They can fret but they don't dwell on things. Deer pretty much live for the moment."

"You make it sound like they don't think."

"Well, deer do think some. They know where the grass is green and where to find water. They seem to remember when a water source has dried up and will check back later, but deer don't think like people do. There isn't some Einstein deer out there that is going to suddenly approach some scientist and try to explain the meaning of life to them. Deer know about grass and what trees are edible when the grass is gone and how to stay warm in the snow. They are only smart in the areas they need to be. Their world is very small. Patrick, why do you worry about what the deer think?"

"Because… they matter too."

I could hear Rusty's dad telling me, "Every life is precious." I guess Patrick had decided the same thing.

"I'm glad you think that way, but don't worry about them. The deer get along fine and they will be back. Now Uncle Rusty is going to shower and get dressed in the bathroom so we can put peanuts in the platform feeder and watch the birds."

Patrick followed me outside to where I kept the bins of birdseed. After filling one bird feeder with wild birdseed, I had Patrick put a scoop of peanuts in the platform feeder. I needed to buy suet and wished I'd known earlier how much Patrick liked watching the birds. With the right seed I could probably draw in a few acorn woodpeckers, maybe some flickers.

It didn't take long for the birds to realize there was food out there. I set Patrick up in the bay window with his bird book opened to jays and a bookmark in place for the sparrows and finches. I went to the kitchen and started preparing breakfast. Every once in a while I went to the bedroom and put my ear to the bathroom door.

"What are you doing?" Patrick asked.

"Checking the time," I told him. "When Uncle Rusty starts shaving I know it's time to start making his breakfast. If I start too soon it will be cold before he finishes." I returned to the kitchen and puttered around, waiting for the right time to start cooking.

"Ooo! Ooo!" I heard down the hall. "It's a jay! It's a jay! I don't have any jays checked off!" Then later, "Darn, house finches and purple finches are both red. How do you tell light red from dark red?" And then later, "Aaaah! Aunt Cassidy! A big bird got one of the little ones!" He ran into the kitchen. "A big bird got one of the little ones!" he repeated.

"Some big birds eat little birds," I replied calmly. "It's just a fact of life. What kind of big bird was it? A hawk? An owl? It was probably a hawk if it was out in the daytime."

We went back to the bay window to see if the hawk was perched somewhere close by, eating his breakfast, but it was nowhere to be seen.

"Did you notice how big it was? What color? Any patterns, especially on the tail? Did it have a cute little mask on? Sparrow hawks have really striking facial markings."

"I don't know. I was so mad at it I didn't think of finding it in the bird book."

"Well, look up hawks and read about them. See which ones live in this area, which ones eat small birds. Maybe you can narrow it down." And so the bird detective went to work. He sat at the dining room table poring through a book that had been written for adults. I guess he was used to not understanding all of it because he never asked questions except to get the pronunciation of the names. Rusty came into the kitchen for breakfast and saw Patrick engrossed in the bird book.

"I think you'll have to watch and see if it comes back and then remember to watch its markings," I told him.

"I don't want it to come back," he said. "Not if it eats the little birds!"

"You said you wanted to see birds. You didn't say what kind. Hawks are like the bobcats and lynxes of the air. Just like wildcats eat rabbits, hawks eat small birds. Surely you've seen hawks at the ranch."

"Mom and Dad don't pay much attention to the birds. They're too busy. I think they are missing a lot because they don't bother to look around them. It's just get this done and get that done. So I watch the birds and go stalking by myself. But it's hard because I can't leave the yard. It is so boring. Schoolwork and the yard, that's all I get to do."

I could empathize. At six, he was pretty much stuck under Jesse's watchful eye. He wanted to stalk deer but was limited to watching birds and rabbits. I'd always pushed the rules when I was growing up, but that was the reason for much of the trouble I'd gotten into.

Rusty and I sat at the dining room table watching Patrick deeply engrossed in the book.

"How old were you when you started reading?" Rusty asked me.

"I read easy books in first grade. It was when I realized that people wrote about all the things that interested me that I really started reading. It was mostly books just like that one. Field guides, survival books, horse books. Whatever interested me at the time, I wanted to know as much as possible about it. My father would buy me the books and then my mom would hide and watch as I tried all the things I read about. Of course, the older I got the more adventurous I became. My mom was afraid to get me any more books, but my dad wasn't. He fed my imagination with more and more adventures to try. One time I…" oops, nope I better not tell Rusty that particular story with Patrick listening because I didn't want to try and find him if he pulled the same thing. "I'll tell you some other time."

"Aw, Aunt Cassidy, that's mean!"

"And that's precisely why I won't tell him. Because you'd listen. And then you'd try it."

"Try what?"

"I'm not falling for that. You think I didn't try that when I was a kid? By the way, that works really good on Zack and Randy. Zack forgets right away that he wasn't going to say something. Randy just likes to talk. If you do that to Old Frank he just glares at you and says, 'I weren't born yestidy, y'know.'"

"What does Steve do?"

"Steve doesn't have to do anything."

When Rusty left for work Patrick and I stood in the entryway looking at each other with a "Now what?" expression on our faces. Here we were in a nice warm, quiet house and the deer had come and gone for the morning.

"I need to get out. Let's go visit some friends."

"Do we have to? When Mom goes to visit friends she ends up drinking tea and I have to play some baby game with Sammy and Richie."

"I don't have those kinds of friends, at least not yet. Let's go visit the rangers up in the mountains. I haven't seen some of them in a long time. You remember Mr. Green don't you?"

His eyes brightened at the prospect of having some guy talk. He might even get to see some more birds for his checklist.

"Bring your bird book and some binoculars. You're not getting out of the Jeep without a coat on. It might even be a little snowy up there."

"Snow? Yahoo!" He ran to get his book then grabbed his coat off the back of a chair while I searched for hiking boots, another coat and binoculars.

"What do you use that thing for?" he asked.

"You've never used binoculars before?"

"No. Why do you have them?"

"Every first-rate birdwatcher needs a good pair of binoculars. Look through these lenses and then turn this little wheel until it's in focus. It makes far away things look bigger and you can see details. So if there's a bird in a tree you can see it better. If you see a bird that you want to look at, tell me to stop and maybe we can get a better look at it."

I took him to the end of the driveway.

"See that sign on the Mireau's house? Look at it through the binoculars and you'll be able to read it."

He looked and fiddled with the wheel.

"Oh, cool! Can I use these? Really?"

"Yeah, that's why I brought them, so you could see the birds. Just don't drop them."

It didn't take long for me to wish I'd never brought the binoculars.

"Aunt Cassidy! Stop!" he yelled.

I thought I was about to drive off a cliff or hit the general in my Jeep or something. I screeched to a halt.

"What is it, Pat?" I worriedly asked.

"Can you back up? I think it was by that tree."

Backing the Jeep up we watched as a quail quickly scurried into the brush and vanished.

"Patrick, if it's just a bird sighting, don't panic. Let's try this. First of all watch ahead of the car. Then, if you see a bird, say 'bird at three o'clock' or wherever it is."

"Three o'clock?"

"Picture a clock face. You're facing twelve o'clock. So, as you go around the clock you have one o'clock, two o'clock and three o'clock is directly to your right. Six o'clock is directly behind you. Nine o'clock is to your left. Can you do that? Then I will know it's not an emergency." I pointed to each direction as I said it. The plan was semi-successful. He couldn't think through the clock theory fast enough to stop me from passing the birds so he settled for "bird on my side" and "bird ahead" and that worked for me.

After about a dozen bird stops we pulled into the ranger station. They had a feeder filled with birdseed and Patrick watched it as we walked up, trying to decide if there were any new birds. As soon as we got close they all flew away in a flurry. We stepped into the warmth of the station but all was quiet.

"Hello?" I called out. "Anybody home?"

Paul came out of the back room. He was pudgier and balder than I remembered him.

"Cassidy! Where have you been all this time? You don't stop by like you used to. Did you move away or something?"

"No, I'm still around. You came to my wedding and you've seen the news."

"I just haven't seen you. And, sorry, I didn't make it to the wedding."

"This is my nephew, Patrick. Pat, this is Paul. He's never told me his last name so you can just call him Paul."

"Are you a real ranger?" Patrick asked.

"Yeah," Paul said. "There's just not much rangering to do this time of year. We are between seasons so we do a lot of maintenance work. Usually the office isn't even open and I guess it's not open to the public. I just had it unlocked because I'm expecting a bunch of guys in here any minute."

"We're up here looking for deer and birds. And we'd like to say 'hi' to Kelly if he's handy. Pat, why don't you *slowly* walk up to the window so you won't scare the birds away, then you can see if they are in the book."

As Patrick stalked up to the window Paul's eyes got big.

"Don't tell me you're teaching him to track. I swear it's just like watching a miniature you," he commented.

"Umm, yes and no. He just seems to take after me and I promised him I'd take him deer stalking if he touched a wild rabbit. Well, he did, so his mom brought him down here to stalk deer in my backyard."

"Oh! Aunt Cassidy, how do you tell a Mexican jay from a scrub jay?" Patrick called out.

"It's a scrub jay," I said. "Mexican jays don't live here."

"He can read that book?" Paul asked.

"Some of it, some of it he has trouble with. *Mexican* is easy to sound out."

Pat ran over and opened his book to a list in the back and checked off scrub jay.

"You might find deer, birds and Kelly all fairly close together if you head for Jasper Flats. Sometimes the deer feed in that big clearing. Kelly's doing maintenance work on Glen Hollow Campground."

I looked over the map on the counter and planned my route.

"Okay, thanks."

Patrick was back at the window. He couldn't decide if the birds he was watching were house finches or purple finches. I'd never been able to tell the difference either.

"How come scrub jays don't come to the feeder?" Patrick asked.

"Because they eat bugs. Bug eaters won't come to the feeders much. You have to see them in the wild. Birds eat all kinds of things. Big birds eat little birds. Some birds eat seeds. Some eat bugs. Roadrunners eat snakes and lizards," I added. "And many birds eat fish."

"We can't put fish out for the birds, can we?"

"It wouldn't work. The birds that eat fish like to catch their own. Okay, we're off to Glen Hollow Campground. Watch for quail and meadowlarks on the side of the road. Meadowlarks have bright yellow breasts and they wear a black necklace."

"Good luck," Paul called out, "and don't be such a stranger. Stop in again soon."

"I will."

A meadowlark and two coveys of quail later, we pulled into Glen Hollow. It was just as deserted as its name implied. We drove around looking for Kelly or his light green ranger truck and saw that the campground was in sad shape. We found Kelly hard at work painting over graffiti on overturned picnic tables. He smiled broadly as we drove up. As I got out of the Jeep Kelly's big black lab galloped up. I jumped back into the Jeep and slammed the door shut. Kelly shot me an odd look as he leaned up against the hood of the Jeep. I leaned back in the seat and started counting to twenty. Then I looked down into the dog's big brown eyes. Okay, Cass, you know this dog is harmless. Just get out. It's easy. He may jump on you, but he's friendly. I psyched myself up and then slowly opened the door. Kelly commanded his dog to sit and he obeyed, but I could sense the tension just under the surface. Friendly tension, Cass. He just wants to say 'hi'. I slid out of the Jeep. By now Patrick had run around our vehicle and was enthusiastically petting the big black dog. I reached down and patted the massive head. Flashbacks echoed in my mind. Dogs rushing at me. I tried to put it away. I knew this dog wouldn't hurt me. I had played with Amos many times on visits with Rusty to Kelly's house. But right now I couldn't. I just couldn't force myself to be close to the dog for any length of time. I hoped that would change, but right now it was a sharp fear that made my heart pound and my flight mode kick in.

"Hey kiddo," Kelly said. "You okay? Amos won't hurt you."

"I know. Big dogs just trigger something in me. Rusty doesn't understand it either, how I always loved dogs and then after one trouble attack I'm scared of them. But he never saw the dogs the way I saw them. The fear will fade with time. I know most dogs are friendly."

"What are you doing way up here?"

"Keeping Patrick out of trouble. He gets bored at home. Did Rusty tell you what he did yesterday?"

"No, I haven't talked to Rusty in a week."

"We're up here looking for birds and deer. Patrick has a checklist and he's found several birds today that he'd never seen before. Here, Patrick, take the binoculars and see if you can find any new birds. Just stay where we can see you."

Patrick walked around the campground staring into the bushes and trees.

"So, now that he's out of earshot, what did Patrick do yesterday?"

"Mark came over to the house to stalk deer and Patrick, seeing a man sneaking around the backyard, thought he was a prowler. The deer bypassed my house, maybe because they saw Mark there. Anyway, Patrick grabbed my cell phone and called 911 as he followed Mark home. When he got to Mark's house he read the address off a sign on their house. I tracked down Patrick right before the police came screaming up the road. It was embarrassing. I was glad both officers knew me."

Kelly laughed loudly. "What did you do to him?"

"Nothing, I couldn't fault the kid for doing what he thought was right. He thought Mark was a bad guy stalking me. What's a kid to think when bad guys regularly *do* stalk me? It was the logical conclusion for a six-year-old to reach. He's heard all the stories. How was he supposed to know that some men sneak around my backyard and are welcomed there?"

"Is everything okay at the ranch? Why is he here?"

"He tagged a rabbit."

"Already?"

"Yup, surprised me, too. I thought it would be at least another year before I'd be taking him deer stalking."

"Aunt Cassidy! Can you still see me?" Patrick called from a distance. I looked around. No Patrick.

"No, Pat, stay closer."

"Aw, how come, I can see you!" he called back.

"Where are you?"

"Look up!"

My heart skipped a beat. Oh, hell. "Patrick! What are you doing way up there? You get down here, right now!"

"I'm stalking a bird. A little brown bird that goes hop, hop, hop around the tree. Can you find it in the book? I couldn't climb with the book so I thought I'd see it real good and then look it up after I get down." He struggled to hold onto the tree and the binoculars at the same time. Kelly gawked up into the tree, then shot me a worried look.

"Get down *now*! If your mom saw you up there she'd strangle me!"

"Okay!" Then suddenly, "Ahh, I can't!"

Sigh. Kelly and I exchanged glances.

"Got a rope?" I asked.

"I always have a rope."

"Can I use it?"

"What are you going to do?"

"I'm going to climb up there, fashion a harness out of the rope and then lower him down to you."

"No way."

"Why?"

"Because if Rusty saw you way up there he'd strangle me."

"We won't tell Rusty you were here. Besides, your paint is drying."

"To hell with the paint. Paint is supposed to dry eventually."

"Not in the can. I'll be fine."

We found the rope and Kelly followed me to the tree.

"Kelly, no, look, he's my responsibility. I'll get him down." We had a short stare down. I stood tall and put all my twenty-six years of being daddy's girl into it.

"Cassidy, how do you do that?" he asked, backing down with a sheepish grin on his face.

We coiled and tied the rope so I could wear it and still climb. I draped it over my shoulder and started climbing. I was maybe six feet off the ground when I noticed I was covered in sap. Anything that came remotely close to touching the tree became sappy.

"Patrick? Did you get sap all over you?"

"What's sap?"

"Sticky stuff."

"Yeah, it was on the tree."

"Oh, Pat, that stuff doesn't wash out of anything. We're both going to be sticky for the rest of our lives."

"Can I go to school sticky?"

"Yeah, but you might stick to your desk and then you won't be able to go home."

"I better not go to school. I might get the other kids sticky."

"Sorry, buddy, sap isn't an excuse to skip school."

"How come the birds don't stick to the tree? I remember Dad put up this sticky paper and flies got stuck to it. It freaked me out hearing the poor flies stuck on the paper, buzzing until they died there. I felt sorry for them."

"The birds know where to go so they don't get sappy."

Kelly laughed quietly at the bottom of the tree while I climbed higher and higher.

"How did you get this high up?" I asked Patrick.

"I told you, I followed a little bird. I wasn't thinking about how far it was."

The branches were bending uncomfortably now. Patrick was able to climb higher because he weighed less. I stood on a branch looking for a sturdy way up and it broke out from under me. I grabbed the next branch on my way down and pulled myself up, unsteadily. I sat on the branch catching my breath.

"Kelly?"

"Yeah?"

"We're going to do a sort of belay."

I tied the rope around my waist and formed the rest of the rope into a bundle that I could fling over a sturdy fork in the tree above where Patrick was stranded. I tossed the bundle up and over Patrick's head. When it finally landed on the other side, I pulled in the bundle of rope and untied it, lowering the end down through the branches to Kelly.

"Just take up the slack as I climb," I called down.

I climbed up to Patrick's level holding onto the sturdy middle trunk, then inched out along the branch. Kelly reluctantly fed me more rope.

"Pat, I can't come any further without breaking the branch. You know what it means if the branch breaks. Reach out to me. When you do, grab my wrist, not my hand. Grab the wrist. Got it?"

Six inches. Four inches. With each movement the branch bobbed more and more. I leaned out, grabbed Patrick's wrist and pulled him to me. With that, the branch snapped and fell tumbling downward, bouncing off lower branches as it went. I instinctively grasped Patrick's wrist and held on as we rode the rope straight into the trunk of the tree.

Patrick yelled, "Ahhhhhhhhh," as though he was falling off a cliff but the bounce off the trunk stopped him short. I took the brunt of it, having been on the inside of the fall.

"Cassidy! Are you okay?" Kelly shouted up the tree.

I finished bouncing and swinging around before I answered.

"Yeah, give us some rope."

He slowly lowered us to a sturdy branch where I untied the rope and made a harness for Patrick.

"Use your hands and feet to ward off the branches and just ride it down," I told him. "Ready?" I called out to Kelly.

"Ready," he called back.

I lifted Patrick and lowered him over the branch.

"Take up slack," I called down.

When the roped felt taut I released Patrick, and Kelly lowered him to the ground. I began climbing down. Kelly would have lowered me down too, but I didn't feel like accepting any more help today. When I had my feet safely on the ground I glared down at Pat.

"New rule," I said. "Keep your feet on the ground unless specifically told to do otherwise."

He stared at his feet. "Yes, Ma'am," he said softly.

"Okay, now that we got our daily disaster over with let's look up that bird. I know what it was but you need to figure it out for yourself. I'll give you a hint. Look in amongst the birds like the nuthatch. It should be close to those birds in your book. Remember, it looks like tree bark and it has a long curvy bill so it can pick bugs out of the crevasses of the bark. The name starts with a B."

"Cassidy," Kelly said, "you have the patience of an angel. I would have tanned his hide."

"You never tan *my* hide," I replied and blushed after realizing what I'd said. "I mean…"

Kelly was smiling broadly, enjoying my predicament.

"He was just doing what I would have done. Now he knows not to go so high. Why punish him more?"

"Here it is," Patrick said. "A brown creeper. I would have named it a bark backed beaky bird. I don't get some of these names. I get why they named this one a brown creeper, but, what about the gallinule? Who thought up that? And why did they think gallinule when they saw a bird?"

"I don't know Pat. If you become an ornithologist and discover a new species you can name it whatever you want."

"I could?"

"Yeah, it's just really hard to discover new species because they may have all been discovered already. You'd have to go to college and get a degree in ornithology and then travel to some remote island where nobody has seen birds yet. After that you'd have to actually find one that hasn't been categorized yet… it's a hard job to discover a new species. Now, let me see you. Any scrapes we need to doctor? Nope? You were lucky. I think our trip to the mountains is over for today. We should go home to try and wash off all this sap. We can't do much of anything with all this sap on us."

"Aww, I don't want to go home."

"We need to get back before four o'clock anyway just in case the deer come down to eat. After we've had our baths maybe the deer will come. I'll take you to town and get you some greasy fast food on the way."

"Do we have to?"

"I guess we don't have to right away. I'll give you half an hour to find another bird for your checklist and then when I say 'load up' I really mean it."

Pat started to race off. "Stay in sight, no climbing!" He began prowling through the brush scaring off every bird within half a mile. I visited with Kelly while he finished painting the picnic table and trashcan.

"Want me to pull it back over with my winch?" I asked.

"It's gotta dry first or all the dirt stirred up will stick to it."

We heard giggling from the brush. "It's an Austin Powers bird!" Patrick laughed. He flipped this way and that in his book. Kelly and I looked at each other again. An Austin Powers bird? What in the world was an Austin Powers bird? I snuck through the brush.

"What is it?" he whispered.

"It's a flicker," I laughed. How appropriate was that? "Is it a red shafted or a yellow shafted flicker? When it flies and you can see it's under parts that will tell you."

He rattled the branches and the flicker flew away, revealing red under parts.

"It's a red shafted flicker," I informed him. "It's a kind of woodpecker."

We crawled out of the brush. Leaves had stuck to the sap. I tried to brush them off but they just broke off, leaving little bits of leaf imbedded in the sap.

"Why do you think it's an Austin Powers bird?" I asked.

"It has a big black spot on its chest just like Austin Powers."

Kelly roared with laughter. He seemed to see the humor in everything. "It makes as much sense and it's just as good a visual picture as red shafted flicker!"

"Only if you've seen Austin Powers without a shirt on," I added. "Was that a new bird too?"

"Yeah! I checked off western meadowlark, California quail, scrub jay and red shafted flicker today!"

"And brown creeper," I added. "You don't want to forget that one after all the trouble you went through to see it."

"Can I call Mom when we get home?"

"What are you going to tell her?" I asked, wary about what a call home might entail.

He thought for a minute. "Maybe I better not."

"She'd love to get a call from you. Just tell her you got to stalk the deer and you went bird watching and you saw some new kinds of birds. You don't have to tell her everything."

"If I tell her I got to stalk the deer she'll want me to come home."

"I can't take you home until Friday, that's settled. You'll have more chances to stalk deer. Especially if we go home and get cleaned up."

We pulled into the Carl's Jr parking lot and both of us jumped out of the Jeep ready for a Western Bacon Cheeseburger, but I took one look at Patrick and stopped.

"Look at you, you can't eat in there looking like that."

"Why?"

"You look like you've been tarred and feathered!"

"What's that mean?"

"You've got leaves stuck all over you. And I have little leaf bits stuck all over me too. We'll have to use the drive through and eat at home."

"Aww, I wanted to crawl around in the play place."

"You'd stick to it and then you'd have to live at Carl's Jr forever."

"Okay!"

"Not okay, Rusty and I would miss you. So would your mom, dad, Wyatt, Grandma and Grandpa. Come on, we're driving through, eating at home and taking a long bath to get rid of the sap, then we'll watch for the deer."

"What is sap?"

"It's like tree blood."

"Ewe, I have tree blood on me?"

"Sort of."

"Why was the tree bleeding?"

"Trees just do that. It doesn't hurt them. Okay what do you want?"

"What's the kid's meal prize?"

"Pat, you don't choose your meal according to the toy you might get. If you can eat a big people's meal, I'll buy one. If not, we'll get you a kid's meal."

"Can I get a kid's meal with a Jr Bacon Cheeseburger?"

"I'll check."

Patrick's lunch was eaten before we were half way home. I heard about it each time he found a perfectly cooked French fry. I ran a bath for him when we got home and he closed the shower curtain and played in the water while I ate my lunch.

"Use soap!" I called out.

"Aw, rats."

"Shampoo too!"

"I always get it in my eyes."

"I'll help if you don't mind me coming in."

"I'll try."

"If you feel it running down your head, catch it with the washcloth."

Just monitoring the kid's bath was wearing me out. A hundred questions a day. Discussing the merits of a kid's meal. And just think, if I were his mom I'd be in there shampooing his hair. Keeping track of his whereabouts twenty-four/seven. I wasn't sure I could handle real parenthood.

After his bath, we looked at the platform feeder and found it empty. We put another scoop of peanuts in it and I left him with orders to stay in the house while I showered. Then I took the fastest shower I could remember outside of the Marines.

"Are you still as sticky as me?" I asked after I showered and dressed in the bathroom.

"Yeah, will we really be sticky for the rest of our lives?"

"No, but we will for a few days anyway. At least we will smell more outdoorsy for the deer."

"Except for the soapy smell and the shampooy smell and the fabric softener smell from the towel."

"Well, yeah, there is that. Should we go roll around in the dirt?"

"Yeah!"

"Then you'd need another bath tonight. Have you read a book today?"

"The bird book."

"Okay. Just so you read a little bit every day."

"How come you want me to read but you don't care if I do math?"

"Because you do math anyway."

"I do not."

"Yes, you do. You were doing math when you were trying to figure out the clock. Here, stand up. Show me where three o'clock is."

He thought for a second.

"Twelve is straight ahead?"

"Yeah."

"Then three is that way," he said, pointing right.

"Good, where's six o'clock?"

He pointed behind him.

"Where's four o'clock?"

He pointed to his right and slightly behind him.

"Good! All that is math. It's like a circular number line. How many birds did you see today?"

"Lots!"

"How many did you identify for your checklist?"

He counted. "Five."

"And how many got away before you could figure out what they were?"

He thought a minute. "Six."

I thought it was more than that but I just needed a number.

"So if you had identified all those birds how many checks would you have in your book?"

"Six and five?"

"Yeah."

He thought while counting and decided he didn't have that many fingers. "Eleven?"

"Right! And now you just did math again. You did math the whole time you were measuring ingredients for the cookies. That time you were doing fractions. When you were stalking the deer you were thinking about how far away they were and how much distance you still needed to cross. All that is math, too."

"What about science?"

"You learned science today too. You know birds eat seeds, bugs, smaller birds, snakes and lizards. That's all science."

"What about history?"

"You made your hamburger history. So see?"

"I don't think that counts."

"Well, you're on vacation. I don't expect you to do all your subjects each day you're on vacation. Tell your mom you studied ornithology today. She always likes when you use new words. I bet she doesn't even know what ornithology is."

"What is it again?"

"The study of birds."

"Oh, yeah. Can I call her?"

"Sure."

I tried not to listen as Pat spoke to his parents, but I was worried that he'd go into detail about the past two days. If Jesse really knew what had happened, she'd be down here before nightfall.

"Mom wants to talk to you," Pat said when he was finished.

Gulp. "Hey Jess! Is your house really, really quiet?"

"You wouldn't believe."

"Yes I would."

"Pat is having a great time. I hope he isn't too much trouble."

"No, not at all. Hopefully he'll have better luck stalking the deer this afternoon."

"He was really proud of the fact that he got to have pizza and fast food two days in a row."

"That's a kid for you. I assure you, though, he's been eating other things too." I think. Okay, maybe not yet, hmmm.

"Do you have to teach him big words? I'm not going to be able to understand him when he comes home. What's orthinology?"

I laughed. "I didn't do too good a job. It's orni-thology. The study of birds. He's been working on his bird list."

"Oh yeah, that. I don't see what he sees in it. He spends hours sitting at his window and checking that book."

"It's good for him. It improves his memory to keep track of the bird's markings. It involves categorizing and reading. All those things are important."

"Cassidy, you really should be a mom and have your own kid to teach."

"Me? A mom? I don't think so. I think I'll stick to being an aunt."

"No, you need a baby. Mom needs a new grandchild. Rusty would make a great dad, too."

"I don't need a baby and I wouldn't know what to do with one. I'm perfectly happy the way things are."

"Okay, you don't know what you're missing, though. A baby would help keep you out of trouble too."

Yeah, I thought, I'd be too busy explaining things to the police and climbing three story tall trees to get into trouble.

"Patrick can call you whenever he wants. He was excited about seeing new birds today. He wanted to tell you about it. Are you going to survive until Friday?"

"Yeah, but it *sure is quiet*. I have too much time on my hands. I didn't realize how quiet Wyatt is until Patrick was gone. Sometimes I even wonder if Wyatt's still in the house, he's so quiet."

Yeah, I had wondered the same thing about Pat, except during those moments he usually *wasn't* in the house!

"It's almost four o'clock, time to start the next deer watch."

"Okay, see ya Friday?"

"Yeah."

"Okay, bye."

"Bye."

Whew! Patrick was smarter than I thought. Either that or Jesse was testing me.

"Are the deer coming?" Patrick asked as I hung up the phone.

"We just have to wait and see. Sometimes they do and sometimes they don't. Did you invite them?"

"Yeah, I asked them to come back this morning but they didn't say anything."

"They acted like they had other things to do. Hey, maybe they took off this morning for reasons we don't know about. Maybe if we go back in the trees we'll find out there were predators out there that the deer needed to get away from. If we'd gone to look this morning we could have done some tracking."

"I'm glad we went to the mountains but wish I'd seen snow. I've only seen snow falling. I've never seen it all over the ground."

"I sure have. Once the rainy season starts, the mountains get a lot of snow and then skiers get lost behind the ski resort and I help find them. We wear snowshoes and heavy coats and sometimes our gear freezes. Most people think southern California is all beaches and sunshine, but believe me, it gets cold in spots. Go see if the deer are coming yet."

Patrick went to the den window and peeked out, then he ran to the bedroom and sat in the bay window watching the bird feeder and the hills. When the deer started coming I didn't tell Patrick about it. I wanted the deer to gather outside and get settled before we went out. If everything was calm and settled before leaving the house we'd have better luck. It didn't work. Pat saw the deer coming, too.

"Shoes, coat and gloves," I reminded him. Then I took my time finding my own coat.

"Come *on*, Aunt Cassidy!"

"Pat, one of the things you need to learn in stalking is patience. If you rush things you'll push the deer away. The more settled you let them get in the yard, the calmer they will be when you stalk them. Try it this way just once, and if it doesn't work better than yesterday, we'll go back to your way. Have a cookie while you are waiting. After we go stalking I'm going to make fudge. And we need to cook dinner and have vegetables tonight. You told your mom you'd been eating pizza and fast food so now she thinks I'm spoiling you. I'll make spaghetti. You like that, right?"

"Yeah!"

I looked out the back window.

"Just a few more minutes. The deer are doing good. There are four of them out on the grass and I bet there's another couple still in the trees. Paul was pretty impressed when he saw you sneak up to the window at the ranger station. He thought you'd be good at stalking because of the way you snuck up to the window."

Patrick gave me a surprised look.

"The ranger said that?"

"Well, what he really said was that you stalked like me, but he was impressed or he wouldn't have said anything at all."

A cold wind had come up while we'd been in the house and it was freezing as we stepped outside to stalk. We started out from the back door this time, since the deer took note of us as soon as we stepped out. Crossing the patio was easy. We just waited until the deer were distracted and quietly skimmed over the cement before we stopped at the grass. This angle proved to be easier than starting at the barn. We could use the house and some bushes for cover before actually standing out in the open.

The deer seemed very intent on eating which made me wonder if bad weather was coming. In Joshua hills the winter weather pattern was three days of sunshine followed by several days of wind. The wind would blow in a storm. The high desert version of a storm could be anything from a light drizzle to a hard downpour. If it came out of the east, we'd have rain. If it came from the north, there was a chance of a snowfall. If it came from the west, we'd probably get snow in the foothills but none would fall in town. If the wind was blowing in a storm, the deer might be preparing for it. We might get a real good stalking day in if the deer had a plan.

Now I'm thinking like Patrick, I thought. The deer have a plan; yeah, right. But I couldn't ignore the fact that animals did prepare for bad weather.

I watched the deer. Their heads stayed down so we inched closer. Heads up, freeze. The deer stared at us, daring us to try anything, then they relaxed and looked around for any other dangers. One by one they went back to feeding so we took two more long smooth steps. I signaled Patrick to get down, down, down. We knelt in the grass, just watching the deer. I thought maybe if he rested his legs in a sitting position, he'd have more patience in long still times later in the stalk. Suddenly his expression brightened. He had an idea, but he knew not to share it now. He looked at me and his movement caused the deer to startle. They all jumped slightly and Patrick checked himself, embarrassed that he had slipped. We had to wait for them to settle down again before we smoothly went from our sitting position to a low crouch.

Click, buzz, click, buzz. Mark was here, behind the barn. I hoped he knew to stay out of sight. Patrick didn't seem to notice the camera noises, but the deer did. They stared at the barn, which allowed us to get another step closer. Inch by inch, we crept closer until I noticed a movement in the trees. Now it was my turn to stare off in distraction. What was it? It didn't move like a deer. It was too big to be a coyote. I'd never seen a wolf in the foothills. I'd only seen coyotes and…uh oh…and a mountain lion.

"Pst," I signaled Patrick quietly.

He waited until the deer were distracted then looked at me. With my eyes I signaled, "This way." He gave me a look that said, "Aw, why?" I stared at him with a "Don't question me" look and he replied with an "Okay" look. We stalked over to the side of the house and found a place against the wall. Patrick didn't understand my actions at all. We probably left Mark puzzling about it too. I was hoping my instincts would prove valuable. I signaled for Pat to sit next to me. We curled up small just watching the deer. I saw the movement again and pointed it out to Patrick. He gave me a "What is it?" look and I signaled to just keep watching.

The big cat crouched behind a juniper, watching the deer. Patrick's eyes got real big. I gave him the "hush" signal. The mountain lion was silently planning his stalk, singling out one deer, the weaker one. Patrick gave a "No!" look. He didn't want the mountain lion to catch a deer. I didn't blame him, but mountain lions have to eat, too. I wondered if Jesse would want Patrick to witness the attack but decided to wait and see what happened. If I stood up at the last minute it would throw off the cat and the deer would run away. I felt a little sorry for Mark, missing a great photo opportunity. Before

I could decide anything, the huge cat rushed forward. At the same time, Patrick jumped up and yelled "No!" The deer all scattered and the mountain lion bounded after his target doe. "No! Leave her alone!" he wailed.

We never saw if the mountain lion got dinner that day. Patrick was upset. The deer were gone. Mark came out of hiding, disappointed but elated at the same time.

We were freezing so we all went back inside and I started heating water for hot chocolate.

"That was awesome!" Mark exclaimed.

"Did you get pictures of the mountain lion?" I asked.

"You know how that is. I'll develop them and let you know. I want to give you the pictures of Patrick so he can take them home with him. Moms like pictures of their kids."

"Mr. Mireau is a nature photographer," I told Patrick. "There are posters and calendars and note cards with his pictures on them. He even has a studio in Toronto where he sells prints. He took the pictures in the living room on a trip to Santa Cruz Island."

"I thought those pictures were of you," Patrick said.

I paused. It was odd that Patrick knew the pictures were of me, especially since adults usually didn't recognize me in those pictures.

"They are," I told him. "I was on Santa Cruz Island, too. Pat, you can't get upset whenever you see an animal hunting. Mountain lions need to eat too, you know. How is a mountain lion supposed to eat if it can't catch a deer?"

"I just hate to see one of them die."

"I know, sport, but it's just the way nature works. I was really excited to see a mountain lion. I'd only seen one once before. Do you understand now why I called off the stalking?"

"Yeah, I guess."

"I didn't want the mountain lion to decide you were easier to catch than a deer. Now that we know there's a mountain lion in this area, you can't play outside by yourself. Mountain lions are too dangerous."

"Do you think he caught one of the deer?"

"I don't know, Pat. If you really want to find out we can track him tomorrow. I don't want to track him today because he might still be close by. In the morning, we'll see if we can track him."

"What if we see a dead deer?"

"We don't have to track it if you don't want to, but I'd like to anyway. I don't get to track mountain lions very often."

Mark perked up at the mention of tracking.

"You're going to track the cougar? Can I tag along?"

"Sure, what time can you be over here?"

"Nine?"

"Okay, we can stalk deer in the morning, get Rusty off to work, and then track the mountain lion."

Patrick wasn't sure he wanted to track the mountain lion. His mind was still on the deer. I puzzled over what to do. I didn't want to leave Patrick home alone while I went out tracking.

I started a pot of spaghetti sauce. It was simmering nicely when Rusty arrived home a little early. What a break!

"Can you watch Patrick for about half an hour?" I asked him.

"Sure, I guess, why?"

"We had a little adventure today and I want to see the results of it. Can I borrow your rifle?"

My words brought raised eyebrows.

"I don't expect to use it but my 9mm would be useless."

More raised eyebrows.

"I'm tracking a mountain lion just to see if Patrick can try tracking it with me tomorrow. He doesn't want to track it if he has to see a dead deer so I'm tracking it a little ways to see if the deer is out there. If it's not, then I'll take him with me tomorrow. If it is, we'll skip the tracking. I'm only taking the rifle to be on the safe side."

I called Mark. "I'm doing some pretracking tracking. Want to go? Get over here before it gets dark."

Mark drove up as I was pulling the rifle out of the Explorer.

"And we are doing this, why?" he asked.

"If it's all clear, I'll let Pat do some tracking tomorrow. If there's a dead deer out there, Patrick doesn't want to go."

He followed me to the backyard and I quickly found the place where the cougar had crouched. I pointed out the big cat paw prints in the sand. The tracks showed up well in the evening light.

"Put your hand next to the track so we can get an idea of the scale," Mark said and then photographed my hand next to the paw print in the sand.

I heard the frequent *click, buzz* of Mark's camera as I tracked the cougar. It had chased the herd past the corral and off into the junipers towards the Mireau's house. Then the trail turned downhill and into more open ground where the deer could bound. It didn't take the cougar long to give up the chase and this now seemed like a good trail for Patrick to track, so I happily returned home to report that the deer had gotten away. Patrick brightened noticeably when he knew the deer were safe. Rusty however wasn't as pleased.

"Take the rifle when you go out tomorrow. If there's a hungry cat out there, I don't want you relying on that pistol."

"You might need it for work," I protested.

"Take it, or you're not going out. I won't need it tomorrow. The day is pretty much set." I recognized that tone of voice. He seldom used it with me, but I knew not to question it.

When Patrick was talking and tracking, I had to remind myself that he was only six. When he was eating spaghetti, however, it was a different story. He placed a mound of spaghetti noodles on his plate, hollowed out a hole in the middle and poured the red lava into the noodle volcano until it overflowed and wiped out a forest of asparagus. Rusty and I watched him, wondering how he would manage to eat even half of the food on his plate. He ate a few trees just to say he had vegetables and then started on the volcano. When Rusty and I had clean plates he still had a mountain of food.

"I'm full," he complained.

"It's okay, you don't have to eat it all. I thought you took more than you could eat anyway."

He seemed relieved. After dinner he was bored. It sure didn't take kids long to get bored. I wondered what I did when I got bored and realized I couldn't do that with Patrick around. When Patrick wasn't around I visited with Rusty and then one thing led to another and pretty soon we weren't bored at all.

"Patrick, why don't you tell Uncle Rusty what you did today?" I suggested.

"Do I hafta tell him everything?"

"He's not like your mom. Besides, you didn't break any rules. You just… well, tell Uncle Rusty about it."

So Patrick went into a long monologue telling Rusty all about his day and recounting each bird sighting and how he followed the brown creeper up into the tree. He ran to get his bird book and showed Rusty all the new checkmarks, which, oddly enough, looked a lot like the old checkmarks. If there was one thing Patrick could do it was talk and that seemed to be the one area where he took after his mother. When he got to the afternoon's deer stalking, he became very quiet and tense. The mountain lion had scared him. I wasn't sure if he was scared for the deer or for his own safety. I also wasn't sure what exactly he had seen as we sat next to the house. I personally saw a huge tawny cat bounding across the yard and startled deer leaping away. A tan blur went by, but everything happened so fast I was only able to capture a quick snapshot in my mind. Patrick's snapshot could have been totally different from my own. I soon realized how strongly it had affected him when he ran crying from his room in the middle of the night and launched himself onto our bed. Rusty awoke in action mode, and found himself instantly standing next to the bed.

It took me a few seconds to figure out what had happened. Patrick was frantically burrowing under the covers, hiding from the thing in his dream. Rusty was standing by the bed. I reached over trying to determine which end of Patrick was which.

"Pat, it's okay, come here. There's nothing to be scared of."

"The mountain lion came again!" he cried. "It was killing all the deer and I couldn't stop him! He was after the deer and they were running all over the place and the mountain lion was just catching them all."

"It was just a dream. Mountain lions don't really hunt like that. They only get one deer and that is their food for the next few days. They don't kill just to kill. They only kill to eat or defend themselves."

"I don't like them, they're scary!"

"I know mountain lions look scary. They are big and powerful, but they are just a part of nature. They have to eat, too."

"Nature is mean! Why does it have to be mean?"

Rusty finally relaxed again and sat next to us on the bed.

"It just seems that way to you, Pat. When you have to chase down bad guys who do terrible things for no good reason, nature doesn't seem so bad," Rusty said gently.

"Now that you know it was all just a bad dream, let's go back to bed. If we're going to stalk deer in the morning, you're going to have to get up early."

"What if the mountain lion comes back?"

"It won't hurt us. I'll have the rifle."

"You can't shoot it!" he cried.

"I wouldn't shoot it unless it came after us."

"What if it came after the deer? Would you shoot it?"

"No, it has to eat to survive. It can hunt the deer."

"Then I don't want to stalk the deer. If the mountain lion is going to come, I don't want to see it hunt the deer."

"Come on, let's go to bed. You'll feel better after a good night's rest."

"Are we going to stalk the deer tomorrow?"

"Only if you want to. I won't make you. I'd like to show you the tracks though. You could learn a thing or two from the tracks."

"How come you like nature so much if there's scary things out there?"

"Lay down and close your eyes and I'll tell you. Now relax. I like nature because it is peaceful a lot more often than it is violent. I like to lie in the grass while the deer graze around me. I like to watch the squirrels playing in the treetops. I sometimes like to sit under a tree holding nuts in my hand until a chipmunk gets brave enough to eat right from my hand. I like colorful birds and I enjoy following a little animal when it runs under the brush where mice and voles live. And I like listening to the coyotes or wolves at night. If I could visit other countries I'd want to follow giraffes through the savannah. I think they are so funny looking. And I like foxes. They try to act dignified like a wolf but they are actually quite funny and more playful like a kitten. I've seen dolphins leap out of the water once and watched seals and sea lions too…" I rambled on and on until he started getting drowsy from the monotone and the repetition and then I quietly said good night and slipped away.

"Do you think he'll stay?" Rusty whispered.

"Shh, not if we talk."

Chapter 10

Five a.m. came way too early. At least that's how it felt after spending half the night calming the frayed nerves of a frightened boy. I dragged myself out of bed knowing we likely wouldn't be stalking the deer, but wanting to be ready just in case. Five-thirty rolled around, no sign of Pat. Six o'clock came and went and he slept on.

There were no deer in the yard. They knew the mountain lion had my yard scoped out and wouldn't show this morning. I was halfway glad as it was icy cold and the wind cut through my coat, freezing me to the bone.

Rusty got up at six-thirty and showered. I had breakfast ready for him when he came out. The house was quiet. I checked to make sure Patrick was really still in bed, and he was.

"What are you doing with Patrick today?" Rusty's asked.

"Maybe we'll go into town and do some last minute Christmas shopping."

"Are you going to stop by the station?"

"I think we should save a trip to the station for emergencies." I thought about my words and quickly backtracked. "Not that kind of emergency. Boredom emergencies. After Christmas shopping I don't know what to do with him. What do you want Santa Claus to bring you?"

"How about a cute little number from Victoria's Secret?"

"What size?"

"Five."

"You'll never get it on."

"Oh, yeah, I will," he said with a wink.

"I don't know if Patrick does Victoria's Secret."

"If he goes shopping with Jesse, I bet he does Victoria's Secret."

First we had planned to go tracking with Mark who rang the doorbell promptly at nine a.m. I'd awakened Patrick at eight and made sure he ate a good breakfast.

"I want to show you these tracks. It always pays to be able to recognize different tracks when you go camping and hiking."

I took him to the sandy area near the corral.

"Look, the back paw prints are here. Where do you think the front paw prints are?"

He looked at the huge tracks, the splayed toes of a running cougar. The wind had weathered the tracks over night but they were still there. We all shivered under layers of coats. Patrick noted the direction of the tracks and stepped forward looking for the front paws. He stepped forward again, and again.

"Wow," he said, "the mountain lion's steps are longer than me!" He crouched examining the front paw prints, then relatively close the next set of back paw prints.

"He was running, that's why they are so far apart. A walking trail is a lot different. We will see that, too. Follow the tracks."

Pat came to a sudden lunge in a different direction and got stuck.

"See how the tracks twist this way? I bet there is a matching sideways leap that the deer also made."

"Are you sure he didn't get it?" Patrick asked with concern.

"I didn't see any dead deer, only that the deer bounded away and the mountain lion eventually gave up."

He followed the mountain lion tracks and I followed him, rifle slung across my back. Mark watched from a distance, camera at the ready. Every once in a while I heard the familiar *click, buzz* as he took pictures.

Track led to track and after the running leaps slowed to a walk, I showed Patrick the trail of a mountain lion on the move.

"Where did he go?" Pat asked.

"I don't know. I don't want to track all the way to the mountain lion. It isn't safe, even with the rifle. I wouldn't want to have to shoot him, but we could follow him for a while."

"Can I do it?" he asked.

"Sure, that's why I brought you out here, to give you practice tracking. Did you notice that you can't see the claws on cat tracks? That's because their claws are retractable."

"What does retractable mean?"

"It means they can pull them in."

"Where do the claws go if they pull them in?"

"Inside their toes."

"Ouch."

"It doesn't hurt them. They don't poke the cat."

"How can it not poke to have pokey things in your toes?"

"They probably stay in a sheath of some kind. And the points face out."

Mark smiled at the stream of questions and my attempted answers. Patrick continued to follow the mountain lion's tracks. One thing about mountain lions, they leave a pretty distinct trail with their big paws, plenty of weight, and the nice desert sand. This was a perfect track for Patrick. I followed patiently as he puzzled it through, keeping an eye on the brush and trees. I still didn't trust the cat to stay away. In fact, as we followed it disturbed me to see the cat had turned back toward the house. I didn't want Patrick to notice that so I changed the topic.

"Patrick, do you know how mule deer run away from mountain lions?"

"No, I guess they run. I would run if I were them."

"Did you notice what the deer did when they ran out of our yard? At first they ran but when they really wanted to go fast they bounded."

"Bounded?"

"They jump like Tigger."

"You mean they bounce? Tigger bounces. He wouldn't like to say that he bounds. That sounds too classy for a Tigger. Tiggers bounce."

"Yeah," I said, "they bounce, in a classy way. Look at the tracks. See how far they can bounce?"

We found a set of mule deer tracks. "See? When they bounce, all four feet hit the ground at the same time and they go *sproing* all the way to…where?"

He walked, looking around, then walked some more.

"Where is it?"

"Keep going."

About fifteen feet away from the first set he found the second set, all four hoof prints again.

"Wow! It bounced *that* far?"

"Yeah, when they are in a hurry they can leap anywhere from six to fifteen feet, and they are really fast bouncers."

"I wish I could watch them do it. I bet they go really high, too. I bet they could jump right over me!"

"I bet they could too."

He tracked the deer until it became monotonous.

Mark came up beside me. "He doesn't morph into Dangerous Tracker Boy but it's spooky how much he resembles you when he's concentrating on a track."

"Maybe tracking just has a certain look to it. You ought to go see if Chase Downing will take you tracking. He's an interesting character."

I looked around.

"Patrick?" I called.

He answered from several feet away. Whew! The wind was picking up, so I suggested we go back to the house and warm up. We all blew in through the back door at the same time and I headed for the hot chocolate.

"Aunt Cassidy? I hear Santa Claus but it's not Christmas yet," Patrick said.

"What do you mean you hear Santa Claus?"

"I heard footsteps on the front porch and then they went away and now I hear jingle bells."

I listened carefully. Okay, there was a slight jingling noise coming from somewhere. It sounded like small jingle bells swaying in the wind. I followed the sound to the front porch, opened the door and there stood a brightly wrapped box with jingle bells tied to it. No tag. Just a box wrapped in Santa Claus wrapping paper with a big red Christmas bow, and the jingle bell decorations were swaying in the breeze making a light, cheerful tinkling noise. Now where did that come from?

"Mark? Is this box from you?" I asked.

"Me? No. Why? Should it be?" he answered.

"No, it's just that I'm not expecting anything."

"Open it!" Patrick exclaimed.

"I don't know who it's for or who it's from, and I'd rather not open something if it's not for me."

"You don't have any bad guys after you right now, do you?" Patrick asked. "It might be a trick."

"All the bad guys I can think of are either in jail or dead."

"How many can you think of?" Mark asked hesitantly.

"Too many. You've heard some of the stories, haven't you?"

"A few, I didn't know whether to believe them or not."

"You can probably believe them. I know they may sound farfetched, but that's the kind of life I lead. Just don't ask Rusty to tell them to you, but Patrick wouldn't mind. He's heard most of them, but you'll get a tamer version from him."

"What do you mean a tamer version?" Patrick asked accusingly.

"There's some things little boys shouldn't hear and you really wouldn't want to know."

"Are you holding out on me?" he asked, sounding very much like Steve or Rusty.

"Yeah, there are some things you don't need to know."

Pat appeared a little put out, but he didn't push for more.

"So," Mark said to Patrick, "you want to tell me some stories? I'll tell you one as well, for example how about the day I met your aunt. That's a pretty interesting story."

They walked into the kitchen where Mark turned off the stove and began pouring hot chocolate into mugs. I stood in the doorway debating what to do with the box. Should a Christmas gift be considered a suspicious package? Only to a few select people. Was I one of them? Sometimes, yes. Right now? I wasn't sure and decided it was best to leave the wrapped box where it was until Rusty arrived home.

The stories were flying back and forth over the dining room table when I returned to the kitchen. I listened to their conversation while I planned our activities for the next few days. Shopping today, stalking at four. Then what about tomorrow? A trip to the police station? Schroeder wouldn't involve Rusty in any more new cases if he was going out of town on Friday. The police station would only kill half a day, though. Maybe we could find some snow. One of the rangers should know the location of a good snowy spot.

"Aunt Cassidy? Who was the carjacker guy trying to shoot when Uncle Rusty had to shoot him?"

"I'm not sure, Rusty or me, but he missed us both. I wasn't armed, so I was diving for cover."

"So, you met Rusty because of a carjacking?" Mark asked.

"Yeah, Pat, how did you remember that? You heard that story a year ago."

"I know. It's one of my favoritest ones, too. It's interesting. And I like the story about when your parachute didn't open and you had to spend five days in the woods without food and water. And you saw a bear! And a moose!"

"Mark heard that one. That happened right before we met."

Mark told Patrick about how we had met while I finished my hot chocolate and changed clothes to go to the mall.

The mall was a mad house. It was the week before Christmas with thousands of desperate shoppers looking for last minute presents. There were gifts ranging from the remnants of mismatched gloves and scarves to silly stuffed animals that vibrated while playing irritating versions of Jingle Bells. Patrick and I were stuck in the middle of a slow shuffle down the mall which, in about ten minutes, was going to drive me batty. Crowds had never been my favorite place. Whenever Rusty and I were in a crowd like this I just held onto his arm and followed. People always made way for Rusty. Women stopped and stared and men hurried out of his way but not so for me, I didn't command the same presence. Patrick looked like he felt the same. He stared at the person in front of him. I so seldom shopped at the mall that I didn't know where any of the stores were located. I just started at one end and walked the whole mall searching for the store I had in mind.

"Aunt Cassidy?"

I bet he needs to go to the bathroom, I thought. It was three hours of slow shuffle behind us.

"Aunt Cassidy?" he repeated.

"What is it Patrick?"

"Bad guy at eleven o'clock."

My zombied brain kicked into gear. I watched the guy at eleven o'clock.

Pat was right. After a while I became aware of his odd behavior too. He was watching purses and bags, looking for an easy take and a quick getaway. There was no way to make a quick getaway in this crowd though, not without bulldozing his way through.

"Thanks Pat," I said. "That was a good catch."

"What are you going to do?"

"Watch for mall security and keep my eye on him."

"Can I have some gum?" Patrick asked.

"I don't know if I have any, but you can look," I said, handing down my pack for him to look through. There was no telling what he'd find in there.

The crowd broke up into smaller groups as we made our way through a large intersection and found a way around the booth where kids had their picture taken with Santa Claus.

The guy saw an opportunity and lunged forward, but I grabbed the hood of his black sweatshirt.

"I wouldn't do that if I were you," I said in my academy voice of authority that always backfired on me. It backfired again as he spun around and looked me in the eye.

"Oh yeah? Well, what about this?"

He looked around for my purse and saw that Patrick had it. Even better, he thought, an easy take. He grabbed the loop on top and dashed away. Pat held on for dear life and I watched in horror as he was dragged down the mall.

"Patrick! Let go!" I yelled as I dashed after the fleeing purse snatcher.

People scattered and I heard a lady yell, "Stop that man!"

Patrick was, at least, slowing the thief down. I caught up to him and took a flying leap for his ankles. As I made a grab for any available body part the man staggered face first into Santa's mailbox. With a roar he got to his feet and gave me a hard shove which left me staggering backwards, landing right in Santa's very padded lap. The camera went *flash* and Santa looked me right in the eye and asked, "And my dear, what would *you* like for Christmas?"

"A normal life," I replied before taking off again after the purse-snatcher. I grabbed Patrick, who was still searching through my pack, then gazed up and down the mall looking for the thief. Think, Cass, where's the path of least resistance?

"Excuse me, Ma'am." Mall security.

The office of the mall was stark, business gray. A tinfoil tree with shiny red ornaments and a blue star were the only visible Christmas decoration.

"Are we in trouble?" Patrick asked as he fished out M&Ms from the bag of trail mix.

"Yes and no. We didn't do anything wrong so I don't know what kind of trouble we could be in."

"Are you going to buy the picture of you on Santa Claus's lap?"

"I don't think so."

"I think we should go look at it. It might be funny."

"Thanks Pat."

"If you don't want it, can I buy it?"

"Why would you want a picture of me on Santa's lap?"

"So I can tell Mom about it."

"No."

"Aw, come on, it'll be funny."

"Do you really want your mom to know you were almost kidnapped at the mall by a purse snatcher?"

"She would think you were a hero. You rescued me."

"Real heroes keep things like that from happening in the first place. Your mom is a hero. Bad things never happen around your mom."

A man wearing a gray business suit entered the waiting area.

"Is this the same mall where you tackled the bank robber?" Patrick asked.

"Yeah, strange things always happen to me when I go to the mall."

The man fiddled with a coat button, cocked his head with a puzzled look, and disappeared. Another wait and then he returned accompanied by a second man and a woman.

"Miss, I am Nyle Galen and these are my associates Cheryl Chaney and Richard Beaumont. Could you step this way, please?"

We followed them into a bare room with a long table and several chairs. It looked like a suitable place to detain purse-snatchers until they got their free ride to the police station, a fact that apparently was not lost on Pat.

"Do you think we should call Uncle Rusty?" he asked.

"It's okay."

"I apologize for the accommodations," Nyle Galen said, "this is the only room with enough chairs to seat everybody. Please sit down."

I took a seat. Patrick climbed into the chair next to mine and knelt so he'd be taller.

Mr. Galen pulled out a file.

There's a file on me at the mall? I wondered. He took out several sheets of paper and spread them out on the table.

"Is this you?" he asked, then stood back with his hands in his pockets. He exchanged glances with Richard Beaumont who nodded his agreement.

Oh shit, these were old pictures of the bank robbery, taken from the security tapes.

"That case has been closed for a long time," I said. "Why would you bring it up now?"

"I think you are the person in these pictures. Richard and I have a bet going whether or not we'd ever find the person who stopped that bank robber. I told him there was no way. He insisted the reward would bring you out. It didn't work."

"There was a reward?" Patrick said in awe. "Why didn't you collect your reward, Aunt Cassidy?"

"Because I hate TV cameras and it was all over the news."

Richard smiled smugly.

"And I wasn't interested in the money. I just saw the bank robber at work and I was in the right place to catch him, so I did. It was that simple. So, why are you keeping me here? Your bet is settled. I hope this doesn't get to the news again. The accident out there was not my fault. A man tried to steal my daypack. My nephew was holding it at the time and when I tried to chase the guy down he threw me into Santa's lap. It's that simple. I hope Santa wasn't hurt."

Galen tossed another photo onto the table. It was me landing on Santa's lap, my eyes wide in surprise, feet still up in the air. Patrick started laughing out loud.

"That's even better than the one of me… and I pulled off Santa's beard right before the flash went off," he giggled.

"Pat! You didn't!" I scolded.

"Can I have it, *please*?" Patrick asked, looking up at me with big hound doggy eyes.

"This picture belongs to Mr. Galen," I said.

He tossed another one on the table. "You can keep that one," he said.

Patrick's eyes lit up with excitement.

Beaumont walked over to a telephone by the door and spoke quickly into the receiver. In a minute two officers wrestled the purse-snatcher through the door.

"Is this the man who tried to steal your purse?" Beaumont asked.

"No question about it," I stated.

The officer holding onto the purse-snatcher laughed. He turned to the other officer and smirked, "Wait until Michaels hears his grand theft auto was detained at the mall by a little blonde woman with a kid."

"No! Please!" I cried, almost jumping from my chair. "You can't do that. Turn him loose first."

They both gawked at me. I didn't know the mall cops. I hardly ever came to the mall. They worked somewhat separated from the other officers and didn't know me yet.

"Why?" the officer asked suspiciously.

"Because, Rusty Michaels is my husband and… and I accidentally do this to him a lot. Don't embarrass him. I can't help it if all the guys on his most wanted list show up where I am. It just happens that way."

The two men grinned broadly; to them this was getting better all the time.

"Just tell him you have the woman's name and she's willing to testify. He'll figure the rest out."

"At least we didn't get in trouble," Patrick observed as we left the mall office. "And we're five hundred dollars richer!" he said in glee.

"And we have a $50 mall gift card so now I have to spend it. I guess I ought do something to make it up to Rusty when they bring in his grand theft auto."

"Where are we going? When Mom wants to make up with Dad she either goes to Victoria's Secret or Sears."

"What does she buy at Sears?"

"Some tool Dad's been wanting. How come you don't ask what she buys at Victoria's Secret?"

"That's kind of obvious," I told him.

"Oh, yeah."

After all that, I figured it was safe to go to Victoria's Secret. I was wrong. Patrick walked around the store with his eyes closed bumping into racks. After righting and sorting three racks of teddies, I stopped him.

"Patrick, watch where you're going!" I scolded. "I'll only be a minute if you will open your eyes and let me shop."

He opened his eyes a little, saw the mannequin wearing nothing but see-through underwear, and his eyes got big before he shut them again.

"Pat, it's just a mannequin. It's not a person. Open your eyes. What does your mom do with you when she shops?"

"She lets me ride around in a race car so I can close my eyes."

"Smart mom," I said quietly.

"Sometimes Grandma takes me to the toy store while Mom shops, but I never see anything interesting in there. It's all kiddy toys."

"Pat, you're a kid, you're supposed to like kiddy toys."

"I can't help it if I've got *refined taste*," he said with a dignified air.

I laughed. "You have what?" I asked.

"Refined taste. That's what Grandma says I have because I like real toys, not play toys."

"Leave it to a Grandma to justify every little quirk of her grandkids."

I chose a short nightgown made with romantic, light blue, clingy lace. Patrick started flipping through a display of panties.

"Look," he said, holding up two pairs. One was skin colored and the other was camouflage. "Which one is really camouflage?" he asked. "You couldn't see the skin colored ones but the camouflage ones, I guess, are for if you want your private parts to not be seen *outside*. And the skin colored ones are for if you don't want them to be seen *inside*."

I shook my head. Let's get out of here, I thought.

Easier said than done. I stood in a long line of men and women, all of whom continued shopping while they were waiting. The men were unsure of sizes and the women kept seeing new and more interesting things than the ones they had already selected. One woman started out with light pink panties but traded them for a bright red teddy and then traded that for a black leather gartered contraption. Finally she returned to her original choice of pink panties but, embarrassed by her indecision, looked around sheepishly to see if anyone had noticed.

"These are for my daughter," she explained, holding up the pink panties and leaving everyone curious as to whom the black gartered contraption might have been for.

"Going to the mall is a lot more interesting with you," Patrick observed as we left the store. "Shopping with Mom is boring. She never has interesting things happen to her."

I went to the leather store and passed by all the expensive leather coats, purses, gloves, wallets, vests, lampshades, remote control holders… how many things could they make out of leather? We headed to a counter all the way in the back of the store and patiently waited for a clerk to appear.

"I'd like to buy some leather," I stated, obviously. Fortunately this place knew me. I didn't come here often, but there were only a few customers who came in specifically to buy leather, not leather products, so we kind of stood out. The clerk laid out several pieces of leather.

"What color moccasins do you want?" I asked Patrick.

"I get to pick?"

"Well, up to a point. Some leather doesn't make good moccasins, but you can choose."

He felt the leather, turned it over and felt the other side. Patrick picked up a corner and bent it. He seemed to discard one piece as too stiff and another as too flimsy. When he'd narrowed his choices down to three, he started going by color.

"I like this one. My feet will blend in with the sand that way," he stated.

"Good choice," I told him. "Do you have other pieces?" I asked the clerk, and two more pieces were laid out.

"I like your sand colored choice," I told Pat. "Is it okay if I get the same color as you?"

"I don't care."

So I bought leather for two pairs of moccasins and planned on making them tomorrow.

We were both starving, so we ate in the food court. Patrick took advantage of the situation by ordering a corn dog and then grabbing a handful of ketchup packets. I realized it was time to stop buying him fast food. Rusty and I would be eating nothing but grilled cheese sandwiches for a week straight if I didn't start cooking for Patrick. He downed his corn dog in record time and then asked if he could play in the play area.

"Sure," I answered, "but when I call you, you have to come. We should be home by three-thirty or we'll be too late for the stalking."

A woman seated next to me gasped in horror.

"Not *that kind* of stalking," I explained. "We're not, like, dangerous or anything. He likes to see how close he can get to the deer in my yard. It's called stalking, to sneak up on something."

She glared at me then backed away. I wondered if we'd be dealing with mall security again.

"Look, since when are women and six-year-old boys dangerous stalkers? Believe me, I know all about dangerous stalkers. I've been stalked myself in this very mall!"

The woman looked around apprehensively. This lady was just a suspicious character, I concluded. There was simply no helping some people.

I finished my teriyaki bowl and then thought about what to do next. I considered the gifts I'd bought for Rusty's family and wondered if they were enough. I had never been to a Michaels Christmas before and Rusty never mentioned if they had small, tidy Christmases or big flamboyant ones like we enjoyed at the ranch. If they were anything like Rusty I imagined his family had medium-sized semi-neat Christmases. There would be smaller gifts with wrapping paper appearing around the house for days afterwards. His family would have cheerful hearts and a warm house, then I thought over our intended gifts again and wondered if I'd gotten enough for Rusty.

I decided I never had enough for Rusty, but it was hopeless, though, because he didn't need anything or have any real interests. His favorite thing in the whole world seemed to be… well… okay I'd gotten that at Victoria's Secret. Maybe I could sneak back, I thought. What if I got him something *I* thought was sexy? No, that wouldn't work; he was sexy in a suit . He was sexy in jeans. I couldn't think of anytime I'd seen Rusty and not thought he was sexy. Shoot. When was he at his sexiest? It had nothing to do with what he was wearing, I decided, it was simply *that look.* A few seconds of *that look* and I was doomed. You can't buy that. You can't bottle it. It's either there or it's not. Fortunately, it was there a lot. Quit it, I thought, you're getting nowhere with this and if anything, your expression's getting all mushy. Now *you're* the one giving off *that look* and then that strange lady is going to *run* to mall security.

"Patrick? We need to go," I called out. No answer. I went to the bottom of the play area and shouted up a bright orange tube, "Patrick?" Then I went over to the bright blue tube, "Patrick, it's time to go." No answer. Next the bright red tube, "Pat, come down, I mean it." The bright yellow tube produced a little girl with bright red hair in pigtails. "Excuse me, is there a little boy in there in a colorful western shirt with shiny white snaps on it?"

"There was," she answered. "He's cute. He isn't ready for a commitment."

I gawked at her. Okay, this is California, girls are like that here.

"He's from out of town anyway," I said. "There'd be no point in starting a long distance relationship at your age."

She seemed put off.

I looked around and around. Okay, Cass, time to take the plunge. I knelt down and began climbing up the yellow tube. I quickly realized it was a slide when a three-year-old came speeding down towards me. She shrieked as we collided and slid down together landing in a tangled mess.

"How dare you!" an angry mother screamed at me. "Can't you read! The sign says you have to be shorter than this sign to play in the playground. Stay away from my child!"

Yikes! I looked around for Patrick again. Where could he be? I searched through all the rides, on the train, in the arcade and finally found him in a racecar game. He had been crashing a lot and obviously hadn't heard a thing.

"Pat!" I yelled above the din of the sound effects. "I've been looking all over for you!"

One final crash and he turned to me. "Is she gone?" he asked.

"No, she's probably still out there, but maybe if we sneak out quietly we can get out of here in one piece."

Patrick stalked to the door of the arcade and looked out. "Just act normal. There's already one woman who considers me dangerous, another who thinks I'm after her kid, and several women who think I'm a sexual pervert. I think we better just leave quietly."

He couldn't help it. I tried not to attract attention next to my stealth mode nephew, but I really couldn't blame him for being leery of the little girl with red pigtails. She had really scared him. We were almost clear of the food court area when we were met by another officer. Why couldn't he have been one of the other two security officers we'd met earlier? The ones who thought I was a hero for running down a bank robber. Before we knew what happened, Pat and I were in a car on the way to the station for questioning.

"Are we in trouble this time?" Patrick asked.

"I don't think so. We'll get to see Uncle Rusty and he'll think this is all very funny. But it's not, it's embarrassing."

"Why? I think it's cool! Mr. officer? Can you turn on the siren?"

"No."

"Aw, shucks."

Rusty walked into the interrogation room with a smirk on his face.

"Cassidy, what did you get yourself into this time?"

"It's half your fault," I burst out.

"How is this my fault?"

The words tumbled out and bounced around on the table and I totally forgot that another officer was standing in the corner guarding the door.

"I went to the mall and we ate at the food court. Patrick wanted to play while I finished eating my lunch so he climbed up into the play area and when I got through eating I called to him to come down. But he didn't answer. I told him to come down because we needed to go stalking and this paranoid lady standing next to me must have assumed I meant *people stalking*, not stalking deer. She got all worried and then I tried to climb up and find Patrick and I got all tangled up with some kid sliding down and her mom assumed I was doing something wrong and screamed at me to leave her child alone. In the meantime Patrick had met this little girl who developed a quick crush on him and he escaped to the arcade to get away from her, so I was looking all over the place for Patrick. Then Patrick didn't want to get caught by the little girl so he was hiding from her as we walked down the mall and all these moms banded together and called security and they packed me up and here I am. Not to mention I was trying to think of what to get you for Christmas and I was trying to think of something sexy that *I* could buy *you* and I got all hot under the collar and that didn't help matters much. So now they all think I'm a sexual pervert who stalks kids in mall playgrounds."

Rusty smirked and took a sudden interest in his shoes, then glanced over his shoulder at the officer who was standing by the door, red faced. The flush from his face clashed with his uniform, very unbecoming to an officer.

"And to think half an hour before I was given a reward for capturing a bank robber and a $50 gift card. It was part of a bet that the reward would never be claimed. I'm sorry about detaining your grand theft auto. It wasn't my fault that he tried to steal my pack. If it was just the pack then he could have kept it, but Patrick was looking for something in it and when it was grabbed the guy hauled Patrick along too. So I couldn't just let him take off with it. I had to chase him down."

"Can I show him the picture?" Patrick interrupted enthusiastically.

"Yeah, Pat, I think now would be a fitting time to show Uncle Rusty the picture."

"Yay!" He whipped the zipper around my pack and pulled out the picture with lightning speed and proudly displayed it for Rusty's inspection.

Rusty tried not to laugh, and I had to give him credit for that, but he couldn't help it. His smirk started spreading and then he started quietly laughing as he handed the picture to the other officer. "What did you ask Santa Claus for while you were sitting on his lap?" Both men roared with laughter.

"A normal life! Rusty, I promise I don't try to do these things. It's just what comes when I try to go to the mall. I should just stay out of malls. I should be banned from them. Don't they make little tracking devices that keep people within bounds? Maybe I need one of those."

"So," he said in a serious tone, "what were you going to book her for?"

"Let's just forget it Michaels," the officer said. "Don't forget to watch the news."

Whew!

"Do we *have* to watch the news tonight?" Patrick whined. "The news is boring."

"Why should we watch the news? The only time we watch the news is when Cassidy gets in trouble," Rusty stated.

"Or when big mall mysteries are finally solved?" the officer said. "Beaumont called the news people right after Cassidy left to see if they were interested in a follow up."

"A year late?" I asked.

"The more time passes, the more mysterious it gets."

"Oh, man, I hope they didn't latch onto that one."

Unfortunately that's exactly what happened. They showed footage from the original takedown and rehashed the entire story. Nyle Galen and Richard Beaumont enjoyed their short interview time. They also explained how I had detained a man wanted for multiple crimes in the area during an attempted purse snatching. Then Patrick had his time in the limelight as they revealed how they discovered who had nabbed the bank robber because of a little kid who let slip in front of the wrong person. They showed the picture of me sprawled out on Santa's lap and zoomed in on my shocked expression. I hid in shame until the phone started ringing. Landon Wilson called first, followed by Kelly Green. I turned Kelly over to Rusty and endured a lengthy teasing by Landon. Then I stopped answering the phone which rang every half hour until ten o'clock that night. Why did we need cell phones and a house phone, too? It sounded as if we were living in a clock shop where all the clocks chime on the hour. Each time the phone rang I glanced at the caller ID and ignored the interruption... until Jesse called. Gulp, had this made the news all the way up there? Please, no.

"Hello?" I answered tentatively.

"Hi, Cassidy! How's it going?"

"Umm, fine! We didn't get to stalk deer today. They didn't show up this morning and then we got tied up at the mall."

"There's always tomorrow. Can I talk to Patrick?"

"Umm, sure, he's right here."

I handed the phone over to Patrick who looked at me with a million questions that I couldn't answer out loud. Just wing it, I thought. Carefully. Wing it carefully.

"Hi, Mom!" I heard as I walked down the hall. I had no control over what Patrick would say to his mother. I would just deal with the consequences later.

After work Rusty brought the mysterious Christmas package into the house and it stood in the den haunting me. What was it? How did it get here? Who sent it? Who was it for?

"Open it," Rusty said.

"I don't know anything about it. I don't even know whose it is. What if it's not even mine? What if it got delivered to the wrong house?"

"It didn't get delivered to the wrong house and I have a feeling it's yours."

"If it's mine and it's not from you, then I don't trust it."

"Cassidy, I wouldn't tell you to open something if I thought it was dangerous. I hefted it, heard some noises, and felt it shift around in the box. I think I know what it is. If I'm right then I also think I know who sent it. Just open it."

Patrick walked in and handed over the phone. "Mom says I hafta eat vegetables tonight if it kills me. Just don't make it Brussels sprouts. Did you figure out where the box came from?"

"Rusty wants me to open it," I answered.

"What if a bad guy sent it? What if it's a bomb?" Patrick asked.

"It's not a bomb," Rusty told him.

I picked it up and shook the box. It was about the size of a small, flat suitcase. The jingle bells jangled cheerily again.

"Okay, here goes," I said with an air of desolation. I grabbed a loose piece of paper and tore, revealing a white corrugated box. After pulling the paper back I peeled off the little bits that were taped down. I pulled out my pocketknife and slit the packaging tape. Then I lifted the flaps revealing...

tissue paper. There was a note: “I heard you could use one of these,” followed by the signature of Philip Cranston. I handed the note to Rusty and his expression told me he’d guessed correctly. After pulling the tissue paper away, there sat a bulletproof vest. Not just any bulletproof vest. It was a fancy Kevlar vest, easy to move in yet powerful enough to stop almost anything.

“What is it?” Patrick asked.

“Body armor,” I answered. “It’s a bulletproof vest.”

“Does somebody think you might get shot at?” Patrick surmised.

“No, somebody just knows it’s a possibility.”

“Who is it from?” Pat asked.

“It’s from the father of a man I tracked down. He wanted to do something for me because I found his son. Problem is I couldn’t accept his gift because, well Pat, because I found his son too late and I was just too sad. If I didn’t know any better, I’d have thought this gift was from Mark. I told him if I ended up making anything off his current photography project that I was planning to save up for one of these. But it’s not from Mark and now I know it’s from Philip Cranston. How can I thank him for it without stirring things back up again?”

“Let me see that box.” Rusty took the box and emptied it while I tried on the vest. He then showed me the inside of the box where a small black device had been stuck to the bottom.

“A bug? The box was bugged? If the box was bugged what else was, too?” I thought back. The little black dress? Nah. My sweater? My purse? The Jeep? It had to be the purse. That was all I had with me when I’d been talking to Mark. I went and found the purse I’d carried to the memorial service and discovered my panties were still inside from the Christmas party. I snuck them out, sticking them in between the cushions of the couch before emptying the rest of the contents. Nothing. I turned the bag inside out and felt my finger catch on something stuck to the underside and there it was. Philip Cranston had listened to everything that had happened to me that day. The trip to the station, the meeting at the bar, the flirting at the party, the trip to the bathroom. I wondered if he’d understood the conversation at the antique store better than I had myself. My ears burned as the list grew. I flopped down next to Rusty.

“My purse was bugged. The box is bugged. What else is bugged? It’s not like bugs grow on trees. A person has to go to some trouble to plant a bug and they need sophisticated equipment to listen in. Why would Philip Cranston want to know what I was up to?”

“He just wanted to find out what he could do that would be of value to you and decided that the Kevlar vest was right. I don’t think you need to worry about it."

I picked up the box and put my face into it and said, "Philip Cranston? You are a dirty, rotten, no good sneak. I hope you had fun listening in at the Christmas party, umm and afterwards." Gosh, I forgot about that! "But I've had experience being shot at and I'm a *terrible* trouble magnet. Maybe with this vest I can keep from being shot again. Sooo… thanks…I'm going to squash this bug now."

Rusty added, "Yeah, Philip, thanks."

Patrick asked, "Why are you talking to a box?"

I went to the garage and found a hammer, then placed the box on the floor and gave the bug a good whack.

"Hey," Rusty said when I tried on the vest, "it fits you like a glove. Philip Cranston really knew what he was doing when he chose that for you."

"I wonder if he knew how much I'd think about his son when he bought this for me."

"Was his son little, like me?" Patrick asked.

"No, Pat, he was a grown up, but he was a daddy and his kids were your age," I sniffed. "And he was a good daddy too. I could tell by the pictures they showed at his funeral."

"Aunt Cassidy, please, don't be sad," Patrick said forlornly. "I can't stand it when you're sad."

"It's okay, Pat, there's times when it's good to be sad."

Chapter 11

Patrick awoke early again Thursday morning. He had obviously slept well and not been frightened by nightmares. Unfortunately, I had not been as lucky. I dreamed of Carl Cranston, tracking the entire search in my sleep, knowing I'd find him dead. As I tracked, I became more and more despondent and, oddly, the sadder I became the more often Rusty was with me. Rusty hadn't been on the real search. Why would he be in the dream version? Because, admit it Cass, he's always been there when you were sad or hurt. We shared a bond and sadness deepened it. After I thought about it the dream seemed more comforting than troubling. Rusty was there. He would always be there.

The temperature hovered around ten degrees and the wind blew relentlessly. Clouds scudded across the sky and ominous, heavy storm clouds gathered on the horizon to the north. Last night when we listened to the news we should have waited for the weather forecast, too.

"We need to do some serious stalking today, Pat. Today's your last chance to stalk the deer. You have to go home tomorrow."

"But I don't want to go home."

"Oh come on, admit it, you miss your mom, dad and Wyatt. You'll be glad to be back in your familiar house with all the things you like around you. I bet you even miss your mom's vegetables."

"I can still not want to go home. Why can't you move closer to the ranch?"

"Because Rusty's job is here. We're settled here. You can visit any time your parents let you, just like I can visit the ranch whenever I want."

"But you never want to."

"That's not true. I'd like to visit the ranch more often, but there are people counting on me here. It might not be a job, but it's a responsibility. Let's get you some breakfast and then we'll see if the deer show up."

"Can I go talk to the deer?"

"Go get your coat and I'll go out with you. I don't trust that mountain lion to stay away."

"Okay, but you have to be peaceful, respectful and talk gently."

"I will."

We put on our coats and gloves and then went out to the edge of the yard where Patrick knelt down in the grass to invite the deer to breakfast at our house. The wind whipped our hair around and crept up under our coats which made me wonder how long we'd be able to continue stalking out there. I wondered if Patrick had made the deer any promises about the mountain lion not showing up or if he had given the mountain lion a good silent scolding. It was hard to tell, but he went through his little ritual and seemed to feel better for it.

I made omelets for breakfast, filling them with cheese, bell peppers, onions and ham. I was determined to give Patrick three nutritious meals today. We would stalk deer, bake Christmas goodies then make our moccasins and, hopefully, stalk deer again in the afternoon. No trouble today. It would be nice and peaceful in our comfy, toasty warm house.

By six o'clock when the deer still hadn't shown up, I couldn't blame them one bit. The wind howled around the house and through the junipers. I hoped nobody was out in this weather because if I had to track them down there would be no tracks left to follow. We made a batch of Christmas candy. Patrick measured out the ingredients and I explained again how measuring was math. We determined how many total cups of ingredients we had added, a quarter cup of this and two thirds of a cup of that. He didn't seem to notice that fractions were difficult to understand. They were just parts of something. Parts of cups were easy to figure out. And so we made candy by using math and then we rolled the dough into little balls. Patrick dipped them in chocolate candy coating and we set them out on a piece of waxed paper to harden. Every ten minutes or so he checked for deer.

"The deer are probably hunkered down out of the wind," I told him and he agreed.

We brought out the leather and I traced around his foot to figure out the right size to cut the soles of his moccasins.

"My feet aren't that big, he said, watching me cut way beyond the traced lines."

"We need to allow space for the stitching. If I cut it on the line they will turn out too small."

I used the sole to calculate the other pieces of the shoe and then drew them on the leather with a pencil and cut them out.

"Leather is really thick. You can't push a needle through it so you need to poke sewing holes all the way around the sole."

I gave him a block of wood, a nail and a hammer, and he went to work driving the nail through the leather every eighth of an inch. When he tired of the task he would check on the deer and I took over, aware it was tedious, hard work for a six-year-old to hammer that many tiny holes. And that was just for the sole. He had to do more for the other pieces, too. The further along we got, the more frequently he checked for deer. Every time he checked for deer, the fiercer the wind howled.

"Can I go out just to look for them?" Pat asked.

I glanced out the sliding glass door at the trees thrashing in the wind and thought of the freezing temperature outside. It made me want to light a fire instead of venturing out there, but I gave in anyway. I insisted Pat pull the hood up on his coat and I tied it down around his ears. I wore my search and rescue coat and when we were finally bundled up enough I opened the back door. The wind whipped inside, lifting the curtains and sending a chill down my back.

"Are you sure?" I asked.

"I just want to go look. Even if the deer don't come, I want to tell them that I like them and I would like to see them again. I understand if they can't come in this weather."

Poor kid came all this way to stalk deer, and look what happened. Okay, so I'd go out there with him.

The yard was swept clean. There were no leaves to rake. They were long gone. A tumbleweed rolled by at fifty miles an hour. I leaned down, "Hold my hand. That wind is really strong. I don't want you blowing away."

We crept out into the yard and I instantly froze. I was used to cold weather, but this wind had a way of reaching through the layers. Threatening clouds were closing in. I followed Patrick, hand in hand. He led the way out into the yard, looking, looking, sensing. He didn't walk to the edge of the yard and kneel as I had expected, but appeared to have something else in mind. He watched the ground and so I watched it too. I didn't expect to see anything. I thought the wind would have erased any signs of deer. Patrick bent down.

"Sharp means new, right?"

"Right," I said, kneeling down. The tracks were rounded on top from the wind, but the tips of them were sharp and distinct. I hadn't even bothered looking for them, yet Pat did, as though he had been expecting them. He followed the tracks but didn't have to go far. The tracks ambled a little bit but led around the barn. There, huddled out of the wind, were three does, all curled up and sleeping with their backs to the barn.

I gave Pat the go ahead signal and his eyes shone with admiration. I guessed it was for the deer and this gift that they had given to him on his last day here. They had come out in this dreadful weather and waited for him. He went forward on silent feet, crouched low. When he was about ten feet away, a doe awoke, suddenly alert. He froze, staring at the doe eye to eye. Had he dashed forward he probably could have touched a sleeping doe, but he had respect for them and that wasn't in his plan. He wasn't going to take advantage of them. He simply accepted the gift of their presence without intruding.

As we stood there, a fine snow began falling, blowing in sideways from the north. I forced myself to relax. Shivering was not permitted when stalking deer. I don't know how long Pat stood there. I was a Popsicle by the time he broke eye contact, and the doe quickly rose to her feet. When she moved, the other does awoke with a start and suddenly Pat had three deer towering over him. He didn't get scared, though. He knelt down on the freezing ground and thanked them for coming then quietly backed away. I hoped they would settle back down again because I wanted them to remain sheltered. If I thought they would go in the barn, I'd have opened the door for them, but knew the odor of machinery and woodworking would prevent them from entering.

When Pat had backed away from the deer and joined me again we quietly returned to the house.

"That was so cool!" he exclaimed once we were indoors shedding coats.

"That *was* cool!" I agreed. "I'm glad we went out there. We might have missed them completely today if we'd only watched from the house."

The snowflakes were bigger now, still blowing in from the north. I lit some logs in the fireplace, then turned on the TV and searched for a news station. We had never watched much TV in our home when I was younger as the ranch was too busy for television. I had to give it some thought before remembering our TV set had been kept in an extra bedroom with a couch and bookshelves. I had a small library in there of field guides and survival books. My sister had a small collection of romance novels. My mother had read quite a few of the novels but her section of the shelves contained mostly cookbooks. My dad's books were in his office where I would invade one small section of maps, but other than that I avoided his bookshelves. His books lined the wall behind his desk from corner to corner. He encouraged me to read maps, but the rest of his office was intimidating, and behind the desk was forbidden territory.

Rusty had a TV, but before we met he'd been a workaholic. I wasn't sure what happened after our meeting. His work habits changed dramatically, but our time at home rarely involved TV. We kept tabs on the Dodgers and sometimes when I felt lonely I turned on the TV for background noise. But I bet the TV was lonelier than I was. It was neglected and deprived of normal TV activities. No sitcoms, no soaps… here we go, the weather. Patrick plunked down on the couch.

"What are you doing?" he asked.

"Seeing how much snow might fall. Think we can build a snowman before we drive you back home?"

"We can try!"

I was more worried about the going home part since the weather forecast was not encouraging. A huge storm had come down the coast from the arctic, dumping snow on everything from Redding to Atascadero. That was ranch land and the storm was now moving south. We were only seeing the beginning of it. Even Joshua Hills might receive a measureable amount of snow. The entire time I'd lived in town I'd only seen a few short flurries. One of the things I'd hoped for when we bought our home in the foothills was more weather. I love storms. I love to hear thunder rolling and I love the way fog creeps in silently. The tapping of rain never fails to draw me to a window, and falling snow was better than a good movie. I stood by the window and saw there was already a dusting of snow in the yard. I felt a pang of guilt and began pulling on my coat and gloves again.

"Where are you going?" Pat asked, knowing I didn't want to be outside in the wind.

"It's going to be hard for the birds to find food. I'm going to go fill up the feeders so when it is calm enough for them to come out, they can eat. Stay here. The wind is blowing like crazy and I can't hold onto you and fill the feeders at the same time."

I stepped outside and instantly wished for the warmth of the den. I bent my head into the wind and ducked down to keep the wind from stinging my eyes. I went around to the feeders and poured several scoops of seed into the two feeders, then filled the platform feeder with peanuts. I flung a scoop of seed on the ground, knowing the junkos and quail preferred ground feeding. I put the scoop back in the bin and snuck out to the barn. The deer had settled back down, sheltered from the snow. Again I wished they would go in the barn. I went to the big doors and pulled one open. It was stiff pulling against the wind. The door shoved me into the dark, calm and relatively warm interior. I sniffed around wondering how much it smelled of man and machinery to a deer. Maybe if I opened the back door the deer would feel better about entering, knowing they were out of sight of the house. I opened the door that bent south and held on for dear life as it opened all the way. Pushing the door that opened north was another matter. I pushed as hard as I could until it was firmly against the back wall of the barn, then stopped a minute to rest before going back to the house. I stood there looking into the barn, trying to think like a deer when the barn door hit me broadside. It felt like being hit by a train. I noticed the sparkly white crystals of snow falling as I hit the ground in slow motion and then everything was snowy, my vision first, then my senses.

Patrick told me later what had happened. He'd waited for a while inside the house, just like I told him to. He knew I had no desire to be out in the storm for such a long time. After looking out the windows and seeing the full feeders, he watched the clock and looked out the windows again before putting on his coat and venturing into the storm to find me. Once outside, he was unable to walk in the wind. It nearly blew him away and he crawled through the snow to get back to the house. He was crying when he got through to Rusty. Something was wrong. He didn't know what and he couldn't go out. What should he do? What *could* he do? Rusty kept him on the phone as he quickly drove home. The closer he got to the foothills the fiercer the storm grew. Big flakes sliced the air and the roads became slick, and then snowy and then deeper.

People in southern California don't know how to drive in snow but they don't seem to know it. They drive the same no matter what the weather is like. The speed limits are fast and the drivers drive faster, even in the snow. Rusty saw cars off the road, the drivers victims of their own carelessness. He rushed home talking to Patrick, trying to calm them both as the fear rose and the storm clamped down.

By the time Rusty got home, he had the whole story and there wasn't much to it. Aunt Cassidy went out to feed the birds… an hour ago. Rusty tried telling Patrick all the things that could have happened, but it didn't work.

Walking around the yard things looked normal, just snowy. The wind howled. The snow continued to slice through the property. The feeders remained full. The deer had fled, scared away by the slamming of the barn door. The barn doors facing the house were closed. The yard held no hints, no footprints, no sign of my being there. Rusty didn't even know that the barn had back doors since he wasn't familiar with barn construction. He didn't know how handy it was having doors opening in both directions. He only knew I was nowhere to be seen and it was awfully cold.

I was lucky. When the door slammed shut it had knocked me into the barn, out of the wind and the snow. I came to wondering if I was freezing to death because I could have sworn my bones felt frozen. My first thoughts were of Patrick. How long had I been gone? I tried getting up but was too cold and too numb. I crawled to the front doors of the barn and pushed. The door swung open about a foot before the wind pushed back slamming it closed again with a loud bang. I pulled myself up again, determined to reach the house. I took a tentative step and, although I couldn't feel my feet, I didn't fall over either. I walked wooden-legged out the back door of the barn, then felt my way numbly down the side of the building, slipping awkwardly on the slick snow. Snowflakes plastered themselves to every square inch of me, clinging to my eyelashes, coating me with a thin, frosty layer of snow. I staggered to the sliding back door of the house, but was unable to open it. Was it locked? I hadn't locked it. It couldn't be locked from the outside. Patrick?

I felt myself starting to fade again. The snow swirling all around seemed to me like the snow on a TV screen. I couldn't make sense of it. I leaned against the sliding glass door just as it was opened from the inside. I tumbled in, landing in a limp, wet pile at Rusty's feet. Snowflakes whipped up into the air and settled around me melting into the carpet in the family room.

Rusty stood there for a second, shock registering in every movement. Patrick stood in the den echoing Rusty's fear.

A quick trip to the couch. He brushed the snow off my face. He started peeling off layers. My coat. Everything was cold and damp.

"What're you doing?" Pat asked.

"She needs warmth and her clothes are all wet from the snow."

Patrick thought for a minute and then disappeared down the hall. Rusty peeled off my gloves cupping my frozen fingers in his hands and blowing into them. He finally decided dryness was more important than the fire, carried me to the bedroom and closed the door. He stripped off the rest of my clothes and bundled me up in the comforter on the bed.

There was a tentative knock. "Uncle Rusty?"

"Patrick, just find something to do for a little while. Go turn on the TV."

"I got the dry clothes out of the dryer. They're still warm."

Surprise crossed Rusty's face and he pulled the basket into the room. He dumped the warm laundry under the comforter, then went to his dresser drawer and dumped its contents of t-shirts and underwear into the basket.

"Here Pat, go put these in the dryer. That was good thinking."

"I put a sleeping bag in there. I'll dry these next." Again, a look of surprise.

Rusty pulled his cell phone from his pocket. He quickly selected a number from the address book and hit call. After a second, "Wilson, you've gotta help me… Hell, no… Turn that thing off. I need real help. It's Cass… I don't know… She was outside in the storm for an hour or more… I'm trying… I don't know what happened… sort of… No, I don't think it's life threatening. I just don't know what the danger signs are… You can't get up here. It's snowing too hard. We've got an inch of snow and it's not letting up."

The clothes were cooling off again and I started shivering. My toes burned. My fingers burned. My nose burned. I was trying to figure out if my ears burned. I curled up in a little ball. Rusty noted the movement.

"Cassidy? Babe, can you hear me?"

"Yeah, I c-can hear everything. W-what happened?"

"I was hoping you could tell us that."

"The barn."

"What about the barn?"

"I was standing there one second and, and I don't know."

"Did you pass out?"

"No, it was hard and big. Knocked me across the barn. The door. The door blew shut." Gradually the pieces were coming together.

"Are you getting any of this?" Rusty asked Landon.

"The door knocked me flat."

He ruffled my hair checking for bumps.

"This reminds me of when I got run over by a racehorse. Felt like a bulldozer. The fastest bulldozer in the west. Wham!"

"Landon wants to know how long you were out there," Rusty said.

"I don't know. Ask Patrick."

"It was at least an hour," he said into the phone. "Patrick got worried first, and then he called me and I drove up from the station, so it had to be at least an hour… He's our nephew. Cassidy was supposed to help him stalk deer. Yeah," he said gazing into my eyes, "her eyes seem okay. Neither one seems to be dilated."

He flipped the phone closed.

"Come on, babe, Landon needs more information. He said to get you into warm clothes, get you up and around, find something warm to drink. Patrick needs to see you. He's worried. Sooo… clothes first."

He started sorting through the mess of clothing on top of me, but it was mostly his own laundry. He went to the closet, found a thermal shirt and lounge pants. Something comfortable. I didn't want to move. My hands and feet burned from the cold. He ran his hands over my skin trying to determine if I was back to a normal body temperature. Under his touch, I was heating up real quick. I wasn't getting *the look* though. I guess I couldn't really expect his mind to be on sex under the circumstances, especially with Patrick in the house. He pulled the shirt over my head and tried sticking my hands through the sleeves. I jerked my hands back. Any contact with my hands felt like pins and needles. The pants were easier, but standing was difficult. The skin on my feet was still recovering from the fire and now it was frozen too. There was no way I would be able to stand on my feet. Rusty pulled all the laundry to the other side of the bed and stood back, reassessing the situation. He seemed to feel better about it because he went to the bedroom door and opened it. Patrick ran down the hall.

"I kept the fire going," he reported. "The sleeping bag is warm. I've got hot water on the stove."

"You used the stove?" Rusty asked.

"My mom taught me how to make hot chocolate and grilled cheese sandwiches. Want me to make grilled cheese sandwiches?"

"Have you had lunch yet?" Rusty asked him.

"No, all this started right before lunch time."

"You're sure you know how to do it?"

"Yeah."

"Go ahead and give it a try. We'll be out there in a minute to help. Can you get the sleeping bag first?"

Pat turned and made a run for the dryer while Rusty examined my hands and feet. He started massaging my feet, but it hurt like crazy. He worked his way up my ankle and my calf. Mmm, that was better. Back down to my feet.

Patrick ran in with the sleeping bag and I wrapped up in it, luxuriating in the warmth.

"Okay, we're off to the den. Come on."

He offered me a hand up but my hands burned and I couldn't even hold onto the sleeping bag. I rolled out of bed and nearly screamed when my feet hit the floor. It felt like walking on stinging nettles, but I toughened up inside and stepped forward.

Cass, you're turning into a wimp, I thought as Rusty lifted me up and I wrapped my arms and legs around his torso. He buried his face in my dirty, damp hair and carried me out to the den. He sat on the coffee table, rubbing my feet, and I sat on the couch trying not to cry. But at the same time, it was homey and comfortable and the sleeping bag felt warm. Patrick was busy in the kitchen and eventually came in sloshing hot chocolate. Rusty took the cup from him.

"Can we have a hot pad to go with it?" he asked and Patrick ran back to the kitchen. Rusty wrapped the warm cup up in the hot pad and handed it to me. My fingers didn't want to bend, but I managed to drink as I watched the fire and Rusty rubbed the needle jabs out of my feet. I started relaxing as my feet eventually stopped hurting and returned to normal. I handed the empty mug to Rusty and fell asleep to the smell of grilled cheese sandwiches burning in the kitchen. Rusty went to supervise. I roused when he came back and began rubbing my hands. They were a normal temperature but still felt stiff. I tried to ignore him, but simply couldn't. Having Rusty close was hard to ignore, even if he was just worriedly rubbing my fingers.

"I have to call Wilson back. So, tell me, what happened. Are we keeping all the fingers and toes? Are you back in the world of the living?"

I told him about going out to feed the birds and worrying about the deer, then about the barn.

"I didn't even know we had a back door on the barn," he said. "I walked around out there looking for you and calling your name, but I didn't think to walk around the barn. Are you sure you're okay?"

"I've had worse happen to me. A knock on the head isn't going to kill me."

"Maybe not, but an hour laying in a freezing cold barn could have. What if Patrick hadn't called? What if he'd tried to go after you?"

"I did try," Patrick said, "but I couldn't." He bowed his head in shame. "The wind was too strong."

"You have nothing to be ashamed of, Pat. You did everything a kid could be expected to do, and you did a great job. You used your head and thought of ways to help even before I did. We're proud of you and you should be proud of yourself, too," Rusty said. "Are we ready to call Jesse and tell her every road between here and the ranch is closed until the storm ends? We already have three inches of snow and it's still coming down. It's worse to the north and inland, so there's no way we can take Patrick home tomorrow."

Somehow Patrick managed to look pleased and disappointed at the same time. There was just something about the ranch, especially Christmas at the ranch, that was special. He really wanted to be home for Christmas.

"Pat, we'll keep an eye on the news and try tomorrow. But do you know what it means if you don't get to go home tomorrow?"

"It means I gotta spend Christmas here."

"No, it means you will have to go to San Diego with us on Saturday."

"San Diego?" he wailed. "How will Santa Claus know where I am if I'm in San Diego?"

Good question, I thought, although we had our gift for him. Santa may have a hard time coming up with surprises at the last minute, especially for a kid who didn't play with toys. I didn't even know if one of us could drive into town to shop. Rusty and I looked at each other. Then I took a big risk.

"Pat, Santa Claus knows where the kids are. He doesn't have to be told. No matter where you are, Santa Claus will find you."

He didn't seem convinced, and now his disappointment was definitely showing.

Rusty disappeared to call Landon back while I continued talking to Patrick.

"Pat, Christmas isn't just opening presents, it's also about what you give, and you are a very generous boy. You have a sharp mind and willing heart. I could tell that just from today. Tell me, what did you ask Santa Claus for?"

"I asked him to send deer to the ranch, just like he sends them to your house. And I asked him for roller blades and for, for a baby cousin, and for everybody to be together."

"That's all?" I asked, swallowing a big lump in my throat. "Pat, the baby cousin is entirely out of Santa's hands. He doesn't control things like that.

And it looks like the whole family won't be together for Christmas this year. Even if we took you home, we'd have to go to San Diego on Saturday."

"I know," he said sadly.

"I think Santa can handle the roller blades. But, what are you going to do with roller blades at the ranch? It's all dirt."

"Not the porch on the ranch house. It's big and it goes halfway around the house. I could learn on that and Ricky lives in town. I could skate at his house."

Sounded good to me. I was glad to find out what he really wanted and I made a mental note to check his shoe size later.

"Lookit the snow!" he said with admiration. "I've never seen so much snow before. Can we build a snowman?"

"If the wind settles down and we can get my coat dried out, we can definitely build a snowman. If we use the snow from the side yard then the deer will be able to eat the grass, too."

"Can I put your coat in the dryer?"

"It probably won't hurt it to be in there for a little while."

He dashed off and pretty soon I heard the rumble of the clothes dryer humming in the background.

"I think I managed to convince Wilson you would live to see another search," Rusty said as he walked in. "Where's Patrick?"

"I told him we could build a snowman if the wind settled down and our coats were dry enough to wear. So now he is drying my coat."

"I've been thinking. If we have to take him to San Diego then we need to do some serious shopping. That's your department," he said in a serious tone of voice. "I have tomorrow off to take Patrick home, but he could come with me to the station and I can show him around while you shop. Are you going to be up for an intense day of Christmas shopping?"

"I need ideas more than anything. I've got a short list of things to look for but I don't know what kind of Christmas he's used to."

"He knows not to expect it to be the same. How are those fingers feeling?"

"I don't know, hand me something to feel and we can test them out."

"Mmmm," he said contemplating. "Need a test subject? I'll let you know how good they are feeling."

I laughed at his suggestion and he looked back at me wearing his mischievous smile.

"I need to pack. If I don't pack, we can't use our bed tonight."

Standing in the doorway of the bedroom we noted the mountain of clothing covering the bed. Okay, first things first, all the laundry needed to be rewashed. If I'd picked up that much dirt lying in the barn I could only imagine what my coat must look like. The dryer. ARG! In the laundry room I opened the dryer to find it coated with half dried mud. The coat was mostly dry, but dirty from tumbling around with dirt, sticks and dried grass. He's only six, I told myself. He's only six. It will wash off. I got a bucket of warm water and a rag and began washing the inside of the dryer.

"What are you doing, Aunt Cassidy?" Pat asked innocently.

"You aren't supposed to put dirty things in the dryer. Only clean clothes go in here."

"But you said…"

"I know, Pat, but I didn't realize how dirty my coat was when I told you to use the dryer. I just need to wash it, then wash all the clothes on the bed before I start packing. While I am at it I might as well wash your dirty clothes, too. Can you put them in a pile for me?"

After cleaning out the dryer and sorting the laundry it looked more like a week's worth of clothes which had to be washed, dried and packed by morning. I shook my coat out the back door then passed by Rusty as I headed for the washroom.

"Cass, do you think every time you nearly die that you need to do extra to prove you're still alive? Relax."

"That's easy for you to say, but I have to get three people ready to spend five days in San Diego by morning."

"We aren't going anywhere until Saturday. The whole inland part of California is snowbound."

"Then I have more time but there are also more things to do. I promised Pat we'd build a snowman, and we have to go to town."

He sighed. "Okay, tell me what I can do and then we'll get everything done."

"It's mostly all of the laundry and I'm the one who has to do it."

"There must be something."

"Okay, go get the suitcases. I'll start packing. Maybe I can cut back to only the necessary laundry."

"That's what I mean, you're always trying to do everything, even when it's not necessary. I'm sure we have five days worth of clothes somewhere around here."

In my frustration I replied, "It's not just a matter of finding five sets of clothes. It's finding a beach set, a mall set, the right clothes for Christmas dinner and then something for goofing off around town. I need a set for tracking with Chase. Every activity requires a change of clothes. I can't wear a pantsuit to see Cody and I refuse to wear shorts with a tank top to see Sandy. Maybe you can, but I won't because there are certain things that will be expected of me. And what about Pat? We can't just take him along. It's rude to drop in with unexpected guests."

"Not at my house," Rusty pointed out.

"I can't just force them to take in another person. I need to call them and make sure it's okay first."

"Okay, so call them," Rusty said nonchalantly as though it was the easiest thing in the world. Maybe he was right. Maybe it was easy, but it didn't feel easy to me. I'd wait to see what tomorrow would bring. We packed and as it turned out I really only had to do two loads of laundry, and that was mostly because Patrick was almost out of clothes and because I wouldn't wash lights and darks together.

Friday morning brought more snow. The storm had come to a halt right on top of us and the snow was now fluttering down lazily in huge delicate flakes. I looked out the window and there were six inches on the ground and three more inches on the north side of everything in sight. That made nine inches or did the three inches count?

Rusty turned on the TV. North was impossible. South was doable if we took the Jeep, and headed for the coast ASAP. I was hoping we wouldn't need the winch, but I was glad we had one just in case. West was safe but there was no way of traveling anywhere north or east. Sigh, time to call Bev. Then Jesse.

Bev answered the phone on the fourth ring. "Hello?"

"Good morning, Bev, this is Cassidy," I said. She might be my mother-in-law, but so far we hadn't spoken on the phone much.

"Well, hello dear! How are you and Rusty? I do hope you're coming for Christmas."

"That is what I was calling about. I have my nephew here and we were supposed to take him home today but the roads are all blocked. So… I was wondering… if you'd mind if he came with us to San Diego."

A long pause. Uh oh, I was afraid of this kind of reaction, which was why I felt it best to call first.

"You're bringing a *child* with you?"

"Only if it's okay. He's a very polite, well behaved boy. You won't have any trouble out of him. He…"

"Cassidy! That's the most wonderful Christmas present you could give us this year! We haven't had a child in the house for years! It'll be more Christmasy with a child here. I can't wait."

"You're sure you won't mind?"

"Mind? I'm thrilled! Bill and Cody will be, too. You wouldn't think it, but Cody's great with children. He's like a big kid himself and the kids at the beach just flock to him."

I could believe that, particularly twelve-year-old girls.

"Tell me all about him so I can go shopping!"

"That really isn't necessary," I insisted. "He doesn't expect any gifts."

"Nonsense, a kid's got to have presents to open."

"We'll bring some along, besides, this isn't exactly your everyday six-year-old. He doesn't play with toys much. He lives on a ranch and he takes after me. So he likes to get out in the hills to track and stalk animals. It's not a personality type that is easy to shop for but don't worry, he is very easy to please."

"And what is your nephew's name?"

"Patrick. He was the ring bearer at our wedding."

"Oh yes! Darling boy. He kept his tux on longer than any kid I've ever seen in a wedding. Usually you see their image changing as they walk back down the aisle."

"And you're sure you don't mind if he comes with us?"

"No! I can't wait! It'll be like having *grandkids*!"

Oh, great. Just what we needed: parents wanting grandkids.

My sister was next. She answered on the first ring.

"Hey Cass! When do you think you can be here?"

"Umm, well, have you seen the news? How much snow is up there?"

"Oh, it's beautiful! You were right, the inflatable snowmen fit right in. We have a few inches of snow on the ground. The ranch looks so different in the snow! You won't believe it when you see it!"

"There's one problem with that. I won't be seeing it. Jesse, the storm went south and it's been dumping snow on every highway between here and there. It's been snowing for two days and we have six inches of snow here. Rusty says there's no way to get up there and we are due in San Diego tomorrow."

There was silence on the line. How can you tell a sad silence from a happy silence? Rusty's worried silence was particularly recognizable. I could tell Jesse was almost in tears, but she hadn't said a word.

"Pat's not coming home today? Not coming home for Christmas? He's never been gone for Christmas! He can't be gone for Christmas! He's only six! Six-year-olds have to be home for Christmas! It's a rule! If they aren't home for Christmas their moms…"

"Jesse, he'll get Christmas. Don't worry. I already called Rusty's mom. She's thrilled to have a kid coming for Christmas. She can't wait and she'll spoil him rotten."

"But *I* wanted to spoil him rotten. It's my job! I'm his mom! You can't understand because you're not a mom."

"And I'm not superman either. I can't clear the roads and make the storm go away. All I can do is say I'm sorry and promise to take lots of pictures. I'll make sure he has plenty of presents and, really, he'll get two Christmases out of it; one in San Diego and another when he gets home. We'll drive straight from San Diego to your house. I'll get him home as soon as the roads are safe. We have to stay in San Diego through Tuesday, and then he'll be home Wednesday, I promise."

"Can I talk to him?"

"Jess, I don't think that's a good idea. If you talk to him right now, you'll get him all upset about it, too. You need to hang up, go have a good cry, calm down, get used to the idea, and then call us back. I'll keep my cell phone on me. I promised Pat we'd make a snowman today."

"It's no fair. You get to play with him in his first real snowfall. It's no fair."

"Jess, you sound more like a six-year-old than Patrick does. You'll feel better after you think it through, and I'll talk to you later."

She sniffed, "Okay." And we said our goodbyes.

Golly, I never expected such a strong a reaction from her! I knew Jesse would be disappointed but I never expected her to whine and carry on. What did motherhood do to a once perfectly reasonable woman?

As soon as I turned around to track down my guys, the phone rang.

"Put him on a plane," Jesse demanded.

"You want him to fly through a snowstorm to an airport you can't even drive to? Jesse, hang up the phone, turn on the weather channel and see for yourself."

"You're mean!" she cried as she hung up the phone.

Rusty stood before me bundled up in a coat, gloves and scarf. A scarf? Rusty in a scarf? I'd known him for over a year and I'd never seen him wear a scarf. He looked rather dashing and comfy, and it made me want to throw snowballs at him.

"Jesse wasn't too happy about the news," he observed.

"That's an understatement! She was as crushed as your mom was thrilled. You've got to do something to stop her. She's going to go nuts."

"What do you mean?"

"She wants to buy Pat Christmas presents. I told her he didn't need or expect a gift and that we'd be bringing some for him."

Rusty just grinned. "Oh, let her have some fun. Let's go build a snowman. You know this is our first real snowfall together, too. You got to see lots of snow last winter but I didn't get to see any of it. I was either stuck in an office in town or out in the desert wind. I never saw one snowflake all year."

"I need to find my cold weather gear. I'll be ready in ten minutes."

In the bedroom I pulled on long johns, heavy socks, a t-shirt, a flannel shirt, snow pants and finally my coat. I was glad I was used to moving in all these layers. I had to dress like this for snow rescues. There had been many snow rescues last year, but they involved me mostly for training purposes. They usually didn't need a tracker when there was snow. They'd call me if they needed me, but the other teams got called more often. I put on all the gear because I still felt cold in the house. I even found my snowshoes. I didn't need them in the yard, but wondered if Patrick would like to try them. I grabbed a camera on my way out and found the guys working on the base of the snowman. I took a picture of Patrick rolling the ball through the snow. Rusty took over when the ball became too heavy to push. It might be cold out, but it warmed my heart to see Rusty out there playing in the snow with Patrick. It just felt right and he looked so comfortable. I tried to pin the feeling down and realized it was very much the way I was while tracking. It seemed to me that Rusty was a natural born mentor. Whether it involved work, play or even sitting beside a bedridden person, Rusty was there, supporting, and effortlessly giving it his all without even trying. And now he was playing and I was enjoying every minute of it.

"Come on, Cass!" he called.

I waded out through the snow. "Look what I've got, Patrick!"

"What are they?"

"Snowshoes! Want to try them? I wear them for snow rescues. They let you walk on top of the snow."

"Cool!"

Rusty pulled him out of the snow and placed him on top of the snowshoes while I strapped them to his feet.

"Don't walk yet!" I warned. "You can't take normal steps. You have to shuffle. Do you ever scoot your feet on the carpet to build up static electricity so you can sneak up and shock someone?"

"Not any more. Wyatt gave me a bloody nose."

"Well, walk like that in the snowshoes."

He started scooting across the snow, scooping up snow with the tips.

"Raise the tips a little more and sort of scoot and jog at the same time."

When Patrick shuffled across the snow Shadow got excited. A sheep on the run! He started running around, trying to herd Patrick but the snow was too deep for Shadow to keep up so he gave up the chase. Shadow brought his black head up out of the snow and had a pile of snow on his nose. I quickly snapped a picture and then took one of Patrick snowshoeing. Patrick stepped on the tip of his snowshoe and tripped, landing in a heap in the snow. Rusty retrieved him.

I took note of where the snowman's body had ended up and tried to push it further. It was too heavy.

"The base is big enough," Rusty said. "If we make it bigger it's going to be hard to lift the other balls up on top of it."

"But it needs to be about ten feet further," I explained. "What's the use of building a snowman if it's not visible from the road?"

He grinned again. I'd do anything to see Rusty smile like that. His job was so serious that sometimes he had trouble grinning. It warmed my heart that today he'd be free to grin all he wanted.

"Okay, help me push," he said leaning into the huge snowball, like I could add much power to his two hundred plus pounds. I calculated that moving the ball ten feet had added at least ten pounds of snow to it. But our snowman would look cute from the road. We wouldn't be here to see it, but at least other people would. Our snowman would greet Hazel and Wally as they drove into town. We called Patrick over to start the second ball of snow and then, when it got too heavy for Patrick, I handed Rusty the camera and took over. I pushed it towards the larger ball but it stopped and wouldn't budge before I got halfway there, so Rusty took over.

"Come on everybody, I need some help," he called as he hefted the big ball of snow up onto the base. We grabbed handfuls of snow and pressed it into the seam between the two balls sealing them together. Then we patted and smoothed the snow so the snowman would be nice and round.

Patrick was just about able to make the head all by himself, but he didn't want to put the head on right away.

"We need to decide what kind of a man our snowman is," he insisted.

"What kind of a snowman do you want him to be?" I asked him.

"How about a policeman?"

"How do you make a snow policeman?" Rusty asked.

"Maybe a snow cowboy?" Patrick suggested.

"And exactly how do you make a snow cowboy?" I asked.

"We could put a cowboy hat on him and tie a bandana around his neck."

"Your cowboy hat is for dressing up. You're not putting it on a snowman that is going to turn into a puddle."

"We can make a hat. Do you have a piece of cardboard?"

"Yeah, how are you going to make a hat out of a piece of cardboard?"

"With scissors."

He seemed to have something in mind so I found a piece of cardboard and a pair of scissors and let him get to work. He cut a brim out of the cardboard and then cut off the top of the snowman's head so it would look like the hat was tilted a little. He placed the brim on the head and bent the edges so they curled a little. Then he packed snow on top of it to make the crown of the hat.

"What do you think?" he asked.

"I think he needs a face," I suggested.

"What kind of a face? A nice face? A mean face?"

"I think when you find things to make a face out of he'll develop his own personality."

Rusty lifted the snowball carefully to the top and we sealed the two snowballs together and then smoothed them like the first two. Patrick ran up with two sprigs from the junipers, two rocks that he found in the barn, and a pinecone. Rusty lifted him up so he could put the face on the snowman. Bushy eyebrows and bulbous nose and piercing eyes. Patrick laughed with delight at his creation.

"He looks like Old Frank! Old Frank, the snowman, was a creaky, grouchy soul…" he sang, making up his own version of the "Frosty the Snowman" song.

"Pat, that's not very nice."

"Aw, okay, but it still looks like Old Frank. Do you have a bandana?"

"Yeah, I think he'll need two though."

I went inside and found two red bandanas and we made them into a necktie for our Old Frank snowman. Patrick made him a nametag and we took his picture, then took more shots with us all standing around our Old Frank snowman. Jesse would like these pictures for her scrapbooking hobby. Patrick's first snow and I was able to share it. He marveled at it and played in it and tried to catch snowflakes on his tongue. It was glorious watching him, and I felt sorry for Jesse having missed it. She would have enjoyed this too, so to make up for her loss I took lots of pictures.

"Okay, it's my turn to try the snowshoes," Rusty announced.

"You've never tried snowshoes?"

"No, the only use these have ever seen is on rescues."

Rusty strapped on the snowshoes and went shuffling off around the side of the house. I picked up some snow and formed it into a loose snowball so I could clobber him with it when he came around the house. Instead, a snowball whacked me on the shoulder from behind.

"Ha ha! I snuck up on you!" he yelled jubilantly. Rusty had been trying for over a year to sneak up on me, and was successful simply because I'd been playing and not paying attention. He took off around the house again while I ran in the other direction. The snow was still falling and sticking to our hats, shoulders and hair. We all looked like one big frosty family and I thought to myself, you know, Cass, if this was the storm of the century, then your kids have missed it. They may never see snow like this because you were selfish and didn't want to share your personal time. You didn't want the responsibility and so they've missed it. But there are lots of things they haven't missed. You can still enjoy lots of things with a family if you can just quit being selfish. Open your eyes and see what you're missing.

"Cass!" I heard in the distance, it was Rusty. I followed his voice until I found him out in the junipers head first in a snow bank. I'd never have guessed there would be a snow bank out here large enough to swallow up Rusty but here it was, his snow shoed feet sticking up out of it. First I laughed at him. Then I took his picture. Then I started digging him out. His face appeared all red from the cold and he was mad at himself but the grin was still there. He pulled me down into the snow and planted a big kiss on me, lingering.

"Ewe, mush!" yelled Patrick and quickly lunged for the camera. "Do it again!" he said. "Mom will love this."

Rusty kissed me again while Patrick took a quick picture of us. He then ran up to Rusty and announced, "Tag, you're it!" before running away. Rusty scrambled to his feet and took off after him, shuffling through the snow. They were about evenly matched, Rusty forced to shuffle, Pat struggling to wade through nearly knee-deep snow. I jogged after the two of them. When I caught up with them, I reminded them that we still had to make a trip into town that day.

"Where are we going in town?" Pat asked.

"We thought you'd like to go to the police station, while I do a little last minute shopping."

We had to creep along in the Jeep, watching carefully for the turns in the road. Everybody on Lost Hills Road seemed to be staying indoors, waiting for the snow to melt. We couldn't afford to do that. Santa Claus was needed in San Diego. It was important; important enough for four-wheel drive and a slow trek to town. As we came down out of the foothills the snow was shallower and we were able to drive more easily. We came to more traveled roads and by the time we'd reached town the streets were nearly bare. I dropped off the guys at the station and then took off with a list of stores and the quickest shopping trip I could manage. Roller blades first, binoculars, a field guide to animal tracks, another bird book, and a couple of children's books about birds and forest animals. I found a simple wooden bird feeder kit, a big Lego construction set, a backgammon board and dominoes. He wouldn't even think about math as he played and they weren't kiddy games. Even I would play with the Legos. I thought I could count on Rusty's family to provide Wyatt with a second Christmas. Patrick would open up the toys and politely thank everybody for them and then when he got home Wyatt would be the one playing with them.

The stores were crowded and the lines were long. Every time I got tied up in a long line I worried about the guys, bored stiff at the police station, reduced to playing Solitaire on Rusty's computer. After my last stop, I stashed all the bags out of sight and drove to the station. I found Rusty and Patrick both in Rusty's office, but they weren't bored. Schroeder and Kent Jacobsen were with them, too. Patrick was sitting on top of Rusty's desk cross-legged, coloring in a book, and Jacobsen was telling stories which hopefully weren't about me. I knocked lightly then peeked in the window like I always did and Patrick looked up expectantly. I opened the door and joined the group.

"Aunt Cassidy, I got to color in Uncle Rusty's special coloring book!"

"He has a special coloring book? What's special about it? It looks like an ordinary book to me."

"It isn't. It's a reminder book."

I had a feeling I was about to learn something rather significant. I felt alarm bells go off, but not frightening ones. Oh, man, how can I explain it? I have this propensity for seeing the odd in amongst the normal. It helps me spot kidnappers in restaurants. Mostly it is a pain in the butt. I don't like seeing bad guys everywhere I go. But it also helps when I track, and on rare occasions I see a simple comment as something it is not. A reminder book. That phrase stood out. I pushed aside my racing thoughts and returned to the situation at hand.

"Can I see?" I asked.

Patrick handed over the book willingly, proud that he had a chance to add a picture to Rusty's reminder book. I looked at Patrick's page.

"You did a really great job on your picture!" I praised. "You stayed in the lines and everything!"

"I'm not finished yet. I need to shade it so you can see the shapes of stuff. Look at the other pages."

I browsed through the book. Some pages were scribbles, some were sloppy and a few pages were only colored in black. The black pages spoke volumes. I saw neat pages, and some that were half-finished. Each page was signed, either by a parent or the child. Only a first name and a date. Reuben, July 16, 2006. Marshal, with a star next to his name, July 23, 2005.

"And look what Uncle Rusty gave me," he said, handing me a small object. It was a Matchbox car, a police car. "He has a whole drawer full of them, but I liked the police car to remind me of my trip."

I don't know what I must have looked like at that moment, putting two and two together, doing emotional math in my head, but Schroeder and Jacobsen excused themselves hastily and left.

Rusty loved kids. I thought of the other desks up and down the hall. Did they have Matchbox cars, coloring books and old, used up crayons in their desk drawers, too? I didn't think so. I wasn't sure how to get a handle on my feelings, so I started the only way I could.

"Who's Reuben?" I asked.

"Let me see the book," Rusty said. He flipped to Reuben's page, a picture of a toy airplane and a hangar made out of blocks. Rusty studied the picture for a few seconds and handed the book to Patrick so he could finish his picture.

"Reuben was a little Mexican boy who came in with his mom. His mother had finally decided she would press charges against an abusive boyfriend. I had the case because the boyfriend also sold drugs and tended to steal large, valuable objects from people's homes. Reuben didn't like the guy. And he didn't want to sit in a stuffy office and listen to his mom talk about the guy. So he colored that page and then went home with a red racecar. Sometimes when parents talk their kids get bored."

"What about the dark pages?"

"I don't look at the dark pages much, only when I'm tempted to quit. Then I get sad and buckle down and get back to work again. It's a reminder book. Some things, dark things, I need reminders of, too. Sometimes I want pleasant reminders. Patrick is making me one of those right now."

My face felt flush from my pent up emotions. Usually when I felt like this a good run took care of it, or a bout with the punching bag but that wasn't an option for me at the moment. So I just reminded them, "We need to get home before dark. We could barely see the road in the light."

"Can I take it home to finish it?" Patrick asked.

"Sure," Rusty answered, "I'm not going to be back for a while anyway. Did you want to color in one of the other books, too? It's going to be a long drive to San Diego."

He opened a drawer and took out three more reminder books. Patrick chose a harder book about the coast of California. He read the captions aloud as we drove home.

"Show Aunt Cassidy the middle page of that book," Rusty said as he drove.

Patrick handed me the book and I looked at the picture. Jade, December 3, 2006. It was a beach scene with the sun shining and gulls circling over a pounding surf. Umbrellas dotted the shoreline in the distance. She'd also drawn in a mom and a girl walking down the beach. On the hills way in the background she colored in a bright orange fire, not enough to scare anybody, just serving as a reminder.

"Terry Brooks borrowed the book when she questioned Jade," Rusty explained.

"Looks like they talked for a long time," I observed.

"To me the page looks hopeful."

I studied the picture; the fire had been drawn in the distance. The colors were bright and cheerful. He was right, it *did* look hopeful.

"A pleasant reminder and a reminder about you, too. I was glad to have that picture in my book."

We had to slow down again as we drove up into the foothills. The snow had stopped falling, but the road was still hidden under a blanket of snow. There were tire treads from a few other cars that had tried to leave after we had passed earlier.

We stomped our way into the house, met a hyper Shadow, and started shedding clothes. Everybody except Patrick.

"Can I go see if the deer came?" he asked.

I started putting my coat back on.

"I'll go," said Rusty. "You have things you need to do."

He was right, I did and I needed to start dinner. I also had to bring in the gifts, wrap them and hide them in some way to bring them down to San Diego without Patrick noticing. Getting anything past Patrick was going to be tough. Fortunately, he hadn't asked for a bicycle. I put meat in the microwave to defrost then put on my coat and brought the gifts in and stashed them in our closet. I'd never had a walk-in closet before. They sure were handy for times like these.

I had just set all the bags down when Patrick ran in and announced behind me, "Aunt Cassidy! The deer are in the barn! They went in! I went to see if they were lying beside the barn and we tracked them to the back door. One deer went and it took her a *long* time to decide to go in. You can see her tracks full of snow where she stood there a long time deciding. If you go out there you can see that each deer took long enough to follow that the snow covered up the first deer's tracks. I bet we can figure out who the brave one is if we go in there," he said with a mischievous look in his eye.

"You don't want to scare them. Let them be nice and warm in there. I'm glad they went in. It was worth getting clobbered by the barn door if they will shelter there."

I closed the door behind me and went to the kitchen to start dinner while Patrick finished his picture in Rusty's reminder book. He signed and dated it. As things simmered in the kitchen I took time to look through the book. I wondered what stories Rusty had hidden away about the many people he had spoken with at work. Had he really dealt with so many kids? He had four coloring books in his drawer. Were they all as full as this one? This one had pages dating back four years. How many Matchbox cars had he given away? My big tough detective husband collected kid's crayon pictures and handed out toy cars. It was a revelation to me.

"Cassidy, you look like you just discovered I'd been having an affair or something. Why so serious?"

"You love kids," I observed simply.

"Yeah, I do," he replied wrapping me in that hug I'd grown to love so much. I slipped my hands under his coat and snuggled in, checking my emotions.

"You want a family," I continued cautiously.

"Maybe. Do you?" He was treading on thin ice and he knew it.

"Rusty, this is something we should have discussed before we were married. This is serious. I don't know. Sometimes I do, and sometimes I get selfish, and sometimes the job just looks too big to handle."

"That's good enough for me. You just see things realistically. For now you're enough like a kid that I get the best of both worlds. I have a twelve-year-old throwing snowballs at me in play and I get a twenty-six-year-old hot babe to play with at night all wrapped up in one luscious package. And if, for some reason, we never have kids, every now and then I'll just borrow someone else's."

"You don't make faces and silly noises whenever you get near a baby, do you?"

"Not every time. Only if they flirt with me. One-year-old girls can be terrible flirts."

"I can't believe I've known you this long and I've never seen you make goo goo eyes at a baby in a restaurant."

"I was very careful for a very long time. I was worried about scaring you off, pushing too hard. You'd stand up to drug dealers and stalkers, but you wouldn't stand up to your own feelings. I wanted your feelings to be right. I wanted you to be comfortable with them, not something I pushed for. Admit it, if I'd played peek-a-boo with a baby in a restaurant you'd have thought I was nuts."

"Well, not nuts, maybe, but it would have seemed awfully strange. Some people I can picture doing that easily. I bet Kelly does and Victor, too, because he's a dad. Some guys just don't seem like the peek-a-boo type."

"You'd be surprised. I can play a mean game of peek-a-boo," he said with a wink.

"I bet you can."

The phone rang and I picked it up on my way back to the kitchen. It was Chase.

Chapter 12

"Bring your gear along," he said with no prior greeting. This wasn't unusual for Chase.

"What am I doing that I need to bring gear along?"

Rusty raised his eyebrows.

"Maybe nothing."

"Hey, I got a new bulletproof vest. Should I bring that along, too?"

"Wouldn't hurt, might help."

"Chase, I can't go tracking for more than one day. I'm bringing my nephew, Patrick, along."

"Is everything okay at the ranch?"

"Yeah, he's just stranded down here because of the snowstorm. He's been at our house stalking deer."

"How's he doing on the deer?"

"As good as can be expected. When we get there, though, I need to talk to you about his tracking. I need some advice."

"Shoot."

"I can't discuss this over the phone. I'm supposed to be cooking dinner."

"Can you give me some clue?"

"I'm not sure how to teach Patrick how to track. He does things I didn't know how to do until years later. He needs guidance, but he has tremendous insight. He profiles as he tracks and reads the ages of tracks. Maybe not accurately, but he does it unconsciously. He has the talent, but he needs a teacher and I live too far away to do it. He asks questions about tracks he saw weeks ago and so far I've known the answers, but just the fact that he's able to keep tracks in his head amazes me. And he has the trouble gene. He sent the police after a friend and he was nearly hauled off by a purse snatcher at the mall. Then he got stuck near the top of a tree, all just in this one week! What am I going to do?"

"Bring your gear. We can talk on a trail."

It's as simple as that. Chase was a man of few words and infinite wisdom in a few areas. His social skills were unpredictable and his manners were terse. His heart was big. His hair was long. He was a sixty plus year old hippie, but he could surf with the kids in San Diego and keep up with the best of them. Chase had retired from the police force so he could concentrate on his real talent, which was tracking. He had a heart for tracking, and he worried that it was becoming a dying art, until he met me. He'd kind of taken me under his wing, and when he found out Patrick had inherited tracking tendencies as well, we automatically fell under his watchful eye. I could count on his help, if not his presence.

After dinner I checked the suitcases, found a storage box and placed Patrick's gifts on the bottom, out of sight, leaving Rusty's parent's gifts on top in plain sight. Then I grabbed my pack full of camping gear, my tracking tools, and my brand new bulletproof vest. I looked at the pile of everything we were taking to San Diego and knew there was no way we were taking the Jeep. We would have to take the Explorer. More room, more comfort, no four-wheel drive, no winch.

"We should be fine after we leave the foothills. The 18 and the 15 should be clear," Rusty said.

I agreed, though we watched the news again that night to be sure.

"Have they ever had snow in San Diego?" I asked.

"Not that I know of," Rusty answered. "It doesn't get cold enough."

When I put Patrick to bed that night he seemed apprehensive. "Are you sure Santa Claus will know where I am?"

"Yes, Pat, he keeps track of all the kids. It might be a little different there but Santa Claus will plan accordingly."

"Is it far?"

"Not as far as driving from the ranch to here. You'll get a couple more pictures colored on the way. Rusty's family is real nice and they are really excited to have a kid there for Christmas. You get to be their honorary grandkid."

"Do I hafta call them Grandma and Grandpa?"

"I doubt it. Start out calling them Mr. and Mrs. Michaels, but I bet they tell you to call them Bill and Bev. You know Cody and you know you can call him by his first name. And you will probably see Chase Downing there. Call him Mr. Downing until he tells you different. Rusty has a sister named Sandy. I don't know if his other brother will be there or not, but his name is Tony."

"Do they have a dog or a cat?"

"Nope, no pets."

"What will I do there? Do they have birds? Do they have kids?"

"Sorry, Pat, I don't know. We will find something to do. Have you ever gone tracking at the beach? There are a hundred different sets of tracks all in the sand."

I read to him from one of the longer books and within two chapters he had fallen asleep.

"We lucked out," I said, joining Rusty in the den. "He's asleep." I snuggled up to Rusty on the couch. "Today was a good day. I'm glad we got to play in the snow. I'm glad Santa Claus will make it to San Diego. I'm especially glad I'm married to you."

"You are?"

"Yes, if we have kids are they going to catch us kissing in the snow?"

"I hope so."

"And what'll we do if eleven o'clock rolls around and they're still not in bed?"

"Then I'll just kiss you good and hard and start taking your clothes off and they'll go to bed out of embarrassment."

"You wouldn't."

"Hey, they need to learn the facts of life. The fact is Daddy loves Mommy. Let me see your hands."

We were snuggled pretty tight, so it took some squirming around to bring my hands around in front of me. He took my hands in his and inspected them, then brought my hands to his lips and began kissing my fingertips.

"How do they feel?"

"They're fine. Why? Do you think I need to test them out?"

"Yeah, I think you need to make sure they feel everything like they should."

"Think I can find a willing test subject?"

"Yeah, I think so."

My stomach fluttered just at the thought of running my hands over Rusty.

"In the den? With Patrick in the next room?"

"No," he said softly. "Under the Christmas tree. You said it was magic to lie under the Christmas tree."

I peeled myself away and led him into the living room. Turning on the Christmas tree lights I lay underneath the tree, looking up through all the lights, watching the bright red and cozy green reflections of the lights dance off the ornaments.

I pulled Rusty down onto the floor. "Look up, right through there. It looks like fairies could dance. It looks like Christmas spirit formed into light." He lay there on his back gazing up through the tree, so I straddled him and slipped my hands up under his shirt. Oh, yeah.

"Skin," I said. "This is skin and hard muscle." I let my fingers dance and tease over the muscles. "Hair," I said. "I feel hair and more skin." And more muscle. I brushed the stubble of his beard. Traced his lips. He reached up and kissed my finger as it passed by. "Kisses, I feel kisses." I knew it wouldn't take long and he'd have to test out his fingers, too.

Okay, Cass, this is just a ruse so you'd make love with him under the Christmas tree. So, make love to him. Touch him. Oh, yeah. I slipped off him and gave him a deep kiss. A shiver went up my spine and the kiss became more insistent. To hell with the fingers. I needed contact, full body contact. I pulled off my t-shirt and started undoing his buttons. As I made my way down his shirt, his hands were making their way up my body. It seemed to me that men's shirts were designed to torture women with their little buttons and minuscule buttonholes. Time consuming little buttons, especially hard to handle with raging hormones. He grabbed the shirttails and pulled it over his head. Why hadn't I thought of that?

A tumble under the Christmas tree. I wondered if Santa ever took a tumble with Mrs. Claus under their tree. Of course he did. It was Christmas at the North Pole year around, right? So he must have. Christmas just wasn't the same without a tumble under the Christmas tree.

My fingers felt fine. Everything felt wonderful but I thought my vision was going hokey. While the lights were dancing all around us my feelings seemed to merge with the lights. With amusement I realized our timing matched the twinkling of the lights above us. I let it flow into me and through me, marveling at all the many forms Christmas spirit could take.

Next thing I knew, daylight was streaming through the windows. Yikes!

"Rusty! Damn it. Put some clothes on! It's morning, and we have a kid in the house."

I yanked on my pants, t-shirt, grabbed my underwear and made a run for the bedroom.

"Huh?" he said behind me.

I returned more calmly once I realized the house was still quiet.

"We need to get ready to leave. Come on. Finger test is over. Everything feels great, but it's morning. I'm going to shower."

"Do you need help?" he asked, still sounding drowsy.

"We need to get on the road and it's going to take longer to get there with Patrick along. You can't expect a six-year-old to sit still for three hours. We'll have to stop to stretch and then we'll have to stop again for lunch. We need to drop Shadow off at the kennel. Come on, we have a lot to do."

"Okay," he said, "I'm moving."

I showered first, then picked a pair of newer jeans and a cute sweater. Jesse called it a boyfriend sweater. I thought Rusty would like it, and it was a little on the dressy side so I felt dressed up for Rusty's parents.

Patrick woke up and I made him take a quick bath then laid out his clothes and made all the beds. After feeding Shadow I packed up his food, leash and toys for his stay in the kennel. I went through Patrick's room making sure everything had been packed for the trip to San Diego and his return trip home again.

After a million small details were finally done, we settled in the Explorer, ready to go. We picked our way out of the foothills noticing more and more foothill residents had given up waiting on the snow to clear. We dropped Shadow off at the kennel and took Route 18, heading east to join I-15. We stopped at Ontario Mills and took Patrick to the Rain Forest Café.

"The fishes are real but the other animals are stuffed," he announced. "I like the rain, though. You get the storm without getting wet. Can I buy Wyatt a t-shirt from here? He'd like one with that funny looking frog on it."

"Sure, that sounds like a good idea," I answered.

We had just finished our lunch when all the servers suddenly stopped as a waiter rushed through the restaurant carrying a plate held high. "Volcano!" they shouted one at a time as the dessert sped by and was plunked down right in front of Patrick. He looked at it in wide-eyed amazement. The dessert looked like a huge chocolate volcano. Fudge lava overflowed onto the plate. It was more chocolate than Patrick had eaten all year. I looked at Rusty and he just grinned.

"You know, he's going to make himself sick on that," I said.

The waiter handed Patrick a long thin spoon. Two minutes later Rusty and I helped him finish it. Rusty ate most of it. Patrick and I had to quit.

"Chocolate wimps," Rusty called us, but he was right, we *were* chocolate wimps.

We continued down the I-15 until we reached La Jolla and then Rusty left the freeway and drove through the beach town until he found a small beach with a sea wall protecting the shore. This looked like a place where we could let Patrick run around and track as much as he liked. Patrick had been to the beach years ago, before he'd been old enough to track and now he found it fascinating.

"Look!" he said excitedly. "Here's a family just like mine! A mom, dad and two little kids. Only I think the kids are younger because the tracks are smaller, see?" He placed his foot next to the track and his shoe was a little bigger.

"I bet if you took your shoe off it would be about the same size," I observed.

He took off his shoe and did another comparison then followed the family of tracks with one shoe off and the other one on.

"I think it's a girl, not a boy," he decided.

I agreed.

"The one my age is a girl and the one littler than Wyatt is a boy and the dad is fat. Or he's carrying something big. Probably both. I bet it's an ice chest full of beer. Mom says beer makes guys fat… Dad's not fat though."

"Rusty's not fat, but he doesn't drink much beer."

We pulled into the driveway at Rusty's parent's house by mid-afternoon and Bev rushed out to greet us.

"It's so good to see you!" she squealed. And then to Patrick, "Look how much you've grown! You're getting so big!"

"You just saw him in July," I said.

"I know, but six-year-old boys grow fast. If you put them up to a growth chart every day you get to make a new mark."

"I'm in first grade!" Patrick said proudly. "I can read!"

"I bet you can," Bev said. "Do you like school?"

"Most of the time, but they make us read baby books."

"I doubt that. Maybe they just need some books that are interesting to small boys."

"I think he decided he wanted to learn how to read because I promised to buy him a survival guide when he was big enough to understand it. He's going to be able to read one long before he's old enough to try a survival trip, though."

"Take Patrick up to the attic. I dug out some of the kids' old games and toys. He can stay up there and you two can have the spare bedroom."

After taking one look at the attic I knew there was no way Patrick would be sleeping up there. It was wall-to-wall toys, but that held little appeal for him. What caught his eye immediately was a huge erector set. The pieces from several sets had been collected in a big plastic bin and for Patrick that was heaven. He looked through the pieces, not quite understanding their purpose but definitely seeing their potential.

He looked through the bookcases and picked a western book that looked like something his grandpa would read.

"Bev," I said, "it's nice of you to do all this for Patrick but it's better if Rusty and I stay up here. If it was Patrick's room he'd play all night."

"Nonsense, I can't let you sleep up here with only a mattress on the floor."

"It'll be fine, really." Rusty and I can play all night, I thought to myself. "I worry that Patrick might try climbing down the ladder to the pool. He's good at stuff like that. He got stuck in a tree when I took him bird watching. He followed a little bird all the way to the top. It took me climbing up there with ropes to get him down. I'd feel better if he slept in the bedroom."

"Aw, Aunt Cassidy, that's no fair."

"You can play up here all day but at night it's time to sleep. You can take a toy or a book to bed with you but it's to sleep, not play, especially on Christmas Eve. Santa Claus won't come until you are sleeping. Now, I have one, very important rule for you. You cannot go out the back door. The backyard only has a swimming pool in it. No toys, no space to play. It's too cold to swim and pools are dangerous for little kids. So… no going in the backyard for any reason. Got that?"

"Yes Ma'am, I'm not allowed in the backyard."

"Good, and you don't have to be so formal with me. A simple yes or no is fine."

There was a great big thump as the front door opened and Cody came through carrying his red bicycle. Patrick's eyes got big with delight.

"You've got a bike!"

"Yeah, I've got a bike," Cody said, giving him a high five. "Don't tell me you don't have one, every kid should have a bike."

"I don't have a bike because there's nowhere to ride one," Patrick answered. "We walk to the ranch and the highway is too busy. So I don't have a bike."

"Aw dude, we'll see if you can ride this one. Do you know how to skateboard?"

"No, we don't have cement at home. But Santa's going to bring me rollerblades!"

"Cool! Then you can rollerblade on our street. Just don't go too fast down the hill because Mrs. Rathburn hates calling 911 to get kids out of her rosebushes. Last kid broke his arm. The kid before that broke his ankle. Every kid in the neighborhood has landed in those rose bushes at one time or another. She especially hates it when kids do that in the fall when she is trying to grow the perfect rose to enter into the county fair. She always gets the perfect rose grown and then some kid knocks all the petals off it."

"I didn't break anything when I went through her rosebushes," Rusty said. "I dented her aluminum siding with my hard head."

"That was you?" Cody asked. "The dent's still there. When I did it, I had quick reflexes and skidded my bike sideways and plowed a perfect trench right through her yard. She made me rake it all back out and sprinkle fresh grass seed down."

"When I went down that hill," Bev added, "I didn't make it to the rosebushes, I went face first into the yard and skinned my nose on the ground."

We all stared at her in surprise. Rusty's mom had landed in Mrs. Rathburn's yard too? Wow.

"How did you do that?" Cody asked his mom.

"On rollerblades. My wheels locked on a tiny rock and I just went flying!"

"When?" Patrick asked.

"Oh, it was a long time ago. It's been two, maybe three years."

"Well, Patrick, looks like we have a tradition to live up to," I said.

"Oh no you don't," Rusty and Cody said in unison.

"Has Mr. Chase landed in the rosebushes?" Patrick asked.

Cody looked over the group like he was wondering whether or not Chase would want this story told. "Yeah, he nearly killed us both. Tommy York called Chase an old man. Then Chase bet him he could skateboard down the hill and make it back up without falling. To make it hard he had me kneel down towards the bottom of the hill. He was going to skateboard down the hill, send the skateboard under me and jump over, turn the board around and then come back up. I'd seen him skateboard. I knew he could do the hill, get the board through the hole, and jump over me. What I didn't count on was Chase coming down on the wrong end of the skateboard, sending it up into my ribs and then rolling through Mrs. Rathburn's yard. He put a little dent in her siding, right next to Rusty's."

"Oh, Cody, you should have stopped him," Bev said.

"Nobody can stop Chase once he decides to do something."

"What did Tommy get for winning his bet?" Patrick asked.

"Nothing. He got scared and ran home and we didn't see him for a week. But he doesn't call Chase an old man any more."

"But he *is* an old man," Patrick said.

"Kid, only his skin is old, the rest of him refuses to age."

"Did Mr. Michaels land in Mrs. Rathburn's rosebushes?" Patrick asked.

"I don't know, we'll have to ask him at dinner," Rusty answered. "I doubt it."

We heard the rest of the tales of Mrs. Rathburn's rosebushes during dinner. Bill returned home from the golf course and Sandy came for dinner. The dining room table was filled to capacity. It normally sat six, and that made the little dining corner behind the stairs cozy. The extended family had increased it to seven and that made it downright cramped. We may have been overcrowded but at least it created a warm and friendly atmosphere.

"Do you remember that Barbie bicycle I had when I was five years old?" Sandy asked.

"No," all the guys said, but Bev brightened immediately. "Yes! And you looked so cute on it with your brown pigtails flying in the breeze."

"The day the training wheels came off that thing I landed in Mrs. Rathburn's rosebushes. I was head to toe scratches."

"Oh, yes, I remember now," Bev said. "You were mad because you lost the little glittery license plate off your bike. We never did find it."

Everybody looked at Bill.

"Well, Dad," Cody said, "we've heard all the stories except yours."

Bill sighed. He thought about it, but didn't want to admit he'd also landed in Mrs. Rathburn's rosebushes.

"I didn't land in the rosebushes," he finally said, "I landed in the hedges on the side of her house."

"How did you manage that?" Cody asked.

"I was chasing a teenager up the street. She had been part of a group of kids that vandalized the school a few years ago. I was on her tail and keeping up pretty good. Some of the other guys were lagging behind. Suddenly the kid turns on me and does this fast kickboxing maneuver and I went flying into the bushes. She took off and I was struggling to get up out of the bushes. All the other guys saw the bushes thrashing around and aimed their guns at me, yelling at me to stand up quietly with my hands behind my head. It was embarrassing."

"Did Mrs. Rathburn come out and yell at you?" Sandy asked.

"You know Mrs. Rathburn. She isn't a bad lady. She came out, saw all the policemen in her front yard and just said, 'What is this world coming to?' and then went back inside."

Patrick looked around the table and smiled smugly. "This is an interesting family," he finally said.

"If I remember right, that's what Chase said when he first met *your* family," Cody added. "Did you bring your hat with the gopher snake hatband?"

"Yeah, but I only wear it for dress up and Aunt Cassidy said you probably don't dress up for Christmas dinner." Then he brightened and added, "Do you want to hear how I got the hatband, though? Aunt Cassidy killed the snake on a survival trip because she had to eat and then she saved the skin for me. My dad made it into a hatband for me. Isn't that cool? You want to see it?"

Sandy's complexion turned green. Bev's eyes got big. "Oh, you poor dear, reduced to eating gopher snake. You must have been starved." Bill sat back with his hands folded over his chest. He filed the story away, knowing one day he'd understand this odd little daughter-in-law of his. Cody seemed to be enjoying the women's reactions. Patrick left the table and ran out to the Explorer to retrieve his cowboy hat from the box in the back. He returned wearing it tilted at an angle, a mischievous cowboy glint in his eyes. Too bad he couldn't sing. He was such a good looking kid that all the girls would faint if he became a country star.

"Oh, my, would you look at the boy! We need to go to the mall and have your picture taken in that hat! Your mom will love it! Sandy, do you want to go to the mall after dinner?"

"Sure," she answered.

I put Patrick in his outfit for dress up occasions and the two women went nuts.

"I know just the place to go!" Sandy said. "They have this backdrop with aspen trees and they have a saddle prop."

Patrick looked at me for help but he knew he'd been the one who had started it.

Just before Bev and Sandy left to have Patrick's picture taken I warned them, "Don't let him out of your sight for a second, and if he points out a bad guy, he means it. Run in the opposite direction."

"She's not kidding," Rusty added for emphasis.

As they disappeared down the walk, I asked Rusty, "Do you think one of us should go too?"

"Nah, they can handle him."

"But can they handle what happens when he goes to the mall? Remember last time I took him to the mall? Maybe I should go along."

"That would just double the trouble. They'll be fine."

"You don't think we should warn them?"

"We already did, they'll be fine."

"Okay, I guess we can use the time to bring in his presents and hide them. Then I'll take a little time for myself and stop worrying about the trouble he may be getting into."

Chapter 13

Rusty, Bill and I were in the attic playing a game of Nine Ball when we heard the group returning from the mall. They made Cody sound like a mute.

"HA, ha! That was so funny! You'd think they never saw a rope before! That was so fun! Are we really going back tomorrow?" Patrick said, his voice carrying all the way upstairs and bouncing off the rafters.

"It depends on how bad you want to earn the money. I'd say go for it!" Sandy said. "It looks like an easy buck to me."

"Do I hafta autograph pictures again?"

Rusty and I exchanged glances then both turned and looked at Bill.

"I think I better go see what happened. You can finish the game without me," I said.

Sandy was still laughing when I appeared downstairs. "Cassidy! You should have warned us!" she cackled.

"Warned you about what?"

"What a flirt this guy is! It was hilarious!"

"Patrick! What did you do this time?" I asked. I didn't want to get angry unless I had a good reason, so I was withholding judgment, but my question must have still sounded stern.

"I didn't do anything! I promise!"

"You should have been there!" Sandy guffawed.

I'd never seen my sister-in-law laugh hysterically before. Sandy was very proper and professional with a history of always wearing matching pantsuits with high heel shoes and diamond jewelry. And now she was rolling on the couch in hysterical laughter which was only making me worry more.

"We went to the photography studio in the mall and they had the aspen backdrop and the saddle just like I remembered. They had to adjust the cameras so we were waiting for them to be ready and Patrick picks up the rope lying on the saddle. He starts twirling the rope around his head like a real cowboy! And, and the photographer starts to say, 'Don't touch that!' but when he saw what Patrick was doing he puts him in the picture and starts shooting pictures of him twirling the rope. They usually take six shots at this place and then you have to choose two that you want reprints of. This guy must have taken at least fifty pictures and he brings them up on a computer and prints out his favorite ones. Then he asks Patrick if he can do some more tricks."

"He called it a trick!" Patrick said, sounding offended. "Dad says I can't be a real cowboy until I can handle a rope so I have to work with the rope every day. I open the loop and close the loop and turn it different ways and I lasso fence posts. But this guy at the mall said it was a *trick* and it wasn't. I just got bored so I was practicing. They really need to break in their rope. It was real stiff and hard to twirl but I got it to work a little bit."

"A little bit!" Sandy exclaimed. "You made that rope dance!"

"Then they asked me if I would do it out in the mall and I thought they were nuts. Why would I want to practice with a rope in a mall? But I said I would do it because everybody was so interested. So I went out in the mall and I twirled it up and then I figured out how to twirl it down. At home with a real rope the practice gets boring so I try jumping into the loop and then out of it. And when I did that the crowd went wild. The people would watch for a while and then wander around and look in the shops and then come back. So the shop people offered me money to stay there and twirl the rope! And then the photography place taped my picture up on their window. Lots of kids stopped to have their pictures taken and now the photographer wants me to do it again tomorrow. This lady said she was from Georgia and asked if I was a movie star. Another person asked if I had any autographed pictures. They all thought I was famous or something. Heck, I was just doing stuff I do every day at home and I'm not even a real cowboy yet, but they thought it was great. You'd think they'd never seen a person twirl a rope before!"

"Did you give that person an autographed picture?" I asked.

"The photographer printed out a bunch of pictures on plain paper and I just signed my first name and he handed them out to anybody who wanted one. He stapled a business card to each one. It was kind of fun but I didn't understand what the big deal was. Now they want me to come back and do it again tomorrow. They said if I filled out a form they would pay me to do it."

"Can I go too? I can twirl a rope," I asked.

"I think they were just amazed because Patrick is so little and cute," Bev said.

I looked at Pat in his white pinstriped shirt, pressed jeans, shiny boots, string tie, big black snakeskin trimmed cowboy hat and laughed to myself. This was normal where he came from, but it was a show in San Diego. My father, Big Wayne Gordon, kept the old west alive on the ranch. If it weren't for him, it would be just like any other ranch in California. But it wasn't; it was a cowboy ranch, and all the kids grew up like cowboys.

"They gave us a big batch of pictures almost for free, and even when we were walking around the mall people kept asking me for my autograph. I signed notebooks, shopping bags, jeans and hats. Hats are hard to write on though. Those people are going to be mad when they find out there's no famous kid named Patrick."

"They won't be mad at you," I told him, "because they asked you to do it. It's not like you did something bad. At least you didn't see any purse snatchers and end up in the office again."

"Yeah," he said, taking my words into consideration, "I don't know what was worse, thinking we were going to jail or having to do a rope twirling act at the mall. I think I'll stay away from malls."

I could sympathize with the kid. It came with having the trouble gene. Some trouble was definitely bad news, but then sometimes it was just interesting, like what happened to Pat at the mall. At least he hadn't had a boring time.

"Mr. Michaels? Do you have a real rope I could use?"

"We'll go look," Rusty said.

A little later, I heard cursing coming from the front yard. Looking out of the window, I saw Cody and Patrick standing side by side with Cody tangled in the rope.

"You have to do it smooth and regular like. You're not doing it smoothly. Every time you jerk your hand you have to fix the wobble. If you're spending your time fixing wobbles, you'll never learn anything else."

"I am not wobbling. I'm a smooth dude," Cody insisted.

"You might be a smooth dude, but you aren't a smooth roper. Aunt Cassidy can lasso a calf from a running horse, flank him and tie him in ten seconds."

"Well, in ten seconds she doesn't have time to *wobble*," Cody complained.

"Aw, shit, you'll never learn if you won't listen to me!" Patrick complained. "I think it's time for you to teach me to ride your bike."

"Okay, but no wobbling. Wobbling hurts worse on a bike than it does with a rope. And we aren't going down the hill yet, we're starting out at Cabrillo Court."

Cody's bike was a little too big for Patrick, but it was way too small for Cody. He looked silly riding it, but it seemed to suit his personality and he could sling it over his shoulder and carry it if he got a flat tire. Cody and his red bike were almost inseparable. He rode it to work, up and down the boardwalk during breaks, and then later would ride it back home. I tried to remember if I'd ever seen him drive a car.

Cody jogged into the house and then up the steps to his room, which always blared music even when he wasn't in it. He came out carrying the bike and then jogged back down the stairs somehow managing not to bump into the stairway or walls. He turned the corner and was out the front door before you could say Jack Robinson.

"You better go take some pictures or Jesse's going to be mad," Rusty suggested to me.

"She'll probably be mad that Pat learned how to ride a bike without her anyway," I replied. "At least she will like having some pictures of Cody, too."

I was half convinced that if Jesse wasn't already married to James she might have packed up and relocated to San Diego to put the moves on Rusty's little brother. Fortunately, she was very settled into her ranch life with a good husband and two wonderful kids. I doubt she'd budge for a suntanned cruise line poster boy. But I was sure she wouldn't mind having a few pictures of him with her son either.

By the time I caught up with them Cody was pushing Patrick around the circle. Cabrillo Court was a cul de sac just three houses long and looked like a good place to practice.

"No training wheels. Training wheels are for sissies, besides there haven't been training wheels at our house for twenty years. Learning to balance is the key. And it's easier to balance the faster you go."

"It hurts more to crash the faster you go!" Patrick wailed.

"That's why you learn to balance faster!" Cody said. "Plus, the bike will take wobbles easier the faster you go so pedal, come on pedal!"

"I *am* pedaling but pedaling causes wobbling!"

"Pedal smoothly, if you spend your time fixing wobbles you'll never learn to ride a bike."

Turn a rope, pedal a bike, all you've got to do is get the wobbles out.

That first night getting Patrick to bed was easier than back home. After a day of traveling, visiting, going to the mall, and bike riding, all the activity had added up. I let him take the western book to bed with him, knowing he'd get bored with it and fall asleep. I was wrong.

"Aunt Cassidy…" I heard from his room.

"What is it, Patrick?" I called back.

"How long is a sidewinder?"

Sigh, okay, more questions. I got up and went to his bedroom.

"Baby ones are little, adult ones are three or four feet. I bet some of them get longer. Why?"

He looked at me in disbelief. "I was just wondering," he said. "I read the word in this book and I didn't know."

"Well, read the sentence to me and we'll figure it out."

He read aloud, "He was mean, slick and sneaky as an old coyote and I bet his dick was as long as a sidewinder. Maybe that's why…"

"Patrick! I think you need to stick to kids books. Where did you get this?"

"Upstairs," he said innocently.

I took the book, let it fall open, and started reading. Oh my gosh! This book was *not* intended for kids.

"I'll go up and get you one that your mom won't be mad about," I said and went to the attic. I looked through the books and found a Louis L'Amour book that I thought I had read as a kid, and brought it down to him. "Here, I think this one is safe."

"Is the other one dangerous?"

"You need to be older to read that one. Your mom will probably let you read it when you get to be, oh, twenty-one, or married, whichever comes first."

"Aw, that's no fair."

"It is too. Every kid has to wait for some books. It's rule number eighteen."

"Yeah, right."

"It's time for you to try and get some sleep. Goodnight, Patrick."

"I think we need to censor the books upstairs," I said to the adults downstairs. "Did you hear what his question was about?"

"No, but I think it's wonderful when children ask questions. It makes it so much easier to talk about difficult subjects," Bev said.

"Oh yeah?" I asked. "He wanted to know how long a sidewinder is."

"Did you tell him?"

"Yeah, he wanted to know because of this sentence in a book that he read." I handed her the book and pointed to the sentence.

"Oh, dear," she said. "He's doing very well if he knew how to read the words *coyote* and *sidewinder*." I smiled at her, my mother-in-law, always the eternal optimist.

The book got passed around and the grins passed along with it. I noticed, though, that nobody claimed to have already read the book.

"Do you mind sleeping in the attic? I thought if Patrick stayed up here there would be too many temptations to play."

"No, I don't mind. It's more comfortable than that stuffy bedroom and we don't have to worry about the bed frame creaking. Plus we're adults, and we can play all night if we want to. It's one of the advantages of growing up," Rusty said as he smiled at me.

"Would you play all night with me?" I asked.

I slipped out of my clothes and into the "cute little number" from

Victoria's Secret. He took me in his arms.

"Mmm, I think I might be persuaded."

"How much persuasion do you need?"

"How much can I get?"

Chapter 14

It was barely light out when I awoke because of a sound near my head. I was sleeping in a strange house so I didn't overreact, just suddenly came awake, senses alert, assessing my situation without moving. Was I clothed? No. Was I covered? Mostly. Good, because the noise wasn't Rusty. I listened carefully and sensed there was another person in the room. It wasn't Patrick. Patrick would have spoken before he approached our bed. Rusty's family knew to stay out of the attic. In my mind I ran down the list. Chase. He knelt beside the mattress, waiting. He signaled with his eyes. Downstairs. Then he silently crept down the pull-down stairs, avoiding the creaky step, and went to the living room silent as fog. I got up, slipped into lounge pants and a t-shirt and went downstairs too, not nearly as quietly as Chase. I just didn't want to wake anybody although they knew I was in the house and wouldn't mind me being up.

"How did you get in here?" I whispered loudly.

"This house is easy to break into," he stated simply.

"A cop's house and you find it easy to break into?"

"I don't break into it often. I usually come in through the front door. After someone opens it for me."

"So why are you breaking in this morning?"

"I need some help."

"What kind of help? Tracking help? Scouting help?"

He briefly looked me up and down. "I need a sixteen-year-old girl."

"You're right, you do need help. And you're ten years too late."

"Not that kind of help. I heard about Stan."

I paused.

"I heard this happens to you a lot. You draw people out. I need a seventeen-year-old boy drawn out."

"Chase, Rusty will kill me if I go along with you."

"Nice private school. One kid dealing drugs. One lonely girl being abandoned to boarding school by her mean old dad. One lonely girl who just needs a fix to deal with the situation. You'd have him in two seconds. The school would be free of him. What do you say?"

"What happened to your last narc?"

"They have bigger fish to catch. This is a small school. Nearly everybody's gone for the holidays. Ten kids there, tops. One in particular we're after. There's a quota he's got to meet and he'll take some extra risks right now. All you gotta do is buy something from him and your daddy will arrest his sorry butt and get him out of there."

"Are you my daddy?" I asked sarcastically.

"No, I'm too old. But I got someone who wants to be your daddy."

I stood up to him, looked him eye to eye and said simply, "I don't trust you."

"Good, you shouldn't," he answered.

ARGH, I was going to be really sorry for getting involved in Chase's harebrained scheme. I knew it. This situation had trouble written all over it. TROUBLE with a bright neon pink marker. I was going to get lynched, and if not lynched then Rusty would kill me. If Rusty didn't kill me, I'd be grounded for life.

"Here," Chase said as he handed me a bundle of clothes, "you'll need these."

"You went through my things?" I accused.

"I knew what you'd need and what you'd pick. They didn't match up, so I made some decisions for you."

"And why am I going to need these?" I asked, holding up a pair of panties made out of lace and a few ribbons.

"I just liked the look of them. I don't expect you to need them."

"Will you talk to me about Patrick on the way?"

"I will."

Sigh, I noticed my badge was in the bundle along with my bulletproof vest but my gun was missing. What kind of a deal was I making here?

"When will I be back?"

"Noon, tops, your dad is going to ask you to just spend a few hours talking to the kids about the school. You're not going to like it but you don't have any choice. He'll leave you right where he needs you to be. He'll appear to leave, but we'll have guys stationed in the empty classrooms. All you gotta do is act angry, miserable and cute and you'll have him eating out of your hand."

"I can't lie. I'm a terrible liar."

"Then don't. Tell him you want to go back to the ranch. You don't want to live in San Diego. And slip in a line about how you knew where to get a fix in your nice little town. That you'll die in the big city. Just think of something."

"Give me fifteen minutes. I need to changes clothes and tell Rusty what I'm up to."

He looked at me with raised eyebrows. "You really think you'll make it out of this house if you tell Rusty what you're up to?"

"Yeah."

I took the bundle upstairs, showered and changed clothes quietly. Rusty was used to me getting up before him so it was no big deal. I put on some make-up because I thought sixteen-year-old girls would wear make-up. I curled my hair. Then I took my purse along, because I thought a sixteen-year-old wouldn't be caught dead without her purse.

I sat beside Rusty and stroked his arm. He was awake in an instant. I hoped he wasn't too awake.

"Chase is here. He wants to talk about Patrick. I'll be back in a few hours. If I'm not back by noon, send out a search party."

"Where are you going?"

"I'm not sure."

"What should I do with Patrick?"

"If he wants to go back to the mall, ask Sandy about it. He might need a bodyguard. If Cody will let you, teach him to ride the bicycle. I'll try not to be too long. And I'm serious about the noon bit. I'll see you soon." I kissed him then beat a hasty retreat.

"You know, if I end up back in the hospital after this, Rusty is going to tan your hide," I said as we slipped out of the house and got into his light blue Baja bug. For a dune buggy it ran surprisingly quiet and we slipped out of the neighborhood without a rumble.

"Not me," he answered.

"Oh ya? Then who?"

"Slick Whitman. It's his case."

"This is sounding more and more like someone else's job. Not mine. Slick Whitman? Sounds like a used car salesman."

"He could sell glasses to eagles, a mop to Sponge Bob Squarepants, a vacuum cleaner to a cat."

"Then why didn't *he* come talk to me about this case?"

"Because you'd have said 'no'."

"Wait a minute…"

"You'd have seen through him. You're smarter than Sponge Bob."

"Well, gee, thanks, I think."

"I came because Rusty and Slick don't exactly get along. Slick's the reason Rusty's in Joshua Hills, not San Diego. Slick's got more arrests than anybody in the city and he doesn't mind stepping on a few toes or taking a few risks. That's because he lives up to his name, he's slick"

"Risking a few people he shouldn't?"

"You can still say no. Is it true about Stan?"

"Yeah, it's true. I didn't do anything, just sat at a bar and waited for Rusty, then Stan walks up, blows his cover, and gets hauled off slick as a whistle."

"Is it true about Alfonso?"

"Yeah, although that one wasn't as easy."

"Is it true about the purse snatcher at the mall?"

"Wait a minute, that was only a few days ago. How could you know about that?"

"News travels fast."

"That wasn't me so much as Patrick. Remember I told you he takes after me? Well, it's showing up more and more."

"You're expecting too much out of him."

"Me? I'm not expecting anything out of him! He's the one who keeps doing these uncharacteristically advanced things. He still talks about them like a kid. He called the purse snatcher a bad guy. But just the fact that he sees these things at all is amazing. I worry about letting it go without any guidance."

"What about you? You just grew up into a tracker with very little guidance."

"It was just chance."

"So what is it with Patrick?"

"I just wonder how far he could go if he had more help than I did, but I can't move to the ranch to teach him. My dad would hire another hand if they could help Patrick learn to track. If someone would mentor him while he was out of school, my dad would hire them no questions asked. All I would have to do is talk to Jesse and my dad."

"I'd give him a few years at least. He won't be old enough to turn loose in the hills for a few years, so wait until that time to get serious about it. He still needs to learn at his own rate. By then we will know how serious he is about it."

"That's another thing. If he had me to keep him motivated then he'd stay interested. What if he loses interest?"

"You'd like to see him get serious about tracking?"

"I'd like to see him use his talent, whether he ends up in college studying science or working on the ranch training horses. Tracking isn't exactly a high paying position. He has to have other interests as well."

"I think you're worrying about nothing. Just keep tabs on him. Give him a new goal. What can he do around the ranch that's more advanced than tagging rabbits?"

"That's just it. Jesse won't let him out of the yard, so rabbits and birds are the only animals he has access to. He asked Santa Claus to send deer, but I doubt Santa has that kind of power. Santa works more on the level of rollerblades."

"Have him keep track of all the different animals that come around the house. All the people, all the animals, even the birds. Stress that it doesn't have to just involve tracks. Any sign can be used. That will get him to thinking about the fact that cracked seeds could mean birds… or mice or squirrels. If he starts noticing scat, he can learn to distinguish one kind from another. All these skills are useful in building other skills. The most important thing you can do is create an inquiring mind."

"That's a good idea, although I doubt if he writes them all down. I got him a field guide to animal tracks, maybe he'll use it to check off animals like he does in his bird book."

We arrived at the station and I followed Chase through to an office. He knocked quickly and walked in without waiting for a response. I didn't follow. It seemed rude. Chase turned around and waved me in. I didn't want to appear timid so I squared my shoulders and strode in confidently. Whitman stood when I walked in and looked me over.

"Well, well, well," he said to Chase, "you were right." No introductions, no pleasantries. I was being sized up for a job, no more, no less. I didn't like it. I got the feeling I was disposable and somehow I thought being Rusty's wife in this situation was a distinct disadvantage. I wondered if he knew who I was.

"How old are you?" he asked.

"It's good to meet you too, Mr. Whitman," I said, and Chase hid a grin.

Chapter 15

Whitman took a step back and reconsidered his next move. I felt like a used car. He was going to kick my tires and I was going to say something not very nice. I thought I should call Rusty and get a ride home.

"How old are you?" Whitman repeated.

"I'm out of here," I said to Chase. "I'll get a ride, no problem."

"Cassidy, it's six a.m. How are you going to get a ride back?"

"I'll call, or I'll walk. I don't care. I'd do just about anything for you, Chase, but I won't walk into a dangerous situation for someone who won't even say 'hello' to me. If all I am to him is a person to plant in a school, he can find somebody else."

Then I turned and walked out. It wasn't like me to just walk out so I had to do it quickly and kept walking without looking back. Chase caught up with me.

"I know, he isn't Mr. Tact but the problem is still there."

"No he isn't, he's following us."

Chase looked behind him while I kept walking. Problem was I had followed Chase coming in and I didn't know the way out. I looked at the ends of the halls for exit signs.

"Cassidy, I've never seen you like this. Why are you doing this?"

"Because, my trouble radar is going off like crazy. I've nearly died enough times that I tend to listen to it. I don't want some drug dealing high school kid to try and knock me off because I'm a cop. I'm not even a *real cop*. And we agreed a long time ago that I would never make it to cophood. So why all of a sudden is everyone trying to put me in that position? I'm going to go in there and say something wrong and the mob is going to come get me, shoot me and all I can do is hope they aim for my heart and don't drop me off a pier because I finally got a Kevlar vest, and I think I could fake my way out but…"

"Cassidy, stop. Do you think I'd tell you about the job if I didn't think you could do it? Do you think I'd have you do it if I thought it was dangerous? The only reason I brought you here is because you fit the job. You *can* do it and you'll have backup."

"Chase, I'm not a cop. The badge means nothing. Zip, zilch. I follow tracks. That's what I do. I follow tracks until I find my man. That's what I'm good at. I haven't had a very good time of it lately, but I've found my man. Shit, where's the punching bag in this place?"

He steered me through some double doors and there was the exercise room. I punched the bag, sending it rocking.

"Whitman's in charge of this?"

"Yup." *Wham.*

"I'm not working with Whitman."

"So I see."

"You think this is going to be like the Stan case, but it's not."

"Same mindset, different age group. Bet you weren't a high school kid when Stan tried to pick you up."

"It's hard for me not to look like a high school kid."

"What were you wearing?"

"Little black dress."

"Ah, that would explain it."

"Don't get me thinking about the little black dress. I wore it to a funeral for a ten sixty-five."

He went quiet, just holding the bag. He understood how tough it must have been for me since it was my first. The past year began bubbling, percolating in my mind. The kidnappings, the traps, being shot, beaten and attacked, all the tracking, the searches, the fire. What had I gotten myself into and what was I fixing to walk into now? Nobody knew. They were all bright and cheerful about it now, but how would it look if I stared down the barrel of a revolver or got dumped in the bay just for being a cop in the wrong place at the wrong time? And I couldn't do it. I couldn't sneak off with Chase to do some foolhardy and dangerous stunt. I was a wife now and it was time to start behaving like a wife. I had Rusty to think of and Patrick to consider. I couldn't go through with this without at least a phone call. I pulled out my cell phone and speed dialed Rusty.

He answered on the second ring alert for trouble. He was in cop mode.

"Cass?"

"Yeah, it's me."

"What is it?"

"Are you awake? I need you."

"Yeah, what's wrong?"

"Nothing and everything."

"Would you like to elaborate a little bit?"

"Chase and I discussed Patrick and it was a good talk. I know what to do now. But we ended up at the station and… And there's a case going on that they would like some help with."

The line went quiet.

"They say all I need to do is go to a school, pretend my dad is thinking of starting me there, and whine about my situation so a kid will sell me some drugs and get arrested. It sounds doable and straightforward but my trouble radar is going off like crazy. And I don't like this guy who's in charge at all, but maybe I'm just being biased. Chase isn't pushing. He knows I have to decide for myself. I want to help, but this just feels all wrong so I thought I should call."

"Tell Slick I'm going to bust his balls for even thinking of asking you to go on a narcotics bust. Then drag Chase back here by his overgrown ponytail so I can…"

"Rusty, no one is forcing me to do anything. But, what about the kids at the school? It doesn't sound dangerous, but I want a partner I can trust and I don't trust this guy."

"Put Chase on."

"I don't think Whitman knows who I am. He just thinks I'm a reserve deputy who matches their requirements. But that brings up a question of rank."

"Not until you are working on the case. As a volunteer, you have a choice until you place yourself under their command. After that, you have to follow orders. But to hell with that. I don't care what's happened. I want you out of there."

Chase motioned for the phone.

"It's not what it looks like," he told Rusty. "This is a cushy school. Ten rich kids left at boarding school over the holidays. No weapons are allowed… I know that. We're talking real cushy. Tennis courts, riding school. The cars in student parking are Porsches and Corvettes… If you come down here it's going to be World War Three…" He snapped the phone closed. "He's coming down here."

Rusty knew San Diego well and that included the police station layout inside and out. He was standing there very cross and agitated within half an hour.

"Where is he?" he demanded.

"In his office," Chase said.

Rusty looked me up and down. Curly hair, make-up.

"You knew. You knew when you left this morning that something was up. You let me think you were just talking to Chase and you were going to do a drug bust instead?"

He felt betrayed. I could see it. And I felt like a heel.

"I wanted to help but once we were here I knew I couldn't walk into this without your knowledge. I'll leave with you right now if you don't want me to do it. If you think this is doable then you choose who I go with. What about Patrick?"

"Patrick was still asleep. When he wakes up Mom is going to let him help her make Mickey Mouse shaped waffles. You should have thought of that before you went out."

"I did, we talked about it."

He stalked off to Whitman's office and I followed. Whitman had his pitch ready. Four guys in swat team black lined the room. On the whiteboard was a sketch of the first floor of the school. What Whitman hadn't counted on was Rusty getting involved.

"What're you doing here?" he snapped.

"You're stuck with me, Slick."

"And why is that?"

"When you involve my family, you involve me."

Whitman looked alarmed.

"She's…"

"My wife," Rusty said bluntly.

Slick shot dagger looks towards Chase. I worried a little about a physical confrontation, but Slick turned back to the matter at hand and kept his cool.

"If she goes in, I go in," Rusty demanded.

"You? You want to be her dad? How ironic."

Whitman started writing names on the board. In one room he wrote Mo, in another room he wrote Gib. Then Mac, and Guss, ending with Slick in an office to the side.

"These are classrooms. You see your positions. This is the lobby and this is the cafeteria. If we can get down there before the kids eat breakfast, we can be in and out by lunchtime."

Rusty approved of the men. I didn't know who they were, but each name meant something to him. Slick tapped a picture posted on the whiteboard. "This is Shawn the Shark Martell. He chose the name Shark because Martell means 'hammerer'. He thinks of himself like a hammerhead shark."

"Great," I mumbled, "now I'm shark bait."

"Cassidy, is it?"

"Yeah," I said, still suspicious of Whitman.

"You'll be Cassandra today. I assume people shorten your name to Cass?"

"Not if they know what's good for them. The people who shorten it have earned the right." I was going to demand every ounce of respect I could drag out of this guy.

"Yes, well, if your new boyfriend happens to call you Cass, don't slug him. We need him to follow through with this."

"My new boyfriend?"

"I've heard this guy is quick. That works in our favor."

"*Your* favor. What should I do if he makes advances?"

"Just do whatever comes naturally. You already have a boyfriend. Tell him that. Just don't let him leave the school."

"How am I supposed to stop him?"

"Lie, tell him your dad will be back in a few hours and if you're not there he'll be furious."

I was getting cold feet and felt tempted to walk out again. I toughened myself up, deciding that cold feet were a sure sign of weakness.

"Here," Slick said, handing me a wad of cash. "Put this in your wallet."

"What?"

"How are you supposed to buy drugs if you don't have money?"

"I have money," I said.

"Not this kind of money. You want to be able to buy as much as he's willing to sell you. Kids at this school have a thousand dollars to blow. Plus, these bills are all recorded. Only pay for his drugs with these bills so we can match them up afterwards. Let's go."

When we reached the parking lot, Slick tossed some car keys to Rusty. He pushed the button and the lights to a brand new Stingray flashed amongst the cars in the parking lot.

"I was looking forward to driving that. Take good care of it," Slick said.

"At least I get to drive a classy car," Rusty said as he opened the car door for me.

He drove in silence and I could feel the tension building between us. I decided the tension worked in my favor and would help in putting on this act. I was supposed to be stressed out and mad at my dad. Well, I was getting there.

"You know what you need to do?" he asked.

"Yeah, get him to sell me some drugs ASAP."

"Don't rush it or he'll get suspicious. It has to flow naturally in the conversation." He pulled a pin from his pocket and attached it to my shirt, letting his fingers linger a little. "It's a bug. Take care of my girl out there."

"I will."

"Remember, I'm Dad, not Rusty. Dad. Got that?"

"Got it," I answered grimly.

"And one more thing," he added hesitantly.

"Yeah?"

"Hon, I need your wedding ring. You can't be a married high school kid."

We both stared down at the ring I'd chosen as a symbol of our union. I didn't want to take it off, but I knew he was right. Just taking it off made me feel a hint of betrayal. I pressed it into his hand. He closed his hand around mine.

"Please, babe, make sure I get to put this back on," he said.

"I will," I answered quietly. "Today."

It wasn't going to require much acting to pull off this job. All I had to do was remember my lines. I felt like an emotional time bomb and it wouldn't take much to set me off.

It was getting close to eight a.m. and I started wondering what Patrick was up to. I wanted a Mickey Mouse waffle with grape jam and a side of peanut butter myself, but knew I wouldn't be getting one. Okay, Cass, think like a stubborn teenager. I sullenly followed Rusty through the big, wide, double doors and into a fancy lobby. It looked like a ritzy hotel. A crystal chandelier hung in the middle of the room and double curved staircases spiraled down from the second floor. A girl sat on a sofa and a boy entered from a side door. They were still wearing school uniforms, even though they were on their Christmas break. A huge Christmas tree filled one end of the lobby. Under the tree there were several gifts professionally wrapped in department store paper and tied in bows. They were probably gifts from parents who hadn't taken the time to wrap their own kids' presents.

Shawn Martell came down the left staircase and instantly an icy feeling raced down my back. Even my toes felt cold. Cass, you really are a wimp. It was show time. I turned on Rusty, my dad, and angrily stomped my foot.

"I don't want to live in San Diego!" I whined. "I don't want to go to a fancy school!"

"You have to," he replied calmly. "I'm not letting you stay on that god forsaken ranch to grow up to be a redneck. You're going to be enrolled here to learn some class."

I knew Rusty was only acting and giving me a history to work with, but his words made me angry and that helped my performance.

"I love the ranch!" I cried. "I want to go back. I don't want to live in the city."

"Stop it," he scolded. "You're making a scene. Just stay here for a few hours. That's all I'm asking. Talk to the kids. Find out what they think of the school. Ask about the riding school. Maybe you can ride real horses here. Do dressage here, something classy."

"Don't leave me here," I begged, knowing it would tear him up.

"It's just for a few hours. You can have a good breakfast, talk to the kids. I'm going to the office to tell them you're here, then I'm going to my office downtown to check my messages. I'll be back in time for lunch. Be good," he said and gave me a kiss on the cheek. He walked into the office where I imagined he threatened Slick to within an inch of his life if this backfired. Once he was out of earshot I let loose.

"Shit!" I said and kicked at the nearest piece of furniture. I looked helplessly in the direction where Rusty had disappeared.

"Better not let any of the staff hear you talk like that or you'll be reprimanded," Martell said.

"He just doesn't get it. I don't want to move. I don't want to go to school here. I don't care what you guys say about it. I want to go home."

"Aw, come on," he said, sizing me up. "You want to see the riding school? I'll show you the riding school, the tennis courts and the indoor swimming pool."

"You have an indoor swimming pool?"

"We have everything, we even have *freedom*. Don't worry about being stuck here. The rules in this place are so lax. I only spend class time here, then I sign myself out and drive to town. And San Diego isn't such a bad city. There's lots of things to do here. I bet you'll like it once you get used to it."

His words were contrived. His little speech was all an act, too, but I followed along.

"What do you do for fun here? At home I hung out with friends. We partied. It was great. My mom got mad at me staying out all night but I didn't get into any trouble. I just, you know… we were just having fun."

The fact that I wouldn't voice just *how* we were having fun allowed him to jump to his own conclusions.

"You ever experiment?"

"Not any more. I nearly died once, so I backed off from it. But that's another reason I don't want to move. Back home I knew the ins and outs. I knew where I could get what and here I don't know anything. I'm going to go nuts. I can't stay here."

I paced back and forth acting antsy, looking for a way out. I pictured the guys listening to my performance and wondered what they thought about it. I didn't know what I was doing and thought the subject came up awfully quick. I fought an impulse to run out the door and keep going until one of the cops picked me up. My toes still felt icy cold and my mind was racing a hundred miles an hour. I walked to the front windows looking for the Stingray, but it was gone. I realized it didn't mean that Rusty had left. I knew he'd be around here somewhere.

"You want some fun and you're supposed to have a look at the school? I'll show you."

"Isn't it time for breakfast? You haven't eaten yet," I said, stalling.

"We'll get breakfast in time. Come on."

I followed him out the back doors of the lobby and down a short brick stairway to a parking garage under the building.

"This isn't student parking," I said. "My dad showed me student parking."

"The teachers are all gone. So, I borrowed a spot. Nobody notices."

"I can't leave. My dad will be back in a few hours. If I'm not here he'll call out the National Guard. He'll sue the school for negligence. He'll..."

"We'll be back in a few hours. Your dad will never know."

"You don't know my dad. I won't go."

"You'll stay out all night and sneak in but you won't leave a school for two hours while he's at his office banging his secretary?"

"He is not! How could you say a thing like that?"

"You're cute when you're riled. Get in the car."

"No! Hell, I'm feeling bad. I can't take this anymore." I let my hands tremble.

He moved around to my side. I thought he was going to open the door and make me get in but he pinned me against the car then leaned in closer.

"Stop it!" I said, feeling even more like I was betraying my husband. I imagined him sitting tensely in the van listening. "I've taken self defense classes. You know the first thing they tell girls in self defense classes?"

"Yeah," he answered, backing off.

"There you go, now I can get more leverage."

He backed off some more, calculating the length of my legs.

"Okay, so you're not ready to get it on. I can understand that. I'll give you a few weeks."

"I won't be here in a few weeks, unless I can figure out a way to get my old lifestyle back. I need a source. I need friends. I need wheels."

"I can help with some of that. You got cash? I got what you need. But not here. The walls have ears. That's why I go to town after class. Get in the car, I'll show you a source. I'll help you with the wheels. I'll be your best friend if you'll let me. You have to let me."

"Let you what?"

"You'll see. First step, find the source. Come on. Do you trust me? I'll have you back in time for your old man to pick you up."

Oh, man! I was told not to leave, but to get to the drugs we *had* to leave the school. What do I do now? I couldn't blow my cover. He'd kill me. I couldn't leave the school, I'd lose all my backup! I had to trust him. To finish this assignment I had to trust him. And I had to keep the police informed. I became intensely thankful for the bug on my shirt. I tried to remember what it looked like. It must have resembled an ordinary pin of some kind.

"No," I admitted, "I don't trust you. You move too fast. I'm just supposed to talk to the kids at school. So, let's go back inside. Let's talk."

"You don't want to talk to them. They'll tell you all about trigonometry and biology."

"Why, are those classes interesting?"

"Just get in the car. I'll show you what's interesting."

"How long have you had your license? My dad won't let me go out with anybody who hasn't had their license for at least six months. He said they need driving experience first."

"I've got plenty of driving experience. This is my third car," he said, opening the door on a black Carrera.

Great, like that was supposed to make me feel better. I could feel time slipping away. I had to be back by lunch. I needed to find the drugs. Okay, I'd stalled enough. I'd go. The police had plenty of time to see this coming. They'd be on our tail.

He drove around the school grounds, pointing out the tennis courts, the stables, the gym, then he took a service road out the back of the school and down a hill.

"Where are we going?" I asked nervously. "If my dad gets back and I'm not at the school…"

"I know, I know, he'll call out the National Guard. We're going to town. You can see that San Diego isn't such a bad place."

"I never thought of San Diego being such a hilly place," I said, trying to hand out hints as we drove along. It helped a little that I was supposed to be unfamiliar with the city. I could ask lots of dumb questions.

He got on the freeway.

"I hate freeways," I cringed. "We don't have them where I come from. We get on a highway, but it's nothing like this. I'll *never* learn the freeways here. Which one is this?"

"This is the eight."

I started reciting the names of the exits to myself. "I have to learn the city if I am going to get around. It seems huge. I doubt I'll ever venture out on the freeway. I didn't even have a freeway to practice on in driving school. Just a two lane highway."

"So how long have you had your license?"

"Not long. I hate driving. If I had my choice I'd stick to horses."

"But you have your license, don't you?"

"Yeah, I have my license."

"Can I see it?"

"No!" I exclaimed a bit too quickly. "I… hate the picture on it. I look like I'm on drugs or something."

"Were you?"

"No! Not that time. I wouldn't do drugs right before a driving test. I wanted to look serious on my driver's license and my sister was trying to make me smile so the picture is awful."

I looked in the rearview mirrors for a van or a Stingray or a patrol car, but I couldn't see anything and I didn't want to look too often.

He reached into his pocket and pulled out a metal object. He flicked it and a sharp four-inch blade slid out.

"Shawn, put that thing away. You're scaring me. Take me back to the school. Please, take me back."

His look suddenly hardened.

"How did you know my name? I never told you my name."

"Of course you did," I said, nearly panicking. Did he? When? I couldn't remember.

"Then, tell me, what's yours? You never told me *your* name."

"My name?" I decided the truth would work better just in case he got his hands on an ID. "My name is Cassidy."

"How did you know my name?" he repeated harshly.

"You told it to me."

"No…" he said, pausing for emphasis, "I didn't. I guard my name very carefully."

He flicked the knife blade in and out and I wanted to say, "Look Patrick, that's what *retractable* means!" but I didn't. Then I wondered if I'd ever see Patrick again.

"Show me your driver's license," Shawn demanded. "Better yet, empty your purse."

"I don't think I brought my driver's license because I knew my dad would be driving. I didn't need it."

"Empty it anyway," he said, holding the knife where he could easily jab it into my leg. I started emptying my purse, wishing I was a girly girl with lots of stuff to dump out of it. Checkbook, wallet, pen, a card reminding me to refill my birth control pills. He took the wallet, hefted it, then flipped it open.

"Twenty-six, you're twenty-six? What are you? Some fucking cop? Tell me!" he shouted. He looked me over and finally noticed the pin. "Oh shit." He ripped the pin off my shirt, rolled down his window and threw the bug out before stepping on the gas. The Carrera shot forward. He weaved in and out of cars on the freeway watching for a tail. "Damn it, Cassidy, you really screwed yourself good when you messed with me!"

"Getting rid of me isn't going to solve your problem," I said. "It only adds to it."

"How many of them were there?"

"Six, that I know of. When it was just a drug problem, they only wanted to arrest you. Now that it's become a kidnapping, they will shoot you. Turn it back into a drug problem if you want to live. At least that saves your skin. I don't know where you were going and I can't send them after you. I just came to San Diego to visit my in-laws. I got recruited for this because I look like a kid. I'm not even a real cop. I'm just qualified as one when they choose to use me. I'm really a housewife and tracker. I find missing people when they get lost in the woods."

"You got kids?"

"Not yet, although my nephew came with us on this trip. He's waiting for me at my in-law's house. He's only six."

I was hoping to appeal to his sense of compassion, if he had any.

"Show me where he is."

"No, I won't allow you to use anyone else in this mess you've made for yourself. You've got to stop now and count your losses. Look on the bright side, you never showed me where the drugs are. You didn't get caught with those. So far all you can be charged with is kidnapping and I'll drop that if you let me go."

"Would you shut the fuck up!" he yelled. "It's Christmas Eve, all I want is a normal life. I get sent off to boarding school and what happens? I get forgotten there, so I try and make a life for myself on my own. I try to stick with school. I try to finish and some Barbie Doll cop comes along and screws it all up."

"Actually, most people think I look like Skipper," I interjected.

"Shit."

"Why do you sell drugs if you're trying to make a life for yourself? Drugs just mess up people's lives. They are messing up yours. But you don't have to let them. You can do better than that."

"The hell I can. I didn't have anything till I started selling. Now I can buy cars. I won't have to have a job when I get out of school. Just keep dealing. It's good money."

"And a bad health risk. You'll always be worried about the cops. This is just the beginning of your life with the police after you. You'll either be running from them or in jail. Neither of those options sounds like much fun."

"I suppose you have a better plan?"

Just keep him talking, Cass, you can talk your way out.

"What did you want to be when you started school? I'm sure you didn't start school thinking you were going to sell drugs to the kids there."

"I wanted to be something fast and dangerous, well, not really dangerous. Like, glamorous. I wanted to be like the cops on TV solving crimes or like firemen or ambulance workers. I wanted to be in the thick of things."

"Those jobs aren't nearly as glamorous as you think. I work with a lot of people like that. On the news you see all the lights and the uniforms, but do you ever actually notice the real people? Nobody does. They only see the glamorous side. If you want to be a cop, a fireman or even an ambulance driver, you've got to get out of this drug dealing before you're arrested. You won't become any of those things if you have a felony on your record. Right now you're heading down a dead end street. You have to stop and turn around and choose a different way. You have to. Eventually. When you see the dead end, will you be seventeen? Twenty? Thirty? At seventeen, you still have a chance to make a good life for yourself, but every year you refuse to see the dead end, the harder it will be to turn your life around."

"How do you know?"

"Because I've been searching for what I want to be all my life. I've been a cowgirl. I really did grow up on a ranch, but I'm not a redneck, at least I don't think people see me that way. Then I joined the Marines. I think that's why I didn't freak out when things turned ugly. For a while I was a widow. Now I'm a tracker. You might have seen me on TV. Remember the two people who were stuck in the mine right after the earthquake in LA?"

"Yeah, that was big news. Everybody was talking about it."

"That was me and a little boy from Texas, named…"

"Trevor," he interrupted. "Did you ever get married to that detective?"

"Yeah, I did, about five months ago."

"He's a detective, right?"

"Right."

"So where is he when all this is going on? Why isn't he tailing us right now?"

"Because you threw the bug away and lost him."

He looked like he felt a little guilty about that. Here he had some guy's wife and he was out there looking for her.

"Do you have a girlfriend?" I asked.

"Yes, and no. If I did I wouldn't have put the moves on you. But there's a girl I like."

"How would you like it if some crazy high school kid took off with her and you didn't know what his intentions were? What if you thought he might kill her? What would you do?"

"I'd kill him."

"Then you might want to rethink your plan about what you're going to do to me. My husband is a patient man, but you're kind of trying his patience right now. What time is it?"

"About ten."

"How about you take me back to the school?"

"I'll get arrested and kicked out."

"Then how about if you take me to the police station?"

"Then I'll get arrested and I *might* get kicked out."

"What if you just drop me off? You have no use for me. I have no use for you. We can just go our separate ways and then the police are left hanging again."

"I wouldn't be able to go back to the school."

"Then what do you think you should do?"

"Aw, hell. Where are you staying?"

"At my in-law's house."

"Where's that?"

"Hudson Road."

He did a U-turn and headed west, then he got back on a freeway. I got lost. I didn't know San Diego and started reading off exits again.

"What are you doing? You don't have another bug on you, do you?"

"No, I really don't know the city and it can't hurt to know my way around."

Once he exited the freeway I started recognizing streets again. He drove around and around and we read the street signs. After passing a street named Pizzaro Place I told him, "We're closing in on it."

Suddenly, from out of nowhere, a kid appeared on a bike. His eyes got big as he pictured himself plastered on the side of a black sports car. It was Patrick! Cody was on the curb, ready to help him avoid Mrs. Rathburn's rosebushes. Shawn jabbed the brakes and jerked the wheel, bouncing into Mrs. Rathburn's yard. Then Patrick jerked the handlebars, leaving a three foot long gash on the side of the Carrera. He went up Mrs. Rathburn's driveway and into her poinsettia by the front door. Cody jumped out of the way and Mrs. Rathburn came out of the door wearing her housecoat and cursing up a storm. I opened the car door into the rosebushes and squeezed my way out. Shawn got out and surveyed the damage.

"Cody! Run home and call Rusty on his cell. Tell him we're in Mrs. Rathburn's rosebushes! Oh, and tell him not to worry, we're fine."

I ran over and picked Patrick up. "Pat! Are you okay buddy? I'm sorry about the car. Come on, show me you're okay. Please, Patrick, please be okay."

"Aunt Cassidy! What are you doing here?"

"Getting kidnapped. What are you doing?"

"Learning to ride a bike."

Shawn was looking around as though he was contemplating making a break for it.

"Shawn, don't even think about running. Believe it or not, I can catch you and take you down. So far you're in minimal trouble. Don't push it."

Three police cars converged on Mrs. Rathburn's yard. Officers jumped out, guns at the ready. We all stood around looking at them except for Shawn who was ready to run.

"It won't work, Shawn. Just wait for Detective Whitman to get here," I warned him.

"Aw, Slick," one of the officers muttered under his breath. None of the men looked pleased.

Cody jogged down the hill then stood there, hands in pockets. "Cassidy, you don't do anything halfway, do you? I told you that Mrs. Rathburn wouldn't be happy with you."

"I wasn't driving!" I answered.

Cody looked the car over. "Can I?"

"No!"

Patrick piped up, "I missed the rosebushes. Does the flower tree count?"

"You don't really have to crash into Mrs. Rathburn's rosebushes to be part of the family," Cody told him. "You can be an adopted nephew. Or a nephew-in-law."

"Are all of you related?" one of the officers asked.

"Everybody except him," Cody said, pointing to Shawn.

"How does he fit into this situation?" the officer asked.

"Ask Slick," I replied.

"Do we have to?"

"Why don't you start writing your traffic report?" I suggested.

The Stingray pulled up and Slick Whitman sauntered up. Then the surveillance van pulled up and Rusty jumped out. He looked at the Carrera, then at me and finally at Mrs. Rathburn's rosebushes.

"It was an accident, I swear! Shawn was trying to take me home and Patrick appeared out of nowhere and Shawn went into the rosebushes trying to miss Patrick."

"Shawn was taking you home. Just like that. He's a drug dealing kidnapper and he was taking you home."

"Yeah. I talked to him. He didn't want to go back to the school and get kicked out. And he didn't want to go to the station and get arrested. So he was taking me home. Then at least he'd avoid the kidnapping charge. And he never showed me where the drugs were or sold me any, so you can't get him on that. About all you can pin on him is property damage. And I think the damage to the car is going to cost more than the damage to the yard."

"Cassidy, how do you get into these things?" Rusty asked.

"You know exactly how I got into this one. If you haven't figured it out, ask Chase. Where is Chase anyway?"

"He'll be along shortly."

Slick sauntered up. He was good at sauntering. Had it down pat. "I told you to stay at the school."

"One, I did everything a high school girl could do without getting into a fist fight to stay at the school. Two, the drugs weren't at the school. To get him on the drug charge required a trip to wherever they were being held. Three, I had no authorization to use force and I didn't have a weapon along, anyway. Tell me how I was supposed to stay on school grounds."

Slick considered it for a minute and finally gave up.

I remembered something. "Hey, Shawn, can I borrow your knife?"

"Yeah, why?"

"I want to show it to my nephew." He handed over the stiletto. "Look, Patrick, this is what *retractable* means. See, it pops out, and then it pulls back. It retracts. Just like a mountain lion's claws. If the handle curved it would still pop out and retract but it wouldn't hurt the handle, just like claws don't hurt the mountain lion."

"Cool! Can I see it? I want one."

"Sorry, Patrick," Rusty said, "these are illegal street fighting knives. Cassidy, you didn't disarm him after the accident?"

"No, I didn't think of it as a weapon. I thought of it more as a teaching tool."

"How did you get through the Marines and reserve academy without thinking of a stiletto as an illegal weapon?" Rusty asked.

"I thought we already agreed that I'll never be a cop. I'm a tracker. When I see something, I see its uses, not the legalities of it. When I saw it, I immediately knew I could show Patrick what *retractable* meant. I was really excited to actually find an example to show him."

"See why I was reluctant to get her involved?" Chase asked, turning to Slick.

Slick added, "She's cute, but dangerous. Too bad she isn't dangerous to anyone besides herself."

My anger flared and I said, "You're welcome to call me if you need a tracker. But don't call me to be cute. If it involves following tracks on the ground, I haven't lost a trail yet and can find your man without fouling up. I'm not a cop, I'll never be a cop and I don't want to be a cop. But I can track. I can even track Chase, spend a week on the trail, and live off the land if necessary, but I'm not a cop and I'm *not* cute."

There, I wasn't mad anymore. I'd had my say. However, I doubted they would call me because they had Chase.

"She's still cute," Slick said as I walked away.

"Hey, cutie," Rusty said, and I almost didn't turn around. I only did because it was Rusty calling. "I have something special to give you."

With Shawn the Shark, all the officers, Cody, Patrick, and Mrs. Rathburn standing around I thought this wasn't the place to be given something special, but I turned anyway. From his pocket he drew out my wedding ring, stepped forward, and slid it over my finger.

"Thanks for taking care of my girl," he said. "I knew you could do it."

Chapter 16

"Patrick you are the world's worst ham. You really want to go back there?"

"Yeah! It was fun. You should have been there the first time. There was a hundred people gathered around watching. You want to come see?"

"Of course I will, and I'll take your picture so your mom will believe it when you tell her all about San Diego. You really need to call her tonight. She is going to be awfully lonely without you home on Christmas Eve."

"I know. I just hope she doesn't cry. I can't stand to see a grown woman cry."

"Well, have patience with her. She's had patience with you all these years. Babies cry a lot too, you know, and you were a baby not too long ago."

"But I'm growing. I can even ride a bike now. I went down the hill and back up without crashing into Mrs. Rathburn's bushes."

"That's good, and I hope you start watching for cross traffic on Coronado Street because you could have gotten killed today."

"I am careful. It was my very first try and I was busy being scared when I crashed into you. Now I'm not scared, so I look both ways first."

I tied his string tie and shined his boots.

"There, are you ready to go?"

"Yeah!"

"Go ask Uncle Rusty if he wants to come, too."

The mall was packed. I didn't see how they could make room for a kid to do rope tricks in the middle of the corridor, but the manager of the photography studio waded through the crowd and posted a barricade in a circle and put a table at one end. He placed two chairs at the table and set down a stack of pictures of Patrick printed on typing paper. Patrick signed about twenty of them and then stood in the middle of the circle and loosened up for his performance. He'd brought Bill's rope this time and opened a small loop, then began turning the rope smoothly and consistently. No wobbles. People were looking at him as they went about their holiday shopping. He ignored them, concentrating on getting into the rhythm. I understood what he was doing, but Rusty was already fascinated. As Patrick became more comfortable with it, he turned the rope to his side, brought it over his head, then down to his feet. He started stepping into the loop and then out of it, turning it, while keeping it moving. I had to admit the kid was good for a six-year-old. He must have been *really* bored practicing at home. I wasn't sure why James had him only lassoing fence posts when he really should have been out catching colts. That was about all the roping we did at the ranch. Patrick could be catching colts, then gently leading them around to get used to being led. Or he could catch the horses when the hands needed them for a chore. Then he would get used to a moving target and the horses would get to know Patrick better.

People were stopping to watch now, but Patrick concentrated on the rope. If he became distracted by the crowd then his rope wobbled. So he twirled the rope, then jumped and turned some more. Pretty soon a woman noticed the stack of pictures and asked me for one. The twenty pictures that Patrick had signed went quickly and people kept asking for more. I told them that if they wanted a signed one, they would have to wait. A few people took unsigned ones, but many people wanted their picture autographed.

"I'm going to buy him a soda. He's going to need one pretty soon," Rusty said, and then disappeared into the shopping crowd. Fifteen minutes later two large sodas appeared on the table but Rusty vanished again. Patrick stopped, relieved to see the cups sitting there. He took a long drink and started signing pictures.

"Are you his agent?" a woman asked me.

"No, I'm his aunt."

"Well, would you give his agent this card?" she asked.

"I'll give it to his mom. He doesn't have an agent and doesn't really need one either. He's just a kid."

"Well!" she said in a huff, and walked away with a signed picture. Two minutes later she was back. "This business card is for the photography studio. Can I have Patrick's business card?"

"My nephew doesn't have a business card. He's only six years old. Six year old kids don't need business cards."

"How did he get this gig if he doesn't have an agent and he doesn't have business cards?"

"This isn't a gig. He came here to have his picture taken and the studio was surprised to see he could turn a rope, so they set him up out here to draw customers. He's a ham, so he did it. That's it."

"Well!" she said again and left.

"Are you a movie star?" a teenage girl asked Patrick.

"No, my dad's a horse trainer. He taught me how to use a rope."

Use a rope. It was as simple as that. These weren't tricks to him.

"That is so amazing!" a woman gushed at him. "How did you learn to do that?"

"My dad made me practice roping and I got bored so I made it a little more interesting."

"I'm going to buy my Jimmy a rope. Maybe he can do that, too."

"Have I seen you on TV?" a man asked.

"No, but my aunt has been on TV," Patrick answered.

The man turned to me, "Can I have your autograph?" he asked.

"Not that kind of TV. I've just been on the news because of my work. I'm not an actress."

"I bet you are so proud of him!" a grandmotherly woman said, giving me a hug.

I am, I thought. He was able to read and recognize a mule deer track, ride a bike and twirl a rope. He's a ranch kid. Sheesh. But I really was proud of Patrick because he was smart, cute and happy, but then even one of those qualities would have done it for me.

"Three down, one to go," Rusty said as he sat down next to me. "Can you take a walk around the crowd and find him?"

"What?"

"Pickpockets. If you spot him, point him out to a security guard. I'll stay with Patrick."

I walked the perimeter of the crowd. It took me two laps around the outskirts before spotting her. She was a punk girl with orange and black hair, thick eyeliner and wore low rider leather pants. After watching for a few moments I knew she was clearly working the crowd. I went to a security guard and pointed her out. She spotted me with the guard, raised a pink glittery box over her head and yelled, "Torpedo Toys has Tabatha Twisty dolls! They found a box in the back!"

The crowd turned as one and stampeded in the direction of Torpedo Toys. The barricade around Patrick came down. The girl took off into the crowd. The pictures went flying. A few kids left behind in the rush stood crying. Frantic mothers ran back, angry about the delay. When we looked up, Patrick sat in a heap, pictures settling to the floor around him.

"Up staged by Tabatha Twisty," he said in disgust.

"Yeah, and I bet they don't even really have them," I said. "That was just a pickpocket causing a distraction so she could get away."

"It wasn't a total loss, I got offered a part in a soap opera," Rusty said.

"You aren't going to do it, are you?" I asked.

"No, I have no desire to get into acting. My performance today at the school was more than I wanted to do."

"What did you do at the school?" Patrick asked, curious.

"I had to pretend to be Cassidy's daddy."

Patrick thought that was funny. "You had to pretend to be *Grandpa*? He's old!"

"Gee, thanks, Patrick."

We returned to the Michaels' home where Patrick called his parents to wish them a Merry Christmas. Whenever he called his mother I expected to catch hell from Jesse. It seemed she had adjusted to the fact that Patrick was in San Diego until Wednesday. I began to wonder what Patrick was actually telling her because normally he didn't smooth things over. If anything, his bright enthusiasm made his adventures appear even more outlandish than they really were. I sat with Rusty in the living room, visiting with his parents, Bill and Bev. Cody was working at Tacky T-shirts. He must really have been stuck on that girl who worked there. He'd managed to keep the job for months. With Patrick on the phone the house seemed nice and peaceful.

"It's so much fun having kids in the house again," Bev said. "I can't wait to have a whole houseful of kids for the holidays. Patrick is such a character."

"Yeah, but after spending a week with him now I'm afraid to have kids!"

"Oh, dear, don't say that. When you have your own children you grow with them. Anybody would be exhausted suddenly given the care of a six-year- old boy. When you have a baby, it'll be different. Just wait and see."

"It's been half an hour. It's too quiet. What is he telling her? I hope he didn't tell her about getting stuck in the top of the tree, or being dragged across the mall by a purse-snatcher. I know I'm going to catch hell from Jessie when we take him back home."

Then we heard the sound of small steps coming down the attic stairs.

"Mr. Michaels, sir?"

"You can call me Bill," he said with a smile as Patrick entered the room.

Patrick seemed to relax a little after hearing that. "Do you have a little bitty wrench?"

"A little wrench? What do you need a little wrench for?"

"I'm trying to build something with the metal things in the attic."

"That's great! I'm sure we can find a little wrench somewhere," Bill said as he disappeared up the attic stairs with Patrick. We then heard the two of them moving erector set pieces around, searching for the tools that went with it. There was a small avalanche followed by the sound of plastic boxes being opened, and finally Bill returned to the living room. "I think I'll stay upstairs for a while," he said, appearing a little embarrassed to be more interested in Pat's project than our conversation below.

"He's a sucker for building things," Bev told me.

As the afternoon wore on, Bev and I turned to the kitchen while Rusty wandered up to the attic. I helped with the dinner preparations by peeling potatoes and carrots.

"There's no telling how many we will have for dinner tonight. I always hate for Chase to spend the holidays alone so he has an open invitation, and Sandy will probably be here. She will come Christmas morning, too, but we won't wait for her if Patrick is ready to open presents. I know how hard it is for a kid to wait on Christmas morning."

"What was Rusty like on Christmas?"

"Oh, he was the quiet one. He always seemed thoughtful and never exclaimed or got excited. That was Sandy and Cody. They would carry on terribly if they had to wait or go to bed before they were ready. Those two would always get so excited when they got a gift they were hoping for. With Rusty, it was more like a quiet affirmation. I never knew if he really liked his gifts or not. I waited to see if he used them and he always remembered to thank us for them. He was just quiet about it."

"I know what you mean. The first year we celebrated his birthday I bought him a new computer desk and decorated his office. He was so quiet I thought I'd done something wrong."

"I bet he liked it though. In his heart he is very appreciative of any little thing you do."

"What about Tony? I don't know very much about him."

"Tony was a middle child in every way. He was the average of the two other personality types. He was more focused, especially when it came to sports. It seemed to me that Tony was interested in a new sport every Christmas. Baseball, soccer, basketball, football, lacrosse... I think he tried them all."

"I was a lot like Rusty," I admitted. "There wasn't very much I needed or wanted as a kid. Freedom to explore was tops on my list, and that's something you can't package. As long as I was free to follow where my curiosity led me I was happy. So Christmas wasn't a big deal. As I grew up my favorite gifts were my horse because that added miles to my exploration and a friend to do it all with, and books that helped me understand what I was seeing out there."

"Oh, my, what did your parents do?"

"They bought me all the toys that the other kids wished for. I thanked Mom for all the gifts, and then let my sister play with them. I was glad the toys were around for others, but I didn't care for them myself. I've always liked useful things, so now Christmas is a little easier. There's always something I can use around the house, and Rusty has helped instill a little bit of fashion sense in me. You should have seen me when we first met. My wardrobe consisted of camouflage, khakis and jeans. I've grown in so many ways because of him. He's the best thing that has ever have happened to me."

"Have you told him that?"

"No, I guess I haven't, but I know he sees it. He knows I'm happier, more settled and far more comfortable with myself. I don't run for the woods now whenever something scary happens and he's the reason for those changes."

"You're good for him too, you know. He'd do anything for you."

"He's always been kind like that, even before I really knew him."

Bev slid dinner into the oven and we went upstairs to see what the guys were doing. Bill and Rusty were in conversation and watching Patrick building something elaborate. Patrick was bent over his creation, his brow creased in concentration.

"What are you building, Pat? It looks like a brace for an elephant trunk!"

"You wouldn't believe it if we told you." Bill answered. "He's building a ball return for the pool table."

"Wow! Now that you've told me what it is, I can see it. What made you think of building that?"

"Nothing, I don't even know if it'll work, or if I'll even have enough pieces, but I thought it couldn't hurt to try." Patrick answered.

I thought to myself that his parents had no idea what they were really dealing with here. When he complained about the baby books he was forced to read at school, they weren't able to see that he was bored. They only saw a whiney first grader. Jesse would have thought a ball return for the pool table was a silly idea. She'd say there was no way that atrocious looking contraption would be going on *her* pool table. She'd tell him to go brush his teeth and then put on his good clothes for dinner. And he'd do it while his mind went numb with boredom. I reminded myself that Jesse wasn't a bad mom and James wasn't a bad dad, they were simply unaware of Patrick's potential. I vowed right then and there that if my kids ever wanted an erector set ball return on our pool table, I would encourage them and be proud to have one. I'd see the intelligence behind their complaints; I'd challenge my kids, not smother them with emotions and stiff dinner dress. Whenever they wanted to explore I would go and explore with them. They'd wear play clothes and make mud pies, and crawl around in fields stalking deer and following game trails.

"Hello, earth calling Cassidy. You there, hon?"

"Oh, yeah, sorry."

"Look, Aunt Cassidy, the screws for the erector set fit right into the screw holes from the fancy pockets. I only have one done so it works, but I know how to do it now. Should we make the balls go to one end or the middle? It would be shorter tubes to go to the middle but it would be easier getting the balls out if it went to the end. We could make them go to the side of the middle. That would solve both problems."

"The little engineer," Bev commented.

"At pool halls the balls go to the end of the table where you rack them so it's easier to rack up the balls," Rusty explained.

"I don't know if there's enough pieces to do that," Patrick countered.

"Well, start at one end and work your way to the other. Then, if you run out of pieces, we'll just make up new rules and only use the pockets with ball returns on them. That'll make the game more challenging, too."

"Four kids' erector sets plus some and it might not be enough," Bev observed. "You've got big aspirations, kid."

"Use the big pieces for the long tubes and the short ones for the short tubes," Rusty advised.

"Let him figure it out for himself," Bev scolded. "He's doing a fine job."

I heard a light click downstairs.

"Chase is here," I told them.

"I didn't hear the bell," Bev said.

"He didn't ring the doorbell. He knew we were expecting him."

Chase climbed the stairs to the attic.

"What are we all doing up here?" he asked.

"Building a ball return for the pool table," Rusty pointed out.

"It seems to take a lot of supervision to build a ball return for a pool table," Chase observed.

"Okay, send a ball down," Patrick instructed.

Chase picked up the four ball and rolled it into the pocket where it gently followed the track and dropped into a plastic box at the end. Patrick crawled out from under the table and peeked over the top grinning.

"It worked!" he said brightly.

We spent the afternoon talking around the pool table, sitting on the floor, watching Patrick build. It went quicker once Patrick discovered he didn't need to build tubes, he could build troughs.

Sandy arrived but nobody noticed. We were trying to figure out how to get the trough a certain shape so it would reach the box without jamming. Sandy stood there arms on hips watching us.

"It *looks* like it should work," I said.

"It's getting stuck right here," Patrick said, pointing. "It's hard to move just one piece of it. If I move one I have to move almost all of them."

"Well, there's nothing you can do. It's got to move so you'll have to take it off and try again," Bill advised.

Sandy said, "This reminds me of that old junker Tony had. All four guys were under that thing every weekend trying to figure something out. Did it ever work good enough to pass the smog test?"

"No, it was just a dud car. We sold it to a junkyard for scrap," Bill replied. "But it wasn't a total dud. We all learned a lot from that old car."

"Speaking of learning things," Chase added, "I think I finally convinced Slick there's a few people who won't do his bidding. Cassidy convinced him that matters were not always in his hands. He wanted to pack that kid off to jail on Christmas Eve, clean up the school, and be done with it. He's got a lot more work ahead of him now. He's probably going to spend Christmas trying to figure out how to break up this drug ring Shawn got pulled into. That kid was low man on the totem pole. He's signed up for special counseling at the school and they'll keep tabs on him until he graduates. They have a college placement office and he spent the afternoon in that office taking personality profile tests. Now he's chosen a course of action. Can't say I agree with all those surveys and some of the questions are very… umm… questionable, but at least it's a start. When I took one of those tests, it said I should be a chef. Can you imagine me as a chef? If I wasn't here, my Christmas dinner would be a hamburger and French fries. I might add a slice of cake for a special occasion. I might go buy a six-pack but can you imagine me *a chef*?"

"Slick shouldn't spend Christmas working, and he must have something better to do than that." I may not have cared for the guy but I didn't want him spending Christmas alone in his office. I also didn't like the idea of him scouring bad neighborhoods for people who just wanted to have a peaceful holiday. It may seem a little naïve but I'd rather believe that criminals don't work on holidays. So why should detectives? "Rusty, he can't spend Christmas all alone."

"He spends Christmas how he chooses," Rusty said. He knew what I was thinking, and he didn't like it.

"Okay," said Patrick, "I think we're ready to try again." He carefully screwed the trough to the pool table and Chase sent down the nine ball. It threatened to get stuck just because it lost momentum, but it finally made it all the way down the trough and into the box. "I'll try again if there's time, but it works good enough for now."

Patrick started on the next pocket, but each ball return had to be slightly different, so he wasn't able to simply build six identical troughs and attach them. Each had to be fitted to the pocket it attached to and then be tweaked until it hit the box at the right angle. It was quite a feat for a kid, but he didn't see it that way. It was just something to do and he thought it was interesting. I wasn't going to throw geometry and physics into his fun, but it was tempting.

After dinner, seven adults and one kid played three-pocket pool. The balls were supposed to go in the ball return pockets. A target ball in a different pocket was a scratch and meant ball in hand. We never knew who won because there wasn't really a rule about that. If we counted the balls everybody sank, then Chase won easily. Patrick declared his project a success and told everybody he'd finish the job the next day, but there would be little chance of that happening after all the presents had been opened.

"Now you have to go right to sleep or Santa Claus won't be able to come. He needs plenty of time to deliver all the presents."

"I'll try. It's no fair that kids have to fall asleep on the hardest night there is to sleep."

"I know, but you'll survive. I did and so did Uncle Rusty. It's just part of being a kid."

"Why don't adults have to go to bed? Does Santa come while adults are awake? Have any adults seen Santa?"

"I haven't. I always thought Santa preferred to work alone, so I never tried to see him. Time for sleep. Just give it a try. I'm going to bed soon, too."

I went downstairs to join everyone in the living room watching an old movie, but fell asleep halfway through it. Rusty finally woke me up when the movie ended.

"Come on, Mrs. Claus, we still have work to do."

We pulled out our box of gifts and placed them all under the tree, then filled one of those fuzzy red and white stockings with candy and little doodads. It wasn't his Christmas stocking from home but then he knew not to expect that. Bev brought out her gifts and added them under the tree. Many of them were labeled from Santa Claus rather than from Bill and herself. Cody then added his gifts to the pile.

"Chase, it's nearly midnight," Bev said. "You can stay if you want to. There won't be much for you to do in the morning but at least you'll already be here. I know there are a few things for you under the tree, but we buried them."

"Who's staying in the attic?"

"Rusty and Cassidy."

"Is the hammock put away for the winter?"

Bev nodded. "It's the couch or floor but I'm sure we can come up with something. You don't want to drive all the way home and wake up in that cold trailer. You know you'll just come back in the morning anyway."

"Are you making cinnamon rolls?"

"I doubled the recipe."

"First one up turns on the Christmas lights," Bill said as he headed up the stairs to bed.

Rusty stood in the attic and dropped down a bundle of comforters for Chase. Then we all turned in, knowing it would be a very short night. We all expected Patrick to be up before dawn.

Chapter 17

Dawn was just beginning to color the horizon when I crept downstairs and saw that the Christmas lights were already on. Chase was up and had already shaved. I peeked into Patrick's room to discover his bed was empty and he was gone.

"Chase, where's Patrick?" I asked.

"He isn't up yet," Chase answered.

"Yes he is. He isn't in bed."

Chase looked alarmed. To think Patrick was up and we hadn't heard him was hard to believe. Chase was like me and prided himself in being aware of what was going on around him at all times. We checked the downstairs. I checked the bathroom, then the forbidden backyard. I climbed the stairs to the attic where Rusty was still sleeping. There were a dozen nooks and crannies up there but Patrick wasn't in any of them. I checked the balcony overlooking the pool, opened the doors and stepped out. The ladder was still on the balcony.

"Rusty, wake up," I said worriedly. "It's morning and I can't find Patrick."

"What? Where could he be? A kid on Christmas morning heads for the tree. It's a rule. The tree is a kid magnet."

"I still can't find him. I've checked the house and the backyard."

"Did you check Cody's room? Mom and Dad's? Maybe he got scared and they took him in?"

Rusty checked his brother's room first but Cody hadn't seen Patrick and the bike was still there. Bill and Bev were next but they hadn't seen or heard from Patrick either. We had six adults searching a small house for one boy and we all came up empty. Chase and I then did what came naturally. We headed outside and looked at the ground, cursing the cement and grass. The first hint was easy enough to find.

"Chase, look, the flower bed has been dug into. Tonight?"

"No, yesterday. The tracks are shoes and Patrick's shoes are by his bed. Patrick did it, but why? What would he want with a pail of dirt?"

We walked a large circle around the house looking for soil dropped on the sidewalk or in the grass. Then we searched the backyard again, but I wasn't expecting to find him back there. He knew the rules. Chase and I both ruled out the backyard. The adults ruled out the house. It was nearly light outside, but still no sign of Patrick.

"Come on Cassidy, we have one hint. Missing dirt. It's got to be out front somewhere. Our missing clue has to be this way."

We made wider and wider circles, ending all the way down the hill almost in Mrs. Rathburn's roses. We turned and looked back up the hill. A big silly grin crept across Chase's face and I knew he'd found Patrick. At least he was smiling. That was a good sign. I followed his gaze and it became obvious why we hadn't been able to find him. Patrick was up on the roof!

"I don't believe it," I said. "How did he get up there?"

"I don't know, but I can't wait to find out. However he did it, it was sneaky and smart and I want to find out."

We rushed into the house.

"He's on the roof!" I announced to everyone.

Rusty rushed down from the attic. "How could he be on the roof? We'd have heard him up there last night. He had no way up."

"We saw him up there. Got a ladder?"

We retrieved a ladder from the garage and Rusty climbed up. The adults stood in silence on the ground below. He approached Patrick cautiously, not wanting to scare him and have him tumble off.

"He's just sleeping," Rusty called down. "Hey Pat, what are you doing on the roof, buddy? Be careful. Don't fall. What are you doing way up here?"

Pat sat up sleepily. "Aw, I missed it!" he said sounding disappointed. He got up and Rusty held his hand as he went to the chimney and examined the area. I saw a smile cross Rusty's face. I knew this was going to be good. Patrick's eyes got big. "Santa's magic!" he exclaimed. "He doesn't leave footprints! Did Santa come?"

"Of course he came. If you were downstairs, like you should be, you'd see all the presents."

"He came and he doesn't leave footprints. That means he's magic."

We couldn't disagree with the logic of it. Now how had he gotten up there?

Rusty started down the ladder and then had Patrick follow him so Rusty could catch him if he fell. There was no need for Rusty's precautions, especially after we found out how he'd gotten up there. Jesse must *never* hear about this, I thought when he showed us what he did. I couldn't believe he could do it, but he showed us how it was done and how the plan had failed.

The attic rope ladder, with hooks on both ends, was to be used to escape the attic in the event of a fire. Patrick had snuck through the attic to the balcony in stocking feet. He had hooked the ladder as high as he could reach and then pulled up the bottom of it. He then climbed half the ladder and hooked the other end even higher. He alternated ends of the ladder until he hooked it to the eves of the house and finally pulled himself over and onto the roof. Yup, Jesse would definitely kill me. Patrick brought up the bucket of dirt and spread it on the roof around the chimney, just to be able to track Santa Claus. He did it with Rusty and I sleeping just underfoot and we hadn't heard a thing. He was going to pull the ladder up and go down the easy way but he dropped the end. Being stuck on the roof hadn't scared him, it had simply created a new opportunity. Now he could actually catch Santa Claus in the act! Only problem being that Santa only arrives once kids are sleeping, so he must have come to our house about four a.m.

"Patrick," I scolded, "you know better than to go up on the roof! You could have fallen off."

"You said not to go in the backyard and I didn't. I only went over it a little."

"When you got stuck in the tree, I told you to keep your feet on the ground unless you were told otherwise."

"Oh, yeah. But I told you I was going to track Santa Claus this Christmas. I told you and you said it was a good idea!"

I looked at Rusty. "Did I do that?"

"You sure did. But that was when you thought he was spending Christmas at *his* house." Oh the joys of eating my own words.

While we were investigating Patrick's night time adventures, Bev began baking cinnamon rolls and their scent from the oven brought everybody into the house. Patrick entered the living room and stood in awe before the ten foot tall Christmas tree. Adorned with twinkling lights and sparkling ornaments, it had been totally decked out in his honor. With a kid finally in Bev and Bill's home for Christmas, they had spared no expense to please him. Patrick's stocking had been filled with candy and had little toys poking out from the top. We had a kid who thought Santa was magic. It truly was Christmas!

Everybody staked out a corner of the living room. The coffee table was shoved aside and Chase appointed himself as the official gift-hander-outer. He crawled around under the tree, reading tags and then handing out the gifts. He helped Patrick with heavily taped packages, then handed his pocketknife around to anyone who needed to cut tape. At first I felt sorry for Chase, but he watched over Patrick's shoulder and his eyes crinkled with joy when he saw the familiar, simple things that kids enjoy. He also approved when Pat opened the adult-sized field guide to animal tracks. After opening the book and leafing through the pages, Pat stopped at the section on canines.

He examined the dog track and the coyote track and read.

"Now do you think you can tell the difference?" Chase asked him.

"Sometimes. I can tell a coyote from a little dog or from a big dog, but I don't know if I could tell the difference between a coyote and a medium sized dog."

"A lot depends on where you see the track. If it looks like a medium sized dog track and it's in the middle of the desert, it's probably a coyote. If it's near a house, it's probably a dog."

"It sounds easy when they say to look at the size of the middle toes, but out in the dirt the tracks get smeared around and it's hard to tell if the middle toes are bigger than the other toes or not."

"I know. That'll come with time and practice."

"Cassidy, he can't possibly read that book." Bev said.

"It doesn't matter. It's only important that he wants to discover what's inside. If he wants to learn, he'll figure out how. Oh my, Cody, umm, thank you. Rusty's going to like this."

"What is it?" Bev asked.

"It's something really cute! That Rusty will like." Get the hint?

"Oh, look!" Patrick shouted with delight. "Aunt Cassidy! Santa *did* bring me rollerblades! Look out Mrs. Rathburn!"

"You're not starting out on the hill. You'll practice close to the house first," I warned him.

"Cody, do you have rollerblades?" Patrick asked.

"Of course. You can't be a cool dude without a bike, a skateboard and rollerblades."

"How do you skate on them?"

"You balance and try not to wobble, just like the bike, except the balance is different."

The pile of wrapping paper, boxes and ribbons gradually grew and finally fell over.

"Rusty, where in the world did you find these?" Cody asked, holding up the three records.

"I didn't. Cassidy found them."

"Okay, it's story time and you're going to get a kick out of this," I started. "I had to go to a funeral. It was for one of my ten sixty-fives and I was really down in the dumps. Punching bag at the station kind of down in the dumps, but I couldn't do the punching bag because I was wearing a little black dress and all I got was hoots and hollers from the guys there." All the guys looked at each other, wondering if the others got the same mental picture they did. I smiled to myself and continued speaking. "So Rusty sent me to the antique mall to look for records except I didn't know what I was looking for. All the workers there had names from old songs. The two women working there were Miss Molly and Rhonda, and the guy who showed me where the record booth was said his name was Henery. Henery left me alone to look and I didn't even know where to start. So then I flagged down Rhonda. 'Help me Rhonda!' is what I said, and they thought that was so funny. Then they launched into this really weird conversation that I took completely seriously. One of them said they had too much to dream that night and I agreed, saying me too, not even aware they were speaking in lyrics from an old song. It kind of went down hill from there, and I was feeling blonder by the minute, but it definitely got my mind off the funeral. You'll have to show me your collection so next time I'll know what to look for."

"'Cause you still haven't found what you're looking for?" Cody asked, laughing at me.

"I don't know but I was hoping to find out. If these records don't fit into your collection, let me know and I'll try again."

"No! This is great! You'll have to show me where you got them next time I visit."

"You better not go there. They had boxes and boxes of old records. I barely started looking through them. Right after that was when I ran into Stan the High Way Man. It was an interesting day."

"Yeah, then we went to a Christmas party at the Schroeder's house. Great party," Rusty said with a wink.

"Pat, what do you have there?" Bev asked.

"It's binoculars," Pat said as he unwound the strap and fiddled with the knob. "They help you see things that are far away. If you look in these little holes and turn this little knob you can see things far away!"

"Why would Santa Claus bring you binoculars?"

"Because he knows I like to look at birds. I have a list!"

"He added five or six birds to his list when he was at our place, and he learned how to use Rusty's binoculars. I wonder how Santa knew you needed a pair of binoculars, though."

"'Cause he's smart!" Patrick said, sure that Santa knew everything now.

Books, Lego blocks, coloring books, markers, rollerblades… once everything had been opened and stacked up we sat back to admire the plunder.

"I have one more thing for you Cass, but it's not a Christmas present because I know you don't want to use it. But I want you to have one. I would have just left it at home, but I knew the guys would want to see it, maybe try it out." Rusty left the house and went out to the Explorer and brought in a rifle in a case. He took it out, removed the trigger lock and handed it to me.

"It's not loaded. I chose that particular gun because it was small and lightweight, but big enough to pack some real firepower. You'll need some heavy ammunition if you need to take down a mountain lion. Your 9mm just won't do it." He didn't mention stalkers, kidnappers or apprehensions because he knew better. I checked the magazine to make sure it wasn't loaded, then sighted down the rifle. I hefted it. I could actually hike with this rifle. Not that I couldn't hike with any rifle. Anybody who hikes armed will tell you there are rifles you can hike with and rifles that turn into a pain in the ass. This one was carefully chosen with the trail in mind, with ease of use, with minimum size and maximum stopping power. A gun a small person like me could use. It would take some practice and getting used to. I was used to the guns at the ranch, the military issue, and the standard police weapons. Although I was able to shoot almost anything, I'd be comfortable once the rifle became more natural to me. Then I'd be able to aim and fire without hesitation.

"Christmas day is a lousy time to go to the firing range. Every guy that got a new gun is there trying it out," Chase said. "Later maybe we can drive to my place. There's plenty of room to shoot out there, and I can show Patrick some tracks, too."

A trip to Chase's place? That sounded interesting. What kind of a place would Chase choose to live in? Then I started wondering if it would be safe to bring Patrick there.

It was a wonderful day, watching Patrick trying to learn how to rollerblade without wobbling, watching Cody skate circles around him. He was able to skate backwards while holding Patrick's hands. Cabrillo Court was well used that day. The little Kentaro girl received a new scooter and the Mason's oldest child had a new tricycle. Mrs. Rathburn sat in her front yard, daring anybody to attempt the hill on their first day riding on shaky wheels. She was wearing a brand new robe with slippers on her feet and sitting in a well worn patio chair holding a steaming cup of coffee.

"Your nephew is a scallywag," she told me. "He tries things before he should. He's going to get into a lot of trouble if you don't keep a close watch on him."

"He's a good kid, though. I didn't really know him that well until he visited us a few weeks ago. Now I'm going to miss him when he goes home."

"How long until I can quit worrying about the little ruffian?"

"Wednesday morning."

"That's just one of them though. I bet a dozen kids got wheels for Christmas. Happens every year."

"I know what you need. You could use one of those inflatable Christmas lawn ornaments. At least it would make a soft landing spot."

"Can't do that. Those things cost a fortune. Plus, the kids would think I was getting soft. Can't let them think that."

At least my suggestion was worth a try. As I walked back up the hill I noticed two cars parked on the street. Inside the cars teenagers watched the activity on the street. Normally a kid in a car using a cell phone was a common everyday thing to see in any neighborhood, but for some reason it didn't feel right to me. These teenagers didn't seem to be just talking to friends. They appeared to have their own agenda. I wondered if they were looking for a house to break into and felt grateful that Patrick was safe with Rusty and Cody. When I reached the top of the hill I saw Patrick skating by himself, still mighty wobbly, but improving. At least now he was able to balance on his own. Cody had traded in his rollerblades for the red bike and was riding circles around Patrick.

"Cody!" The Kentaro girl called out. "Do a wheelie! Do a wheelie!"

Cody popped his front tire into the air and rode around for a bit on one wheel. The little girl jumped up and down clapping with excitement.

Later we drove to Chase's house to try out the rifle. Considering the number of cops involved, we decided to bring more firepower, so Bill dug out his rifles and Chase assured everyone that he had a couple more rifles at his house. We packed our ear protection and added at least one cinnamon roll apiece before heading out.

Chase lived outside the city limits and he was right, he had plenty of space for target practice.

"Are you sure it's really legal to shoot out here?" Rusty asked. Just because Chase was a retired cop didn't mean he didn't stretch the law a bit if nobody was going to notice.

"Sign says no hunting. Doesn't say anything about target practice."

"Those are your signs," Rusty pointed out.

"Yeah, well they mean it."

Chase's place looked like a country western song gone bad. It was an old tan mobile home parked out in the desert. I wondered if the trailer was trying to disappear into the flat desert land surrounding it. It had skirting at some point in time, but many of the panels had fallen off and many were missing completely. An Indian dream catcher swayed in the breeze. Other Indian artifacts were visible around the property. An old wooden table held some pieces of pottery, several arrowheads, a motorcycle helmet, and a cat bowl with a water dish. Approaching the trailer, the sorriest looking cat I'd ever seen crawled out from under the mobile home and began pitifully meowing at Chase. He got a box of cat food and poured out a portion for the cat. Chase poked the reservoir bottle attached to the water dish and it gurgled, indicating the bottle was still half full. He reached out to pet the cat but it hissed and batted at his hand.

"Ornery critter. I think he's still mad at me for having him fixed. Hasn't talked to me since. That was seven years ago."

"What happened to his eye?" Patrick asked.

"Rattlesnake," Chase answered simply.

"What's his name?" Patrick asked.

"He doesn't have one. He's just a cat. He didn't name me, so why should I name him?"

"You had to tell them a name at the vet," Patrick pointed out.

"They just wrote down Cat."

"Hey, Cat," Patrick said. The cat hissed and backed away.

"I wouldn't touch him," Chase advised. "Not if you value your hand. Darn critter only lives out of orneriness. When I leave on searches I fill the dish. After that, he lives on mice. He never comes in the house. He's just a tough old cat. Can't do nothing with him except let him stay."

He dug around beside the mobile home and brought out a stack of what looked like signs. He tossed them into a rack on top of his Baja Bug, then drove out away from his home. He placed each sign out in the desert and stapled a target to each one. It looked as though he did this often.

Bev disappeared into the mobile home. I was almost curious enough to follow her, but it didn't feel right just walking into Chase's home while he was off doing something else. Why not, I asked myself, he walks into your house when you're not home, but that still didn't make it right for me. I'd wait for an invitation of some kind.

"Cass?" It was Rusty, calling me to try my hand with the rifle.

He produced a loaded clip from his pocket.

"Is there a strap for it?" I asked.

"Yeah, but I didn't think you'd want to mess with it."

"If I have to mess with it on the trail then I want to practice with it. I want to feel how all the pieces work together. I don't want to be able to shoot it perfectly and then get tangled in the strap when it counts."

"I guess that makes sense."

"Let me take a few shots with your rifle so I can compare the new rifle to one I am familiar with."

Rusty handed me his service rifle and I took my time squeezing off five shots. Then I took my time with the new rifle. My accuracy was not as good with the new rifle. That was partly due to my unfamiliarity with the weapon and partly because of the shorter barrel.

"Where did you learn to shoot like that?" Cody asked.

"On the ranch. Then it became more refined in the Marines. I graduated from sniper school. That's where I got a lot of experience with the bigger guns. I had lots of practice in reserve academy, too. After all that time shooting, it comes pretty naturally."

"Yeah," added Patrick. "She had a BB gun when she was a little kid. I wish my mom would let me have a BB gun."

"Stay behind the shooters, Patrick. You know better than that."

"Can I shoot too?" Patrick asked.

"If your mom and dad say it's okay, and if you let Uncle Rusty help you, then you can shoot, too."

"Oh boy!" he said, and ran off with my cell phone to call his parents. I could see the wheels turning, Pat knew them well and realized only his dad would grant permission. Problem was how to speak to his dad alone without involving his mom? The ranch. Call the ranch office and then Old Frank would find James.

"All right! Hi, Steve! I hafta ask my dad a question…. Yeah, I know. I'll call her as soon as we get home again… We're shooting… I hafta ask my dad if I can shoot, too… Merry Christmas." There was a long pause. "Daddy? Aunt Cassidy says I have to ask before I can shoot a gun. I knew Mom would say no, but can I shoot the gun, too? Please? It's safe. Aunt Cassidy and Uncle Rusty both know all about shooting. I'm obeying the rules… I don't know, what's a caliber?… Okay." He handed the phone to Rusty.

"Merry Christmas, James… Cassidy's shooting forty-five's right now… I know. If you let Patrick shoot we'll hunt down a twenty-two… Yeah, I'll be right there with him… No problem… You got it. We'll see you Wednesday evening. Two days. Thanks. If Jesse says anything, I'll back you up. Enjoy the rest of your holiday. Bye." He closed the phone and pocketed it. "Chase, do you have a twenty-two hiding in that rat trap of yours?"

"A twenty-two?"

"Yipee!" Patrick said, jumping up and down.

"I think so, but it's got to be a hundred years old. I haven't shot one since I was a teenager."

"Told you he was old," Patrick whispered loudly to Cody. I glanced towards Chase hoping he hadn't heard.

"Can we look it over and make sure it's safe?" Rusty asked.

Patrick received a very limited shooting lesson. It took some searching to find the twenty-two and then even more searching to find bullets for it. Rusty dusted the weapon off, did a quick cleaning job on it then looked over the bullets.

"How old are these things?" he asked Chase.

Chase just shrugged.

Rusty squeezed off two shots, hoping for the best. He led Patrick away from the group where he could instruct easier. I saw him demonstrating how a rifle kicked and how to hold it right up against his shoulder so it would just push him, not hammer him when the shot went off. He demonstrated how to site along the barrel, match up the point and the V, then how to squeeze off a shot without jerking. Rusty further explained what would happen if he didn't do it right. When it was finally time for Patrick to actually shoot the weapon Rusty knelt behind him helping him to stand steady. It was awkward for Patrick and took him a while to line up the site correctly. I knew it would take several years of practice before shooting a gun became more natural to him. Jesse would limit his use of firearms. Jesse wasn't against them and had also shot a twenty-two when she was Patrick's age. She knew the family and the ranch hands would all teach Patrick correctly, but to her, it was always too soon. He was growing up too quickly… So it would take a while for shooting to come naturally to Pat.

"Hold your fire!" Rusty yelled over the din of the other guns. He waited for all firing to stop before he ran out to the target and brought it in close for Patrick. "Okay!" he yelled, giving everyone permission to shoot again. "Now, line it up carefully."

I watched as Patrick aimed, squeezed, closed his eyes and fired.

"Keep your eye on the target," Rusty instructed.

"The noise scares me."

"Closing your eyes won't stop the noise. You have to see where you are shooting. It's important. Be alert when you shoot. Closing your eyes leaves you less prepared for your next shot. Always be ready for whatever you decide to do next, whether it's to take another shot or not. Always be alert and careful. Never point a gun at a person."

"You do."

"If you become a policeman, you will be taught exactly when you can point your gun at a person and when you can't. For now, never point a gun at anyone. Policemen are trained not to point a gun at a person during practice, and that's what we are doing, just practicing."

Bang! Thunk. Bang! Thunk. I heard my bullets hit wood. I didn't have a good feel for it because the rifle felt light to me. I was shooting high because I expected more weight. It was going to take practice to gain accuracy. I could defend myself with the rifle now, but that wasn't good enough for me. There were times I needed to hit exactly where I wanted. It was important for me to be able to hit what I was aiming for. When it really counted, inches mattered a great deal. I always took my shooting seriously.

Bev came out with a bag of trash. Cody ran to help his mom.

"For a full trash bag there's not much here," he commented.

"It's all fast food wrappers and take out boxes," she said with disapproval. I began to see why Chase showed up at the Michaels' house so regularly. It was probably the only home cooked food he ever ate.

I heard the click of an empty chamber. "Sorry, Pat, that's all there is. Your dad said you could only shoot the twenty-two. We have to obey the rules. Next time we will call before we go shooting and pick up the ammo we need. Today we have to just use what we have on hand and none of the stores are open. Now remember to stay behind the people who are shooting."

"Hey, Patrick, you want to go find some tracks? I know a place to track animals and you can ride in my Bug."

"Can I, Aunt Cassidy?"

"You know how quick he gets into trouble?" I asked Chase.

"I know. I'll watch him. Unless he takes off in the Bug, there's nothing out there for him to get into. The Bug's not automatic, so I doubt he can even start it." They got into the Bug with Chase asking, "Have you ever seen a javelina?"

"Cassidy?" Bev called from the steps of the mobile home. "Can you help me a second?"

Chase's living room looked like forty years worth of bachelorhood. It was still cluttered even after Bev had removed all the fast food wrappers and take out boxes. After looking at it more closely I decided it was an organized clutter which made me wonder if Bev had something to do with it.

"What are you trying to do?" I asked.

"Can you empty the dishwasher while I wash pots and pans? Then we'll fill it up again."

"Sure. How can he live like this?"

It took me a while to figure out where to put things. His cupboards were empty. Every dish had been used, so I just guessed where everything went. I thought about where would be handiest and just started stacking.

"I get out here a couple of times a year and it's always just like this. When he sees it all straightened up he starts cooking again. Nothing fancy, but stews and things he can use for leftovers. Once everything is a mess, the job looks too big and he opts for take out. I'll strip his bed and take a bag full of laundry home, too."

"Doesn't he get upset having his home invaded and rearranged?"

"He was embarrassed the first time, but he knows he can't stop me. I don't want to shoot, and I need something to do, so now he just lets me work."

"He's always so neat at my house."

"He's respectful, but that's what he is. He isn't a homemaker, but he's good at what he does. You're lucky to have him on your side. He loves

Patrick, too. I hope your family doesn't mind."

"Doesn't mind?"

"If he keeps tabs on him. Chase keeps tabs on you. Did you know that? He talks to Lou Strickland and gets stories from the station. He knows more than you think he does and he also knows what not to talk about. I can see through his stories though, and know you've had some rough times. I know when he told me about your honeymoon something else had happened, and I know when he says you are fine, it means you are fine, for now, again. I don't know what you did on your honeymoon, but thank you. Thank you for watching out for Rusty."

"Why would you think I was watching out for Rusty? He's the big, strong detective. I'm…"

"Wise in the ways of the woods. I know you went to the woods. Rusty is comfortable in the wilderness. He can get along, but he isn't woods wise. You can't fool me."

"We watch out for each other."

"Did you know the difference between you two even shows up in pictures?"

"So I've been told. I've got a photographer friend trying to figure out what it is about my stalking that shows up in pictures. He wants to try and sell pictures of me stalking."

"Pictures of Rusty in the woods say, 'Isn't this great? I'm out in the woods having a great time.' Pictures of you say, 'Isn't this great? I'm out in the woods having a great time. See the deer behind me? I know you can't, but he's there. And there's a mouse trying to decide if he wants to check out my shoe. I'd point out the raccoon, but I'd scare him away.'"

"Bev, that's silly. A picture can't do that."

"Maybe not, but you do."

"What I know about the woods, Rusty knows about the city. He watches out for me in the city and I watch out for him in the woods."

"There, if we run this second batch and empty it Chase ought to be set for a while."

She began stacking up magazines and books in the living room. In her sorting she uncovered a moose hide on the floor. A moose hide rug. What other surprises were underfoot?

"He's going to burn this place down one day," Bev commented. "To think he put a wood burning stove in this tinderbox. Where does he even find wood when there's not a stick of wood within ten miles?"

I started looking at the pictures on the walls. I'd never thought of Chase as the sentimental type. There were old black and white pictures of him when he was a kid. In the background I frequently saw a white man and also an

Indian man. The white man appeared to always look indifferent, or possibly he didn't want to be photographed. The Indian always seemed focused, either on Chase or something very close by. He was relaxed in a tense manner. I wondered if that was what people saw in me when I was in the woods.

We stripped the bed and gathered up the clothes that were obviously dirty. Things hung in the closet, so I knew Chase would have something to wear despite the growing piles that Bev had sacked up. We put fresh sheets on the bed from a tiny linen closet in the hall. The sheets were threadbare and the towels had holes.

"You're going to wash all this? It's going to take you a week."

"It's okay. It's about the only thing I can do for Chase. I think of it like a Christmas present, a gift of time. I doubt if he ever sorts it when he does his own laundry. The only thing he pays close attention to is his uniform. If you've never seen him in uniform, it is always spotless."

"Actually I have, he was one of my teachers at academy. I barely recognized him the first time I saw him out of uniform."

"Was academy hard for you? I've seen big strapping men say it was like hell."

"It was challenging, in odd ways."

"What do you mean, odd ways?"

"Well, you have to remember I'd already been through Marine boot camp and sniper school. Then my husband passed away and I took to the woods. I ran for a long time and trouble tagged along wherever I went. I'd spent days without food in the mountains. I'd had drug dealers chase me through the woods. I knew academy was coming up, so I trained for it. The hard part was trying to act like a real officer. I'm not the action hero type. So many people get into academy because they have this glorified vision of what they will be like as an officer. That wasn't me. I was just there so I would be allowed to track. All the drills on capture and arrest were what the other cadets thrived on and what I dreaded. I was the odd man out all the time. Physically it was demanding. Academically it was challenging. That was where I worked the hardest, trying to pass the tests. I never was one to sit around studying books and writing reports."

"You don't like writing?"

"No, not usually. I can do it, if it's important. I've really applied myself to a few police reports, trying to make sure everything is told just so. But in general I don't write much."

"That's too bad. I think the stories of your adventures would be fascinating reading."

"You do? There's no way I could do that. I wrote a ten page term paper in high school and thought it was going to kill me. Besides, who would believe all the crazy things that have happened to me?"

"There's a difference between researching a term paper and writing about your personal experiences. You have such a lively imagination. I bet you could do it."

"Well, thank you," I said, a little embarrassed. "I appreciate your faith in me."

"Okay," she said with a relieved sigh, "dishes done, laundry packaged up, floor found. What else can we do before the guys are ready to go?"

"I don't want to look in his bathroom," I said, knowing it needed a good cleaning without even going in there. "Does he even own any cleanser or 409? Windex?"

"I'm sure he keeps it somewhere, even if he doesn't use it. I'll tackle the toilet if you'll do the shower, first one finished can take on the sink."

Bev found three different bottles of cleaning fluids and a scrub brush under the kitchen sink. I was hoping for a cleanser with bleach in it. She cleaned the toilet while I scrubbed the shower. Later she dust mopped all the gray hair off the floor. When Bev finished the sink I was still scrubbing in the shower.

"Is there room for two in there?" she asked.

"I don't think so," I answered truthfully. It was barely a one man shower.

"Well, take these old paper towels out to the trash and see what the guys are up to. I don't hear shooting anymore. See how much time we have left."

Bill, Cody and Rusty were talking and sitting at an ancient picnic table in back of the mobile home.

"What job did Mom recruit you for?" Cody asked.

"Dishes, we're working on the bathroom now."

"Oh, man, I hope nothing eats her alive. It's spooky in there."

"Bev wants to know how long we'll be here. She's wondering if there's enough time to tackle another job."

"Right now we're just waiting for Chase and Patrick to get back," Bill answered. "How long they are gone depends on what they found to track."

"Why are you wearing your vest?" Rusty asked me.

"I thought I better get used to moving in it. I'm most likely to need it when I am scouting and that's when I have to move smoothly. I need to be able to shoot in it. I didn't count on doing dishes or scrubbing showers in it."

"Typical American housewife, washing dishes in a bulletproof vest," Rusty quipped. "You think that rifle will work for you?"

"Yeah! I need to spend some time at the firing range getting used to the weight. I can tell you spent a long time looking for just the right one. A gun like that isn't easy to find. Thank you."

"I like the service rifle better," Cody added.

"It's what I'm used to," I admitted, "but I don't hike with one because it is too bulky. If you weighed a hundred fifteen pounds and had to carry a thirty-pound pack and a rifle all day, you might appreciate a rifle that packs well. Chase told me to bring my gear. Strap on that pack and a rifle then see which one you end up with in three or four miles."

Cody went to the back of the Explorer and pulled out my pack.

"You track in this getup?"

"Yeah, in winter add snowshoes and three layers of clothes to it. I need to get back in there and help Bev. She has her hands full."

Bev had taken my place and was still cleaning the shower. Once she finished we mopped the kitchen and bathroom floors. She was tired and tempted to quit, but we still had one job to tackle. The refrigerator. I took a peek and found a mess of more takeout boxes. Using a trash bag I removed the ones that were growing science experiments. The vegetable bins were the worst. I just dumped them out and washed them, nothing worth saving in there.

"Well, it isn't perfect, but there's more space anyway," I said as I joined Bev and the guys.

"I don't expect Chase to be much longer. He's probably noticed the shooting has stopped," Bill said.

Patrick came back very excited.

"Aunt Cassidy! I tracked javelina! They are little pigs and they live in the desert. There was a bunch of them! And I found out that snakes do leave tracks but the track we saw was old. It looked like a hose had gotten pulled through the dirt."

"That's great, Pat! I've never seen javelina tracks before."

"They look like tiny round deer tracks."

"I'll have to remember that. Did you check javelina off in your tracks book?"

"No, but I better when we get home. I can check off javelina, mule deer and mountain lion! I would check off the snake but we don't know what kind it was." We all piled into the Explorer and Chase's Bug and drove back to the Michaels' house. Patrick had been bitten by the dune buggy bug and wanted to ride with Chase in the Bug. I thought it would wear off once he was back on the ranch.

As we pulled onto Hudson Street I had an uncomfortable feeling that we were being watched. Half asleep teenagers, parked in cars, perked up one by one as we drove to the house and parked.

"Rusty?"

"Yeah?"

"Take a short walk with me," I said.

"What's wrong?"

"I want to show you something."

As we walked, I quietly pointed out cars to him.

"Look at the red Honda and the silver Acura." We walked a block down the street and nonchalantly passed the two cars, trying to look like a couple out for a stroll. We crossed the street and walked back, passing the house. "Now look at the little black car across the street and the red one on this side. We didn't pass them on the way in so I don't know the makes."

"Your trouble radar going off?"

"No, not yet, more like caution radar. I wonder if a uniform could discourage them. Have there been any break-ins on this street?"

"I don't know, but it would be easy enough to find out."

We went into the house and Rusty talked to Bill who then picked up the phone. An hour later the doorbell rang and an officer entered the living room.

"First kid said he was waiting for a friend. While I was talking to him two cars quietly drove away. The second kid said he was trying to find Pizzaro Street and so he'd pulled over to call someone for directions. I bet if I go out there they'll both be gone."

"And I bet a few hours later four more will be back," I added. "There were cars posted out there yesterday too."

"I'll drive by in a few hours and see. You say there were four of them?"

"Yeah, all sitting quietly, watching the street, trying not to stand out."

The officer looked at me like, 'Why am I talking to you when there's a detective and a cop handy?' So I backed off. I went upstairs and caught Patrick checking off animals in his tracking book.

"I can't find *javelina*," he said, puzzled.

"Look in the j's. If it isn't there, look up peccary. It's the same animal, but it has two different names."

He thumbed through the index then turned to the right page.

"Here it is. I have to ask Chase a question." He ran downstairs and a quick discussion about wild pigs occurred, then he returned and placed a check next to collared peccary.

"Aunt Cassidy, why do you answer my questions?"

"Because that's how you learn stuff."

"Then how come my mom won't answer my questions?"

"It's not that she won't. It's because moms get busy and because your questions are often about things your mom doesn't know about. She can't answer very well if she doesn't know the answer."

"Then, why does she want me to read baby books like at school?"

"It's because she doesn't know how smart you are. She thinks six year olds are supposed to be just so smart and so she only expects you to be as smart as other kids your age."

That started him thinking. "You mean I'm smarter than other six-year-old kids?"

"Yes, Patrick, you are very intelligent. You learn things easily and very quickly. You think like a much older kid. Only problem is, your age will never match your intelligence. You will always want to do more than you are allowed to do because your mind will figure things out before you are old enough to do them."

"Mom and dad know I'm smart."

"Of course they do, but they don't know how smart you really are. They expect you to be a typical first grader. That's why they can't understand why you're bored at school. Does your mom know you can twirl a rope and jump in and out of it?"

"I don't think so. She uses my practice time to do crafts."

"Does your dad?"

"He's usually at work."

"Does your mom know you can read the bird book?"

"Sort of, but she thinks it's dumb so she doesn't pay attention."

"Do they realize you can make a ball return for a pool table?"

"No, I don't have toys like that at home."

"What do you have at home that interests you, that would show your mom and dad how smart you are?"

"Nothing. What interests me doesn't interest them, so they think it's dumb."

"We've got to do something to get them out of that mindset. Just because you like something different doesn't mean it's dumb. If they knew how smart you were, they would encourage you to learn and I think they would let you do more around the ranch. Only problem is, they worry about you doing things that are dangerous, like driving the truck. I'm afraid that little stunt you pulled at Thanksgiving made them think you do stuff without thinking. They couldn't get past it to see how smart you were for knowing how the truck worked. So you have to choose the way you use that brain of yours very carefully. Don't do things that can hurt you. A truck is a dangerous thing in the hands of a six-year-old. Choose smarter things to do that show your parents that you can think like a big kid. That way they will be more likely to let you do big kid things. For Christmas you got a kit to help you make a birdfeeder. Your dad will have to help you build it, but don't let him help too much. You read the directions out loud to show him that you can read well. Try to put it together with as little help as possible. I bet it will surprise him just how much you can do on your own. Once he sees that you are able to make a birdfeeder, maybe he will find other interesting projects for you to build."

"Chase gave me a project to do at home. He said I should watch for any signs of people or animals around the house. He told me to watch for tracks and scat. I had to ask him what scat was and then I had to ask him why I should be interested in animal poop. Once he explained, it made sense to me. He said to watch for feathers or hairs in the weeds or overturned rocks and crushed or nibbled plants. And he told me to ask myself questions about everything I see so maybe I can figure out what animals came in the yard. He said it might sound boring, but the closer I look, the more I will see. He said I'd be surprised what animals really come there that I don't know about."

"And he's right, but you will have to be patient. It is a learning process. Once you find one thing, it will get you thinking about other possibilities. You won't see lots of sign at first, but as you learn to recognize it you'll start seeing more and more. It gets to be very interesting after it clicks, and then you will start seeing all kinds of things you didn't know to look for before."

"Can we do that here? Can you show me?"

"We can try, but I really need to help Mrs. Michaels with dinner pretty soon."

We went out in the front yard and started poking around in the flowerbeds.

"We are looking for anything that looks like it is from an animal or a man. Oh, look! Something has been digging in the flowerbed! What do you think it was? The dirt is disturbed here. There are little tracks. Come look!"

He bent over the spot. "That's just me," he said with disappointment.

"So we identified one thing that has been in the yard. One small boy. Keep looking. Maybe we can find more."

A long shadow appeared over us.

"What are you doing?" Rusty asked, amused. It didn't seem strange to him to find his wife crawling around in the flowerbeds. He was just curious what we were up to.

"Tracking, small scale."

"Aunt Cassidy, look," Patrick said.

"Ooo, what is it?" I asked, fascinated with his find.

"It's fur of some kind."

"Okay, what did Chase say to do next?"

"Ask myself questions."

"So what is your first question?"

"What kind of fur is it?"

"And?"

"It's dog or cat fur."

"How do you know?"

"I think it's cat fur because cats are more likely to be in flower beds. Dogs like to be out in the open where they can see people."

"Good thinking, but how can we learn more?"

"It's long and a little wavy."

"What color?"

"Gray."

"Long, a little wavy, gray. I bet Cody would know if a neighbor has a gray Persian cat. Go ask him and see if you're right."

"Cassidy, you're nuts," Rusty said in a teasing voice.

"Why? I'm just showing him how to teach himself. It could save his sanity if Jesse doesn't ease up a bit. Plus it'll teach him new ways to look at things. It'll come in very handy later for tracking."

A small black car cruised by. The young driver watched as he passed. I felt a little bit silly laying in the yard looking under a bush.

"It is a cat," Patrick said when he returned. "His name is Smoky and he lives across the street."

"Can you find any cat tracks in the dirt?"

Sandy drove up and eyed us warily as she went into the house. She greeted everybody inside and then came back out front.

"What are you doing?" she asked, appalled that her sister-in-law would be caught crawling around in the dirt.

"Tracking. Small scale," I repeated for her. "Small scale neighborhood tracking that kids can do to teach themselves more."

"And you want kids to do this… why?" she asked.

"It teaches them to be observant. It gets them thinking about the world around them. It's good for them."

"He's going to get filthy down there crawling around in the dirt."

"Yeah, me too."

Patrick bent over the ground and followed the flowerbed.

"The cat came from the grass and he went in the flower bed. Then he scratched around in the dirt and after he was through he rubbed up against the bush. That's where we first saw sign. The fur in the bush. Then he followed the front of the flowerbed and went back into the grass again. How do you follow a cat in the grass?"

"It's pretty tough. I think the hints in the flowerbed are the most information we can get from this cat. But you did pretty well! Tell me, how can you tell a cat track from a dog track."

"No claws."

"Right, anything else?"

"Most dogs are bigger than cats."

"True. Some dogs are smaller than cats, too, but most dogs are larger."

"And cat tracks are rounder and more… the toes are closer together. Dog's feet are longer and the toes spread out more when they walk."

"Right. Good job!"

"Is there a reason he needs to know that?" Sandy asked.

"If he's going to be a tracker he needs to build up a library of tracks in his brain. And there are hundreds of variations for each type of track. Weather tears them down. The actions of people or animals vary a lot. So it's not just a track to memorize. There's a wide array of tracks and actions and variations and quirks for each kind of animal. The sooner he gets started, the more he can learn."

"Patrick, do you want to be a tracker when you grow up?" Sandy asked him.

"I can't," he said sadly.

"Why not?" Sandy asked.

"Because my mom says I need a real job and tracking doesn't pay anything."

"Don't let that stop you," I told him. "Learn everything you can. Anything you are interested in, learn as much as possible about it. I don't care if it's birds or tracks or cars or outer space. Just pack that brain full of information. The more learning you do, the easier it will be to learn more. Stay curious and search for your own answers and you will always be smart. Intelligent people find a way to make their brains work for them."

"You track, but you don't get paid for it."

"That's true, but if I had a job I would still track. I track to help find people. Finding people is more important to me than a job. Especially after Carl Cranston. It's even more important that I do my very best. Because sometimes… sometimes even my very best isn't good enough." Oh, shoot, I'd done it again. I waited, willing the sharp pang of guilt and sorrow away, but it wasn't working. I looked to Rusty. Why did I allow myself to become emotional over one mistake? It wasn't a mistake, Cass. The old argument started again in my head and this time I couldn't stop it.

"Can you watch Patrick for a bit?" I asked, and then headed for the house. I ran up to the attic, pulled up the stairs and threw myself down on the mattress Rusty and I had been using as a bed. Comforters *floofed* up around me as I landed and settled back down in disarray. No tears, please, don't cry, Cass, just wait and it'll go away. Just wait. I heard a noise and tried to ignore it, but it walked over to the mattress and sat down beside our bed on the floor. It was my brother-in-law.

"Cody, please, go away."

"Okay, when you really want me to go away tell me again. In the meantime, tell me what happened."

"Nothing. Nothing happened. I was just reminded of something upsetting and I needed a time out."

"You're one tough cookie. What did you do this time? Last time I saw you like this you'd killed somebody."

Cody's words were too close to the truth for me. "Would you please just think a little before you say things like that?"

"Cassidy, you didn't."

My emotions were battling it out inside me. I was still wearing my vest which was rubbing and making me feel uncomfortable but I couldn't change with Cody in the room. I couldn't talk about the Cranston search without making things worse and I refused to cry in front of him. I needed some space. Pushing the stairs back down slowly so I wouldn't hit anybody, I grabbed my purse in case I needed my cell phone or some money. I didn't know where I was heading but I was going somewhere, then I took off out the front door again. Cody followed. I ran.

"Cassidy, I'm sorry," he called as he ran after me. I cut across the street and suddenly a car pulled out. I jumped, trying to get out of the way, but it hit my leg and sent me sprawling across the hood. Two guys jumped out, stuffed me in the backseat and drove away.

Chapter 18

At first I was too full of pent up emotions to be scared. I looked out the car window as Cody raced down the street. Patrick ran out, then went up to the Explorer and wrote something in the dust on the vehicle's side. The car turned the corner and the men bound my wrists together, then tied a gag around my head.

What in the world was going on? I forced myself to think. Part of me refused to believe this was happening. It was Christmas Day. What were these kids doing out on Christmas Day? Watching the street, obviously. But why? I had thought they were looking for a house that was an easy victim for a burglary. But that was obviously not the case. Why would they be watching the Michaels' house? Because of the connection with the police? Then why take me? Because of Shawn the Shark? Oh, shit. Maybe it was because of Shawn the Shark. It was the only connection I could come up with.

I looked at the faces of my captors and memorized their features in case I had a chance to identify them later. They appeared to be young. They were tough. They were the forgotten. That's why they were out on Christmas Day. They didn't have families close enough to keep them home even on Christmas. They had each other and too many ways to get into trouble.

I yanked the gag off, partly because it was bugging me and partly because I wanted to see their reaction.

"Hey, you get that thing back on," the boy sitting on my feet said. He moved to tie it back on and I got a foot loose. I kicked him against the car door. The car rocked.

"Woohoo! We got us a live one! Can we have some fun with her? What do you think?" he said turning to me. "We gonna have some fun wit' you?"

"Not if you value your life," I replied.

"Ooo, I'm scared," he said mocking me, waving around a long, black pistol.

"Dang it, Butcher, if you want them to keep that rag in you gotta tie their hands *behind* them."

"Where are you taking me?" I demanded to know.

"Where the Shark should have taken you in the first place," the driver answered. "Soon's he found out you were a narc he should'a brought you to us. We'd'a fixed you up right then."

"I'm not a narc. I'm a tracker visiting family in San Diego for Christmas. I don't know anything about narcotics. I don't know anything about your little ring. The more you do to me the more I'm learning. If I know anything about it at all it's because of you. So don't go blaming me or Shawn. Shawn didn't tell me anything."

"So you admit you're the narc Shawn picked up?"

Dang it. "I told you I'm not a narc. You guys have it all wrong."

"Well, it don't matter now. We got you. We're gonna have some fun with you, long as we got you."

I turned my thoughts to getting out of this dilemma and what I could expect from the police. I was pretty sure Patrick had written down the license plate number on the Explorer. I wasn't sure why he'd thought to do that, but I was very grateful. What a kid, a thinker, that's for sure. He didn't freak out; he thought about what to do and did it. I looked out the window. The driver turned out of the neighborhood, with a screeching of tires, and the landscape changed to a busy commercial street. The driver expected to be followed. His eyes kept flicking to his rearview mirrors.

"Tell me again, where we're going," I demanded. I needed some clues. Any tiny facts I could pull from my captors might help. If I got away I wanted to know where I was, and what I might be dealing with.

"To town, just like the Shark told you. You wanted a fix? We're gonna fix you. We're gonna fix you good."

"That sounds like a waste of good drugs to me. Seems like you could line your pockets a little, save the drugs and just shoot me."

"We might do that, too."

"If I have a choice between being shot and being shot. I'd rather be shot."

"Huh?"

"With guns."

"I'll keep that in mind, chicken. You taking the chicken way out."

No, I thought, I'm keeping my mind straight right up until the end. If my mind was sharp I could watch for breaks.

"We're going downtown?" I asked. "Aren't there an awful lot of people downtown?"

"Not today, plus this part of downtown is used to a bit of action. A few shots won't mean much to them. Bet we can even recruit a little help if we need it."

"I like the lighting effects. Little fog, eerie lights, good place to die."

"We kinda like it."

They pulled into a back alley and the eerie light faded. I counted the backs of the buildings so I'd know how far away my freedom was. Graffiti adorned the brick walls. Some had been painted over by local merchants while other tags were more recent. I tried to memorize the letters I saw. Any clues were useful. They stopped the car and yanked me out.

"347 dim alley," I quipped, reading the number off the back of the building.

"Yeah, a dim alley leading to nowhere for you. What's your name?" the driver asked.

"Cassidy," I answered, determined to see if they'd use the information against me later. It didn't take them long.

"Cassidy, as in Butch Cassidy?"

"You got it, exactly. My dad likes the old west."

He busted out laughing. "Hey, Butcher, you lucked out. I think you ought to get first shot at miss narc bitch here."

I could see why they called him Butcher. He actually looked like he'd butchered a few. A few *what* I didn't want to try and guess. Butcher closed in and I backed off. Two men moved in behind me. I stopped.

I heard sirens in the background and wondered if they were off on some other case or actually looking for me. But that was dumb. They had no way of knowing where I was.

Butcher grabbed my arm and pulled me towards a building. He unlocked a deadbolt and shoved me into the rear of the building. I found myself in the back room of a business. I was surrounded by three men and another three entered the room behind us. One of the guys was Shawn the Shark, but he wasn't looking much like a predator at the moment. He was looking apologetic.

"Okay, Shark, now I want you to see exactly what we do to narcs around here. Even little baby narcs. Narcs… don't… live. Got it? Butcher? Choose your weapon."

"She said she didn't want to get shot. She don' say nuthin' 'bout pills or sniffin'"

"You can't make me!" I said, backing away. As soon as the men closed in I stopped. I didn't want them to touch me. So far they seemed rather clueless, and I wanted them to stay that way.

"Then it's a shot. You said you wanted to be shot if you had a choice."

"You know what I meant!" I said, getting even more worried.

"Butcher, no!" Shawn called out. "She's never done drugs. You'll kill her with that. I thought you wanted to have some fun with her."

"Then, just a little bit. That'll make her less fun but more cooperative."

He started filling a needle and I nearly panicked. I kicked the needle and bottle out of his hand. The sirens grew closer. Their eyes flicked back and forth like a half dozen Felix the Cat clocks.

"I don't like this. How do the cops know? We need to do her in and get out of here."

Flashing lights went by the front windows of the business. The men all ducked for cover even though little could be seen through the single door leading out to the main room. Butcher grabbed the needle off the floor, jabbed it into my leg and pushed the plunger on it, then he pushed me to the back alley. All the men looked uneasy as a black and white cruised by the end of the alley.

I could feel the drugs seep through my system. Focus, Cassidy, stay focused. Your life depends on it.

"I say, just do her. We gotta get out of here."

I could feel ice creeping up my leg. I didn't know what they shot me with, but it felt like ice and I could feel my will slipping away. Out in the alley they lined up. Four had guns. They took careful aim.

The driver of the black car looked at Shawn. "Narcs don't live. Got it?"

"No!" Shawn yelled.

"Narcs… don't… live!" Butcher shouted at Shawn. He swung his weapon in Shawn's direction, but there wasn't anything that he could do. Shawn couldn't take on four guys and he knew it. The weapon swung in my direction again.

It was all I could do to not hit the ground. I knew to move meant death. Point blank range. Forty-fives. They couldn't miss. I was counting on them not to miss. I needed them to hit where they were aiming.

Go for the heart.

A sharp explosion, blast that shook me to the core, then all went dark.

"Cassidy! Please, please, babe, breathe, breathe! You can't do this to me."

Frantic rubbing. Jostling. Rusty. I was breathing again but he was in such a panic that he didn't see it. When I tried to move he finally stopped. A few seconds of tense waiting and then he realized that I was breathing and gathered me up in his arms. I felt his face next to my neck. The quick ragged breaths of fear.

Something was important. Something I had to tell him. What was it? The drugs.

"Rus…"

"Shh, babe, just relax. It'll clear soon."

"No, they shot me."

"I know, babe, it'll be okay soon. Four shots are going to leave quite a bruise."

"No, they shot me… with drugs. Bottle on floor inside."

His movements stopped. His relief crumbled. "What is it?"

"Don' know, don' know how much. Icy, felt icy. Don' go."

"I have to, babe, we have to know what that stuff was."

I didn't know what was happening to me, but I was scared. If Rusty left, I felt like everything would fall on me. I'd die. Part of me said it was a bad reaction to the drugs. Part of me was scared to death. I tried to get up, but the alley tilted and I fell. I couldn't stay here! Had to get out! I staggered for the end of the alley. I'd counted the buildings. How many were there? I stumbled out of the alley and into the street. I heard running feet. They were after me! I tried to run but my coordination was gone. Men surrounded me again. No!

"No, Rusty… please come back." I couldn't catch my breath. All I knew was that men were going to kill me. Then the drugs took me completely and I fell.

My mind wandered down dark alleys. People were after me. I ran in my dreams. I hid in alleyways. Shots. Must get away. Over and over again. Can't let them catch me. Have to run. I relived that last shot over and over, relived the fear that I'd fall before the last shot hit.

"Rusty…"

Nothing.

Then again later. Searching. Trying to find my way back. "Rus?"

"Oh, babe, you're back. Please tell me you're back."

"Rusty…"

"It's going to take a while. Don't push."

I faded in and out. The dreams were the worst. I held onto the brief moments of clarity as long as I could. When, at last, I felt like I was fully conscious, I gripped the feeling like a life ring, refusing to be pulled down into the murky depths of the drugs. I opened my eyes and Rusty stood, studying my face, looking for a sign, hoping, just hoping.

"Cass?"

"Yeah."

A huge sigh of relief. "Think you can stick around this time?"

"I'll try. Talk to me."

"You gave everybody a big scare this time."

"Patrick? How's Patrick?"

"He's okay. He's been good for Mom. If he weren't there she'd be frantic, but he keeps her busy. He asks about you and trying to answer his questions makes her work it out in her own mind."

"How did the police find me so quick?"

"They didn't. I did."

"How did you know?"

"Remember when we squashed the bug in the box with your bulletproof vest?"

"Yeah."

"We forgot about the one on your purse. A guy from Cranston's office was told to keep tabs on you and Phillip Cranston backed off. They called Phillip in when we were out doing target practice, but they figured out that those shots were okay. They called him again when you were taken and the conversation was suspicious. Phillip called me as I was trying to tail the black Honda. He passed along the information that leaked through. You gave Cranston Security just enough hints we could use to close in. Eerie lights, fog, a building number. It was just enough. We headed for the gas lamp district. I turned the corner at the end of the alley when they fired at you." A long pause. "I forgot you were wearing the vest. I saw the shooting, saw you fall and my life ended. There was no way they could have missed. The men shot you, made sure you were laying still and took off up the fire escapes. I was stupid. I was scared and I didn't care about myself anymore; I had to be there, I had to be with you, no matter what happened. I ran down the alley and picked you up, felt the vest." He shook his head with a nervous, weary laugh. "Wearing that vest today was the best Christmas present you could have given me. Looking at you, I could see you took quite a blast. I wasn't sure the vest was enough protection. I tried to remember that it's normal to not breathe after a hit like that. I told myself that you'd breathe when the shock wore off. But I couldn't wait. It felt too long. It felt like eons."

"Have you ever had four guys standing ten feet away from you, knowing they were going to shoot? It was so hard, knowing I couldn't move or else. I had to just take it. It was my only way out. I thought they were scared enough to shoot and leave me for dead, so I was counting on them not missing."

"Why did you take off?"

"I… I just freaked out. In my imagination they were coming. When you left, I got scared and had to run. I thought I'd die. I didn't know the footsteps I heard were the police. I was only half there and had to run."

"Okay, that makes sense now, considering what you were on. Slick was able to get four of the guys in the alley. He knows where to pick up Shawn. There's only one guy missing."

"Shawn didn't shoot. Tell Slick not to pin that on Shawn. He stood up for me. They were going to shoot me full of drugs and they backed off because of Shawn and shot me instead. He didn't know he was pulling me from the frying pan into the fire, and he didn't know it would save my life, but he kept them from doing something worse."

"Do you know any names?"

"Only Shawn and a guy named Butcher. Butcher was the one they put in charge of my execution because of my name. They thought it was funny that

I was named after Butch Cassidy and they had a Butch handy. So they gave him the job."

"They must have owed Butcher a favor. Who seemed to be the leader of the group?"

"The driver of the black car."

"I'll tell Slick."

"You're getting along with Slick okay?"

"No. We're just controlling ourselves for the sake of the case. He apologized for 'using my wife', though. Claimed he didn't know."

"Well, if it helps any, I don't feel used. I feel shot. But that's not his fault."

"He should have checked your file before he sent you into that school. That's one reason we never got along. He uses people. It wouldn't be so bad if he used experienced people, trained officers, but he uses anybody. You had the looks and the little piece of paper. He had all his boxes checked so it was a go in his eyes. The only reason I let you go through with it was because you were staying on campus. Shawn couldn't do much on campus, but then it got out of hand when you let him leave."

"Did Patrick really copy the plate number onto the side of the Explorer?"

"Yeah, he did. He even thought up an acronym for the letters so he wouldn't forget them. Patrick will be okay. This has been really rough for Chase. He's taking the blame for dragging you into this in the first place. He was right behind me when I found you. He covered me while I was in the alley and then joined a group of cops in the hunt. He was mad. He was ready to shoot somebody. When he saw what they'd done to you he was ready to see some heads roll."

"I'm glad he hasn't been around for some of my other disasters then. This one was mild in comparison."

"None of them are mild in comparison. All of them scare me spitless. Maybe this one seemed milder because you thought you knew what would happen. But *I* certainly didn't."

"Okay, I know the drill. Tests run in the morning to make sure I'll live. What was the guess on when they'd let me go?"

"Before lunch. Since you were unconscious at the time, I thought that was pushing it, but now that you're awake and making sense and nothing is broken, it looks pretty good."

"Good, I'll clean up my perky blond act and I'll be out of here by ten. Where's my hairbrush. Do I have clothes?"

"You have jeans, a see through tank top, shoes and socks. The blouse and vest got damaged in the shooting. I had to take them off when you weren't breathing."

"You mean I staggered out of the alley in only jeans and a see through tank top?"

"Yeah, but all the cops in San Diego know who you are now."

"That makes me feel *so* much better."

"Why does Slick get to capture his own felons?" he asked, half kidding.

"I can only hand them over one at a time. Six is pushing it. I did round them up for him and it's not my fault they got away."

"Are you going to be okay if I run home and pick up some things for you?"

"Yeah, why don't you get some sleep and fill everybody in and then bring the stuff with you in the morning?"

"You're sure?"

"You've spent so many nights in hospital chairs. Nothing's going to happen while you are gone. We're both just going to sleep so you might as well do it in a bed. Your mom will know everything's okay if you're willing to stay there."

"I'm not worried about my mom."

"And there's no reason to worry about me either. You know I won't stop you from staying here. I just think you'd be more comfortable at home."

When I woke up in the morning I wasn't surprised to see Rusty sleeping in the chair next to my bed. Chase showed up bright and early as well.

Other than all the nurses assuming I had a drug problem, the stay was uneventful. They ran their tests and the doctors visited late in the morning to pronounce me fit. One of them even asked why I was there and had to read my chart to be convinced. I thought the bruises across my chest were a gimme on the shooting. And I guess the drug reaction was worse than the actual physical effects on my body. Maybe I stressed the perky blonde act too much if they had to ask what was wrong with me. Rusty and Chase didn't have the luxury of wondering. They still worried. Rusty brought me home and fussed over me. Patrick sat in my lap. He didn't seem worried, but it was unusual for him to be physically close, so I took it as a sign that he needed comfort. Rusty's family tried to act as though nothing had happened. They didn't pry, but I could tell they were curious. I let Rusty handle the questions unless they were directed specifically to me.

Patrick didn't want to play outside. He was content building Lego buildings and little cars. We colored, but he insisted on coloring in Rusty's reminder books. So I colored a picture for Rusty too. I signed it and dated it just like all the kids did.

"I'm going nuts sitting around the house," I announced suddenly. "Cody, what size are your rollerblades?"

"Men's nine."

"Hmm, too big. And the bike is too small."

"Too small? You're smaller than me," he argued.

"Still too small. Can I try your skateboard?"

"Do you know how to skateboard?"

"Yes and no. I've never done it, but that doesn't mean I can't try."

Bev said, "Cassidy, are you sure that's wise? You just got out of the hospital."

"I just got shot at and drugged. It's not like I just had a body cast removed."

Patrick asked, "What if the bad guys come back?"

"There are not enough of them left to take me, and I think they've learned their lesson."

The entire family came out front to supervise my first skateboarding attempt. The guys hovered around me like news helicopters on a car chase. Rusty kept watch. Patrick rode the bike. Cody rollerbladed. Bill and Bev watched from patio chairs with Bev cringing whenever I went over a bump or had to jump off. I started out easy, just coasting down the driveway. Even that took some practice. Eventually I tried coasting down the driveway, crossing the street, and trying to go up the neighbor's driveway. The front wheels made it up the short curb but the back wheels stuck and sent me lurching off the front of the skateboard. I got back on and tried it in the other direction. This time, with a little more speed, I made it up the driveway. Time to try turning. I coasted down the driveway, turned down the hill and everybody yelled at once, "No! Not the hill yet!"

"I'm just turning at the first driveway!" I called back. With my back to the house I pointed the skateboard down the hill, concentrating on the first driveway. Cody followed ready to give me a hand if I needed to bail out. Patrick was riding up and down the sidewalk. Rusty was in police mode. I heard a car approaching from behind so I started my turn to get out of the way. Patrick gasped, which made me think I was going to run into something.

"Uncle Rusty! Bad guy at six o'clock!" Patrick yelled.

I turned to see what Patrick was yelling about and saw the car smoothly drive down the street. The driver's gun was leveled on me. Rusty turned, drew, fired. A tire blew on the car and it sped up. I looked for cover but couldn't see any, so I ducked. The skateboard flew out from under me and careened down the hill. I crashed to the asphalt, startled, then rolled to my feet in time to see the car still coming, narrowing the gap.

Bev hid her eyes.

Bill jumped to his feet and grabbed Patrick.

Rusty took out another tire but he was at the wrong angle to get the driver.

I jumped onto the hood of the car, threw myself onto the windshield and grabbed the driver's gun hand, sticking out the window. I forced it down and away from me and squeezed off shots until I heard a hollow click. I rolled off the car, twisting the gunman's arm with my fall. I heard a crunch and he screamed. I held on for dear life and the car began drifting as the driver had less and less control. He hit the curb at the end of the street, glanced off and then hit a parked car. Rusty ran up, gun at the ready. The driver dropped his weapon when ordered to and spread eagled as best he could on the hood of the car. Rusty held him there until the officers arrived, Slick right behind them.

Mrs. Rathburn marched up, waggled her finger at me and said, "And I thought your *nephew* was a scallywag!"

Neighbors poured out of houses and a group gathered at the end of the street. We gave Slick the rundown and when things became boring, we went home to let him sort the rest out. If he had more questions, he knew where to look. I went into the house to check on Patrick but Rusty gathered me up into his arms and walked over to the couch to sit down. He pulled me close, not caring that his parents were watching. He buried his face in my hair and took two deep breaths to steady his nerves.

"Cass, never, never go into the line of fire," he said quietly, relief mixed with worry.

"I had to make a choice. The car was on top of me. I had to go up or down, and I thought I'd have better luck going up than getting run over. Then once I was up there, I had to deal with the driver."

"You could have been killed in half a dozen different ways. I know. While I couldn't shoot I was counting. Are you all right?"

"Yeah… I'm fine."

Patrick stood there, hands on hips, and asked, "*Now* can we stay inside and quietly play Legos?"

"Six out of six, Pat. The bad guys are all accounted for, now."

The doorbell rang and Chase walked in. "Did you know there's a big to-do at the end of the street?" He looked at Rusty and I sitting together on the couch. "Okay, you know. Do I get the story firsthand or do I have to pry it out of everybody at the station?"

Chase got his story from three different angles and then he got dinner.

"I knew you were leaving in the morning so I wanted to come say goodbye. Maybe things will calm down and get boring again."

"You have to admit, things are never boring with Cassidy around," Bev said.

"That's true," Chase acknowledged, "but I'd settle for mildly interesting rather than terrifyingly interesting. Patrick, you've got my number, right?"

"Yeah."

"Don't hesitate to call if you have questions. Just ask your mom or dad first."

"Chase, you don't know what you're asking for."

"I think I do."

"What if you're busy policing or tracking?" Pat asked.

"Just leave a message and I'll call you back. Remember, if I'm tracking I might be gone for a few days."

Goodbyes in the morning were rough. Bev got attached to Patrick and knew she might never see him again. And she was beginning to think the same thing about me, for different reasons. There were hugs all around.

"You take care," Bill admonished me.

"I always try," I answered.

"Thanks for everything," Cody said, "the interesting Christmas, the records, letting me see the honeymoon pictures."

The honeymoon pictures? I glared at Rusty. I guess I should have known.

"Thank you, for letting me stay with you for Christmas and for all the cool presents," Patrick said, well aware that his mother would ask if he had thanked the Michaels. "My mom will help me write a thank you note after I get home."

"Not that you need help. I'm going to frame that picture you had taken at the mall and add it to the collection in the bedroom," Bev said.

We climbed into our packed Explorer and headed for the freeway. It was going to be a long drive. Patrick was all set up with coloring books, reading books and Lego blocks. I could barely see him back there in amongst the toys.

"Are you all settled in for a long drive? It's going to take most of the day to get to the ranch."

"Yeah, ready."

We stopped in Santa Monica for lunch, then in Solvang to stretch our legs in the tourist shops, finally we had a brief stop in San Luis Obispo for a snack. The drive took all day. We finally pulled into the ranch around dusk. After driving slowly past Patrick's house we realized everyone had gathered at the ranch house. We walked in to see another Christmas waiting for us all over again. Behind the tree was a bright red bicycle. I bent down and pointed it out to Patrick.

"Do me a favor, Pat, wobble a little for your mom when she teaches you to ride it."

He nodded, eyes big, and said, “It’s almost like Cody’s, except newer.”

“Oooooo, you’re home!” Jesse squealed as she rushed to greet us. She gathered up Patrick and started hugging and kissing him until he squirmed. “Let me look at you!” She turned Patrick this way and that. “You spent nearly two weeks with Cassidy and you’re still in one piece! It’s a miracle!”

“Yeah,” I mumbled, “a miracle.”

“Rusty, Cassidy, you’re looking good,” she added.

“Thanks.”

“Now do we get to? Now do we get to?” asked Wyatt.

“After dinner, Wyatt. Martha is putting it on the table right now.”

We all crowded around the huge table to enjoy a ranch Christmas feast.

“What did Santa Claus bring you in San Diego?” Jesse asked Patrick.

“I got rollerblades, lots of books and binoculars. They make it so you can see things far away. Aunt Cassidy showed me how to look at birds with them. And I got Legos and a remote control car. The car was from Mr. and Mrs. Michaels. I got lots of stuff!”

“What was your favorite present?”

Patrick thought a minute then said, “I got new friends and had adventures. That’s my favorite things. Can we visit San Diego some day?”

“I don’t know Pat, that’s far away. What kind of adventures did you have?”

Uh oh, I thought, here it comes.

“I got to see a mountain lion and we tracked it after it was gone. And I got to go bird watching. We found lots of birds that were in my bird book! And I helped catch a purse snatcher at the mall. And I did a show at the mall in San Diego. They thought it was cool that I could twirl a rope and they had me do it in the mall for people to stop and see. Everybody thought I was a movie star. I handed out autographed pictures and everything.”

“Yeah, if a woman calls and asks for his agent, just tell her you’re not interested.” I added.

“I tracked javelina and I got to shoot a twenty-two. Aunt Cassidy made me call and ask first. So I wasn’t breaking any rules. Uncle Rusty helped me. And I tracked Santa Claus and found out he was magic! He doesn’t leave footprints.”

“Of course Santa leaves footprints,” Jesse said.

“No, he doesn’t. We looked and there were no footprints.”

“Trust me, Jesse, we know for sure now. Patrick and Rusty both checked it out together.”

It was wonderful having Christmas dinner at the ranch with all the hands present, the house decorated, the warmth of family and friends, the excitement of the kids. Everyone ate, opened gifts and enjoyed our time together.

“Thanks for the sweaters,” I told Jesse once we were finally alone. “Rusty will really like them.” Why did everybody buy me clothes with Rusty in mind? “Jesse, I need to talk to you about Pat.”

“Why, he wasn’t any trouble was he? If he was I’ll tan his hide.”

“No! He was no trouble. He was great. But I worry about him. Does he like school?”

“Sometimes. He complains about it a lot.”

“It’s not school he’s complaining about. He isn’t challenged there. When he says they make him read baby books, it’s because he can read at a much higher level. You’ve got to find ways to challenge that kid’s brain. When he was at our place he was reading the bird book, no problem. So I got him a field guide to animal tracks, too. He read a novel at the Michaels’ house, a western like Dad reads. And he built a ball return out of an old erector set for their pool table. He’s very intelligent, but he needs your support. I’m concerned Pat may stop trying, and if that happens then he’ll stop learning.”

“He built a ball return for a pool table. And you let him?”

“Rusty’s dad let him. They just took the fancy pockets off and Patrick went to town on it.”

“Cassidy! How could you let him do that? Do you know how much a pool table costs?”

“And that’s where I’m worried. You’re more concerned about a pool table than you are about letting Patrick use his talents. Bill and Bev thought it was great. We even made up a special version of pool to match the pockets he’d made ball returns for. They were proud of his accomplishment. Why can’t you see his intelligence for what it is? He wasn’t trying to ruin a pool table. He was thinking. When we go back there, I bet the rest of the pool table has erector set ball returns on the pockets. I’m sure it will take Bill a lot longer to figure it out than it did Patrick. Pat has intelligence, talents, skills and interests that are different than yours, but they are valuable and should be encouraged.”

“He gets into trouble when we encourage him. What about the truck?”

“You see the truck incident as a dumb thing for Patrick to do. Did it occur to you that it takes some thinking for a six-year-old to drive a truck? He had to figure out how to start it, what makes it go and stop. The only reason he took out the fence was because he was too little to drive. You choose to see the bad in his actions, and I have trouble with that. You need to look behind what he does and see the brainpower that it took to do it. I agree, driving the truck was a bad thing to do and his punishment was fair. I’m just asking you to be a little more broadminded. I want you to see him in a different light. In San Diego I ran into some trouble. When everybody was freaking out, Patrick was writing the license plate number on the side of the truck. He thinks, Jess. He reasons things out in a way that a kid shouldn't be able to do. When he does things that seem odd, ask him questions. Find out why he came to the conclusion he did. You'll be very surprised."

"Why are you doing this? You've never taken the time to talk to me about Patrick before."

"That's because I'd never been around him long enough to see how complex he is. I've never had enough time with him to love him for who he is. But now that we've been together for awhile, I feel like I need to speak up for him. If you see him crawling around in the yard looking at the ends of grasses and finding hairs in the bushes and reading difficult books, don't stop him. He's studying the world in a way that interests him. The dirt washes off, but the knowledge doesn't. Let him learn."

"What about you? Did you learn anything from all this? Are you ready to be a mom or did Patrick scare motherhood right out of you?"

"I learned volumes but I'm not ready to be a mom. I'm more open to it though. I want to be a tracker and a wife before I'm a mom. What would you think if Patrick wanted to be a tracker? I know. Tracking doesn't pay and he needs a real job. But what if he just wanted to develop that side of himself? He loves animals. He loves tracking. Patrick could become really good at it, better than me. Would you support him in that?"

"You taught him to track?"

"Only a little, enough to see he has a lot of potential. He tracked a mountain lion, a mule deer, and a person. Then Chase took him out to track javelina. He did exceptionally well for a six-year-old. I talked to Chase about how to teach Pat and he's been giving me some guidance."

"He can learn to track. Nobody's stopping him."

"Pat needs to get out more to track. When he's limited to the yard it's really hard on him."

"That's why we bought him the bike. Once he learns to ride it well I'll have new boundaries for him. He'll be able to explore between our house and the ranch. He can follow the road behind the ranch. There's a gate back there he has to stay behind. I think that might help."

"Yes, definitely! He'll be happier with more space. He really does enjoy learning. We practiced math, reading and science while he was with us and he seemed very open to it. Just keep an open mind, look for the intelligence behind Pat's actions and complaints, and ask him questions when you don't understand him. Don't automatically think he's weird when he's just being different. Someday when Wyatt is a little older I'll keep him for a week too. I bet he's an entirely different little person and even smarter than he looks as well."

"You need your own little person to teach," she reminded me.

"I know. Maybe someday."

That evening I had a job to do. I wasn't sure if anyone would cooperate, but was hoping a few would. I gathered a small group of our family and ranch hands in the living room and told them about the vest and the drug dealers. Then I explained how Phillip Cranston had kept tabs on me through the bug and how he had helped the police to find me. Finally I showed them my purse, hoping to convince everyone that it wasn't as strange as they may have first thought to speak to an inanimate object.

"Phillip? This is Cassidy. If Phillip isn't available then whoever is listening please take a message, or set your sneaky recording device, or whatever it is you do." I gave them time to find a notepad and pen, or Phillip, then continued. "I don't know if you heard the outcome of my latest little escapade. I wanted to thank you, but I don't really know how. I tested the vest. It worked and I'm still alive because of it. Because of you, maybe I'll see another Christmas. So, thank you. I'll never forget you or Carl. I hope you got to play slot cars with the boys. Have a Happy New Year, this is Cassidy, signing off."

My dad stepped forward and said, "Mr. Cranston? This Wayne Gordon of Gordon Quarter Horses. I'm Cassidy's father and I'd like to say thank you. Thank you for giving my daughter back to me. She's a whole heck of trouble, but we love her anyway."

"I'm Randy, I work at the ranch and Cassidy is like my little sister. Don't know what I'd do without her. So, thank you, sir, for being there when she needed you."

"Mr. Cranston? I'm Jesse. I'm Cassidy's sister and, and hell, I'm terrible at these things. I'm going to cry, I know it."

One by one, several of them said a few words. I didn't know if Phillip got it all. I hoped he got the gist of it. When everybody was through, I peeled off the bug and squashed it, closing that chapter of my life and ending my link to the Cranston family. The bug left a sticky square of glue on my purse. Reminders of Carl would be with me forever, I thought. Next time I'll track faster. I'll get there sooner. I'll find that ten sixty-five or my name isn't Cassidy Michaels, Dangerous Tracker Woman.

Chapter 19

I got up early the next morning. We had to go home but I hadn't even said 'hi' to Shasta, my gray quarter horse. I saddled him up in western gear and rode him around the corral. The hands kept him working on the ranch while I was gone, so he stayed in good form. Once we'd been reacquainted I rolled barrels out into the corral in a cloverleaf. Rusty joined me in setting up the barrels, then stood at the fence with Steve watching as I spurred Shasta into a traditional barrel racing run. It was good feeling my horse underneath me again. I galloped Shasta around the ring a few times just because he liked to run and then joined the guys.

"Do you want to go for a trail ride?" Rusty asked me. It was an unusual question for him because he wasn't used to riding horseback yet.

"Okay, I'll saddle a horse. Why?"

"Because I love watching you ride. You are so at ease in the saddle. I need to see you be happy and free for just a little while."

We rode off into the hills behind the ranch. I put Shasta into a canter and pulled ahead of Rusty, just so he could watch me ride, then I circled back around and joined him on the trail. We shared small talk, both wondering if life would ever be the same after Patrick. I thought not. Patrick had affected us whether he meant to or not. There was an empty spot that we couldn't really identify, and a memory of giving of ourselves to a child, of devoting ourselves to a child, and there really wasn't anything to compare with it. Were we ready to become parents? I wasn't, and yet… Nope, I thought, I need time. Time to be a wife and a tracker. Time to put at least a few successful searches behind me. I couldn't let Carl Cranston overshadow my life forever. I wasn't ready for parenthood just yet, but maybe someday.

The house was quiet. Eerily quiet. I didn't think I'd ever get used to our home being this silent again. I missed Patrick. I was glad he was getting the dose of freedom he so desperately yearned for. It opened up a whole new world for him, but I still pictured him home quietly being stifled into a nice, obedient, clean, average six-year-old boy and that grated on me.

Mark came by with pictures and Strict called to see if I was ready to go out on searches. Landon called to get the scoop on what happened in San Diego.

"I got the part about the transparent tank top, but I missed what led up to that."

"That's because the only people who saw it were six drug dealers, and then Rusty and Chase." I told him what happened and he took it all in stride.

"Sounds like it was a normal Christmas, for you. Next time you have a disaster in a transparent tank top make sure it's on my call."